A NORTON CRITICAL EDITION

HERMAN MELVILLE

MOBY-DICK

AN AUTHORITATIVE TEXT
REVIEWS AND LETTERS BY MELVILLE
ANALOGUES AND SOURCES
CRITICISM

Edited by

HARRISON HAYFORD
NORTHWESTERN UNIVERSITY

HERSHEL PARKER
UNIVERSITY OF
SOUTHERN CALIFORNIA

PICTORIAL MATERIALS PREPARED BY
JOHN B. PUTNAM

W · W · NORTON & COMPANY

New York · London

COPYRIGHT © 1967 BY W. W. NORTON & COMPANY, INC.

Library of Congress Catalog Card No. 66–11309

W. W. Norton & Company, Inc., 500 Fifth Avenue, New York, NY 10110
W. W. Norton & Company Ltd., 10 Coptic Street London WC1A 1PU

PRINTED IN THE UNITED STATES OF AMERICA

8 9 0

ISBN 0-393-04284-7 CL
ISBN 0-393-09670-X PBK

Contents

Analogues and Sources

Criticism

Foreword

During the last half-century *Moby-Dick* has been recognized, and is now widely studied, as one of the world's great books. This Norton Critical Edition of it is designed for use in college literature courses.

We have annotated the text sparingly, most often when a passage presents a problem of identification or recognition which a reader cannot solve with the aid of a desk dictionary, or when a reader might not become aware that there *is* a problem, and so might miss the point of a passage. There are no footnotes which propound a particular interpretation of the book. We believe that most college students using this Norton Critical Edition, many of them reading *Moby-Dick* for the first time, do not need many footnotes. The allusions in the book come thick and fast, but they normally reveal their relevant denotative and connotative meanings by their contexts. For example, what is important about Cato in the first paragraph of Chapter 1 is not his birth date and death date but the philosophical flourish with which he commits suicide, and the contrast of Ishmael's less desperate substitute. Footnotes to such limited allusions are irrelevant, and sometimes they defeat Melville's (or Ishmael's) purposes. Footnotes which identify all of the allusions in "The Whiteness of the Whale" do more than destroy the sense of Ishmael as the storyteller—they frustrate his appeal to the reader to follow him *imaginatively*: "But in a matter like this, subtlety appeals to subtlety, and without imagination no man can follow another into these halls."

The text is preceded by two maps prepared by John B. Putnam. It is followed by a glossary of nautical terms; an essay, "Whaling and Whalecraft: A Pictorial Account," especially written and illustrated by Mr. Putnam; and a group of contemporary engravings.

Moby-Dick deserves and will reward close attention to its verbal detail, and we believe the textual evidence in "The Text: History, Variants, and Emendations" will show that such attention can again and again have the effect of enhancing a reader's appreciation of Melville's literary powers. He was a writer capable both of imagining what Hawthorne called "his grand conception of the white whale" and of working out that conception into minute details, even while becoming impatient of the "minute gnat-like torments" of the mechanical matters involved in preparing a consistent manuscript and reading proofs for its published form. This section contains a discussion of the textual problems of *Moby-Dick* and a full collation of the differences in wording between the first American and the first English editions, as well as briefer sections listing all our emendations. Both the collation table and the lists of emendations are designed to make clear just what we have done or not done to the text; hence they are arranged for clarity rather than economy of presentation.

Reviews and letters written by Melville just before and during the years *Moby-Dick* was in process are given in the next section; they furnish clues to its biographical and literary backgrounds. The analogues and sources, in the section following, represent something of the popular knowledge of whaling legends in Melville's time and also document some of his particular borrowings and characteristic ways of reshaping them.

The last section offers several valid critical perspectives in which *Moby-Dick* may be viewed. It is not meant to provide a historical overview of critical opinion or a conspectus of conflicting interpretations. Still, the major critical problems of the book are dealt with: its genesis, in relation to Melville's life and his way of writing; its peculiar, organic form, in relation to the standard fictional genres, epic, tragedy, comedy, the novel, and their characteristic "spirit" or "vision"; its meaning; and its art and technique. None of the critical pieces is to be taken as definitive or as requiring the reader's agreement. By design, they will be found to express rather different views as to the critical problems involved.

NOTE ON THE TEXT

This text of *Moby-Dick* has been specially prepared for the Norton Critical Edition by the present editors.

It is like all recent scholarly texts of *Moby-Dick* in following as its copy-text the first American edition (New York, 1851), which is the source closest to Melville's non-extant manuscript. But it is unlike any previous edition in that it is not a slightly corrected reproduction of the first American text but a *critical*, constructed text—that is, one which attempts to come closer than the first edition did to the author's final intention by correcting errors and adopting his own later revisions. As such, it is based on current editorial principles and procedures. (See, for example, the brief article "Textual Criticism," by Fredson Bowers in the pamphlet *The Aims and Methods of Scholarship in Modern Languages and Literatures*, edited by James Thorpe [Modern Language Association of America, New York, 1963].) Hence, it differs from previous editions in two respects. (1) We identify and correct many more scribal and compositorial errors in the first American text than any previous editors. A large number of these misreadings were corrected in the first English edition, some of them unquestionably by Melville; other errors not corrected there have already been pointed out and a few of them corrected by previous editors, but we make many corrections for the first time in the present edition. (2) We emend the first American text with many readings from the first English edition, *The Whale* (London, 1851), because—as we are the first editors to recognize—it was Melville himself who made many of the numerous changes that appear in the English edition.

This Norton Critical Edition, we wish to emphasize, is not offered as "definitive," but as going further than any other to date in recovering and presenting Melville's own final intentions for the text. Since preparing it, we have become engaged, as general editor and associate general editor, upon the new complete edition of Melville's works now being prepared at Northwestern University and The Newberry Library under a contract from the United States Office of Education. The text of *Moby-Dick* for that edition has not yet been prepared, but it will follow the same general principles as this Norton text, and hence will incorporate many of the same features. However, its preparation will involve further collations of multiple copies of the various editions and issues as well as further intensive consideration of the range of possible emendations and of bibliographical problems not yet exhaustively treated. The present edition is presented in a form designed to help readers think about its text. We offer it as opening up, not as closing, the textual problems of *Moby-Dick*, and we solicit the criticisms and suggestions of its readers.

HARRISON HAYFORD
HERSHEL PARKER

The Text of
Moby-Dick;
or,
The Whale.

"There Leviathan,
Hugest of living creatures, in the deep
Stretch'd like a promontory sleeps or swims,
And seems a moving land; and at his gills
Draws in, and at his breath spouts out a sea."
PARADISE LOST.

IN TOKEN

OF MY ADMIRATION FOR HIS GENIUS,

𝕿𝖍𝖎𝖘 𝕭𝖔𝖔𝖐 𝖎𝖘 𝕴𝖓𝖘𝖈𝖗𝖎𝖇𝖊𝖉

TO

NATHANIEL HAWTHORNE.

Contents of Moby-Dick

Chapters 118-126

Melville's Voyages, 1841-1844

Legend

Track of Pequod

Melville's voyages:

Outward bound ------

Homeward bound ....

Sperm-whaling grounds ////

Principal ports of southeastern
New England in the mid-1800's

Those noted for whaling shown in roman

Others shown in italics

Salem

Boston

Provincetown

Plymouth

New
Bedford

Fairhaven

Newport

Providence

Nantucket

Martha's Vineyard

Block Island

Mystic

New
London

Sag Harbor

ETYMOLOGY.

(SUPPLIED BY A LATE CONSUMPTIVE USHER TO A
GRAMMAR SCHOOL.)

[THE pale Usher [1]—threadbare in coat, heart, body, and brain;
I see him now. He was ever dusting his old lexicons and grammars,
with a queer handkerchief, mockingly embellished with all the gay
flags of all the known nations of the world. He loved to dust his old
grammars; it somehow mildly reminded him of his mortality.]

"While you take in hand to school others, and to teach them by
what name a whale-fish is to be called in our tongue, leaving out,
through ignorance, the letter H, which almost alone maketh up the
signification of the word, you deliver that which is not true."
Hackluyt.

"WHALE. * * * Sw. and Dan. *hval.* This animal is named from
roundness or rolling; for in Dan. *hvalt* is arched or vaulted."
Webster's Dictionary.

"WHALE. * * * It is more immediately from the Dut. and Ger.
Wallen; A.S. *Walw-ian*, to roll, to wallow."
Richardson's Dictionary.

הן,	*Hebrew.*
χητος,	*Greek.*
CETUS,	*Latin.*
WHŒL,	*Anglo-Saxon.*
HVALT,	*Danish.*
WAL,	*Dutch.*
HWAL,	*Swedish.*
WHALE,	*Icelandic.*
WHALE,	*English.*
BALEINE,	*French.*
BALLENA,	*Spanish.*
PEKEE-NUEE-NUEE,	*Fegee.*
PEHEE-NUEE-NUEE,	*Erromangoan.*

---

1 Assistant schoolmaster.

EXTRACTS.

(SUPPLIED BY A SUB-SUB-LIBRARIAN.)

[It will be seen that this mere painstaking burrower and grub-worm of a poor devil of a Sub-Sub appears to have gone through the long Vaticans [1] and street-stalls of the earth, picking up whatever random allusions to whales he could anyways find in any book whatsoever, sacred or profane. Therefore you must not, in every case at least, take the higgledy-piggledy whale statements, however authentic, in these extracts, for veritable gospel cetology. Far from it. As touching the ancient authors generally, as well as the poets here appearing, these extracts are solely valuable or entertaining, as affording a glancing bird's eye view of what has been promiscuously said, thought, fancied, and sung of Leviathan, by many nations and generations, including our own.

So fare thee well, poor devil of a Sub-Sub, whose commentator I am. Thou belongest to that hopeless, sallow tribe which no wine of this world will ever warm; and for whom even Pale Sherry would be too rosy-strong; but with whom one sometimes loves to sit, and feel poor-devilish, too; and grow convivial upon tears; and say to them bluntly, with full eyes and empty glasses, and in not altogether unpleasant sadness—Give it up, Sub-Subs! For by how much the more pains ye take to please the world, by so much the more shall ye for ever go thankless! Would that I could clear out Hampton Court and the Tuileries for ye! But gulp down your tears and hie aloft to the royal-mast with your hearts; for your friends who have gone before are clearing out the seven-storied heavens, and making refugees of long-pampered Gabriel, Michael, and Raphael,[2] against your coming. Here ye strike but splintered hearts together—there, ye shall strike unsplinterable glasses!]

"And God created great whales."
Genesis.

"Leviathan maketh a path to shine after him;
One would think the deep to be hoary."
Job.

"Now the Lord had prepared a great fish to swallow up Jonah."
Jonah.

"There go the ships; there is that Leviathan whom thou hast made to play therein."
Psalms.

"In that day, the Lord with his sore, and great, and strong sword, shall punish Leviathan the piercing serpent, even Leviathan that crooked serpent; and he shall slay the dragon that is in the sea."
Isaiah.

1. Great libraries (like that of the Vatican).　2. Archangels.

"And what thing soever besides cometh within the chaos of this monster's mouth, be it beast, boat, or stone, down it goes all incontinently that foul great swallow of his, and perisheth in the bottomless gulf of his paunch."

Holland's Plutarch's Morals.

"The Indian Sea breedeth the most and the biggest fishes that are: among which the Whales and 'Whirlpooles called Balæne, take up as much in length as four acres or arpens of land."

Holland's Pliny.

"Scarcely had we proceeded two days on the sea, when about sunrise a great many Whales and other monsters of the sea, appeared. Among the former, one was of a most monstrous size. * * This came towards us, open-mouthed, raising the waves on all sides, and beating the sea before him into a foam."

Tooke's Lucian.
"The True History."

"He visited this country also with a view of catching horse-whales, which had bones of very great value for their teeth, of which he brought some to the king. * * * The best whales were catched in his own country, of which some were forty-eight, some fifty yards long. He said that he was one of six who had killed sixty in two days."

Other or Octher's verbal narrative taken down
from his mouth by King Alfred. A. D. 890.

"And whereas all the other things, whether beast or vessel, that enter into the dreadful gulf of this monster's (whale's) mouth, are immediately lost and swallowed up, the sea-gudgeon retires into it in great security, and there sleeps."

MONTAIGNE.—*Apology for Raimond Sebond.*

"Let us fly, let us fly! Old Nick take me if it is not Leviathan described by the noble prophet Moses in the life of patient Job."

Rabelais.

"This whale's liver was two cart-loads."

Stowe's Annals.

"The great Leviathan that maketh the seas to seethe like a boiling pan." *Lord Bacon's Version of the Psalms.*

"Touching that monstrous bulk of the whale or ork we have received nothing certain. They grow exceeding fat, insomuch that an incredible quantity of oil will be extracted out of one whale."

Ibid "History of Life and Death."

"The sovereignest thing on earth is parmacetti for an inward bruise." *King Henry.*

"Very like a whale." *Hamlet.*

"Which to secure, no skill of leach's art
Mote him availle, but to returne againe
To his wound's worker, that with lowly dart,
Dinting his breast, had bred his restless paine,
Like as the wounded whale to shore flies thro' the
maine."   *The Fairie Queen.*

"Immense as whales, the motion of whose vast bodies can in a
peaceful calm trouble the ocean till it boil."
                    Sir William Davenant. Preface to Gondibert.

"What spermacetti is, men might justly doubt, since the learned
Hofmannus in his work of thirty years, saith plainly, *Nescio quid
sit.*" [1]
                              *Sir T. Browne. Of Sperma Ceti and the
                                  Sperma Ceti Whale. Vide his V. E.*

"Like Spencer's Talus with his modern flail
He threatens ruin with his ponderous tail.
    *   *   *   *   *
Their fixed jav'lins in his side he wears,
And on his back a grove of pikes appears."
                          Waller's Battle of the Summer Islands.

"By art is created that great Leviathan, called a Commonwealth
or State—(in Latin, Civitas) which is but an artificial man."
                          Opening sentence of Hobbes's Leviathan.

"Silly Mansoul swallowed it without chewing, as if it had been
a sprat in the mouth of a whale."   *Holy War.*

            "That sea beast
Leviathan, which God of all his works
Created hugest that swim the ocean stream."
                                              Paradise Lost.

            ——— "There Leviathan,
Hugest of living creatures, in the deep
Stretched like a promontory sleeps or swims,
And seems a moving land; and at his gills
Draws in, and at his breath spouts out a sea."
                                                      Ibid.

"The mighty whales which swim in a sea of water, and have a
sea of oil swimming in them."
                          Fuller's Profane and Holy State.

"So close behind some promontory lie
The huge Leviathans to attend their prey,
And give no chace, but swallow in the fry,
    Which through their gaping jaws mistake the way."
                                Dryden's Annus Mirabilis.

---

1. "I do not know what it is."

"While the whale is floating at the stern of the ship, they cut off his head, and tow it with a boat as near the shore as it will come; but it will be aground in twelve or thirteen feet water."
Thomas Edge's Ten Voyages to Spitzbergen, in Purchass.

"In their way they saw many whales sporting in the ocean, and in wantonness fuzzing up the water through their pipes and vents, which nature has placed on their shoulders."
Sir T. Herbert's Voyages into Asia and Africa.
Harris Coll.

"Here they saw such huge troops of whales, that they were forced to proceed with a great deal of caution for fear they should run their ship upon them."
Schouten's Sixth Circumnavigation.

"We set sail from the Elbe, wind N. E. in the ship called The Jonas-in-the-Whale. * * *
Some say the whale can't open his mouth, but that is a fable. * * *
They frequently climb up the masts to see whether they can see a whale, for the first discoverer has a ducat for his pains. * * *
I was told of a whale taken near Shetland, that had above a barrel of herrings in his belly. * * *
One of our harpooneers told me that he caught once a whale in Spitzbergen that was white all over."
A Voyage to Greenland, A.D. 1671.
Harris Coll.

"Several whales have come in upon this coast (Fife). Anno 1652, one eighty feet in length of the whale-bone kind came in, which, (as I was informed) besides a vast quantity of oil, did afford 500 weight of baleen. The jaws of it stand for a gate in the garden of Pitferren."
Sibbald's Fife and Kinross.

"Myself have agreed to try whether I can master and kill this Sperma-ceti whale, for I could never hear of any of that sort that was killed by any man, such is his fierceness and swiftness."
Richard Strafford's Letter from the Bermudas.
Phil. Trans. A. D. 1668.

"Whales in the sea
God's voice obey."
N. E. Primer.

"We saw also abundance of large whales, there being more in those southern seas, as I may say, by a hundred to one; than we have to the northward of us."
Captain Cowley's Voyage round the Globe. A. D. 1729.

* * * * * "and the breath of the whale is frequently attended with such an insupportable smell, as to bring on a disorder of the brain." *Ulloa's South America.*

6 · *Moby-Dick*

> "To fifty chosen sylphs of special note,
> We trust the important charge, the petticoat.
> Oft have we known that seven-fold fence to fail,
> Tho' stiff with hoops and armed with ribs of whale."
>
> *Rape of the Lock.*

"If we compare land animals in respect to magnitude, with those that take up their abode in the deep, we shall find they will appear contemptible in the comparison. The whale is doubtless the largest animal in creation."

Goldsmith's Nat. Hist.

"If you should write a fable for little fishes, you would make them speak like great whales."

Goldsmith to Johnson.

"In the afternoon we saw what was supposed to be a rock, but it was found to be a dead whale, which some Asiatics had killed, and were then towing ashore. They seemed to endeavor to conceal themselves behind the whale, in order to avoid being seen by us."

Cook's Voyages.

"The larger whales, they seldom venture to attack. They stand in so great dread of some of them, that when out at sea they are afraid to mention even their names, and carry dung, lime-stone, juniper-wood, and some other articles of the same nature in their boats, in order to terrify and prevent their too near approach."

Uno Von Troil's Letters on Banks's and Solander's Voyage to Iceland in 1772.

"The Spermacetti Whale found by the Nantuckois, is an active, fierce animal, and requires vast address and boldness in the fishermen."

Thomas Jefferson's Whale Memorial to the French minister in 1778.

"And pray, sir, what in the world is equal to it?"

Edmund Burke's reference in Parliament to the Nantucket Whale-Fishery.

"Spain——a great whale stranded on the shores of Europe."

Edmund Burke. (somewhere.)

"A tenth branch of the king's ordinary revenue, said to be grounded on the consideration of his guarding and protecting the seas from pirates and robbers, is the right to *royal* fish, which are whale and sturgeon. And these, when either thrown ashore or caught near the coast, are the property of the king."

Blackstone.

> "Soon to the sport of death the crews repair:
> Rodmond unerring o'er his head suspends
> The barbed steel, and every turn attends."
>
> *Falconer's Shipwreck.*

"Bright shone the roofs, the domes, the spires,
　And rockets blew self driven,
To hang their momentary fire
Around the vault of heaven.

"So fire with water to compare,
　The ocean serves on high,
Up-spouted by a whale in air,
To express unwieldy joy."
　　　　Cowper, on the Queen's Visit to London.

"Ten or fifteen gallons of blood are thrown out of the heart at a stroke, with immense velocity."
　　　　John Hunter's account of the dissection
　　　　　　of a whale. (A small sized one.)

"The aorta of a whale is larger in the bore than the main pipe of the water-works at London Bridge, and the water roaring in its passage through that pipe is inferior in impetus and velocity to the blood gushing from the whale's heart."
　　　　Paley's Theology.

"The whale is a mammiferous animal without hind feet."
　　　　Baron Cuvier.

"In 40 degrees south, we saw Spermacetti Whales, but did not take any till the first of May, the sea being then covered with them."
　　　　Colnett's Voyage for the Purpose of
　　　　　　Extending the Spermacetti Whale Fishery.

"In the free element beneath me swam,
　Floundered and dived, in play, in chace, in battle,
Fishes of every color, form, and kind;
Which language cannot paint, and mariner
Had never seen; from dread Leviathan
To insect millions peopling every wave:
Gather'd in shoals immense, like floating islands,
Led by mysterious instincts through that waste
And trackless region, though on every side
Assaulted by voracious enemies,
Whales, sharks, and monsters, arm'd in front or jaw.
With swords, saws, spiral horns, or hooked fangs."
　　　　Montgomery's World before the Flood.

"Io! Pæan! Io! sing,
　To the finny people's king.
Not a mightier whale than this
In the vast Atlantic is;
Not a fatter fish than he,
Flounders round the Polar Sea."
　　　　Charles Lamb's Triumph of the Whale.

"In the year 1690 some persons were on a high hill observing the whales spouting and sporting with each other, when one observed; there—pointing to the sea—is a green pasture where our children's grand-children will go for bread."

Obed Macy's History of Nantucket.

"I built a cottage for Susan and myself and made a gateway in the form of a Gothic Arch, by setting up a whale's jaw bones."

Hawthorne's Twice Told Tales.

"She came to bespeak a monument for her first love, who had been killed by a whale in the Pacific ocean, no less than forty years ago."   *Ibid.*

"No, Sir, 'tis a Right Whale," answered Tom; "I saw his spout; he threw up a pair of as pretty rainbows as a Christian would wish to look at. He's a raal oil-butt, that fellow!"

Cooper's Pilot.

"The papers were brought in, and we saw in the Berlin Gazette that whales had been introduced on the stage there."

Eckermann's Conversations with Goethe.

"My God! Mr. Chase, what is the matter?" I answered, "we have been stove by a whale."

"Narrative of the Shipwreck of the Whale Ship Essex of Nantucket, which was attacked and finally destroyed by a large Sperm Whale in the Pacific Ocean." By Owen Chase of Nantucket, first mate of said vessel. New York. 1821.

"A mariner sat in the shrouds one night,
   The wind was piping free;
Now bright, now dimmed, was the moonlight pale,
And the phospher gleamed in the wake of the whale,
   As it floundered in the sea."

Elizabeth Oakes Smith.

"The quantity of line withdrawn from the different boats engaged in the capture of this one whale, amounted altogether to 10,440 yards or nearly six English miles." * * *

"Sometimes the whale shakes its tremendous tail in the air, which, cracking like a whip, resounds to the distance of three or four miles."   *Scoresby.*

"Mad with the agonies he endures from these fresh attacks, the infuriated Sperm Whale rolls over and over; he rears his enormous head, and with wide expanded jaws snaps at everything around him; he rushes at the boats with his head; they are propelled before him with vast swiftness, and sometimes utterly destroyed.

* * * It is a matter of great astonishment that the considera-

tion of the habits of so interesting, and, in a commercial point of view, of so important an animal (as the Sperm Whale) should have been so entirely neglected, or should have excited so little curiosity among the numerous, and many of them competent observers, that of late years must have possessed the most abundant and the most convenient opportunities of witnessing their habitudes."

Thomas Beale's History of the Sperm Whale, 1839.

"The Cachalot" (Sperm Whale) "is not only better armed than the True Whale" (Greenland or Right Whale) "in possessing a formidable weapon at either extremity of its body, but also more frequently displays a disposition to employ these weapons offensively, and in a manner at once so artful, bold, and mischievous, as to lead to its being regarded as the most dangerous to attack of all the known species of the whale tribe."

Frederick Debell Bennett's Whaling
Voyage Round the Globe. 1840.

October 13. "There she blows," was sung out from the mast-head.
"Where away?" demanded the captain.
"Three points off the lee bow, sir."
"Raise up your wheel. Steady!"
"Steady, sir."
"Mast-head ahoy! Do you see that whale now?"
"Ay ay, sir! A shoal of Sperm Whales! There she blows! There she breaches!"
"Sing out! sing out every time!"
"Ay ay, sir! There she blows! there—there—*thar* she blows—bowes—bo-o-o-s!"
"How far off?"
"Two miles and a half."
"Thunder and lightning! so near! Call all hands!"

J. Ross Browne's Etchings
of a Whaling Cruise. 1846.

"The Whale-ship Globe, on board of which vessel occurred the horrid transactions we are about to relate, belonged to the island of Nantucket."

"Narrative of the Globe Mutiny," by
Lay and Hussey survivors. A. D. 1828.

"Being once pursued by a whale which he had wounded, he parried the assault for some time with a lance; but the furious monster at length rushed on the boat; himself and comrades only being preserved by leaping into the water when they saw the onset was inevitable."

Missionary Journal of Tyerman and Bennett.

"Nantucket itself," said Mr. Webster, "is a very striking and peculiar portion of the National interest. There is a population of eight or nine thousand persons, living here in the sea, adding largely every year to the National wealth by the boldest and most persevering industry."

> *Report of Daniel Webster's Speech in the U. S. Senate, on the application for the Erection of a Breakwater at Nantucket. 1828.*

"The whale fell directly over him, and probably killed him in a moment."

> *"The Whale and his Captors, or The Whaleman's Adventures and the Whale's Biography, gathered on the Homeward Cruise of the Commodore Preble." By Rev. Henry T. Cheever.*

"If you make the least damn bit of noise," replied Samuel, "I will send you to hell."

> *Life of Samuel Comstock (the mutineer), by his brother, William Comstock. Another Version of the whale-ship Globe narrative.*

"The voyages of the Dutch and English to the Northern Ocean, in order, if possible, to discover a passage through it to India, though they failed of their main object, laid open the haunts of the whale."

> *McCulloch's Commercial Dictionary.*

"These things are reciprocal; the ball rebounds, only to bound forward again; for now in laying open the haunts of the whale, the whalemen seem to have indirectly hit upon new clews to that same mystic North-West Passage."

> *From "Something" unpublished.*

"It is impossible to meet a whale-ship on the ocean without being struck by her mere appearance. The vessel under short sail, with look-outs at the mast-heads, eagerly scanning the wide expanse around them, has a totally different air from those engaged in a regular voyage."

> *Currents and Whaling. U. S. Ex. Ex.*

"Pedestrians in the vicinity of London and elsewhere may recollect having seen large curved bones set upright in the earth, either to form arches over gateways, or entrances to alcoves, and they may perhaps have been told that these were the ribs of whales."

> *Tales of a Whale Voyager to the Arctic Ocean.*

"It was not till the boats returned from the pursuit of these whales, that the whites saw their ship in bloody possession of the savages enrolled among the crew."

> *Newspaper Account of the Taking and Retaking of the Whale-ship Hobomack.*

"It is generally well known that out of the crews of Whaling vessels (American) few ever return in the ships on board of which they departed."   *Cruise in a Whale Boat.*

"Suddenly a mighty mass emerged from the water, and shot up perpendicularly into the air. It was the whale."
                              Miriam Coffin or the Whale Fisherman.

"The Whale is harpooned to be sure; but bethink you, how you would manage a powerful unbroken colt, with the mere appliance of a rope tied to the root of his tail."
                              A Chapter on Whaling in Ribs and Trucks.

"On one occasion I saw two of these monsters (whales) probably male and female, slowly swimming, one after the other, within less than a stone's throw of the shore" (Terra Del Fuego), "over which the beech tree extended its branches."
                              Darwin's Voyage of a Naturalist.

" 'Stern all!' exclaimed the mate, as upon turning his head, he saw the distended jaws of a large Sperm Whale close to the head of the boat, threatening it with instant destruction;—'Stern all, for your lives!' "
                              Wharton the Whale Killer.

"So be cheery, my lads, let your hearts never fail,
  While the bold harpooneer is striking the whale!"
                              Nantucket Song.

"Oh, the rare old Whale, mid storm and gale
    In his ocean home will be
  A giant in might, where might is right,
    And King of the boundless sea."
                              Whale Song.

Chapter 1

Call me Ishmael.[1] Some years ago—never mind how long precisely—having little or no money in my purse, and nothing particular to interest me on shore, I thought I would sail about a little and see the watery part of the world. It is a way I have of driving off the spleen, and regulating the circulation. Whenever I find myself growing grim about the mouth; whenever it is a damp, drizzly November in my soul; whenever I find myself involuntarily pausing before coffin warehouses, and bringing up the rear of every funeral I meet; and especially whenever my hypos[2] get such an upper hand of me, that it requires a strong moral principle to prevent me from deliberately stepping into the street, and methodically knocking people's hats off—then, I account it high time to get to sea as soon as I can. This is my substitute for pistol and ball. With a philosophical flourish Cato throws himself upon his sword; I quietly take to the ship. There is nothing surprising in this. If they but knew it, almost all men in their degree, some time or other, cherish very nearly the same feelings towards the ocean with me.

There now is your insular city of the Manhattoes,[3] belted round by wharves as Indian isles by coral reefs—commerce surrounds it with her surf. Right and left, the streets take you waterward. Its extreme down-town is the Battery, where that noble mole is washed by waves, and cooled by breezes, which a few hours previous were out of sight of land. Look at the crowds of water-gazers there.

Circumambulate the city of a dreamy Sabbath afternoon. Go from Corlears Hook to Coenties Slip, and from thence, by Whitehall, northward.[4] What do you see?—Posted like silent sentinels all around the town, stand thousands upon thousands of mortal men fixed in ocean reveries. Some leaning against the spiles; some seated upon the pier-heads; some looking over the bulwarks of ships from China; some high aloft in the rigging, as if striving to get a still better seaward peep. But these are all landsmen; of week days pent up in lath and plaster—tied to counters, nailed to

1. The biblical Ishmael was the son of Abraham by the bondservant Hagar, an Egyptian. Ishmael was disinherited and cast out in favor of his younger half-brother Isaac, Abraham's son by his wife Sarah. An angel prophesies to Hagar: "And he will be a wild man; and every man's hand against him." See Genesis 16-25. The name was in common use to mean an exile or outcast.
2. Short for "hypochondria," a state of depression somewhat more chronic and morbid than our "blues."
3. The people of Manhattan Island, so referred to by Irving in *Knickerbocker History of New York* who also refers to "the ancient city of Manhattoes" in "The Legend of Sleepy Hollow."
4. That is, go from a point (or "hook") on the East River near the present Williamsburg Bridge, round the Battery and walk northward on Whitehall along the Hudson River.

benches, clinched to desks. How then is this? Are the green fields gone? What do they here?

But look! here come more crowds, pacing straight for the water, and seemingly bound for a dive. Strange! Nothing will content them but the extremest limit of the land; loitering under the shady lee of yonder warehouses will not suffice. No. They must get just as nigh the water as they possibly can without falling in. And there they stand—miles of them—leagues. Inlanders all, they come from lanes and alleys, streets and avenues—north, east, south, and west. Yet here they all unite. Tell me, does the magnetic virtue in the needles of the compasses of all those ships attract them thither?

Once more. Say, you are in the country; in some high land of lakes. Take almost any path you please, and ten to one it carries you down in a dale, and leaves you there by a pool in the stream. There is magic in it. Let the most absent-minded of men be plunged in his deepest reveries—stand that man on his legs, set his feet a-going, and he will infallibly lead you to water, if water there be in all that region. Should you ever be athirst in the great American desert, try this experiment, if your caravan happen to be supplied with a metaphysical professor. Yes, as every one knows, meditation and water are wedded for ever.

But here is an artist. He desires to paint you the dreamiest, shadiest, quietest, most enchanting bit of romantic landscape in all the valley of the Saco. What is the chief element he employs? There stand his trees, each with a hollow trunk, as if a hermit and a crucifix were within; and here sleeps his meadow, and there sleep his cattle; and up from yonder cottage goes a sleepy smoke. Deep into distant woodlands winds a mazy way, reaching to overlapping spurs of mountains bathed in their hill-side blue. But though the picture lies thus tranced, and though this pine-tree shakes down its sighs like leaves upon this shepherd's head, yet all were vain, unless the shepherd's eye were fixed upon the magic stream before him. Go visit the Prairies in June, when for scores on scores of miles you wade knee-deep among Tiger-lilies—what is the one charm wanting?—Water—there is not a drop of water there! Were Niagara but a cataract of sand, would you travel your thousand miles to see it? Why did the poor poet of Tennessee, upon suddenly receiving two handfuls of silver, deliberate whether to buy him a coat, which he sadly needed, or invest his money in a pedestrian trip to Rockaway Beach? Why is almost every robust healthy boy with a robust healthy soul in him, at some time or other crazy to go to sea? Why upon your first voyage as a passenger, did you yourself feel such a mystical vibration, when first told that you and your ship were now out of sight of land?

Why did the old Persians hold the sea holy? Why did the Greeks give it a separate deity,[5] and make him the own brother of Jove? Surely all this is not without meaning. And still deeper the meaning of that story of Narcissus,[6] who because he could not grasp the tormenting, mild image he saw in the fountain, plunged into it and was drowned. But that same image, we ourselves see in all rivers and oceans. It is the image of the ungraspable phantom of life; and this is the key to it all.

Now, when I say that I am in the habit of going to sea whenever I begin to grow hazy about the eyes, and begin to be over conscious of my lungs, I do not mean to have it inferred that I ever go to sea as a passenger. For to go as a passenger you must needs have a purse, and a purse is but a rag unless you have something in it. Besides, passengers get sea-sick—grow quarrelsome—don't sleep of nights—do not enjoy themselves much, as a general thing;—no, I never go as a passenger; nor, though I am something of a salt, do I ever go to sea as a Commodore, or a Captain, or a Cook. I abandon the glory and distinction of such offices to those who like them. For my part, I abominate all honorable respectable toils, trials, and tribulations of every kind whatsoever. It is quite as much as I can do to take care of myself, without taking care of ships, barques, brigs, schooners, and what not. And as for going as cook,—though I confess there is considerable glory in that, a cook being a sort of officer on ship-board—yet, somehow, I never fancied broiling fowls;—though once broiled, judiciously buttered, and judgmatically salted and peppered, there is no one who will speak more respectfully, not to say reverentially, of a broiled fowl than I will. It is out of the idolatrous dotings of the old Egyptians upon broiled ibis and roasted river horse, that you see the mummies of those creatures in their huge bake-houses the pyramids.

No, when I go to sea, I go as a simple sailor, right before the mast, plumb down into the forecastle, aloft there to the royal mast-head. True, they rather order me about some, and make me jump from spar to spar, like a grasshopper in a May meadow. And at first, this sort of thing is unpleasant enough. It touches one's sense of honor, particularly if you come of an old established family in the land, the Van Rensselaers, or Randolphs, or Hardicanutes.[7] And more than all, if just previous to putting your hand into the tar-pot, you have been lording it as a country schoolmaster, making the tallest boys stand in awe of you. The transition is a keen one, I assure you, from a schoolmaster to a sailor, and

---

5. Poseidon.
6. A Greek youth condemned to pine away for love of his own reflection in a spring; at his death he became a narcissus.
7. Dominant in New York, in Virginia, and in eleventh-century Denmark and England.

requires a strong decoction of Seneca and the Stoics to enable you to grin and bear it. But even this wears off in time.

What of it, if some old hunks [8] of a sea-captain orders me to get a broom and sweep down the decks? What does that indignity amount to, weighed, I mean, in the scales of the New Testament? Do you think the archangel Gabriel thinks anything the less of me, because I promptly and respectfully obey that old hunks in that particular instance? Who aint a slave? Tell me that. Well, then, however the old sea-captains may order me about—however they may thump and punch me about, I have the satisfaction of knowing that it is all right; that everybody else is one way or other served in much the same way—either in a physical or metaphysical point of view, that is; and so the universal thump is passed round, and all hands should rub each other's shoulder-blades, and be content.

Again, I always go to sea as a sailor, because they make a point of paying me for my trouble, whereas they never pay passengers a single penny that I ever heard of. On the contrary, passengers themselves must pay. And there is all the difference in the world between paying and being paid. The act of paying is perhaps the most uncomfortable infliction that the two orchard thieves entailed upon us. But *being paid*,—what will compare with it? The urbane activity with which a man receives money is really marvellous, considering that we so earnestly believe money to be the root of all earthly ills, and that on no account can a monied man enter heaven. Ah! how cheerfully we consign ourselves to perdition!

Finally, I always go to sea as a sailor, because of the wholesome exercise and pure air of the forecastle deck. For as in this world, head winds are far more prevalent than winds from astern (that is, if you never violate the Pythagorean maxim),[9] so for the most part the Commodore on the quarter-deck gets his atmosphere at second hand from the sailors on the forecastle. He thinks he breathes it first; but not so. In much the same way do the commonalty lead their leaders in many other things, at the same time that the leaders little suspect it. But wherefore it was that after having repeatedly smelt the sea as a merchant sailor, I should now take it into my head to go on a whaling voyage; this the invisible police officer of the Fates,[1] who has the constant surveillance of me, and secretly dogs me, and influences me in some unaccountable way—he can better answer than any one else. And, doubtless, my going on this whaling voyage, formed part of the

8. A surly, crusty fellow.
9. The Pythagorean injunction is to avoid eating beans, which cause flatulence.

1. Three goddesses who control human destiny and life. Clotho spins the thread of life; Lachesis determines its length; and Atropos cuts it off.

grand programme of Providence that was drawn up a long time ago. It came in as a sort of brief interlude and solo between more extensive performances. I take it that this part of the bill must have run something like this:

"*Grand Contested Election for the Presidency*
of the United States.
"WHALING VOYAGE BY ONE ISHMAEL.
"BLOODY BATTLE IN AFFGHANISTAN."

Though I cannot tell why it was exactly that those stage managers, the Fates, put me down for this shabby part of a whaling voyage, when others were set down for magnificent parts in high tragedies, and short and easy parts in genteel comedies, and jolly parts in farces—though I cannot tell why this was exactly; yet, now that I recall all the circumstances, I think I can see a little into the springs and motives which being cunningly presented to me under various disguises, induced me to set about performing the part I did, besides cajoling me into the delusion that it was a choice resulting from my own unbiased freewill and discriminating judgment.

Chief among these motives was the overwhelming idea of the great whale himself. Such a portentous and mysterious monster roused all my curiosity. Then the wild and distant seas where he rolled his island bulk; the undeliverable, nameless perils of the whale; these, with all the attending marvels of a thousand Patagonian sights and sounds, helped to sway me to my wish. With other men, perhaps, such things would not have been inducements; but as for me, I am tormented with an everlasting itch for things remote. I love to sail forbidden seas, and land on barbarous coasts. Not ignoring what is good, I am quick to perceive a horror, and could still be social with it—would they let me—since it is but well to be on friendly terms with all the inmates of the place one lodges in.

By reason of these things, then, the whaling voyage was welcome; the great flood-gates of the wonder-world swung open, and in the wild conceits that swayed me to my purpose, two and two there floated into my inmost soul, endless processions of the whale, and, midmost of them all, one grand hooded phantom, like a snow hill in the air.

Chapter 2

THE CARPET-BAG

I stuffed a shirt or two into my old carpet-bag, tucked it under my arm, and started for Cape Horn and the Pacific. Quitting the good city of old Manhatto, I duly arrived in New Bedford. It was on a Saturday night in December. Much was I disappointed upon learning that the little packet for Nantucket had already sailed, and that no way of reaching that place would offer, till the following Monday.

As most young candidates for the pains and penalties of whaling stop at this same New Bedford, thence to embark on their voyage, it may as well be related that I, for one, had no idea of so doing. For my mind was made up to sail in no other than a Nantucket craft, because there was a fine, boisterous something about everything connected with that famous old island, which amazingly pleased me. Besides though New Bedford has of late been gradually monopolizing the business of whaling, and though in this matter poor old Nantucket is now much behind her, yet Nantucket was her great original—the Tyre of this Carthage;— the place where the first dead American whale was stranded. Where else but from Nantucket did those aboriginal whalemen, the Red-Men, first sally out in canoes to give chase to the Leviathan? And where but from Nantucket, too, did that first adventurous little sloop put forth, partly laden with imported cobble-stones—so goes the story—to throw at the whales, in order to discover when they were nigh enough to risk a harpoon from the bowsprit?

Now having a night, a day, and still another night following before me in New Bedford, ere I could embark for my destined port, it became a matter of concernment where I was to eat and sleep meanwhile. It was a very dubious-looking, nay, a very dark and dismal night, bitingly cold and cheerless. I knew no one in the place. With anxious grapnels I had sounded my pocket, and only brought up a few pieces of silver,—So, wherever you go, Ishmael, said I to myself, as I stood in the middle of a dreary street shouldering my bag, and comparing the gloom towards the north with the darkness towards the south—wherever in your wisdom you may conclude to lodge for the night, my dear Ishmael, be sure to inquire the price, and don't be too particular.

With halting steps I paced the streets, and passed the sign of "The Crossed Harpoons"—but it looked too expensive and jolly there. Further on, from the bright red windows of the "Sword-Fish Inn," there came such fervent rays, that it seemed to have melted the packed snow and ice from before the house, for everywhere else the congealed frost lay ten inches thick in a hard, asphaltic pavement,—rather weary for me, when I struck my foot against the flinty projections, because from hard, remorseless service the soles of my boots were in a most miserable plight. Too expensive and jolly, again thought I, pausing one moment to watch the broad glare in the street, and hear the sounds of the tinkling glasses within. But go on, Ishmael, said I at last; don't you hear? get away from before the door; your patched boots are stopping the way. So on I went. I now by instinct followed the streets that took me waterward, for there, doubtless, were the cheapest, if not the cheeriest inns.

Such dreary streets! blocks of blackness, not houses, on either hand, and here and there a candle, like a candle moving about in a tomb. At this hour of the night, of the last day of the week, that quarter of the town proved all but deserted. But presently I came to a smoky light proceeding from a low, wide building, the door of which stood invitingly open. It had a careless look, as if it were meant for the uses of the public; so, entering, the first thing I did was to stumble over an ash-box in the porch. Ha! thought I, ha, as the flying particles almost choked me, are these ashes from that destroyed city, Gomorrah? [1] But "The Crossed Harpoons," and "The Sword-Fish?"—this, then, must needs be the sign of "The Trap." However, I picked myself up and hearing a loud voice within, pushed on and opened a second, interior door.

It seemed the great Black Parliament sitting in Tophet.[2] A hundred black faces turned round in their rows to peer; and beyond, a black Angel of Doom was beating a book in a pulpit. It was a negro church; and the preacher's text was about the blackness of darkness, and the weeping and wailing and teeth-gnashing there. Ha, Ishmael, muttered I, backing out, Wretched entertainment at the sign of "The Trap!"

Moving on, I at last came to a dim sort of out-hanging light not far from the docks, and heard a forlorn creaking in the air; and looking up, saw a swinging sign over the door with a white painting upon it, faintly representing a tall straight jet of misty spray, and these words underneath—"The Spouter-Inn:—Peter Coffin."

Coffin? — Spouter? — Rather ominous in that particular connexion, thought I. But it is a common name in Nantucket, they say, and I suppose this Peter here is an emigrant from there. As the light looked so dim, and the place, for the time, looked quiet enough, and the dilapidated little wooden house itself looked as if it might have been carted here from the ruins of some burnt district, and as the swinging sign had a poverty-stricken sort of creak to it, I thought that here was the very spot for cheap lodgings, and the best of pea coffee.

It was a queer sort of place—a gable-ended old house, one side

1. In Genesis 19, God destroys Sodom and Gomorrah, the wicked cities of the plain, by raining fire and brimstone upon them.
2. Hell.

palsied as it were, and leaning over sadly. It stood on a sharp bleak corner, where that tempestuous wind Euroclydon kept up a worse howling than ever it did about poor Paul's tossed craft. Euroclydon,[3] nevertheless, is a mighty pleasant zephyr to any one in-doors, with his feet on the hob quietly toasting for bed. "In judging of that tempestuous wind called Euroclydon," says an old writer—of whose works I possess the only copy extant—"it maketh a marvellous difference, whether thou lookest out at it from a glass window where the frost is all on the outside, or whether thou observest it from that sashless window, where the frost is on both sides, and of which the wight Death is the only glazier." True enough, thought I, as this passage occurred to my mind—old black-letter,[4] thou reasonest well. Yes, these eyes are windows, and this body of mine is the house. What a pity they didn't stop up the chinks and the crannies though, and thrust in a little lint here and there. But it's too late to make any improvements now. The universe is finished; the copestone is on, and the chips were carted off a million years ago. Poor Lazarus[5] there, chattering his teeth against the curbstone for his pillow, and shaking off his tatters with his shiverings, he might plug up both ears with rags, and put a corn-cob into his mouth, and yet that would not keep out the tempestuous Euroclydon. Euroclydon! says old Dives, in his red silken wrapper (he had a redder one afterwards)—pooh, pooh! What a fine frosty night; how Orion glitters; what northern lights! Let them talk of their oriental summer climes of everlasting conservatories; give me the privilege of making my own summer with my own coals.

But what thinks Lazarus? Can he warm his blue hands by holding them up to the grand northern lights? Would not Lazarus rather be in Sumatra than here? Would he not far rather lay him down lengthwise along the line of the equator; yea, ye gods! go down to the fiery pit itself, in order to keep out this frost?

Now, that Lazarus should lie stranded there on the curbstone before the door of Dives, this is more wonderful than that an iceberg should be moored to one of the Moluccas. Yet Dives himself, he too lives like a Czar in an ice palace made of frozen sighs, and being a president of a temperance society, he only drinks the tepid tears of orphans.

But no more of this blubbering now, we are going a-whaling,

3. A "tempestuous wind, called Euroclydon," buffets Paul's ship in Acts 27. The old writer is presumably Ishmael's invention.
4. From the name of the type in the earliest printed books, resembling the script of medieval manuscripts.
5. In the biblical parable Lazarus is a beggar who is saved, while a rich man (Dives) is damned to the fires of Hell. See Luke 16: 19-31.

and there is plenty of that yet to come. Let us scrape the ice from our frosted feet, and see what sort of a place this "Spouter" may be.

Chapter 3

THE SPOUTER-INN

Entering that gable-ended Spouter-Inn, you found yourself in a wide, low, straggling entry with old-fashioned wainscots, reminding one of the bulwarks of some condemned old craft. On one side hung a very large oil-painting so thoroughly be-smoked, and every way defaced, that in the unequal cross-lights by which you viewed it, it was only by diligent study and a series of systematic visits to it, and careful inquiry of the neighbors, that you could any way arrive at an understanding of its purpose. Such unaccountable masses of shades and shadows, that at first you almost thought some ambitious young artist, in the time of the New England hags, had endeavored to delineate chaos bewitched. But by dint of much and earnest contemplation, and oft repeated ponderings, and especially by throwing open the little window towards the back of the entry, you at last came to the conclusion that such an idea, however wild, might not be altogether unwarranted.

But what most puzzled and confounded you was a long, limber, portentous, black mass of something hovering in the centre of the picture over three blue, dim, perpendicular lines floating in a nameless yeast. A boggy, soggy, squitchy picture truly, enough to drive a nervous man distracted. Yet was there a sort of indefinite, half-attained, unimaginable sublimity about it that fairly froze you to it, till you involuntarily took an oath with yourself to find out what that marvellous painting meant. Ever and anon a bright, but, alas, deceptive idea would dart you through.—It's the Black Sea in a midnight gale.—It's the unnatural combat of the four primal elements.—It's a blasted heath.—It's a Hyperborean winter scene.—It's the breaking-up of the ice-bound stream of Time. But at last all these fancies yielded to that one portentous something in the picture's midst. *That* once found out, and all the rest were plain. But stop; does it not bear a faint resemblance to a gigantic fish? even the great leviathan himself?

In fact, the artist's design seemed this: a final theory of my own, partly based upon the aggregated opinions of many aged persons with whom I conversed upon the subject. The picture represents a Cape-Horner in a great hurricane; the half-foundered ship weltering there with its three dismantled masts alone visible; and an exasperated whale, purposing to spring clean over the craft,

is in the enormous act of impaling himself upon the three mast-
heads.

The opposite wall of this entry was hung all over with a heathenish array of monstrous clubs and spears. Some were thickly
set with glittering teeth resembling ivory saws; others were tufted
with knots of human hair; and one was sickle-shaped, with a vast
handle sweeping round like the segment made in the new-mown
grass by a long-armed mower. You shuddered as you gazed, and
wondered what monstrous cannibal and savage could ever have gone
a death-harvesting with such a hacking, horrifying implement.
Mixed with these were rusty old whaling lances and harpoons all
broken and deformed. Some were storied weapons. With this once
long lance, now wildly elbowed, fifty years ago did Nathan Swain
kill fifteen whales between a sunrise and a sunset. And that harpoon—so like a corkscrew now—was flung in Javan seas, and run
away with by a whale, years afterwards slain off the Cape of Blanco.
The original iron entered nigh the tail, and, like a restless needle
sojourning in the body of a man, travelled full forty feet, and at
last was found imbedded in the hump.

Crossing this dusky entry, and on through yon low-arched way
—cut through what in old times must have been a great central
chimney with fire-places all round—you enter the public room. A
still duskier place is this, with such low ponderous beams above,
and such old wrinkled planks beneath, that you would almost
fancy you trod some old craft's cockpits, especially of such a howling night, when this corner-anchored old ark rocked so furiously.
On one side stood a long, low, shelf-like table covered with
cracked glass cases, filled with dusty rarities gathered from this
wide world's remotest nooks. Projecting from the further angle
of the room stands a dark-looking den—the bar—a rude attempt
at a right whale's head. Be that how it may, there stands the vast
arched bone of the whale's jaw, so wide, a coach might almost
drive beneath it. Within are shabby shelves, ranged round with
old decanters, bottles, flasks; and in those jaws of swift destruction,
like another cursed Jonah [1] (by which name indeed they called
him), bustles a little withered old man, who, for their money,
dearly sells the sailors deliriums and death.

Abominable are the tumblers into which he pours his poison.
Though true cylinders without—within, the villanous green gog-
gling glasses deceitfully tapered downwards to a cheating bottom.
Parallel meridians rudely pecked into the glass, surround these
footpads' goblets. Fill to *this* mark, and your charge is but a penny;

1. See Jonah 1-2.

to *this* a penny more; and so on to the full glass—the Cape Horn measure, which you may gulp down for a shilling.

Upon entering the place I found a number of young seamen gathered about a table, examining by a dim light divers specimens of *skrimshander*.[2] I sought the landlord, and telling him I desired to be accommodated with a room, received for answer that his house was full—not a bed unoccupied. "But avast," he added, tapping his forehead, "you haint no objections to sharing a harpooneer's blanket, have ye? I s'pose you are goin' a whalin', so you'd better get used to that sort of thing."

I told him that I never liked to sleep two in a bed; that if I should ever do so, it would depend upon who the harpooneer might be, and that if he (the landlord) really had no other place for me, and the harpooneer was not decidedly objectionable, why rather than wander further about a strange town on so bitter a night, I would put up with the half of any decent man's blanket.

"I thought so. All right; take a seat. Supper?—you want supper? Supper 'll be ready directly."

I sat down on an old wooden settle, carved all over like a bench on the Battery. At one end a ruminating tar was still further adorning it with his jack-knife, stooping over and diligently working away at the space between his legs. He was trying his hand at a ship under full sail, but he didn't make much headway, I thought.

At last some four or five of us were summoned to our meal in an adjoining room. It was cold as Iceland—no fire at all—the landlord said he couldn't afford it. Nothing but two dismal tallow candles, each in a winding sheet. We were fain to button up our monkey jackets, and hold to our lips cups of scalding tea with our half frozen fingers. But the fare was of the most substantial kind —not only meat and potatoes, but dumplings; good heavens! dumplings for supper! One young fellow in a green box coat, addressed himself to these dumplings in a most direful manner.

"My boy," said the landlord, "you'll have the nightmare to a dead sartainty."

"Landlord," I whispered, "that aint the harpooneer, is it?"

"Oh, no," said he, looking a sort of diabolically funny, "the harpooner is a dark complexioned chap. He never eats dumplings, he don't—he eats nothing but steaks, and likes 'em rare."

"The devil he does," says I. "Where is that harpooneer? Is he here?"

"He'll be here afore long," was the answer.

I could not help it, but I began to feel suspicious of this "dark complexioned" harpooneer. At any rate, I made up my mind that

2. Also called scrimshaw. See Melville's definition, Chapter 57, paragraph two.

if it so turned out that we should sleep together, he must undress and get into bed before I did.

Supper over, the company went back to the bar-room, when, knowing not what else to do with myself, I resolved to spend the rest of the evening as a looker on.

Presently a rioting noise was heard without. Starting up, the landlord cried, "That's the Grampus's crew. I seed her reported in the offing this morning; a three years' voyage, and a full ship. Hurrah, boys; now we'll have the latest news from the Feegees."

A tramping of sea boots was heard in the entry; the door was flung open, and in rolled a wild set of mariners enough. Enveloped in their shaggy watch coats, and with their heads muffled in woollen comforters, all bedarned and ragged, and their beards stiff with icicles, they seemed an eruption of bears from Labrador. They had just landed from their boat, and this was the first house they entered. No wonder, then, that they made a straight wake for the whale's mouth—the bar—when the wrinkled little old Jonah, there officiating, soon poured them out brimmers all round. One complained of a bad cold in his head, upon which Jonah mixed him a pitch-like potion of gin and molasses, which he swore was a sovereign cure for all colds and catarrhs whatsoever, never mind of how long standing, or whether caught off the coast of Labrador, or on the weather side of an ice-island.

The liquor soon mounted into their heads, as it generally does even with the arrantest topers newly landed from sea, and they began capering about most obstreperously.

I observed, however, that one of them held somewhat aloof, and though he seemed desirous not to spoil the hilarity of his shipmates by his own sober face, yet upon the whole he refrained from making as much noise as the rest. This man interested me at once; and since the sea-gods had ordained that he should soon become my shipmate (though but a sleeping-partner [3] one, so far as this narrative is concerned), I will here venture upon a little description of him. He stood full six feet in height, with noble shoulders, and a chest like a coffer-dam.[4] I have seldom seen such brawn in a man. His face was deeply brown and burnt, making his white teeth dazzling by the contrast; while in the deep shadows of his eyes floated some reminiscences that did not seem to give him much joy. His voice at once announced that he was a Southerner, and from his fine stature, I thought he must be one of those tall mountaineers from the Alleghanian Ridge in Virginia. When the revelry of his companions had mounted to its height, this man slipped away unobserved, and I saw no more of him till he

3. Not bunkmate but a "silent partner," that is a partner who takes no visible part in the business.

4. A watertight structure from which repairs can be made on a ship below the waterline.

became my comrade on the sea. In a few minutes, however, he was missed by his shipmates, and being, it seems, for some reason a huge favorite with them, they raised a cry of "Bulkington! Bulkington! where's Bulkington?" and darted out of the house in pursuit of him.

It was now about nine o'clock, and the room seeming almost supernaturally quiet after these orgies, I began to congratulate myself upon a little plan that had occurred to me just previous to the entrance of the seamen.

No man prefers to sleep two in a bed. In fact, you would a good deal rather not sleep with your own brother. I don't know how it is, but people like to be private when they are sleeping. And when it comes to sleeping with an unknown stranger, in a strange inn, in a strange town, and that stranger a harpooneer, then your objections indefinitely multiply. Nor was there any earthly reason why I as a sailor should sleep two in a bed, more than anybody else; for sailors no more sleep two in a bed at sea, than bachelor Kings do ashore. To be sure they all sleep together in one apartment, but you have your own hammock, and cover yourself with your own blanket, and sleep in your own skin.

The more I pondered over this harpooneer, the more I abominated the thought of sleeping with him. It was fair to presume that being a harpooneer, his linen or woollen, as the case might be, would not be of the tidiest, certainly none of the finest. I began to twitch all over. Besides, it was getting late, and any decent harpooneer ought to be home and going bed-wards. Suppose now, he should tumble in upon me at midnight—how could I tell from what vile hole he had been coming?

"Landlord! I've changed my mind about that harpooneer.—I shan't sleep with him. I'll try the bench here."

"Just as you please; I'm sorry I cant spare ye a table-cloth for a mattress, and it's a plaguy rough board here"—feeling of the knots and notches. "But wait a bit, Skrimshander; I've got a carpenter's plane there in the bar—wait, I say, and I'll make ye snug enough." So saying he procured the plane; and with his old silk handkerchief first dusting the bench, vigorously set to planing away at my bed, the while grinning like an ape. The shavings flew right and left; till at last the plane-iron came bump against an indestructible knot. The landlord was near spraining his wrist, and I told him for heaven's sake to quit—the bed was soft enough to suit me, and I did not know how all the planing in the world could make eider down of a pine plank. So gathering up the shavings with another grin, and throwing them into the great stove in the middle of the room, he went about his business, and left me in a brown study.

I now took the measure of the bench, and found that it was a foot too short; but that could be mended with a chair. But it was a foot too narrow, and the other bench in the room was about four inches higher than the planed one—so there was no yoking them. I then placed the first bench lengthwise along the only clear space against the wall, leaving a little interval between, for my back to settle down in. But I soon found that there came such a draught of cold air over me from under the sill of the window, that this plan would never do at all, especially as another current from the rickety door met the one from the window, and both together formed a series of small whirlwinds in the immediate vicinity of the spot where I had thought to spend the night.

The devil fetch that harpooneer, thought I, but stop, couldn't I steal a march on him—bolt his door inside, and jump into his bed, not to be wakened by the most violent knockings? It seemed no bad idea; but upon second thoughts I dismissed it. For who could tell but what the next morning, so soon as I popped out of the room, the harpooneer might be standing in the entry, all ready to knock me down!

Still, looking round me again, and seeing no possible chance of spending a sufferable night unless in some other person's bed, I began to think that after all I might be cherishing unwarrantable prejudices against this unknown harpooneer. Thinks I, I'll wait awhile; he must be dropping in before long. I'll have a good look at him then, and perhaps we may become jolly good bedfellows after all—there's no telling.

But though the other boarders kept coming in by ones, twos, and threes, and going to bed, yet no sign of my harpooneer.

"Landlord!" said I, "what sort of a chap is he—does he always keep such late hours?" It was now hard upon twelve o'clock.

The landlord chuckled again with his lean chuckle, and seemed to be mightily tickled at something beyond my comprehension. "No," he answered, "generally he's an airley bird—airley to bed and airley to rise—yes, he's the bird what catches the worm.—But to-night he went out a peddling, you see, and I don't see what on airth keeps him so late, unless, may be, he can't sell his head."

"Can't sell his head?—What sort of a bamboozling story is this you are telling me?" getting into a towering rage. "Do you pretend to say, landlord, that this harpooneer is actually engaged this blessed Saturday night, or rather Sunday morning, in peddling his head around this town?"

"That's precisely it," said the landlord, "and I told him he couldn't sell it here, the market's overstocked."

"With what?" shouted I.

"With heads to be sure; ain't there too many heads in the world?"

"I tell you what it is, landlord," said I, quite calmly, "you'd better stop spinning that yarn to me—I'm not green."

"May be not," taking out a stick and whittling a toothpick, "but I rayther guess you'll be done *brown* if that ere harpooneer hears you a slanderin' his head."

"I'll break it for him," said I, now flying into a passion again at this unaccountable farrago of the landlord's.

"It's broke a'ready," said he.

"Broke," said I—"*broke,* do you mean?"

"Sartain, and that's the very reason he can't sell it, I guess."

"Landlord," said I, going up to him as cool as Mt. Hecla in a snow storm,[5]—"landlord, stop whittling. You and I must understand one another, and that too without delay. I come to your house and want a bed; you tell me you can only give me half a one; that the other half belongs to a certain harpooneer. And about this harpooneer, whom I have not yet seen, you persist in telling me the most mystifying and exasperating stories, tending to beget in me an uncomfortable feeling towards the man whom you design for my bedfellow—a sort of connexion, landlord, which is an intimate and confidential one in the highest degree. I now demand of you to speak out and tell me who and what this harpooneer is, and whether I shall be in all respects safe to spend the night with him. And in the first place, you will be so good as to unsay that story about selling his head, which if true I take to be good evidence that this harpooneer is stark mad, and I've no idea of sleeping with a madman; and you, sir, *you* I mean, landlord, *you,* sir, by trying to induce me to do so knowingly, would thereby render yourself liable to a criminal prosecution."

"Wall," said the landlord, fetching a long breath, "that's a purty long sarmon for a chap that rips a little now and then. But be easy, be easy, this here harpooneer I have been tellin' you of has just arrived from the south seas, where he bought up a lot of 'balmed New Zealand heads (great curios, you know), and he's sold all on 'em but one, and that one he's trying to sell to-night, cause to-morrow's Sunday, and it would not do to be sellin' human heads about the streets when folks is goin' to churches. He wanted to, last Sunday, but I stopped him just as he was goin' out of the door with four heads strung on a string, for all the airth like a string of onions."

This account cleared up the otherwise unaccountable mystery, and showed that the landlord, after all, had had no idea of fooling me—but at the same time what could I think of a harpooneer who stayed out of a Saturday night clean into the holy Sabbath,

---

5. Externally cool but inwardly furious.   an active volcano.
Mt. Hecla, in Iceland, well known as

engaged in such a cannibal business as selling the heads of dead idolators?

"Depend upon it, landlord, that harpooneer is a dangerous man."

"He pays reg'lar," was the rejoinder. "But come, it's getting dreadful late, you had better be turning flukes—it's a nice bed: Sal and me slept in that ere bed the night we were spliced. There's plenty room for two to kick about in that bed; it's an almighty big bed that. Why, afore we give it up, Sal used to put our Sam and little Johnny in the foot of it. But I got a dreaming and sprawling about one night, and somehow, Sam got pitched on the floor, and came near breaking his arm. Arter that, Sal said it wouldn't do. Come along here, I'll give ye a glim in a jiffy;" and so saying he lighted a candle and held it towards me, offering to lead the way. But I stood irresolute; when looking at a clock in the corner, he exclaimed, "I vum it's Sunday—you won't see that harpooneer to-night; he's come to anchor somewhere—come along then; *do* come; *won't* ye come?"

I considered the matter a moment, and then up stairs we went, and I was ushered into a small room, cold as a clam, and furnished, sure enough, with a prodigious bed, almost big enough indeed for any four harpooneers to sleep abreast.

"There," said the landlord, placing the candle on a crazy old sea chest that did double duty as a wash-stand and centre table; "there, make yourself comfortable now, and good night to ye." I turned round from eyeing the bed, but he had disappeared.

Folding back the counterpane, I stooped over the bed. Though none of the most elegant, it yet stood the scrutiny tolerably well. I then glanced round the room; and besides the bedstead and centre table, could see no other furniture belonging to the place, but a rude shelf, the four walls, and a papered fireboard representing a man striking a whale. Of things not properly belonging to the room, there was a hammock lashed up, and thrown upon the floor in one corner; also a large seaman's bag, containing the harpooneer's wardrobe, no doubt in lieu of a land trunk. Likewise, there was a parcel of outlandish bone fish hooks on the shelf over the fire-place, and a tall harpoon standing at the head of the bed.

But what is this on the chest? I took it up, and held it close to the light, and felt it, and smelt it, and tried every way possible to arrive at some satisfactory conclusion concerning it. I can compare it to nothing but a large door mat, ornamented at the edges with little tinkling tags something like the stained porcupine quills round an Indian moccasin. There was a hole or slit in the middle of this mat, the same as in South American ponchos. But could it be possible that any sober harpooneer would get into a door mat, and parade the streets of any Christian town in that sort of guise? I put it on, to try it, and it weighed me down like a hamper, being uncommonly shaggy and thick, and I thought a little damp, as though this mysterious harpooneer had been wearing it of a rainy day. I went up in it to a bit of glass stuck against the wall, and I never saw such a sight in my life. I tore myself out of it in such a hurry that I gave myself a kink in the neck.

I sat down on the side of the bed, and commenced thinking about this head-peddling harpooneer, and his door mat. After thinking some time on the bed-side, I got up and took off my monkey jacket, and then stood in the middle of the room thinking. I then took off my coat, and thought a little more in my shirt sleeves. But beginning to feel very cold now, half undressed as I was, and remembering what the landlord said about the harpooneer's not coming home at all that night, it being so very late, I made no more ado, but jumped out of my pantaloons and boots, and then blowing out the light tumbled into bed, and commended myself to the care of heaven.

Whether that mattress was stuffed with corn-cobs or broken crockery, there is no telling, but I rolled about a good deal, and could not sleep for a long time. At last I slid off into a light doze, and had pretty nearly made a good offing towards the land of Nod, when I heard a heavy footfall in the passage, and saw a glimmer of light come into the room from under the door.

Lord save me, thinks I, that must be the harpooneer, the infernal head-peddler. But I lay perfectly still, and resolved not to say a word till spoken to. Holding a light in one hand, and that identical New Zealand head in the other, the stranger entered the room, and without looking towards the bed, placed his candle a good way off from me on the floor in one corner, and then began working away at the knotted cords of the large bag I before spoke of as being in the room. I was all eagerness to see his face, but he kept it averted for some time while employed in unlacing the bag's mouth. This accomplished, however, he turned round—when, good heavens! what a sight! Such a face! It was of a dark, purplish, yellow color, here and there stuck over with large, blackish looking squares. Yes, it's just as I thought, he's a terrible bedfellow; he's been in a fight, got dreadfully cut, and here he is, just from the surgeon. But at that moment he chanced to turn his face so towards the light, that I plainly saw they could not be sticking-plasters at all, those black squares on his cheeks. They were stains of some sort or other. At first I knew not what to make of this; but soon an inkling of the truth occurred to me. I remembered a story of a white man—a whaleman too—who, falling among the cannibals, had been tattooed by them. I concluded that this harpooneer, in the course of his distant voyages, must have met with a similar adventure. And what is it, thought I, after all! It's only his outside; a man can be honest in any sort of skin. But then, what to make of his unearthly complexion, that part of it, I mean, lying round about, and completely independent of the squares of tattooing. To be sure, it might be nothing but a good coat of tropical tanning; but I never heard of a hot sun's tanning a white man into a purplish yellow one. However, I had never been in the South Seas; and perhaps the sun there produced these extraordinary effects upon the skin. Now, while all these ideas were passing through me like lightning, this harpooneer never noticed me at all. But, after some difficulty having opened his bag, he commenced fumbling in it, and presently pulled out a sort of tomahawk, and a seal-skin wallet with the hair on. Placing these on the old chest in the middle of the room, he then took the New Zealand head—a ghastly thing enough—and crammed it down into the bag. He now took off his hat—a new beaver hat—when I came nigh singing out with fresh surprise. There was no hair on his head—none to speak of at least—nothing but a small scalp-knot twisted up on his forehead. His bald purplish head now looked for all the world like a mildewed skull. Had not the stranger stood between me and the door, I would have bolted out of it quicker than ever I bolted a dinner.

Even as it was, I thought something of slipping out of the window, but it was the second floor back. I am no coward, but what to make of this head-peddling purple rascal altogether passed my comprehension. Ignorance is the parent of fear, and being completely nonplussed and confounded about the stranger, I confess I was now as much afraid of him as if it was the devil himself who had thus broken into my room at the dead of night. In fact, I was so afraid of him that I was not game enough just then to address him, and demand a satisfactory answer concerning what seemed inexplicable in him.

Meanwhile, he continued the business of undressing, and at last showed his chest and arms. As I live, these covered parts of him were checkered with the same squares as his face; his back, too, was all over the same dark squares; he seemed to have been in a Thirty Years' War, and just escaped from it with a sticking-plaster shirt. Still more, his very legs were marked, as if a parcel of dark green frogs were running up the trunks of young palms. It was now quite plain that he must be some abominable savage or other shipped aboard of a whaleman in the South

Seas, and so landed in this Christian country. I quaked to think of it. A peddler of heads too—perhaps the heads of his own brothers. He might take a fancy to mine—heavens! look at that tomahawk!

But there was no time for shuddering, for now the savage went about something that completely fascinated my attention, and convinced me that he must indeed be a heathen. Going to his heavy grego, or wrapall, or dreadnaught, which he had previously hung on a chair, he fumbled in the pockets, and produced at length a curious little deformed image with a hunch on its back, and exactly the color of a three days' old Congo baby. Remembering the embalmed head, at first I almost thought that this black manikin was a real baby preserved in some similar manner. But seeing that it was not at all limber, and that it glistened a good deal like polished ebony, I concluded that it must be nothing but a wooden idol, which indeed it proved to be. For now the savage goes up to the empty fire-place, and removing the papered fire-board, sets up this little hunchbacked image, like a tenpin, between the andirons. The chimney jambs and all the bricks inside were very sooty, so that I thought this fire-place made a very appropriate little shrine or chapel for his Congo idol.

I now screwed my eyes hard towards the half hidden image, feeling but ill at ease meantime—to see what was next to follow. First he takes about a double handful of shavings out of his grego pocket, and places them carefully before the idol; then laying a bit of ship biscuit on top and applying the flame from the lamp, he kindled the shavings into a sacrificial blaze. Presently, after many hasty snatches into the fire, and still hastier withdrawals of his fingers (whereby he seemed to be scorching them badly), he at last succeeded in drawing out the biscuit; then blowing off the heat and ashes a little, he made a polite offer of it to the little negro. But the little devil did not seem to fancy such dry sort of fare at all; he never moved his lips. All these strange antics were accompanied by still stranger guttural noises from the devotee, who seemed to be praying in a sing-song or else singing some pagan psalmody or other, during which his face twitched about in the most unnatural manner. At last extinguishing the fire, he took the idol up very unceremoniously, and bagged it again in his grego pocket as carelessly as if he were a sportsman bagging a dead woodcock.

All these queer proceedings increased my uncomfortableness, and seeing him now exhibiting strong symptoms of concluding his business operations, and jumping into bed with me, I thought it was high time, now or never, before the light was put out, to break the spell in which I had so long been bound.

But the interval I spent in deliberating what to say, was a fatal one. Taking up his tomahawk from the table, he examined the head of it for an instant, and then holding it to the light, with his mouth at the handle, he puffed out great clouds of tobacco smoke. The next moment the light was extinguished, and this wild cannibal, tomahawk between his teeth, sprang into bed with me. I sang out, I could not help it now; and giving a sudden grunt of astonishment he began feeling me.

Stammering out something, I knew not what, I rolled away from him against the wall, and then conjured him, whoever or whatever he might be, to keep quiet, and let me get up and light the lamp again. But his guttural responses satisfied me at once that he but ill comprehended my meaning.

"Who-e debel you?"—he at last said—"you no speak-e, damme, I kill-e." And so saying the lighted tomahawk began flourishing about me in the dark.

"Landlord, for God's sake, Peter Coffin!" shouted I. "Landlord! Watch! Coffin! Angels! save me!"

"Speak-e! tell-ee me who-ee be, or dam-me, I kill-e!" again growled the cannibal, while his horrid flourishings of the tomahawk scattered the hot tobacco ashes about me till I thought my linen would get on fire. But thank heaven, at that moment the landlord came into the room light in hand, and leaping from the bed I ran up to him.

"Don't be afraid now," said he, grinning again. "Queequeg here wouldn't harm a hair of your head."

"Stop your grinning," shouted I, "and why didn't you tell me that that infernal harpooneer was a cannibal?"

"I thought ye know'd it;—didn't I tell ye, he was a peddlin' heads around town?—but turn flukes again and go to sleep. Queequeg, look here—you sabbee me, I sabbee you—this man sleepe you—you sabbee?"—

"Me sabbee plenty"—grunted Queequeg, puffing away at his pipe and sitting up in bed.

"You gettee in," he added, motioning to me with his tomahawk, and throwing the clothes to one side. He really did this in not only a civil but a really kind and charitable way. I stood looking at him a moment. For all his tattooings he was on the whole a clean, comely looking cannibal. What's all this fuss I have been making about, thought I to myself—the man's a human being just as I am: he has just as much reason to fear me, as I have to be afraid of him. Better sleep with a sober cannibal than a drunken Christian.

"Landlord," said I, "tell him to stash his tomahawk there, or pipe, or whatever you call it; tell him to stop smoking, in short, and I will turn in with him. But I don't fancy having a man smoking in bed with me. It's dangerous. Besides, I aint insured."

This being told to Queequeg, he at once complied, and again politely motioned me to get into bed—rolling over to one side as much as to say—I wont touch a leg of ye.

"Good night, landlord," said I, "you may go."

I turned in, and never slept better in my life.

Chapter 4

THE COUNTERPANE

Upon waking next morning about daylight, I found Queequeg's arm thrown over me in the most loving and affectionate manner. You had almost thought I had been his wife. The counterpane was of patchwork, full of odd little parti-colored squares and triangles; and this arm of his tattooed all over with an interminable Cretan labyrinth [1] of a figure, no two parts of which were of one precise shade—owing I suppose to his keeping his arm at sea unmethodically in sun and shade, his shirt sleeves irregularly rolled up at various times—this same arm of his, I say, looked for all the world like a strip of that same patchwork quilt. Indeed, partly lying on it as the arm did when I first awoke, I could hardly tell it from the quilt, they so blended their hues together; and it was only by the sense of weight and pressure that I could tell that Queequeg was hugging me.

My sensations were strange. Let me try to explain them. When I was a child, I well remember a somewhat similar circumstance that befell me; whether it was a reality or a dream, I never could entirely settle. The circumstance was this. I had been cutting up some caper or other—I think it was trying to crawl up the chimney, as I had seen a little sweep do a few days previous; and my step-mother who, somehow or other, was all the time whipping me, or sending me to bed supperless,—my mother dragged me by the legs out of the chimney and packed me off to bed, though it was only two o'clock in the afternoon of the 21st June, the longest day in the year in our hemisphere. I felt dreadfully. But there was no help for it, so up stairs I went to my little room in the third floor, undressed myself as slowly as possible so as to kill time, and with a bitter sigh got between the sheets.

I lay there dismally calculating that sixteen entire hours must elapse before I could hope for a resurrection. Sixteen hours in bed! the small of my back ached to think of it. And it was so light too; the sun shining in at the window, and a great rattling of coaches

1. In Greek mythology, the maze that   Minotaur.
imprisoned the half-human, half-bull

in the streets, and the sound of gay voices all over the house. I felt
worse and worse—at last I got up, dressed, and softly going down
in my stockinged feet, sought out my stepmother, and suddenly
threw myself at her feet, beseeching her as a particular favor to give
me a good slippering for my misbehavior; anything indeed but
condemning me to lie abed such an unendurable length of time.
But she was the best and most conscientious of stepmothers, and
back I had to go to my room. For several hours I lay there broad
awake, feeling a great deal worse than I have ever done since, even
from the greatest subsequent misfortunes. At last I must have
fallen into a troubled nightmare of a doze; and slowly waking from
it—half steeped in dreams—I opened my eyes, and the before sun-
lit room was now wrapped in outer darkness. Instantly I felt a
shock running through all my frame; nothing was to be seen, and
nothing was to be heard; but a supernatural hand seemed placed
in mine. My arm hung over the counterpane, and the nameless,
unimaginable, silent form or phantom, to which the hand belonged, seemed closely seated by my bed-side. For what seemed ages
piled on ages, I lay there, frozen with the most awful fears, not
daring to drag away my hand; yet ever thinking that if I could but
stir it one single inch, the horrid spell would be broken. I knew not
how this consciousness at last glided away from me; but waking
in the morning, I shudderingly remembered it all, and for days and
weeks and months afterwards I lost myself in confounding attempts
to explain the mystery. Nay, to this very hour, I often puzzle myself with it.

Now, take away the awful fear, and my sensations at feeling the
supernatural hand in mine were very similar, in their strangeness, to
those which I experienced on waking up and seeing Queequeg's
pagan arm thrown round me. But at length all the past night's
events soberly recurred, one by one, in fixed reality, and then I
lay only alive to the comical predicament. For though I tried to
move his arm—unlock his bridegroom clasp—yet, sleeping as he
was, he still hugged me tightly, as though naught but death
should part us twain. I now strove to rouse him—"Queequeg!"—
but his only answer was a snore. I then rolled over, my neck
feeling as if it were in a horse-collar; and suddenly felt a slight
scratch. Throwing aside the counterpane, there lay the tomahawk
sleeping by the savage's side, as if it were a hatchet-faced baby. A
pretty pickle, truly, thought I; abed here in a strange house in the
broad day, with a cannibal and a tomahawk! "Queequeg!—in the
name of goodness, Queequeg, wake!" At length, by dint of much
wriggling, and loud and incessant expostulations upon the unbe-
comingness of his hugging a fellow male in that matrimonial sort

of style, I succeeded in extracting a grunt; and presently, he drew back his arm, shook himself all over like a Newfoundland dog just from the water, and sat up in bed, stiff as a pike-staff, looking at me, and rubbing his eyes as if he did not altogether remember how I came to be there, though a dim consciousness of knowing something about me seemed slowly dawning over him. Meanwhile, I lay quietly eyeing him, having no serious misgivings now, and bent upon narrowly observing so curious a creature. When, at last, his mind seemed made up touching the character of his bedfellow, and he became, as it were, reconciled to the fact; he jumped out upon the floor, and by certain signs and sounds gave me to understand that, if it pleased me, he would dress first and then leave me to dress afterwards, having the whole apartment to myself. Thinks I, Queequeg, under the circumstances, this is a very civilized overture; but, the truth is, these savages have an innate sense of delicacy, say what you will; it is marvellous how essentially polite they are. I pay this particular compliment to Queequeg, because he treated me with so much civility and consideration, while I was guilty of great rudeness; staring at him from the bed, and watching all his toilette motions; for the time my curiosity getting the better of my breeding. Nevertheless, a man like Queequeg you don't see every day, he and his ways were well worth unusual regarding.

He commenced dressing at top by donning his beaver hat, a very tall one, by the by, and then—still minus his trowsers—he hunted up his boots. What under the heavens he did it for, I cannot tell, but his next movement was to crush himself—boots in hand, and hat on—under the bed; when, from sundry violent gaspings and strainings, I inferred he was hard at work booting himself; though by no law of propriety that I ever heard of, is any man required to be private when putting on his boots. But Queequeg, do you see, was a creature in the transition state—neither caterpillar nor butterfly. He was just enough civilized to show off his outlandishness in the strangest possible manner. His education was not yet completed. He was an undergraduate. If he had not been a small degree civilized, he very probably would not have troubled himself with boots at all; but then, if he had not been still a savage, he never would have dreamt of getting under the bed to put them on. At last, he emerged with his hat very much dented and crushed down over his eyes, and began creaking and limping about the room, as if, not being much accustomed to boots, his pair of damp, wrinkled cowhide ones—probably not made to order either—rather pinched and tormented him at the first go off of a bitter cold morning.

Seeing, now, that there were no curtains to the window, and that the street being very narrow, the house opposite commanded a plain view into the room, and observing more and more the indecorous figure that Queequeg made, staving about with little else but his hat and boots on; I begged him as well as I could, to accelerate his toilet somewhat, and particularly to get into his pantaloons as soon as possible. He complied, and then proceeded to wash himself. At that time in the morning any Christian would have washed his face; but Queequeg, to my amazement, contented himself with restricting his ablutions to his chest, arms, and hands. He then donned his waistcoat, and taking up a piece of hard soap on the wash-stand centre-table, dipped it into water and commenced lathering his face. I was watching to see where he kept his razor, when lo and behold, he takes the harpoon from the bed corner, slips out the long wooden stock, unsheathes the head, whets it a little on his boot, and striding up to the bit of mirror against the wall, begins a vigorous scraping, or rather harpooning of his cheeks. Thinks I, Queequeg, this is using Rogers's best cutlery with a vengeance. Afterwards I wondered the less at this operation when I came to know of what fine steel the head of a harpoon is made, and how exceedingly sharp the long straight edges are always kept.

The rest of his toilet was soon achieved, and he proudly marched out of the room, wrapped up in his great pilot monkey jacket, and sporting his harpoon like a marshal's baton.

Chapter 5

BREAKFAST

I quickly followed suit, and descending into the bar-room accosted the grinning landlord very pleasantly. I cherished no malice towards him, though he had been skylarking with me not a little in the matter of my bedfellow.

However, a good laugh is a mighty good thing, and rather too scarce a good thing; the more's the pity. So, if any one man, in his own proper person, afford stuff for a good joke to anybody, let him not be backward, but let him cheerfully allow himself to spend and be spent in that way. And the man that has anything bountifully laughable about him, be sure there is more in that man than you perhaps think for.

The bar-room was now full of the boarders who had been dropping in the night previous, and whom I had not as yet had a good look at. They were nearly all whalemen; chief mates, and second mates, and third mates, and sea carpenters, and sea coopers, and sea blacksmiths, and harpooneers, and ship keepers; a brown and brawny company, with bosky beards; an unshorn, shaggy set, all wearing monkey jackets for morning gowns.

You could pretty plainly tell how long each one had been ashore. This young fellow's healthy cheek is like a sun-toasted pear in hue, and would seem to smell almost as musky; he cannot have been three days landed from his Indian voyage. That man next him looks a few shades lighter; you might say a touch of satin wood is in him. In the complexion of a third still lingers a tropic tawn, but slightly bleached withal; he doubtless has tarried whole weeks ashore. But who could show a cheek like Queequeg? which, barred with various tints, seemed like the Andes' western slope, to show forth in one array, contrasting climates, zone by zone.

"Grub, ho!" now cried the landlord, flinging open a door, and in we went to breakfast.

They say that men who have seen the world, thereby become quite at ease in manner, quite self-possessed in company. Not always, though: Ledyard, the great New England traveller, and Mungo Park,[1] the Scotch one; of all men, they possessed the least assurance in the parlor. But perhaps the mere crossing of Siberia in a sledge drawn by dogs as Ledyard did, or the taking a long solitary walk on an empty stomach, in the negro heart of Africa, which was the sum of poor Mungo's performances—this kind of travel, I say, may not be the very best mode of attaining a high social polish. Still, for the most part, that sort of thing is to be had anywhere.

These reflections just here are occasioned by the circumstance that after we were all seated at the table, and I was preparing to hear some good stories about whaling; to my no small surprise, nearly every man maintained a profound silence. And not only that, but they looked embarrassed. Yes, here were a set of sea-dogs, many of whom without the slightest bashfulness had boarded great whales on the high seas—entire strangers to them—and duelled them dead without winking; and yet, here they sat at a social breakfast table—all of the same calling, all of kindred tastes—looking round as sheepishly at each other as though they had never been out of sight of some sheepfold among the Green Mountains. A curious sight; these bashful bears, these timid warrior whalemen!

But as for Queequeg—why, Queequeg sat there among them—at the head of the table, too, it so chanced; as cool as an icicle.

1. Ledyard and Mungo Park were late eighteenth-century explorers.

To be sure I cannot say much for his breeding. His greatest admirer could not have cordially justified his bringing his harpoon into breakfast with him, and using it there without ceremony; reaching over the table with it, to the imminent jeopardy of many heads, and grappling the beefsteaks towards him. But *that* was certainly very coolly done by him, and every one knows that in most people's estimation, to do anything coolly is to do it genteelly.

We will not speak of all Queequeg's peculiarities here; how he eschewed coffee and hot rolls, and applied his undivided attention to beefsteaks, done rare. Enough, that when breakfast was over he withdrew like the rest into the public room, lighted his toma-hawk-pipe, and was sitting there quietly digesting and smoking with his inseparable hat on, when I sallied out for a stroll.

Chapter 6

THE STREET

If I had been astonished at first catching a glimpse of so out-landish an individual as Queequeg circulating among the polite society of a civilized town, that astonishment soon departed upon taking my first daylight stroll through the streets of New Bedford.

In thoroughfares nigh the docks, any considerable seaport will frequently offer to view the queerest looking nondescripts from foreign parts. Even in Broadway and Chestnut streets, Mediter-ranean mariners will sometimes jostle the affrighted ladies. Re-gent street is not unknown to Lascars and Malays; and at Bombay, in the Apollo Green, live Yankees have often scared the natives. But New Bedford beats all Water street and Wapping.[1] In these last-mentioned haunts you see only sailors; but in New Bedford, actual cannibals stand chatting at street corners; savages outright; many of whom yet carry on their bones unholy flesh. It makes a stranger stare.

But, besides the Feegeeans, Tongatabooans, Erromanggoans, Pannangians, and Brighggians, and, besides the wild specimens of the whaling-craft which unheeded reel about the streets, you will see other sights still more curious, certainly more comical. There weekly arrive in this town scores of green Vermonters and New Hampshire men, all athirst for gain and glory in the fishery. They are mostly young, of stalwart frames; fellows who have felled forests, and now seek to drop the axe and snatch the whale-lance. Many are as green as the Green Mountains whence they come. In some things you would think them but a few hours old. Look

1. Broadway is in New York, Chestnut in Philadelphia, Regent and Wapping in London, and Water Street in Liver-pool.

there! that chap strutting round the corner. He wears a beaver hat and swallow-tailed coat, girdled with a sailor-belt and sheath-knife. Here comes another with a sou'-wester and a bombazine cloak.

No town-bred dandy will compare with a country-bred one—I mean a downright bumpkin dandy—a fellow that, in the dog-days, will mow his two acres in buckskin gloves for fear of tanning his hands. Now when a country dandy like this takes it into his head to make a distinguished reputation, and joins the great whale-fishery, you should see the comical things he does upon reaching the seaport. In bespeaking his sea-outfit, he orders bell-buttons to his waistcoats; straps[2] to his canvas trowsers. Ah, poor Hay-Seed! how bitterly will burst those straps in the first howling gale, when thou art driven, straps, buttons, and all, down the throat of the tempest.

But think not that this famous town has only harpooneers, cannibals, and bumpkins to show her visitors. Not at all. Still New Bedford is a queer place. Had it not been for us whalemen, that tract of land would this day perhaps have been in as howling condition as the coast of Labrador. As it is, parts of her back country are enough to frighten one, they look so bony. The town itself is perhaps the dearest place to live in, in all New England. It is a land of oil, true enough: but not like Canaan, a land, also, of corn and wine. The streets do not run with milk; nor in the spring-time do they pave them with fresh eggs. Yet, in spite of this, nowhere in all America will you find more patrician-like houses, parks and gardens more opulent, than in New Bedford. Whence came they? how planted upon this once scraggy scoria of a country?

Go and gaze upon the iron emblematical harpoons round yonder lofty mansion, and your question will be answered. Yes; all these brave houses and flowery gardens came from the Atlantic, Pacific, and Indian oceans. One and all, they were harpooned and dragged up hither from the bottom of the sea. Can Herr Alexander[3] perform a feat like that?

In New Bedford, fathers, they say, give whales for dowers to their daughters, and portion off their nieces with a few porpoises a-piece. You must go to New Bedford to see a brilliant wedding; for, they say, they have reservoirs of oil in every house, and every night recklessly burn their lengths in spermaceti candles.

In summer time, the town is sweet to see; full of fine maples—long avenues of green and gold. And in August, high in air, the beautiful and bountiful horse-chestnuts, candelabra-wise, proffer the passer-by their tapering upright cones of congregated blossoms.

---

2. Suspenders, or galluses.
3. A German magician who performed   in the United States in the 1840's.

So omnipotent is art; which in many a district of New Bedford has superinduced bright terraces of flowers upon the barren refuse rocks thrown aside at creation's final day.

And the women of New Bedford, they bloom like their own red roses. But roses only bloom in summer; whereas the fine carnation of their cheeks is perennial as sunlight in the seventh heavens. Elsewhere match that bloom of theirs, ye cannot, save in Salem, where they tell me the young girls breathe such musk, their sailor sweethearts smell them miles off shore, as though they were drawing nigh the odorous Moluccas instead of the Puritanic sands.

Chapter 7

THE CHAPEL

In this same New Bedford there stands a Whaleman's Chapel, and few are the moody fishermen, shortly bound for the Indian Ocean or Pacific, who fail to make a Sunday visit to the spot. I am sure that I did not.

Returning from my first morning stroll, I again sallied out upon this special errand. The sky had changed from clear, sunny cold, to driving sleet and mist. Wrapping myself in my shaggy jacket of the cloth called bearskin, I fought my way against the stubborn storm. Entering, I found a small scattered congregation of sailors, and sailors' wives and widows. A muffled silence reigned, only broken at times by the shrieks of the storm. Each silent worshipper seemed purposely sitting apart from the other, as if each silent grief were insular and incommunicable. The chaplain had not yet arrived; and there these silent islands of men and women sat steadfastly eyeing several marble tablets, with black borders, masoned into the wall on either side the pulpit. Three of them ran something like the following, but I do not pretend to quote:—

SACRED

To the Memory

OF

JOHN TALBOT,

Who, at the age of eighteen, was lost overboard,
Near the Isle of Desolation, off Patagonia,
November 1st, 1836.

THIS TABLET

Is erected to his Memory

BY HIS SISTER.

SACRED
To the Memory
OF
ROBERT LONG, WILLIS ELLERY,
NATHAN COLEMAN, WALTER CANNY,
SETH MACY, AND SAMUEL GLEIG,
Forming one of the boats' crews
OF
THE SHIP ELIZA,
Who were towed out of sight by a Whale,
On the Off-shore Ground in the
PACIFIC,
December 31st, 1839.
THIS MARBLE
Is here placed by their surviving
Shipmates.

———————

SACRED
To the Memory
OF
The late
CAPTAIN EZEKIEL HARDY,
Who in the bows of his boat was killed by a
Sperm Whale on the coast of Japan,
August 3d, 1833.
THIS TABLET
Is erected to his Memory

BY

HIS WIDOW.

Shaking off the sleet from my ice-glazed hat and jacket, I seated myself near the door, and turning sideways was surprised to see Queequeg near me. Affected by the solemnity of the scene, there was a wondering gaze of incredulous curiosity in his countenance. This savage was the only person present who seemed to notice my entrance; because he was the only one who could not read, and, therefore, was not reading those frigid inscriptions on the wall. Whether any of the relatives of the seamen whose names appeared there were now among the congregation, I knew not; but so many are the unrecorded accidents in the fishery, and so plainly did several women present wear the countenance if not the trappings of some unceasing grief, that I feel sure that here before me were assembled those, in whose unhealing hearts the sight of those bleak tablets sympathetically caused the old wounds to bleed afresh.

Oh! ye whose dead lie buried beneath the green grass; who standing among flowers can say—here, *here* lies my beloved; ye know not the desolation that broods in bosoms like these. What bitter blanks in those black-bordered marbles which cover no ashes! What despair in those immovable inscriptions! What deadly voids and unbidden infidelities in the lines that seem to gnaw upon all Faith, and refuse resurrections to the beings who have placelessly perished without a grave. As well might those tablets stand in the cave of Elephanta[1] as here.

In what census of living creatures, the dead of mankind are included; why it is that a universal proverb says of them, that they tell no tales, though containing more secrets than the Goodwin Sands; how it is that to his name who yesterday departed for the other world, we prefix so significant and infidel a word, and yet do not thus entitle him, if he but embarks for the remotest Indies of this living earth; why the Life Insurance Companies pay death-forfeitures upon immortals; in what eternal, unstirring paralysis, and deadly, hopeless trance, yet lies antique Adam who died sixty round centuries ago; how it is that we still refuse to be comforted for those who we nevertheless maintain are dwelling in unspeakable bliss; why all the living so strive to hush all the dead; wherefore but the rumor of a knocking in a tomb will terrify a whole city. All these things are not without their meanings.

But Faith, like a jackal, feeds among the tombs, and even from these dead doubts she gathers her most vital hope.

It needs scarcely to be told, with what feelings, on the eve of a Nantucket voyage, I regarded those marble tablets, and by the murky light of that darkened, doleful day read the fate of the whalemen who had gone before me. Yes, Ishmael, the same fate may be thine. But somehow I grew merry again. Delightful inducements to embark, fine chance for promotion, it seems—aye, a stove boat will make me an immortal by brevet.[2] Yes, there is death in this business of whaling—a speechlessly quick chaotic bundling of a man into Eternity. But what then? Methinks we have hugely mistaken this matter of Life and Death. Methinks that what they call my shadow here on earth is my true substance. Methinks that in looking at things spiritual, we are too much like oysters observing the sun through the water, and thinking that thick water the thinnest of air. Methinks my body is but the lees of my better being. In fact take my body who will, take it I say, it is not me. And therefore three cheers for Nantucket; and come a stove boat and stove body when they will, for stave my soul, Jove himself cannot.

---

1. An immense cave temple on an island in the Bay of Bombay.

2. By an unexpected, on-the-spot promotion.

Chapter 8

THE PULPIT

I had not been seated very long ere a man of a certain vene-rable robustness entered; immediately as the storm-pelted door flew back upon admitting him, a quick regardful eyeing of him by all the congregation, sufficiently attested that this fine old man was the chaplain. Yes, it was the famous Father Mapple, so called by the whalemen, among whom he was a very great favorite. He had been a sailor and a harpooneer in his youth, but for many years past had dedicated his life to the ministry. At the time I now write of, Father Mapple was in the hardy winter of a healthy old age; that sort of old age which seems merging into a second flower-ing youth, for among all the fissures of his wrinkles, there shone certain mild gleams of a newly developing bloom—the spring verdure peeping forth even beneath February's snow. No one having previously heard his history, could for the first time behold Father Mapple without the utmost interest, because there were certain engrafted clerical peculiarities[1] about him, imputable to that adventurous maritime life he had led. When he entered I observed that he carried no umbrella, and certainly had not come in his carriage, for his tarpaulin hat ran down with melting sleet, and his great pilot cloth jacket seemed almost to drag him to the floor with the weight of the water it had absorbed. However, hat and coat and overshoes were one by one removed, and hung up in a little space in an adjacent corner; when, arrayed in a decent suit, he quietly approached the pulpit.

Like most old fashioned pulpits, it was a very lofty one, and since a regular stairs to such a height would, by its long angle with the floor, seriously contract the already small area of the chapel, the architect, it seemed, had acted upon the hint of Father Mapple, and finished the pulpit without a stairs, substituting a perpendicular side ladder, like those used in mounting a ship from a boat at sea. The wife of a whaling captain had provided the chapel with a handsome pair of red worsted man-ropes for this ladder, which, being itself nicely headed, and stained with a mahog-any color, the whole contrivance, considering what manner of chapel it was, seemed by no means in bad taste. Halting for an instant at the foot of the ladder, and with both hands grasping the ornamental knobs of the man-ropes, Father Mapple cast a look upwards, and then with a truly sailor-like but still reverential dexterity, hand over hand, mounted the steps as if ascending the main-top of his vessel.

1. Habitual mannerisms peculiar in a cleric.

The perpendicular parts of this side ladder, as is usually the case with swinging ones, were of cloth-covered rope, only the rounds were of wood, so that at every step there was a joint. At my first glimpse of the pulpit, it had not escaped me that however convenient for a ship, these joints in the present instance seemed unnecessary. For I was not prepared to see Father Mapple after gaining the height, slowly turn round, and stooping over the pulpit, deliberately drag up the ladder step by step, till the whole was deposited within, leaving him impregnable in his little Quebec.[2] *(fortres)* *Nebucanezar's city was impregna—*

I pondered some time without fully comprehending the reason for this. Father Mapple enjoyed such a wide reputation for sincerity and sanctity, that I could not suspect him of courting notoriety by any mere tricks of the stage. No, thought I, there must be some sober reason for this thing; furthermore, it must symbolize something unseen. Can it be, then, that by that act of physical isolation, he signifies his spiritual withdrawal for the time, from all outward worldly ties and connexions? Yes, for replenished with the meat and wine of the word, to the faithful man of God, this pulpit, I see, is a self-containing strong-hold—a lofty Ehrenbreitstein,[3] with a perennial well of water within the walls.

But the side ladder was not the only strange feature of the place, borrowed from the chaplain's former sea-farings. Between the marble cenotaphs on either hand of the pulpit, the wall which formed its back was adorned with a large painting representing a gallant ship beating against a terrible storm off a lee coast of black rocks and snowy breakers. But high above the flying scud and dark-rolling clouds, there floated a little isle of sunlight, from which beamed forth an angel's face; and this bright face shed a distinct spot of radiance upon the ship's tossed deck, something like that silver plate now inserted into the Victory's plank where Nelson fell. "Ah, noble ship," the angel seemed to say, "beat on, beat on, thou noble ship, and bear a hardy helm; for lo! the sun is breaking through; the clouds are rolling off—serenest azure is at hand."

Nor was the pulpit itself without a trace of the same sea-taste that had achieved the ladder and the picture. Its panelled front was in the likeness of a ship's bluff bows, and the Holy Bible rested on a projecting piece of scroll work, fashioned after a ship's fiddle-headed beak.

What could be more full of meaning?—for the pulpit is ever this earth's foremost part; all the rest comes in its rear; the pulpit

2. Fortress.   3. A fortress on the Rhine.

leads the world. From thence it is the storm of God's quick
wrath is first descried, and the bow must bear the earliest brunt.
From thence it is the God of breezes fair or foul is first
invoked for favorable winds. Yes, the world's a ship on its passage
out, and not a voyage complete; and the pulpit is its prow.

Chapter 9

THE SERMON

Father Mapple rose, and in a mild voice of unassuming authority
ordered the scattered people to condense. "Starboard gangway,
there! side away to larboard—larboard gangway to starboard!
Midships! midships!"

There was a low rumbling of heavy sea-boots among the
benches, and a still slighter shuffling of women's shoes, and all
was quiet again, and every eye on the preacher.

He paused a little; then kneeling in the pulpit's bows, folded
his large brown hands across his chest, uplifted his closed eyes, and
offered a prayer so deeply devout that he seemed kneeling and
praying at the bottom of the sea.

This ended, in prolonged solemn tones, like the continual toll-
ing of a bell in a ship that is foundering at sea in a fog—in such
tones he commenced reading the following hymn; but changing
his manner towards the concluding stanzas, burst forth with a
pealing exultation and joy—

> "The ribs and terrors in the whale,
>   Arched over me a dismal gloom,
> While all God's sun-lit waves rolled by,
>   And left me deepening down to doom.
>
> "I saw the open maw of hell,
>   With endless pains and sorrows there;
> Which none but they that feel can tell—
>   Oh, I was plunging to despair.
>
> "In black distress, I called my God,
>   When I could scarce believe him mine,
> He bowed his ear to my complaints—
>   No more the whale did me confine.
>
> "With speed he flew to my relief,
>   As on a radiant dolphin borne;
> Awful, yet bright, as lightning shone
>   The face of my Deliverer God.
>
> "My song for ever shall record
>   That terrible, that joyful hour;
> I give the glory to my God,
>   His all the mercy and the power."

Nearly all joined in singing this hymn, which swelled high above the howling of the storm. A brief pause ensued; the preacher slowly turned over the leaves of the Bible, and at last, folding his hand down upon the proper page, said: "Beloved shipmates, clinch the last verse of the first chapter of Jonah—'And God had prepared a great fish to swallow up Jonah.'

"Shipmates, this book, containing only four chapters—four yarns—is one of the smallest strands in the mighty cable of the Scriptures. Yet what depths of the soul does Jonah's deep sea-line sound! what a pregnant lesson to us is this prophet! What a noble thing is that canticle in the fish's belly! How billow-like and boisterously grand! We feel the floods surging over us; we sound with him to the kelpy bottom of the waters; sea-weed and all the slime of the sea is about us! But *what* is this lesson that the book of Jonah teaches? Shipmates, it is a two-stranded lesson; a lesson to us all as sinful men, and a lesson to me as a pilot of the living God. As sinful men, it is a lesson to us all, because it is a story of the sin, hard-heartedness, suddenly awakened fears, the swift punishment, repentance, prayers, and finally the deliverance and joy of Jonah. As with all sinners among men, the sin of this son of Amittai was in his wilful disobedience of the command of God—never mind now what that command was, or how conveyed—which he found a hard command. But all the things that God would have us do are hard for us to do—remember that—and hence, he oftener commands us than endeavors to persuade. And if we obey God, we must disobey ourselves; and it is in this disobeying ourselves, wherein the hardness of obeying God consists.

"With this sin of disobedience in him, Jonah still further flouts at God, by seeking to flee from Him. He thinks that a ship made by men, will carry him into countries where God does not reign, but only the Captains of this earth. He skulks about the wharves of Joppa, and seeks a ship that's bound for Tarshish. There lurks, perhaps, a hitherto unheeded meaning here. By all accounts Tarshish could have been no other city than the modern Cadiz. That's the opinion of learned men. And where is Cadiz, shipmates? Cadiz is in Spain; as far by water, from Joppa, as Jonah could possibly have sailed in those ancient days, when the Atlantic was an almost unknown sea. Because Joppa, the modern Jaffa, shipmates, is on the most easterly coast of the Mediterranean, the Syrian; and Tarshish or Cadiz more than two thousand miles to the westward from that, just outside the Straits of Gibraltar. See ye not then, shipmates, that Jonah sought to flee world-wide from God? Miserable man! Oh! most contemptible and worthy of all scorn; with slouched hat and guilty eye, skulking from his God;

prowling among the shipping like a vile burglar hastening to cross the seas. So disordered, self-condemning is his look, that had there been policemen in those days, Jonah, on the mere suspicion of something wrong, had been arrested ere he touched a deck. How plainly he's a fugitive! no baggage, not a hat-box, valise, or carpet-bag,—no friends accompany him to the wharf with their adieux. At last, after much dodging search, he finds the Tarshish ship receiving the last items of her cargo; and as he steps on board to see its Captain in the cabin, all the sailors for the moment desist from hoisting in the goods, to mark the stranger's evil eye. Jonah sees this; but in vain he tries to look all ease and confidence; in vain essays his wretched smile. Strong intuitions of the man assure the mariners he can be no innocent. In their gamesome but still serious way, one whispers to the other—'Jack, he's robbed a widow;' or, 'Joe, do you mark him; he's a bigamist;' or, 'Harry lad, I guess he's the adulterer that broke jail in old Gomorrah, or belike, one of the missing murderers from Sodom.' Another runs to read the bill that's stuck against the spile upon the wharf to which the ship is moored, offering five hundred gold coins for the apprehension of a parricide, and containing a description of his person. He reads, and looks from Jonah to the bill; while all his sympathetic shipmates now crowd round Jonah, prepared to lay their hands upon him. Frighted Jonah trembles, and summoning all his boldness to his face, only looks so much the more a coward. He will not confess himself suspected; but that itself is strong suspicion. So he makes the best of it; and when the sailors find him not to be the man that is advertised, they let him pass, and he descends into the cabin.

" 'Who's there?' cries the Captain at his busy desk, hurriedly making out his papers for the Customs—'Who's there?' Oh! how that harmless question mangles Jonah! For the instant he almost turns to flee again. But he rallies. 'I seek a passage in this ship to Tarshish; how soon sail ye, sir?' Thus far the busy Captain had not looked up to Jonah, though the man now stands before him; but no sooner does he hear that hollow voice, than he darts a scrutinizing glance. 'We sail with the next coming tide,' at last he slowly answered, still intently eyeing him. 'No sooner, sir?'— 'Soon enough for any honest man that goes a passenger.' Ha! Jonah, that's another stab. But he swiftly calls away the Captain from that scent. 'I'll sail with ye,'—he says,—'the passage money, how much is that?—I'll pay now.' For it is particularly written, shipmates, as if it were a thing not to be overlooked in this history, 'that he paid the fare thereof' ere the craft did sail. And taken with the context, this is full of meaning.

"Now Jonah's Captain, shipmates, was one whose discernment

detects crime in any, but whose cupidity exposes it only in the penniless. In this world, shipmates, sin that pays its way can travel freely, and without a passport; whereas Virtue, if a pauper, is stopped at all frontiers. So Jonah's Captain prepares to test the length of Jonah's purse, ere he judge him openly. He charges him thrice the usual sum; and it's assented to. Then the Captain knows that Jonah is a fugitive; but at the same time resolves to help a flight that paves its rear with gold. Yet when Jonah fairly takes out his purse, prudent suspicions still molest the Captain. He rings every coin to find a counterfeit. Not a forger, any way, he mutters; and Jonah is put down for his passage. 'Point out my state-room, Sir,' says Jonah now, 'I'm travel-weary; I need sleep.' 'Thou look'st like it,' says the Captain, 'there's thy room.' Jonah enters, and would lock the door, but the lock contains no key. Hearing him foolishly fumbling there, the Captain laughs lowly to himself, and mutters something about the doors of convicts' cells being never allowed to be locked within. All dressed and dusty as he is, Jonah throws himself into his berth, and finds the little state-room ceiling almost resting on his forehead. The air is close, and Jonah gasps. Then, in that contracted hole, sunk, too, beneath the ship's water-line, Jonah feels the heralding presentiment of that stifling hour, when the whale shall hold him in the smallest of his bowel's wards.

"Screwed at its axis against the side, a swinging lamp slightly oscillates in Jonah's room; and the ship, heeling over towards the wharf with the weight of the last bales received, the lamp, flame and all, though in slight motion, still maintains a permanent obliquity with reference to the room; though, in truth, infallibly straight itself, it but made obvious the false, lying levels among which it hung. The lamp alarms and frightens Jonah; as lying in his berth his tormented eyes roll round the place, and this thus far successful fugitive finds no refuge for his restless glance. But that contradiction in the lamp more and more appals him. The floor, the ceiling, and the side, are all awry. 'Oh! so my conscience hangs in me!' he groans, 'straight upward, so it burns; but the chambers of my soul are all in crookedness!'

"Like one who after a night of drunken revelry hies to his bed, still reeling, but with conscience yet pricking him, as the plungings of the Roman race-horse but so much the more strike his steel tags into him; as one who in that miserable plight still turns and turns in giddy anguish, praying God for annihilation until the fit be passed; and at last amid the whirl of woe he feels, a deep stupor steals over him, as over the man who bleeds to death, for conscience is the wound, and there's naught to staunch it; so, after sore wrestlings in his berth, Jonah's prodigy of ponderous misery drags him drowning down to sleep.

"And now the time of tide has come; the ship casts off her cables; and from the deserted wharf the uncheered ship for Tarshish, all careening, glides to sea. That ship, my friends, was the first of recorded smugglers! the contraband was Jonah. But the sea rebels; he will not bear the wicked burden. A dreadful storm comes on, the ship is like to break. But now when the boatswain calls all hands to lighten her; when boxes, bales, and jars are clattering overboard; when the wind is shrieking, and the men are yelling, and every plank thunders with trampling feet right over Jonah's head; in all this raging tumult, Jonah sleeps his hideous sleep. He sees no black sky and raging sea, feels not the reeling timbers, and little hears he or heeds he the far rush of the mighty whale, which even now with open mouth is cleaving the seas after him. Aye, shipmates, Jonah was gone down into the sides of the ship— a berth in the cabin as I have taken it, and was fast asleep. But the frightened master comes to him, and shrieks in his dead ear, 'What meanest thou, O sleeper! arise!' Startled from his lethargy by that direful cry, Jonah staggers to his feet, and stumbling to the deck, grasps a shroud, to look out upon the sea. But at that moment he is sprung upon by a panther billow leaping over the bulwarks. Wave after wave thus leaps into the ship, and finding no speedy vent runs roaring fore and aft, till the mariners come nigh to drowning while yet afloat. And ever, as the white moon shows her affrighted face from the steep gullies in the blackness overhead, aghast Jonah sees the rearing bowsprit pointing high upward, but soon beat downward again towards the tormented deep.

"Terrors upon terrors run shouting through his soul. In all his cringing attitudes, the God-fugitive is now too plainly known. The sailors mark him; more and more certain grow their suspicions of him, and at last, fully to test the truth, by referring the whole matter to high Heaven, they fall to casting lots, to see for whose cause this great tempest was upon them. The lot is Jonah's; that discovered, then how furiously they mob him with their questions. 'What is thine occupation? Whence comest thou? Thy country? What people?' But mark now, my shipmates, the behavior of poor Jonah. The eager mariners but ask him who he is, and where from; whereas, they not only receive an answer to those questions, but likewise another answer to a question not put by them, but the unsolicited answer is forced from Jonah by the hard hand of God that is upon him.

" 'I am a Hebrew,' he cries—and then—'I fear the Lord the God of Heaven who hath made the sea and the dry land!' Fear him, O Jonah? Aye, well mightest thou fear the Lord God *then!*

Straightway, he now goes on to make a full confession; whereupon the mariners become more and more appalled, but still are pitiful. For when Jonah, not yet supplicating God for mercy, since he but too well knew the darkness of his deserts,—when wretched Jonah cries out to them to take him and cast him forth into the sea, for he knew that for *his* sake this great tempest was upon them; they mercifully turn from him, and seek by other means to save the ship. But all in vain; the indignant gale howls louder; then, with one hand raised invokingly to God, with the other they not unreluctantly lay hold of Jonah.

"And now behold Jonah taken up as an anchor and dropped into the sea; when instantly an oily calmness floats out from the east, and the sea is still, as Jonah carries down the gale with him, leaving smooth water behind. He goes down in the whirling heart of such a masterless commotion that he scarce heeds the moment when he drops seething into the yawning jaws awaiting him; and the whale shoots-to all his ivory teeth, like so many white bolts, upon his prison. Then Jonah prayed unto the Lord out of the fish's belly. But observe his prayer, and learn a weighty lesson. For sinful as he is, Jonah does not weep and wail for direct deliverance. He feels that his dreadful punishment is just. He leaves all his deliverance to God, contenting himself with this, that spite of all his pains and pangs, he will still look towards His holy temple. And here, shipmates, is true and faithful repentance; not clamorous for pardon, but grateful for punishment. And how pleasing to God was this conduct in Jonah, is shown in the eventual deliverance of him from the sea and the whale. Shipmates, I do not place Jonah before you to be copied for his sin but I do place him before you as a model for repentance. Sin not; but if you do, take heed to repent of it like Jonah."

While he was speaking these words, the howling of the shrieking, slanting storm without seemed to add new power to the preacher, who, when describing Jonah's sea-storm, seemed tossed by a storm himself. His deep chest heaved as with a ground-swell; his tossed arms seemed the warring elements at work; and the thunders that rolled away from off his swarthy brow, and the light leaping from his eye, made all his simple hearers look on him with a quick fear that was strange to them.

There now came a lull in his look, as he silently turned over the leaves of the Book once more; and, at last, standing motionless, with closed eyes, for the moment, seemed communing with God and himself.

But again he leaned over towards the people, and bowing his head lowly, with an aspect of the deepest yet manliest humility, he spake these words:

"Shipmates, God has laid but one hand upon you; both his hands press upon me. I have read ye by what murky light may be mine the lesson that Jonah teaches to all sinners; and therefore to ye, and still more to me, for I am a greater sinner than ye. And now how gladly would I come down from this mast-head and sit on the hatches there where you sit, and listen as you listen, while some one of you reads *me* that other and more awful lesson which Jonah teaches to *me*, as a pilot of the living God. How being an anointed pilot-prophet, or speaker of true things, and bidden by the Lord to sound those unwelcome truths in the ears of a wicked Nineveh, Jonah, appalled at the hostility he should raise, fled from his mission, and sought to escape his duty and his God by taking ship at Joppa. But God is everywhere; Tarshish he never reached. As we have seen, God came upon him in the whale, and swallowed him down to living gulfs of doom, and with swift slantings tore him along 'into the midst of the seas,' where the eddying depths sucked him ten thousand fathoms down, and 'the weeds were wrapped about his head,' and all the watery world of woe bowled over him. Yet even then beyond the reach of any plummet—'out of the belly of hell'—when the whale grounded upon the ocean's utmost bones, even then, God heard the engulphed, repenting prophet when he cried. Then God spake unto the fish; and from the shuddering cold and blackness of the sea, the whale came breeching up towards the warm and pleasant sun, and all the delights of air and earth; and 'vomited out Jonah upon the dry land;' when the word of the Lord came a second time; and Jonah, bruised and beaten—his ears, like two sea-shells, still multitudinously murmuring of the ocean—Jonah did the Almighty's bidding. And what was that, shipmates? To preach the Truth to the face of Falsehood! That was it!

"This, shipmates, this is that other lesson; and woe to that pilot of the living God who slights it. Woe to him whom this world charms from Gospel duty! Woe to him who seeks to pour oil upon the waters when God has brewed them into a gale! Woe to him who seeks to please rather than to appal! Woe to him whose good name is more to him than goodness! Woe to him who, in this world, courts not dishonor! Woe to him who would not be true, even though to be false were salvation! Yea, woe to him who, as the great Pilot Paul has it, while preaching to others is himself a castaway!"

He drooped and fell away from himself for a moment; then lifting his face to them again, showed a deep joy in his eyes, as he cried out with a heavenly enthusiasm,—"But oh! shipmates! on the starboard hand of every woe, there is a sure delight; and higher the top of that delight, than the bottom of the woe is deep.

Is not the main-truck higher than the kelson is low? Delight is to
him—a far, far upward, and inward delight—who against the proud
gods and commodores of this earth, ever stands forth his own inexorable self. Delight is to him whose strong arms yet support
him, when the ship of this base treacherous world has gone down
beneath him. Delight is to him, who gives no quarter in the truth,
and kills, burns, and destroys all sin though he pluck it out from
under the robes of Senators and Judges. Delight,—top-
gallant delight is to him, who acknowledges no law or lord, but
the Lord his God, and is only a patriot to heaven. Delight is to
him, whom all the waves of the billows of the seas of the boisterous
mob can never shake from this sure Keel of the Ages. And eternal
delight and deliciousness will be his, who coming to lay him down,
can say with his final breath—O Father!—chiefly known to me by
Thy rod—mortal or immortal, here I die. I have striven to be
Thine, more than to be this world's, or mine own. Yet this is
nothing; I leave eternity to Thee; for what is man that he should
live out the lifetime of his God?"

He said no more, but slowly waving a benediction, covered his
face with his hands, and so remained, kneeling, till all the people
had departed, and he was left alone in the place.

Chapter 10

A BOSOM FRIEND

Returning to the Spouter-Inn from the Chapel, I found Queequeg there quite alone; he having left the Chapel before the
benediction some time. He was sitting on a bench before the fire,
with his feet on the stove hearth, and in one hand was holding
close up to his face that little negro idol of his; peering hard into
its face, and with a jack-knife gently whittling away at its nose,
meanwhile humming to himself in his heathenish way.

But being now interrupted, he put up the image; and pretty
soon, going to the table, took up a large book there, and placing
it on his lap began counting the pages with deliberate regularity;
at every fiftieth page—as I fancied—stopping a moment, looking
vacantly around him, and giving utterance to a long-drawn gurgling
whistle of astonishment. He would then begin again at the next
fifty; seeming to commence at number one each time, as though
he could not count more than fifty, and it was only by such a large
number of fifties being found together, that his astonishment at
the multitude of pages was excited.

With much interest I sat watching him. Savage though he was,
and hideously marred about the face—at least to my taste—his
countenance yet had a something in it which was by no means

disagreeable. You cannot hide the soul. Through all his unearthly tattooings, I thought I saw the traces of a simple honest heart; and in his large, deep eyes, fiery black and bold, there seemed tokens of a spirit that would dare a thousand devils. And besides all this, there was a certain lofty bearing about the Pagan, which even his uncouthness could not altogether maim. He looked like a man who had never cringed and never had had a creditor. Whether it was, too, that his head being shaved, his forehead was drawn out in freer and brighter relief, and looked more expansive than it otherwise would, this I will not venture to decide; but certain it was his head was phrenologically[1] an excellent one. It may seem ridiculous, but it reminded me of General Washington's head, as seen in the popular busts of him. It had the same long regularly graded retreating slope from above the brows, which were likewise very projecting, like two long promontories thickly wooded on top. Queequeg was George Washington cannibalistically developed.

Whilst I was thus closely scanning him, half-pretending meanwhile to be looking out at the storm from the casement, he never heeded my presence, never troubled himself with so much as a single glance; but appeared wholly occupied with counting the pages of the marvellous book. Considering how sociably we had been sleeping together the night previous, and especially considering the affectionate arm I had found thrown over me upon waking in the morning, I thought this indifference of his very strange. But savages are strange beings; at times you do not know exactly how to take them. At first they are overawing; their calm self-collectedness of simplicity seems a Socratic wisdom. I had noticed also that Queequeg never consorted at all, or but very little, with the other seamen in the inn. He made no advances whatever; appeared to have no desire to enlarge the circle of his acquaintances. All this struck me as mighty singular; yet, upon second thoughts, there was something almost sublime in it. Here was a man some twenty thousand miles from home, by the way of Cape Horn, that is—which was the only way he could get there—thrown among people as strange to him as though he were in the planet Jupiter; and yet he seemed entirely at his ease; preserving the utmost serenity; content with his own companionship; always equal to himself. Surely this was a touch of fine philosophy; though no doubt he had never heard there was such a thing as that. But, perhaps, to be true philosophers, we mortals should not be conscious of so living or so striving. So soon as I hear that such or such a man gives himself out for a philosopher, I conclude that,

1. Phrenology was a fashionable pseudoscience that claimed to gauge particular traits and abilities by measuring conformations of the skull.

like the dyspeptic old woman, he must have "broken his digester."

As I sat there in that now lonely room; the fire burning low, in that mild stage when, after its first intensity has warmed the air, it then only glows to be looked at; the evening shades and phantoms gathering round the casements, and peering in upon us silent, solitary twain; the storm booming without in solemn swells; I began to be sensible of strange feelings. I felt a melting in me. No more my splintered heart and maddened hand were turned against the wolfish world. This soothing savage had redeemed it. There he sat, his very indifference speaking a nature in which there lurked no civilized hypocrisies and bland deceits. Wild he was; a very sight of sights to see; yet I began to feel myself mysteriously drawn towards him. And those same things that would have repelled most others, they were the very magnets that thus drew me. I'll try a pagan friend, thought I, since Christian kindness has proved but hollow courtesy. I drew my bench near him, and made some friendly signs and hints, doing my best to talk with him meanwhile. At first he little noticed these advances; but presently, upon my referring to his last night's hospitalities, he made out to ask me whether we were again to be bedfellows. I told him yes; whereat I thought he looked pleased, perhaps a little complimented.

We then turned over the book together, and I endeavored to explain to him the purpose of the printing, and the meaning of the few pictures that were in it. Thus I soon engaged his interest; and from that we went to jabbering the best we could about the various outer sights to be seen in this famous town. Soon I proposed a social smoke; and, producing his pouch and tomahawk, he quietly offered me a puff. And then we sat exchanging puffs from that wild pipe of his, and keeping it regularly passing between us.

If there yet lurked any ice of indifference towards me in the Pagan's breast, this pleasant, genial smoke we had, soon thawed it out, and left us cronies. He seemed to take to me quite as naturally and unbiddenly as I to him; and when our smoke was over, he pressed his forehead against mine, clasped me round the waist, and said that henceforth we were married; meaning, in his country's phrase, that we were bosom friends; he would gladly die for me, if need should be. In a countryman, this sudden flame of friendship would have seemed far too premature, a thing to be much distrusted; but in this simple savage those old rules would not apply.

After supper, and another social chat and smoke, we went to our room together. He made me a present of his embalmed head; took out his enormous tobacco wallet, and groping under the tobacco, drew out some thirty dollars in silver; then spreading them on the table, and mechanically dividing them into two equal portions, pushed one of them towards me, and said it was mine. I was going to remonstrate; but he silenced me by pouring them into my trowsers' pockets. I let them stay. He then went about his evening prayers, took out his idol, and removed the paper fireboard. By certain signs and symptoms, I thought he seemed anxious for me to join him; but well knowing what was to follow, I deliberated a moment whether, in case he invited me, I would comply or otherwise.

I was a good Christian; born and bred in the bosom of the infallible Presbyterian Church. How then could I unite with this wild idolator in worshipping his piece of wood? But what is worship? thought I. Do you suppose now, Ishmael, that the magnanimous God of heaven and earth—pagans and all included —can possibly be jealous of an insignificant bit of black wood? Impossible! But what is worship?—to do the will of God—*that* is worship. And what is the will of God?—to do to my fellow man what I would have my fellow man to do to me—*that* is the will of God. Now, Queequeg is my fellow man. And what do I wish that this Queequeg would do to me? Why, unite with me in my particular Presbyterian form of worship. Consequently, I must then unite with him in his; ergo, I must turn idolator. So I kindled the shavings; helped prop up the innocent little idol; offered him burnt biscuit with Queequeg; salaamed before him twice or thrice; kissed his nose; and that done, we undressed and went to bed, at peace with our own consciences and all the world. But we did not go to sleep without some little chat.

How it is I know not; but there is no place like a bed for confidential disclosures between friends. Man and wife, they say, there open the very bottom of their souls to each other; and some old couples often lie and chat over old times till nearly morning. Thus, then, in our hearts' honeymoon, lay I and Queequeg—a cosy, loving pair.

Chapter 11

NIGHTGOWN

We had lain thus in bed, chatting and napping at short intervals, and Queequeg now and then affectionately throwing his brown tattooed legs over mine, and then drawing them back; so entirely sociable and free and easy were we; when, at last, by reason of our confabulations, what little nappishness remained in us altogether departed, and we felt like getting up again, though daybreak was yet some way down the future.

Yes, we became very wakeful; so much so that our recumbent

position began to grow wearisome, and by little and little we found ourselves sitting up; the clothes well tucked around us, leaning against the head-board with our four knees drawn up close together, and our two noses bending over them, as if our knee-pans were warming-pans. We felt very nice and snug, the more so since it was so chilly out of doors; indeed out of bed-clothes too, seeing that there was no fire in the room. The more so, I say, because truly to enjoy bodily warmth, some small part of you must be cold, for there is no quality in this world that is not what it is merely by contrast. Nothing exists in itself. If you flatter yourself that you are all over comfortable, and have been so a long time, then you cannot be said to be comfortable any more. But if, like Queequeg and me in the bed, the tip of your nose or the crown of your head be slightly chilled, why then, indeed, in the general consciousness you feel most delightfully and unmistakably warm. For this reason a sleeping apartment should never be furnished with a fire, which is one of the luxurious discomforts of the rich. For the height of this sort of deliciousness is to have nothing but the blanket between you and your snugness and the cold of the outer air. Then there you lie like the one warm spark in the heart of an arctic crystal.

We had been sitting in this crouching manner for some time, when all at once I thought I would open my eyes; for when between sheets, whether by day or by night, and whether asleep or awake, I have a way of always keeping my eyes shut, in order the more to concentrate the snugness of being in bed. Because no man can ever feel his own identity aright except his eyes be closed; as if darkness were indeed the proper element of our essences, though light be more congenial to our clayey part. Upon opening my eyes then, and coming out of my own pleasant and self-created darkness into the imposed and coarse outer gloom of the unilluminated twelve-o'clock-at-night, I experienced a disagreeable revulsion. Nor did I at all object to the hint from Queequeg that perhaps it were best to strike a light, seeing that we were so wide awake; and besides he felt a strong desire to have a few quiet puffs from his Tomahawk. Be it said, that though I had felt such a strong repugnance to his smoking in the bed the night before, yet see how elastic our stiff prejudices grow when love once comes to bend them. For now I liked nothing better than to have Queequeg smoking by me, even in bed, because he seemed to be full of such serene household joy then. I no more felt unduly concerned for the landlord's policy of insurance. I was only alive to the condensed confidential comfortableness of sharing a pipe and a blanket with a real friend. With our shaggy jackets drawn about our shoulders, we now passed the Tomahawk from one to the other, till slowly there grew over us a blue hanging tester of smoke, illuminated by the flame of the new-lit lamp.

Whether it was that this undulating tester rolled the savage away to far distant scenes, I know not, but he now spoke of his native island; and, eager to hear his history, I begged him to go on and tell it. He gladly complied. Though at the time I but ill comprehended not a few of his words, yet subsequent disclosures, when I had become more familiar with his broken phraseology, now enable me to present the whole story such as it may prove in the mere skeleton I give.

Chapter 12

BIOGRAPHICAL

Queequeg was a native of Kokovoko, an island far away to the West and South. It is not down in any map; true places never are.

While yet a new-hatched savage running wild about his native woodlands in a grass clout, followed by the nibbling goats, as if he were a green sapling; even then, in Queequeg's ambitious soul, lurked a strong desire to see something more of Christendom than a specimen whaler or two. His father was a High Chief, a King; his uncle a High Priest; and on the maternal side he boasted aunts who were the wives of unconquerable warriors. There was excellent blood in his veins—royal stuff; though sadly vitiated, I fear, by the cannibal propensity he nourished in his untutored youth.

A Sag Harbor[1] ship visited his father's bay, and Queequeg sought a passage to Christian lands. But the ship, having her full complement of seamen, spurned his suit; and not all the King his father's influence could prevail. But Queequeg vowed a vow. Alone in his canoe, he paddled off to a distant strait, which he knew the ship must pass through when she quitted the island. On one side was a coral reef; on the other a low tongue of land, covered with mangrove thickets that grew out into the water. Hiding his canoe, still afloat, among these thickets, with its prow seaward, he sat down in the stern, paddle low in hand; and when the ship was gliding by, like a flash he darted out; gained her side; with one backward dash of his foot capsized and sank his canoe; climbed up the chains; and throwing himself at full length upon the deck, grappled a ring-bolt there, and swore not to let it go, though hacked in pieces.

In vain the captain threatened to throw him overboard; suspended a cutlass over his naked wrists; Queequeg was the son of

---

1. Sag Harbor, on Long Island, a major whaling port.

a King, and Queequeg budged not. Struck by his desperate daunt-
lessness, and his wild desire to visit Christendom, the captain at
last relented, and told him he might make himself at home. But
this fine young savage—this sea Prince of Wales, never saw the
captain's cabin. They put him down among the sailors, and made
a whaleman of him. But like Czar Peter content to toil in the
shipyards of foreign cities, Queequeg disdained no seeming ig-
nominy, if thereby he might haply gain the power of enlightening
his untutored countrymen. For at bottom—so he told me—he was
actuated by a profound desire to learn among the Christians, the
arts whereby to make his people still happier than they were; and
more than that, still better than they were. But, alas! the practices
of whalemen soon convinced him that even Christians could be
both miserable and wicked; infinitely more so, than all his father's
heathens. Arrived at last in old Sag Harbor; and seeing what the
sailors did there; and then going on to Nantucket, and seeing how
they spent their wages in *that* place also, poor Queequeg gave it
up for lost. Thought he, it's a wicked world in all meridians; I'll
die a pagan.

And thus an old idolator at heart, he yet lived among these
Christians, wore their clothes, and tried to talk their gibberish.
Hence the queer ways about him, though now some time from
home.

By hints, I asked him whether he did not propose going back,
and having a coronation; since he might now consider his father
dead and gone, he being very old and feeble at the last accounts.
He answered no, not yet; and added that he was fearful Christianity, or rather Christians, had unfitted him for ascending the
pure and undefiled throne of thirty pagan Kings before him. But
by and by, he said, he would return,—as soon as he felt himself
baptized again. For the nonce, however, he proposed to sail
about, and sow his wild oats in all four oceans. They had made a
harpooneer of him, and that barbed iron was in lieu of a sceptre
now.

I asked him what might be his immediate purpose, touching
his future movements. He answered, to go to sea again, in his old
vocation. Upon this, I told him that whaling was my own design,
and informed him of my intention to sail out of Nantucket, as
being the most promising port for an adventurous whaleman to
embark from. He at once resolved to accompany me to that island,
ship aboard the same vessel, get into the same watch, the same
boat, the same mess with me, in short to share my every hap;
with both my hands in his, boldly dip into the Potluck of both
worlds. To all this I joyously assented; for besides the affection I
now felt for Queequeg, he was an experienced harpooneer, and

as such, could not fail to be of great usefulness to one, who, like me, was wholly ignorant of the mysteries of whaling, though well acquainted with the sea, as known to merchant seamen.

His story being ended with his pipe's last dying puff, Queequeg embraced me, pressed his forehead against mine, and blowing out the light, we rolled over from each other, this way and that, and very soon were sleeping.

Chapter 13

WHEELBARROW

Next morning, Monday, after disposing of the embalmed head to a barber, for a block,[1] I settled my own and comrade's bill; using, however, my comrade's money. The grinning landlord, as well as the boarders, seemed amazingly tickled at the sudden friendship which had sprung up between me and Queequeg—especially as Peter Coffin's cock and bull stories about him had previously so much alarmed me concerning the very person whom I now companied with.

We borrowed a wheelbarrow, and embarking our things, including my own poor carpet-bag, and Queequeg's canvas sack and hammock, away we went down to the "Moss," the little Nantucket packet schooner moored at the wharf. As we were going along the people stared; not at Queequeg so much—for they were used to seeing cannibals like him in their streets,—but at seeing him and me upon such confidential terms. But we heeded them not, going along wheeling the barrow by turns, and Queequeg now and then stopping to adjust the sheath on his harpoon barbs. I asked him why he carried such a troublesome thing with him ashore, and whether all whaling ships did not find[2] their own harpoons. To this, in substance, he replied, that though what I hinted was true enough, yet he had a particular affection for his own harpoon, because it was of assured stuff, well tried in many a mortal combat, and deeply intimate with the hearts of whales. In short, like many inland reapers and mowers, who go into the farmers' meadows armed with their own scythes—though in no wise obliged to furnish them—even so, Queequeg, for his own private reasons, preferred his own harpoon.

Shifting the barrow from my hand to his, he told me a funny story about the first wheelbarrow he had ever seen. It was in Sag Harbor. The owners of his ship, it seems, had lent him one, in which to carry his heavy chest to his boarding house. Not to seem ignorant about the thing—though in truth he was entirely so, concerning the precise way in which to manage the barrow—

1. A form on which to keep a wig.   2. Furnish, supply.

Queequeg puts his chest upon it; lashes it fast; and then shoulders the barrow and marches up the wharf. "Why," said I, "Queequeg, you might have known better than that, one would think. Didn't the people laugh?"

Upon this, he told me another story. The people of his island of Kokovoko, it seems, at their wedding feasts express the fragrant water of young cocoanuts into a large stained calabash like a punchbowl; and this punchbowl always forms the great central ornament on the braided mat where the feast is held. Now a certain grand merchant ship once touched at Kokovoko, and its commander—from all accounts, a very stately punctilious gentleman, at least for a sea captain—this commander was invited to the wedding feast of Queequeg's sister, a pretty young princess just turned of ten. Well; when all the wedding guests were assembled at the bride's bamboo cottage, this Captain marches in, and being assigned the post of honor, placed himself over against the punchbowl, and between the High Priest and his majesty the King, Queequeg's father. Grace being said,—for those people have their grace as well as we—though Queequeg told me that unlike us, who at such times look downwards to our platters, they, on the contrary, copying the ducks, glance upwards to the great Giver of all feasts—Grace, I say, being said, the High Priest opens the banquet by the immemorial ceremony of the island; that is, dipping his consecrated and consecrating fingers into the bowl before the blessed beverage circulates. Seeing himself placed next the Priest, and noting the ceremony, and thinking himself—being Captain of a ship—as having plain precedence over a mere island King, especially in the King's own house—the Captain coolly proceeds to wash his hands in the punch bowl;—taking it I suppose for a huge finger-glass. "Now," said Queequeg, "what you tink now?—Didn't our people laugh?"

At last, passage paid, and luggage safe, we stood on board the schooner. Hoisting sail, it glided down the Acushnet river. On one side, New Bedford rose in terraces of streets, their ice-covered trees all glittering in the clear, cold air. Huge hills and mountains of casks on casks were piled upon her wharves, and side by side the world-wandering whale ships lay silent and safely moored at last; while from others came a sound of carpenters and coopers, with blended noises of fires and forges to melt the pitch, all betokening that new cruises were on the start; that one most perilous and long voyage ended, only begins a second; and a second ended, only begins a third, and so on, for ever and for aye. Such is the endlessness, yea, the intolerableness of all earthly effort.

Gaining the more open water, the bracing breeze waxed fresh; the little Moss tossed the quick foam from her bows, as a young colt his snortings. How I snuffed that Tartar air!—how I spurned that turnpike earth!—that common highway all over dented with the marks of slavish heels and hoofs; and turned me to admire the magnanimity of the sea which will permit no records.

At the same foam-fountain, Queequeg seemed to drink and reel with me. His dusky nostrils swelled apart; he showed his filed and pointed teeth. On, on we flew; and our offing gained, the Moss did homage to the blast; ducked and dived her bows as a slave before the Sultan. Sideways leaning, we sideways darted; every ropeyarn tingling like a wire; the two tall masts buckling like Indian canes in land tornadoes. So full of this reeling scene were we, as we stood by the plunging bowsprit, that for some time we did not notice the jeering glances of the passengers, a lubber-like assembly, who marvelled that two fellow beings should be so companionable; as though a white man were anything more dignified than a whitewashed negro. But there were some boobies and bumpkins there, who, by their intense greenness, must have come from the heart and centre of all verdure. Queequeg caught one of these young saplings mimicking him behind his back. I thought the bumpkin's hour of doom was come. Dropping his harpoon, the brawny savage caught him in his arms, and by an almost miraculous dexterity and strength, sent him high up bodily into the air; then slightly tapping his stern in mid-somerset, the fellow landed with bursting lungs upon his feet, while Queequeg, turning his back upon him, lighted his tomahawk pipe and passed it to me for a puff.

"Capting! Capting!" yelled the bumpkin, running towards that officer; "Capting, Capting, here's the devil."

"Hallo, *you* sir," cried the Captain, a gaunt rib of the sea, stalking up to Queequeg, "what in thunder do you mean by that? Don't you know you might have killed that chap?"

"What him say?" said Queequeg, as he mildly turned to me.

"He say," said I, "that you came near kill-e that man there," pointing to the still shivering greenhorn.

"Kill-e," cried Queequeg, twisting his tattooed face into an unearthly expression of disdain, "ah! him bery small-e fish-e; Queequeg no kill-e so small-e fish-e; Queequeg kill-e big whale!"

"Look you," roared the Captain, "I'll kill-e *you*, you cannibal, if you try any more of your tricks aboard here; so mind your eye."

But it so happened just then, that it was high time for the Captain to mind his own eye. The prodigious strain upon the main-sail had parted the weather-sheet, and the tremendous boom was now flying from side to side, completely sweeping the entire after part of the deck. The poor fellow whom Queequeg had handled so roughly, was swept overboard; all hands were in a panic; and to attempt snatching at the boom to stay it, seemed madness. It flew from right to left, and back again, almost in one ticking of a watch, and every instant seemed on the point of snapping into splinters. Nothing was done, and nothing seemed capable of being done; those on deck rushed towards the bows, and stood eyeing the boom as if it were the lower jaw of an exasperated whale. In the midst of this consternation, Queequeg dropped deftly to his knees, and crawling under the path of the boom, whipped hold of a rope, secured one end to the bulwarks, and then flinging the other like a lasso, caught it round the boom as it swept over his head, and at the next jerk, the spar was that way trapped, and all was safe. The schooner was run into the wind, and while the hands were clearing away the stern boat, Queequeg, stripped to the waist, darted from the side with a long living arc of a leap. For three minutes or more he was seen swimming like a dog, throwing his long arms straight out before him, and by turns revealing his brawny shoulders through the freezing foam. I looked at the grand and glorious fellow, but saw no one to be saved. The greenhorn had gone down. Shooting himself perpendicularly from the water, Queequeg now took an instant's glance around him, and seeming to see just how matters were, dived down and disappeared. A few minutes more, and he rose again, one arm still striking out, and with the other dragging a lifeless form. The boat soon picked them up. The poor bumpkin was restored. All hands voted Queequeg a noble trump; the captain begged his pardon. From that hour I clove to Queequeg like a barnacle; yea, till poor Queequeg took his last long dive.

Was there ever such unconsciousness? [3] He did not seem to think that he at all deserved a medal from the Humane and Magnanimous Societies. He only asked for water—fresh water—something to wipe the brine off; that done, he put on dry clothes, lighted his pipe, and leaning against the bulwarks, and mildly eyeing those around him, seemed to be saying to himself—"It's a mutual, joint-stock world, in all meridians. We cannibals must help these Christians."

Chapter 14

NANTUCKET

Nothing more happened on the passage worthy the mentioning; so, after a fine run, we safely arrived in Nantucket.

Nantucket! Take out your map and look at it. See what a real corner of the world it occupies; how it stands there, away off

---

3. Lack of self-consciousness.

shore, more lonely than the Eddystone lighthouse. Look at it—a mere hillock, and elbow of sand; all beach, without a background. There is more sand there than you would use in twenty years as a substitute for blotting paper. Some gamesome wights will tell you that they have to plant weeds there, they don't grow naturally; that they import Canada thistles; that they have to send beyond seas for a spile to stop a leak in an oil cask; that pieces of wood in Nantucket are carried about like bits of the true cross in Rome; that people there plant toadstools before their houses, to get under the shade in summer time; that one blade of grass makes an oasis, three blades in a day's walk a prairie; that they wear quicksand shoes, something like Laplander snow-shoes; that they are so shut up, belted about, every way inclosed, surrounded, and made an utter island of by the ocean, that to their very chairs and tables small clams will sometimes be found adhering, as to the backs of sea turtles. But these extravaganzas only show that Nantucket is no Illinois.

Look now at the wondrous traditional story of how this island was settled by the red-men. Thus goes the legend. In olden times an eagle swooped down upon the New England coast, and carried off an infant Indian in his talons. With loud lament the parents saw their child borne out of sight over the wide waters. They resolved to follow in the same direction. Setting out in their canoes, after a perilous passage they discovered the island, and there they found an empty ivory casket,—the poor little Indian's skeleton.

What wonder, then, that these Nantucketers, born on a beach, should take to the sea for a livelihood! They first caught crabs and quohogs in the sand; grown bolder, they waded out with nets for mackerel; more experienced, they pushed off in boats and captured cod; and at last, launching a navy of great ships on the sea, explored this watery world; put an incessant belt of circumnavigations round it; peeped in at Behring's Straits; and in all seasons and all oceans declared everlasting war with the mightiest animated mass that has survived the flood; most monstrous and most mountainous! That Himmalehan, salt-sea Mastodon, clothed with such portentousness of unconscious power, that his very panics are more to be dreaded than his most fearless and malicious assaults!

And thus have these naked Nantucketers, these sea hermits, issuing from their ant-hill in the sea, overrun and conquered the watery world like so many Alexanders; parcelling out among them the Atlantic, Pacific, and Indian oceans, as the three pirate powers [1] did Poland. Let America add Mexico to Texas, and pile Cuba upon Canada; let the English overswarm all India, and hang

1. Russia, Austria, and Prussia.

out their blazing banner from the sun; two thirds of this ter-
raqueous globe are the Nantucketer's. For the sea is his; he owns
it, as Emperors own empires; other seamen having but a right of
way through it. Merchant ships are but extension bridges; armed
ones but floating forts; even pirates and privateers, though following the sea as highwaymen the road, they but plunder other
ships, other fragments of the land like themselves, without seeking
to draw their living from the bottomless deep itself. The Nantucketer, he alone resides and riots on the sea; he alone, in Bible
language, goes down to it in ships; to and fro ploughing it as
his own special plantation. *There* is his home; *there* lies his business, which a Noah's flood would not interrupt, though it overwhelmed all the millions in China. He lives on the sea, as prairie
cocks in the prairie; he hides among the waves, he climbs them
as chamois hunters climb the Alps. For years he knows not the
land; so that when he comes to it at last, it smells like another
world, more strangely than the moon would to an Earthsman.
With the landless gull, that at sunset folds her wings and is
rocked to sleep between billows; so at nightfall, the Nantucketer,
out of sight of land, furls his sails, and lays him to his rest, while
under his very pillow rush herds of walruses and whales.

Chapter 15

CHOWDER

It was quite late in the evening when the little Moss came
snugly to anchor, and Queequeg and I went ashore; so we could
attend to no business that day, at least none but a supper and a
bed. The landlord of the Spouter-Inn had recommended us to his
cousin Hosea Hussey of the Try Pots, whom he asserted to be the
proprietor of one of the best kept hotels in all Nantucket, and
moreover he had assured us that cousin Hosea, as he called him,
was famous for his chowders. In short, he plainly hinted that we
could not possibly do better than try pot-luck at the Try Pots.
But the directions he had given us about keeping a yellow warehouse on our starboard hand till we opened [1] a white church to
the larboard, and then keeping that on the larboard hand till we
made a corner three points to the starboard, and that done, then
ask the first man we met where the place was: these crooked directions of his very much puzzled us at first, especially as, at the
outset, Queequeg insisted that the yellow warehouse—our first
point of departure—must be left on the larboard hand, whereas I
had understood Peter Coffin to say it was on the starboard. However, by dint of beating about a little in the dark, and now and

1. Sighted.

then knocking up a peaceable inhabitant to inquire the way, we at last came to something which there was no mistaking.

Two enormous wooden pots painted black, and suspended by asses' ears, swung from the cross-trees of an old top-mast, planted in front of an old doorway. The horns of the cross-trees were sawed off on the other side, so that this old top-mast looked not a little like a gallows. Perhaps I was over sensitive to such impressions at the time, but I could not help staring at this gallows with a vague misgiving. A sort of crick was in my neck as I gazed up to the two remaining horns; yes, *two* of them, one for Queequeg, and one for me. It's ominous, thinks I. A Coffin my Inn-keeper upon landing in my first whaling port; tombstones staring at me in the whalemen's chapel; and here a gallows! and a pair of prodigious black pots too! Are these last throwing out oblique hints touching Tophet?

I was called from these reflections by the sight of a freckled woman with yellow hair and a yellow gown, standing in the porch of the inn, under a dull red lamp swinging there, that looked much like an injured eye, and carrying on a brisk scolding with a man in a purple woollen shirt.

"Get along with ye," said she to the man, "or I'll be combing ye!"

"Come on, Queequeg," said I, "all right. There's Mrs. Hussey."

And so it turned out; Mr. Hosea Hussey being from home, but leaving Mrs. Hussey entirely competent to attend to all his affairs. Upon making known our desires for a supper and a bed, Mrs. Hussey, postponing further scolding for the present, ushered us into a little room, and seating us at a table spread with the relics of a recently concluded repast, turned round to us and said— "Clam or Cod?"

"What's that about Cods, ma'am?" said I, with much politeness.

"Clam or Cod?" she repeated.

"A clam for supper? a cold clam; is *that* what you mean, Mrs. Hussey?" says I; "but that's a rather cold and clammy reception in the winter time, ain't it, Mrs. Hussey?"

But being in a great hurry to resume scolding the man in the purple shirt, who was waiting for it in the entry, and seeming to hear nothing but the word "clam," Mrs. Hussey hurried towards an open door leading to the kitchen, and bawling out "clam for two," disappeared.

"Queequeg," said I, "do you think that we can make out a supper for us both on one clam?"

However, a warm savory steam from the kitchen served to belie the apparently cheerless prospect before us. But when that smoking chowder came in, the mystery was delightfully explained. Oh, sweet friends! hearken to me. It was made of small juicy clams, scarcely bigger than hazel nuts, mixed with pounded ship biscuit, and salted pork cut up into little flakes; the whole enriched with butter, and plentifully seasoned with pepper and salt. Our appetites being sharpened by the frosty voyage, and in particular, Queequeg seeing his favorite fishing food before him, and the chowder being surpassingly excellent, we despatched it with great expedition: when leaning back a moment and bethinking me of Mrs. Hussey's clam and cod announcement, I thought I would try a little experiment. Stepping to the kitchen door, I uttered the word "cod" with great emphasis, and resumed my seat. In a few moments the savory steam came forth again, but with a different flavor, and in good time a fine cod-chowder was placed before us.

We resumed business; and while plying our spoons in the bowl, thinks I to myself, I wonder now if this here has any effect on the head? What's that stultifying saying about chowder-headed people? "But look, Queequeg, ain't that a live eel in your bowl? Where's your harpoon?"

Fishiest of all fishy places was the Try Pots, which well deserved its name; for the pots there were always boiling chowders. Chowder for breakfast, and chowder for dinner, and chowder for supper, till you began to look for fish-bones coming through your clothes. The area before the house was paved with clam-shells. Mrs. Hussey wore a polished necklace of codfish vertebræ; and Hosea Hussey had his account books bound in superior old sharkskin. There was a fishy flavor to the milk, too, which I could not at all account for, till one morning happening to take a stroll along the beach among some fishermen's boats, I saw Hosea's brindled cow feeding on fish remnants, and marching along the sand with each foot in a cod's decapitated head, looking very slip-shod, I assure ye.

Supper concluded, we received a lamp, and directions from Mrs. Hussey concerning the nearest way to bed; but, as Queequeg was about to precede me up the stairs, the lady reached forth her arm, and demanded his harpoon; she allowed no harpoon in her chambers. "Why not?" said I; "every true whaleman sleeps with his harpoon—but why not?" "Because it's dangerous," says she. "Ever since young Stiggs coming from that unfort'nate v'y'ge of his, when he was gone four years and a half, with ony three barrels of *ile*, was found dead in my first floor back, with his harpoon in his side; ever since then I allow no boarders to take sich dangerous weepons in their rooms a-night. So, Mr. Queequeg" (for she had learned his name), "I will just take this here iron, and keep it for you till morning. But the chowder; clam or cod to-morrow for breakfast, men?"

"Both," says I; "and let's have a couple of smoked herring by
way of variety."

Chapter 16

THE SHIP

In bed we concocted our plans for the morrow. But to my surprise and no small concern, Queequeg now gave me to understand, that he had been diligently consulting Yojo—the name of
his black little god—and Yojo had told him two or three times
over, and strongly insisted upon it everyway, that instead of our
going together among the whaling-fleet in harbor, and in concert
selecting our craft; instead of this, I say, Yojo earnestly enjoined
that the selection of the ship should rest wholly with me, inasmuch as Yojo purposed befriending us; and, in order to do so,
had already pitched upon a vessel, which, if left to myself, I,
Ishmael, should infallibly light upon, for all the world as though
it had turned out by chance; and in that vessel I must immediately
ship myself, for the present irrespective of Queequeg.

I have forgotten to mention that, in many things, Queequeg
placed great confidence in the excellence of Yojo's judgment
and surprising forecast of things; and cherished Yojo with considerable esteem, as a rather good sort of god, who perhaps meant well
enough upon the whole, but in all cases did not succeed in his
benevolent designs.

Now, this plan of Queequeg's, or rather Yojo's, touching the
selection of our craft; I did not like that plan at all. I had not a
little relied upon Queequeg's sagacity to point out the whaler best
fitted to carry us and our fortunes securely. But as all my re-
monstrances produced no effect upon Queequeg, I was obliged to
acquiesce; and accordingly prepared to set about this business with
a determined rushing sort of energy and vigor, that should quickly
settle that trifling little affair. Next morning early, leaving Queequeg shut up with Yojo in our little bedroom—for it seemed that
it was some sort of Lent or Ramadan, or day of fasting, humiliation,
and prayer with Queequeg and Yojo that day; *how* it was I
never could find out, for, though I applied myself to it several
times, I never could master his liturgies and XXXIX Articles [1]—
leaving Queequeg, then, fasting on his tomahawk pipe, and Yojo
warming himself at his sacrificial fire of shavings, I sallied out
among the shipping. After much prolonged sauntering and many
random inquiries, I learnt that there were three ships up for
three-years' voyages—The Devil-dam, the Tit-bit, and the Pequod.

1. Points of doctrine, so-called from the Articles of Faith of the Church of England.

Devil-Dam, I do not know the origin of; *Tit-bit* is obvious; *Pequod*, you will no doubt remember, was the name of a celebrated tribe of Massachusetts Indians, now extinct as the ancient Medes. I peered and pryed about the Devil-Dam; from her, hopped over to the Tit-bit; and, finally, going on board the Pequod, looked around her for a moment, and then decided that this was the very ship for us.

You may have seen many a quaint craft in your day, for aught I know;—square-toed luggers; mountainous Japanese junks; butter-box galliots, and what not; but take my word for it, you never saw such a rare old craft as this same rare old Pequod. She was a ship of the old school, rather small if anything; with an old fashioned claw-footed look about her. Long seasoned and weather-stained in the typhoons and calms of all four oceans, her old hull's complexion was darkened like a French grenadier's, who has alike fought in Egypt and Siberia. Her venerable bows looked bearded. Her masts—cut somewhere on the coast of Japan, where her original ones were lost overboard in a gale—her masts stood stiffly up like the spines of the three old kings of Cologne.[2] Her ancient decks were worn and wrinkled, like the pilgrim-worshipped flag-stone in Canterbury Cathedral where Becket bled. But to all these her old antiquities, were added new and marvellous features, per-taining to the wild business that for more than half a century she had followed. Old Captain Peleg, many years her chief-mate, before he commanded another vessel of his own, and now a re-tired seaman, and one of the principal owners of the Pequod,—this old Peleg, during the term of his chief-mateship, had built upon her original grotesqueness, and inlaid it, all over, with a quaintness both of material and device, unmatched by anything except it be Thorkill-Hake's carved buckler or bedstead.[3] She was apparelled like any barbaric Ethiopian emperor, his neck heavy with pendants of polished ivory. She was a thing of trophies. A cannibal of a craft, tricking herself forth in the chased bones of her enemies. All round, her unpanelled, open bulwarks were garnished like one continuous jaw, with the long sharp teeth of the sperm whale, inserted there for pins, to fasten her old hempen thews and tendons to. Those thews ran not through base blocks of land wood, but deftly travelled over sheaves of sea-ivory. Scorning a turnstile wheel at her reverend helm, she sported there a tiller; and that tiller was in one mass, curiously carved from the long narrow lower jaw of her hereditary foe. The helmsman who steered by that tiller in a tempest, felt like the Tartar, when he

2. The three Magi, whose purported re-mains were exhibited at the Cathedral of Cologne.
3. Thorkill-Hake was an eleventh-century Icelandic hero who had his shield and bedstead carved with illus-trations of his exploits.

holds back his fiery steed by clutching its jaw. A noble craft, but somehow a most melancholy! All noble things are touched with that.

Now when I looked about the quarter-deck, for some one having authority, in order to propose myself as a candidate for the voyage, at first I saw nobody; but I could not well overlook a strange sort of tent, or rather wigwam, pitched a little behind the main-mast. It seemed only a temporary erection used in port. It was of a conical shape, some ten feet high; consisting of the long, huge slabs of limber black bone taken from the middle and highest part of the jaws of the right-whale. Planted with their broad ends on the deck, a circle of these slabs laced together, mutually sloped towards each other, and at the apex united in a tufted point, where the loose hairy fibres waved to and fro like the top-knot on some old Pottowottamie Sachem's head. A triangular opening faced towards the bows of the ship, so that the insider commanded a complete view forward.

And half concealed in this queer tenement, I at length found one who by his aspect seemed to have authority; and who, it being noon, and the ship's work suspended, was now enjoying respite from the burden of command. He was seated on an old-fashioned oaken chair, wriggling all over with curious carving; and the bottom of which was formed of a stout interlacing of the same elastic stuff of which the wigwam was constructed.

There was nothing so very particular, perhaps, about the appearance of the elderly man I saw; he was brown and brawny, like most old seamen, and heavily rolled up in blue pilot-cloth, cut in the Quaker style; only there was a fine and almost microscopic net-work of the minutest wrinkles interlacing round his eyes, which must have arisen from his continual sailings in many hard gales, and always looking to windward;—for this causes the muscles about the eyes to become pursed together. Such eye-wrinkles are very effectual in a scowl.

"Is this the Captain of the Pequod?" said I, advancing to the door of the tent.

"Supposing it be the Captain of the Pequod, what dost thou want of him?" he demanded.

"I was thinking of shipping."

"Thou wast, wast thou? I see thou art no Nantucketer—ever been in a stove boat?"

"No, Sir, I never have."

"Dost know nothing at all about whaling, I dare say—eh?"

"Nothing, Sir; but I have no doubt I shall soon learn. I've been several voyages in the merchant service, and I think that——"

"Marchant service be damned. Talk not that lingo to me. Dost see that leg?—I'll take that leg away from thy stern, if ever thou talkest of the marchant service to me again. Marchant service indeed! I suppose now ye feel considerable proud of having served in those marchant ships. But flukes! man, what makes thee want to go a whaling, eh?—it looks a little suspicious, don't it, eh?— Hast not been a pirate, hast thou?—Didst not rob thy last Captain, didst thou?—Dost not think of murdering the officers when thou gettest to sea?"

I protested my innocence of these things. I saw that under the mask of these half humorous innuendoes, this old seaman, as an insulated Quakerish Nantucketer, was full of his insular prejudices, and rather distrustful of all aliens, unless they hailed from Cape Cod or the Vineyard.

"But what takes thee a-whaling? I want to know that before I think of shipping ye."

"Well, sir, I want to see what whaling is. I want to see the world."

"Want to see what whaling is, eh? Have ye clapped eye on Captain Ahab?" [4]

"Who is Captain Ahab, sir?"

"Aye, aye, I thought so. Captain Ahab is the Captain of this ship."

"I am mistaken then. I thought I was speaking to the Captain himself."

"Thou art speaking to Captain Peleg—that's who ye are speaking to, young man. It belongs to me and Captain Bildad to see the Pequod fitted out for the voyage, and supplied with all her needs, including crew. We are part owners and agents. But as I was going to say, if thou wantest to know what whaling is, as thou tellest ye do, I can put ye in a way of finding it out before ye bind yourself to it, past backing out. Clap eye on Captain Ahab, young man, and thou wilt find that he has only one leg."

"What do you mean, sir? Was the other one lost by a whale?"

"Lost by a whale! Young man, come nearer to me: it was devoured, chewed up, crunched by the monstrousest parmacetty that ever chipped a boat!—ah, ah!"

I was a little alarmed by his energy, perhaps also a little touched at the hearty grief in his concluding exclamation, but said as calmly as I could, "What you say is no doubt true enough, sir; but how could I know there was any peculiar ferocity in that particular whale, though indeed I might have inferred as much from the simple fact of the accident."

"Look ye now, young man, thy lungs are a sort of soft, d'ye see; thou dost not talk shark a bit. *Sure*, ye've been to sea before

4. The story of the idolatrous King Ahab is told in I Kings 16–22. The biblical account stresses his evil in the sight of the Lord.

now; sure of that?"

"Sir," said I, "I thought I told you that I had been four voyages in the merchant——"

"Hard down out of that! Mind what I said about the marchant service—don't aggravate me—I won't have it. But let us understand each other. I have given thee a hint about what whaling is; do ye yet feel inclined for it?"

"I do, sir."

"Very good. Now, art thou the man to pitch a harpoon down a live whale's throat, and then jump after it? Answer, quick!"

"I am, sir, if it should be positively indispensable to do so; not to be got rid of, that is; which I don't take to be the fact."

"Good again. Now then, thou not only wantest to go a-whaling, to find out by experience what whaling is, but ye also want to go in order to see the world? Was not that what ye said? I thought so. Well then, just step forward there, and take a peep over the weather-bow, and then back to me and tell me what ye see there."

For a moment I stood a little puzzled by this curious request, not knowing exactly how to take it, whether humorously or in earnest. But concentrating all his crow's feet into one scowl, Captain Peleg started me on the errand.

Going forward and glancing over the weather bow, I perceived that the ship swinging to her anchor with the flood-tide, was now obliquely pointing towards the open ocean. The prospect was unlimited, but exceedingly monotonous and forbidding; not the slightest variety that I could see.

"Well, what's the report?" said Peleg when I came back; "what did ye see?"

"Not much," I replied—"nothing but water; considerable horizon though, and there's a squall coming up, I think."

"Well, what dost thou think then of seeing the world? Do ye wish to go round Cape Horn to see any more of it, eh? Can't ye see the world where you stand?"

I was a little staggered, but go a-whaling I must, and I would; and the Pequod was as good a ship as any—I thought the best—and all this I now repeated to Peleg. Seeing me so determined, he expressed his willingness to ship me.

"And thou mayest as well sign the papers right off," he added —"come along with ye." And so saying, he led the way below deck into the cabin.

Seated on the transom [5] was what seemed to me a most uncommon and surprising figure. It turned out to be Captain Bildad, [6] who along with Captain Peleg was one of the largest

---

5. A crossbeam in the stern used as a seat.

6. Bildad is the name of one of Job's "comforters."

owners of the vessel; the other shares, as is sometimes the case in these ports, being held by a crowd of old annuitants; widows, fatherless children, and chancery wards; each owning about the value of a timber head, or a foot of plank, or a nail or two in the ship. People in Nantucket invest their money in whaling vessels, the same way that you do yours in approved state stocks bringing in good interest.

Now, Bildad, like Peleg, and indeed many other Nantucketers, was a Quaker, the island having been originally settled by that sect; and to this day its inhabitants in general retain in an uncommon measure the peculiarities of the Quaker, only variously and anomalously modified by things altogether alien and heterogeneous. For some of these same Quakers are the most sanguinary of all sailors and whale-hunters. They are fighting Quakers; they are Quakers with a vengeance.

So that there are instances among them of men, who, named with Scripture names—a singularly common fashion on the island —and in childhood naturally imbibing the stately dramatic *thee* and *thou* of the Quaker idiom; still, from the audacious, daring, and boundless adventure of their subsequent lives, strangely blend with these unoutgrown peculiarities, a thousand bold dashes of character, not unworthy a Scandinavian sea-king, or a poetical Pagan Roman. And when these things unite in a man of greatly superior natural force, with a globular brain and a ponderous heart; who has also by the stillness and seclusion of many long night-watches in the remotest waters, and beneath constellations never seen here at the north, been led to think untraditionally and independently; receiving all nature's sweet or savage impressions fresh from her own virgin, voluntary, and confiding breast, and thereby chiefly, but with some help from accidental advantages, to learn a bold and nervous lofty language—that man makes one in a whole nation's census—a mighty pageant creature, formed for noble tragedies. Nor will it at all detract from him, dramatically regarded, if either by birth or other circumstances, he have what seems a half wilful over-ruling morbidness at the bottom of his nature. For all men tragically great are made so through a certain morbidness. Be sure of this, O young ambition, all mortal greatness is but disease. But, as yet we have not to do with such an one, but with quite another; and still a man, who, if indeed peculiar, it only results again from another phase of the Quaker, modified by individual circumstances.

Like Captain Peleg, Captain Bildad was a well-to-do, retired whaleman. But unlike Captain Peleg—who cared not a rush for what are called serious things, and indeed deemed those self-same serious things the veriest of all trifles—Captain Bildad had not only been originally educated according to the strictest sect of Nantucket Quakerism, but all his subsequent ocean life, and the sight of many unclad, lovely island creatures, round the Horn—all that had not moved this native born Quaker one single jot, had not so much as altered one angle of his vest. Still, for all this immutableness, was there some lack of common consistency about worthy Captain Bildad. Though refusing, from conscientious scruples, to bear arms against land invaders, yet himself had illimitably invaded the Atlantic and Pacific; and though a sworn foe to human bloodshed, yet had he in his straight-bodied coat, spilled tuns[7] upon tuns of leviathan gore. How now in the contemplative evening of his days, the pious Bildad reconciled these things in the reminiscence, I do not know; but it did not seem to concern him much, and very probably he had long since come to the sage and sensible conclusion that a man's religion is one thing, and this practical world quite another. This world pays dividends. Rising from a little cabin-boy in short clothes of the drabbest drab, to a harpooneer in a broad shad-bellied waistcoat; from that becoming boat-header, chief-mate, and captain, and finally a ship-owner; Bildad, as I hinted before, had concluded his adventurous career by wholly retiring from active life at the goodly age of sixty, and dedicating his remaining days to the quiet receiving of his well-earned income.

Now Bildad, I am sorry to say, had the reputation of being an incorrigible old hunks, and in his sea-going days, a bitter, hard task-master. They told me in Nantucket, though it certainly seems a curious story, that when he sailed the old Categut whaleman, his crew, upon arriving home, were mostly all carried ashore to the hospital, sore exhausted and worn out. For a pious man, especially for a Quaker, he was certainly rather hard-hearted, to say the least. He never used to swear, though, at his men, they said; but somehow he got an inordinate quantity of cruel, unmitigated hard work out of them. When Bildad was a chief-mate, to have his drab-colored eye intently looking at you, made you feel completely nervous, till you could clutch something—a hammer or a marling-spike, and go to work like mad, at something or other, never mind what. Indolence and idleness perished from before him. His own person was the exact embodiment of his utilitarian character. On his long, gaunt body, he carried no spare flesh, no superfluous beard, his chin having a soft, economical nap to it, like the worn nap of his broad-brimmed hat.

Such, then, was the person that I saw seated on the transom when I followed Captain Peleg down into the cabin. The space

7. A tun is a large barrel containing two hundred and fifty-two gallons. See the title of Chapter 77.

between the decks was small; and there, bolt-upright, sat old Bildad, who always sat so, and never leaned, and this to save his coat tails. His broad-brim was placed beside him; his legs were stiffly crossed; his drab vesture was buttoned up to his chin; and spectacles on nose, he seemed absorbed in reading from a ponderous volume.

"Bildad," cried Captain Peleg, "at it again, Bildad, eh? Ye have been studying those Scriptures, now, for the last thirty years, to my certain knowledge. How far ye got, Bildad?"

As if long habituated to such profane talk from his old shipmate, Bildad, without noticing his present irreverence, quietly looked up, and seeing me, glanced again inquiringly towards Peleg.

"He says he's our man, Bildad," said Peleg, "he wants to ship."

"Dost thee?" said Bildad, in a hollow tone, and turning round to me.

"I *dost*," said I unconsciously, he was so intense a Quaker.

"What do ye think of him, Bildad?" said Peleg.

"He'll do," said Bildad, eyeing me, and then went on spelling away at his book in a mumbling tone quite audible.

I thought him the queerest old Quaker I ever saw, especially as Peleg, his friend and old shipmate, seemed such a blusterer. But I said nothing, only looking round me sharply. Peleg now threw open a chest, and drawing forth the ship's articles, placed pen and ink before him, and seated himself at a little table. I began to think it was high time to settle with myself at what terms I would be willing to engage for the voyage. I was already aware that in the whaling business they paid no wages; but all hands, including the captain, received certain shares of the profits called *lays*, and that these lays were proportioned to the degree of importance pertaining to the respective duties of the ship's company. I was also aware that being a green hand at whaling, my own lay would not be very large; but considering that I was used to the sea, could steer a ship, splice a rope, and all that, I made no doubt that from all I had heard I should be offered at least the 275th lay—that is, the 275th part of the clear net proceeds of the voyage, whatever that might eventually amount to. And though the 275th lay was what they call a rather *long lay*, yet it was better than nothing; and if we had a lucky voyage, might pretty nearly pay for the clothing I would wear out on it, not to speak of my three years' beef and board, for which I would not have to pay one stiver.

It might be thought that this was a poor way to accumulate a princely fortune—and so it was, a very poor way indeed. But I am one of those that never take on about princely fortunes, and am quite content if the world is ready to board and lodge me, while I am putting up at this grim sign of the Thunder

Cloud. Upon the whole, I thought that the 275th lay would be about the fair thing, but would not have been surprised had I been offered the 200th, considering I was of a broad-shouldered make.

But one thing, nevertheless, that made me a little distrustful about receiving a generous share òf the profits was this: Ashore, I had heard something of both Captain Peleg and his unaccountable old crony Bildad; how that they being the principal proprietors of the Pequod, therefore the other and more inconsiderable and scattered owners, left nearly the whole management of the ship's affairs to these two. And I did not know but what the stingy old Bildad might have a mighty deal to say about shipping hands, especially as I now found him on board the Pequod, quite at home there in the cabin, and reading his Bible as if at his own fireside. Now while Peleg was vainly trying to mend a pen with his jack-knife, old Bildad, to my no small surprise, considering that he was such an interested party in these proceedings; Bildad never heeded us, but went on mumbling to himself out of his book, " '*Lay* not up for yourselves treasures upon earth, where moth—' " [8]

"Well, Captain Bildad," interrupted Peleg, "what d'ye say, what lay shall we give this young man?"

"Thou knowest best," was the sepulchral reply, "the seven hundred and seventy-seventh wouldn't be too much, would it?— 'where moth and rust do corrupt, but *lay*—' "

Lay, indeed, thought I, and such a lay! the seven hundred and seventy-seventh! Well, old Bildad, you are determined that I, for one, shall not *lay* up many *lays* here below, where moth and rust do corrupt. It was an exceedingly *long lay* that, indeed; and though from the magnitude of the figure it might at first deceive a landsman, yet the slightest consideration will show that though seven hundred and seventy-seven is a pretty large number, yet, when you come to make a *teenth* of it, you will then see, I say, that the seven hundred and seventy-seventh part of a farthing is a good deal less than seven hundred and seventy-seven gold doubloons; and so I thought at the time.

"Why, blast your eyes, Bildad," cried Peleg, "thou dost not want to swindle this young man! he must have more than that."

"Seven hundred and seventy-seventh," again said Bildad, without lifting his eyes; and then went on mumbling—" 'for where your treasure is, there will your heart be also.' "

"I am going to put him down for the three hundredth," said Peleg, "do ye hear that, Bildad! The three hundredth lay, I say."

8. Matthew 6:19–21.

Bildad laid down his book, and turning solemnly towards him said, "Captain Peleg, thou hast a generous heart; but thou must consider the duty thou owest to the other owners of this ship— widows and orphans, many of them—and that if we too abundantly reward the labors of this young man, we may be taking the bread from those widows and those orphans. The seven hundred and seventy-seventh lay, Captain Peleg."

"Thou Bildad!" roared Peleg, starting up and clattering about the cabin. "Blast ye, Captain Bildad, if I had followed thy advice in these matters, I would afore now had a conscience to lug about that would be heavy enough to founder the largest ship that ever sailed round Cape Horn."

"Captain Peleg," said Bildad steadily, "thy conscience may be drawing ten inches of water, or ten fathoms, I can't tell; but as thou art still an impenitent man, Captain Peleg, I greatly fear lest thy conscience be but a leaky one; and will in the end sink thee foundering down to the fiery pit, Captain Peleg."

"Fiery pit! fiery pit! ye insult me, man; past all natural bearing, ye insult me. It's an all-fired outrage to tell any human creature that he's bound to hell. Flukes and flames! Bildad, say that again to me, and start my soul-bolts, but I'll—I'll—yes, I'll swallow a live goat with all his hair and horns on. Out of the cabin, ye canting, drab-colored son of a wooden gun—a straight wake with ye!"

As he thundered out this he made a rush at Bildad, but with a marvellous oblique, sliding celerity, Bildad for that time eluded him.

Alarmed at this terrible outburst between the two principal and responsible owners of the ship, and feeling half a mind to give up all idea of sailing in a vessel so questionably owned and temporarily commanded, I stepped aside from the door to give egress to Bildad, who, I made no doubt, was all eagerness to vanish from before the awakened wrath of Peleg. But to my astonishment, he sat down again on the transom very quietly, and seemed to have not the slightest intention of withdrawing. He seemed quite used to impenitent Peleg and his ways. As for Peleg, after letting off his rage as he had, there seemed no more left in him, and he, too, sat down like a lamb, though he twitched a little as if still nervously agitated. "Whew!" he whistled at last—"the squall's gone off to leeward, I think. Bildad, thou used to be good at sharpening a lance, mend that pen, will ye. My jack-knife here needs the grindstone. Thank ye; thank ye, Bildad. Now then, my young man, Ishmael's thy name, didn't ye say? Well then, down ye go here, Ishmael, for the three hundredth lay."

"Captain Peleg," said I, "I have a friend with me who wants to ship too—shall I bring him down to-morrow?"

"To be sure," said Peleg. "Fetch him along, and we'll look at him."

"What lay does *he* want?" groaned Bildad, glancing up from the book in which he had again been burying himself.

"Oh! never thee mind about that, Bildad," said Peleg. "Has he ever whaled it any?" turning to me.

"Killed more whales than I can count, Captain Peleg."

"Well, bring him along then."

And, after signing the papers, off I went; nothing doubting but that I had done a good morning's work, and that the Pequod was the identical ship that Yojo had provided to carry Queequeg and me round the Cape.

But I had not proceeded far, when I began to bethink me that the captain with whom I was to sail yet remained unseen by me; though, indeed, in many cases, a whale-ship will be completely fitted out, and receive all her crew on board, ere the captain makes himself visible by arriving to take command; for sometimes these voyages are so prolonged, and the shore intervals at home so exceedingly brief, that if the captain have a family, or any absorbing concernment of that sort, he does not trouble himself much about his ship in port, but leaves her to the owners till all is ready for sea. However, it is always as well to have a look at him before irrevocably committing yourself into his hands. Turning back I accosted Captain Peleg, inquiring where Captain Ahab was to be found.

"And what dost thou want of Captain Ahab? It's all right enough; thou art shipped."

"Yes, but I should like to see him."

"But I don't think thou wilt be able to at present. I don't know exactly what's the matter with him; but he keeps close inside the house; a sort of sick, and yet he don't look so. In fact, he ain't sick; but no, he isn't well either. Any how, young man, he won't always see me, so I don't suppose he will thee. He's a queer man, Captain Ahab—so some think—but a good one. Oh, thou'lt like him well enough; no fear, no fear. He's a grand, ungodly, god-like man, Captain Ahab; doesn't speak much; but, when he does speak, then you may well listen. Mark ye, be forewarned; Ahab's above the common; Ahab's been in colleges, as well as 'mong the cannibals; been used to deeper wonders than the waves; fixed his fiery lance in mightier, stranger foes than whales. His lance! aye, the keenest and the surest that, out of all our isle! Oh! he ain't Captain Bildad; no, and he ain't Captain Peleg; *he's Ahab*, boy; and Ahab of old, thou knowest, was a crowned king!"

"And a very vile one. When that wicked king was slain, the dogs, did they not lick his blood?"

"Come hither to me—hither, hither," said Peleg, with a significance in his eye that almost startled me. "Look ye, lad; never say that on board the Pequod. Never say it anywhere. Captain Ahab did not name himself. 'Twas a foolish, ignorant whim of his crazy, widowed mother, who died when he was only a twelvemonth old. And yet the old squaw Tistig, at Gay-head,[9] said that the name would somehow prove prophetic. And, perhaps, other fools like her may tell thee the same. I wish to warn thee. It's a lie. I know Captain Ahab well; I've sailed with him as mate years ago; I know what he is—a good man—not a pious, good man, like Bildad, but a swearing good man—something like me—only there's a good deal more of him. Aye, aye, I know that he was never very jolly; and I know that on the passage home, he was a little out of his mind for a spell; but it was the sharp shooting pains in his bleeding stump that brought that about, as any one might see. I know, too, that ever since he lost his leg last voyage by that accursed whale, he's been a kind of moody—desperate moody, and savage sometimes; but that will all pass off. And once for all, let me tell thee and assure thee, young man, it's better to sail with a moody good captain than a laughing bad one. So good-bye to thee—and wrong not Captain Ahab, because he happens to have a wicked name. Besides, my boy, he has a wife—not three voyages wedded—a sweet, resigned girl. Think of that; by that sweet girl that old man has a child: hold ye then there can be any utter, hopeless harm in Ahab? No, no, my lad; stricken, blasted, if he be, Ahab has his humanities!"

As I walked away, I was full of thoughtfulness; what had been incidentally revealed to me of Captain Ahab, filled me with a certain wild vagueness of painfulness concerning him. And somehow, at the time, I felt a sympathy and a sorrow for him, but for I don't know what, unless it was the cruel loss of his leg. And yet I also felt a strange awe of him; but that sort of awe, which I cannot at all describe, was not exactly awe; I do not know what it was. But I felt it; and it did not disincline me towards him; though I felt impatience at what seemed like mystery in him, so imperfectly as he was known to me then. However, my thoughts were at length carried in other directions, so that for the present dark Ahab slipped my mind.

9. The "most westerly promontory of Martha's Vineyard" (Chap. 27).

Chapter 17

THE RAMADAN

As Queequeg's Ramadan. or Fasting and Humiliation, was to continue all day, I did not choose to disturb him till towards night-fall; for I cherish the greatest respect towards everybody's religious obligations, never mind how comical, and could not find it in my heart to undervalue even a congregation of ants worshipping a toad-stool; or those other creatures in certain parts of our earth, who with a degree of footmanism quite unprecedented in other planets, bow down before the torso of a deceased landed proprietor merely on account of the inordinate possessions yet owned and rented in his name.

I say, we good Presbyterian Christians should be charitable in these things, and not fancy ourselves so vastly superior to other mortals, pagans and what not, because of their half-crazy conceits on these subjects. There was Queequeg, now, certainly entertaining the most absurd notions about Yojo and his Ramadan;—but what of that? Queequeg thought he knew what he was about, I suppose; he seemed to be content; and there let him rest. All our arguing with him would not avail; let him be, I say: and Heaven have mercy on us all—Presbyterians and Pagans alike— for we are all somehow dreadfully cracked about the head, and sadly need mending.

Towards evening, when I felt assured that all his performances and rituals must be over, I went up to his room and knocked at the door; but no answer. I tried to open it, but it was fastened inside. "Queequeg," said I softly through the key-hole:—all silent. "I say, Queequeg! why don't you speak? It's I—Ishmael." But all remained still as before. I began to grow alarmed. I had allowed him such abundant time; I thought he might have had an apoplectic fit. I looked through the key-hole; but the door opening into an odd corner of the room, the key-hole prospect was but a crooked and sinister one. I could only see part of the foot-board of the bed and a line of the wall, but nothing more. I was surprised to behold resting against the wall the wooden shaft of Queequeg's harpoon, which the landlady the evening previous had taken from him, before our mounting to the chamber. That's strange, thought I; but at any rate, since the harpoon stands yonder, and he seldom or never goes abroad without it, therefore he must be inside here, and no possible mistake.

"Queequeg!—Queequeg!"—all still. Something must have happened. Apoplexy! I tried to burst open the door; but it stubbornly resisted. Running down stairs, I quickly stated my suspicions to the first person I met—the chamber-maid. "La! La!" she cried, "I thought something must be the matter. I went to make the bed after breakfast, and the door was locked; and not a mouse to be heard; and it's been just so silent ever since. But I thought, may be, you had both gone off and locked your baggage in for safe keeping. La! La, ma'am!—Mistress! murder! Mrs. Hussey! apoplexy!"—and with these cries, she ran towards the kitchen, I following."

Mrs. Hussey soon appeared, with a mustard-pot in one hand and a vinegar-cruet in the other, having just broken away from the occupation of attending to the castors,[1] and scolding her little black boy meantime.

"Wood-house!" cried I, "which way to it! Run for God's sake, and fetch something to pry open the door—the axe!—the axe!—he's had a stroke; depend upon it!"—and so saying I was unmethodically rushing up stairs again empty-handed, when Mrs. Hussey interposed the mustard-pot and vinegar-cruet, and the entire castor of her countenance.

"What's the matter with you, young man?"

"Get the axe! For God's sake, run for the doctor, some one, while I pry it open!"

"Look here," said the landlady, quickly putting down the vinegar-cruet, so as to have one hand free; "look here; are you talking about prying open any of my doors?"—and with that she seized my arm. "What's the matter with you? What's the matter with you, shipmate?"

In as calm, but rapid a manner as possible, I gave her to understand the whole case. Unconsciously clapping the vinegar-cruet to one side of her nose, she ruminated for an instant; then exclaimed—"No! I haven't seen it since I put it there." Running to a little closet under the landing of the stairs, she glanced in, and returning, told me that Queequeg's harpoon was missing. "He's killed himself," she cried. "It's unfort'nate Stiggs done over again—there goes another counterpane—God pity his poor mother! —it will be the ruin of my house. Has the poor lad a sister? Where's that girl?—there, Betty, go to Snarles the Painter, and tell him to paint me a sign, with—'no suicides permitted here, and no smoking in the parlor;'—might as well kill both birds at once. Kill? The Lord be merciful to his ghost! What's that noise there? You, young man, avast there!"

And running up after me, she caught me as I was again trying to force open the door.

"I won't allow it; I won't have my premises spoiled. Go for the locksmith, there's one about a mile from here. But avast!"

---

1. Also spelled "casters"—containers for condiments.

putting her hand in her side-pocket, "here's a key that'll fit, I guess; let's see." And with that, she turned it in the lock; but, alas! Queequeg's supplemental bolt remained unwithdrawn within.

"Have to burst it open," said I, and was running down the entry a little, for a good start, when the landlady caught at me, again vowing I should not break down her premises; but I tore from her, and with a sudden bodily rush dashed myself full against the mark.

With a prodigious noise the door flew open, and the knob slamming against the wall, sent the plaster to the ceiling; and there, good heavens! there sat Queequeg, altogether cool and self-collected; right in the middle of the room; squatting on his hams, and holding Yojo on top of his head. He looked neither one way nor the other way, but sat like a carved image with scarce a sign of active life.

"Queequeg," said I, going up to him, "Queequeg, what's the matter with you?"

"He hain't been a sittin' so all day, has he?" said the landlady.

But all we said, not a word could we drag out of him; I almost felt like pushing him over, so as to change his position, for it was almost intolerable, it seemed so painfully and unnaturally constrained; especially, as in all probability he had been sitting so for upwards of eight or ten hours, going too without his regular meals.

"Mrs. Hussey," said I, "he's *alive* at all events; so leave us, if you please, and I will see to this strange affair myself."

Closing the door upon the landlady, I endeavored to prevail upon Queequeg to take a chair; but in vain. There he sat; and all I could do—for all my polite arts and blandishments—he would not move a peg, nor say a single word, nor even look at me, nor notice my presence in any the slightest way.

I wonder, thought I, if this can possibly be a part of his Ramadan; do they fast on their hams that way in his native island? It must be so; yes, it's part of his creed, I suppose; well, then, let him rest; he'll get up sooner or later, no doubt. It can't last for ever, thank God, and his Ramadan only comes once a year; and I don't believe it's very punctual then.

I went down to supper. After sitting a long time listening to the long stories of some sailors who had just come from a plum-pudding voyage, as they called it (that is, a short whaling-voyage in a schooner or brig, confined to the north of the line, in the Atlantic Ocean only); after listening to these plum-puddingers till nearly eleven o'clock, I went up stairs to go to bed, feeling quite sure by this time Queequeg must certainly have brought his Ramadan to a termination. But no; there he was just where I had left him; he had not stirred an inch. I began to grow vexed with him; it seemed so downright senseless and insane to be sitting there all day and half the night on his hams in a cold room, holding a piece of wood on his head.

"For heaven's sake, Queequeg, get up and shake yourself; get up and have some supper. You'll starve; you'll kill yourself, Queequeg." But not a word did he reply.

Despairing of him, therefore, I determined to go to bed and to sleep; and no doubt, before a great while, he would follow me. But previous to turning in, I took my heavy bearskin jacket, and threw it over him, as it promised to be a very cold night; and he had nothing but his ordinary round jacket on. For some time, do all I would, I could not get into the faintest doze. I had blown out the candle; and the mere thought of Queequeg—not four feet off—sitting there in that uneasy position, stark alone in the cold and dark; this made me really wretched. Think of it; sleeping all night in the same room with a wide awake pagan on his hams in this dreary, unaccountable Ramadan!

But somehow I dropped off at last, and knew nothing more till break of day; when, looking over the bedside, there squatted Queequeg, as if he had been screwed down to the floor. But as soon as the first glimpse of sun entered the window, up he got, with stiff and grating joints, but with a cheerful look; limped towards me where I lay; pressed his forehead again against mine; and said his Ramadan was over.

Now, as I before hinted, I have no objection to any person's religion, be it what it may, so long as that person does not kill or insult any other person, because that other person don't believe it also. But when a man's religion becomes really frantic; when it is a positive torment to him; and, in fine, makes this earth of ours an uncomfortable inn to lodge in; then I think it high time to take that individual aside and argue the point with him.

And just so I now did with Queequeg. "Queequeg," said I, "get into bed now, and lie and listen to me." I then went on, beginning with the rise and progress of the primitive religions, and coming down to the various religions of the present time, during which time I labored to show Queequeg that all these Lents, Ramadans, and prolonged ham-squattings in cold, cheerless rooms were stark nonsense; bad for the health; useless for the soul; opposed, in short, to the obvious laws of Hygiene and common sense. I told him, too, that he being in other things such an extremely sensible and sagacious savage, it pained me, very badly pained me, to see him now so deplorably foolish about this ridiculous Ramadan of his. Besides, argued I, fasting makes the body cave in; hence the spirit caves in; and all thoughts born of a fast must necessarily be half-starved. This is the reason why most dyspeptic religionists cherish such melancholy notions about their hereafters. In one word, Queequeg, said I, rather digressively; hell is an idea first born on an undigested apple-dumpling; and since then perpetuated through the hereditary dyspepsias nurtured by Ramadans.

I then asked Queequeg whether he himself was ever troubled with dyspepsia; expressing the idea very plainly, so that he could take it in. He said no; only upon one memorable occasion. It was after a great feast given by his father the king, on the gaining of a great battle wherein fifty of the enemy had been killed by about two o'clock in the afternoon, and all cooked and eaten that very evening.

"No more, Queequeg," said I, shuddering; "that will do;" for I knew the inferences without his further hinting them. I had seen a sailor who had visited that very island, and he told me that it was the custom, when a great battle had been gained there, to barbecue all the slain in the yard or garden of the victor; and then, one by one, they were placed in great wooden trenchers, and garnished round like a pilau, with breadfruit and cocoanuts; and with some parsley in their mouths, were sent round with the victor's compliments to all his friends, just as though these presents were so many Christmas turkeys.

After all, I do not think that my remarks about religion made much impression upon Queequeg. Because, in the first place, he somehow seemed dull of hearing on that important subject, unless considered from his own point of view; and, in the second place, he did not more than one third understand me, couch my ideas simply as I would; and, finally, he no doubt thought he knew a good deal more about the true religion than I did. He looked at me with a sort of condescending concern and compassion, as though he thought it a great pity that such a sensible young man should be so hopelessly lost to evangelical pagan piety.

At last we rose and dressed; and Queequeg, taking a prodigiously hearty breakfast of chowders of all sorts, so that the landlady should not make much profit by reason of his Ramadan, we sallied out to board the Pequod, sauntering along, and picking our teeth with halibut bones.

Chapter 18

HIS MARK

As we were walking down the end of the wharf towards the ship, Queequeg carrying his harpoon, Captain Peleg in his gruff voice loudly hailed us from his wigwam, saying he had not suspected my friend was a cannibal, and furthermore announcing that he let no cannibals on board that craft, unless they previously produced their papers.

"What do you mean by that, Captain Peleg?" said I, now jumping on the bulwarks, and leaving my comrade standing on the wharf.

"I mean," he replied, "he must show his papers."

"Yea," said Captain Bildad in his hollow voice, sticking his head from behind Peleg's, out of the wigwam. "He must show that he's converted. Son of darkness," he added, turning to Queequeg, "art thou at present in communion with any Christian church?"

"Why," said I, "he's a member of the First Congregational Church." Here be it said, that many tattooed savages sailing in Nantucket ships at last come to be converted into the churches.

"First Congregational Church," cried Bildad, "what! that worships in Deacon Deuteronomy Coleman's meeting-house?" and so saying, taking out his spectacles, he rubbed them with his great yellow bandana handkerchief, and putting them on very carefully, came out of the wigwam, and leaning stiffly over the bulwarks, took a good long look at Queequeg.

"How long hath he been a member?" he then said, turning to me; "not very long, I rather guess, young man."

"No," said Peleg, "and he hasn't been baptized right either, or it would have washed some of that devil's blue off his face."

"Do tell, now," cried Bildad, "is this Philistine a regular member of Deacon Deuteronomy's meeting? I never saw him going there, and I pass it every Lord's day."

"I don't know anything about Deacon Deuteronomy or his meeting," said I, "all I know is, that Queequeg here is a born member of the First Congregational Church. He is a deacon himself, Queequeg is."

"Young man," said Bildad sternly, "thou art skylarking with me —explain thyself, thou young Hittite. What church dost thee mean? answer me."

Finding myself thus hard pushed, I replied. "I mean, sir, the same ancient Catholic Church to which you and I, and Captain Peleg there, and Queequeg here, and all of us, and every mother's son and soul of us belong; the great and everlasting First Congregation of this whole worshipping world; we all belong to that; only some of us cherish some queer crotchets noways touching the grand belief; in *that* we all join hands."

"Splice, thou mean'st *splice* hands," cried Peleg, drawing nearer. "Young man, you'd better ship for a missionary, instead of a fore-mast hand; I never heard a better sermon. Deacon Deuteronomy—why Father Mapple himself couldn't beat it, and he's reckoned something. Come aboard, come aboard; never mind about the papers. I say, tell Quohog [1] there—what's that you call him? tell Quohog to step along. By the great anchor, what a harpoon he's got there! looks like good stuff that; and he handles it about right. I say, Quohog, or whatever your name is, did you ever stand in the head of a whale-boat? did you ever strike a fish?"

Without saying a word, Queequeg, in his wild sort of way, jumped upon the bulwarks, from thence into the bows of one of the whale-boats hanging to the side; and then bracing his left knee, and poising his harpoon, cried out in some such way as this:—

"Cap'ain, you see him small drop tar on water dere? You see him? well, spose him one whale eye, well, den!" and taking sharp aim at it, he darted the iron right over old Bildad's broad brim, clean across the ship's decks, and struck the glistening tar spot out of sight.

"Now," said Queequeg, quietly hauling in the line, "spos-ee him whale-e eye; why, dad whale dead."

"Quick, Bildad," said Peleg, to his partner, who, aghast at the close vicinity of the flying harpoon, had retreated towards the cabin gangway. "Quick, I say, you Bildad, and get the ship's papers. We must have Hedgehog there, I mean Quohog, in one of our boats. Look ye, Quohog, we'll give ye the ninetieth lay, and that's more than ever was given a harpooneer yet out of Nantucket."

So down we went into the cabin, and to my great joy Queequeg was soon enrolled among the same ship's company to which I myself belonged.

When all preliminaries were over and Peleg had got everything ready for signing, he turned to me and said, "I guess, Quohog there don't know how to write, does he? I say, Quohog, blast ye! dost thou sign thy name or make thy mark?"

But at this question, Queequeg, who had twice or thrice before taken part in similar ceremonies, looked no ways abashed; but taking the offered pen, copied upon the paper, in the proper place, an exact counterpart of a queer round figure [2] which was tattooed upon his arm; so that through Captain Peleg's obstinate mistake touching his appellative, it stood something like this:—

Quohog.
his ✠ mark.

Meanwhile Captain Bildad sat earnestly and steadfastly eyeing Queequeg, and at last rising solemnly and fumbling in the huge

---

1. Peleg deals with Queequeg's strange name by using a familiar similar word, quohog (or quahog), a kind of local clam (mentioned in Chap. 14).
2. The cross printed in the American edition as Queequeg's mark (and imitated here) is not "a queer round figure," and was probably supplied by the original typesetter in place of the figure Melville had drawn in his manuscript.

pockets of his broad-skirted drab coat, took out a bundle of tracts, and selecting one entitled "The Latter Day Coming; or No Time to Lose," placed it in Queequeg's hands, and then grasping them and the book with both his, looked earnestly into his eyes, and said, "Son of darkness, I must do my duty by thee; I am part owner of this ship, and feel concerned for the souls of all its crew; if thou still clingest to thy Pagan ways, which I sadly fear, I beseech thee, remain not for aye a Belial bondsman. Spurn the idol Bel, and the hideous dragon; turn from the wrath to come; mind thine eye, I say; oh! goodness gracious! steer clear of the fiery pit!"

Something of the salt sea yet lingered in old Bildad's language, heterogeneously mixed with Scriptural and domestic phrases.

"Avast there, avast there, Bildad, avast now spoiling our harpooneer," cried Peleg. "Pious harpooneers never make good voyagers—it takes the shark out of 'em; no harpooneer is worth a straw who aint pretty sharkish. There was young Nat Swaine, once the bravest boat-header out of all Nantucket and the Vineyard; he joined the meeting, and never came to good. He got so frightened about his plaguy soul, that he shrinked and sheered away from whales, for fear of after-claps, in case he got stove and went to Davy Jones."

"Peleg! Peleg!" said Bildad, lifting his eyes and hands, "thou thyself, as I myself, hast seen many a perilous time; thou knowest, Peleg, what it is to have the fear of death; how, then, can'st thou prate in this ungodly guise. Thou beliest thine own heart, Peleg. Tell me, when this same Pequod here had her three masts overboard in that typhoon off Japan, that same voyage when thou went mate with Captain Ahab, did'st thou not think of Death and the Judgment then?"

"Hear him, hear him now," cried Peleg, marching across the cabin, and thrusting his hands far down into his pockets,—"hear him, all of ye. Think of that! When every moment we thought the ship would sink! Death and the Judgment then? What? With all three masts making such an everlasting thundering against the side; and every sea breaking over us, fore and aft. Think of Death and the Judgment then? No! no time to think about Death then. Life was what Captain Ahab and I was thinking of; and how to save all hands—how to rig jury-masts—how to get into the nearest port; that was what I was thinking of."

Bildad said no more, but buttoning up his coat, stalked on deck, where we followed him. There he stood, very quietly overlooking some sail-makers who were mending a top-sail in the waist. Now and then he stooped to pick up a patch, or save an end of the tarred twine, which otherwise might have been wasted.

Chapter 19

THE PROPHET

"Shipmates, have ye shipped in that ship?"

Queequeg and I had just left the Pequod, and were sauntering away from the water, for the moment each occupied with his own thoughts, when the above words were put to us by a stranger, who, pausing before us, levelled his massive forefinger at the vessel in question. He was but shabbily apparelled in faded jacket and patched trowsers; a rag of a black handkerchief investing his neck. A confluent small-pox had in all directions flowed over his face, and left it like the complicated ribbed bed of a torrent, when the rushing waters have been dried up.

"Have ye shipped in her?" he repeated.

"You mean the ship Pequod, I suppose," said I, trying to gain a little more time for an uninterrupted look at him.

"Aye, the Pequod—that ship there," he said, drawing back his whole arm, and then rapidly shoving it straight out from him, with a fixed bayonet of his pointed finger darted full at the object.

"Yes," said I, "we have just signed the articles."

"Anything down there about your souls?"

"About what?"

"Oh, perhaps you hav'n't got any," he said quickly. "No matter though, I know many chaps that hav'n't got any,—good luck to 'em; and they are all the better off for it. A soul's a sort of a fifth wheel to a wagon."

"What are you jabbering about, shipmate?" said I.

"*He's* got enough, though, to make up for all deficiencies of that sort in other chaps," abruptly said the stranger, placing a nervous emphasis upon the word *he*.

"Queequeg," said I, "let's go; this fellow has broken loose from somewhere; he's talking about something and somebody we don't know."

"Stop!" cried the stranger. "Ye said true—ye hav'n't seen Old Thunder yet, have ye?"

"Who's Old Thunder?" said I, again riveted with the insane earnestness of his manner.

"Captain Ahab."

"What! the captain of our ship, the Pequod?"

"Aye, among some of us old sailor chaps, he goes by that name. Ye hav'n't seen him yet, have ye?"

"No, we hav'n't. He's sick they say, but is getting better, and will be all right again before long."

"All right again before long!" laughed the stranger, with a

solemnly derisive sort of laugh. "Look ye; when Captain Ahab is all right, then this left arm of mine will be all right; not before."

"What do you know about him?"

"What did they *tell* you about him? Say that!"

"They didn't tell much of anything about him; only I've heard that he's a good whale-hunter, and a good captain to his crew."

"That's true, that's true—yes, both true enough. But you must jump when he gives an order. Step and growl; growl and go— that's the word with Captain Ahab. But nothing about that thing that happened to him off Cape Horn, long ago, when he lay like dead for three days and nights; nothing about that deadly skrimmage with the Spaniard afore the altar in Santa?—heard nothing about that, eh? Nothing about the silver calabash he spat into? And nothing about his losing his leg last voyage, according to the prophecy? Didn't ye hear a word about them matters and something more, eh? No, I don't think ye did; how could ye? Who knows it? Not all Nantucket, I guess. But hows'ever, mayhap, ye've heard tell about the leg, and how he lost it; aye, ye have heard of that, I dare say. Oh yes, *that* every one knows a'most—I mean they know he's only one leg; and that a parmacetti took the other off."

"My friend," said I, "what all this gibberish of yours is about, I don't know, and I don't much care; for it seems to me that you must be a little damaged in the head. But if you are speaking of Captain Ahab, of that ship there, the Pequod, then let me tell you, that I know all about the loss of his leg."

"*All* about it, eh—sure you do?—all?"

"Pretty sure."

With finger pointed and eye levelled at the Pequod, the beggar-like stranger stood a moment, as if in a troubled reverie; then starting a little, turned and said:—"Ye've shipped, have ye? Names down on the papers? Well, well, what's signed, is signed; and what's to be, will be; and then again, perhaps it wont be, after all. Any how, it's all fixed and arranged a'ready; and some sailors or other must go with him, I suppose; as well these as any other men, God pity 'em! Morning to ye, shipmates, morning; the ineffable heavens bless ye; I'm sorry I stopped ye."

"Look here, friend," said I, "if you have anything important to tell us, out with it; but if you are only trying to bamboozle us, you are mistaken in your game; that's all I have to say."

"And it's said very well, and I like to hear a chap talk up that way; you are just the man for him—the likes of ye. Morning to ye, shipmates, morning! Oh! when ye get there, tell 'em I've concluded not to make one of 'em."

"Ah, my dear fellow, you can't fool us that way—you can't

fool us. It is the easiest thing in the world for a man to look as if he had a great secret in him."

"Morning to ye, shipmates, morning."

"Morning it is," said I. "Come along, Queequeg, let's leave this crazy man. But stop, tell me your name, will you?"

"Elijah." [1]

Elijah! thought I, and we walked away, both commenting, after each other's fashion, upon this ragged old sailor; and agreed that he was nothing but a humbug, trying to be a bugbear. But we had not gone perhaps above a hundred yards, when chancing to turn a corner, and looking back as I did so, who should be seen but Elijah following us, though at a distance. Somehow, the sight of him struck me so, that I said nothing to Queequeg of his being behind, but passed on with my comrade, anxious to see whether the stranger would turn the same corner that we did. He did; and then it seemed to me that he was dogging us, but with what intent I could not for the life of me imagine. This circumstance, coupled with his ambiguous, half-hinting, half-revealing, shrouded sort of talk, now begat in me all kinds of vague wonderments and half-apprehensions, and all connected with the Pequod; and Captain Ahab; and the leg he had lost; and the Cape Horn fit; and the silver calabash; and what Captain Peleg had said of him, when I left the ship the day previous; and the prediction of the squaw Tistig; and the voyage we had bound ourselves to sail; and a hundred other shadowy things.

I was resolved to satisfy myself whether this ragged Elijah was really dogging us or not, and with that intent crossed the way with Queequeg, and on that side of it retraced our steps. But Elijah passed on, without seeming to notice us. This relieved me; and once more, and finally as it seemed to me, I pronounced him in my heart, a humbug.

Chapter 20

ALL ASTIR

A day or two passed, and there was great activity aboard the Pequod. Not only were the old sails being mended, but new sails were coming on board, and bolts of canvas, and coils of rigging; in short, everything betokened that the ship's preparations were hurrying to a close. Captain Peleg seldom or never

1. I Kings recounts the prophet Elijah's conflicts with King Ahab and his wife Jezebel, a worshiper of Baal. When Jezebel has Naboth killed in order to obtain his vineyard for Ahab to use as an herb garden, Elijah prophesies to Ahab (as Ishmael recalled above, Chap. 16) that "in the place where dogs licked the blood of Naboth shall dogs lick thy blood, even thine," and that "the dogs shall eat Jezebel by the wall of Jezreel."

went ashore, but sat in his wigwam keeping a sharp look-out upon the hands: Bildad did all the purchasing and providing at the stores; and the men employed in the hold and on the rigging were working till long after night-fall.

On the day following Queequeg's signing the articles, word was given at all the inns where the ship's company were stopping, that their chests must be on board before night, for there was no telling how soon the vessel might be sailing. So Queequeg and I got down our traps, resolving, however, to sleep ashore till the last. But it seems they always give very long notice in these cases, and the ship did not sail for several days. But no wonder; there was a good deal to be done, and there is no telling how many things to be thought of, before the Pequod was fully equipped.

Every one knows what a multitude of things—beds, sauce-pans, knives and forks, shovels and tongs, napkins, nut-crackers, and what not, are indispensable to the business of housekeeping. Just so with whaling, which necessitates a three-years' housekeeping upon the wide ocean, far from all grocers, coster-mongers,[1] doctors, bakers, and bankers. And though this also holds true of merchant vessels, yet not by any means to the same extent as with whalemen. For besides the great length of the whaling voyage, the numerous articles peculiar to the prosecution of the fishery, and the impossibility of replacing them at the remote harbors usually frequented, it must be remembered, that of all ships, whaling vessels are the most exposed to accidents of all kinds, and especially to the destruction and loss of the very things upon which the success of the voyage most depends. Hence, the spare boats, spare spars, and spare lines and harpoons, and spare everythings, almost, but a spare Captain and duplicate ship.

At the period of our arrival at the Island, the heaviest stowage of the Pequod had been almost completed; comprising her beef, bread, water, fuel, and iron hoops and staves. But, as before hinted, for some time there was a continual fetching and carrying on board of divers odds and ends of things, both large and small.

Chief among those who did this fetching and carrying was Captain Bildad's sister,[2] a lean old lady of a most determined and indefatigable spirit, but withal very kindhearted, who seemed resolved that, if *she* could help it, nothing should be found wanting in the Pequod, after once fairly getting to sea. At one time

1. Hawkers of fruits or vegetables.
2. If Aunt Charity is Bildad's sister and Stubb is her brother-in-law (See Chap. 22, first paragraph), then Stubb has a wife, who is also her and Bildad's sister, and Stubb is Bildad's brother-in-law—facts not mentioned or developed elsewhere. There are a number of such curious details in the book.

she would come on board with a jar of pickles for the steward's pantry; another time with a bunch of quills for the chief mate's desk, where he kept his log; a third time with a roll of flannel for the small of some one's rheumatic back. Never did any woman better deserve her name, which was Charity—Aunt Charity, as everybody called her. And like a sister of charity did this charitable Aunt Charity bustle about hither and thither, ready to turn her hand and heart to anything that promised to yield safety, comfort, and consolation to all on board a ship in which her beloved brother Bildad was concerned, and in which she herself owned a score or two of well-saved dollars.

But it was startling to see this excellent hearted Quakeress coming on board, as she did the last day, with a long oil-ladle in one hand, and a still longer whaling lance in the other. Nor was Bildad himself nor Captain Peleg at all backward. As for Bildad, he carried about with him a long list of the articles needed, and at every fresh arrival, down went his mark opposite that article upon the paper. Every once and a while Peleg came running out of his whalebone den, roaring at the men down the hatchways, roaring up to the riggers at the mast-head, and then concluded by roaring back into his wigwam.

During these days of preparation, Queequeg and I often visited the craft, and as often I asked about Captain Ahab, and how he was, and when he was going to come on board his ship. To these questions they would answer, that he was getting better and better, and was expected aboard every day; meantime, the two Captains, Peleg and Bildad, could attend to everything necessary to fit the vessel for the voyage. If I had been downright honest with myself, I would have seen very plainly in my heart that I did but half fancy being committed this way to so long a voyage, without once laying my eyes on the man who was to be the absolute dictator of it, so soon as the ship sailed out upon the open sea. But when a man suspects any wrong, it sometimes happens that if he be already involved in the matter, he insensibly strives to cover up his suspicions even from himself. And much this way it was with me. I said nothing, and tried to think nothing.

At last it was given out that some time next day the ship would certainly sail. So next morning, Queequeg and I took a very early start.

Chapter 21
GOING ABOARD

It was nearly six o'clock, but only grey imperfect misty dawn, when we drew nigh the wharf.

"There are some sailors running ahead there, if I see right," said I to Queequeg, "it can't be shadows; she's off by sunrise, I guess; come on!"

"Avast!" cried a voice, whose owner at the same time coming close behind us, laid a hand upon both our shoulders, and then insinuating himself between us, stood stooping forward a little, in the uncertain twilight, strangely peering from Queequeg to me. It was Elijah.

"Going aboard?"

"Hands off, will you," said I.

"Lookee here," said Queequeg, shaking himself, "go 'way!"

"Aint going aboard, then?"

"Yes, we are," said I, "but what business is that of yours? Do you know, Mr. Elijah, that I consider you a little impertinent?"

"No, no, no; I wasn't aware of that," said Elijah, slowly and wonderingly looking from me to Queequeg, with the most unaccountable glances.

"Elijah," said I, "you will oblige my friend and me by withdrawing. We are going to the Indian and Pacific Oceans, and would prefer not to be detained."

"Ye be, be ye? Coming back afore breakfast?"

"He's cracked, Queequeg," said I, "come on."

"Holloa!" cried stationary Elijah, hailing us when we had removed a few paces.

"Never mind him," said I, "Queequeg, come on."

But he stole up to us again, and suddenly clapping his hand on my shoulder, said—"Did ye see anything looking like men going towards that ship a while ago?"

Struck by this plain matter-of-fact question, I answered, saying, "Yes, I thought I did see four or five men; but it was too dim to be sure."

"Very dim, very dim," said Elijah. "Morning to ye."

Once more we quitted him; but once more he came softly after us; and touching my shoulder again, said, "See if you can find 'em now, will ye?"

"Find who?"

"Morning to ye! morning to ye!" he rejoined, again moving off. "Oh! I was going to warn ye against—but never mind, never mind —it's all one, all in the family too;—sharp frost this morning, ain't it? Good bye to ye. Shan't see ye again very soon, I guess; unless it's before the Grand Jury." And with these cracked words he finally departed, leaving me, for the moment, in no small wonderment at his frantic impudence.

At last, stepping on board the Pequod, we found everything in profound quiet, not a soul moving. The cabin entrance was locked within; the hatches were all on, and lumbered with coils of rigging. Going forward to the forecastle, we found the slide of the scuttle open. Seeing a light, we went down, and found only an old rigger there, wrapped in a tattered pea-jacket. He was thrown at whole length upon two chests, his face downwards and inclosed in his folded arms. The profoundest slumber slept upon him.

"Those sailors we saw, Queequeg, where can they have gone to?" said I, looking dubiously at the sleeper. But it seemed that, when on the wharf, Queequeg had not at all noticed what I now alluded to; hence I would have thought myself to have been optically deceived in that matter, were it not for Elijah's otherwise inexplicable question. But I beat the thing down; and again marking the sleeper, jocularly hinted to Queequeg that perhaps we had best sit up with the body; telling him to establish himself accordingly. He put his hand upon the sleeper's rear, as though feeling if it was soft enough; and then, without more ado, sat quietly down there.

"Gracious! Queequeg, don't sit there," said I.

"Oh! perry dood seat," said Queequeg, "my country way; won't hurt him face."

"Face!" said I, "call that his face? very benevolent countenance then; but how hard he breathes, he's heaving himself; get off, Queequeg, you are heavy, it's grinding the face of the poor. Get off, Queequeg! Look, he'll twitch you off soon. I wonder he don't wake."

Queequeg removed himself to just beyond the head of the sleeper, and lighted his tomahawk pipe. I sat at the feet. We kept the pipe passing over the sleeper, from one to the other. Meanwhile, upon questioning him, in his broken fashion Queequeg gave me to understand that, in his land, owing to the absence of settees and sofas of all sorts, the king, chiefs, and great people generally, were in the custom of fattening some of the lower orders for ottomans; and to furnish a house comfortably in that respect, you had only to buy up eight or ten lazy fellows, and lay them round in the piers and alcoves. Besides, it was very convenient on an excursion; much better than those garden-chairs which are convertible into walking-sticks; upon occasion, a chief calling his attendant, and desiring him to make a settee of himself under a spreading tree, perhaps in some damp marshy place.

While narrating these things, every time Queequeg received the tomahawk from me, he flourished the hatchet-side of it over the sleeper's head.

"What's that for, Queequeg?"

"Perry easy, kill-e; oh! perry easy!"

He was going on with some wild reminiscences about his toma-hawk-pipe, which, it seemed, had in its two uses both brained his foes and soothed his soul, when we were directly attracted to the sleeping rigger. The strong vapor now completely filling the contracted hole, it began to tell upon him. He breathed with a sort of muffledness; then seemed troubled in the nose; then revolved over once or twice; then sat up and rubbed his eyes.

"Holloa!" he breathed at last, "who be ye smokers?"

"Shipped men," answered I, "when does she sail?"

"Aye, aye, ye are going in her, be ye? She sails to-day. The Captain came aboard last night."

"What Captain?—Ahab?"

"Who but him indeed?"

I was going to ask him some further questions concerning Ahab, when we heard a noise on deck.

"Holloa! Starbuck's astir," said the rigger. "He's a lively chief mate, that; good man, and a pious; but all alive now, I must turn to." And so saying he went on deck, and we followed.

It was now clear sunrise. Soon the crew came on board in twos and threes; the riggers bestirred themselves; the mates were actively engaged; and several of the shore people were busy in bringing various last things on board. Meanwhile Captain Ahab remained invisibly enshrined within his cabin.

Chapter 22

MERRY CHRISTMAS

At length, towards noon, upon the final dismissal of the ship's riggers, and after the Pequod had been hauled out from the wharf, and after the ever-thoughtful Charity had come off in a whaleboat, with her last gifts—a night-cap for Stubb, the second mate, her brother-in-law, and a spare Bible for the steward—after all this, the two captains, Peleg and Bildad, issued from the cabin, and turning to the chief mate, Peleg said:

"Now, Mr. Starbuck, are you sure everything is right? Captain Ahab is all ready—just spoke to him—nothing more to be got from shore, eh? Well, call all hands, then. Muster 'em aft here—blast 'em!"

"No need of profane words, however great the hurry, Peleg," said Bildad, "but away with thee, friend Starbuck, and do our bidding."

How now! Here upon the very point of starting for the voyage, Captain Peleg and Captain Bildad were going it with a high hand on the quarter-deck, just as if they were to be joint-commanders at sea, as well as to all appearances in port. And, as for Captain Ahab, no sign of him was yet to be seen; only, they said he was in the cabin. But then, the idea was, that his presence was by no means necessary in getting the ship under weigh, and steering her well out to sea. Indeed, as that was not at all his proper business, but the pilot's; and as he was not yet completely recovered—so they said—therefore, Captain Ahab stayed below. And all this seemed natural enough; especially as in the merchant service many captains never show themselves on deck for a considerable time after heaving up the anchor, but remain over the cabin table, having a farewell merry-making with their shore friends, before they quit the ship for good with the pilot.

But there was not much chance to think over the matter, for Captain Peleg was now all alive. He seemed to do most of the talking and commanding, and not Bildad.

"Aft here, ye sons of bachelors," he cried, as the sailors lingered at the main-mast. "Mr. Starbuck, drive 'em aft."

"Strike the tent there!"—was the next order. As I hinted before, this whalebone marquee was never pitched except in port; and on board the Pequod, for thirty years, the order to strike the tent was well known to be the next thing to heaving up the anchor.

"Man the capstan! Blood and thunder!—jump!"—was the next command, and the crew sprang for the handspikes.

Now, in getting under weigh, the station generally occupied by the pilot is the forward part of the ship. And here Bildad, who, with Peleg, be it known, in addition to his other offices, was one of the licensed pilots of the port—he being suspected to have got himself made a pilot in order to save the Nantucket pilot-fee to all the ships he was concerned in, for he never piloted any other craft—Bildad, I say, might now be seen actively engaged in looking over the bows for the approaching anchor, and at intervals singing what seemed a dismal stave of psalmody, to cheer the hands at the windlass, who roared forth some sort of a chorus about the girls in Booble Alley, with hearty good will. Nevertheless, not three days previous, Bildad had told them that no profane songs would be allowed on board the Pequod, particularly in getting under weigh; and Charity, his sister, had placed a small choice copy of Watts [1] in each seaman's berth.

Meantime, overseeing the other part of the ship, Captain Peleg ripped and swore astern in the most frightful manner. I almost thought he would sink the ship before the anchor could be got up; involuntarily I paused on my handspike, and told Queequeg

1. Isaac Watts (1674–1748), writer of hymns and versions of the psalms.

to do the same, thinking of the perils we both ran, in starting
on the voyage with such a devil for a pilot. I was comforting myself, however, with the thought that in pious Bildad might be
found some salvation, spite of his seven hundred and seventy-
seventh lay; when I felt a sudden sharp poke in my rear, and
turning round, was horrified at the apparition of Captain Peleg
in the act of withdrawing his leg from my immediate vicinity.
That was my first kick.

"Is that the way they heave in the marchant service?" he roared.
"Spring, thou sheep-head; spring, and break thy backbone! Why
don't ye spring, I say, all of ye—spring! Quohog! spring, thou
chap with the red whiskers; spring there, Scotch-cap; spring, thou
green pants. Spring, I say, all of ye, and spring your eyes out!"
And so saying, he moved along the windlass, here and there using
his leg very freely, while imperturbable Bildad kept leading
off with his psalmody. Thinks I, Captain Peleg must have been
drinking something to-day.

At last the anchor was up, the sails were set, and off we glided.
It was a short, cold Christmas; and as the short northern day
merged into night, we found ourselves almost broad upon the
wintry ocean, whose freezing spray cased us in ice, as in polished
armor. The long rows of teeth on the bulwarks glistened in the
moonlight; and like the white ivory tusks of some huge elephant,
vast curving icicles depended from the bows.

Lank Bildad, as pilot, headed the first watch, and ever and anon,
as the old craft deep dived into the green seas, and sent the
shivering frost all over her, and the winds howled, and the cordage rang, his steady notes were heard,—

> "Sweet fields beyond the swelling flood,
>   Stand dressed in living green.
> So to the Jews old Canaan stood,
>   While Jordan rolled between."

Never did those sweet words sound more sweetly to me than
then. They were full of hope and fruition. Spite of this frigid
winter night in the boisterous Atlantic, spite of my wet feet and
wetter jacket, there was yet, it then seemed to me, many a pleasant haven in store; and meads and glades so eternally vernal, that
the grass shot up by the spring, untrodden, unwilted, remains at
midsummer.

At last we gained such an offing, that the two pilots were
needed no longer. The stout sail-boat that had accompanied us
began ranging alongside.

It was curious and not unpleasing, how Peleg and Bildad were affected at this juncture, especially Captain Bildad. For loath to depart, yet; very loath to leave, for good, a ship bound on so long and perilous a voyage—beyond both stormy Capes; a ship in which some thousands of his hard earned dollars were invested; a ship, in which an old shipmate sailed as captain; a man almost as old as he, once more starting to encounter all the terrors of the pitiless jaw; loath to say good-bye to a thing so every way brimful of every interest to him,—poor old Bildad lingered long; paced the deck with anxious strides; ran down into the cabin to speak another farewell word there; again came on deck, and looked to windward; looked towards the wide and endless waters, only bounded by the far-off unseen Eastern Continents; looked towards the land; looked aloft; looked right and left; looked everywhere and nowhere; and at last, mechanically coiling a rope upon its pin, convulsively grasped stout Peleg by the hand, and holding up a lantern, for a moment stood gazing heroically in his face, as much as to say, "Nevertheless, friend Peleg, I can stand it; yes, I can."

As for Peleg himself, he took it more like a philosopher; but for all his philosophy, there was a tear twinkling in his eye, when the lantern came too near. And he, too, did not a little run from cabin to deck—now a word below, and now a word with Starbuck, the chief mate.

But, at last, he turned to his comrade, with a final sort of look about him,—"Captain Bildad—come, old shipmate, we must go. Back the main-yard there! Boat ahoy! Stand by to come close alongside, now! Careful, careful!—come, Bildad, boy—say your last. Luck to ye, Starbuck—luck to ye, Mr. Stubb—luck to ye, Mr. Flask—good-bye, and good luck to ye all—and this day three years I'll have a hot supper smoking for ye in old Nantucket. Hurrah and away!"

"God bless ye, and have ye in His holy keeping, men," murmured old Bildad, almost incoherently. "I hope ye'll have fine weather now, so that Captain Ahab may soon be moving among ye—a pleasant sun is all he needs, and ye'll have plenty of them in the tropic voyage ye go. Be careful in the hunt, ye mates. Don't stave the boats needlessly, ye harpooneers; good white cedar plank is raised full three per cent. within the year. Don't forget your prayers, either. Mr. Starbuck, mind that cooper don't waste the spare staves. Oh! the sail-needles are in the green locker! Don't whale it too much a' Lord's days, men; but don't miss a fair chance either, that's rejecting Heaven's good gifts. Have an eye to the molasses tierce, Mr. Stubb; it was a little leaky, I thought. If ye touch at the islands, Mr. Flask, beware of fornication. Good-bye, good-bye! Don't keep that cheese too long down in the hold, Mr. Starbuck; it'll spoil. Be careful with the butter —twenty cents the pound it was, and mind ye, if—"

"Come, come, Captain Bildad; stop palavering,—away!" and with that, Peleg hurried him over the side, and both dropt into the boat.

Ship and boat diverged; the cold, damp night breeze blew between; a screaming gull flew overhead; the two hulls wildly rolled; we gave three heavy-hearted cheers, and blindly plunged like fate into the lone Atlantic.

Chapter 23

THE LEE SHORE

Some chapters back, one Bulkington was spoken of, a tall, new-landed mariner, encountered in New Bedford at the inn.

When on that shivering winter's night, the Pequod thrust her vindictive bows into the cold malicious waves, who should I see standing at her helm but Bulkington! I looked with sympathetic awe and fearfulness upon the man, who in mid-winter just landed from a four years' dangerous voyage, could so unrestingly push off again for still another tempestuous term. The land seemed scorching to his feet. Wonderfullest things are ever the unmentionable; deep memories yield no epitaphs; this six-inch chapter is the stoneless grave of Bulkington. Let me only say that it fared with him as with the storm-tossed ship, that miserably drives along the leeward land. The port would fain give succor; the port is pitiful; in the port is safety, comfort, hearthstone, supper, warm blankets, friends, all that's kind to our mortalities. But in that gale, the port, the land, is that ship's direst jeopardy; she must fly all hospitality; one touch of land, though it but graze the keel, would make her shudder through and through. With all her might she crowds all sail off shore; in so doing, fights 'gainst the very winds that fain would blow her homeward; seeks all the lashed sea's landlessness again; for refuge's sake forlornly rushing into peril; her only friend her bitterest foe!

Know ye, now, Bulkington? Glimpses do ye seem to see of that mortally intolerable truth; that all deep, earnest thinking is but the intrepid effort of the soul to keep the open independence of her sea; while the wildest winds of heaven and earth conspire to cast her on the treacherous, slavish shore?

But as in landlessness alone resides the highest truth, shoreless, indefinite as God—so, better is it to perish in that howling infinite, than be ingloriously dashed upon the lee, even if that were safety! For worm-like, then, oh! who would craven crawl to land!

Terrors of the terrible! is all this agony so vain? Take heart, take heart, O Bulkington! Bear thee grimly, demigod! Up from the spray of thy ocean-perishing—straight up, leaps thy apotheosis!

Chapter 24

THE ADVOCATE [1]

As Queequeg and I are now fairly embarked in this business of whaling; and as this business of whaling has somehow come to be regarded among landsmen as a rather unpoetical and disreputable pursuit; therefore, I am all anxiety to convince ye, ye landsmen, of the injustice hereby done to us hunters of whales.

In the first place, it may be deemed almost superfluous to establish the fact, that among people at large, the business of whaling is not accounted on a level with what are called the liberal professions. If a stranger were introduced into any miscellaneous metropolitan society, it would but slightly advance the general opinion of his merits, were he presented to the company as a harpooneer, say; and if in emulation of the naval officers he should append the initials S. W. F. (Sperm Whale Fishery) to his visiting card, such a procedure would be deemed pre-eminently presuming and ridiculous.

Doubtless one leading reason why the world declines honoring us whalemen, is this: they think that, at best, our vocation amounts to a butchering sort of business; and that when actively engaged therein, we are surrounded by all manner of defilements. Butchers we are, that is true. But butchers, also, and butchers of the bloodiest badge have been all Martial Commanders whom the world invariably delights to honor. And as for the matter of the alleged uncleanliness of our business, ye shall soon be initiated into certain facts hitherto pretty generally unknown, and which, upon the whole, will triumphantly plant the sperm whale-ship at least among the cleanliest things of this tidy earth. But even granting the charge in question to be true; what disordered slippery decks of a whale-ship are comparable to the unspeakable carrion of those battle-fields from which so many soldiers return to drink in all ladies' plaudits? And if the idea of peril so much enhances the popular conceit of the soldier's profession; let me assure ye that many a veteran who has freely marched up to a battery, would

1. Mansfield and Vincent point out that the "bulk of this chapter was derived in spirit and in ideas" from Thomas Beale's *The Natural History of the Sperm Whale* (London, 1839) but that William Scoresby, Jr's, *An Account of the Arctic Regions, with a History and Description of the Northern Whale-Fishery*, 2 vols., (Edinburgh, 1820) and J. Ross Browne's *Etchings of a Whaling Cruise* . . . (New York, 1846) "also furnished suggestions."

quickly recoil at the apparition of the sperm whale's vast tail, fanning into eddies the air over his head. For what are the comprehensible terrors of man compared with the interlinked terrors and wonders of God!

But, though the world scouts at us whale hunters, yet does it unwittingly pay us the profoundest homage; yea, an all-abounding adoration! for almost all the tapers, lamps, and candles that burn round the globe, burn, as before so many shrines, to our glory!

But look at this matter in other lights; weigh it in all sorts of scales; see what we whalemen are, and have been.

Why did the Dutch in De Witt's time [2] have admirals of their whaling fleets? Why did Louis XVI. of France, at his own personal expense, fit out whaling ships from Dunkirk, and politely invite to that town some score or two of families from our own island of Nantucket? Why did Britain between the years 1750 and 1788 pay to her whalemen in bounties upwards of £1,000,000? And lastly, how comes it that we whalemen of America now outnumber all the rest of the banded whalemen in the world; sail a navy of upwards of seven hundred vessels; manned by eighteen thousand men; yearly consuming 4,000,000 of dollars; the ships worth, at the time of sailing, $20,000,000; and every year importing into our harbors a well reaped harvest of $7,000,000. How comes all this, if there be not something puissant in whaling?

But this is not the half; look again.

I freely assert, that the cosmopolite philosopher cannot, for his life, point out one single peaceful influence, which within the last sixty years has operated more potentially upon the whole broad world, taken in one aggregate, than the high and mighty business of whaling. One way and another, it has begotten events so remarkable in themselves, and so continuously momentous in their sequential issues, that whaling may well be regarded as that Egyptian mother, who bore offspring themselves pregnant from her womb. It would be a hopeless, endless task to catalogue all these things. Let a handful suffice. For many years past the whale-ship has been the pioneer in ferreting out the remotest and least known parts of the earth. She has explored seas and archipelagoes which had no chart, where no Cook or Vancouver had ever sailed. If American and European men-of-war now peacefully ride in once savage harbors, let them fire salutes to the honor and the glory of the whale-ship, which originally showed them the way, and first interpreted between them and the savages. They may celebrate as they will the heroes of Exploring Expeditions,

2. In the mid-seventeenth century, under the Dutch statesman Jan de Witt.

your Cooks, your Krusensterns; but I say that scores of anonymous Captains have sailed out of Nantucket, that were as great, and greater than your Cook and your Krusenstern. For in their succorless empty-handedness, they, in the heathenish sharked waters, and by the beaches of unrecorded, javelin islands, battled with virgin wonders and terrors that Cook with all his marines and muskets would not willingly have dared. All that is made such a flourish of in the old South Sea Voyages, those things were but the lifetime commonplaces of our heroic Nantucketers. Often, adventures which Vancouver dedicates three chapters to, these men accounted unworthy of being set down in the ship's common log. Ah, the world! Oh, the world!

Until the whale fishery rounded Cape Horn, no commerce but colonial, scarcely any intercourse but colonial, was carried on between Europe and the long line of the opulent Spanish provinces on the Pacific coast. It was the whaleman who first broke through the jealous policy of the Spanish crown, touching those colonies; and, if space permitted, it might be distinctly shown how from those whalemen at last eventuated the liberation of Peru, Chili, and Bolivia from the yoke of Old Spain, and the establishment of the eternal democracy in those parts.

That great America on the other side of the sphere, Australia, was given to the enlightened world by the whalemen. After its first blunder-born discovery by a Dutchman, all other ships long shunned those shores as pestiferously barbarous; but the whaleship touched there. The whale-ship is the true mother of that now mighty colony. Moreover, in the infancy of the first Australian settlement, the emigrants were several times saved from starvation by the benevolent biscuit of the whale-ship luckily dropping an anchor in their waters. The uncounted isles of all Polynesia confess the same truth, and do commercial homage to the whale-ship, that cleared the way for the missionary and the merchant, and in many cases carried the primitive missionaries to their first destinations. If that double-bolted land, Japan, is ever to become hospitable, it is the whale-ship alone to whom the credit will be due; for already she is on the threshold.

But if, in the face of all this, you still declare that whaling has no æsthetically noble associations connected with it, then am I ready to shiver fifty lances with you there, and unhorse you with a split helmet every time.

The whale has no famous author, and whaling no famous chronicler, you will say.

The whale no famous author, and whaling no famous chronicler? Who wrote the first account of our Leviathan? Who but mighty Job! And who composed the first narrative of a whaling-voyage?

Who, but no less a prince than Alfred the Great, who, with his own royal pen, took down the words from Other, the Norwegian whale-hunter of those times! And who pronounced our glowing eulogy in Parliament? Who, but Edmund Burke!

True enough, but then whalemen themselves are poor devils; they have no good blood in their veins.

No good blood in their veins? They have something better than royal blood there. The grandmother of Benjamin Franklin was Mary Morrel; afterwards, by marriage, Mary Folger, one of the old settlers of Nantucket, and the ancestress to a long line of Folgers and harpooneers—all kith and kin to noble Benjamin— this day darting the barbed iron from one side of the world to the other.

Good again; but then all confess that somehow whaling is not respectable.

Whaling not respectable? Whaling is imperial! By old English statutory law, the whale is declared "a royal fish." *

Oh, that's only nominal! The whale himself has never figured in any grand imposing way.

The whale never figured in any grand imposing way? In one of the mighty triumphs given to a Roman general upon his entering the world's capital, the bones of a whale, brought all the way from the Syrian coast, were the most conspicuous object in the cymballed procession.*

Grant it, since you cite it; but, say what you will, there is no real dignity in whaling.

No dignity in whaling? The dignity of our calling the very heavens attest. Cetus is a constellation in the South! No more! Drive down your hat in presence of the Czar, and take it off to Queequeg! No more! I know a man that, in his lifetime, has taken three hundred and fifty whales. I account that man more honorable than that great captain of antiquity who boasted of taking as many walled towns.

And, as for me, if, by any possibility, there be any as yet un-discovered prime thing in me; if I shall ever deserve any real repute in that small but high hushed world which I might not be unreasonably ambitious of; if hereafter I shall do anything that, upon the whole, a man might rather have done than to have left undone; if, at my death, my executors, or more properly my creditors, find any precious MSS. in my desk, then here I pro-spectively ascribe all the honor and the glory to whaling; for a whale-ship was my Yale College and my Harvard.

---

* See subsequent chapters for something more on this head [Melville's note: he refers to chapters 82 and 90].

Chapter 25

POSTSCRIPT

In behalf of the dignity of whaling, I would fain advance naught but substantiated facts. But after embattling his facts, an advocate who should wholly suppress a not unreasonable surmise, which might tell eloquently upon his cause—such an advocate, would he not be blameworthy?

It is well known that at the coronation of kings and queens, even modern ones, a certain curious process of seasoning them for their functions is gone through. There is a saltcellar of state, so called, and there may be a caster of state. How they use the salt, precisely—who knows? Certain I am, however, that a king's head is solemnly oiled at his coronation, even as a head of salad. Can it be, though, that they anoint it with a view of making its interior run well, as they anoint machinery? Much might be ruminated here, concerning the essential dignity of this regal process, because in common life we esteem but meanly and contemptibly a fellow who anoints his hair, and palpably smells of that anointing. In truth, a mature man who uses hair-oil, unless medicinally, that man has probably got a quoggy spot in him somewhere. As a general rule, he can't amount to much in his totality.

But the only thing to be considered here, is this—what kind of oil is used at coronations? Certainly it cannot be olive oil, nor macassar oil, nor castor oil, nor bear's oil, nor train oil, nor cod-liver oil. What then can it possibly be, but sperm oil in its un-manufactured, unpolluted state, the sweetest of all oils?

Think of that, ye loyal Britons! we whalemen supply your kings and queens with coronation stuff!

Chapter 26

KNIGHTS AND SQUIRES

The chief mate of the Pequod was Starbuck, a native of Nantucket, and a Quaker by descent. He was a long, earnest man, and though born on an icy coast, seemed well adapted to endure hot latitudes, his flesh being hard as twice-baked biscuit. Transported to the Indies, his live blood would not spoil like bottled ale. He must have been born in some time of general drought and famine, or upon one of those fast days for which his state is famous. Only some thirty arid summers had he seen; those summers had dried up all his physical superfluousness. But this, his thinness, so to speak, seemed no more the token of wasting anxieties and cares, than it seemed the indication of any bodily blight. It was merely the condensation of the man. He was by no means ill-looking; quite the contrary. His pure tight skin was an excellent fit; and closely wrapped up in it, and embalmed with inner health and strength, like a revivified Egyptian, this Starbuck seemed prepared to endure for long ages to come, and to endure always, as now; for be it Polar snow or torrid sun, like a patent chronometer, his interior vitality was warranted to do well in all climates. Looking into his eyes, you seemed to see there the yet lingering images of those thousand-fold perils he had calmly confronted through life. A staid, steadfast man, whose life for the most part was a telling pantomime of action, and not a tame chapter of sounds. Yet, for all his hardy sobriety and fortitude, there were certain qualities in him which at times affected, and in some cases seemed well nigh to overbalance all the rest. Uncommonly conscientious for a seaman, and endued with a deep natural reverence, the wild watery loneliness of his life did therefore strongly incline him to superstition; but to that sort of superstition, which in some organizations seems rather to spring, somehow, from intelligence than from ignorance. Outward portents and inward presentiments were his. And if at times these things bent the welded iron of his soul, much more did his far-away domestic memories of his young Cape wife and child, tend to bend him still more from the original ruggedness of his nature, and open him still further to those latent influences which, in some honest-hearted men, restrain the gush of dare-devil daring, so often evinced by others in the more perilous vicissitudes of the fishery. "I will have no man in my boat," said Starbuck, "who is not afraid of a whale." By this, he seemed to mean, not only that the most reliable and useful courage is that which arises from the fair estimation of the encountered peril, but that an utterly fearless man is a far more dangerous comrade than a coward.

"Aye, aye," said Stubb, the second mate, "Starbuck, there, is as careful a man as you'll find anywhere in this fishery." But we shall ere long see what that word "careful" precisely means when used by a man like Stubb, or almost any other whale hunter.

Starbuck was no crusader after perils; in him courage was not a sentiment; but a thing simply useful to him, and always at hand upon all mortally practical occasions. Besides, he thought, perhaps, that in this business of whaling, courage was one of the great staple outfits of the ship, like her beef and her bread, and not to be foolishly wasted. Wherefore he had no fancy for lowering for whales after sun-down; nor for persisting in fighting a fish that too much persisted in fighting him. For, thought Starbuck, I am here in this critical ocean to kill whales for my living, and not to be killed by them for theirs; and that hundreds of men had been so killed Starbuck well knew. What doom was his own father's? Where, in the bottomless deeps, could he find the torn limbs of his brother?

With memories like these in him, and, moreover, given to a certain superstitiousness, as has been said; the courage of this Starbuck which could, nevertheless, still flourish, must indeed have been extreme. But it was not in reasonable nature that a man so organized, and with such terrible experiences and re-membrances as he had; it was not in nature that these things should fail in latently engendering an element in him, which, under suitable circumstances, would break out from its confine-ment, and burn all his courage up. And brave as he might be, it was that sort of bravery, chiefly visible in some intrepid men, which, while generally abiding firm in the conflict with seas, or winds, or whales, or any of the ordinary irrational horrors of the world, yet cannot withstand those more terrific, because more spiritual terrors, which sometimes menace you from the concen-trating brow of an enraged and mighty man.

But were the coming narrative to reveal, in any instance, the complete abasement of poor Starbuck's fortitude, scarce might I have the heart to write it; for it is a thing most sorrowful, nay shocking, to expose the fall of valor in the soul. Men may seem detestable as joint stock-companies and nations; knaves, fools, and murderers there may be; men may have mean and meagre faces; but man, in the ideal, is so noble and so sparkling, such a grand and glowing creature, that over any ignominious blemish in him all his fellows should run to throw their costliest robes. That im-maculate manliness we feel within ourselves, so far within us, that it remains intact though all the outer character seem gone; bleeds with keenest anguish at the undraped spectacle of a valor-ruined man. Nor can piety itself, at such a shameful sight, completely stifle her upbraidings against the permitting stars. But this august dignity I treat of, is not the dignity of kings and robes, but that abounding dignity which has no robed investiture. Thou shalt see it shining in the arm that wields a pick or drives a spike; that dem-ocratic dignity which, on all hands, radiates without end from God; Himself! The great God absolute! The centre and circum-ference of all democracy! His omnipresence, our divine equality!

If, then, to meanest mariners, and renegades and castaways, I shall hereafter ascribe high qualities, though dark; weave round them tragic graces; if even the most mournful, perchance the most abased, among them all, shall at times lift himself to the exalted mounts; if I shall touch that workman's arm with some ethereal light; if I shall spread a rainbow over his disastrous set of

sun; then against all mortal critics bear me out in it, thou just
Spirit of Equality, which hast spread one royal mantle of humanity over all my kind! Bear me out in it, thou great democratic God! who didst not refuse to the swart convict, Bunyan, the
pale, poetic pearl; Thou who didst clothe with doubly hammered
leaves of finest gold, the stumped and paupered arm of old Cervantes; Thou who didst pick up Andrew Jackson from the pebbles;
who didst hurl him upon a warhorse; who didst thunder him
higher than a throne! Thou who, in all Thy mighty earthly marchings, ever cullest Thy selectest champions from the kingly commons; bear me out in it, O God!

Chapter 27

KNIGHTS AND SQUIRES

Stubb was the second mate. He was a native of Cape Cod; and
hence, according to local usage, was called a Cape-Cod-man. A
happy-go-lucky; neither craven nor valiant; taking perils as they
came with an indifferent air; and while engaged in the most imminent crisis of the chase, toiling away, calm and collected as a
journeyman joiner engaged for the year. Good-humored, easy, and
careless, he presided over his whale-boat as if the most deadly encounter were but a dinner, and his crew all invited guests. He
was as particular about the comfortable arrangement of his part
of the boat, as an old stage-driver is about the snugness of his
box. When close to the whale, in the very death-lock of the fight,
he handled his unpitying lance coolly and off-handedly, as a whistling tinker his hammer. He would hum over his old rigadig tunes
while flank and flank with the most exasperated monster. Long
usage had, for this Stubb, converted the jaws of death into an
easy chair. What he thought of death itself, there is no telling.
Whether he ever thought of it at all, might be a question; but, if
he ever did chance to cast his mind that way after a comfortable
dinner, no doubt, like a good sailor, he took it to be a sort of call
of the watch to tumble aloft, and bestir themselves there, about
something which he would find out when he obeyed the order,
and not sooner.

What, perhaps, with other things, made Stubb such an easygoing, unfearing man, so cheerily trudging off with the burden of
life in a world full of grave peddlers, all bowed to the ground
with their packs; what helped to bring about that almost impious
good-humor of his; that thing must have been his pipe. For, like
his nose, his short, black little pipe was one of the regular features
of his face. You would almost as soon have expected him to turn
out of his bunk without his nose as without his pipe. He kept a

whole row of pipes there ready loaded, stuck in a rack, within easy reach of his hand; and, whenever he turned in, he smoked them all out in succession, lighting one from the other to the end of the chapter; then loading them again to be in readiness anew. For, when Stubb dressed, instead of first putting his legs into his trowsers, he put his pipe into his mouth.

I say this continual smoking must have been one cause, at least, of his peculiar disposition; for every one knows that this earthly air, whether ashore or afloat, is terribly infected with the nameless miseries of the numberless mortals who have died exhaling it; and as in time of the cholera, some people go about with a camphorated handkerchief to their mouths; so, likewise, against all mortal tribulations, Stubb's tobacco smoke might have operated as a sort of disinfecting agent.

The third mate was Flask, a native of Tisbury, in Martha's Vineyard. A short, stout, ruddy young fellow, very pugnacious concerning whales, who somehow seemed to think that the great Leviathans had personally and hereditarily affronted him; and therefore it was a sort of point of honor with him, to destroy them whenever encountered. So utterly lost was he to all sense of reverence for the many marvels of their majestic bulk and mystic ways; and so dead to anything like an apprehension of any possible danger from encountering them; that in his poor opinion, the wondrous whale was but a species of magnified mouse, or at least water-rat, requiring only a little circumvention and some small application of time and trouble in order to kill and boil. This ignorant, unconscious fearlessness of his made him a little waggish in the matter of whales; he followed these fish for the fun of it; and a three years' voyage round Cape Horn was only a jolly joke that lasted that length of time. As a carpenter's nails are divided into wrought nails and cut nails; so mankind may be similarly divided. Little Flask was one of the wrought ones; made to clinch tight and last long. They called him King-Post on board of the Pequod; because, in form, he could be well likened to the short, square timber known by that name in Arctic whalers; and which by the means of many radiating side timbers inserted into it, serves to brace the ship against the icy concussions of those battering seas.

Now these three mates—Starbuck, Stubb, and Flask, were momentous men. They it was who by universal prescription commanded three of the Pequod's boats as headsmen. In that grand order of battle in which Captain Ahab would probably marshal his forces to descend on the whales, these three headsmen were as captains of companies. Or, being armed with their long keen whaling spears, they were as a picked trio of lancers; even as the harpooneers were flingers of javelins.

And since in this famous fishery, each mate or headsman, like a Gothic Knight of old, is always accompanied by his boat-steerer or harpooneer, who in certain conjunctures provides him with a fresh lance, when the former one has been badly twisted, or elbowed in the assault; and moreover, as there generally subsists between the two, a close intimacy and friendliness; it is therefore but meet, that in this place we set down who the Pequod's harpooneers were, and to what headsman each of them belonged.

First of all was Queequeg, whom Starbuck, the chief mate, had selected for his squire. But Queequeg is already known.

Next was Tashtego, an unmixed Indian from Gay Head, the most westerly promontory of Martha's Vineyard, where there still exists the last remnant of a village of red men, which has long supplied the neighboring island of Nantucket with many of her most daring harpooneers. In the fishery, they usually go by the generic name of Gay-Headers. Tashtego's long, lean, sable hair, his high cheek bones, and black rounding eyes—for an Indian, Oriental in their largeness, but Antarctic in their glittering expression—all this sufficiently proclaimed him an inheritor of the unvitiated blood of those proud warrior hunters, who, in quest of the great New England moose, had scoured, bow in hand, the aboriginal forests of the main. But no longer snuffing in the trail of the wild beasts of the woodland, Tashtego now hunted in the wake of the great whales of the sea; the unerring harpoon of the son fitly replacing the infallible arrow of the sires. To look at the tawny brawn of his lithe snaky limbs, you would almost have credited the superstitions of some of the earlier Puritans, and half believed this wild Indian to be a son of the Prince of the Powers of the Air.[1] Tashtego was Stubb the second mate's squire.

Third among the harpooneers was Daggoo, a gigantic, coal-black negro-savage, with a lion-like tread—an Ahasuerus[2] to behold. Suspended from his ears were two golden hoops, so large that the sailors called them ring-bolts, and would talk of securing the top-sail halyards to them. In his youth Daggoo had voluntarily shipped on board of a whaler, lying in a lonely bay on his native coast. And never having been anywhere in the world but in Africa, Nantucket, and the pagan harbors most frequented by whalemen; and having now led for many years the bold life of the fishery in the ships of owners uncommonly heedful of what manner of men they shipped; Daggoo retained all his barbaric virtues, and erect as a giraffe, moved about the decks in all the pomp of six feet

1. The Devil; see Ephesians 2:2.
2. In the book of Esther the King of Persia who is said to have reigned over provinces "from India even unto Ethiopia."

five in his socks. There was a corporeal humility in looking up at
him; and a white man standing before him seemed a white flag
come to beg truce of a fortress. Curious to tell, this imperial negro,
Ahasuerus Daggoo, was the Squire of little Flask, who looked like
a chess-man beside him. As for the residue of the Pequod's company, be it said, that at the present day not one in two of the
many thousand men before the mast employed in the American
whale fishery, are Americans born, though pretty nearly all the officers are. Herein it is the same with the American whale fishery
as with the American army and military and merchant navies, and
the engineering forces employed in the construction of the American Canals and Railroads. The same, I say, because in all these
cases the native American liberally provides the brains, the rest
of the world as generously supplying the muscles. No small number of these whaling seamen belong to the Azores, where the outward bound Nantucket whalers frequently touch to augment their
crews from the hardy peasants of those rocky shores. In like manner, the Greenland whalers sailing out of Hull or London, put in
at the Shetland Islands, to receive the full complement of their
crew. Upon the passage homewards, they drop them there again.
How it is, there is no telling, but Islanders seem to make the
best whalemen. They were nearly all Islanders in the Pequod,
Isolatoes too, I call such, not acknowledging the common continent of men, but each *Isolato* living on a separate continent of
his own. Yet now, federated along one keel, what a set these
Isolatoes were! An Anacharsis Clootz deputation [3] from all the
isles of the sea, and all the ends of the earth, accompanying Old
Ahab in the Pequod to lay the world's grievances before that
bar from which not very many of them ever came back. Black
Little Pip—he never did! Poor Alabama boy! On the grim Pequod's forecastle, ye shall ere long see him, beating his tambourine; prelusive of the eternal time, when sent for, to the great
quarter-deck on high, he was bid strike in with angels, and beat
his tambourine in glory; called a coward here, hailed a hero there!

Chapter 28

AHAB

For several days after leaving Nantucket, nothing above hatches
was seen of Captain Ahab. The mates regularly relieved each
other at the watches, and for aught that could be seen to the contrary, they seemed to be the only commanders of the ship; only

3. Composed of men of different nations and races, like the motley deputation which Clootz led into the French
National Assembly in 1790 to symbolize all mankind's support of the French
Revolution.

they sometimes issued from the cabin with orders so sudden and peremptory, that after all it was plain they but commanded vicariously. Yes, their supreme lord and dictator was there, though hitherto unseen by any eyes not permitted to penetrate into the now sacred retreat of the cabin.

Every time I ascended to the deck from my watches below, I instantly gazed aft to mark if any strange face were visible; for my first vague disquietude touching the unknown captain, now in the seclusion of the sea, became almost a perturbation. This was strangely heightened at times by the ragged Elijah's diabolical incoherences uninvitedly recurring to me, with a subtle energy I could not have before conceived of. But poorly could I withstand them, much as in other moods I was almost ready to smile at the solemn whimsicalities of that outlandish prophet of the wharves. But whatever it was of apprehensiveness or uneasiness— to call it so—which I felt, yet whenever I came to look about me in the ship, it seemed against all warranty to cherish such emotions. For though the harpooneers, with the great body of the crew, were a far more barbaric, heathenish, and motley set than any of the tame merchant-ship companies which my previous experiences had made me acquainted with, still I ascribed this— and rightly ascribed it—to the fierce uniqueness of the very nature of that wild Scandinavian vocation in which I had so abandonedly embarked. But it was especially the aspect of the three chief officers of the ship, the mates, which was most forcibly calculated to allay these colorless misgivings, and induce confidence and cheerfulness in every presentment of the voyage. Three better, more likely sea-officers and men, each in his own different way, could not readily be found, and they were every one of them Americans; a Nantucketer, a Vineyarder, a Cape man. Now, it being Christmas when the ship shot from out her harbor, for a space we had biting Polar weather, though all the time running away from it to the southward; and by every degree and minute of latitude which we sailed, gradually leaving that merciless winter, and all its intolerable weather behind us. It was one of those less lowering, but still grey and gloomy enough mornings of the transition, when with a fair wind the ship was rushing through the water with a vindictive sort of leaping and melancholy rapidity, that as I mounted to the deck at the call of the forenoon watch, so soon as I levelled my glance towards the taffrail, foreboding shivers ran over me. Reality outran apprehension; Captain Ahab stood upon his quarter-deck.

There seemed no sign of common bodily illness about him, nor of the recovery from any. He looked like a man cut away from the stake, when the fire has overrunningly wasted all the limbs without consuming them, or taking away one particle from their compacted aged robustness. His whole high, broad form, seemed made of solid bronze, and shaped in an unalterable mould, like Cellini's cast Perseus. Threading its way out from among his grey hairs, and continuing right down one side of his tawny scorched face and neck, till it disappeared in his clothing, you saw a slender rod-like mark, lividly whitish. It resembled that perpendicular seam sometimes made in the straight, lofty trunk of a great tree, when the upper lightning tearingly darts down it, and without wrenching a single twig, peels and grooves out the bark from top to bottom, ere running off into the soil, leaving the tree still greenly alive, but branded. Whether that mark was born with him, or whether it was the scar left by some desperate wound, no one could certainly say. By some tacit consent, throughout the voyage little or no allusion was made to it, especially by the mates. But once Tashtego's senior, an old Gay-Head Indian among the crew, superstitiously asserted that not till he was full forty years old did Ahab become that way branded, and then it came upon him, not in the fury of any mortal fray, but in an elemental strife at sea. Yet, this wild hint seemed inferentially negatived, by what a grey Manxman insinuated, an old sepulchral man, who, having never before sailed out of Nantucket, had never ere this laid eye upon wild Ahab. Nevertheless, the old sea-traditions, the immemorial credulities, popularly invested this old Manxman with preternatural powers of discernment. So that no white sailor seriously contradicted him when he said that if ever Captain Ahab should be tranquilly laid out—which might hardly come to pass, so he muttered—then, whoever should do that last office for the dead, would find a birth-mark on him from crown to sole.

So powerfully did the whole grim aspect of Ahab affect me, and the livid brand which streaked it, that for the first few moments I hardly noted that not a little of this overbearing grimness was owing to the barbaric white leg upon which he partly stood. It had previously come to me that this ivory leg had at sea been fashioned from the polished bone of the sperm whale's jaw. "Aye, he was dismasted off Japan," said the old Gay-Head Indian once; "but like his dismasted craft, he shipped another mast without coming home for it. He has a quiver of 'em."

I was struck with the singular posture he maintained. Upon each side of the Pequod's quarter deck, and pretty close to the mizen shrouds, there was an auger hole, bored about half an inch or so, into the plank. His bone leg steadied in that hole; one arm elevated, and holding by a shroud; Captain Ahab stood erect, looking straight out beyond the ship's ever-pitching prow. There was an infinity of firmest fortitude, a determinate, unsurrenderable wilfulness, in the fixed and fearless, forward dedication of that glance. Not a word he spoke; nor did his officers say aught to him; though by all their minutest gestures and expressions, they plainly showed the uneasy, if not painful, consciousness of being under a troubled master-eye. And not only that, but moody stricken Ahab stood before them with a crucifixion in his face; in all the nameless regal overbearing dignity of some mighty woe.

Ere long, from his first visit in the air, he withdrew into his cabin. But after that morning, he was every day visible to the crew; either standing in his pivot-hole, or seated upon an ivory stool he had; or heavily walking the deck. As the sky grew less gloomy; indeed, began to grow a little genial, he became still less and less a recluse; as if, when the ship had sailed from home, nothing but the dead wintry bleakness of the sea had then kept him so secluded. And, by and by, it came to pass, that he was almost continually in the air; but, as yet, for all that he said, or perceptibly did, on the at last sunny deck, he seemed as unnecessary there as another mast. But the Pequod was only making a passage now; not regularly cruising; nearly all whaling preparatives needing supervision the mates were fully competent to, so that there was little or nothing, out of himself to employ or excite Ahab, now; and thus chase away, for that one interval, the clouds that layer upon layer were piled upon his brow, as ever all clouds choose the loftiest peaks to pile themselves upon.

Nevertheless, ere long, the warm, warbling persuasiveness of the pleasant, holiday weather we came to, seemed gradually to charm him from his mood. For, as when the red-cheeked, dancing girls, April and May, trip home to the wintry, misanthropic woods; even the barest, ruggedest, most thunder-cloven old oak will at least send forth some few green sprouts, to welcome such glad-hearted visitants; so Ahab did, in the end, a little respond to the playful allurings of that girlish air. More than once did he put forth the faint blossom of a look, which, in any other man, would have soon flowered out in a smile.

Chapter 29

ENTER AHAB; TO HIM, STUBB

Some days elapsed, and ice and icebergs all astern, the Pequod now went rolling through the bright Quito spring, which, at sea, almost perpetually reigns on the threshold of the eternal August of the Tropic. The warmly cool, clear, ringing, perfumed, overflowing, redundant days, were as crystal goblets of Persian sherbet, heaped up—flaked up, with rose-water snow. The starred and stately nights seemed haughty dames in jewelled velvets, nursing at home in lonely pride, the memory of their absent conquering Earls, the golden helmeted suns! For sleeping man, 'twas hard to choose between such winsome days and such seducing nights. But all the witcheries of that unwaning weather did not merely lend new spells and potencies to the outward world. Inward they turned upon the soul, especially when the still mild hours of eve came on; then, memory shot her crystals as the clear ice most forms of noiseless twilights. And all these subtle agencies, more and more they wrought on Ahab's texture.

Old age is always wakeful; as if, the longer linked with life, the less man has to do with aught that looks like death. Among seacommanders, the old greybeards will oftenest leave their berths to visit the night-cloaked deck. It was so with Ahab; only that now, of late, he seemed so much to live in the open air, that truly speaking, his visits were more to the cabin, than from the cabin to the planks. "It feels like going down into one's tomb,"—he would mutter to himself,—"for an old captain like me to be descending this narrow scuttle, to go to my grave-dug berth."

So, almost every twenty-four hours, when the watches of the night were set, and the band on deck sentinelled the slumbers of the band below; and when if a rope was to be hauled upon the forecastle, the sailors flung it not rudely down, as by day, but with some cautiousness dropt it to its place, for fear of disturbing their slumbering shipmates; when this sort of steady quietude would begin to prevail, habitually, the silent steersman would watch the cabin-scuttle; and ere long the old man would emerge, griping at the iron banister, to help his crippled way. Some considerating touch of humanity was in him; for at times like these, he usually abstained from patrolling the quarter-deck; because to his wearied mates, seeking repose within six inches of his ivory heel, such would have been the reverberating crack and din of that bony step, that their dreams would have been of the crunching teeth of sharks. But once, the mood was on him too deep for common regardings; and as with heavy, lumberlike pace he was measuring the ship from taffrail to mainmast, Stubb, the odd second mate, came up from below, and with a certain unassured, deprecating humorousness, hinted that if Captain Ahab was pleased to walk the planks, then, no one could say nay; but there might be some way of muffling the noise; hinting something indistinctly and hesitatingly about a globe of tow, and the insertion into it, of the ivory heel. Ah! Stubb, thou did'st not know Ahab then.

"Am I a cannon-ball, Stubb," said Ahab, "that thou wouldst

wad me that fashion? But go thy ways; I had forgot. Below to thy nightly grave; where such as ye sleep between shrouds, to use ye to the filling one at last.—Down, dog, and kennel!"

Starting at the unforeseen concluding exclamation of the so suddenly scornful old man, Stubb was speechless a moment; then said excitedly, "I am not used to be spoken to that way, sir; I do but less than half like it, sir."

"Avast!" gritted Ahab between his set teeth, and violently moving away, as if to avoid some passionate temptation.

"No, sir; not yet," said Stubb, emboldened, "I will not tamely be called a dog, sir."

"Then be called ten times a donkey, and a mule, and an ass, and begone, or I'll clear the world of thee!"

As he said this, Ahab advanced upon him with such overbearing terrors in his aspect, that Stubb involuntarily retreated.

"I was never served so before without giving a hard blow for it," muttered Stubb, as he found himself descending the cabin-scuttle. "It's very queer. Stop, Stubb; somehow, now, I don't well know whether to go back and strike him, or—what's that?—down here on my knees and pray for him? Yes, that was the thought coming up in me; but it would be the first time I ever *did* pray. It's queer; very queer; and he's queer too; aye, take him fore and aft, he's about the queerest old man Stubb ever sailed with. How he flashed at me!—his eyes like powder-pans! is he mad? Anyway there's something on his mind, as sure as there must be something on a deck when it cracks. He aint in his bed now, either, more than three hours out of the twenty-four; and he don't sleep then. Didn't that Dough-Boy, the steward, tell me that of a morning he always finds the old man's hammock clothes all rumpled and tumbled, and the sheets down at the foot, and the coverlid almost tied into knots, and the pillow a sort of frightful hot, as though a baked brick had been on it? A hot old man! I guess he's got what some folks ashore call a conscience; it's a kind of Tic-Dolly-row [1] they say—worse nor a toothache. Well, well; I don't know what it is, but the Lord keep me from catching it. He's full of riddles; I wonder what he goes into the after hold for, every night, as Dough-Boy tells me he suspects; what's that for, I should like to know? Who's made appointments with him in the hold? Ain't that queer, now? But there's no telling, it's the old game—Here goes for a snooze. Damn me, it's worth a fellow's while to be born into the world, if only to fall right asleep. And now that I think of it, that's about the first thing babies do, and that's a sort of queer, too. Damn me, but all things are queer, come to think of 'em. But that's against my

1. *Tic douloureux,* a painful facial twitching.

principles. Think not, is my eleventh commandment; and sleep when you can, is my twelfth—So here goes again. But how's that? didn't he call me a dog? blazes! he called me ten times a donkey, and piled a lot of jackasses on top of *that!* He might as well have kicked me, and done with it. Maybe he *did* kick me, and I didn't observe it, I was so taken all aback with his brow, somehow. It flashed like a bleached bone. What the devil's the matter with me? I don't stand right on my legs. Coming afoul of that old man has a sort of turned me wrong side out. By the Lord, I must have beem dreaming, though—How? how? how?—but the only way's to stash it; so here goes to hammock again; and in the morning, I'll see how this plaguy juggling thinks over by daylight."

Chapter 30

THE PIPE

When Stubb had departed, Ahab stood for a while leaning over the bulwarks; and then, as had been usual with him of late, calling a sailor of the watch, he sent him below for his ivory stool, and also his pipe. Lighting the pipe at the binnacle lamp and planting the stool on the weather side of the deck, he sat and smoked.

In old Norse times, the thrones of the sea-loving Danish kings were fabricated, saith tradition, of the tusks of the narwhale. How could one look at Ahab then, seated on that tripod of bones, without bethinking him of the royalty it symbolized? For a Khan of the plank, and a king of the sea, and a great lord of Leviathans was Ahab.

Some moments passed, during which the thick vapor came from his mouth in quick and constant puffs, which blew back again into his face. "How now," he soliloquized at last, withdrawing the tube, "this smoking no longer soothes. Oh, my pipe! hard must it go with me if thy charm be gone! Here have I been unconsciously toiling, not pleasuring,—aye, and ignorantly smoking to windward all the while; to windward, and with such nervous whiffs, as if, like the dying whale, my final jets were the strongest and fullest of trouble. What business have I with this pipe? This thing that is meant for sereneness, to send up mild white vapors among mild white hairs, not among torn iron-grey locks like mine. I'll smoke no more—"

He tossed the still lighted pipe into the sea. The fire hissed in the waves; the same instant the ship shot by the bubble the sinking pipe made. With slouched hat, Ahab lurchingly paced the planks.

Chapter 31

QUEEN MAB

Next morning Stubb accosted Flask.

"Such a queer dream, King-Post, I never had. You know the old man's ivory leg, well I dreamed he kicked me with it; and when I tried to kick back, upon my soul, my little man, I kicked my leg right off! And then, presto! Ahab seemed a pyramid, and I, like a blazing fool, kept kicking at it. But what was still more curious, Flask—you know how curious all dreams are—through all this rage that I was in, I somehow seemed to be thinking to myself, that after all, it was not much of an insult, that kick from Ahab. 'Why,' thinks I, 'what's the row? It's not a real leg, only a false leg.' And there's a mighty difference between a living thump and a dead thump. That's what makes a blow from the hand, Flask, fifty times more savage to bear than a blow from a cane. The living member—that makes the living insult, my little man. And thinks I to myself all the while, mind, while I was stubbing my silly toes against that cursed pyramid—so confound-edly contradictory was it all, all the while, I say, I was thinking to myself, 'what's his leg now, but a cane—a whalebone cane. Yes,' thinks I, 'it was only a playful cudgelling—in fact, only a whaleboning that he gave me—not a base kick. Besides,' thinks I, 'look at it once; why, the end of it—the foot part—what a small sort of end it is; whereas, if a broad footed farmer kicked me, *there's* a devilish broad insult. But this insult is whittled down to a point only.' But now comes the greatest joke of the dream, Flask. While I was battering away at the pyramid, a sort of badger-haired old merman, with a hump on his back, takes me by the shoulders, and slews me round. 'What are you 'bout?' says he. 'Slid! man, but I was frightened. Such a phiz! But, some-how, next moment I was over the fright. 'What am I about?' says I at last. 'And what business is that of yours, I should like to know, Mr. Humpback? Do *you* want a kick?' By the lord, Flask, I had no sooner said that, than he turned round his stern to me, bent over, and dragging up a lot of seaweed he had for a clout —what do you think, I saw?—why thunder alive, man, his stern was stuck full of marlinspikes, with the points out. Says I, on second thoughts, 'I guess I won't kick you, old fellow.' 'Wise Stubb,' said he, 'wise Stubb;' and kept muttering it all the time, a sort of eating of his own gums like a chimney hag. Seeing he wasn't going to stop saying over his 'wise Stubb, wise Stubb,' I thought I might as well fall to kicking the pyramid again. But I had only just lifted my foot for it, when he roared out,

'Stop that kicking!' 'Halloa,' says I, 'what's the matter now, old fellow?' 'Look ye here,' says he; 'let's argue the insult. Captain Ahab kicked ye, didn't he?' 'Yes, he did,' says I—'right *here* it was.' 'Very good,' says he—'he used his ivory leg, didn't he?' 'Yes, he did,' says I. 'Well then,' says he, 'wise Stubb, what have you to complain of? Didn't he kick with right good will? it wasn't a common pitch pine leg he kicked with, was it? No, you were kicked by a great man, and with a beautiful ivory leg, Stubb. It's an honor; I consider it an honor. Listen, wise Stubb. In old England the greatest lords think it great glory to be slapped by a queen, and made garter-knights of; but, be *your* boast, Stubb, that ye were kicked by old Ahab, and made a wise man of. Remember what I say; *be* kicked by him; account his kicks honors; and on no account kick back; for you can't help yourself, wise Stubb. Don't you see that pyramid?' With that, he all of a sudden seemed somehow, in some queer fashion, to swim off into the air. I snored; rolled over; and there I was in my hammock! Now, what do you think of that dream, Flask?"

"I don't know; it seems a sort of foolish to me, tho'."

"May be; may be. But it's made a wise man of me, Flask. D'ye see Ahab standing there, sideways looking over the stern? Well, the best thing you can do, Flask, is to let that old man alone; never speak quick [1] to him, whatever he says. Halloa! what's that he shouts? Hark!"

"Mast-head, there! Look sharp, all of ye! There are whales hereabouts! If ye see a white one, split your lungs for him!"

"What d'ye think of that now, Flask? ain't there a small drop of something queer about that, eh? A white whale—did ye mark that, man? Look ye—there's something special in the wind. Stand by for it, Flask. Ahab has that that's bloody on his mind. But, mum; he comes this way."

Chapter 32

CETOLOGY

Already we are boldly launched upon the deep; but soon we shall be lost in its unshored, harborless immensities. Ere that come to pass; ere the Pequod's weedy hull rolls side by side with the barnacled hulls of the leviathan; at the outset it is but well to attend to a matter almost indispensable to a thorough appreciative understanding of the more special leviathanic revelations and allusions of all sorts which are to follow.

It is some systematized exhibition of the whale in his broad genera, that I would now fain put before you. Yet is it no easy

1. Never speak angrily to him.

task. The classification of the constituents of a chaos, nothing less is here essayed. Listen to what the best and latest authorities [1] have laid down.

"No branch of Zoology is so much involved as that which is entitled Cetology," says Captain Scoresby, A.D. 1820.

"It is not my intention, were it in my power, to enter into the inquiry as to the true method of dividing the cetacea into groups and families. * * * Utter confusion exists among the historians of this animal" (sperm whale), says Surgeon Beale, A.D. 1839.

"Unfitness to pursue our research in the unfathomable waters." "Impenetrable veil covering our knowledge of the cetacea." "A field strewn with thorns." "All these incomplete indications but serve to torture us naturalists."

Thus speak of the whale, the great Cuvier, and John Hunter, and Lesson, those lights of zoology and anatomy. Nevertheless, though of real knowledge there be little, yet of books there are a plenty; and so in some small degree, with cetology, or the science of whales. Many are the men, small and great, old and new, landsmen and seamen, who have at large or in little, written of the whale. Run over a few:—The Authors of the Bible; Aristotle; Pliny; Aldrovandi; Sir Thomas Browne; Gesner; Ray; Linnæus; Rondeletius; Willoughby; Green; Artedi; Sibbald; Brisson; Marten; Lacépède; Bonneterre; Desmarest; Baron Cuvier; Frederick Cuvier; John Hunter; Owen; Scoresby; Beale; Bennett; J. Ross Browne; the Author of Miriam Coffin; Olmsted; and the Rev. T. Cheever. But to what ultimate generalizing purpose all these have written, the above cited extracts will show.

Of the names in this list of whale authors, only those following Owen ever saw living whales; and but one of them was a real professional harpooneer and whaleman. I mean Captain Scoresby. On the separate subject of the Greenland or right-whale, he is the best existing authority. But Scoresby knew nothing and says nothing of the great sperm whale, compared with which the Greenland whale is almost unworthy mentioning. And here be it said, that the Greenland whale is an usurper upon the throne of the seas. He is not even by any means the largest of the whales. Yet, owing to the long priority of his claims, and the profound ignorance which, till some seventy years back, invested the then fabulous or utterly

1. "These four quotations strikingly illustrate Melville's 'borrowing' practice. The implication of his citations was that he had read the four authorities (and the later ones) in question. But the four quotations had appeared in Beale, on a special page before the title-page, so that Melville's research, here, went no farther than his much used copy of Beale's *Natural History of the Sperm Whale*" (Mansfield-Vincent).

unknown sperm-whale, and which ignorance to this present day still reigns in all but some few scientific retreats and whale-ports; this usurpation has been every way complete. Reference to nearly all the leviathanic allusions in the great poets of past days, will satisfy you that the Greenland whale, without one rival, was to them the monarch of the seas. But the time has at last come for a new proclamation. This is Charing Cross; hear ye! good people all,—the Greenland whale is deposed,—the great sperm whale now reigneth!

There are only two books in being which at all pretend to put the living sperm whale before you, and at the same time, in the remotest degree succeed in the attempt. Those books are Beale's and Bennett's; both in their time surgeons to English South-Sea whale-ships, and both exact and reliable men. The original matter touching the sperm whale to be found in their volumes is necessarily small; but so far as it goes, it is of excellent quality, though mostly confined to scientific description. As yet, however, the sperm whale, scientific or poetic, lives not complete in any literature. Far above all other hunted whales, his is an unwritten life.

Now the various species of whales need some sort of popular comprehensive classification, if only an easy outline one for the present, hereafter to be filled in all its departments by subsequent laborers. As no better man advances to take this matter in hand, I hereupon offer my own poor endeavors. I promise nothing complete; because any human thing supposed to be complete, must for that very reason infallibly be faulty. I shall not pretend to a minute anatomical description of the various species, or—in this place at least—to much of any description. My object here is simply to project the draught [2] of a systematization of cetology. I am the architect, not the builder.

But it is a ponderous task; no ordinary letter-sorter in the Post-office is equal to it. To grope down into the bottom of the sea after them; to have one's hands among the unspeakable foundations, ribs, and very pelvis of the world; this is a fearful thing. What am I that I should essay to hook the nose of this leviathan! The awful tauntings in Job might well appal me. "Will he" (the leviathan) "make a covenant with thee? Behold the hope of him is vain!" But I have swam through libraries and sailed through oceans; I have had to do with whales with these visible hands; I am in earnest; and I will try. There are some preliminaries to settle.

First: The uncertain, unsettled condition of this science of Cetology is in the very vestibule attested by the fact, that in some quarters it still remains a moot point whether a whale be a fish.

2. As in the famous last paragraph of this chapter, draft, or preliminary sketch.

In his System of Nature, A.D. 1776. Linnæus declares, "I hereby separate the whales from the fish." But of my own knowledge, I know that down to the year 1850, sharks and shad, alewives and herring, against Linnæus's express edict, were still found dividing the possession of the same seas with the Leviathan.

The grounds upon which Linnæus would fain have banished the whales from the waters, he states as follows: "On account of their warm bilocular heart, their lungs, their movable eyelids, their hollow ears, penem intrantem feminam mammis lactantem," [3] and finally, "ex lege naturæ jure meritoque." [4] I submitted all this to my friends Simeon Macey and Charley Coffin, of Nantucket, both messmates of mine in a certain voyage, and they united in the opinion that the reasons set forth were altogether insufficient. Charley profanely hinted they were humbug.

Be it known that, waiving all argument, I take the good old fashioned ground that the whale is a fish, and call upon holy Jonah to back me. This fundamental thing settled, the next point is, in what internal respect does the whale differ from other fish. Above, Linnæus has given you those items. But in brief, they are these: lungs and warm blood; whereas, all other fish are lungless and cold blooded.

Next: how shall we define the whale, by his obvious externals, so as conspicuously to label him for all time to come? To be short, then, a whale is *a spouting fish with a horizontal tail*. There you have him. However contracted, that definition is the result of expanded meditation. A walrus spouts much like a whale, but the walrus is not a fish, because he is amphibious. But the last term of the definition is still more cogent, as coupled with the first. Almost any one must have noticed that all the fish familiar to landsmen have not a flat, but a vertical, or up-and-down tail. Whereas, among spouting fish the tail, though it may be similarly shaped, invariably assumes a horizontal position.

By the above definition of what a whale is, I do by no means exclude from the leviathanic brotherhood any sea creature hitherto identified with the whale by the best informed Nantucketers; nor, on the other hand, link with it any fish hitherto authoritatively regarded as alien.* Hence, all the smaller, spouting, and horizontal tailed fish must be included in this ground-plan of Cetology. Now, then, come the grand divisions of the entire whale

3. "A penis that enters the female, who gives milk from breasts."
4. "From the law of nature, justly and deservedly."
* I am aware that down to the present time, the fish styled Lamatins and Dugongs (Pig-fish and Sow-fish of the Coffins of Nantucket) are included by many naturalists among the whales. But as these pig-fish are a nosy, contemptible set, mostly lurking in the mouths of rivers, and feeding on wet hay, and especially as they do not spout, I deny their credentials as whales; and have presented them with their passports to quit the Kingdom of Cetology [Melville's note].

host.

First: According to magnitude I divide the whales into three primary BOOKS (subdivisible into CHAPTERS), and these shall comprehend them all, both small and large.

I. The FOLIO WHALE; II. the OCTAVO WHALE; III. the DUODECIMO WHALE.[5]

As the type of the FOLIO I present the *Sperm Whale*; of the OCTAVO, the *Grampus*; of the DUODECIMO, the *Porpoise*.

FOLIOS. Among these I here include the following chapters;— I. The *Sperm Whale*; II. the *Right Whale*; III. the *Fin Back Whale*; IV, the *Hump-backed Whale*; V. the *Razor Back Whale*; VI. the *Sulphur Bottom Whale*.

BOOK I. (*Folio*), CHAPTER I. (*Sperm Whale*).—This whale, among the English of old vaguely known as the Trumpa whale, and the Physeter whale, and the Anvil Headed whale, is the present Cachalot of the French, and the Pottfisch of the Germans, and the Macrocephalus of the Long Words. He is, without doubt, the largest inhabitant of the globe; the most formidable of all whales to encounter; the most majestic in aspect; and lastly, by far the most valuable in commerce; he being the only creature from which that valuable substance, spermaceti, is obtained. All his peculiarities will, in many other places, be enlarged upon. It is chiefly with his name that I now have to do. Philologically considered, it is absurd. Some centuries ago, when the Sperm whale was almost wholly unknown in his own proper individuality, and when his oil was only accidentally obtained from the stranded fish; in those days spermaceti, it would seem, was popularly supposed to be derived from a creature identical with the one then known in England as the Greenland or Right Whale. It was the idea also, that this same spermaceti was that quickening humor [6] of the Greenland Whale which the first syllable of the word literally expresses. In those times, also, spermaceti was exceedingly scarce, not being used for light, but only as an ointment and medicament. It was only to be had from the druggists as you nowadays buy an ounce of rhubarb. When, as I opine, in the course of time, the true nature of spermaceti became known, its original name was still retained by the dealers; no doubt to enhance its value by a notion so strangely significant of its scarcity. And so the appellation must at last have come to be bestowed upon the whale from which this spermaceti was really derived.

BOOK I. (*Folio*), CHAPTER II. (*Right Whale*).—In one respect this is the most venerable of the leviathans, being the one first

---

5. Folio, octavo, and duodecimo are terms by which printers and booksellers classify the size of books and their pages.
6. Semen.

regularly hunted by man. It yields the article commonly known as whalebone or baleen; and the oil specially known as "whale oil," an inferior article in commerce. Among the fishermen, he is indiscriminately designated by all the following titles: The Whale; the Greenland Whale; the Black Whale; the Great Whale; the True Whale; the Right Whale. There is a deal of obscurity concerning the identity of the species thus multitudinously baptized. What then is the whale, which I include in the second species of my Folios? It is the Great Mysticetus of the English naturalists; the Greenland Whale of the English whalemen; the Baleine Ordinaire of the French whalemen; the Gröndlands Valfisk of the Swedes. It is the whale which for more than two centuries past has been hunted by the Dutch and English in the Arctic seas; it is the whale which the American fishermen have long pursued in the Indian ocean, on the Brazil Banks, on the Nor' West Coast, and various other parts of the world, designated by them Right Whale Cruising Grounds.

Some pretend to see a difference between the Greenland whale of the English and the right whale of the Americans. But they precisely agree in all their grand features; nor has there yet been presented a single determinate fact upon which to ground a radical distinction. It is by endless subdivisions based upon the most inconclusive differences, that some departments of natural history become so repellingly intricate. The right whale will be elsewhere treated of at some length, with reference to elucidating the sperm whale.

BOOK I. (*Folio*), CHAPTER III. (*Fin-Back*).—Under this head I reckon a monster which, by the various names of Fin-Back, Tall-Spout, and Long-John, has been seen almost in every sea and is commonly the whale whose distant jet is so often descried by passengers crossing the Atlantic, in the New York packet-tracks. In the length he attains, and in his baleen, the Fin-back resembles the right whale, but is of a less portly girth, and a lighter color, approaching to olive. His great lips present a cable-like aspect, formed by the intertwisting, slanting folds of large wrinkles. His grand distinguishing feature, the fin, from which he derives his name, is often a conspicuous object. This fin is some three or four feet long, growing vertically from the hinder part of the back, of an angular shape, and with a very sharp pointed end. Even if not the slightest other part of the creature be visible, this isolated fin will, at times, be seen plainly projecting from the surface. When the sea is moderately calm, and slightly marked with spherical ripples, and this gnomon-like fin stands up and casts shadows upon the wrinkled surface, it may well be supposed that the watery circle surrounding it somewhat resembles a dial, with its style and wavy hour-lines graved on it. On that Ahaz-dial the shadow often goes back.[7] The Fin-Back is not gregarious. He seems a whale-hater, as some men are man-haters. Very shy; always going solitary; unexpectedly rising to the surface in the remotest and most sullen waters; his straight and single lofty jet rising like a tall misanthropic spear upon a barren plain; gifted with such wondrous power and velocity in swimming, as to defy all present pursuit from man; this leviathan seems the banished and unconquerable Cain of his race, bearing for his mark that style upon his back. From having the baleen in his mouth, the Fin-Back is sometimes included with the right whale, among a theoretic species denominated *Whalebone whales*, that is, whales with baleen. Of these so called Whalebone whales, there would seem to be several varieties, most of which, however, are little known. Broad-nosed whales and beaked whales; pike-headed whales; bunched whales; underjawed whales and rostrated whales, are the fishermen's names for a few sorts.

In connexion with this appellative of "Whalebone whales," it is of great importance to mention, that however such a nomenclature may be convenient in facilitating allusions to some kind of whales, yet it is in vain to attempt a clear classification of the Leviathan, founded upon either his baleen, or hump, or fin, or teeth; notwithstanding that those marked parts or features very obviously seem better adapted to afford the basis for a regular system of Cetology than any other detached bodily distinctions, which the whale, in his kinds, presents. How then? The baleen, hump, back-fin, and teeth; these are things whose peculiarities are indiscriminately dispersed among all sorts of whales, without any regard to what may be the nature of their structure in other and more essential particulars. Thus, the sperm whale and the humpbacked whale, each has a hump; but there the similitude ceases. Then, this same humpbacked whale and the Greenland whale, each of these has baleen; but there again the similitude ceases. And it is just the same with the other parts above mentioned. In various sorts of whales, they form such irregular combinations; or, in the case of any one of them detached, such an irregular isolation; as utterly to defy all general methodization formed upon such a basis. On this rock every one of the whale-naturalists has split.

But it may possibly be conceived that, in the internal parts of the whale, in his anatomy—there, at least, we shall be able to hit the right classification. Nay; what thing, for example, is there in

7. In Isaiah 38:8 time already marked off by the shadow on the sundial of Ahaz is called back. Here the sense is that the whale's fin looks like the shadow-casting gnomon of a sundial but that the whale's movements would make the shadows it casts on the water show time often moving backward or otherwise irregularly, unlike those of any fixed-gnomon dial, except that of Ahaz when there was a special divine intervention.

the Greenland whale's anatomy more striking than his baleen? Yet we have seen that by his baleen it is impossible correctly to classify the Greenland whale. And if you descend into the bowels of the various leviathans, why there you will not find distinctions a fiftieth part as available to the systematizer as those external ones already enumerated. What then remains? nothing but to take hold of the whales bodily, in their entire liberal volume, and boldly sort them that way. And this is the Bibliographical system here adopted; and it is the only one that can possibly succeed, for it alone is practicable. To proceed.

BOOK I. (*Folio*), CHAPTER IV. (*Hump Back*).—This whale is often seen on the northern American coast. He has been frequently captured there, and towed into harbor. He has a great pack on him like a peddler; or you might call him the Elephant and Castle whale. At any rate, the popular name for him does not sufficiently distinguish him, since the sperm whale also has a hump, though a smaller one. His oil is not very valuable. He has baleen. He is the most gamesome and lighthearted of all the whales, making more gay foam and white water generally than any other of them.

BOOK I. (*Folio*), CHAPTER V. (*Razor Back*).—Of this whale little is known but his name. I have seen him at a distance off Cape Horn. Of a retiring nature, he eludes both hunters and philosophers. Though no coward, he has never yet shown any part of him but his back, which rises in a long sharp ridge. Let him go. I know little more of him, nor does anybody else.

BOOK I. (*Folio*), CHAPTER VI. (*Sulphur Bottom*).—Another retiring gentleman, with a brimstone belly, doubtless got by scraping along the Tartarean tiles in some of his profounder divings. He is seldom seen; at least I have never seen him except in the remoter southern seas, and then always at too great a distance to study his countenance. He is never chased; he would run away with rope-walks of line. Prodigies are told of him. Adieu, Sulphur Bottom! I can say nothing more that is true of ye, nor can the oldest Nantucketer.

Thus ends BOOK I. (*Folio*), and now begins BOOK II. (*Octavo*).

OCTAVOES.* These embrace the whales of middling magnitude, among which at present may be numbered:—I., the *Grampus*; II., the *Black Fish*; III., the *Narwhale*; IV., the *Thrasher*; V., the *Killer*.

---

* Why this book of whales is not denominated the Quarto is very plain. Because, while the whales of this order, though smaller than those of the former order, nevertheless retain a proportionate likeness to them in figure, yet the bookbinder's Quarto volume in its diminished form does not preserve the shape of the Folio volume, but the Octavo volume does [Melville's note].

BOOK II. (*Octavo*), CHAPTER I. (*Grampus*).—Though this fish, whose loud sonorous breathing, or rather blowing, has furnished a proverb to landsmen, is so well known a denizen of the deep, yet is he not popularly classed among whales. But possessing all the grand distinctive features of the leviathan, most naturalists have recognised him for one. He is of moderate octavo size, varying from fifteen to twenty-five feet in length, and of corresponding dimensions round the waist. He swims in herds; he is never regularly hunted, though his oil is considerable in quantity, and pretty good for light. By some fishermen his approach is regarded as premonitory of the advance of the great sperm whale.

BOOK II. (*Octavo*), CHAPTER II. (*Black Fish*).—I give the popular fishermen's names for all these fish, for generally they are the best. Where any name happens to be vague or inexpressive, I shall say so, and suggest another. I do so now, touching the Black Fish, so called, because blackness is the rule among almost all whales. So, call him the Hyena Whale, if you please. His voracity is well known, and from the circumstance that the inner angles of his lips are curved upwards, he carries an everlasting Mephistophelean grin on his face. This whale averages some sixteen or eighteen feet in length. He is found in almost all latitudes. He has a peculiar way of showing his dorsal hooked fin in swimming, which looks something like a Roman nose. When not more profitably employed, the sperm whale hunters sometimes capture the Hyena whale, to keep up the supply of cheap oil for domestic employment—as some frugal housekeepers, in the absence of company, and quite alone by themselves, burn unsavory tallow instead of odorous wax. Though their blubber is very thin, some of these whales will yield you upwards of thirty gallons of oil.

BOOK II. (*Octavo*), CHAPTER III. (*Narwhale*), that is, *Nostril whale*.—Another instance of a curiously named whale, so named I suppose from his peculiar horn being originally mistaken for a peaked nose. The creature is some sixteen feet in length, while its horn averages five feet, though some exceed ten, and even attain to fifteen feet. Strictly speaking, this horn is but a lengthened tusk, growing out from the jaw in a line a little depressed from the horizontal. But it is only found on the sinister side, which has an ill effect, giving its owner something analogous to the aspect of a clumsy left-handed man. What precise purpose this ivory horn or lance answers, it would be hard to say. It does not seem to be used like the blade of the sword-fish and bill-fish; though some sailors tell me that the Narwhale employs it for a rake in turning over the bottom of the sea for food. Charley Coffin said it was used for an ice-piercer; for the Narwhale, rising to the surface of the Polar Sea, and finding it sheeted with ice, thrusts his horn up, and so breaks through. But you cannot prove either of these surmises to be correct. My own opinion is, that however this one-sided horn may really be used by the Narwhale—however that may be—it would certainly be very convenient to him for a folder in reading pamphlets. The Narwhale I have heard called the Tusked whale, the Horned whale, and the Unicorn whale. He is certainly a curious example of the Unicornism to be found in almost every kingdom of animated nature. From certain cloistered old authors I have gathered that this same sea-unicorn's horn was in ancient days regarded as the great antidote against poison, and as such, preparations of it brought immense prices. It was also distilled to a volatile salts for fainting ladies, the same way that the horns of the male deer are manufactured into hartshorn. Originally it was in itself accounted an object of great curiosity. Black Letter tells me that Sir Martin Frobisher on his return from that voyage, when Queen Bess did gallantly wave her jewelled hand to him from a window of Greenwich Palace, as his bold ship sailed down the Thames; "when Sir Martin returned from that voyage," saith Black Letter, "on bended knees he presented to her highness a prodigious long horn of the Narwhale, which for a long period after hung in the castle at Windsor." An Irish author avers that the Earl of Leicester, on bended knees, did likewise present to her highness another horn, pertaining to a land beast of the unicorn nature.[8]

The Narwhale has a very picturesque, leopard-like look, being of a milk-white ground color, dotted with round and oblong spots of black. His oil is very superior, clear and fine; but there is little of it, and he is seldom hunted. He is mostly found in the circumpolar seas.

BOOK II. (*Octavo*), CHAPTER IV. (*Killer*).—Of this whale little is precisely known to the Nantucketer, and nothing at all to the professed naturalist. From what I have seen of him at a distance, I should say that he was about the bigness of a grampus. He is very savage—a sort of Feegee fish. He sometimes takes the great Folio whales by the lip, and hangs there like a leech, till the mighty brute is worried to death. The Killer is never hunted. I never heard what sort of oil he has. Exception might be taken to the name bestowed upon this whale, on the ground of its indistinctness. For we are all killers, on land and on sea; Bonapartes and Sharks included.

BOOK II. (*Octavo*), CHAPTER V. (*Thrasher*).—This gentle-

8. The "land beast" is the Earl of Leicester himself, who was the Queen's favorite.

man is famous for his tail, which he uses for a ferule in thrashing his foes. He mounts the Folio whale's back, and as he swims, he works his passage by flogging him; as some schoolmasters get along in the world by a similar process. Still less is known of the Thrasher than of the Killer. Both are outlaws, even in the lawless seas.

Thus ends BOOK II. (*Octavo*), and begins BOOK III. (*Duodecimo.*)

DUODECIMOES.—These include the smaller whales. I. The Huzza Porpoise. II. The Algerine Porpoise. III. The Mealy-mouthed Porpoise.

To those who have not chanced specially to study the subject, it may possibly seem strange, that fishes not commonly exceeding four or five feet should be marshalled among WHALES—a word, which, in the popular sense, always conveys an idea of hugeness. But the creatures set down above as Duodecimoes are infallibly whales, by the terms of my definition of what a whale is—i. e. a spouting fish, with a horizontal tail.

BOOK III. (*Duodecimo*), CHAPTER I. (*Huzza Porpoise*).—This is the common porpoise found almost all over the globe. The name is of my own bestowal; for there are more than one sort of porpoises, and something must be done to distinguish them. I call him thus, because he always swims in hilarious shoals, which upon the broad sea keep tossing themselves to heaven like caps in a Fourth-of-July crowd. Their appearance is generally hailed with delight by the mariner. Full of fine spirits, they invariably come from the breezy billows to windward. They are the lads that always live before the wind. They are accounted a lucky omen. If you yourself can withstand three cheers at beholding these vivacious fish, then heaven help ye; the spirit of godly gamesomeness is not in ye. A well-fed, plump Huzza Porpoise will yield you one good gallon of good oil. But the fine and delicate fluid extracted from his jaws is exceedingly valuable. It is in request among jewellers and watchmakers. Sailors put it on their hones. Porpoise meat is good eating, you know. It may never have occurred to you that a porpoise spouts. Indeed, his spout is so small that it is not very readily discernible. But the next time you have a chance, watch him; and you will then see the great Sperm whale himself in miniature.

BOOK III. (*Duodecimo*), CHAPTER II. (*Algerine Porpoise*). A pirate. Very savage. He is only found, I think, in the Pacific. He is somewhat larger than the Huzza Porpoise, but much of the same general make. Provoke him, and he will buckle to a shark. I have lowered for him many times, but never yet saw him captured.

BOOK III. (*Duodecimo*), CHAPTER III. (*Mealy-mouthed Por-*

poise).—The largest kind of Porpoise; and only found in the Pacific, so far as it is known. The only English name, by which he has hitherto been designated, is that of the fishers—Right-Whale Porpoise, from the circumstance that he is chiefly found in the vicinity of that Folio. In shape, he differs in some degree from the Huzza Porpoise, being of a less rotund and jolly girth; indeed, he is of quite a neat and gentleman-like figure. He has no fins on his back (most other porpoises have), he has a lovely tail, and sentimental Indian eyes of a hazel hue. But his mealy-mouth spoils all. Though his entire back down to his side fins is of a deep sable, yet a boundary line, distinct as the mark in a ship's hull, called the "bright waist," that line streaks him from stem to stern, with two separate colors, black above and white below. The white comprises part of his head, and the whole of his mouth, which makes him look as if he had just escaped from a felonious visit to a meal-bag. A most mean and mealy aspect! His oil is much like that of the common porpoise.

* * * * * *

Beyond the DUODECIMO, this system does not proceed, inasmuch as the Porpoise is the smallest of the whales. Above, you have all the Leviathans of note. But there are a rabble of uncertain, fugitive, half-fabulous whales, which, as an American whaleman, I know by reputation, but not personally. I shall enumerate them by their forecastle appellations; for possibly such a list may be valuable to future investigators, who may complete what I have here but begun. If any of the following whales, shall hereafter be caught and marked, then he can readily be incorporated into this System, according to his Folio, Octavo, or Duodecimo magnitude:—The Bottle-Nose Whale; the Junk Whale; the Pudding-Headed Whale; the Cape Whale; the Leading Whale; the Cannon Whale; the Scragg Whale; the Coppered Whale; the Elephant Whale; the Iceberg Whale; the Quog Whale; the Blue Whale; &c. From Icelandic, Dutch, and old English authorities, there might be quoted other lists of uncertain whales, blessed with all manner of uncouth names. But I omit them as altogether obsolete; and can hardly help suspecting them for mere sounds, full of Leviathanism, but signifying nothing.

Finally: It was stated at the outset, that this system would not be here, and at once, perfected. You cannot but plainly see that I have kept my word. But I now leave my cetological System standing thus unfinished, even as the great Cathedral of Cologne was left, with the crane still standing upon the top of the uncompleted tower. For small erections may be finished by their first architects; grand ones, true ones, ever leave the copestone to posterity. God keep me from ever completing anything. This whole book is but a draught—nay, but the draught of a draught. Oh, Time, Strength, Cash, and Patience!

Chapter 33

THE SPECKSYNDER

Concerning the officers of the whale-craft, this seems as good a place as any to set down a little domestic peculiarity on ship-board, arising from the existence of the harpooneer class of officers, a class unknown of course in any other marine than the whale-fleet.

The large importance attached to the harpooneer's vocation is evinced by the fact, that originally in the old Dutch Fishery, two centuries and more ago, the command of a whale ship was not wholly lodged in the person now called the captain, but was divided between him and an officer called the Specksynder. Literally this word means Fat-Cutter; usage, however, in time made it equivalent to Chief Harpooneer. In those days, the captain's authority was restricted to the navigation and general management of the vessel: while over the whale-hunting department and all its concerns, the Specksynder or Chief Harpooneer reigned supreme. In the British Greenland Fishery, under the corrupted title of Specksioneer, this old Dutch official is still retained, but his former dignity is sadly abridged. At present he ranks simply as senior Harpooneer; and as such, is but one of the captain's more inferior subalterns. Nevertheless, as upon the good conduct of the harpooneers the success of a whaling voyage largely depends, and since in the American Fishery he is not only an important officer in the boat, but under certain circumstances (night watches on a whaling ground) the command of the ship's deck is also his; therefore the grand political maxim of the sea demands, that he should nominally live apart from the men before the mast, and be in some way distinguished as their professional superior; though always, by them, familiarly regarded as their social equal.

Now, one of the grand distinctions drawn between officer and man at sea, is this—the first lives aft, the last forward. Hence, in whale-ships and merchantmen alike, the mates have their quarters with the captain; and so, too, in most of the American whalers the harpooneers are lodged in the after part of the ship. That is to say, they take their meals in the captain's cabin, and sleep in a place indirectly communicating with it.

Though the long period of a Southern whaling voyage (by far the longest of all voyages now or ever made by man), the peculiar perils of it, and the community of interest prevailing among a company, all of whom, high or low, depend for their profits, not upon fixed wages, but upon their common luck, together with their common vigilance, intrepidity, and hard work; though all these things do in some cases tend to beget a less rigorous discipline than in merchantmen generally; yet, never mind how much like an old Mesopotamian family these whalemen may, in some primitive instances, live together; for all that, the punctilious externals, at least, of the quarter-deck are seldom materially relaxed, and in no instance done away. Indeed, many are the Nantucket ships in which you will see the skipper parading his quarter-deck with an elated grandeur not surpassed in any military navy; nay, extorting almost as much outward homage as if he wore the imperial purple, and not the shabbiest of pilot-cloth.

And though of all men the moody captain of the Pequod was the least given to that sort of shallowest assumption; and though the only homage he ever exacted, was implicit, instantaneous obedience; though he required no man to remove the shoes from his feet ere stepping upon the quarter-deck; and though there were times when, owing to peculiar circumstances connected with events hereafter to be detailed, he addressed them in unusual terms, whether of condescension or *in terrorem*, or otherwise; yet even Captain Ahab was by no means unobservant of the paramount forms and usages of the sea.

Nor, perhaps, will it fail to be eventually perceived, that behind those forms and usages, as it were, he sometimes masked himself; incidentally making use of them for other and more private ends than they were legitimately intended to subserve. That certain sultanism of his brain, which had otherwise in a good degree remained unmanifested; through those forms that same sultanism became incarnate in an irresistible dictatorship. For be a man's intellectual superiority what it will, it can never assume the practical, available supremacy over other men, without the aid of some sort of external arts and entrenchments, always, in themselves, more or less paltry and base. This it is, that for ever keeps God's true princes of the Empire from the world's hustings; and leaves the highest honors that this air can give, to those men who become famous more through their infinite inferiority to the choice hidden handful of the Divine Inert,[1] than through their undoubted superiority over the dead level of the mass. Such large virtue lurks in these small things when extreme political superstitions invest them, that in some royal instances even to idiot imbecility they have imparted potency. But when, as in the case of Nicholas the Czar, the ringed crown of geographical empire encircles an imperial brain; then, the plebeian herds crouch abased before the tremendous centralization. Nor, will the tragic dramatist

1. "God's true princes" who do not seek outward worldly honors or power.

who would depict mortal indomitableness in its fullest sweep and direst swing, ever forget a hint, incidentally so important in his art, as the one now alluded to.

But Ahab, my Captain, still moves before me in all his Nantucket grimness and shagginess; and in this episode touching Emperors and Kings, I must not conceal that I have only to do with a poor old whale-hunter like him; and, therefore, all outward majestical trappings and housings are denied me. Oh, Ahab! what shall be grand in thee, it must needs be plucked at from the skies, and dived for in the deep, and featured in the unbodied air!

Chapter 34

THE CABIN-TABLE

It is noon; and Dough-Boy, the steward, thrusting his pale loaf-of-bread face from the cabin-scuttle, announces dinner to his lord and master; who, sitting in the lee quarter-boat, has just been taking an observation of the sun; and is now mutely reckoning the latitude on the smooth, medallion-shaped tablet, reserved for that daily purpose on the upper part of his ivory leg. From his complete inattention to the tidings, you would think that moody Ahab had not heard his menial. But presently, catching hold of the mizen shrouds, he swings himself to the deck, and in an even, unexhilarated voice, saying, "Dinner, Mr. Starbuck," disappears into the cabin.

When the last echo of his sultan's step has died away, and Starbuck, the first Emir, has every reason to suppose that he is seated, then Starbuck rouses from his quietude, takes a few turns along the planks, and, after a grave peep into the binnacle, says, with some touch of pleasantness, "Dinner, Mr. Stubb," and descends the scuttle. The second Emir lounges about the rigging awhile, and then slightly shaking the main brace, to see whether it be all right with that important rope, he likewise takes up the old burden, and with a rapid "Dinner, Mr. Flask," follows after his predecessors.

But the third Emir, now seeing himself all alone on the quarter-deck, seems to feel relieved from some curious restraint; for, tipping all sorts of knowing winks in all sorts of directions, and kicking off his shoes, he strikes into a sharp but noiseless squall of a hornpipe right over the Grand Turk's head; and then, by a dexterous sleight, pitching his cap up into the mizen-top for a shelf, he goes down rollicking, so far at least as he remains visible from the deck, reversing all other processions, by bringing up the rear with music. But ere stepping into the cabin doorway below, he pauses, ships a new face altogether, and, then, independent, hilarious little Flask enters King Ahab's presence, in the character of Abjectus, or the Slave.

It is not the least among the strange things bred by the intense artificialness of sea-usages, that while in the open air of the deck some officers will, upon provocation, bear themselves boldly and defyingly enough towards their commander; yet, ten to one, let those very officers the next moment go down to their customary dinner in that same commander's cabin, and straightway their inoffensive, not to say deprecatory and humble air towards him, as he sits at the head of the table; this is marvellous, sometimes most comical. Wherefore this difference? A problem? Perhaps not. To have been Belshazzar, King of Babylon; and to have been Belshazzar, not haughtily but courteously, therein certainly must have been some touch of mundane grandeur.[1] But he who in the rightly regal and intelligent spirit presides over his own private dinner-table of invited guests, that man's unchallenged power and dominion of individual influence for the time; that man's royalty of state transcends Belshazzar's, for Belshazzar was not the greatest. Who has but once dined his friends, has tasted what it is to be Cæsar. It is a witchery of social czarship which there is no withstanding. Now, if to this consideration you superadd the official supremacy of a ship-master, then, by inference, you will derive the cause of that peculiarity of sea-life just mentioned.

Over his ivory-inlaid table, Ahab presided like a mute, maned sea-lion on the white coral beach, surrounded by his warlike but still deferential cubs. In his own proper turn, each officer waited to be served. They were as little children before Ahab; and yet, in Ahab, there seemed not to lurk the smallest social arrogance. With one mind, their intent eyes all fastened upon the old man's knife, as he carved the chief dish before him. I do not suppose that for the world they would have profaned that moment with the slightest observation, even upon so neutral a topic as the weather. No! And when reaching out his knife and fork, between which the slice of beef was locked, Ahab thereby motioned Starbuck's plate towards him, the mate received his meat as though receiving alms; and cut it tenderly; and a little started if, perchance, the knife grazed against the plate; and chewed it noiselessly; and swallowed it, not without circumspection. For, like the Coronation banquet at Frankfort, where the German Emperor profoundly dines with the seven Imperial Electors, so these cabin meals were somehow solemn meals, eaten in awful

1. "Belshazzar the king made a great feast to a thousand of his lords, and drank wine before the thousand." Daniel 5: 1

silence; and yet at table old Ahab forbade not conversation; only he himself was dumb. What a relief it was to choking Stubb, when a rat made a sudden racket in the hold below. And poor little Flask, he was the youngest son, and little boy of this weary family party. His were the shinbones of the saline beef; his would have been the drumsticks. For Flask to have presumed to help himself, this must have seemed to him tantamount to larceny in the first degree. Had he helped himself at that table, doubtless, never more would he have been able to hold his head up in this honest world; nevertheless, strange to say, Ahab never forbade him. And had Flask helped himself, the chances were Ahab had never so much as noticed it. Least of all, did Flask presume to help himself to butter. Whether he thought the owners of the ship denied it to him, on account of its clotting his clear, sunny complexion; or whether he deemed that, on so long a voyage in such marketless waters, butter was at a premium, and therefore was not for him, a subaltern; however it was, Flask, alas! was a butterless man!

Another thing. Flask was the last person down at the dinner, and Flask is the first man up. Consider! For hereby Flask's dinner was badly jammed in point of time. Starbuck and Stubb both had the start of him; and yet they also have the privilege of lounging in the rear. If Stubb even, who is but a peg higher than Flask, happens to have but a small appetite, and soon shows symptoms of concluding his repast, then Flask must bestir himself, he will not get more than three mouthfuls that day; for it is against holy usage for Stubb to precede Flask to the deck. Therefore it was that Flask once admitted in private, that ever since he had arisen to the dignity of an officer, from that moment he had never known what it was to be otherwise than hungry, more or less. For what he ate did not so much relieve his hunger, as keep it immortal in him. Peace and satisfaction, thought Flask, have for ever departed from my stomach. I am an officer; but, how I wish I could fist a bit of old-fashioned beef in the forecastle, as I used to when I was before the mast. There's the fruits of promotion now; there's the vanity of glory: there's the insanity of life! Besides, if it were so that any mere sailor of the Pequod had a grudge against Flask in Flask's official capacity, all that sailor had to do, in order to obtain ample vengeance, was to go aft at dinner-time, and get a peep at Flask through the cabin skylight, sitting silly and dumfoundered before awful Ahab.

Now, Ahab and his three mates formed what may be called the first table in the Pequod's cabin. After their departure, taking place in inverted order to their arrival, the canvas cloth was cleared, or rather was restored to some hurried order by the pallid steward. And then the three harpooneers were bidden to the feast, they being its residuary legatees. They made a sort of temporary servants' hall of the high and mighty cabin.

In strange contrast to the hardly tolerable constraint and nameless invisible domineerings of the captain's table, was the entire care-free license and ease, the almost frantic democracy of those inferior fellows the harpooneers. While their masters, the mates, seemed afraid of the sound of the hinges of their own jaws, the harpooneers chewed their food with such a relish that there was a report to it. They dined like lords; they filled their bellies like Indian ships all day loading with spices. Such portentous appetites had Queequeg and Tashtego, that to fill out the vacancies made by the previous repast, often the pale Dough-Boy was fain to bring on a great baron of salt-junk, seemingly quarried out of the solid ox. And if he were not lively about it, if he did not go with a nimble hop-skip-and-jump, then Tashtego had an ungentlemanly way of accelerating him by darting a fork at his back, harpoon-wise. And once Daggoo, seized with a sudden humor, assisted Dough-Boy's memory by snatching him up bodily, and thrusting his head into a great empty wooden trencher, while Tashtego, knife in hand, began laying out the circle preliminary to scalping him. He was naturally a very nervous, shuddering sort of little fellow, this bread-faced steward; the progeny of a bankrupt baker and a hospital nurse. And what with the standing spectacle of the black terrific Ahab, and the periodical tumultuous visitations of these three savages, Dough-Boy's whole life was one continual lip-quiver. Commonly, after seeing the harpooneers furnished with all things they demanded, he would escape from their clutches into his little pantry adjoining, and fearfully peep out at them through the blinds of its door, till all was over.

It was a sight to see Queequeg seated over against Tashtego, opposing his filed teeth to the Indian's: crosswise to them, Daggoo seated on the floor, for a bench would have brought his hearse-plumed head to the low carlines; at every motion of his colossal limbs, making the low cabin framework to shake, as when an African elephant goes passenger in a ship. But for all this, the great negro was wonderfully abstemious, not to say dainty. It seemed hardly possible that by such comparatively small mouthfuls he could keep up the vitality diffused through so broad, baronial, and superb a person. But, doubtless, this noble savage fed strong and drank deep of the abounding element of air; and through his dilated nostrils snuffed in the sublime life of the worlds. Not by beef or by bread, are giants made or nourished. But Queequeg, he had a mortal, barbaric smack of the lip in eating—an ugly sound enough—so much so, that the trembling Dough-Boy almost looked to see whether any marks of teeth lurked in his own lean arms. And when he would hear Tashtego singing out for him to produce himself, that his bones might be picked, the simple-witted Steward all but shattered the crockery hanging round him in the pantry, by his sudden fits of the palsy. Nor did the whetstones which the harpooneers carried in their pockets, for their lances and other weapons; and with which whetstones, at dinner, they would ostentatiously sharpen their knives; that grating sound did not at all tend to tranquillize poor Dough-Boy. How could he forget that in his Island days, Queequeg, for one, must certainly have been guilty of some murderous, convivial indiscretions. Alas! Dough-Boy! hard fares the white waiter who waits upon cannibals. Not a napkin should he carry on his arm, but a buckler. In good time, though, to his great delight, the three salt-sea warriors would rise and depart; to his credulous, fable-mongering ears, all their martial bones jingling in them at every step, like Moorish scimitars in scabbards.

But, though these barbarians dined in the cabin, and nominally lived there; still, being anything but sedentary in their habits, they were scarcely ever in it except at meal-times, and just before sleeping-time, when they passed through it to their own peculiar quarters.

In this one matter, Ahab seemed no exception to most American whale captains, who, as a set, rather incline to the opinion that by rights the ship's cabin belongs to them; and that it is by courtesy alone that anybody else is, at any time, permitted there. So that, in real truth, the mates and harpooneers of the Pequod might more properly be said to have lived out of the cabin than in it. For when they did enter it, it was something as a street-door enters a house; turning inwards for a moment, only to be turned out the next; and, as a permanent thing, residing in the open air. Nor did they lose much hereby; in the cabin was no companionship; socially, Ahab was inaccessible. Though nominally included in the census of Christendom, he was still an alien to it. He lived in the world, as the last of the Grisly Bears lived in settled Missouri. And as when Spring and Summer had departed, that wild Logan [2] of the woods, burying himself in the hollow of a tree, lived out the winter there, sucking his own paws; so, in his inclement, howling old age, Ahab's soul, shut up in the caved trunk of his body, there fed upon the sullen paws of its gloom!

2. A then-famous eighteenth-century Indian chief noted for his defiance of peace overtures from the whites.

Chapter 35

THE MAST-HEAD

It was during the more pleasant weather, that in due rotation with the other seamen my first mast-head [1] came round.

In most American whalemen the mast-heads are manned almost simultaneously with the vessel's leaving her port; even though she may have fifteen thousand miles, and more, to sail ere reaching her proper cruising ground. And if, after a three, four, or five years' voyage she is drawing nigh home with anything empty in her—say, an empty vial even—then, her mast-heads are kept manned to the last; and not till her skysail-poles sail in among the spires of the port, does she altogether relinquish the hope of capturing one whale more.

Now, as the business of standing mast-heads, ashore or afloat, is a very ancient and interesting one, let us in some measure expatiate here. I take it, that the earliest standers of mast-heads were the old Eygptians; because, in all my researches, I find none prior to them. For though their progenitors, the builders of Babel, must doubtless, by their tower, have intended to rear the loftiest mast-head in all Asia, or Africa either; yet (ere the final truck was put to it) as that great stone mast of theirs may be said to have gone by the board, in the dread gale of God's wrath; therefore, we cannot give these Babel builders priority over the Egyptians. And that the Egyptians were a nation of mast-head standers, is an assertion based upon the general belief among archæologists, that the first pyramids were founded for astronomical purposes: a theory singularly supported by the peculiar stair-like formation of all four sides of those edifices; whereby, with prodigious long upliftings of their legs, those old astronomers were wont to mount to the apex, and sing out for new stars; even as the look-outs of a modern ship sing out for a sail, or a whale just bearing in sight. In Saint Stylites, the famous Christian hermit of old times, who built him a lofty stone pillar in the desert and spent the whole latter portion of his life on its summit, hoisting his food from the ground with a tackle; in him we have a remarkable instance of a dauntless stander-of-mastheads; who was not to be driven from his place by fogs or frosts, rain, hail, or sleet; but valiantly facing everything out to the last, literally died at his post. Of modern standers-of-mastheads we have but a lifeless set; mere stone, iron, and bronze men; who, though well capable of facing out a stiff gale, are still

---

1. The quotation in Mansfield-Vincent reveals Melville's debt to J. Ross Browne's account of his masthead reveries.

entirely incompetent to the business of singing out upon discovering any strange sight. There is Napoleon; who, upon the top of the column of Vendôme, stands with arms folded, some one hundred and fifty feet in the air; careless, now, who rules the decks below; whether Louis Philippe, Louis Blanc, or Louis the Devil.[2] Great Washington, too, stands high aloft on his towering main-mast in Baltimore, and like one of Hercules' pillars, his column marks that point of human grandeur beyond which few mortals will go. Admiral Nelson, also, on a capstan of gun-metal, stands his mast-head in Trafalgar Square; and even when most obscured by that London smoke, token is yet given that a hidden hero is there; for where there is smoke, must be fire. But neither great Washington, nor Napoleon, nor Nelson, will answer a single hail from below, however madly invoked to befriend by their counsels the distracted decks upon which they gaze; however, it may be surmised, that their spirits penetrate through the thick haze of the future, and descry what shoals and what rocks must be shunned.

It may seem unwarrantable to couple in any respect the mast-head standers of the land with those of the sea; but that in truth it is not so, is plainly evinced by an item for which Obed Macy, the sole historian of Nantucket, stands accountable. The worthy Obed tells us, that in the early times of the whale fishery, ere ships were regularly launched in pursuit of the game, the people of that island erected lofty spars along the sea-coast, to which the look-outs ascended by means of nailed cleats, something as fowls go upstairs in a hen-house. A few years ago this same plan was adopted by the Bay whalemen of New Zealand, who, upon descrying the game, gave notice to the ready-manned boats nigh the beach. But this custom has now become obsolete; turn we then to the one proper mast-head, that of a whale-ship at sea.

The three mast-heads are kept manned from sun-rise to sun-set; the seamen taking their regular turns (as at the helm), and relieving each other every two hours. In the serene weather of the tropics it is exceedingly pleasant—the mast-head; nay, to a dreamy meditative man it is delightful. There you stand, a hundred feet above the silent decks, striding along the deep, as if the masts were gigantic stilts, while beneath you and between your legs, as it were, swim the hugest monsters of the sea, even as ships once sailed between the boots of the famous Colossus at old Rhodes. There you stand, lost in the infinite series of the sea, with nothing

2. Louis Philippe was King of France 1830–1848; Louis Blanc was a nineteenth-century French politician. Louis the Devil presumably refers to Louis Napoleon Bonaparte, President of France (1848–1852) during the writing of *Moby-Dick* and later Emperor; the first English edition reads "Louis Napoleon."

ruffled but the waves. The tranced ship indolently rolls; the drowsy trade winds blow; everything resolves you into languor. For the most part, in this tropic whaling life, a sublime uneventfulness invests you; you hear no news; read no gazettes; extras with startling accounts of commonplaces never delude you into unnecessary excitements; you hear of no domestic afflictions; bankrupt securities; fall of stocks; are never troubled with the thought of what you shall have for dinner—for all your meals for three years and more are snugly stowed in casks, and your bill of fare is immutable.

In one of those southern whalemen, on a long three or four years' voyage, as often happens, the sum of the various hours you spend at the mast-head would amount to several entire months. And it is much to be deplored that the place to which you devote so considerable a portion of the whole term of your natural life, should be so sadly destitute of anything approaching to a cosy inhabitiveness, or adapted to breed a comfortable localness of feeling, such as pertains to a bed, a hammock, a hearse, a sentry box, a pulpit, a coach, or any other of those small and snug contrivances in which men temporarily isolate themselves. Your most usual point of perch is the head of the t' gallant-mast, where you stand upon two thin parallel sticks (almost peculiar to whalemen) called the t' gallant cross-trees. Here, tossed about by the sea, the beginner feels about as cosy as he would standing on a bull's horns. To be sure, in coolish weather you may carry your house aloft with you, in the shape of a watch-coat; but properly speaking the thickest watch-coat is no more of a house than the unclad body; for as the soul is glued inside of its fleshly tabernacle, and cannot freely move about in it, nor even move out of it, without running great risk of perishing (like an ignorant pilgrim crossing the snowy Alps in winter); so a watch-coat is not so much of a house as it is a mere envelope, or additional skin encasing you. You cannot put a shelf or chest of drawers in your body, and no more can you make a convenient closet of your watch-coat.

Concerning all this, it is much to be deplored that the mastheads of a southern whale ship are unprovided with those enviable little tents or pulpits, called *crow's-nests*, in which the lookouts of a Greenland whaler are protected from the inclement weather of the frozen seas. In the fire-side narrative of Captain Sleet,[3] entitled "A Voyage among the Icebergs, in quest of the Greenland Whale, and incidentally for the re-discovery of the Lost Icelandic Colonies of Old Greenland;" in this admirable

3. The first of Melville's comic names for William Scoresby, Jr., whose *An Account of the Arctic Regions* he plundered for *Moby-Dick*. In Scoresby's book the inventor of the crow's-nest is his father, William Scoresby, Sr. Melville's compressed parody attributes the father's invention to the son.

volume, all standers of mast-heads are furnished with a charmingly circumstantial account of the then recently invented *crow's-nest* of the Glacier, which was the name of Captain Sleet's good craft. He called it the *Sleet's crow's-nest*, in honor of himself; he being the original inventor and patentee, and free from all ridiculous false delicacy, and holding that if we call our own children after our own names (we fathers being the original inventors and patentees), so likewise should we denominate after ourselves any other apparatus we may beget. In shape, the Sleet's crow's-nest is something like a large tierce or pipe; it is open above, however, where it is furnished with a movable side-screen to keep to windward of your head in a hard gale. Being fixed on the summit of the mast, you ascend into it through a little trap-hatch in the bottom. On the after side, or side next the stern of the ship, is a comfortable seat, with a locker underneath for umbrellas, comforters, and coats. In front is a leather rack, in which to keep your speaking trumpet, pipe, telescope, and other nautical conveniences. When Captain Sleet in person stood his mast-head in this crow's nest of his, he tells us that he always had a rifle with him (also fixed in the rack), together with a powder flask and shot, for the purpose of popping off the stray narwhales, or vagrant sea unicorns infesting those waters; for you cannot successfully shoot at them from the deck owing to the resistance of the water, but to shoot down upon them is a very different thing. Now, it was plainly a labor of love for Captain Sleet to describe, as he does, all the little detailed conveniences of his crow's-nest; but though he so enlarges upon many of these, and though he treats us to a very scientific account of his experiments in this crow's-nest, with a small compass he kept there for the purpose of counteracting the errors resulting from what is called the "local attraction" of all binnacle magnets; an error ascribable to the horizontal vicinity of the iron in the ship's planks, and in the Glacier's case, perhaps, to there having been so many broken-down black-smiths among her crew; I say, that though the Captain is very discreet and scientific here, yet, for all his learned "binnacle deviations," "azimuth compass observations," and "approximate errors," he knows very well, Captain Sleet, that he was not so much immersed in those profound magnetic meditations, as to fail being attracted occasionally towards that well replenished little case-bottle, so nicely tucked in on one side of his crow's nest, within easy reach of his hand. Though, upon the whole, I greatly admire and even love the brave, the honest, and learned Captain; yet I take it very ill of him that he should so utterly ignore that case-bottle, seeing what a faithful friend and comforter it must have been, while with mittened fingers and hooded head he was studying the mathematics aloft there in that bird's nest within three or four perches of the pole.

But if we Southern whale-fishers are not so snugly housed aloft as Captain Sleet and his Greenland-men were; yet that disadvantage is greatly counterbalanced by the widely contrasting serenity of those seductive seas in which we Southern fishers mostly float. For one, I used to lounge up the rigging very leisurely, resting in the top to have a chat with Queequeg, or any one else off duty whom I might find there; then ascending a little way further, and throwing a lazy leg over the top-sail yard, take a preliminary view of the watery pastures, and so at last mount to my ultimate destination.

Let me make a clean breast of it here, and frankly admit that I kept but sorry guard. With the problem of the universe revolving in me, how could I—being left completely to myself at such a thought-engendering altitude,—how could I but lightly hold my obligations to observe all whale-ships' standing orders, "Keep your weather eye open, and sing out every time."

And let me in this place movingly admonish you, ye ship-owners of Nantucket! Beware of enlisting in your vigilant fisheries any lad with lean brow and hollow eye; given to unseasonable meditativeness; and who offers to ship with the Phædon instead of Bowditch in his head. Beware of such an one, I say: your whales must be seen before they can be killed; and this sunken-eyed young Platonist will tow you ten wakes round the world, and never make you one pint of sperm the richer. Nor are these monitions at all unneeded. For nowadays, the whale-fishery furnishes an asylum for many romantic, melancholy, and absent-minded young men, disgusted with the carking cares of earth, and seeking sentiment in tar and blubber. Childe Harold not unfrequently perches himself upon the mast-head of some luckless disappointed whale-ship, and in moody phrase ejaculates:—

> "Roll on, thou deep and dark blue ocean, roll!
> Ten thousand blubber-hunters sweep over thee in vain." [4]

Very often do the captains of such ships take those absent-minded young philosophers to task, upbraiding them with not feeling sufficient "interest" in the voyage; half-hinting that they are so hopelessly lost to all honorable ambition, as that in their secret souls they would rather not see whales than otherwise. But all in vain; those young Platonists have a notion that their vision is imperfect; they are short-sighted; what use, then, to strain the visual nerve? They have left their opera-glasses at home.

4. Byron, *Childe Harold*, Canto IV, stanza 179. "Ten thousand fleets sweep over thee in vain."

"Why, thou monkey," said a harpooneer to one of these lads, "we've been cruising now hard upon three years, and thou hast not raised a whale yet. Whales are scarce as hen's teeth whenever thou art up here." Perhaps they were; or perhaps there might have been shoals of them in the far horizon; but lulled into such an opium-like listlessness of vacant, unconscious reverie is this absent-minded youth by the blending cadence of waves with thoughts, that at last he loses his identity; takes the mystic ocean at his feet for the visible image of that deep, blue, bottomless soul, pervading mankind and nature; and every strange, half-seen, gliding, beautiful thing that eludes him; every dimly-discovered, uprising fin of some undiscernible form, seems to him the embodiment of those elusive thoughts that only people the soul by continually flitting through it. In this enchanted mood, thy spirit ebbs away to whence it came; becomes diffused through time and space; like Wickliff's [5] sprinkled Pantheistic ashes, forming at last a part of every shore the round globe over.

There is no life in thee, now, except that rocking life imparted by a gently rolling ship; by her, borrowed from the sea; by the sea, from the inscrutable tides of God. But while this sleep, this dream is on ye, move your foot or hand an inch; slip your hold at all; and your identity comes back in horror. Over Descartian vortices you hover. And perhaps, at mid-day, in the fairest weather, with one half-throttled shriek you drop through that transparent air into the summer sea, no more to rise for ever. Heed it well, ye Pantheists!

Chapter 36

THE QUARTER-DECK

(Enter Ahab: Then, all.)

It was not a great while after the affair of the pipe, that one morning shortly after breakfast, Ahab, as was his wont, ascended the cabin-gangway to the deck. There most sea-captains usually walk at that hour, as country gentlemen, after the same meal, take a few turns in the garden.

Soon his steady, ivory stride was heard, as to and fro he paced his old rounds, upon planks so familiar to his tread, that they were all over dented, like geological stones, with the peculiar mark of his walk. Did you fixedly gaze, too, upon that ribbed and dented brow; there also, you would see still stranger foot-prints—the foot-prints of his one unsleeping, ever-pacing thought.

5. The ashes of the martyr William Wickliff were cast into a brook. (The first American edition had the reading "Cranmer's," thus confusing Wickliff with another martyr; in the English edition the error was corrected and its correct reading is adopted here.)

But on the occasion in question, those dents looked deeper, even as his nervous step that morning left a deeper mark. And, so full of his thought was Ahab, that at every uniform turn that he made, now at the main-mast and now at the binnacle, you could almost see that thought turn in him as he turned, and pace in him as he paced; so completely possessing him, indeed, that it all but seemed the inward mould of every outer movement.

"D'ye mark him, Flask?" whispered Stubb; "the chick that's in him pecks the shell. 'Twill soon be out."

The hours wore on;—Ahab now shut up within his cabin; anon, pacing the deck, with the same intense bigotry of purpose [1] in his aspect.

It drew near the close of day. Suddenly he came to a halt by the bulwarks, and inserting his bone leg into the auger-hole there, and with one hand grasping a shroud, he ordered Starbuck to send everybody aft.

"Sir!" said the mate, astonished at an order seldom or never given on ship-board except in some extraordinary case.

"Send everybody aft," repeated Ahab. "Mast-heads, there! come down!"

When the entire ship's company were assembled, and with curious and not wholly unapprehensive faces, were eyeing him, for he looked not unlike the weather horizon when a storm is coming up, Ahab, after rapidly glancing over the bulwarks, and then darting his eyes among the crew, started from his stand-point; and as though not a soul were nigh him resumed his heavy turns upon the deck. With bent head and half-slouched hat he continued to pace, unmindful of the wondering whispering among the men; till Stubb cautiously whispered to Flask, that Ahab must have summoned them there for the purpose of witnessing a pedestrian feat. But this did not last long. Vehemently pausing, he cried:—

"What do ye do when ye see a whale, men?"

"Sing out for him!" was the impulsive rejoinder from a score of clubbed voices.

"Good!" cried Ahab, with a wild approval in his tones; observing the hearty animation into which his unexpected question had so magnetically thrown them.

"And what do ye next, men?"

"Lower away, and after him!"

"And what tune is it ye pull to, men?"

"A dead whale or a stove boat!"

More and more strangely and fiercely glad and approving, grew the countenance of the old man at every shout; while the mariners began to gaze curiously at each other, as if marvelling how it was

1. Intense singlemindedness of purpose.

that they themselves became so excited at such seemingly purpose-less questions.

But, they were all eagerness again, as Ahab, now half-revolving in his pivot-hole, with one hand reaching high up a shroud, and tightly, almost convulsively grasping it, addressed them thus:—

"All ye mast-headers have before now heard me give orders about a white whale. Look ye! d'ye see this Spanish ounce of gold?"— holding up a broad bright coin to the sun—"it is a sixteen dollar piece, men,—a doubloon. D'ye see it? Mr. Starbuck, hand me yon top-maul."

While the mate was getting the hammer, Ahab, without speak-ing, was slowly rubbing the gold piece against the skirts of his jacket, as if to heighten its lustre, and without using any words was meanwhile lowly humming to himself, producing a sound so strangely muffled and inarticulate that it seemed the mechanical humming of the wheels of his vitality in him.

Receiving the top-maul from Starbuck, he advanced towards the main-mast with the hammer uplifted in one hand, exhibiting the gold with the other, and with a high raised voice exclaiming: "Whosoever of ye raises me a white-headed whale with a wrinkled brow and a crooked jaw; whosoever of ye raises me that white-headed whale, with three holes punctured in his starboard fluke— look ye, whosoever of ye raises me that same white whale, he shall have this gold ounce, my boys!"

"Huzza! huzza!" cried the seamen, as with swinging tarpaulins they hailed the act of nailing the gold to the mast.

"It's a white whale, I say," resumed Ahab, as he threw down the top-maul; "a white whale. Skin your eyes for him, men; look sharp for white water; if ye see but a bubble, sing out."

All this while Tashtego, Daggoo, and Queequeg had looked on with even more intense interest and surprise than the rest, and at the mention of the wrinkled brow and crooked jaw they had started as if each was separately touched by some specific recollection.

"Captain Ahab," said Tashtego, "that white whale must be the same that some call Moby Dick."

"Moby Dick?" shouted Ahab. "Do ye know the white whale then, Tash?"

"Does he fan-tail a little curious, sir, before he goes down?" said the Gay-Header deliberately.

"And has he a curious spout, too," said Daggoo, "very bushy, even for a parmacetty, and mighty quick, Captain Ahab?"

"And he have one, two, tree—oh! good many iron in him hide, too, Captain," cried Queequeg disjointedly, "all twiske-tee be-twisk, like him—him—" faltering hard for a word, and screwing his hand round and round as though uncorking a bottle—"like him—him—"

"Corkscrew!" cried Ahab, "aye, Queequeg, the harpoons lie all twisted and wrenched in him; aye, Daggoo, his spout is a big one, like a whole shock of wheat, and white as a pile of our Nantucket wool after the great annual sheep-shearing; aye, Tashtego, and he fan-tails like a split jib in a squall. Death and devils! men, it is Moby Dick ye have seen—Moby Dick—Moby Dick!"

"Captain Ahab," said Starbuck, who, with Stubb and Flask, had thus far been eyeing his superior with increasing surprise, but at last seemed struck with a thought which somewhat explained all the wonder. "Captain Ahab, I have heard of Moby Dick—but it was not Moby Dick that took off thy leg?"

"Who told thee that?" cried Ahab; then pausing, "Aye, Starbuck; aye, my hearties all round; it was Moby Dick that dismasted me; Moby Dick that brought me to this dead stump I stand on now. Aye, aye," he shouted with a terrific, loud, animal sob, like that of a heart-stricken moose; "Aye, aye! it was that accursed white whale that razeed me; made a poor pegging lubber of me for ever and a day!" Then tossing both arms, with measureless imprecations he shouted out: "Aye, aye! and I'll chase him round Good Hope, and round the Horn, and round the Norway Maelstrom, and round perdition's flames before I give him up. And this is what ye have shipped for, men! to chase that white whale on both sides of land, and over all sides of earth, till he spouts black blood and rolls fin out. What say ye, men, will ye splice hands on it, now? I think ye do look brave."

"Aye, aye!" shouted the harpooneers and seamen, running closer to the excited old man: "A sharp eye for the White Whale; a sharp lance for Moby Dick!"

"God bless ye," he seemed to half sob and half shout. "God bless ye, men. Steward! go draw the great measure of grog. But what's this long face about, Mr. Starbuck; wilt thou not chase the white whale? art not game for Moby Dick?"

"I am game for his crooked jaw, and for the jaws of Death too, Captain Ahab, if it fairly comes in the way of the business we follow; but I came here to hunt whales, not my commander's vengeance. How many barrels will thy vengeance yield thee even if thou gettest it, Captain Ahab? it will not fetch thee much in our Nantucket market."

"Nantucket market! Hoot! But come closer, Starbuck; thou requirest a little lower layer. If money's to be the measurer, man, and the accountants have computed their great counting-house the globe, by girdling it with guineas, one to every three parts of an inch; then, let me tell thee, that my vengeance will fetch a great premium *here!*"

"He smites his chest," whispered Stubb, "what's that for? methinks it rings most vast, but hollow."

"Vengeance on a dumb brute!" cried Starbuck, "that simply smote thee from blindest instinct! Madness! To be enraged with a dumb thing, Captain Ahab, seems blasphemous."

"Hark ye yet again,—the little lower layer. All visible objects, man, are but as pasteboard masks. But in each event—in the living act, the undoubted deed—there, some unknown but still reasoning thing puts forth the mouldings of its features from behind the unreasoning mask. If man will strike, strike through the mask! How can the prisoner reach outside except by thrusting through the wall? To me, the white whale is that wall, shoved near to me. Sometimes I think there's naught beyond. But 'tis enough. He tasks me; he heaps me; I see in him outrageous strength, with an inscrutable malice sinewing it. That inscrutable thing is chiefly what I hate; and be the white whale agent, or be the white whale principal, I will wreak that hate upon him. Talk not to me of blasphemy, man; I'd strike the sun if it insulted me. For could the sun do that, then could I do the other; since there is ever a sort of fair play herein, jealousy presiding over all creations. But not my master, man, is even that fair play. Who's over me? Truth hath no confines. Take off thine eye! more intolerable than fiends' glarings is a doltish stare! So, so; thou reddenest and palest; my heat has melted thee to anger-glow. But look ye, Starbuck, what is said in heat, that thing unsays itself. There are men from whom warm words are small indignity. I meant not to incense thee. Let it go. Look! see yonder Turkish cheeks of spotted tawn—living, breathing pictures painted by the sun. The Pagan leopards—the unrecking and unworshipping things, that live; and seek, and give no reasons for the torrid life they feel! The crew, man, the crew! Are they not one and all with Ahab, in this matter of the whale? See Stubb! he laughs! See yonder Chilean! he snorts to think of it. Stand up amid the general hurricane, thy one tost sapling cannot, Starbuck! And what is it? Reckon it. 'Tis but to help strike a fin; no wondrous feat for Starbuck. What is it more? From this one poor hunt, then, the best lance out of all Nantucket, surely he will not hang back, when every foremast-hand has clutched a whetstone? Ah! constrainings seize thee; I see! the billow lifts thee! Speak, but speak!—Aye, aye! thy silence, then, *that* voices thee. (*Aside*) Something shot from my dilated nostrils, he has inhaled it in his lungs. Starbuck now is mine; cannot oppose me now, without rebellion."

"God keep me!—keep us all!" murmured Starbuck, lowly.

But in his joy at the enchanted, tacit acquiescence of the mate,

Ahab did not hear his foreboding invocation; nor yet the low laugh from the hold; nor yet the presaging vibrations of the winds in the cordage; nor yet the hollow flap of the sails against the masts, as for a moment their hearts sank in. For again Starbuck's downcast eyes lighted up with the stubbornness of life; the subterranean laugh died away; the winds blew on; the sails filled out; the ship heaved and rolled as before. Ah, ye admonitions and warnings! why stay ye not when ye come? But rather are ye predictions than warnings, ye shadows! Yet not so much predictions from without, as verifications of the foregoing things within. For with little external to constrain us, the innermost necessities in our being, these still drive us on.

"The measure! the measure!" cried Ahab.

Receiving the brimming pewter, and turning to the harpooneers, he ordered them to produce their weapons. Then ranging them before him near the capstan, with their harpoons in their hands, while his three mates stood at his side with their lances, and the rest of the ship's company formed a circle round the group; he stood for an instant searchingly eyeing every man of his crew. But those wild eyes met his, as the bloodshot eyes of the prairie wolves meet the eye of their leader, ere he rushes on at their head in the trail of the bison; but, alas! only to fall into the hidden snare of the Indian.

"Drink and pass!" he cried, handing the heavy charged flagon to the nearest seaman. "The crew alone now drink. Round with it, round! Short draughts—long swallows, men; 'tis hot as Satan's hoof. So, so; it goes round excellently. It spiralizes in ye; forks out at the serpent-snapping eye. Well done; almost drained. That way it went, this way it comes. Hand it me—here's a hollow! Men, ye seem the years; so brimming life is gulped and gone. Steward, refill!

"Attend now, my braves. I have mustered ye all round this capstan; and ye mates, flank me with your lances; and ye harpooneers, stand there with your irons; and ye, stout mariners, ring me in, that I may in some sort revive a noble custom of my fisherman fathers before me. O men, you will yet see that——Ha! boy, come back? bad pennies come not sooner. Hand it me. Why, now, this pewter had run brimming again, wert not thou St. Vitus' imp—away, thou ague!

"Advance, ye mates! Cross your lances full before me. Well done! Let me touch the axis." So saying, with extended arm, he grasped the three level, radiating lances at their crossed centre; while so doing, suddenly and nervously twitched them; meanwhile, glancing intently from Starbuck to Stubb; from Stubb to Flask. It seemed as though, by some nameless, interior volition, he would fain have shocked into them the same fiery emotion accumulated within the Leyden jar of his own magnetic life. The three mates quailed before his strong, sustained, and mystic aspect. Stubb and Flask looked sideways from him; the honest eye of Starbuck fell downright.

"In vain!" cried Ahab; "but, maybe, 'tis well. For did ye three but once take the full-forced shock, then mine own electric thing, *that* had perhaps expired from out me. Perchance, too, it would have dropped ye dead. Perchance ye need it not. Down lances! And now, ye mates, I do appoint ye three cup-bearers to my three pagan kinsmen there—yon three most honorable gentlemen and noblemen, my valiant harpooneers. Disdain the task? What, when the great Pope washes the feet of beggars, using his tiara for ewer? Oh, my sweet cardinals! your own condescension, *that* shall bend ye to it. I do not order ye; ye will it. Cut your seizings and draw the poles, ye harpooneers!"

Silently obeying the order, the three harpooneers now stood with the detached iron part of their harpoons, some three feet long, held, barbs up, before him.

"Stab me not with that keen steel! Cant them; cant them over! know ye not the goblet end? Turn up the socket! So, so; now, ye cup-bearers, advance. The irons! take them; hold them while I fill!" Forthwith, slowly going from one officer to the other, he brimmed the harpoon sockets with the fiery waters from the pewter.

"Now, three to three, ye stand. Commend the murderous chalices! Bestow them, ye who are now made parties to this indissoluble league. Ha! Starbuck! but the deed is done! Yon ratifying sun now waits to sit upon it. Drink, ye harpooneers! drink and swear, ye men that man the deathful whaleboat's bow—Death to Moby Dick! God hunt us all, if we do not hunt Moby Dick to his death!" The long, barbed steel goblets were lifted; and to cries and maledictions against the white whale, the spirits were simultaneously quaffed down with a hiss. Starbuck paled, and turned, and shivered. Once more, and finally, the replenished pewter went the rounds among the frantic crew; when, waving his free hand to them, they all dispersed; and Ahab retired within his cabin.

Chapter 37

SUNSET

The cabin; by the stern windows; Ahab sitting alone, and gazing out.

I leave a white and turbid wake; pale waters, paler cheeks, where'er I sail. The envious billows sidelong swell to whelm my track; let them; but first I pass.

Yonder, by the ever-brimming goblet's rim, the warm waves blush like wine. The gold brow plumbs the blue. The diver sun —slow dived from noon,—goes down; my soul mounts up! she wearies with her endless hill. Is, then, the crown too heavy that I wear? this Iron Crown of Lombardy.[1] Yet is it bright with many a gem; I, the wearer, see not its far flashings; but darkly feel that I wear that, that dazzlingly confounds. 'Tis iron—that I know—not gold. 'Tis split, too—that I feel; the jagged edge galls me so, my brain seems to beat against the solid metal; aye, steel skull, mine; the sort that needs no helmet in the most brain-battering fight!

Dry heat upon my brow? Oh! time was, when as the sunrise nobly spurred me, so the sunset soothed. No more. This lovely light, it lights not me; all loveliness is anguish to me, since I can ne'er enjoy. Gifted with the high perception, I lack the low, enjoying power; damned, most subtly and most malignantly! damned in the midst of Paradise! Good night—good night! (*waving his hand, he moves from the window.*)

'Twas not so hard a task. I thought to find one stubborn, at the least; but my one cogged circle fits into all their various wheels, and they revolve. Or, if you will, like so many ant-hills of powder, they all stand before me; and I their match. Oh, hard! that to fire others, the match itself must needs be wasting! What I've dared, I've willed; and what I've willed, I'll do! They think me mad—Starbuck does; but I'm demoniac, I am madness maddened! That wild madness that's only calm to comprehend itself! The prophecy was that I should be dismembered; and—Aye! I lost this leg. I now prophesy that I will dismember my dismemberer. Now, then, be the prophet and the fulfiller one. That's more than ye, ye great gods, ever were. I laugh and hoot at ye, ye cricket-players, ye pugilists, ye deaf Burkes and blinded Bendigoes![2] I will not say as schoolboys do to bullies,—Take some one of your own size; don't pommel *me!* No, ye've knocked me down, and I am up again; but *ye* have run and hidden. Come forth from behind your cotton bags! I have no long gun to reach ye. Come, Ahab's compliments to ye; come and see if ye can swerve me. Swerve me? ye cannot swerve me, else ye swerve yourselves! man has ye there. Swerve me? The path to my fixed purpose is laid with iron rails, whereon my soul is grooved to run. Over unsounded gorges, through the rifled hearts of mountains, under torrents' beds, unerringly I rush! Naught's an obstacle, naught's an angle to the iron way!

---

1. A crown used at the coronation of Holy Roman Emperors, said to contain a nail from the Cross.

2. Burke and Bendigo were English boxing champions in the 1830's and 1840's; Bendigo was the nickname of William Thompson.

Chapter 38

DUSK

By the Mainmast; Starbuck leaning against it.

My soul is more than matched; she's overmanned; and by a madman! Insufferable sting, that sanity should ground arms on such a field! But he drilled deep down, and blasted all my reason out of me! I think I see his impious end; but feel that I must help him to it. Will I, nill I, the ineffable thing has tied me to him; tows me with a cable I have no knife to cut. Horrible old man! Who's over him, he cries;—aye, he would be a democrat to all above; look, how he lords it over all below! Oh! I plainly see my miserable office,—to obey, rebelling; and worse yet, to hate with touch of pity! For in his eyes I read some lurid woe would shrivel me up, had I it. Yet is there hope. Time and tide flow wide. The hated whale has the round watery world to swim in, as the small gold-fish has its glassy globe. His heaven-insulting purpose, God may wedge aside. I would up heart, were it not like lead. But my whole clock's run down; my heart the all-controlling weight, I have no key to lift again.

[*A burst of revelry from the forecastle.*

Oh, God! to sail with such a heathen crew that have small touch of human mothers in them! Whelped somewhere by the sharkish sea. The white whale is their demogorgon. Hark! the infernal orgies! that revelry is forward! mark the unfaltering silence aft! Methinks it pictures life. Foremost through the sparkling sea shoots on the gay, embattled, bantering bow, but only to drag dark Ahab after it, where he broods within his sternward cabin, builded over the dead water of the wake, and further on, hunted by its wolfish gurglings. The long howl thrills me through! Peace! ye revellers, and set the watch! Oh, life! 'tis in an hour like this, with soul beat down and held to knowledge,—as wild, untutored things are forced to feed—Oh, life! 'tis now that I do feel the latent horror in thee! but 'tis not me! that horror's out of me! and with the soft feeling of the human in me, yet will I try to fight ye, ye grim, phantom futures! Stand by me, hold me, bind me, O ye blessed influences!

Chapter 39

FIRST NIGHT-WATCH

FORE-TOP

(*Stubb solus, and mending a brace.*)

Ha! ha! ha! ha! hem! clear my throat!—I've been thinking over it ever since, and that ha-ha's the final consequence. Why so?

Because a laugh's the wisest, easiest answer to all that's queer; and come what will, one comfort's always left—that unfailing comfort is, it's all predestinated. I heard not all his talk with Starbuck; but to my poor eye Starbuck then looked something as I the other evening felt. Be sure the old Mogul has fixed him, too. I twigged it, knew it; had had the gift, might readily have prophesied it—for when I clapped my eye upon his skull I saw it. Well, Stubb, *wise* Stubb—that's my title—well, Stubb, what of it, Stubb? Here's a carcase. I know not all that may be coming, but be it what it will, I'll go to it laughing. Such a waggish leering as lurks in all your horribles! I feel funny. Fa, la! lirra, skirra! What's my juicy little pear at home doing now? Crying its eyes out?—Giving a party to the last arrived harpooneers, I dare say, gay as a frigate's pennant, and so am I—fa, la! lirra, skirra! Oh—

> We'll drink to-night with hearts as light,
>   To love, as gay and fleeting
> As bubbles that swim, on the beaker's brim,
>   And break on the lips while meeting.

A brave stave that—who calls? Mr. Starbuck? Aye, aye, sir— (*Aside*) he's my superior, he has his too, if I'm not mistaken.— Aye, aye, sir, just through with this job—coming.

Chapter 40

MIDNIGHT, FORECASTLE

HARPOONEERS AND SAILORS.

(*Foresail rises and discovers the watch standing, lounging, leaning, and lying in various attitudes, all singing in chorus.*)

> Farewell and adieu to you, Spanish ladies!
> Farewell and adieu to you, ladies of Spain!
> Our captain's commanded—

1ST NANTUCKET SAILOR.

Oh, boys, don't be sentimental; it's bad for the digestion! Take a tonic, follow me!

> (*Sings, and all follow.*)
> Our captain stood upon the deck,
>   A spy-glass in his hand,
> A viewing of those gallant whales
>   That blew at every strand.
> Oh, your tubs in your boats, my boys,
>   And by your braces stand,
> And we'll have one of those fine whales,
>   Hand, boys, over hand!
> So, be cheery, my lads! may your hearts never fail!
> While the bold harpooneer is striking the whale!

MATE'S VOICE FROM THE QUARTER-DECK.

Eight bells there, forward!

2D NANTUCKET SAILOR.

Avast the chorus! Eight bells there! d'ye hear, bell-boy? Strike the bell eight, thou Pip! thou blackling! and let me call the watch. I've the sort of mouth for that—the hogshead mouth. So, so, (*thrusts his head down the scuttle*,) Star—bo-l-e-e-n-s, a-h-o-y! Eight bells there below! Tumble up!

DUTCH SAILOR.

Grand snoozing to-night, maty; fat night for that. I mark this in our old Mogul's wine; it's quite as deadening to some as filliping to others. We sing; they sleep—aye, lie down there, like ground-tier butts. At 'em again! There, take this copper-pump, and hail 'em through it. Tell 'em to avast dreaming of their lasses. Tell 'em it's the resurrection; they must kiss their last, and come to judgment. That's the way—*that's* it; thy throat ain't spoiled with eating Amsterdam butter.

FRENCH SAILOR.

Hist, boys! let's have a jig or two before we ride to anchor in Blanket Bay. What say ye? There comes the other watch. Stand by all legs! Pip! little Pip! hurrah with your tambourine!

PIP.

(Sulky and sleepy.)

Don't know where it is.

FRENCH SAILOR.

Beat thy belly, then, and wag thy ears. Jig it, men, I say; merry's the word; hurrah! Damn me, won't you dance? Form, now, Indian-file, and gallop into the double-shuffle? Throw yourselves! Legs! legs!

ICELAND SAILOR.

I don't like your floor, maty; it's too springy to my taste. I'm used to ice-floors. I'm sorry to throw cold water on the subject; but excuse me.

MALTESE SAILOR.

Me too; where's your girls? Who but a fool would take his left hand by his right, and say to himself, how d'ye do? Partners! I must have partners!

SICILIAN SAILOR.

Aye; girls and a green!—then I'll hop with ye; yea, turn grasshopper!

LONG-ISLAND SAILOR.

Well, well, ye sulkies, there's plenty more of us. Hoe corn when you may, say I. All legs go to harvest soon. Ah! here comes the music; now for it!

AZORE SAILOR.

(Ascending, and pitching the tambourine up the scuttle.)
Here you are, Pip; and there's the windlass-bitts; up you mount! Now, boys!

(The half of them dance to the tambourine; some go below; some sleep or lie among the coils of ringing. Oaths a-plenty.)

AZORE SAILOR.
(Dancing.)

Go it, Pip! Bang it, bell-boy! Rig it, dig it, stig it, quig it, bell-boy! Make fire-flies; break the jinglers!

PIP.

Jinglers, you say?—there goes another, dropped off; I pound it so.

CHINA SAILOR.

Rattle thy teeth, then, and pound away; make a pagoda of thyself.

FRENCH SAILOR.

Merry-mad! Hold up thy hoop, Pip, till I jump through it! Split jibs! tear yourselves!

TASHTEGO.
(Quietly smoking.)
That's a white man; he calls that fun: humph! I save my sweat.

OLD MANX SAILOR.

I wonder whether those jolly lads bethink them of what they are dancing over. I'll dance over your grave, I will—that's the bitterest threat of your night-women, that beat head-winds round corners. O Christ! to think of the green navies and the green-skulled crews! Well, well; belike the whole world's one ball, as your scholars have it; and so 'tis right to make one ball-room of it. Dance on, lads, you're young; I was once.

3D NANTUCKET SAILOR.

Spell oh!—whew! this is worse than pulling after whales in a calm—give us a whiff, Tash.

(*They cease dancing, and gather in clusters. Meantime the sky darkens—the wind rises.*)

LASCAR SAILOR.

By Brahma! boys, it'll be douse sail soon. The sky-born, high-tide Ganges turned to wind! Thou showest thy black brow, Seeva!

MALTESE SAILOR.

(*Reclining and shaking his cap.*)

It's the waves'—the snow-caps' turn to jig it now. They'll shake their tassels soon. Now would all the waves were women, then I'd go drown, and chassee with them evermore! There's naught so sweet on earth—heaven may not match it!—as those swift glances of warm, wild bosoms in the dance, when the over-arboring arms hide such ripe, bursting grapes.

SICILIAN SAILOR.

(*Reclining.*)

Tell me not of it! Hark ye, lad—fleet interlacings of the limbs —lithe swayings—coyings—flutterings! lip! heart! hip! all graze: unceasing touch and go! not taste, observe ye, else come satiety. Eh, Pagan? (*Nudging.*)

TAHITIAN SAILOR.

(*Reclining on a mat.*)

Hail, holy nakedness of our dancing girls!—the Heeva-Heeva! Ah! low-valed, high-palmed Tahiti! I still rest me on thy mat, but the soft soil has slid! I saw thee woven in the wood, my mat! green the first day I brought ye thence; now worn and wilted quite. Ah me!—not thou nor I can bear the change! How then, if so be transplanted to yon sky? Hear I the roaring streams from Pirohitee's peak of spears, when they leap down the crags and drown the villages?—The blast! the blast! Up, spine, and meet it! (*Leaps to his feet.*)

PORTUGUESE SAILOR.

How the sea rolls swashing 'gainst the side! Stand by for reefing, hearties! the winds are just crossing swords, pell-mell they'll go lunging presently.

DANISH SAILOR.

Crack, crack, old ship! so long as thou crackest, thou holdest! Well done! The mate there holds ye to it stiffly. He's no more afraid than the isle fort at Cattegat, put there to fight the Baltic with storm-lashed guns, on which the sea-salt cakes!

4TH NANTUCKET SAILOR.

He has his orders, mind ye that. I heard old Ahab tell him he must always kill a squall, something as they burst a water-spout with a pistol—fire your ship right into it!

ENGLISH SAILOR.

Blood! but that old man's a grand old cove! We are the lads to hunt him up his whale!

ALL.

Aye! aye!

OLD MANX SAILOR.

How the three pines shake! Pines are the hardest sort of tree to live when shifted to any other soil, and here there's none but the crew's cursed clay. Steady, helmsman! steady. This is the sort of weather when brave hearts snap ashore, and keeled hulls split at sea. Our captain has his birth-mark; look yonder, boys, there's another in the sky—lurid-like, ye see, all else pitch black.

DAGGOO.

What of that? Who's afraid of black's afraid of me! I'm quarried out of it!

SPANISH SAILOR.

(*Aside.*) He wants to bully, ah!—the old grudge makes me touchy. (*Advancing.*) Aye, harpooneer, thy race is the undeniable dark side of mankind—devilish dark at that. No offence.

DAGGOO (*grimly*).

None.

ST. JAGO'S SAILOR.

That Spaniard's mad or drunk. But that can't be, or else in his one case our old Mogul's fire-waters are somewhat long in working.

5TH NANTUCKET SAILOR.

What's that I saw—lightning? Yes.

SPANISH SAILOR.

No; Daggoo showing his teeth.

DAGGOO (*springing*).

Swallow thine, mannikin! White skin, white liver!

SPANISH SAILOR (*meeting him*).

Knife thee heartily! big frame, small spirit!

ALL.

A row! a row! a row!

TASHTEGO (*with a whiff*).

A row a'low, and a row aloft—gods and men—both brawlers! Humph!

BELFAST SAILOR.

A row! arrah a row! The Virgin be blessed, a row! Plunge in with ye!

ENGLISH SAILOR.

Fair play! Snatch the Spaniard's knife! A ring, a ring!

OLD MANX SAILOR.

Ready formed. There! the ringed horizon. In that ring Cain struck Abel. Sweet work, right work! No? Why then, God, mad'st thou the ring?

MATE'S VOICE FROM THE QUARTER DECK.

Hands by the halyards! in top-gallant sails! Stand by to reef topsails!

ALL.

The squall! the squall! jump, my jollies! (*They scatter.*)

PIP (*shrinking under the windlass*).

Jollies? Lord help such jollies! Crish, crash! there goes the jib-stay! Blang-whang! God! Duck lower, Pip, here comes the royal yard! It's worse than being in the whirled woods, the last day of the year! Who'd go climbing after chestnuts now? But there they go, all cursing, and here I don't. Fine prospects to 'em; they're on the road to heaven. Hold on hard! Jimmini, what a squall! But those chaps there are worse yet—they are your white squalls, they. White squalls? white whale, shirr! shirr! Here have I heard all their chat just now, and the white whale—shirr! shirr!—but spoken of once! and only this evening—it makes me jingle all over like my tambourine—that anaconda of an old man swore 'em in to hunt him! Oh, thou big white God aloft there somewhere in yon darkness, have mercy on this small black boy down here; preserve him from all men that have no bowels to feel fear!

*   *   *   *   *   *

Chapter 41

MOBY DICK

I, Ishmael, was one of that crew; my shouts had gone up with the rest; my oath had been welded with theirs; and stronger I shouted, and more did I hammer and clinch my oath, because of the dread in my soul. A wild, mystical, sympathetical feeling was in me; Ahab's quenchless feud seemed mine. With greedy ears I learned the history of that murderous monster against whom I and all the others had taken our oaths of violence and revenge.

For some time past, though at intervals only, the unaccompanied, secluded White Whale had haunted those uncivilized seas mostly frequented by the Sperm Whale fishermen. But not all of them knew of his existence; only a few of them, comparatively, had knowingly seen him; while the number who as yet had actually and knowingly given battle to him, was small indeed. For, owing to the large number of whale-cruisers; the disorderly way they were sprinkled over the entire watery circumference, many of them adventurously pushing their quest along solitary latitudes, so as seldom or never for a whole twelvemonth or more on a stretch, to encounter a single news-telling sail of any sort; the inordinate length of each separate voyage; the irregularity of the times of sailing from home; all these, with other circumstances, direct and indirect, long obstructed the spread through the whole world-wide whaling-fleet of the special individualizing tidings concerning Moby Dick. It was hardly to be doubted, that several vessels reported to have encountered, at such or such a time, or on such or such a meridian, a Sperm Whale of uncommon magnitude and malignity, which whale, after doing great mischief to his assailants, had completely escaped them; to some minds it was not an unfair presumption, I say, that the whale in question must have been no other than Moby Dick. Yet as of late the Sperm Whale fishery had been marked by various and not unfrequent instances of great ferocity, cunning, and malice in the monster attacked; therefore it was, that those who by accident ignorantly gave battle to Moby Dick; such hunters, perhaps, for the most part, were content to ascribe the peculiar terror he bred, more, as it were, to the perils of the Sperm Whale fishery at large, than to the individual cause. In that way, mostly, the disastrous encounter between Ahab and the whale had hitherto been popularly regarded.

And as for those who, previously hearing of the White Whale, by chance caught sight of him; in the beginning of the thing they had every one of them, almost, as boldly and fearlessly lowered for him, as for any other whale of that species. But at length, such calamities did ensue in these assaults—not restricted to sprained wrists and ancles, broken limbs, or devouring amputations—but fatal to the last degree of fatality; those repeated disastrous repulses, all accumulating and piling their terrors upon Moby Dick; those things had gone far to shake the fortitude of many brave hunters, to whom the story of the White Whale had eventually come.

Nor did wild rumors of all sorts fail to exaggerate, and still the more horrify the true histories of these deadly encounters. For not only do fabulous rumors naturally grow out of the very body of all surprising terrible events,—as the smitten tree gives birth to its fungi; but, in maritime life, far more than in that of terra firma, wild rumors abound, wherever there is any adequate reality for them to cling to. And as the sea surpasses the land in this matter, so the whale fishery surpasses every other sort of maritime life, in the wonderfulness and fearfulness of the rumors which sometimes circulate there. For not only are whalemen as a body unexempt from that ignorance and superstitiousness hereditary to all sailors; but of all sailors, they are by all odds the most directly brought into contact with whatever is appallingly astonishing in the sea; face to face they not only eye its greatest marvels, but, hand to jaw, give battle to them. Alone, in such remotest waters, that though you sailed a thousand miles, and passed a thousand shores, you would not come to any chiselled hearthstone, or aught hospitable beneath that part of the sun; in such latitudes and longitudes, pursuing too such a calling as he does, the whaleman is wrapped by influences all tending to make his fancy pregnant with many a mighty birth.

No wonder, then, that ever gathering volume from the mere transit over the widest watery spaces, the outblown rumors of the White Whale did in the end incorporate with themselves all manner of morbid hints, and half-formed fœtal suggestions of supernatural agencies, which eventually invested Moby Dick with new terrors unborrowed from anything that visibly appears. So that in many cases such a panic did he finally strike, that few who by those rumors, at least, had heard of the White Whale, few of those hunters were willing to encounter the perils of his jaw.

But there were still other and more vital practical influences at work. Not even at the present day has the original prestige of the Sperm Whale, as fearfully distinguished from all other species of the leviathan, died out of the minds of the whalemen as a body. There are those this day among them, who, though intelligent and courageous enough in offering battle to the Greenland or Right whale, would perhaps—either from professional inexperience, or incompetency, or timidity, decline a contest with the Sperm Whale; at any rate, there are plenty of whalemen, especially among those whaling nations not sailing under the American flag, who have never hostilely encountered the Sperm Whale, but whose sole knowledge of the leviathan is restricted to the ignoble monster primitively pursued in the North; seated on their hatches, these men will hearken with a childish fire-side interest and awe, to the wild, strange tales of Southern whaling. Nor is the pre-eminent tremendousness of the great Sperm Whale anywhere more feelingly comprehended, than on board of those prows which stem him.

And as if the now tested reality of his might had in former legendary times thrown its shadow before it; we find some book naturalists—Olafsen and Povelsen—declaring the Sperm Whale not only to be a consternation to every other creature in the sea, but also to be so incredibly ferocious as continually to be athirst for human blood. Nor even down to so late a time as Cuvier's, were these or almost similar impressions effaced. For in his Natural History, the Baron himself affirms that at sight of the Sperm Whale, all fish (sharks included) are "struck with the most lively terrors," and "often in the precipitancy of their flight dash themselves against the rocks with such violence as to cause instantaneous death." And however the general experiences in the fishery may amend such reports as these; yet in their full terribleness, even to the bloodthirsty item of Povelsen, the superstitious belief in them is, in some vicissitudes of their vocation, revived in the minds of the hunters.

So that overawed by the rumors and portents concerning him, not a few of the fishermen recalled, in reference to Moby Dick, the earlier days of the Sperm Whale fishery, when it was oftentimes hard to induce long practised Right whalemen to embark in the perils of this new and daring warfare; such men protesting that although other leviathans might be hopefully pursued, yet to chase and point lance at such an apparition as the Sperm Whale was not for mortal man. That to attempt it, would be inevitably to be torn into a quick eternity. On this head, there are some remarkable documents that may be consulted.

Nevertheless, some there were, who even in the face of these things were ready to give chase to Moby Dick; and a still greater number who, chancing only to hear of him distantly and vaguely, without the specific details of any certain calamity, and without superstitious accompaniments, were sufficiently hardy not to flee from the battle if offered.

One of the wild suggestings referred to, as at last coming to be linked with the White Whale in the minds of the superstitiously inclined, was the unearthly conceit that Moby Dick was ubiquitous; that he had actually been encountered in opposite latitudes at one and the same instant of time.

Nor, credulous as such minds must have been, was this conceit altogether without some faint show of superstitious probability. For as the secrets of the currents in the seas have never yet been divulged, even to the most erudite research; so the hidden ways of the Sperm Whale when beneath the surface remain, in great part, unaccountable to his pursuers; and from time to time have originated the most curious and contradictory speculations regarding them, especially concerning the mystic modes whereby, after sounding to a great depth, he transports himself with such vast swiftness to the most widely distant points.

It is a thing well known to both American and English whaleships, and also a thing placed upon authoritative record years ago by Scoresby, that some whales have been captured far north in the Pacific, in whose bodies have been found the barbs of harpoons darted in the Greenland seas. Nor is it to be gainsaid, that in some of these instances it has been declared that the interval of time between the two assaults could not have exceeded very many days. Hence, by inference, it has been believed by some whalemen, that the Nor' West Passage, so long a problem to man, was never a problem to the whale. So that here, in the real living experience of living men, the prodigies related in old times of the inland Strello mountain in Portugal (near whose top there was said to be a lake in which the wrecks of ships floated up to the surface); and that still more wonderful story of the Arethusa fountain near Syracuse (whose waters were believed to have come from the Holy Land by an underground passage); these fabulous narrations are almost fully equalled by the realities of the whaleman.

Forced into familiarity, then, with such prodigies as these; and knowing that after repeated, intrepid assaults, the White Whale had escaped alive; it cannot be much matter of surprise that some whalemen should go still further in their superstitions; declaring Moby Dick not only ubiquitous, but immortal (for immortality is but ubiquity in time); that though groves of spears should be planted in his flanks, he would still swim away unharmed; or if indeed he should ever be made to spout thick blood, such a sight would be but a ghastly deception; for again in unensanguined billows hundreds of leagues away, his unsullied jet would once more be seen.

But even stripped of these supernatural surmisings, there was enough in the earthly make and incontestable character of the monster to strike the imagination with unwonted power. For, it was not so much his uncommon bulk that so much distinguished him from other sperm whales, but, as was elsewhere thrown out —a peculiar snow-white wrinkled forehead, and a high, pyramidical white hump. These were his prominent features; the tokens whereby, even in the limitless, uncharted seas, he revealed his identity, at a long distance, to those who knew him.

The rest of his body was so streaked, and spotted, and marbled with the same shrouded hue, that, in the end, he had gained his distinctive appellation of the White Whale; a name, indeed, literally justified by his vivid aspect, when seen gliding at high noon through a dark blue sea, leaving a milky-way wake of creamy foam, all spangled with golden gleamings.

Nor was it his unwonted magnitude, nor his remarkable hue, nor yet his deformed lower jaw, that so much invested the whale with natural terror, as that unexampled, intelligent malignity which, according to specific accounts, he had over and over again evinced in his assaults. More than all, his treacherous retreats struck more of dismay than perhaps aught else. For, when swimming before his exulting pursuers, with every apparent symptom of alarm, he had several times been known to turn round suddenly, and, bearing down upon them, either stave their boats to splinters, or drive them back in consternation to their ship.

Already several fatalities had attended his chase. But though similar disasters, however little bruited ashore, were by no means unusual in the fishery; yet, in most instances, such seemed the White Whale's infernal aforethought of ferocity, that every dismembering or death that he caused, was not wholly regarded as having been inflicted by an unintelligent agent.

Judge, then, to what pitches of inflamed, distracted fury the minds of his more desperate hunters were impelled, when amid the chips of chewed boats, and the sinking limbs of torn comrades, they swam out of the white curds of the whale's direful wrath into the serene, exasperating sunlight, that smiled on, as if at a birth or a bridal.

His three boats stove around him, and oars and men both whirling in the eddies; one captain, seizing the line-knife from his broken prow, had dashed at the whale, as an Arkansas duellist at his foe, blindly seeking with a six inch blade to reach the fathom-deep life of the whale. That captain was Ahab. And then it was, that suddenly sweeping his sickle-shaped lower jaw beneath him,

Moby Dick had reaped away Ahab's leg, as a mower a blade of grass in the field. No turbaned Turk, no hired Venetian or Malay, could have smote him with more seeming malice. Small reason was there to doubt, then, that ever since that almost fatal encounter, Ahab had cherished a wild vindictiveness against the whale, all the more fell for that in his frantic morbidness he at last came to identify with him, not only all his bodily woes, but all his intellectual and spiritual exasperations. The White Whale swam before him as the monomaniac incarnation of all those malicious agencies which some deep men feel eating in them, till they are left living on with half a heart and half a lung. That intangible malignity which has been from the beginning; to whose dominion even the modern Christians ascribe one-half of the worlds; which the ancient Ophites of the east reverenced in their statue devil;— Ahab did not fall down and worship it like them; but deliriously transferring its idea to the abhorred white whale, he pitted himself, all mutilated, against it. All that most maddens and torments; all that stirs up the lees of things; all truth with malice in it; all that cracks the sinews and cakes the brain; all the subtle demonisms of life and thought; all evil, to crazy Ahab, were visibly personified, and made practically assailable in Moby Dick. He piled upon the whale's white hump the sum of all the general rage and hate felt by his whole race from Adam down; and then, as if his chest had been a mortar, he burst his hot heart's shell upon it.

It is not probable that this monomania in him took its instant rise at the precise time of his bodily dismemberment. Then, in darting at the monster, knife in hand, he had but given loose to a sudden, passionate, corporal animosity; and when he received the stroke that tore him, he probably but felt the agonizing bodily laceration, but nothing more. Yet, when by this collision forced to turn towards home, and for long months of days and weeks, Ahab and anguish lay stretched together in one hammock, rounding in mid winter that dreary, howling Patagonian Cape; then it was, that his torn body and gashed soul bled into one another; and so interfusing, made him mad. That it was only then, on the homeward voyage, after the encounter, that the final monomania seized him, seems all but certain from the fact that, at intervals during the passage, he was a raving lunatic; and, though unlimbed of a leg, yet such vital strength yet lurked in his Egyptian chest, and was moreover intensified by his delirium, that his mates were forced to lace him fast, even there, as he sailed, raving in his hammock. In a strait-jacket, he swung to the mad rockings of the gales. And, when running into more sufferable latitudes, the ship, with mild stun'sails spread, floated across the tranquil tropics, and, to all appearances, the old man's delirium seemed left behind him with the Cape Horn swells, and he came forth from his dark den into the blessed light and air; even then, when he bore that firm, collected front, however pale, and issued his calm orders once again; and his mates thanked God the direful madness was now gone; even then, Ahab, in his hidden self, raved on. Human madness is oftentimes a cunning and most feline thing. When you think it fled, it may have but become transfigured into some still subtler form. Ahab's full lunacy subsided not, but deepeningly contracted; like the unabated Hudson, when that noble Northman flows narrowly, but unfathomably through the Highland gorge. But, as in his narrow-flowing monomania, not one jot of Ahab's broad madness had been left behind; so in that broad madness, not one jot of his great natural intellect had perished. That before living agent, now became the living instrument. If such a furious trope may stand, his special lunacy stormed his general sanity, and carried it, and turned all its concentred cannon upon its own mad mark; so that far from having lost his strength, Ahab, to that one end, did now possess a thousand fold more potency than ever he had sanely brought to bear upon any one reasonable object.

This is much; yet Ahab's larger, darker, deeper part remains unhinted. But vain to popularize profundities, and all truth is profound. Winding far down from within the very heart of this spiked Hotel de Cluny[1] where we here stand—however grand and wonderful, now quit it;—and take your way, ye nobler, sadder souls, to those vast Roman halls of Thermes; where far beneath the fantastic towers of man's upper earth, his root of grandeur, his whole awful essence sits in bearded state; an antique buried beneath antiquities, and throned on torsoes! So with a broken throne, the great gods mock that captive king; so like a Caryatid, he patient sits, upholding on his frozen brow the piled entablatures of ages. Wind ye down there, ye prouder, sadder souls! question that proud, sad king! A family likeness! aye, he did beget ye, ye young exiled royalties; and from your grim sire only will the old State-secret come.

Now, in his heart, Ahab had some glimpse of this, namely: all my means are sane, my motive and my object mad. Yet without power to kill, or change, or shun the fact; he likewise knew that to mankind he did long dissemble; in some sort, did still. But that thing of his dissembling was only subject to his perceptibility, not to his will determinate. Nevertheless, so well did he succeed in that dissembling, that when with ivory leg he stepped ashore at last, no Nantucketer thought him otherwise than but naturally grieved,

1. A late medieval building in Paris (also called Palais des Thermes) beneath which were the ruins of ancient Roman baths (*thermae*).

and that to the quick, with the terrible casualty which had over-taken him.

The report of his undeniable delirium at sea was likewise popularly ascribed to a kindred cause. And so too, all the added moodiness which always afterwards, to the very day of sailing in the Pequod on the present voyage, sat brooding on his brow. Nor is it so very unlikely, that far from distrusting his fitness for another whaling voyage, on account of such dark symptoms, the calculating people of that prudent isle were inclined to harbor the conceit, that for those very reasons he was all the better qualified and set on edge, for a pursuit so full of rage and wildness as the bloody hunt of whales. Gnawed within and scorched without, with the infixed, unrelenting fangs of some incurable idea; such an one, could he be found, would seem the very man to dart his iron and lift his lance against the most appalling of all brutes. Or, if for any reason thought to be corporeally incapacitated for that, yet such an one would seem superlatively competent to cheer and howl on his underlings to the attack. But be all this as it may, certain it is, that with the mad secret of his unabated rage bolted up and keyed in him, Ahab had purposely sailed upon the present voyage with the one only and all-engrossing object of hunting the White Whale. Had any of his old acquaintances on shore but half dreamed of what was lurking in him then, how soon would their aghast and righteous souls have wrenched the ship from such a fiendish man! They were bent on profitable cruises, the profit to be counted down in dollars from the mint. He was intent on an audacious, im-mitigable, and supernatural revenge.

Here, then, was this grey-headed, ungodly old man, chasing with curses a Job's whale round the world, at the head of a crew, too, chiefly made up of mongrel renegades, and castaways, and can-nibals—morally enfeebled also, by the incompetence of mere un-aided virtue or right-mindedness in Starbuck, the invulnerable jollity of indifference and recklessness in Stubb, and the pervading mediocrity in Flask. Such a crew, so officered, seemed specially picked and packed by some infernal fatality to help him to his monomaniac revenge. How it was that they so aboundingly re-sponded to the old man's ire—by what evil magic their souls were possessed, that at times his hate seemed almost theirs; the White Whale as much their insufferable foe as his; how all this came to be—what the White Whale was to them, or how to their uncon-scious understandings, also, in some dim, unsuspected way, he might have seemed the gliding great demon of the seas of life,—all this to explain, would be to dive deeper than Ishmael can go. The subterranean miner that works in us all, how can one tell whither leads his shaft by the ever shifting, muffled sound of his pick? Who does not feel the irresistible arm drag? What skiff in tow of a seventy-four can stand still? For one, I gave myself up to the abandonment of the time and the place; but while yet all a-rush to encounter the whale, could see naught in that brute but the deadliest ill.

Chapter 42

THE WHITENESS OF THE WHALE

What the white whale was to Ahab, has been hinted; what, at times, he was to me, as yet remains unsaid.

Aside from those more obvious considerations touching Moby Dick, which could not but occasionally awaken in any man's soul some alarm, there was another thought, or rather vague, nameless horror concerning him, which at times by its intensity completely overpowered all the rest; and yet so mystical and well nigh ineffable was it, that I almost despair of putting it in a comprehensible form. It was the whiteness of the whale that above all things appalled me. But how can I hope to explain myself here; and yet, in some dim, random way, explain myself I must, else all these chapters might be naught.

Though in many natural objects, whiteness refiningly enhances beauty, as if imparting some special virtue of its own, as in marbles, japonicas, and pearls; and though various nations have in some way recognised a certain royal pre-eminence in this hue; even the barbaric, grand old kings of Pegu placing the title "Lord of the White Elephants" above all their other magniloquent ascriptions of dominion; and the modern kings of Siam unfurling the same snow-white quadruped in the royal standard; and the Hanoverian flag bearing the one figure of a snow-white charger; and the great Austrian Empire, Cæsarian heir to overlording Rome, having for the imperial color the same imperial hue; and though this pre-eminence in it applies to the human race itself, giving the white man ideal mastership over every dusky tribe; and though, besides all this, whiteness has been even made significant of gladness, for among the Romans a white stone marked a joyful day; and though in other mortal sympathies and symbolizings, this same hue is made the emblem of many touching, noble things—the innocence of brides, the benignity of age; though among the Red Men of America the giving of the white belt of wampum was the deepest pledge of honor; though in many climes, whiteness typifies the majesty of Justice in the ermine of the Judge, and contributes to the daily state of kings and queens drawn by milk-white steeds; though even in the higher mysteries of the most august religions it has been made the symbol of the divine spotlessness and power; by the Persian fire worshippers, the white forked flame being held the holiest on the altar; and in the Greek mythologies, Great Jove himself being made incarnate in a snow-white bull; and though to the noble Iroquois, the midwinter sacrifice of the sacred White Dog was by far the holiest festival of their theology, that spotless, faithful creature being held the purest envoy they could send to the Great Spirit with the annual tidings of their own fidelity; and though directly from the Latin word for white, all Christian priests derive the name of one part of their sacred vesture, the alb or tunic, worn beneath the cassock; and though among the holy pomps of the Romish faith, white is specially employed in the celebration of the Passion of our Lord; though in the Vision of St. John,[1] white robes are given to the redeemed, and the four-and-twenty elders stand clothed in white before the great white throne, and the Holy One that sitteth there white like wool; yet for all these accumulated associations, with whatever is sweet, and honorable, and sublime, there yet lurks an elusive something in the innermost idea of this hue, which strikes more of panic to the soul than that redness which affrights in blood.

This elusive quality it is, which causes the thought of whiteness, when divorced from more kindly associations, and coupled with any object terrible in itself, to heighten that terror to the furthest bounds. Witness the white bear of the poles, and the white shark of the tropics; what but their smooth, flaky whiteness makes them the transcendent horrors they are? That ghastly whiteness it is which imparts such an abhorrent mildness, even more loathsome than terrific, to the dumb gloating of their aspect. So that not the fierce-fanged tiger in his heraldic coat can so stagger courage as the white-shrouded bear or shark.*

Bethink thee of the albatross: whence come those clouds of spiritual wonderment and pale dread, in which that white phantom sails in all imaginations? Not Coleridge first threw that spell;

1. The Book of Revelation.

* With reference to the Polar bear, it may possibly be urged by him who would fain go still deeper into this matter, that it is not the whiteness, separately regarded, which heightens the intolerable hideousness of that brute; for, analysed, that heightened hideousness, it might be said, only arises from the circumstance, that the irresponsible ferociousness of the creature stands invested in the fleece of celestial innocence and love; and hence, by bringing together two such opposite emotions in our minds, the Polar bear frightens us with so unnatural a contrast. But even assuming all this to be true; yet, were it not for the whiteness, you would not have that intensified terror.

As for the white shark, the white gliding ghostliness of repose in that creature, when beheld in his ordinary moods, strangely tallies with the same quality in the Polar quadruped. This peculiarity is most vividly hit by the French in the name they bestow upon that fish. The Romish mass for the dead begins with "Requiem eternam" (eternal rest), whence *Requiem* denominating the mass itself, and any other funereal music. Now, in allusion to the white, silent stillness of death in this shark, and the mild deadliness of his habits, the French call him *Requin* [Melville's note].

but God's great, unflattering laureate, Nature.*

Most famous in our Western annals and Indian traditions is that of the White Steed of the Prairies; a magnificent milk-white charger, large-eyed, small-headed, bluff-chested, and with the dignity of a thousand monarchs in his lofty, overscorning carriage. He was the elected Xerxes of vast herds of wild horses, whose pastures in those days were only fenced by the Rocky Mountains and the Alleghanies. At their flaming head he westward trooped it like that chosen star which every evening leads on the hosts of light. The flashing cascade of his mane, the curving comet of his tail, invested him with housings more resplendent than gold and silver-beaters could have furnished him. A most imperial and archangelical apparition of that unfallen, western world, which to the eyes of the old trappers and hunters revived the glories of those primeval times when Adam walked majestic as a god, bluff-bowed and fearless as this mighty steed. Whether marching amid his aides and marshals in the van of countless cohorts that endlessly streamed it over the plains, like an Ohio; or whether with his circumambient subjects browsing all around at the horizon, the White Steed gallopingly reviewed them with warm nostrils reddening through his cool milkiness; in whatever aspect he presented himself, always to the bravest Indians he was the object of trembling reverence and awe. Nor can it be questioned from what stands on legendary record of this noble horse, that it was his

---

* I remember the first albatross I ever saw. It was during a prolonged gale, in waters hard upon the Antarctic seas. From my forenoon watch below, I ascended to the overclouded deck; and there, dashed upon the main hatches, I saw a regal, feathery thing of unspotted whiteness, and with a hooked, Roman bill sublime. At intervals, it arched forth its vast archangel wings, as if to embrace some holy ark. Wondrous flutterings and throbbings shook it. Though bodily unharmed, it uttered cries, as some king's ghost in supernatural distress. Through its inexpressible, strange eyes, methought I peeped to secrets which took hold of God. As Abraham before the angels, I bowed myself; the white thing was so white, its wings so wide, and in those for ever exiled waters, I had lost the miserable warping memories of traditions and of towns. Long I gazed at that prodigy of plumage. I cannot tell, can only hint, the things that darted through me then. But at last I awoke; and turning, asked a sailor what bird was this. A goney, he replied. Goney! I never had heard that name before; is it conceivable that this glorious thing is utterly unknown to men ashore! never! But some time after, I learned that goney was some seaman's name for albatross. So that by no possibility could Coleridge's wild Rhyme have had aught to do with those mystical impressions which were mine, when I saw that bird upon our deck. For neither had I then read the Rhyme, nor knew the bird to be an albatross. Yet, in saying this, I do but indirectly burnish a little brighter the noble merit of the poem and the poet.

I assert, then, that in the wondrous bodily whiteness of the bird chiefly lurks the secret of the spell; a truth the more evinced in this, that by a solecism of terms there are birds called grey albatrosses; and these I have frequently seen, but never with such emotions as when I beheld the Antarctic fowl.

But how had the mystic thing been caught? Whisper it not, and I will tell; with a treacherous hook and line, as the fowl floated on the sea. At last the Captain made a postman of it; tying a lettered, leathern tally round its neck, with the ship's time and place; and then letting it escape. But I doubt not, that leathern tally, meant for man, was taken off in Heaven, when the white fowl flew to join the wing-folding, the invoking, and adoring cherubim! [Melville's note] spiritual whiteness chiefly, which so clothed him with divineness; and that this divineness had that in it which, though commanding worship, at the same time enforced a certain nameless terror.

But there are other instances where this whiteness loses all that accessory and strange glory which invests it in the White Steed and Albatross.

What is it that in the Albino man so peculiarly repels and often shocks the eye, as that sometimes he is loathed by his own kith and kin! It is that whiteness which invests him, a thing expressed by the name he bears. The Albino is as well made as other men —has no substantive deformity—and yet this mere aspect of all-pervading whiteness makes him more strangely hideous than the ugliest abortion. Why should this be so?

Nor, in quite other aspects, does Nature in her least palpable but not the less malicious agencies, fail to enlist among her forces this crowning attribute of the terrible. From its snowy aspect, the gauntleted ghost of the Southern Seas has been denominated the White Squall. Nor, in some historic instances, has the art of human malice omitted so potent an auxiliary. How wildly it heightens the effect of that passage in Froissart, when, masked in the snowy symbol of their faction, the desperate White Hoods of Ghent murder their bailiff in the market-place!

Nor, in some things, does the common, hereditary experience of all mankind fail to bear witness to the supernaturalism of this hue. It cannot well be doubted, that the one visible quality in the aspect of the dead which most appals the gazer, is the marble pallor lingering there; as if indeed that pallor were as much the badge of consternation in the other world, as of mortal trepidation here. And from that pallor of the dead, we borrow the expressive hue of the shroud in which we wrap them. Nor even in our superstitions do we fail to throw the same snowy mantle round our phantoms; all ghosts rising in a milk-white fog—Yea, while these terrors seize us, let us add, that even the king of terrors, when personified by the evangelist, rides on his pallid horse.[2]

Therefore, in his other moods, symbolize whatever grand or gracious thing he will by whiteness, no man can deny that in its profoundest idealized significance it calls up a peculiar apparition to the soul.

But though without dissent this point be fixed, how is mortal man to account for it? To analyse it, would seem impossible. Can we, then, by the citation of some of those instances wherein this thing of whiteness—though for the time either wholly or in great part stripped of all direct associations calculated to impart

2. "And I looked, and behold a pale horse: and his name that sat upon him was Death. . . ." Revelation 6:8.

to it aught fearful, but, nevertheless, is found to exert over us the same sorcery, however modified;—can we thus hope to light upon some chance clue to conduct us to the hidden cause we seek?

Let us try. But in a matter like this, subtlety appeals to subtlety, and without imagination no man can follow another into these halls. And though, doubtless, some at least of the imaginative impressions about to be presented may have been shared by most men, yet few perhaps were entirely conscious of them at the time, and therefore may not be able to recall them now.

Why to the man of untutored ideality, who happens to be but loosely acquainted with the peculiar character of the day, does the bare mention of Whitsuntide marshal in the fancy such long, dreary, speechless processions of slow-pacing pilgrims, down-cast and hooded with new-fallen snow? Or, to the unread, unsophisticated Protestant of the Middle American States,[3] why does the passing mention of a White Friar or a White Nun, evoke such an eyeless statue in the soul?

Or what is there apart from the traditions of dungeoned warriors and kings (which will not wholly account for it) that makes the White Tower of London tell so much more strongly on the imagination of an untravelled American, than those other storied structures, its neighbors—the Byward Tower, or even the Bloody? And those sublimer towers, the White Mountains of New Hampshire, whence, in peculiar moods, comes that gigantic ghostliness over the soul at the bare mention of that name, while the thought of Virginia's Blue Ridge is full of a soft, dewy, distant dreaminess? Or why, irrespective of all latitudes and longitudes, does the name of the White Sea exert such a spectralness over the fancy, while that of the Yellow Sea lulls us with mortal thoughts of long lacquered mild afternoons on the waves, followed by the gaudiest and yet sleepiest of sunsets? Or, to choose a wholly unsubstantial instance, purely addressed to the fancy, why, in reading the old fairy tales of Central Europe, does "the tall pale man" of the Hartz forests, whose changeless pallor unrustlingly glides through the green of the groves—why is this phantom more terrible than all the whooping imps of the Blocksburg?

Nor is it, altogether, the remembrance of her cathedral-toppling earthquakes; nor the stampedoes of her frantic seas; nor the tearlessness of arid skies that never rain; nor the sight of her wide field of leaning spires, wrenched cope-stones, and crosses all adroop (like canted yards of anchored fleets); and her suburban avenues of house-walls lying over upon each other, as a tossed pack of cards; —it is not these things alone which make tearless Lima, the

3. The Middle Atlantic States.

strangest, saddest city thou can'st see. For Lima has taken the white veil; and there is a higher horror in this whiteness of her woe. Old as Pizarro, this whiteness keeps her ruins for ever new; admits not the cheerful greenness of complete decay; spreads over her broken ramparts the rigid pallor of an apoplexy that fixes its own distortions.

I know that, to the common apprehension, this phenomenon of whiteness is not confessed to be the prime agent in exaggerating the terror of objects otherwise terrible; nor to the unimaginative mind is there aught of terror in those appearances whose awfulness to another mind almost solely consists in this one phenomenon, especially when exhibited under any form at all approaching to muteness or universality. What I mean by these two statements may perhaps be respectively elucidated by the following examples.

First: The mariner, when drawing nigh the coasts of foreign lands, if by night he hear the roar of breakers, starts to vigilance, and feels just enough of trepidation to sharpen all his faculties; but under precisely similar circumstances, let him be called from his hammock to view his ship sailing through a midnight sea of milky whiteness—as if from encircling headlands shoals of combed white bears were swimming round him, then he feels a silent, superstitious dread; the shrouded phantom of the whitened waters is horrible to him as a real ghost; in vain the lead assures him he is still off soundings; heart and helm they both go down; he never rests till blue water is under him again. Yet where is the mariner who will tell thee, "Sir, it was not so much the fear of striking hidden rocks, as the fear of that hideous whiteness that so stirred me"?

Second: To the native Indian of Peru, the continual sight of the snow-howdahed Andes conveys naught of dread, except, perhaps, in the mere fancying of the eternal frosted desolateness reigning at such vast altitudes, and the natural conceit of what a fearfulness it would be to lose oneself in such inhuman solitudes. Much the same is it with the backwoodsman of the West, who with comparative indifference views an unbounded prairie sheeted with driven snow, no shadow of tree or twig to break the fixed trance of whiteness. Not so the sailor, beholding the scenery of the Antarctic seas; where at times, by some infernal trick of legerdemain in the powers of frost and air, he, shivering and half shipwrecked, instead of rainbows speaking hope and solace to his misery, views what seems a boundless church-yard grinning upon him with its lean ice monuments and splintered crosses.

But thou sayest, methinks this white-lead[4] chapter about whiteness is but a white flag hung out from a craven soul; thou

4. White powder used in making paint.

surrenderest to a hypo, Ishmael.

Tell me, why this strong young colt, foaled in some peaceful valley of Vermont, far removed from all beasts of prey—why is it that upon the sunniest day, if you but shake a fresh buffalo robe behind him, so that he cannot even see it, but only smells its wild animal muskiness—why will he start, snort, and with bursting eyes paw the ground in phrensies of affright? There is no remembrance in him of any gorings of wild creatures in his green northern home, so that the strange muskiness he smells cannot recall to him anything associated with the experience of former perils; for what knows he, this New England colt, of the black bisons of distant Oregon?

No: but here thou beholdest even in a dumb brute, the instinct of the knowledge of the demonism in the world. Though thousands of miles from Oregon, still when he smells that savage musk, the rending, goring bison herds are as present as to the deserted wild foal of the prairies, which this instant they may be trampling into dust.

Thus, then, the muffled rollings of a milky sea; the bleak rustlings of the festooned frosts of mountains; the desolate shiftings of the windrowed snows of prairies; all these, to Ishmael, are as the shaking of that buffalo robe to the frightened colt!

Though neither knows where lie the nameless things of which the mystic sign gives forth such hints; yet with me, as with the colt, somewhere those things must exist. Though in many of its aspects this visible world seems formed in love, the invisible spheres were formed in fright.

But not yet have we solved the incantation of this whiteness, and learned why it appeals with such power to the soul; and more strange and far more portentous—why, as we have seen, it is at once the most meaning symbol of spiritual things, nay, the very veil of the Christian's Deity; and yet should be as it is, the intensifying agent in things the most appalling to mankind.

Is it that by its indefiniteness it shadows forth the heartless voids and immensities of the universe, and thus stabs us from behind with the thought of annihilation, when beholding the white depths of the milky way? Or is it, that as in essence whiteness is not so much a color as the visible absence of color, and at the same time the concrete of all colors; is it for these reasons that there is such a dumb blankness, full of meaning, in a wide landscape of snows—a colorless, all-color of atheism from which we shrink? And when we consider that other theory of the natural philosophers, that all other earthly hues—every stately or lovely emblazoning—the sweet tinges of sunset skies and woods; yea, and the gilded velvets of butterflies, and the butterfly cheeks of young girls; all these are but subtile deceits, not actually inherent in substances, but only laid on from without; so that all deified Nature absolutely paints like the harlot, whose allurements cover nothing but the charnel-house within; and when we proceed further, and consider that the mystical cosmetic which produces every one of her hues, the great principle of light, for ever remains white or colorless in itself, and if operating without medium upon matter, would touch all objects, even tulips and roses, with its own blank tinge—pondering all this, the palsied universe lies before us a leper; and like wilful travellers in Lapland, who refuse to wear colored and coloring glasses upon their eyes, so the wretched infidel[5] gazes himself blind at the monumental white shroud that wraps all the prospect around him. And of all these things the Albino whale was the symbol. Wonder ye then at the fiery hunt?

Chapter 43

HARK!

"Hist! Did you hear that noise, Cabaco?"

It was the middle-watch: a fair moonlight; the seamen were standing in a cordon, extending from one of the fresh-water butts in the waist, to the scuttle-butt near the taffrail. In this manner, they passed the buckets to fill the scuttle-butt. Standing, for the most part, on the hallowed precincts of the quarter-deck, they were careful not to speak or rustle their feet. From hand to hand, the buckets went in the deepest silence, only broken by the occasional flap of a sail, and the steady hum of the unceasingly advancing keel.

It was in the midst of this repose, that Archy, one of the cordon, whose post was near the after-hatches, whispered to his neighbor, a Cholo, the words above.

"Hist! did you hear that noise, Cabaco?"

"Take the bucket, will ye, Archy? what noise d'ye mean?"

"There it is again—under the hatches—don't you hear it—a cough—it sounded like a cough."

"Cough be damned! Pass along that return bucket."

"There again—there it is!—it sounds like two or three sleepers turning over, now!"

"Caramba! have done, shipmate, will ye? It's the three soaked biscuits ye eat for supper turning over inside of ye—nothing else. Look to the bucket!"

"Say what ye will, shipmate; I've sharp ears."

"Aye, you are the chap, ain't ye, that heard the hum of the

5. Unbeliever, atheist.

old Quakeress's knitting-needles fifty miles at sea from Nantucket; you're the chap."

"Grin away; we'll see what turns up. Hark ye, Cabaco, there is somebody down in the after-hold that has not yet been seen on deck; and I suspect our old Mogul knows something of it too. I heard Stubb tell Flask, one morning watch, that there was something of that sort in the wind."

"Tish! the bucket!"

Chapter 44

THE CHART [1]

Had you followed Captain Ahab down into his cabin after the squall that took place on the night succeeding that wild ratification of his purpose with his crew, you would have seen him go to a locker in the transom, and bringing out a large wrinkled roll of yellowish sea charts, spread them before him on his screwed-down table. Then seating himself before it, you would have seen him intently study the various lines and shadings which there met his eye; and with slow but steady pencil trace additional courses over spaces that before were blank. At intervals, he would refer to piles of old log-books beside him, wherein were set down the seasons and places in which, on various former voyages of various ships, sperm whales had been captured or seen.

While thus employed, the heavy pewter lamp suspended in chains over his head, continually rocked with the motion of the ship, and for ever threw shifting gleams and shadows of lines upon his wrinkled brow, till it almost seemed that while he himself was marking out lines and courses on the wrinkled charts, some invisible pencil was also tracing lines and courses upon the deeply marked chart of his forehead.

But it was not this night in particular that, in the solitude of his cabin, Ahab thus pondered over his charts. Almost every night they were brought out; almost every night some pencil marks were effaced, and others were substituted. For with the charts of all four oceans before him, Ahab was threading a maze of currents and eddies, with a view to the more certain accomplishment of that monomaniac thought of his soul.

Now, to any one not fully acquainted with the ways of the leviathans, it might seem an absurdly hopeless task thus to seek out one solitary creature in the unhooped oceans of this planet. But not so did it seem to Ahab, who knew the sets of all tides and currents; and thereby calculating the driftings of the sperm

---

1. Mansfield and Vincent point out that most of this chapter "had its inception in Commodore Charles Wilkes' *Narrative of the United States Exploring Expedition . . . . 1838–1842* (Philadelphia, 1845)."

whale's food; and, also, calling to mind the regular, ascertained seasons for hunting him in particular latitudes; could arrive at reasonable surmises, almost approaching to certainties, concerning the timeliest day to be upon this or that ground in search of his prey.

So assured, indeed, is the fact concerning the periodicalness of the sperm whale's resorting to given waters, that many hunters believe that, could he be closely observed and studied throughout the world; were the logs for one voyage of the entire whale fleet carefully collated, then the migrations of the sperm whale would be found to correspond in invariability to those of the herring-shoals or the flights of swallows. On this hint, attempts have been made to construct elaborate migratory charts of the sperm whale.*

Besides, when making a passage from one feeding-ground to another, the sperm whales, guided by some infallible instinct—say, rather, secret intelligence from the Deity—mostly swim in *veins*, as they are called; continuing their way along a given ocean-line with such undeviating exactitude, that no ship ever sailed her course, by any chart, with one tithe of such marvellous precision. Though, in these cases, the direction taken by any one whale be straight as a surveyor's parallel, and though the line of advance be strictly confined to its own unavoidable, straight wake, yet the arbitrary *vein* in which at these times he is said to swim, generally embraces some few miles in width (more or less, as the vein is presumed to expand or contract); but never exceeds the visual sweep from the whale-ship's mast-heads, when circumspectly gliding along this magic zone. The sum is, that at particular seasons within that breadth and along that path, migrating whales may with great confidence be looked for.

And hence not only at substantiated times, upon well known separate feeding-grounds, could Ahab hope to encounter his prey; but in crossing the widest expanses of water between those grounds he could, by his art, so place and time himself on his way, as even then not to be wholly without prospect of a meeting.

There was a circumstance which at first sight seemed to entangle his delirious but still methodical scheme. But not so in the reality, perhaps. Though the gregarious sperm whales have

* Since the above was written, the statement is happily borne out by an official circular, issued by Lieutenant Maury, of the National Observatory, Washington, April 16th, 1851. By that circular, it appears that precisely such a chart is in course of completion; and portions of it are presented in the circular. "This chart divides the ocean into districts of five degrees of latitude by five degrees of longitude; perpendicularly through each of which' districts are twelve columns for the twelve months; and horizontally through each of which districts are three lines; one to show the number of days that have been spent in each month in every district, and the two others to show the number of days in which whales, sperm or right, have been seen" [Melville's note].

their regular seasons for particular grounds, yet in general you cannot conclude that the herds which haunted such and such a latitude or longitude this year, say, will turn out to be identically the same with those that were found there the preceding season; though there are peculiar and unquestionable instances where the contrary of this has proved true. In general, the same remark, only within a less wide limit, applies to the solitaries and hermits among the matured, aged sperm whales. So that though Moby Dick had in a former year been seen, for example, on what is called the Seychelle ground in the Indian ocean, or Volcano Bay on the Japanese Coast; yet it did not follow, that were the Pequod to visit either of those spots at any subsequent corresponding season, she would infallibly encounter him there. So, too, with some other feeding grounds, where he had at times revealed himself. But all these seemed only his casual stopping-places and ocean-inns, so to speak, not his places of prolonged abode. And where Ahab's chances of accomplishing his object have hitherto been spoken of, allusion has only been made to whatever way-side, antecedent, extra prospects were his, ere a particular set time and place were attained, when all possibilities would become probabilities, and, as Ahab fondly thought, every possibility the next thing to a certainty. That particular set time and place were conjoined in the one technical phrase—the Season-on-the-Line. For there and then, for several consecutive years, Moby Dick had been periodically descried, lingering in those waters for awhile, as the sun, in its annual round, loiters for a predicted interval in any one sign of the Zodiac. There it was, too, that most of the deadly encounters with the white whale had taken place; there the waves were storied with his deeds; there also was that tragic spot where the monomaniac old man had found the awful motive to his vengeance. But in the cautious comprehensiveness and unloitering vigilance with which Ahab threw his brooding soul into this unfaltering hunt, he would not permit himself to rest all his hopes upon the one crowning fact above mentioned, however flattering it might be to those hopes; nor in the sleeplessness of his vow could he so tranquillize his unquiet heart as to postpone all intervening quest.

Now, the Pequod had sailed from Nantucket at the very beginning of the Season-on-the-Line. No possible endeavor then could enable her commander to make the great passage southwards, double Cape Horn, and then running down sixty degrees of latitude arrive in the equatorial Pacific in time to cruise there. Therefore, he must wait for the next ensuing season. Yet the premature hour of the Pequod's sailing had, perhaps, been covertly selected by Ahab, with a view to this very complexion of things. Because, an interval of three hundred and sixty-five days and nights was before him; an interval which, instead of impatiently enduring ashore, he would spend in a miscellaneous hunt; if by chance the White Whale, spending his vacation in seas far remote from his periodical feeding-grounds, should turn up his wrinkled brow off the Persian Gulf, or in the Bengal Bay, or China Seas, or in any other waters haunted by his race. So that Monsoons, Pampas, Nor-Westers, Harmattans, Trades; any wind but the Levanter and Simoom, might blow Moby Dick into the devious zig-zag world-circle of the Pequod's circumnavigating wake.

But granting all this; yet, regarded discreetly and coolly, seems it not but a mad idea, this; that in the broad boundless ocean, one solitary whale, even if encountered, should be thought capable of individual recognition from his hunter, even as a white-bearded Mufti in the thronged thoroughfares of Constantinople? No. For the peculiar snow-white brow of Moby Dick, and his snow-white hump, could not but be unmistakable. And have I not tallied the whale, Ahab would mutter to himself, as after poring over his charts till long after midnight he would throw himself back in reveries—tallied him, and shall he escape? His broad fins are bored, and scalloped out like a lost sheep's ear! And here, his mad mind would run on in a breathless race; till a weariness and faintness of pondering came over him; and in the open air of the deck he would seek to recover his strength. Ah, God! what trances of torments does that man endure who is consumed with one unachieved revengeful desire. He sleeps with clenched hands; and wakes with his own bloody nails in his palms.

Often, when forced from his hammock by exhausting and intolerably vivid dreams of the night, which, resuming his own intense thoughts through the day, carried them on amid a clashing of phrensies, and whirled them round and round in his blazing brain, till the very throbbing of his life-spot became insufferable anguish; and when, as was sometimes the case, these spiritual throes in him heaved his being up from its base, and a chasm seemed opening in him, from which forked flames and lightnings shot up, and accursed fiends beckoned him to leap down among them; when this hell in himself yawned beneath him, a wild cry would be heard through the ship; and with glaring eyes Ahab would burst from his state room, as though escaping from a bed that was on fire. Yet these, perhaps, instead of being the unsuppressable symptoms of some latent weakness, or fright at his own resolve, were but the plainest tokens of its intensity. For, at such times, crazy Ahab, the scheming, unappeasedly steadfast hunter of the white whale; this Ahab that had gone to his hammock, was not the agent that so caused him to burst from it in horror again. The latter was the eternal, living principle or soul in him; and in sleep, being for the time dissociated from the characterizing mind, which at other times employed it for its outer vehicle or agent, it spontaneously sought escape from the scorching contiguity of the frantic thing, of which, for the time, it was no longer an integral. But as the mind does not exist unless leagued with the soul, therefore it must have been that, in Ahab's case, yielding up all his thoughts and fancies to his one supreme purpose; that purpose, by its own sheer inveteracy of will, forced itself against gods and devils into a kind of self-assumed, independent being of its own. Nay, could grimly live and burn, while the common vitality to which it was conjoined, fled horror-stricken from the unbidden and unfathered birth. Therefore, the tormented spirit that glared out of bodily eyes, when what seemed Ahab rushed from his room, was for the time but a vacated thing, a formless somnambulistic being, a ray of living light, to be sure, but without an object to color, and therefore a blankness in itself. God help thee, old man, thy thoughts have created a creature in thee; and he whose intense thinking thus makes him a Prometheus; [2] a vulture feeds upon that heart for ever; that vulture the very creature he creates.

Chapter 45

THE AFFIDAVIT

So far as what there may be of a narrative in this book; and, indeed, as indirectly touching one or two very interesting and curious particulars in the habits of sperm whales, the foregoing chapter, in its earlier part, is as important a one as will be found in this volume; but the leading matter of it requires to be still further and more familiarly enlarged upon, in order to be adequately understood, and moreover to take away any incredulity which a profound ignorance of the entire subject may induce in some minds, as to the natural verity of the main points of this affair.

I care not to perform this part of my task methodically; but shall be content to produce the desired impression by separate citations of items, practically or reliably known to me as a whaleman; and from these citations, I take it—the conclusion aimed at will naturally follow of itself.

First: I have personally known three instances where a whale,

2. One of the Titans, who stole fire from heaven and gave it to mankind; Zeus punished him for this theft by chaining him to a rock where daily a vulture devoured his liver, which each night was made whole again.

after receiving a harpoon, has effected a complete escape; and, after an interval (in one instance of three years), has been again struck by the same hand, and slain; when the two irons, both marked by the same private cypher, have been taken from the body. In the instance where three years intervened between the flinging of the two harpoons; and I think it may have been something more than that; the man who darted them happening, in the interval, to go in a trading ship on a voyage to Africa, went ashore there, joined a discovery party, and penetrated far into the interior, where he travelled for a period of nearly two years, often endangered by serpents, savages, tigers, poisonous miasmas, with all the other common perils incident to wandering in the heart of unknown regions. Meanwhile, the whale he had struck must also have been on its travels; no doubt it had thrice circumnavigated the globe, brushing with its flanks all the coasts of Africa; but to no purpose. This man and this whale again came together, and the one vanquished the other. I say I, myself, have known three instances similar to this; that is in two of them I saw the whales struck; and, upon the second attack, saw the two irons with the respective marks cut in them, afterwards taken from the dead fish. In the three-year instance, it so fell out that I was in the boat both times, first and last, and the last time distinctly recognized a peculiar sort of huge mole under the whale's eye, which I had observed there three years previous. I say three years, but I am pretty sure it was more than that. Here are three instances, then, which I personally know the truth of; but I have heard of many other instances from persons whose veracity in the matter there is no good ground to impeach.

Secondly: It is well known in the Sperm Whale Fishery, however ignorant the world ashore may be of it, that there have been several memorable historical instances where a particular whale in the ocean has been at distant times and places popularly cognisable. Why such a whale became thus marked was not altogether and originally owing to his bodily peculiarities as distinguished from other whales; for however peculiar in that respect any chance whale may be, they soon put an end to his peculiarities by killing him, and boiling him down into a peculiarly valuable oil. No: the reason was this: that from the fatal experiences of the fishery there hung a terrible prestige of perilousness about such a whale as there did about Rinaldo Rinaldini, insomuch that most fishermen were content to recognise him by merely touching their tarpaulins when he would be discovered lounging by them on the sea, without seeking to cultivate a more intimate acquaintance. Like some poor devils ashore that happen to know an irascible great man, they make distant unobtrusive salutations to him in the street, lest if they pursued the acquaintance further, they might receive a summary thump for their presumption.

But not only did each of these famous whales enjoy great individual celebrity—nay, you may call it an ocean-wide renown; not only was he famous in life and now is immortal in forecastle stories after death, but he was admitted into all the rights, privileges, and distinctions of a name; had as much a name indeed as Cambyses or Cæsar. Was it not so, O Timor Tom! thou famed leviathan, scarred like an iceberg, who so long did'st lurk in the Oriental straits of that name, whose spout was oft seen from the palmy beach of Ombay? Was it not so, O New Zealand Jack! thou terror of all cruisers that crossed their wakes in the vicinity of the Tattoo Land? Was it not so, O Morquan! King of Japan, whose lofty jet they say at times assumed the semblance of a snow-white cross against the sky? Was it not so, O Don Miguel! thou Chilean whale, marked like an old tortoise with mystic hieroglyphics upon the back! In plain prose, here are four whales as well known to the students of Cetacean History as Marius or Sylla to the classic scholar.

But this is not all. New Zealand Jack and Don Miguel, after at various times creating great havoc among the boats of different vessels, were finally gone in quest of, systematically hunted out, chased and killed by valiant whaling captains, who heaved up their anchors with that express object as much in view, as in setting out through the Narragansett Woods, Captain Butler of old had it in his mind to capture that notorious murderous savage Annawon,[1] the headmost warrior of the Indian King Philip.

I do not know where I can find a better place than just here, to make mention of one or two other things, which to me seem important, as in printed form establishing in all respects the reasonableness of the whole story of the White Whale, more especially the catastrophe. For this is one of those disheartening instances where truth requires full as much bolstering as error. So ignorant are most landsmen of some of the plainest and most palpable wonders of the world, that without some hints touching the plain facts, historical and otherwise, of the fishery, they might scout at Moby Dick as a monstrous fable, or still worse and more detestable, a hideous and intolerable allegory.

First: Though most men have some vague flitting ideas of the general perils of the grand fishery, yet they have nothing like a fixed, vivid conception of those perils, and the frequency with which they recur. One reason perhaps is, that not one in fifty of the actual disasters and deaths by casualties in the fishery, ever

1. Annawon was captured in 1676 by Captain Benjamin Church. Lieutenant Colonel William Butler pursued another Indian leader in 1778.

finds a public record at home, however transient and immediately forgotten that record. Do you suppose that that poor fellow there, who this moment perhaps caught by the whale-line off the coast of New Guinea, is being carried down to the bottom of the sea by the sounding leviathan—do you suppose that that poor fellow's name will appear in the newspaper obituary you will read to-morrow at your breakfast? No: because the mails are very irregular between here and New Guinea. In fact, did you ever hear what might be called regular news direct or indirect from New Guinea? Yet I tell you that upon one particular voyage which I made to the Pacific, among many others, we spoke thirty different ships, every one of which had had a death by a whale, some of them more than one, and three that had each lost a boat's crew. For God's sake, be economical with your lamps and candles! not a gallon you burn, but at least one drop of man's blood was spilled for it.

Secondly: People ashore have indeed some indefinite idea that a whale is an enormous creature of enormous power; but I have ever found that when narrating to them some specific example of this two-fold enormousness, they have significantly complimented me upon my facetiousness; when, I declare upon my soul, I had no more idea of being facetious than Moses, when he wrote the history of the plagues of Egypt.

But fortunately the special point I here seek can be established upon testimony entirely independent of my own. That point is this: The Sperm Whale is in some cases sufficiently powerful, knowing, and judiciously malicious, as with direct aforethought to stave in, utterly destroy, and sink a large ship; and what is more, the Sperm Whale *has* done it.

First: In the year 1820 the ship Essex, Captain Pollard, of Nantucket, was cruising in the Pacific Ocean. One day she saw spouts, lowered her boats, and gave chase to a shoal of sperm whales. Ere long, several of the whales were wounded; when, suddenly, a very large whale escaping from the boats, issued from the shoal, and bore directly down upon the ship. Dashing his forehead against her hull, he so stove her in, that in less than "ten minutes" she settled down and fell over. Not a surviving plank of her has been seen since. After the severest exposure, part of the crew reached the land in their boats. Being returned home at last, Captain Pollard once more sailed for the Pacific in command of another ship, but the gods shipwrecked him again upon unknown rocks and breakers; for the second time his ship was utterly lost, and forthwith forswearing the sea, he has never tempted it since. At this day Captain Pollard is a resident of Nantucket. I have seen Owen Chase, who was chief mate of the Essex at the time of the tragedy; I have read his plain and faithful narrative; I have conversed with his son; and all this within a few miles of the scene of the catastrophe.*

Secondly: The ship Union, also of Nantucket, was in the year 1807 totally lost off the Azores by a similar onset, but the authentic particulars of this catastrophe I have never chanced to encounter, though from the whale hunters I have now and then heard casual allusions to it.

Thirdly: Some eighteen or twenty years ago Commodore J—— then commanding an American sloop-of-war of the first class, happened to be dining with a party of whaling captains, on board a Nantucket ship in the harbor of Oahu, Sandwich Islands. Conversation turning upon whales, the Commodore was pleased to be sceptical touching the amazing strength ascribed to them by the professional gentlemen present. He peremptorily denied for example, that any whale could so smite his stout sloop-of-war as to cause her to leak so much as a thimbleful. Very good; but there is more coming. Some weeks after, the Commodore set sail in this impregnable craft for Valparaiso. But he was stopped on the way by a portly sperm whale, that begged a few moments' confidential business with him. That business consisted in fetching the Commodore's craft such a thwack, that with all his pumps going he made straight for the nearest port to heave down and repair. I am not superstitious, but I consider the Commodore's interview with that whale as providential. Was not Saul of Tarsus converted from unbelief by a similar fright? I tell you, the sperm whale will stand no nonsense.

I will now refer you to Langsdorff's Voyages for a little circumstance in point, peculiarly interesting to the writer hereof. Langsdorff, you must know by the way, was attached to the Rus-

---

* The following are extracts from Chase's narrative: "Every fact seemed to warrant me in concluding that it was anything but chance which directed his operations; he made two several attacks upon the ship, at a short interval between them, both of which, according to their direction, were calculated to do us the most injury, by being made ahead, and thereby combining the speed of the two objects for the shock; to effect which, the exact manœuvres which he made were necessary. His aspect was most horrible, and such as indicated resentment and fury. He came directly from the shoal which we had just before entered, and in which we had struck three of his companions, as if fired with revenge for their sufferings." Again: "At all events, the whole circumstances taken together, all happening before my own eyes, and producing, at the time, impressions in my mind of decided, calculating mischief, on the part of the whale (many of which impressions I cannot now recall), induce me to be satisfied that I am correct in my opinion."

Here are his reflections some time after quitting the ship, during a black night in an open boat, when almost despairing of reaching any hospitable shore. "The dark ocean and swelling waters were nothing; the fears of being swallowed up by some dreadful tempest, or dashed upon hidden rocks, with all the other ordinary subjects of fearful contemplation, seemed scarcely entitled to a moment's thought; the dismal looking wreck, and *the horrid aspect and revenge of the whale,* wholly engrossed my reflections, until day again made its appearance."

In another place—p. 45,—he speaks of "*the mysterious and mortal attack of the animal.*" * * * * * * * * * * * * * * * [Melville's note.]

sian Admiral Krusenstern's famous Discovery Expedition in the beginning of the present century. Captain Langsdorff thus begins his seventeenth chapter.

"By the thirteenth of May our ship was ready to sail, and the next day we were out in the open sea, on our way to Ochotsh. The weather was very clear and fine, but so intolerably cold that we were obliged to keep on our fur clothing. For some days we had very little wind; it was not till the nineteenth that a brisk gale from the northwest sprang up. An uncommon large whale, the body of which was larger than the ship itself, lay almost at the surface of the water, but was not perceived by any one on board till the moment when the ship, which was in full sail, was almost upon him, so that it was impossible to prevent its striking against him. We were thus placed in the most imminent danger, as this gigantic creature, setting up its back, raised the ship three feet at least out of the water. The masts reeled, and the sails fell altogether, while we who were below all sprang instantly upon the deck, concluding that we had struck upon some rock; instead of this we saw the monster sailing off with the utmost gravity and solemnity. Captain D'Wolf applied immediately to the pumps to examine whether or not the vessel had received any damage from the shock, but we found that very happily it had escaped entirely uninjured."

Now, the Captain D'Wolf here alluded to as commanding the ship in question, is a New Englander, who, after a long life of unusual adventures as a sea-captain, this day resides in the village of Dorchester near Boston. I have the honor of being a nephew of his. I have particularly questioned him concerning this passage in Langsdorff. He substantiates every word. The ship, however, was by no means a large one: a Russian craft built on the Siberian coast, and purchased by my uncle after bartering away the vessel in which he sailed from home.

In that up and down manly book of old-fashioned adventure, so full, too, of honest wonders—the voyage of Lionel Wafer, one of ancient Dampier's old chums—I found a little matter set down so like that just quoted from Langsdorff, that I cannot forbear inserting it here for a corroborative example, if such be needed.

Lionel, it seems, was on his way to "John Ferdinando," as he calls the modern Juan Fernandez. "In our way thither," he says, "about four o'clock in the morning, when we were about one hundred and fifty leagues from the Main of America, our ship felt a terrible shock, which put our men in such consternation that they could hardly tell where they were or what to think; but every one began to prepare for death. And, indeed, the shock was so sudden

and violent, that we took it for granted the ship had struck against a rock; but when the amazement was a little over, we cast the lead, and sounded, but found no ground.   *   *   *   *
The suddenness of the shock made the guns leap in their carriages, and several of the men were shaken out of their hammocks. Captain Davis, who lay with his head on a gun, was thrown out of his cabin!" Lionel then goes on to impute the shock to an earthquake, and seems to substantiate the imputation by stating that a great earthquake, somewhere about that time, did actually do great mischief along the Spanish land. But I should not much wonder if, in the darkness of that early hour of the morning, the shock was after all caused by an unseen whale vertically bumping the hull from beneath.

I might proceed with several more examples, one way or another known to me, of the great power and malice at times of the sperm whale. In more than one instance, he has been known, not only to chase the assailing boats back to their ships, but to pursue the ship itself, and long withstand all the lances hurled at him from its decks. The English ship Pusie Hall can tell a story on that head; and, as for his strength, let me say, that there have been examples where the lines attached to a running sperm whale have, in a calm, been transferred to the ship, and secured there; the whale towing her great hull through the water, as a horse walks off with a cart. Again, it is very often observed that, if the sperm whale, once struck, is allowed time to rally, he then acts, not so often with blind rage, as with wilful, deliberate designs of destruction to his pursuers; nor is it without conveying some eloquent indication of his character, that upon being attacked he will frequently open his mouth, and retain it in that dread expansion for several consecutive minutes. But I must be content with only one more and a concluding illustration; a remarkable and most significant one, by which you will not fail to see, that not only is the most marvellous event in this book corroborated by plain facts of the present day, but that these marvels (like all marvels) are mere repetitions of the ages; so that for the millionth time we say amen with Solomon—Verily there is nothing new under the sun.

In the sixth Christian century lived Procopius, a Christian magistrate of Constantinople, in the days when Justinian was Emperor and Belisarius general. As many know, he wrote the history of his own times, a work every way of uncommon value. By the best authorities, he has always been considered a most trustworthy and unexaggerating historian, except in some one or two particulars, not at all affecting the matter presently to be mentioned.

Now, in this history of his, Procopius mentions that, during the term of his prefecture at Constantinople, a great sea-monster was captured in the neighboring Propontis, or Sea of Marmora, after having destroyed vessels at intervals in those waters for a period of more than fifty years. A fact thus set down in substantial history cannot easily be gainsaid. Nor is there any reason it should be. Of what precise species this sea-monster was, is not mentioned. But as he destroyed ships, as well as for other reasons, he must have been a whale; and I am strongly inclined to think a sperm whale. And I will tell you why. For a long time I fancied that the sperm whale had been always unknown in the Mediterranean and the deep waters connecting with it. Even now I am certain that those seas are not, and perhaps never can be, in the present constitution of things, a place for his habitual gregarious resort. But further investigations have recently proved to me, that in modern times there have been isolated instances of the presence of the sperm whale in the Mediterranean. I am told, on good authority, that on the Barbary coast, a Commodore Davis of the British navy found the skeleton of a sperm whale. Now, as a vessel of war readily passes through the Dardanelles, hence a sperm whale could, by the same route, pass out of the Mediterranean into the Propontis.

In the Propontis, as far as I can learn, none of that peculiar substance called *brit* is to be found, the aliment of the right whale. But I have every reason to believe that the food of the sperm whale—squid or cuttle-fish—lurks at the bottom of that sea, because large creatures, but by no means the largest of that sort, have been found at its surface. If, then, you properly put these statements together, and reason upon them a bit, you will clearly perceive that, according to all human reasoning, Procopius's sea-monster, that for half a century stove the ships of a Roman Emperor, must in all probability have been a sperm whale.

Chapter 46

SURMISES

Though, consumed with the hot fire of his purpose, Ahab in all his thoughts and actions ever had in view the ultimate capture of Moby Dick; though he seemed ready to sacrifice all mortal interests to that one passion; nevertheless it may have been that he was by nature and long habituation far too wedded to a fiery whaleman's ways, altogether to abandon the collateral prosecution of the voyage. Or at least if this were otherwise, there were not wanting other motives much more influential with him. It would be refining too much, perhaps, even considering his monomania, to hint that his vindictiveness towards the White Whale might have possibly extended itself in some degree to all sperm whales, and that the more monsters he slew by so much the more he multiplied the chances that each subsequently encountered whale would prove to be the hated one he hunted. But if such an hypothesis be indeed exceptionable, there were still additional considerations which, though not so strictly according with the wildness of his ruling passion, yet were by no means incapable of swaying him.

To accomplish his object Ahab must use tools; and of all tools used in the shadow of the moon, men are most apt to get out of order. He knew, for example, that however magnetic his ascendency in some respects was over Starbuck, yet that ascendency did not cover the complete spiritual man any more than mere corporeal superiority involves intellectual mastership; for to the purely spiritual, the intellectual but stands in a sort of corporeal relation. Starbuck's body and Starbuck's coerced will were Ahab's, so long as Ahab kept his magnet at Starbuck's brain; still he knew that for all this the chief mate, in his soul, abhorred his captain's quest, and could he, would joyfully disintegrate himself from it, or even frustrate it. It might be that a long interval would elapse ere the White Whale was seen. During that long interval Starbuck would ever be apt to fall into open relapses of rebellion against his captain's leadership, unless some ordinary, prudential, circumstantial influences were brought to bear upon him. Not only that, but the subtle insanity of Ahab respecting Moby Dick was noways more significantly manifested than in his superlative sense and shrewdness in foreseeing that, for the present, the hunt should in some way be stripped of that strange imaginative impiousness which naturally invested it; that the full terror of the voyage must be kept withdrawn into the obscure background (for few men's courage is proof against protracted meditation unrelieved by action); that when they stood their long night watches, his officers and men must have some nearer things to think of than Moby Dick. For however eagerly and impetuously the savage crew had hailed the announcement of his quest; yet all sailors of all sorts are more or less capricious and unreliable—they live in the varying outer weather, and they inhale its fickleness—and when retained for any object remote and blank in the pursuit, however promissory of life and passion in the end, it is above all things requisite that temporary interests and employments should intervene and hold them healthily suspended for the final dash.

Nor was Ahab unmindful of another thing. In times of strong emotion mankind disdain all base considerations; but such times are evanescent. The permanent constitutional condition of the manufactured man, thought Ahab, is sordidness. Granting that the White Whale fully incites the hearts of this my savage crew, and playing round their savageness even breeds a certain generous knight-errantism in them, still, while for the love of it they give chase to Moby Dick, they must also have food for their more common, daily appetites. For even the high lifted and chivalric Crusaders of old times were not content to traverse two thousand miles of land to fight for their holy sepulchre, without committing burglaries, picking pockets, and gaining other pious perquisites by the way. Had they been strictly held to their one final and romantic object—that final and romantic object, too many would have turned from in disgust. I will not strip these men, thought Ahab, of all hopes of cash—aye, cash. They may scorn cash now; but let some months go by, and no perspective promise of it to them, and then this same quiescent cash all at once mutinying in them, this same cash would soon cashier Ahab.

Nor was there wanting still another precautionary motive more related to Ahab personally. Having impulsively, it is probable, and perhaps somewhat prematurely revealed the prime but private purpose of the Pequod's voyage, Ahab was now entirely conscious that, in so doing, he had indirectly laid himself open to the unanswerable charge of usurpation; and with perfect impunity, both moral and legal, his crew if so disposed, and to that end competent, could refuse all further obedience to him, and even violently wrest from him the command. From even the barely hinted imputation of usurpation, and the possible consequences of such a suppressed impression gaining ground, Ahab must of course have been most anxious to protect himself. That protection could only consist in his own predominating brain and heart and hand, backed by a heedful, closely calculating attention to every minute atmospheric influence which it was possible for his crew to be subjected to.

For all these reasons then, and others perhaps too analytic to be verbally developed here, Ahab plainly saw that he must still in a good degree continue true to the natural, nominal purpose of the Pequod's voyage; observe all customary usages; and not only that, but force himself to evince all his well known passionate interest in the general pursuit of his profession.

Be all this as it may, his voice was now often heard hailing the three mast-heads and admonishing them to keep a bright lookout, and not omit reporting even a porpoise. This vigilance was not long without reward.

Chapter 47

THE MAT-MAKER

It was a cloudy, sultry afternoon; the seamen were lazily lounging about the decks, or vacantly gazing over into the lead-colored waters. Queequeg and I were mildly employed weaving what is called a sword-mat, for an additional lashing to our boat. So still and subdued and yet somehow preluding was all the scene, and such an incantation of revery lurked in the air, that each silent sailor seemed resolved into his own invisible self.

I was the attendant or page of Queequeg, while busy at the mat. As I kept passing and repassing the filling or woof of marline between the long yarns of the warp, using my own hand for the shuttle, and as Queequeg, standing sideways, ever and anon slid his heavy oaken sword between the threads, and idly looking off upon the water, carelessly and unthinkingly drove home every yarn: I say so strange a dreaminess did there then reign all over the ship and all over the sea, only broken by the intermitting dull sound of the sword, that it seemed as if this were the Loom of Time, and I myself were a shuttle mechanically weaving and weaving away at the Fates. There lay the fixed threads of the warp subject to but one single, ever returning, unchanging vibration, and that vibration merely enough to admit of the crosswise interblending of other threads with its own. This warp seemed necessity; and here, thought I, with my own hand I ply my own shuttle and weave my own destiny into these unalterable threads. Meantime, Queequeg's impulsive, indifferent sword, sometimes hitting the woof slantingly, or crookedly, or strongly, or weakly, as the case might be; and by this difference in the concluding blow producing a corresponding contrast in the final aspect of the completed fabric; this savage's sword, thought I, which thus finally shapes and fashions both warp and woof; this easy, indifferent sword must be chance—aye, chance, free will, and necessity—no wise incompatible—all interweavingly working together. The straight warp of necessity, not to be swerved from its ultimate course—its every alternating vibration, indeed, only tending to that; free will still free to ply her shuttle between given threads; and chance, though restrained in its play within the right lines of necessity, and sideways in its motions modified by free will, though thus prescribed to by both, chance by turns rules either, and has the last featuring blow at events.

* * * * * *

Thus we were weaving and weaving away when I started at a sound so strange, long drawn, and musically wild and unearthly, that the ball of free will dropped from my hand, and I stood gazing up at the clouds whence that voice dropped like a wing. High aloft in the cross-trees was that mad Gay-Header, Tashtego. His body was reaching eagerly forward, his hand stretched out like a wand, and at brief sudden intervals he continued his cries. To be sure the same sound was that very moment perhaps being heard all over the seas, from hundreds of whalemen's look-outs perched as high in the air; but from few of those lungs could that accustomed old cry have derived such a marvellous cadence as from Tashtego the Indian's.

As he stood hovering over you half suspended in air, so wildly and eagerly peering towards the horizon, you would have thought him some prophet or seer beholding the shadows of Fate, and by those wild cries announcing their coming.

"There she blows! there! there! there! she blows! she blows!"

"Where-away?"

"On the lee-beam, about two miles off! a school of them!"

Instantly all was commotion.

The Sperm Whale blows as a clock ticks, with the same undeviating and reliable uniformity. And thereby whalemen distinguish this fish from other tribes of his genus.

"There go flukes!" was now the cry from Tashtego; and the whales disappeared.

"Quick, steward!" cried Ahab. "Time! time!"

Dough-Boy hurried below, glanced at the watch, and reported the exact minute to Ahab.

The ship was now kept away from the wind, and she went gently rolling before it. Tashtego reporting that the whales had gone down heading to leeward, we confidently looked to see them again directly in advance of our bows. For that singular craft at times evinced by the Sperm Whale when, sounding with his head in one direction, he nevertheless, while concealed beneath the surface, mills round, and swiftly swims off in the opposite quarter —this deceitfulness of his could not now be in action; for there was no reason to suppose that the fish seen by Tashtego had been in any way alarmed, or indeed knew at all of our vicinity. One of the men selected for shipkeepers—that is, those not appointed to the boats, by this time relieved the Indian at the main-mast head. The sailors at the fore and mizzen had come down; the line tubs were fixed in their places; the cranes were thrust out; the mainyard was backed, and the three boats swung over the sea like three samphire baskets over high cliffs. Outside of the bulwarks their eager crews with one hand clung to the rail, while one foot was expectantly poised on the gunwale. So look the long line of man-of-war's men about to throw themselves on board an enemy's ship.

But at this critical instant a sudden exclamation was heard that took every eye from the whale. With a start all glared at dark Ahab, who was surrounded by five dusky phantoms that seemed fresh formed out of air.

Chapter 48

THE FIRST LOWERING

The phantoms, for so they then seemed, were flitting on the other side of the deck, and, with a noiseless celerity, were casting loose the tackles and bands of the boat which swung there. This boat had always been deemed one of the spare boats, though technically called the captain's, on account of its hanging from the starboard quarter. The figure that now stood by its bows was tall and swart, with one white tooth evilly protruding from its steel-like lips. A rumpled Chinese jacket of black cotton funereally invested him, with wide trowsers of the same dark stuff. But strangely crowning this ebonness was a glistening white plaited turban, the living hair braided and coiled round and round upon his head. Less swart in aspect, the companions of this figure were of that vivid, tiger-yellow complexion peculiar to some of the aboriginal natives of the Manillas;—a race notorious for a certain diabolism of subtilty, and by some honest white mariners supposed to be the paid spies and secret confidential agents on the water of the devil, their lord, whose counting-room they suppose to be elsewhere.

While yet the wondering ship's company were gazing upon these strangers, Ahab cried out to the white-turbaned old man at their head, "All ready there, Fedallah?"

"Ready," was the half-hissed reply.

"Lower away then; d'ye hear?" shouting across the deck. "Lower away there, I say."

Such was the thunder of his voice, that spite of their amazement the men sprang over the rail; the sheaves whirled round in the blocks; with a wallow, the three boats dropped into the sea; while, with a dexterous, off-handed daring, unknown in any other vocation, the sailors, goat-like, leaped down the rolling ship's side into the tossed boats below.

Hardly had they pulled out from under the ship's lee, when a fourth keel, coming from the windward side, pulled round under the stern, and showed the five strangers rowing Ahab, who, standing erect in the stern, loudly hailed Starbuck, Stubb, and Flask, to spread themselves widely, so as to cover a large expanse of water. But with all their eyes again riveted upon the swart Fedallah and his crew, the inmates of the other boats obeyed not the command.

"Captain Ahab?—" said Starbuck.

"Spread yourselves," cried Ahab; "give way, all four boats. Thou, Flask, pull out more to leeward!"

"Aye, aye, sir," cheerily cried little King-Post, sweeping round his great steering oar. "Lay back!" addressing his crew. "There!—there!—there again! There she blows right ahead, boys!—lay back!—Never heed yonder yellow boys, Archy."

"Oh, I don't mind 'em, sir," said Archy; "I knew it all before now. Didn't I hear 'em in the hold? And didn't I tell Cabaco here of it? What say ye, Cabaco? They are stowaways, Mr. Flask."

"Pull, pull, my fine hearts-alive; pull, my children; pull, my little ones," drawlingly and soothingly sighed Stubb to his crew, some of whom still showed signs of uneasiness. "Why don't you break your backbones, my boys? What is it you stare at? Those chaps in yonder boat? Tut! They are only five more hands come to help us—never mind from where—the more the merrier. Pull, then, do pull; never mind the brimstone—devils are good fellows enough. So, so; there you are now; that's the stroke for a thousand pounds; that's the stroke to sweep the stakes! Hurrah for the gold cup of sperm oil, my heroes! Three cheers, men—all hearts alive! Easy, easy; don't be in a hurry—don't be in a hurry. Why don't you snap your oars, you rascals? Bite something, you dogs! So, so, so, then;—softly, softly! That's it—that's it! long and strong. Give way there, give way! The devil fetch ye, ye ragamuffin rapscallions; ye are all asleep. Stop snoring, ye sleepers, and pull. Pull, will ye? pull, can't ye? pull, won't ye? Why in the name of gudgeons and ginger-cakes don't ye pull?—pull and break something! pull, and start your eyes out! Here!" whipping out the sharp knife from his girdle; "every mother's son of ye draw his knife, and pull with the blade between his teeth. That's it—that's it. Now ye do something; that looks like it, my steel-bits. Start her—start her, my silver-spoons! Start her, marling-spikes!"

Stubb's exordium to his crew is given here at large, because he had rather a peculiar way of talking to them in general, and especially in inculcating the religion of rowing. But you must not suppose from this specimen of his sermonizings that he ever flew into downright passions with his congregation. Not at all; and therein consisted his chief peculiarity. He would say the most terrific things to his crew, in a tone so strangely compounded of fun and fury, and the fury seemed so calculated merely as a spice to the fun, that no oarsman could hear such queer invocations without pulling for dear life, and yet pulling for the mere joke of the thing. Besides he all the time looked so easy and indolent himself, so loungingly managed his steering-oar, and so broadly gaped—open-mouthed at times—that the mere sight of such a yawning commander, by sheer force of contrast, acted like a charm upon the crew. Then again, Stubb was one of those odd sort of humorists, whose jollity is sometimes so curiously ambiguous, as to put all inferiors on their guard in the matter of obeying them.

In obedience to a sign from Ahab, Starbuck was now pulling obliquely across Stubb's bow; and when for a minute or so the two boats were pretty near to each other, Stubb hailed the mate.

"Mr. Starbuck! larboard boat there, ahoy! a word with ye, sir, if ye please!"

"Halloa!" returned Starbuck, turning round not a single inch as he spoke; still earnestly but whisperingly urging his crew; his face set like a flint from Stubb's.

"What think ye of those yellow boys, sir!"

"Smuggled on board, somehow, before the ship sailed. (Strong, strong, boys!)" in a whisper to his crew, then speaking out loud again: "A sad business, Mr. Stubb! (seethe her, seethe her, my lads!) but never mind, Mr. Stubb, all for the best. Let all your crew pull strong, come what will. (Spring, my men, spring!) There's hogsheads of sperm ahead, Mr. Stubb, and that's what ye came for. (Pull, my boys!) Sperm, sperm's the play! This at least is duty; duty and profit hand in hand!"

"Aye, aye, I thought as much," soliloquized Stubb, when the boats diverged, "as soon as I clapt eye on 'em, I thought so. Aye, and that's what he went into the after hold for, so often, as Dough-Boy long suspected. They were hidden down there. The White Whale's at the bottom of it. Well, well, so be it! Can't be helped! All right! Give way, men! It ain't the White Whale to-day! Give way!"

Now the advent of these outlandish strangers at such a critical instant as the lowering of the boats from the deck, this had not unreasonably awakened a sort of superstitious amazement in some of the ship's company; but Archy's fancied discovery having some time previous got abroad among them, though indeed not credited then, this had in some small measure prepared them for the event. It took off the extreme edge of their wonder; and so what with all this and Stubb's confident way of accounting for their appearance, they were for the time freed from superstitious surmisings; though the affair still left abundant room for all manner of wild conjectures as to dark Ahab's precise agency in the matter from the beginning. For me, I silently recalled the mysterious shadows I had seen creeping on board the Pequod during the dim Nantucket dawn, as well as the enigmatical hintings of the unaccountable Elijah.

Meantime, Ahab, out of hearing of his officers, having sided the furthest to windward, was still ranging ahead of the other boats; a circumstance bespeaking how potent a crew was pulling him. Those tiger yellow creatures of his seemed all steel and whale-bone; like five trip-hammers they rose and fell with regular strokes of strength, which periodically started the boat along the water like a horizontal burst boiler out of a Mississippi steamer. As for Fedallah, who was seen pulling the harpooneer oar, he had thrown aside his black jacket, and displayed his naked chest with the whole part of his body above the gunwale, clearly cut against the alternating depressions of the watery horizon; while at the other end of the boat Ahab, with one arm, like a fencer's, thrown half backward into the air, as if to counterbalance any tendency to trip; Ahab was seen steadily managing his steering oar as in a thousand boat lowerings ere the White Whale had torn him. All at once the outstretched arm gave a peculiar motion and then remained fixed, while the boat's five oars were seen simultaneously peaked. Boat and crew sat motionless on the sea. Instantly the three spread boats in the rear paused on their way. The whales had irregularly settled bodily down into the blue, thus giving no distantly discernible token of the movement, though from his closer vicinity Ahab had observed it.

"Every man look out along his oar!" cried Starbuck. "Thou, Queequeg, stand up!"

Nimbly springing up on the triangular raised box in the bow, the savage stood erect there, and with intensely eager eyes gazed off towards the spot where the chase had last been descried. Likewise upon the extreme stern of the boat where it was also triangularly platformed level with the gunwale, Starbuck himself was seen coolly and adroitly balancing himself to the jerking tossings of his chip of a craft, and silently eyeing the vast blue eye of the sea.

Not very far distant Flask's boat was also lying breathlessly still; its commander recklessly standing upon the top of the loggerhead, a stout sort of post rooted in the keel, and rising some two feet above the level of the stern platform. It is used for catching turns with the whale line. Its top is not more spacious than the palm of a man's hand, and standing upon such a base as that, Flask seemed perched at the mast-head of some ship which had sunk to all but her trucks. But little King-Post was small and short, and at the same time little King-Post was full of a large and tall ambition, so that this loggerhead stand-point of his did by no means satisfy King-Post.

"I can't see three seas off; tip us up an oar there, and let me on to that."

Upon this, Daggoo, with either hand upon the gunwale to steady his way, swiftly slid aft, and then erecting himself volunteered his lofty shoulders for a pedestal.

"Good a mast-head as any, sir. Will you mount?"

"That I will, and thank ye very much, my fine fellow; only I wish you fifty feet taller."

Whereupon planting his feet firmly against two opposite planks of the boat, the gigantic negro, stooping a little, presented his flat palm to Flask's foot, and then putting Flask's hand on his hearse-plumed head and bidding him spring as he himself should toss, with one dexterous fling landed the little man high and dry on his shoulders. And here was Flask now standing, Daggoo with one lifted arm furnishing him with a breast-band to lean against and steady himself by.

At any time it is a strange sight to the tyro to see with what wondrous habitude of unconscious skill the whaleman will maintain an erect posture in his boat, even when pitched about by the most riotously perverse and cross-running seas. Still more strange to see him giddily perched upon the loggerhead itself, under such circumstances. But the sight of little Flask mounted upon gigantic Daggoo was yet more curious; for sustaining himself with a cool, indifferent, easy, unthought of, barbaric majesty, the noble negro to every roll of the sea harmoniously rolled his fine form. On his broad back, flaxen-haired Flask seemed a snow-flake. The bearer looked nobler than the rider. Though, truly, vivacious, tumultuous, ostentatious little Flask would now and then stamp with impatience; but not one added heave did he thereby give to the negro's lordly chest. So have I seen Passion and Vanity stamping the living magnanimous earth, but the earth did not alter her tides and her seasons for that.

Meanwhile Stubb, the second mate, betrayed no such far-gazing solicitudes. The whales might have made one of their regular soundings, not a temporary dive from mere fright; and if that were the case, Stubb, as his wont in such cases, it seems, was resolved to solace the languishing interval with his pipe. He withdrew it from his hatband, where he always wore it aslant like a feather. He loaded it, and rammed home the loading with his thumb-end; but hardly had he ignited his match across the rough sand-paper of his hand, when Tashtego, his harpooneer, whose eyes had been setting to windward like two fixed stars, suddenly dropped like light from his erect attitude to his seat, crying out in a quick phrensy of hurry, "Down, down all, and give way!— there they are!"

To a landsman, no whale, nor any sign of a herring, would

have been visible at that moment; nothing but a troubled bit of greenish white water, and thin scattered puffs of vapor hovering over it, and suffusingly blowing off to leeward, like the confused scud from white rolling billows. The air around suddenly vibrated and tingled, as it were, like the air over intensely heated plates of iron. Beneath this atmospheric waving and curling, and partially beneath a thin layer of water, also, the whales were swimming. Seen in advance of all the other indications, the puffs of vapor they spouted, seemed their forerunning couriers and detached flying outriders.

All four boats were now in keen pursuit of that one spot of troubled water and air. But it bade fair to outstrip them; it flew on and on, as a mass of interblending bubbles borne down a rapid stream from the hills.

"Pull, pull, my good boys," said Starbuck, in the lowest possible but intensest concentrated whisper to his men; while the sharp fixed glance from his eyes, darted straight ahead of the bow, almost seemed as two visible needles in two unerring binnacle compasses. He did not say much to his crew, though, nor did his crew say anything to him. Only the silence of the boat was at intervals startlingly pierced by one of his peculiar whispers, now harsh with command, now soft with entreaty.

How different the loud little King-Post. "Sing out and say something, my hearties. Roar and pull, my thunderbolts! Beach me, beach me on their black backs, boys; only do that for me, and I'll sign over to you my Martha's Vineyard plantation, boys; including wife and children, boys. Lay me on—lay me on! O Lord, Lord! but I shall go stark, staring mad: See! see that white water!" And so shouting, he pulled his hat from his head, and stamped up and down on it; then picking it up, flirted it far off upon the sea; and finally fell to rearing and plunging in the boat's stern like a crazed colt from the prairie.

"Look at that chap now," philosophically drawled Stubb, who, with his unlighted short pipe, mechanically retained between his teeth, at a short distance, followed after—"He's got fits, that Flask has. Fits? yes, give him fits—that's the very word—pitch fits into 'em. Merrily, merrily, hearts-alive. Pudding for supper, you know;—merry's the word. Pull, babes—pull, sucklings—pull, all. But what the devil are you hurrying about? Softly, softly, and steadily, my men. Only pull, and keep pulling; nothing more. Crack all your backbones, and bite your knives in two—that's all. Take it easy—why don't ye take it easy, I say, and burst all your livers and lungs!"

But what it was that inscrutable Ahab said to that tiger-yellow crew of his—these were words best omitted here; for you live under the blessed light of the evangelical land. Only the infidel sharks in the audacious seas may give ear to such words, when, with tornado brow, and eyes of red murder, and foam-glued lips, Ahab leaped after his prey.

Meanwhile, all the boats tore on. The repeated specific allusions of Flask to "that whale," as he called the fictitious monster which he declared to be incessantly tantalizing his boat's bow with its tail—these allusions of his were at times so vivid and life-like, that they would cause some one or two of his men to snatch a fearful look over the shoulder. But this was against all rule; for the oarsmen must put out their eyes, and ram a skewer through their necks; usage pronouncing that they must have no organs but ears, and no limbs but arms, in these critical moments.

It was a sight full of quick wonder and awe! The vast swells of the omnipotent sea; the surging, hollow roar they made, as they rolled along the eight gunwales, like gigantic bowls in a boundless bowling-green; the brief suspended agony of the boat, as it would tip for an instant on the knife-like edge of the sharper waves, that almost seemed threatening to cut it in two; the sudden profound dip into the watery glens and hollows; the keen spurrings and goadings to gain the top of the opposite hill; the headlong, sled-like slide down its other side;—all these, with the cries of the headsmen and harpooneers, and the shuddering gasps of the oarsmen, with the wondrous sight of the ivory Pequod bearing down upon her boats with outstretched sails, like a wild hen after her screaming brood;—all this was thrilling. Not the raw recruit, marching from the bosom of his wife into the fever heat of his first battle; not the dead man's ghost encountering the first unknown phantom in the other world;—neither of these can feel stranger and stronger emotions than that man does, who for the first time finds himself pulling into the charmed, churned circle of the hunted sperm whale.

The dancing white water made by the chase was now becoming more and more visible, owing to the increasing darkness of the dun cloud-shadows flung upon the sea. The jets of vapor no longer blended, but tilted everywhere to right and left; the whales seemed separating their wakes. The boats were pulled more apart; Starbuck giving chase to three whales running dead to leeward. Our sail was now set, and, with the still rising wind, we rushed along; the boat going with such madness through the water, that the lee oars could scarcely be worked rapidly enough to escape being torn from the row-locks.

Soon we were running through a suffusing wide veil of mist; neither ship nor boat to be seen.

"Give way, men," whispered Starbuck, drawing still further aft the sheet of his sail; "there is time to kill a fish yet before the squall comes. There's white water again!—close to! Spring!"

Soon after, two cries in quick succession on each side of us denoted that the other boats had got fast; but hardly were they overheard, when with a lightning-like hurtling whisper Starbuck said: "Stand up!" and Queequeg, harpoon in hand, sprang to his feet.

Though not one of the oarsmen was then facing the life and death peril so close to them ahead, yet with their eyes on the intense countenance of the mate in the stern of the boat, they knew that the imminent instant had come; they heard, too, an enormous wallowing sound as of fifty elephants stirring in their litter. Meanwhile the boat was still booming through the mist, the waves curling and hissing around us like the erected crests of enraged serpents.

"That's his hump. *There, there*, give it to him!" whispered Starbuck.

A short rushing sound leaped out of the boat; it was the darted iron of Queequeg. Then all in one welded commotion came an invisible push from astern, while forward the boat seemed striking on a ledge; the sail collapsed and exploded; a gush of scalding vapor shot up near by; something rolled and tumbled like an earthquake beneath us. The whole crew were half suffocated as they were tossed helter-skelter into the white curdling cream of the squall. Squall, whale, and harpoon had all blended together; and the whale, merely grazed by the iron, escaped.

Though completely swamped, the boat was nearly unharmed. Swimming round it we picked up the floating oars, and lashing them across the gunwale, tumbled back to our places. There we sat up to our knees in the sea, the water covering every rib and plank, so that to our downward gazing eyes the suspended craft seemed a coral boat grown up to us from the bottom of the ocean.

The wind increased to a howl; the waves dashed their bucklers together; the whole squall roared, forked, and crackled around us like a white fire upon the prairie, in which, unconsumed, we were burning; immortal in these jaws of death! In vain we hailed the other boats; as well roar to the live coals down the chimney of a flaming furnace as hail those boats in that storm. Meanwhile the driving scud, rack, and mist, grew darker with the shadows of night; no sign of the ship could be seen. The rising sea forbade all attempts to bale out the boat. The oars were useless as propellers, performing now the office of life-preservers. So, cutting the lashing of the waterproof match keg, after many failures Starbuck contrived to ignite the lamp in the lantern; then stretching it on a waif pole, handed it to Queequeg as the standard-bearer of this forlorn hope. There, then, he sat, holding up that imbecile candle in the heart of that almighty forlornness. There, then, he sat, the sign and symbol of a man without faith, hopelessly holding up hope in the midst of despair.

Wet, drenched through, and shivering cold, despairing of ship or boat, we lifted up our eyes as the dawn came on. The mist still spread over the sea, the empty lantern lay crushed in the bottom of the boat. Suddenly Queequeg started to his feet, hollowing his hand to his ear. We all heard a faint creaking, as of ropes and yards hitherto muffled by the storm. The sound came nearer and nearer; the thick mists were dimly parted by a huge, vague form. Affrighted, we all sprang into the sea as the ship at last loomed into view, bearing right down upon us within a distance of not much more than its length.

Floating on the waves we saw the abandoned boat, as for one instant it tossed and gaped beneath the ship's bows like a chip at the base of a cataract; and then the vast hull rolled over it, and it was seen no more till it came up weltering astern. Again we swam for it, were dashed against it by the seas, and were at last taken up and safely landed on board. Ere the squall came close to, the other boats had cut loose from their fish and returned to the ship in good time. The ship had given us up, but was still cruising, if haply it might light upon some token of our perishing, —an oar or a lance pole.

Chapter 49

THE HYENA

There are certain queer times and occasions in this strange mixed affair we call life when a man takes this whole universe for a vast practical joke, though the wit thereof he but dimly discerns, and more than suspects that the joke is at nobody's expense but his own. However, nothing dispirits, and nothing seems worth while disputing. He bolts down all events, all creeds, and beliefs, and persuasions, all hard things visible and invisible, never mind how knobby; as an ostrich of potent digestion gobbles down bullets and gun flints. And as for small difficulties and worryings, prospects of sudden disaster, peril of life and limb; all these, and death itself, seem to him only sly, good-natured hits, and jolly punches in the side bestowed by the unseen and unaccountable old joker. That odd sort of wayward mood I am speaking of, comes over a man only in some time of extreme tribulation; it comes in the very midst of his earnestness, so that what just before might have seemed to him a thing most momentous, now seems but a part of the general joke. There is noth-

ing like the perils of whaling to breed this free and easy sort of
genial, desperado philosophy; and with it I now regarded this
whole voyage of the Pequod, and the great White Whale its object.

"Queequeg," said I, when they had dragged me, the last man,
to the deck, and I was still shaking myself in my jacket to fling
off the water; "Queequeg, my fine friend, does this sort of thing
often happen?" Without much emotion, though soaked through
just like me, he gave me to understand that such things did often
happen.

"Mr. Stubb," said I, turning to that worthy, who, buttoned up
in his oil-jacket, was now calmly smoking his pipe in the rain;
"Mr. Stubb, I think I have heard you say that of all whalemen
you ever met, our chief mate, Mr. Starbuck, is by far the most
careful and prudent. I suppose then, that going plump on a
flying whale with your sail set in a foggy squall is the height of
a whaleman's discretion?"

"Certain. I've lowered for whales from a leaking ship in a gale
off Cape Horn."

"Mr. Flask," said I, turning to little King-Post, who was
standing close by; "you are experienced in these things, and I
am not. Will you tell me whether it is an unalterable law in
this fishery, Mr. Flask, for an oarsman to break his own back pulling himself back-foremost into death's jaws?"

"Can't you twist that smaller?" said Flask. "Yes, that's the law.
I should like to see a boat's crew backing water up to a whale
face foremost. Ha, ha! the whale would give them squint for
squint, mind that!"

Here then, from three impartial witnesses, I had a deliberate
statement of the entire case. Considering, therefore, that squalls
and capsizings in the water and consequent bivouacks on the deep,
were matters of common occurrence in this kind of life; considering that at the superlatively critical instant of going on to the
whale I must resign my life into the hands of him who steered
the boat—oftentimes a fellow who at that very moment is in his
impetuousness upon the point of scuttling the craft with his
own frantic stampings; considering that the particular disaster
to our own particular boat was chiefly to be imputed to Starbuck's
driving on to his whale almost in the teeth of a squall, and considering that Starbuck, notwithstanding, was famous for his great
heedfulness in the fishery; considering that I belonged to this uncommonly prudent Starbuck's boat; and finally considering in what
a devil's chase I was implicated, touching the White Whale: taking all things together, I say, I thought I might as well go below
and make a rough draft of my will. "Queequeg," said I, "come
along, you shall be my lawyer, executor, and legatee."

It may seem strange that of all men sailors should be tinkering at their last wills and testaments, but there are no people in
the world more fond of that diversion. This was the fourth time
in my nautical life that I had done the same thing. After the
ceremony was concluded upon the present occasion, I felt all the
easier; a stone was rolled away from my heart. Besides, all the days
I should now live would be as good as the days that Lazarus
lived after his resurrection; a supplementary clean gain of so many
months or weeks as the case might be. I survived myself; my death
and burial were locked up in my chest. I looked round me tranquilly and contentedly, like a quiet ghost with a clean conscience
sitting inside the bars of a snug family vault.

Now then, thought I, unconsciously rolling up the sleeves of my
frock, here goes for a cool, collected dive at death and destruction, and the devil fetch the hindmost.

Chapter 50

AHAB'S BOAT AND CREW. FEDALLAH

"Who would have thought it, Flask!" cried Stubb; "if I had
but one leg you would not catch me in a boat, unless maybe to
stop the plug-hole with my timber toe. Oh! he's a wonderful old
man!"

"I don't think it so strange, after all, on that account," said
Flask. "If his leg were off at the hip, now, it would be a different
thing. That would disable him; but he has one knee, and good
part of the other left, you know."

"I don't know that, my little man; I never yet saw him kneel."

* * * * * *

Among whale-wise people it has often been argued whether,
considering the paramount importance of his life to the success
of the voyage, it is right for a whaling captain to jeopardize that
life in the active perils of the chase. So Tamerlane's soldiers often
argued with tears in their eyes, whether that invaluable life of his
ought to be carried into the thickest of the fight.

But with Ahab the question assumed a modified aspect. Considering that with two legs man is but a hobbling wight in all
times of danger; considering that the pursuit of whales is always
under great and extraordinary difficulties; that every individual
moment, indeed, then comprises a peril; under these circumstances
is it wise for any maimed man to enter a whaleboat in the hunt?
As a general thing, the joint-owners of the Pequod must have
plainly thought not.

Ahab well knew that although his friends at home would
think little of his entering a boat in certain comparatively harmless

vicissitudes of the chase, for the sake of being near the scene of action and giving his orders in person, yet for Captain Ahab to have a boat actually apportioned to him as a regular headsman in the hunt—above all for Captain Ahab to be supplied with five extra men, as that same boat's crew, he well knew that such generous conceits never entered the heads of the owners of the Pequod. Therefore he had not solicited a boat's crew from them, nor had he in any way hinted his desires on that head. Nevertheless he had taken private measures of his own touching all that matter. Until Archy's published discovery, the sailors had little foreseen it, though to be sure when, after being a little while out of port, all hands had concluded the customary business of fitting the whaleboats for service; when some time after this Ahab was now and then found bestirring himself in the matter of making thole-pins with his own hands for what was thought to be one of the spare boats, and even solicitously cutting the small wooden skewers, which when the line is running out are pinned over the groove in the bow: when all this was observed in him, and particularly his solicitude in having an extra coat of sheathing in the bottom of the boat, as if to make it better withstand the pointed pressure of his ivory limb; and also the anxiety he evinced in exactly shaping the thigh board, or clumsy cleat, as it is sometimes called, the horizontal piece in the boat's bow for bracing the knee against in darting or stabbing at the whale; when it was observed how often he stood up in that boat with his solitary knee fixed in the semi-circular depression in the cleat, and with the carpenter's chisel gouged out a little here and straightened it a little there; all these things, I say, had awakened much interest and curiosity at the time. But almost everybody supposed that this particular preparative heedfulness in Ahab must only be with a view to the ultimate chase of Moby Dick; for he had already revealed his intention to hunt that mortal monster in person. But such a supposition did by no means involve the remotest suspicion as to any boat's crew being assigned to that boat.

Now, with the subordinate phantoms, what wonder remained soon waned away; for in a whaler wonders soon wane. Besides, now and then such unaccountable odds and ends of strange nations come up from the unknown nooks and ash-holes of the earth to man these floating outlaws of whalers; and the ships themselves often pick up such queer castaway creatures found tossing about the open sea on planks, bits of wreck, oars, whaleboats, canoes, blown-off Japanese junks, and what not; that Beelzebub himself might climb up the side and step down into the cabin to chat with the captain, and it would not create any unsubduable excitement in the forecastle.

But be all this as it may, certain it is that while the subordinate phantoms soon found their place among the crew, though still as it were somehow distinct from them, yet that hair-turbaned Fedallah remained a muffled mystery to the last. Whence he came in a mannerly world like this, by what sort of unaccountable tie he soon evinced himself to be linked with Ahab's peculiar fortunes; nay, so far as to have some sort of a half-hinted influence; Heaven knows, but it might have been even authority over him; all this none knew. But one cannot sustain an indifferent air concerning Fedallah. He was such a creature as civilized, domestic people in the temperate zone only see in their dreams, and that but dimly; but the like of whom now and then glide among the unchanging Asiatic communities, especially the Oriental isles to the east of the continent—those insulated, immemorial, unalterable countries, which even in these modern days still preserve much of the ghostly aboriginalness of earth's primal generations, when the memory of the first man was a distinct recollection, and all men his descendants, unknowing whence he came, eyed each other as real phantoms, and asked of the sun and the moon why they were created and to what end; when though, according to Genesis, the angels indeed consorted with the daughters of men, the devils also, add the uncanonical Rabbins,[1] indulged in mundane amours.

Chapter 51

THE SPIRIT-SPOUT

Days, weeks passed, and under easy sail, the ivory Pequod had slowly swept across four several cruising-grounds; that off the Azores; off the Cape de Verdes; on the Plate (so called), being off the mouth of the Rio de la Plata; and the Carrol Ground, an unstaked, watery locality, southerly from St. Helena.

It was while gliding through these latter waters that one serene and moonlight night, when all the waves rolled by like scrolls of silver; and, by their soft, suffusing seethings, made what seemed a silvery silence, not a solitude: on such a silent night a silvery jet was seen far in advance of the white bubbles at the bow. Lit up by the moon, it looked celestial; seemed some plumed and glittering god uprising from the sea. Fedallah first descried this jet. For of these moonlight nights, it was his wont to mount to the main-mast head, and stand a look-out there, with the same precision as if it had been day. And yet, though herds of whales were seen by night, not one whaleman in a hundred would venture a

---

1. The Jewish authors of two uncanonical works, the Book of Enoch and Book of Jubilees.

lowering for them. You may think with what emotions, then, the seamen beheld this old Oriental perched aloft at such unusual hours; his turban and the moon, companions in one sky. But when, after spending his uniform interval there for several successive nights without uttering a single sound; when, after all this silence, his unearthly voice was heard announcing that silvery, moon-lit jet, every reclining mariner started to his feet as if some winged spirit had lighted in the rigging, and hailed the mortal crew. "There she blows!" Had the trump of judgment blown, they could not have quivered more; yet still they felt no terror; rather pleasure. For though it was a most unwonted hour, yet so impressive was the cry, and so deliriously exciting, that almost every soul on board instinctively desired a lowering.

Walking the deck with quick, side-lunging strides, Ahab commanded the t'gallant sails and royals to be set, and every stunsail spread. The best man in the ship must take the helm. Then, with every mast-head manned, the piled-up craft rolled down before the wind. The strange, upheaving, lifting tendency of the taffrail breeze filling the hollows of so many sails, made the buoyant, hovering deck to feel like air beneath the feet; while still she rushed along, as if two antagonistic influences were struggling in her—one to mount direct to heaven, the other to drive yawingly to some horizontal goal. And had you watched Ahab's face that night, you would have thought that in him also two different things were warring. While his one live leg made lively echoes along the deck, every stroke of his dead limb sounded like a coffin-tap. On life and death this old man walked. But though the ship so swiftly sped, and though from every eye, like arrows, the eager glances shot, yet the silvery jet was no more seen that night. Every sailor swore he saw it once, but not a second time.

This midnight-spout had almost grown a forgotten thing, when, some days after, lo! at the same silent hour, it was again announced: again it was descried by all; but upon making sail to overtake it, once more it disappeared as if it had never been. And so it served us night after night, till no one heeded it but to wonder at it. Mysteriously jetted into the clear moonlight, or starlight, as the case might be; disappearing again for one whole day, or two days, or three; and somehow seeming at every distinct repetition to be advancing still further and further in our van, this solitary jet seemed for ever alluring us on.

Nor with the immemorial superstition of their race, and in accordance with the preternaturalness, as it seemed, which in many things invested the Pequod, were there wanting some of the seamen who swore that whenever and wherever descried; at however remote times, or in however far apart latitudes and longi-

tudes, that unnearable spout was cast by one self-same whale; and
that whale, Moby Dick. For a time, there reigned, too, a sense of
peculiar dread at this flitting apparition, as if it were treacherously
beckoning us on and on, in order that the monster might turn
round upon us, and rend us at last in the remotest and most
savage seas.

These temporary apprehensions, so vague but so awful, derived
a wondrous potency from the contrasting serenity of the weather,
in which, beneath all its blue blandness, some thought there
lurked a devilish charm, as for days and days we voyaged along,
through seas so wearily, lonesomely mild, that all space, in repugnance to our vengeful errand, seemed vacating itself of life before
our urn-like prow.

But, at last, when turning to the eastward, the Cape winds began howling around us, and we rose and fell upon the long,
troubled seas that are there; when the ivory-tusked Pequod
sharply bowed to the blast, and gored the dark waves in her madness, till, like showers of silver chips, the foam-flakes flew over her
bulwarks; then all this desolate vacuity of life went away, but
gave place to sights more dismal than before.

Close to our bows, strange forms in the water darted hither and
thither before us; while thick in our rear flew the inscrutable sea-
ravens. And every morning, perched on our stays, rows of these
birds were seen; and spite of our hootings, for a long time obstinately clung to the hemp, as though they deemed our ship some
drifting, uninhabited craft; a thing appointed to desolation, and
therefore fit roosting-place for their homeless selves. And heaved and
heaved, still unrestingly heaved the black sea, as if its vast tides
were a conscience; and the great mundane soul were in anguish
and remorse for the long sin and suffering it had bred.

Cape of Good Hope, do they call ye? Rather Cape Tormentoso,[1] as called of yore; for long allured by the perfidious
silences that before had attended us, we found ourselves launched
into this tormented sea, where guilty beings transformed into
those fowls and these fish, seemed condemned to swim on ever-
lastingly without any haven in store, or beat that black air without
any horizon. But calm, snow-white, and unvarying; still directing
its fountain of feathers to the sky; still beckoning us on from before, the solitary jet would at times be descried.

During all this blackness of the elements, Ahab, though assuming for the time the almost continual command of the drenched
and dangerous deck, manifested the gloomiest reserve; and more

1. Tormentoso was the name Bartholomew Diaz gave to the tip of Africa,
which his ruler strategically renamed
the Cape of Good Hope. Melville takes
the word to mean "tormented," not
tempestuous, and the first American
edition spelled the word "Tormentoto,"
here corrected.

seldom than ever addressed his mates. In tempestuous times like these, after everything above and aloft has been secured, nothing more can be done but passively to await the issue of the gale. Then Captain and crew become practical fatalists. So, with his ivory leg inserted into its accustomed hole, and with one hand firmly grasping a shroud, Ahab for hours and hours would stand gazing dead to windward, while an occasional squall of sleet or snow would all but congeal his very eyelashes together. Meantime, the crew driven from the forward part of the ship by the perilous seas that burstingly broke over its bows, stood in a line along the bulwarks in the waist; and the better to guard against the leaping waves, each man had slipped himself into a sort of bowline secured to the rail, in which he swung as in a loosened belt. Few or no words were spoken; and the silent ship, as if manned by painted sailors in wax, day after day tore on through all the swift madness and gladness of the demoniac waves. By night the same muteness of humanity before the shrieks of the ocean prevailed; still in silence the men swung in the bowlines; still wordless Ahab stood up to the blast. Even when wearied nature seemed demanding repose he would not seek that repose in his hammock. Never could Starbuck forget the old man's aspect, when one night going down into the cabin to mark how the barometer stood, he saw him with closed eyes sitting straight in his floor-screwed chair; the rain and half-melted sleet of the storm from which he had some time before emerged, still slowly dripping from the unremoved hat and coat. On the table beside him lay unrolled one of those charts of tides and currents which have previously been spoken of. His lantern swung from his tightly clenched hand. Though the body was erect, the head was thrown back so that the closed eyes were pointed towards the needle of the tell-tale that swung from a beam in the ceiling.*

Terrible old man! thought Starbuck with a shudder, sleeping in this gale, still thou steadfastly eyest thy purpose.

Chapter 52

THE ALBATROSS

South-eastward from the Cape, off the distant Crozets, a good cruising ground for Right Whalemen, a sail loomed ahead, the Goney (Albatross) by name. As she slowly drew nigh, from my lofty perch at the fore-mast-head, I had a good view of that sight so remarkable to a tyro in the far ocean fisheries—a whaler at sea,

---

* The cabin-compass is called the tell-tale, because without going to the compass at the helm, the Captain, while below, can inform himself of the course of the ship [Melville's note].

and long absent from home.

As if the waves had been fullers,[1] this craft was bleached like the skeleton of a stranded walrus. All down her sides, this spectral appearance was traced with long channels of reddened rust, while all her spars and her rigging were like the thick branches of trees furred over with hoar-frost. Only her lower sails were set. A wild sight it was to see her long-bearded look-outs at those three mast-heads. They seemed clad in the skins of beasts, so torn and be-patched the raiment that had survived nearly four years of cruising. Standing in iron hoops nailed to the mast, they swayed and swung over a fathomless sea; and though, when the ship slowly glided close under our stern, we six men in the air came so nigh to each other that we might almost have leaped from the mast-heads of one ship to those of the other; yet, those forlorn-looking fishermen, mildly eyeing us as they passed, said not one word to our own look-outs, while the quarter-deck hail was being heard from below.

"Ship ahoy! Have ye seen the White Whale?"

But as the strange captain, leaning over the pallid bulwarks, was in the act of putting his trumpet to his mouth, it somehow fell from his hand into the sea; and the wind now rising amain, he in vain strove to make himself heard without it. Meantime his ship was still increasing the distance between. While in various silent ways the seamen of the Pequod were evincing their observance of this ominous incident at the first mere mention of the White Whale's name to another ship, Ahab for a moment paused; it al-most seemed as though he would have lowered a boat to board the stranger, had not the threatening wind forbade. But taking ad-vantage of his windward position, he again seized his trumpet, and knowing by her aspect that the stranger vessel was a Nan-tucketer and shortly bound home, he loudly hailed—"Ahoy there! This is the Pequod, bound round the world! Tell them to address all future letters to the Pacific ocean! and this time three years, if I am not at home, tell them to address them to——"

At that moment the two wakes were fairly crossed, and in-stantly, then, in accordance with their singular ways, shoals of small harmless fish, that for some days before had been placidly swimming by our side, darted away with what seemed shuddering fins, and ranged themselves fore and aft with the stranger's flanks. Though in the course of his continual voyagings Ahab must often before have noticed a similar sight, yet, to any monomaniac man, the veriest trifles capriciously carry meanings.

"Swim away from me, do ye?" murmured Ahab, gazing over in-to the water. There seemed but little in the words, but the tone conveyed more of deep helpless sadness than the insane old man

1. Those who full (cleanse) cloth during manufacture.

had ever before evinced. But turning to the steersman, who thus far had been holding the ship in the wind to diminish her head-way, he cried out in his old lion voice,—"Up helm! Keep her off round the world!"

Round the world! There is much in that sound to inspire proud feelings; but whereto does all that circumnavigation con-duct? Only through numberless perils to the very point whence we started, where those that we left behind secure, were all the time before us.

Were this world an endless plain, and by sailing eastward we could for ever reach new distances, and discover sights more sweet and strange than any Cyclades or Islands of King Solomon, then there were promise in the voyage. But in pursuit of those far mysteries we dream of, or in tormented chase of that demon phantom that, some time or other, swims before all human hearts; while chasing such over this round globe, they either lead us on in barren mazes or midway leave us whelmed.

Chapter 53

THE GAM

The ostensible reason why Ahab did not go on board of the whaler we had spoken was this: the wind and sea betokened storms. But even had this not been the case, he would not after all, perhaps, have boarded her—judging by his subsequent con-duct on similar occasions—if so it had been that, by the process of hailing, he had obtained a negative answer to the question he put. For, as it eventually turned out, he cared not to consort, even for five minutes, with any stranger captain, except he could contribute some of that information he so absorbingly sought. But all this might remain inadequately estimated, were not some-thing said here of the peculiar usages of whaling-vessels when meeting each other in foreign seas, and especially on a common cruising-ground.

If two strangers crossing the Pine Barrens in New York State, or the equally desolate Salisbury Plain in England; if casually en-countering each other in such inhospitable wilds, these twain, for the life of them, cannot well avoid a mutual salutation; and stopping for a moment to interchange the news; and, perhaps, sit-ting down for a while and resting in concert: then, how much more natural that upon the illimitable Pine Barrens and Salisbury Plains of the sea, two whaling vessels descrying each other at the ends of the earth—off lone Fanning's Island, or the far away King's Mills; how much more natural, I say, that under such circumstances these ships should not only interchange hails, but come into still closer, more friendly and sociable contact. And especially would this seem to be a matter of course, in the case of vessels owned in one seaport, and whose captains, officers, and not a few of the men are personally known to each other; and consequently, have all sorts of dear domestic things to talk about.

For the long absent ship, the outward-bounder, perhaps, has letters on board; at any rate, she will be sure to let her have some papers of a date a year or two later than the last one on her blurred and thumb-worn files. And in return for that courtesy, the outward-bound ship would receive the latest whaling intelligence from the cruising-ground to which she may be destined, a thing of the utmost importance to her. And in degree, all this will hold true concerning whaling vessels crossing each other's track on the cruising-ground itself, even though they are equally long absent from home. For one of them may have received a transfer of letters from some third, and now far remote vessel; and some of those letters may be for the people of the ship she now meets. Besides, they would exchange the whaling news, and have an agreeable chat. For not only would they meet with all the sympathies of sailors, but likewise with all the peculiar congenialities arising from a common pursuit and mutually shared privations and perils.

Nor would difference of country make any very essential difference; that is, so long as both parties speak one language, as is the case with Americans and English. Though, to be sure, from the small number of English whalers, such meetings do not very often occur, and when they do occur there is too apt to be a sort of shyness between them; for your Englishman is rather reserved, and your Yankee, he does not fancy that sort of thing in anybody but himself. Besides, the English whalers sometimes affect a kind of metropolitan superiority over the American whalers; regarding the long, lean Nantucketer, with his nondescript provincialisms, as a sort of sea-peasant. But where this superiority in the English whalemen does really consist, it would be hard to say, seeing that the Yankees in one day, collectively, kill more whales than all the English, collectively, in ten years. But this is a harmless little foible in the English whale-hunters, which the Nantucketer does not take much to heart; probably, because he knows that he has a few foibles himself.

So, then, we see that of all ships separately sailing the sea, the whalers have most reason to be sociable—and they are so. Whereas, some merchant ships crossing each other's wake in the mid-Atlantic, will oftentimes pass on without so much as a single word of recognition, mutually cutting each other on the high seas, like a brace of dandies in Broadway; and all the time indulging, perhaps, in finical criticism upon each other's rig. As for Men-of-War, when they chance to meet at sea, they first go through such a string of silly bowings and scrapings, such a ducking of ensigns, that there does not seem to be much right-down hearty good-will and brotherly love about it at all. As touching Slave-ships meeting, why, they are in such a prodigious hurry, they run away from each other as soon as possible. And as for Pirates, when they chance to cross each other's cross-bones, the first hail is—"How many skulls?"—the same way that whalers hail—"How many barrels?" And that question once answered, pirates straightway steer apart, for they are infernal villains on both sides, and don't like to see overmuch of each other's villanous likenesses.

But look at the godly, honest, unostentatious, hospitable, sociable, free-and-easy whaler! What does the whaler do when she meets another whaler in any sort of decent weather? She has a *"Gam,"* a thing so utterly unknown to all other ships that they never heard of the name even; and if by chance they should hear of it, they only grin at it, and repeat gamesome stuff about "spouters" and "blubber-boilers," and such like pretty exclamations. Why it is that all Merchant-seamen, and also all Pirates and Man-of-War's men, and Slave-ship sailors, cherish such a scornful feeling towards Whale-ships; this is a question it would be hard to answer. Because, in the case of pirates, say, I should like to know whether that profession of theirs has any peculiar glory about it. It sometimes ends in uncommon elevation, indeed; but only at the gallows. And besides, when a man is elevated in that odd fashion, he has no proper foundation for his superior altitude. Hence, I conclude, that in boasting himself to be high lifted above a whaleman, in that assertion the pirate has no solid basis to stand on.

But what is a *Gam?* You might wear out your index-finger running up and down the columns of dictionaries, and never find the word. Dr. Johnson never attained to that erudition; Noah Webster's ark does not hold it. Nevertheless, this same expressive word has now for many years been in constant use among some fifteen thousand true born Yankees. Certainly, it needs a definition, and should be incorporated into the Lexicon. With that view, let me learnedly define it.[1]

GAM. NOUN—*A social meeting of two (or more) Whale-ships,*

1. Mansfield and Vincent show that Melville was rewriting the definition of gam which Henry T. Cheever gave in *The Whale and his Captors* . . . (New York, 1850).

generally on a cruising-ground; when, after exchanging hails, they exchange visits by boats' crews: the two captains remaining, for the time, on board of one ship, and the two chief mates on the other.

There is another little item about Gamming which must not be forgotten here. All professions have their own little peculiarities of detail; so has the whale fishery. In a pirate, man-of-war, or slave ship, when the captain is rowed anywhere in his boat, he always sits in the stern sheets on a comfortable, sometimes cushioned seat there, and often steers himself with a pretty little milliner's tiller decorated with gay cords and ribbons. But the whale-boat has no seat astern, no sofa of that sort whatever, and no tiller at all. High times indeed, if whaling captains were wheeled about the water on castors like gouty old aldermen in patent chairs. And as for a tiller, the whale-boat never admits of any such effeminacy; and therefore as in gamming a complete boat's crew must leave the ship, and hence as the boat steerer or harpooneer is of the number, that subordinate is the steersman upon the occasion, and the captain, having no place to sit in, is pulled off to his visit all standing like a pine tree. And often you will notice that being conscious of the eyes of the whole visible world resting on him from the sides of the two ships, this standing captain is all alive to the importance of sustaining his dignity by maintaining his legs. Nor is this any very easy matter; for in his rear is the immense projecting steering oar hitting him now and then in the small of his back, the after-oar reciprocating by rapping his knees in front. He is thus completely wedged before and behind, and can only expand himself sideways by settling down on his stretched legs; but a sudden, violent pitch of the boat will often go far to topple him, because length of foundation is nothing without corresponding breadth. Merely make a spread angle of two poles, and you cannot stand them up. Then, again, it would never do in plain sight of the world's riveted eyes, it would never do, I say, for this straddling captain to be seen steadying himself the slightest particle by catching hold of anything with his hands; indeed, as token of his entire, buoyant self-command, he generally carries his hands in his trowsers' pockets; but perhaps being generally very large, heavy hands, he carries them there for ballast. Nevertheless there have occurred instances, well authenticated ones too, where the captain has been known for an uncommonly critical moment or two, in a sudden squall say—to seize hold of the nearest oarsman's hair, and hold on there like grim death.

Chapter 54

THE TOWN-HO'S STORY

(As told at the Golden Inn.)

The Cape of Good Hope, and all the watery region round about there, is much like some noted four corners of a great highway, where you meet more travellers than in any other part.

It was not very long after speaking the Goney that another homeward-bound whaleman, the Town-Ho,* was encountered. She was manned almost wholly by Polynesians. In the short gam that ensued she gave us strong news of Moby Dick. To some the general interest in the White Whale was now wildly heightened by a circumstance of the Town-Ho's story, which seemed obscurely to involve with the whale a certain wondrous, inverted visitation of one of those so called judgments of God which at times are said to overtake some men. This latter circumstance, with its own particular accompaniments, forming what may be called the secret part of the tragedy about to be narrated, never reached the ears of Captain Ahab or his mates. For that secret part of the story was unknown to the captain of the Town-Ho himself. It was the private property of three confederate white seamen of that ship, one of whom, it seems, communicated it to Tashtego with Romish injunctions of secresy, but the following night Tashtego rambled in his sleep, and revealed so much of it in that way, that when he was wakened he could not well withhold the rest. Nevertheless, so potent an influence did this thing have on those seamen in the Pequod who came to the full knowledge of it, and by such a strange delicacy, to call it so, were they governed in this matter, that they kept the secret among themselves so that it never transpired abaft the Pequod's main-mast. Interweaving in its proper place this darker thread with the story as publicly narrated on the ship, the whole of this strange affair I now proceed to put on lasting record.

For my humor's sake, I shall preserve the style in which I once narrated it at Lima, to a lounging circle of my Spanish friends, one saint's eve, smoking upon the thick-gilt tiled piazza of the Golden Inn. Of those fine cavaliers, the young Dons, Pedro and Sebastian, were on the closer terms with me; and hence the interluding questions they occasionally put, and which are duly answered at the time.

"Some two years prior to my first learning the events which I

---

* The ancient whale-cry upon first sighting a whale from the mast-head, still used by whalemen in hunting the famous Gallipagos terrapin [Melville's note].

am about rehearsing to you, gentlemen, the Town-Ho, Sperm Whaler of Nantucket, was cruising in your Pacific here, not very many days' sail westward from the eaves of this good Golden Inn. She was somewhere to the northward of the Line. One morning upon handling the pumps, according to daily usage, it was observed that she made more water in her hold than common. They supposed a sword-fish had stabbed her, gentlemen. But the captain, having some unusual reason for believing that rare good luck awaited him in those latitudes; and therefore being very averse to quit them, and the leak not being then considered at all dangerous, though, indeed, they could not find it after searching the hold as low down as was possible in rather heavy weather, the ship still continued her cruisings, the mariners working at the pumps at wide and easy intervals; but no good luck came; more days went by, and not only was the leak yet undiscovered, but it sensibly increased. So much so, that now taking some alarm, the captain, making all sail, stood away for the nearest harbor among the islands, there to have his hull hove out and repaired.

"Though no small passage was before her, yet, if the commonest chance favored, he did not at all fear that his ship would founder by the way, because his pumps were of the best, and being periodically relieved at them, those six-and-thirty men of his could easily keep the ship free; never mind if the leak should double on her. In truth, well nigh the whole of this passage being attended by very prosperous breezes, the Town-Ho had all but certainly arrived in perfect safety at her port without the occurrence of the least fatality, had it not been for the brutal overbearing of Radney, the mate, a Vineyarder, and the bitterly provoked vengeance of Steelkilt, a Lakeman and desperado from Buffalo."

"Lakeman!—Buffalo! Pray, what is a Lakeman, and where is Buffalo?" said Don Sebastian, rising in his swinging mat of grass.

"On the eastern shore of our Lake Erie, Don; but—I crave your courtesy—may be, you shall soon hear further of all that. Now, gentlemen, in square-sail brigs and three-masted ships, well nigh as large and stout as any that ever sailed out of your old Callao to far Manilla; this Lakeman, in the land-locked heart of our America, had yet been nurtured by all those agrarian freebooting impressions popularly connected with the open ocean. For in their interflowing aggregate, those grand fresh-water seas of ours,—Erie, and Ontario, and Huron, and Superior, and Michigan,—possess an ocean-like expansiveness, with many of the ocean's noblest traits; with many of its rimmed varieties of races and of climes. They contain round archipelagoes of romantic isles, even as the Polynesian waters do; in large part, are shored by two great contrasting nations, as the Atlantic is; they furnish long maritime approaches to our numerous territorial colonies from the East, dotted all round their banks; here and there are frowned upon by batteries, and by the goat-like craggy guns of lofty Mackinaw; they have heard the fleet thunderings of naval victories; at intervals, they yield their beaches to wild barbarians, whose red painted faces flash from out their peltry[1] wigwams; for leagues and leagues are flanked by ancient and unentered forests, where the gaunt pines stand like serried lines of kings in Gothic genealogies; those same woods harboring wild Afric beasts of prey, and silken creatures whose exported furs give robes to Tartar Emperors; they mirror the paved capitals of Buffalo and Cleveland, as well as Winnebago villages; they float alike the full-rigged merchant ship, the armed cruiser of the State, the steamer, and the birch canoe; they are swept by Borean and dismasting blasts as direful as any that lash the salted wave; they know what shipwrecks are, for out of sight of land, however inland, they have drowned full many a midnight ship with all its shrieking crew.

"Thus, gentlemen, though an inlander, Steelkilt was wild-ocean born, and wild-ocean nurtured; as much of an audacious mariner as any. And for Radney, though in his infancy he may have laid him down on the lone Nantucket beach, to nurse at his maternal sea; though in after life he had long followed our austere Atlantic and your contemplative Pacific; yet was he quite as vengeful and full of social quarrel as the backwoods seaman, fresh from the latitudes of buck-horn handled Bowie-knives. Yet was this Nan-tucketer a man with some good-hearted traits; and this Lakeman, a mariner, who though a sort of devil indeed, might yet by inflexible firmness, only tempered by that common decency of hu-man recognition which is the meanest slave's right; thus treated, this Steelkilt had long been retained harmless and docile. At all events, he had proved so thus far; but Radney was doomed and made mad, and Steelkilt—but, gentlemen, you shall hear.

"It was not more than a day or two at the furthest after point-ing her prow for her island haven, that the Town-Ho's leak seemed again increasing, but only so as to require an hour or more at the pumps every day. You must know that in a settled and civilized ocean like our Atlantic, for example, some skippers think little of pumping their whole way across it; though of a still, sleepy night, should the officer of the deck happen to forget his duty in that respect, the probability would be that he and his shipmates would never again remember it, on account of all hands gently subsiding to the bottom. Nor in the solitary and savage seas far from you to the westward, gentlemen, is it altogether unusual for ships to keep clanging at their pump-handles in full chorus even for a voyage of

1. Made of pelts.

considerable length; that is, if it lie along a tolerably accessible coast, or if any other reasonable retreat is afforded them. It is only when a leaky vessel is in some very out of the way part of those waters, some really landless latitude, that her captain begins to feel a little anxious.

"Much this way had it been with the Town-Ho; so when her leak was found gaining once more, there was in truth some small concern manifested by several of her company; especially by Radney the mate. He commanded the upper sails to be well hoisted, sheeted home anew, and every way expanded to the breeze. Now this Radney, I suppose, was as little of a coward, and as little inclined to any sort of nervous apprehensiveness touching his own person as any fearless, unthinking creature on land or on sea that you can conveniently imagine, gentlemen. Therefore when he betrayed this solicitude about the safety of the ship, some of the seamen declared that it was only on account of his being a part owner in her. So when they were working that evening at the pumps, there was on this head no small gamesomeness slily going on among them, as they stood with their feet continually overflowed by the rippling clear water; clear as any mountain spring, gentlemen—that bubbling from the pumps ran across the deck, and poured itself out in steady spouts at the lee scupper-holes.

"Now, as you well know, it is not seldom the case in this conventional world of ours—watery or otherwise; that when a person placed in command over his fellow-men finds one of them to be very significantly his superior in general pride of manhood, straightway against that man he conceives an unconquerable dislike and bitterness; and if he have a chance he will pull down and pulverize that subaltern's tower, and make a little heap of dust of it. Be this conceit of mine as it may, gentlemen, at all events Steelkilt was a tall and noble animal with a head like a Roman, and a flowing golden beard like the tasseled housings of your last viceroy's snorting charger; and a brain, and a heart, and a soul in him, gentlemen, which had made Steelkilt Charlemagne, had he been born son to Charlemagne's father. But Radney, the mate, was ugly as a mule; yet as hardy, as stubborn, as malicious. He did not love Steelkilt, and Steelkilt knew it.

"Espying the mate drawing near as he was toiling at the pump with the rest, the Lakeman affected not to notice him, but unawed, went on with his gay banterings.

"'Aye, aye, my merry lads, it's a lively leak this; hold a cannikin, one of ye, and let's have a taste. By the Lord, it's worth bottling! I tell ye what, men, old Rad's investment must go for it! he had best cut away his part of the hull and tow it home. The fact is, boys, that sword-fish only began the job; he's come back again with a gang of ship-carpenters, saw-fish, and file-fish, and what not; and the whole posse of 'em are now hard at work cutting and slashing at the bottom; making improvements, I suppose. If old Rad were here now, I'd tell him to jump overboard and scatter 'em. They're playing the devil with his estate, I can tell him. But he's a simple old soul,—Rad, and a beauty too. Boys, they say the rest of his property is invested in looking-glasses. I wonder if he'd give a poor devil like me the model of his nose.'

" 'Damn your eyes! what's that pump stopping for?' roared Radney, pretending not to have heard the sailor's talk. 'Thunder away at it!'

" 'Aye, aye, sir,' said Steelkilt, merry as a cricket. 'Lively, boys, lively, now!' And with that the pump clanged like fifty fire-engines; the men tossed their hats off to it, and ere long that peculiar gasping of the lungs was heard which denotes the fullest tension of life's utmost energies.

"Quitting the pump at last, with the rest of his band, the Lakeman went forward all panting, and sat himself down on the windlass; his face fiery red, his eyes bloodshot, and wiping the profuse sweat from his brow. Now what cozening fiend it was, gentlemen, that possessed Radney to meddle with such a man in that corporeally exasperated state, I know not; but so it happened. Intolerably striding along the deck, the mate commanded him to get a broom and sweep down the planks, and also a shovel, and remove some offensive matters consequent upon allowing a pig to run at large.

"Now, gentlemen, sweeping a ship's deck at sea is a piece of household work which in all times but raging gales is regularly attended to every evening; it has been known to be done in the case of ships actually foundering at the time. Such, gentlemen, is the inflexibility of sea-usages and the instinctive love of neatness in seamen; some of whom would not willingly drown without first washing their faces. But in all vessels this broom business is the prescriptive province of the boys, if boys there be aboard. Besides, it was the stronger men in the Town-Ho that had been divided into gangs, taking turns at the pumps; and being the most athletic seaman of them all, Steelkilt had been regularly assigned captain of one of the gangs; consequently he should have been freed from any trivial business not connected with truly nautical duties, such being the case with his comrades. I mention all these particulars so that you may understand exactly how this affair stood between the two men.

"But there was more than this: the order about the shovel was almost as plainly meant to sting and insult Steelkilt, as though Radney had spat in his face. Any man who has gone sailor in a whale-ship will understand this; and all this and doubtless much more, the Lakeman fully comprehended when the mate uttered his command. But as he sat still for a moment, and as he steadfastly looked into the mate's malignant eye and perceived the stacks of powder-casks heaped up in him and the slow-match silently burning along towards them; as he instinctively saw all this, that strange forbearance and unwillingness to stir up the deeper passionateness in any already ireful being—a repugnance most felt, when felt at all, by really valiant men even when aggrieved—this nameless phantom feeling, gentlemen, stole over Steelkilt.

"Therefore, in his ordinary tone, only a little broken by the bodily exhaustion he was temporarily in, he answered him saying that sweeping the deck was not his business, and he would not do it. And then, without at all alluding to the shovel, he pointed to three lads as the customary sweepers; who, not being billeted at the pumps, had done little or nothing all day. To this, Radney replied with an oath, in a most domineering and outrageous manner unconditionally reiterating his command; meanwhile advancing upon the still seated Lakeman, with an uplifted cooper's club hammer which he had snatched from a cask near by.

"Heated and irritated as he was by his spasmodic toil at the pumps, for all his first nameless feeling of forbearance the sweating Steelkilt could but ill brook this bearing in the mate; but somehow still smothering the conflagration within him, without speaking he remained doggedly rooted to his seat, till at last the incensed Radney shook the hammer within a few inches of his face, furiously commanding him to do his bidding.

"Steelkilt rose, and slowly retreating round the windlass, steadily followed by the mate with his menacing hammer, deliberately repeated his intention not to obey. Seeing, however, that his forbearance had not the slightest effect, by an awful and unspeakable intimation with his twisted hand he warned off the foolish and infatuated man; but it was to no purpose. And in this way the two went once slowly round the windlass; when, resolved at last no longer to retreat, bethinking him that he had now forborne as much as comported with his humor, the Lakeman paused on the hatches and thus spoke to the officer:

" 'Mr. Radney, I will not obey you. Take that hammer away, or look to yourself.' But the predestinated mate coming still closer to him, where the Lakeman stood fixed, now shook the heavy hammer within an inch of his teeth; meanwhile repeating a string of insufferable maledictions. Retreating not the thousandth part of an inch; stabbing him in the eye with the unflinching poniard of his glance, Steelkilt, clenching his right hand behind him and creepingly drawing it back, told his persecutor that if the hammer but grazed his cheek he (Steelkilt) would murder him. But, gentlemen, the fool had been branded for the slaughter by the gods. Immediately the hammer touched the cheek; the next instant the lower jaw of the mate was stove in his head; he fell on the hatch spouting blood like a whale.

"Ere the cry could go aft Steelkilt was shaking one of the backstays leading far aloft to where two of his comrades were standing their mast-heads. They were both Canallers."

"Canallers!" cried Don Pedro. "We have seen many whale-ships in our harbors, but never heard of your Canallers. Pardon: who and what are they?"

"Canallers, Don, are the boatmen belonging to our grand Erie Canal. You must have heard of it."

"Nay, Senor; hereabouts in this dull, warm, most lazy, and hereditary land, we know but little of your vigorous North."

"Aye? Well then, Don, refill my cup. Your chicha's very fine; and ere proceeding further I will tell ye what our Canallers are; for such information may throw side-light upon my story.

"For three hundred and sixty miles, gentlemen, through the entire breadth of the state of New York; through numerous populous cities and most thriving villages; through long, dismal, uninhabited swamps, and affluent, cultivated fields, unrivalled for fertility; by billiard-room and bar-room; through the holy-of-holies of great forests; on Roman arches over Indian rivers; through sun and shade; by happy hearts or broken; through all the wide contrasting scenery of those noble Mohawk counties; and especially, by rows of snow-white chapels, whose spires stand almost like milestones, flows one continual stream of Venetianly corrupt and often lawless life. There's your true Ashantee, gentlemen; there howl your pagans; where you ever find them, next door to you; under the long-flung shadow, and the snug patronizing lee of churches. For by some curious fatality, as it is often noted of your metropolitan freebooters that they ever encamp around the halls of justice, so sinners, gentlemen, most abound in holiest vicinities."

"Is that a friar passing?" said Don Pedro, looking downwards into the crowded plaza, with humorous concern.

"Well for our northern friend, Dame Isabella's Inquisition wanes in Lima," laughed Don Sebastian. "Proceed, Senor."

"A moment! Pardon!" cried another of the company. "In the name of all us Limeese, I but desire to express to you, sir sailor, that we have by no means overlooked your delicacy in not substituting present Lima for distant Venice in your corrupt comparison. Oh! do not bow and look surprised; you know the proverb all along this coast—'Corrupt as Lima.' It but bears out your saying, too; churches more plentiful than billiard-tables, and for ever open—and 'Corrupt as Lima.' So, too, Venice; I have been there; the holy city of the blessed evangelist, St. Mark!—St. Dominic,[2] purge it! Your cup! Thanks: here I refill; now, you pour out again."

"Freely depicted in his own vocation, gentlemen, the Canaller would make a fine dramatic hero, so abundantly and picturesquely wicked is he. Like Mark Antony, for days and days along his green-turfed, flowery Nile, he indolently floats, openly toying with his red-cheeked Cleopatra, ripening his apricot thigh upon the sunny deck. But ashore, all this effeminacy is dashed. The brigandish guise which the Canaller so proudly sports; his slouched and gaily-ribboned hat betoken his grand features. A terror to the smiling innocence of the villages through which he floats; his swart visage and bold swagger are not unshunned in cities. Once a vagabond on his own canal, I have received good turns from one of these Canallers; I thank him heartily; would fain be not ungrateful; but it is often one of the prime redeeming qualities of your man of violence, that at times he has as stiff an arm to back a poor stranger in a strait, as to plunder a wealthy one. In sum, gentlemen, what the wildness of this canal life is, is emphatically evinced by this; that our wild whale-fishery contains so many of its most finished graduates, and that scarce any race of mankind, except Sydney men, are so much distrusted by our whaling captains. Nor does it at all diminish the curiousness of this matter, that to many thousands of our rural boys and young men born along its line, the probationary life of the Grand Canal furnishes the sole transition between quietly reaping in a Christian corn-field, and recklessly ploughing the waters of the most barbaric seas."

"I see! I see!" impetuously exclaimed Don Pedro, spilling his chicha upon his silvery ruffles. "No need to travel! The world's one Lima. I had thought, now, that at your temperate North the generations were cold and holy as the hills.—But the story."

"I left off, gentlemen, where the Lakeman shook the backstay. Hardly had he done so, when he was surrounded by the three junior mates and the four harpooneers, who all crowded him to the deck. But sliding down the ropes like baleful comets, the two Canallers rushed into the uproar, and sought to drag their man out of it towards the forecastle. Others of the sailors joined with them in this attempt, and a twisted turmoil ensued; while standing out of harm's way, the valiant captain danced up and down with a whale-pike, calling upon his officers to manhandle that atrocious scoundrel, and smoke him along to the quarter-deck. At intervals, he ran close up to the revolving border of the confusion, and prying into the heart of it with his pike, sought to prick out the object of his resentment. But Steelkilt and his des-

2. Mark is the patron saint of Venice, Dominic of the Cathedral of Lima.

peradoes were too much for them all; they succeeded in gaining the forecastle deck, where, hastily slewing about three or four large casks in a line with the windlass, these sea-Parisians entrenched themselves behind the barricade.''

" 'Come out of that, ye pirates!' roared the captain, now menacing them with a pistol in each hand, just brought to him by the steward. 'Come out of that, ye cut-throats!'

"Steelkilt leaped on the barricade, and striding up and down there, defied the worst the pistols could do; but gave the captain to understand distinctly, that his (Steelkilt's) death would be the signal for a murderous mutiny on the part of all hands. Fearing in his heart lest this might prove but too true, the captain a little desisted, but still commanded the insurgents instantly to return to their duty.

" 'Will you promise not to touch us, if we do?' demanded their ringleader.

" 'Turn to! turn to!—I make no promise;—to your duty! Do you want to sink the ship, by knocking off at a time like this? Turn to!' and he once more raised a pistol.

" 'Sink the ship?' cried Steelkilt. 'Aye, let her sink. Not a man of us turns to, unless you swear not to raise a rope-yarn against us. What say ye, men?' turning to his comrades. A fierce cheer was their response.

"The Lakeman now patrolled the barricade, all the while keeping his eye on the Captain, and jerking out such sentences as these: —'It's not our fault; we didn't want it; I told him to take his hammer away; it was boys' business; he might have known me before this; I told him not to prick the buffalo; I believe I have broken a finger here against his cursed jaw; ain't those mincing knives down in the forecastle there, men? look to those handspikes, my hearties. Captain, by God, look to yourself; say the word; don't be a fool; forget it all; we are ready to turn to; treat us decently, and we're your men; but we won't be flogged.'

" 'Turn to! I make no promises, turn to, I say!'

" 'Look ye, now,' cried the Lakeman, flinging out his arm towards him, 'there are a few of us here (and I am one of them) who have shipped for the cruise, d'ye see; now as you well know, sir, we can claim our discharge as soon as the anchor is down; so we don't want a row; it's not our interest; we want to be peaceable; we are ready to work, but we won't be flogged.'

" 'Turn to!' roared the Captain.

"Steelkilt glanced round him a moment, and then said:—'I tell you what it is now, Captain, rather than kill ye, and be hung for such a shabby rascal, we won't lift a hand against ye unless ye attack us; but till you say the word about not flogging us, we don't do a hand's turn.'

" 'Down into the forecastle then, down with ye, I'll keep ye there till ye're sick of it. Down ye go.'

" 'Shall we?' cried the ringleader to his men. Most of them were against it; but at length, in obedience to Steelkilt, they preceded him down into their dark den, growlingly disappearing, like bears into a cave.

"As the Lakeman's bare head was just level with the planks, the Captain and his posse leaped the barricade, and rapidly drawing over the slide of the scuttle, planted their group of hands upon it, and loudly called for the steward to bring the heavy brass padlock belonging to the companion-way. Then opening the slide a little, the Captain whispered something down the crack, closed it, and turned the key upon them—ten in number—leaving on deck some twenty or more, who thus far had remained neutral.

"All night a wide-awake watch was kept by all the officers, forward and aft, especially about the forecastle scuttle and fore hatchway; at which last place it was feared the insurgents might emerge, after breaking through the bulkhead below. But the hours of darkness passed in peace; the men who still remained at their duty toiling hard at the pumps, whose clinking and clanking at intervals through the dreary night dismally resounded through the ship.

"At sunrise the Captain went forward, and knocking on the deck, summoned the prisoners to work; but with a yell they refused. Water was then lowered down to them, and a couple of handfuls of biscuit were tossed after it; when again turning the key upon them and pocketing it, the Captain returned to the quarter-deck. Twice every day for three days this was repeated; but on the fourth morning a confused wrangling, and then a scuffling was heard, as the customary summons was delivered; and suddenly four men burst up from the forecastle, saying they were ready to turn to. The fetid closeness of the air, and a famishing diet, united perhaps to some fears of ultimate retribution, had constrained them to surrender at discretion. Emboldened by this, the Captain reiterated his demand to the rest, but Steelkilt shouted up to him a terrific hint to stop his babbling and betake himself where he belonged. On the fifth morning three others of the mutineers bolted up into the air from the desperate arms below that sought to restrain them. Only three were left.

" 'Better turn to, now?' said the Captain with a heartless jeer.

" 'Shut us up again, will ye!' cried Steelkilt.

" 'Oh! certainly,' said the Captain, and the key clicked.

"It was at this point, gentlemen, that enraged by the defection of seven of his former associates, and stung by the mocking voice that had last hailed him, and maddened by his long entombment in a place as black as the bowels of despair; it was then that Steelkilt proposed to the two Canallers, thus far apparently of one mind with him, to burst out of their hole, at the next summoning of the garrison; and armed with their keen mincing knives (long, crescentic, heavy implements with a handle at each end) run amuck from the bowsprit to the taffrail; and if by any devilishness of desperation possible, seize the ship. For himself, he would do this, he said, whether they joined him or not. That was the last night he should spend in that den. But the scheme met with no opposition on the part of the other two; they swore they were ready for that, or for any other mad thing, for anything in short but a surrender. And what was more, they each insisted upon being the first man on deck, when the time to make the rush should come. But to this their leader as fiercely objected, reserving that priority for himself; particularly as his two comrades would not yield, the one to the other, in the matter; and both of them could not be first, for the ladder would but admit one man at a time. And here, gentlemen, the foul play of these miscreants must come out.

"Upon hearing the frantic project of their leader, each in his own separate soul had suddenly lighted, it would seem, upon the same piece of treachery, namely: to be foremost in breaking out, in order to be the first of the three, though the last of the ten, to surrender; and thereby secure whatever small chance of pardon such conduct might merit. But when Steelkilt made known his determination still to lead them to the last, they in some way, by some subtle chemistry of villany, mixed their before secret treacheries together; and when their leader fell into a doze, verbally opened their souls to each other in three sentences; and bound the sleeper with cords, and gagged him with cords; and shrieked out for the Captain at midnight.

"Thinking murder at hand, and smelling in the dark for the blood, he and all his armed mates and harpooneers rushed for the forecastle. In a few minutes the scuttle was opened, and, bound hand and foot, the still struggling ringleader was shoved up into the air by his perfidious allies, who at once claimed the honor of securing a man who had been fully ripe for murder. But all three were collared, and dragged along the deck like dead cattle; and, side by side, were seized[3] up into the mizen rigging, like three quarters of meat, and there they hung till morning. 'Damn ye,' cried the Captain, pacing to and fro before them, 'the vultures would not touch ye, ye villains!'

"At sunrise he summoned all hands; and separating those who

3. Lashed, tied.

had rebelled from those who had taken no part in the mutiny, he told the former that he had a good mind to flog them all round— thought, upon the whole, he would do so—he ought to—justice demanded it; but for the present, considering their timely surrender, he would let them go with a reprimand, which he accordingly administered in the vernacular.

" 'But as for you, ye carrion rogues,' turning to the three men in the rigging—'for you, I mean to mince ye up for the try-pots;' and, seizing a rope, he applied it with all his might to the backs of the two traitors, till they yelled no more, but lifelessly hung their heads sideways, as the two crucified thieves are drawn.

" 'My wrist is sprained with ye!' he cried, at last; 'but there is still rope enough left for you, my fine bantam, that wouldn't give up. Take that gag from his mouth, and let us hear what he can say for himself.'

"For a moment the exhausted mutineer made a tremulous motion of his cramped jaws, and then painfully twisting round his head, said in a sort of hiss, 'What I say is this—and mind it well —if you flog me, I murder you!'

" 'Say ye so? then see how ye frighten me'—and the Captain drew off with the rope to strike.

" 'Best not,' hissed the Lakeman.

" 'But I must,'—and the rope was once more drawn back for the stroke.

"Steelkilt here hissed out something, inaudible to all but the Captain; who, to the amazement of all hands, started back, paced the deck rapidly two or three times, and then suddenly throwing down his rope, said, 'I won't do it—let him go—cut him down: d'ye hear?'

"But as the junior mates were hurrying to execute the order, a pale man, with a bandaged head, arrested them—Radney the chief mate. Ever since the blow, he had lain in his berth; but that morning, hearing the tumult on the deck, he had crept out, and thus far had watched the whole scene. Such was the state of his mouth, that he could hardly speak; but mumbling something about *his* being willing and able to do what the captain dared not attempt, he snatched the rope and advanced to his pinioned foe.

" 'You are a coward!' hissed the Lakeman.

" 'So I am, but take that.' The mate was in the very act of striking, when another hiss stayed his uplifted arm. He paused: and then pausing no more, made good his word, spite of Steelkilt's threat, whatever that might have been. The three men were then cut down, all hands were turned to, and, sullenly worked by the moody seamen, the iron pumps clanged as before.

"Just after dark that day, when one watch had retired below, a clamor was heard in the forecastle; and the two trembling traitors running up, besieged the cabin door, saying they durst not consort with the crew. Entreaties, cuffs, and kicks could not drive them back, so at their own instance they were put down in the ship's run for salvation. Still, no sign of mutiny reappeared among the rest. On the contrary, it seemed, that mainly at Steelkilt's instigation, they had resolved to maintain the strictest peacefulness, obey all orders to the last, and, when the ship reached port, desert her in a body. But in order to insure the speediest end to the voyage, they all agreed to another thing—namely, not to sing out for whales, in case any should be discovered. For, spite of her leak, and spite of all her other perils, the Town-Ho still maintained her mast-heads, and her captain was just as willing to lower for a fish that moment, as on the day his craft first struck the cruising ground; and Radney the mate was quite as ready to change his berth for a boat, and with his bandaged mouth seek to gag in death the vital jaw of the whale.

"But though the Lakeman had induced the seamen to adopt this sort of passiveness in their conduct, he kept his own counsel (at least till all was over) concerning his own proper and private revenge upon the man who had stung him in the ventricles of his heart. He was in Radney the chief mate's watch; and as if the infatuated man sought to run more than half way to meet his doom, after the scene at the rigging, he insisted, against the express counsel of the captain, upon resuming the head of his watch at night. Upon this, and one or two other circumstances, Steelkilt systematically built the plan of his revenge.

"During the night, Radney had an unseamanlike way of sitting on the bulwarks of the quarter-deck, and leaning his arm upon the gunwale of the boat which was hoisted up there, a little above the ship's side. In this attitude, it was well known, he sometimes dozed. There was a considerable vacancy between the boat and the ship, and down beneath this was the sea. Steelkilt calculated his time, and found that his next trick at the helm would come round at two o'clock, in the morning of the third day from that in which he had been betrayed. At his leisure, he employed the interval in braiding something very carefully in his watches below.

" 'What are you making there?' said a shipmate.

" 'What do you think? what does it look like?'

" 'Like a lanyard for your bag; but it's an odd one, seems to me.'

" 'Yes, rather oddish,' said the Lakeman, holding it at arm's length before him; 'but I think it will answer. Shipmate, I haven't enough twine,—have you any?'

"But there was none in the forecastle.

" 'Then I must get some from old Rad;' and he rose to go aft.

" 'You don't mean to go a begging to *him!*' said a sailor.

" 'Why not? Do you think he won't do me a turn, when it's to help himself in the end, shipmate?' and going to the mate, he looked at him quietly, and asked him for some twine to mend his hammock. It was given him—neither twine nor lanyard were seen again; but the next night an iron ball, closely netted, partly rolled from the pocket of the Lakeman's monkey jacket, as he was tucking the coat into his hammock for a pillow. Twenty-four hours after, his trick at the silent helm—nigh to the man who was apt to doze over the grave always ready dug to the seaman's hand—that fatal hour was then to come; and in the fore-ordaining soul of Steel-kilt, the mate was already stark and stretched as a corpse, with his forehead crushed in.

"But, gentlemen, a fool saved the would-be murderer from the bloody deed he had planned. Yet complete revenge he had, and without being the avenger. For by a mysterious fatality, Heaven itself seemed to step in to take out of his hands into its own the damning thing he would have done.

"It was just between daybreak and sunrise of the morning of the second day, when they were washing down the decks, that a stupid Teneriffe man, drawing water in the main-chains, all at once shouted out, 'There she rolls! there she rolls! Jesu! what a whale!' It was Moby Dick."

"Moby Dick!" cried Don Sebastian; "St. Dominic! Sir sailor, but do whales have christenings? Whom call you Moby Dick?"

"A very white, and famous, and most deadly immortal monster, Don;—but that would be too long a story."

"How? how?" cried all the young Spaniards, crowding.

"Nay, Dons, Dons—nay, nay! I cannot rehearse that now. Let me get more into the air, Sirs."

"The chicha! the chicha!" cried Don Pedro; "our vigorous friend looks faint;—fill up his empty glass!"

"No need, gentlemen; one moment, and I proceed.—Now, gentlemen, so suddenly perceiving the snowy whale within fifty yards of the ship—forgetful of the compact among the crew—in the excitement of the moment, the Teneriffe man had instinctively and involuntarily lifted his voice for the monster, though for some little time past it had been plainly beheld from the three sullen mast-heads. All was now a phrensy. 'The White Whale—the White Whale!' was the cry from captain, mates, and harpooneers, who, undeterred by fearful rumors, were all anxious to capture so famous and precious a fish; while the dogged crew eyed askance, and with curses, the appalling beauty of the vast milky mass, that lit up by a horizontal spangling sun, shifted and glistened like a living opal in the blue morning sea. Gentlemen, a strange fatality pervades the whole career of these events, as if verily mapped out before the world itself was charted. The mutineer was the bowsman of the mate, and when fast to a fish, it was his duty to sit next him, while Radney stood up with his lance in the prow, and haul in or slacken the line, at the word of command. Moreover, when the four boats were lowered, the mate's got the start; and none howled more fiercely with delight than did Steelkilt, as he strained at his oar. After a stiff pull, their harpooneer got fast, and, spear in hand, Radney sprang to the bow. He was always a furious man, it seems, in a boat. And now his bandaged cry was, to beach him on the whale's topmost back. Nothing loath, his bowsman hauled him up and up, through a blinding foam that blent two whitenesses together; till of a sudden the boat struck as against a sunken ledge, and keeling over, spilled out the standing mate. That instant, as he fell on the whale's slippery back, the boat righted, and was dashed aside by the swell, while Radney was tossed over into the sea, on the other flank of the whale. He struck out through the spray, and, for an instant, was dimly seen through that veil, wildly seeking to remove himself from the eye of Moby Dick. But the whale rushed round in a sudden maelstrom; seized the swimmer between his jaws; and rearing high up with him, plunged headlong again, and went down.

"Meantime, at the first tap of the boat's bottom, the Lakeman had slackened the line, so as to drop astern from the whirlpool; calmly looking on, he thought his own thoughts. But a sudden, terrific, downward jerking of the boat, quickly brought his knife to the line. He cut it; and the whale was free. But, at some distance, Moby Dick rose again, with some tatters of Radney's red woollen shirt, caught in the teeth that had destroyed him. All four boats gave chase again; but the whale eluded them, and finally wholly disappeared.

"In good time, the Town-Ho reached her port—a savage, solitary place—where no civilized creature resided. There, headed by the Lakeman, all but five or six of the foremast-men deliberately deserted among the palms; eventually, as it turned out, seizing a large double war-canoe of the savages, and setting sail for some other harbor.

"The ship's company being reduced to but a handful, the captain called upon the Islanders to assist him in the laborious business of heaving down the ship to stop the leak. But to such unresting vigilance over their dangerous allies was this small band of whites necessitated, both by night and by day, and so extreme was the hard work they underwent, that upon the vessel being ready again for sea, they were in such a weakened condition that the captain durst not put off with them in so heavy a vessel. After taking counsel with his officers, he anchored the ship as far off shore as possible; loaded and ran out his two cannon from the bows; stacked his muskets on the poop; and warning the Islanders not to approach the ship at their peril, took one man with him, and setting the sail of his best whaleboat, steered straight before the wind for Tahiti, five hundred miles distant, to procure a reinforcement to his crew.

"On the fourth day of the sail, a large canoe was descried, which seemed to have touched at a low isle of corals. He steered away from it; but the savage craft bore down on him; and soon the voice of Steelkilt hailed him to heave to, or he would run him under water. The captain presented a pistol. With one foot on each prow of the yoked war-canoes, the Lakeman laughed him to scorn; assuring him that if the pistol so much as clicked in the lock, he would bury him in bubbles and foam.

" 'What do you want of me?' cried the captain.

" 'Where are you bound? and for what are you bound?' demanded Steelkilt; 'no lies.'

" 'I am bound to Tahiti for more men.'

" 'Very good. Let me board you a moment—I come in peace.' With that he leaped from the canoe, swam to the boat; and climbing the gunwale, stood face to face with the captain.

" 'Cross your arms, sir; throw back your head. Now, repeat after me. "As soon as Steelkilt leaves me, I swear to beach this boat on yonder island, and remain there six days. If I do not, may lightnings strike me!" '

" 'A pretty scholar,' laughed the Lakeman. 'Adios, Senor!' and leaping into the sea, he swam back to his comrades.

"Watching the boat till it was fairly beached, and drawn up to the roots of the cocoa-nut trees, Steelkilt made sail again, and in due time arrived at Tahiti, his own place of destination. There, luck befriended him; two ships were about to sail for France, and were providentially in want of precisely that number of men which the sailor headed. They embarked; and so for ever got the start of their former captain, had he been at all minded to work them legal retribution.

"Some ten days after the French ships sailed, the whale-boat arrived, and the captain was forced to enlist some of the more civilized Tahitians, who had been somewhat used to the sea. Chartering a small native schooner, he returned with them to his vessel; and finding all right there, again resumed his cruisings.

"Where Steelkilt now is, gentlemen, none know; but upon the island of Nantucket, the widow of Radney still turns to the sea which refuses to give up its dead; still in dreams sees the awful white whale that destroyed him." * * * * *

"Are you through?" said Don Sebastian, quietly.

"I am, Don."

"Then I entreat you, tell me if to the best of your own convictions, this your story is in substance really true? It is so passing wonderful! Did you get it from an unquestionable source? Bear with me if I seem to press."

"Also bear with all of us, sir sailor; for we all join in Don Sebastian's suit," cried the company, with exceeding interest.

"Is there a copy of the Holy Evangelists [4] in the Golden Inn, gentlemen?"

"Nay," said Don Sebastian; "but I know a worthy priest near by, who will quickly procure one for me. I go for it; but are you well advised? this may grow too serious."

"Will you be so good as to bring the priest also, Don?"

"Though there are no Auto-da-Fés[5] in Lima now," said one of the company to another; "I fear our sailor friend runs risk of the archiepiscopacy. Let us withdraw more out of the moonlight. I see no need of this."

"Excuse me for running after you, Don Sebastian; but may I also beg that you will be particular in procuring the largest sized Evangelists you can."

* * * * * *

"This is the priest, he brings you the Evangelists," said Don Sebastian, gravely, returning with a tall and solemn figure.

"Let me remove my hat. Now, venerable priest, further into the light, and hold the Holy Book before me that I may touch it."

"So help me Heaven, and on my honor, the story I have told ye, gentlemen, is in substance and its great items, true. I know it to be true; it happened on this ball; I trod the ship; I knew the crew; I have seen and talked with Steelkilt since the death of Radney."

Chapter 55

OF THE MONSTROUS PICTURES OF WHALES [1]

I shall ere long paint to you as well as one can without canvas, something like the true form of the whale as he actually appears to the eye of the whaleman when in his own absolute body the whale is moored alongside the whale-ship so that he can be fairly stepped

4. The four Gospels.
5. The ceremonies in which the Inquisition pronounced judgment upon heretics prior to burning them.

1. Suggested by one of Sir Thomas Browne's titles. See Mansfield-Vincent, p. 746.

upon there. It may be worth while, therefore, previously to advert to those curious imaginary portraits of him which even down to the present day confidently challenge the faith of the landsman. It is time to set the world right in this matter, by proving such pictures of the whale all wrong.

It may be that the primal source of all those pictorial delusions will be found among the oldest Hindoo, Egyptian, and Grecian sculptures. For ever since those inventive but unscrupulous times when on the marble panellings of temples, the pedestals of statues, and on shields, medallions, cups, and coins, the dolphin was drawn in scales of chain-armor like Saladin's, and a helmeted head like St. George's; ever since then has something of the same sort of license prevailed, not only in most popular pictures of the whale, but in many scientific presentations of him.

Now, by all odds, the most ancient extant portrait anyways purporting to be the whale's, is to be found in the famous cavern-pagoda of Elephanta, in India. The Brahmins maintain that in the almost endless sculptures of that immemorial pagoda, all the trades and pursuits, every conceivable avocation of man, were pre-figured ages before any of them actually came into being. No wonder then, that in some sort our noble profession of whaling should have been there shadowed forth. The Hindoo whale re-ferred to, occurs in a separate department of the wall, depicting the incarnation of Vishnu in the form of leviathan, learnedly known as the Matse 'Avatar. But though this sculpture is half man and half whale, so as only to give the tail of the latter, yet that small section of him is all wrong. It looks more like the tapering tail of an anaconda, than the broad palms of the true whale's majestic flukes.

But go to the old Galleries, and look now at a great Christian painter's portrait of this fish; for he succeeds no better than the antediluvian Hindoo. It is Guido's picture of Perseus rescuing Andromeda from the sea-monster or whale. Where did Guido get the model of such a strange creature as that? Nor does Hogarth, in painting the same scene in his own "Perseus Descending," make out one whit better. The huge corpulence of that Hogarthian monster undulates on the surface, scarcely drawing one inch of water. It has a sort of howdah on its back, and its distended tusked mouth into which the billows are rolling, might be taken for the Traitors' Gate leading from the Thames by water into the Tower. Then, there are the Prodromus whales of old Scotch Sibbald, and Jonah's whale, as depicted in the prints of old Bibles and the cuts of old primers. What shall be said of these? As for the book-binder's whale winding like a vine-stalk round the stock of a descending anchor—as stamped and gilded on the backs and title-pages of many books both old and new—that is a very picturesque but purely fabulous creature, imitated, I take it, from the like figures on antique vases. Though universally denominated a dolphin, I nevertheless call this book-binder's fish an attempt at a whale; because it was so intended when the device was first introduced. It was introduced by an old Italian publisher somewhere about the 15th century, during the Revival of Learning; and in those days, and even down to a comparatively late period, dolphins were popularly supposed to be a species of the Leviathan.

In the vignettes and other embellishments of some ancient books you will at times meet with very curious touches at the whale, where all manner of spouts, jets d'eau, hot springs and cold, Saratoga and Baden-Baden, come bubbling up from his unexhausted brain. In the title-page of the original edition of the "Advancement of Learning" you will find some curious whales.

But quitting all these unprofessional attempts, let us glance at those pictures of leviathan purporting to be sober, scientific delineations, by those who know. In old Harris's collection of voyages there are some plates of whales extracted from a Dutch book of voyages, A. D. 1671, entitled "A Whaling Voyage to Spitzbergen in the ship Jonas in the Whale, Peter Peterson of Friesland, master." In one of those plates the whales, like great rafts of logs, are represented lying among ice-isles, with white bears running over their living backs. In another plate, the prodigious blunder is made of representing the whale with perpendicular flukes.

Then again, there is an imposing quarto, written by one Captain Colnett, a Post Captain in the English navy, entitled "A Voyage round Cape Horn into the South Seas, for the purpose of extending the Spermaceti Whale Fisheries." In this book is an outline purporting to be a "Picture of a Physeter or Spermaceti whale, drawn by scale from one killed on the coast of Mexico, August, 1793, and hoisted on deck." I doubt not the captain had this veracious picture taken for the benefit of his marines.[2] To mention but one thing about it, let me say that it has an eye which applied, according to the accompanying scale, to a full grown sperm whale, would make the eye of that whale a bow-window some five feet long. Ah, my gallant captain, why did ye not give us Jonah looking out of that eye!

Nor are the most conscientious compilations of Natural History for the benefit of the young and tender, free from the same heinousness of mistake. Look at that popular work "Goldsmith's Animated Nature." In the abridged London edition of 1807,

2. Marines (the soldiers on shipboard) were regarded by sailors as credulous in maritime matters (cf. "Tell it to the Marines").

there are plates of an alleged "whale" and a "narwhale." I do not wish to seem inelegant, but this unsightly whale looks much like an amputated sow; and, as for the narwhale, one glimpse at it is enough to amaze one, that in this nineteenth century such a hippogriff could be palmed for genuine upon any intelligent public of schoolboys.

Then, again, in 1825, Bernard Germain, Count de Lacépède,[3] a great naturalist, published a scientific systemized whale book, wherein are several pictures of the different species of the Leviathan. All these are not only incorrect, but the picture of the Mysticetus or Greenland whale (that is to say, the Right whale), even Scoresby, a long experienced man as touching that species, declares not to have its counterpart in nature.

But the placing of the cap-sheaf to all this blundering business was reserved for the scientific Frederick Cuvier, brother to the famous Baron. In 1836, he published a Natural History of Whales, in which he gives what he calls a picture of the Sperm Whale. Before showing that picture to any Nantucketer, you had best provide for your summary retreat from Nantucket. In a word, Frederick Cuvier's Sperm Whale is not a Sperm Whale, but a squash. Of course, he never had the benefit of a whaling voyage (such men seldom have), but whence he derived that picture, who can tell? Perhaps he got it as his scientific predecessor in the same field, Desmarest, got one of his authentic abortions; that is, from a Chinese drawing. And what sort of lively lads with the pencil those Chinese are, many queer cups and saucers inform us.

As for the sign-painters' whales seen in the streets hanging over the shops of oil-dealers, what shall be said of them? They are generally Richard III. whales, with dromedary humps, and very savage; breakfasting on three or four sailor tarts, that is whaleboats full of mariners: their deformities floundering in seas of blood and blue paint.

But these manifold mistakes in depicting the whale are not so very surprising after all. Consider! Most of the scientific drawings have been taken from the stranded fish; and these are about as correct as a drawing of a wrecked ship, with broken back, would correctly represent the noble animal itself in all its undashed pride of hull and spars. Though elephants have stood for their full-lengths, the living Leviathan has never yet fairly floated himself for his portrait. The living whale, in his full majesty and significance, is only to be seen at sea in unfathomable waters; and afloat the vast bulk of him is out of sight, like a launched line-of-battle

3. Mansfield and Vincent point out that in this paragraph and the next one the references to Lacépède, Frederick Cuvier, and Desmarest are second hand, mainly from Beale.

ship; and out of that element it is a thing eternally impossible for mortal man to hoist him bodily into the air, so as to preserve all his mighty swells and undulations. And, not to speak of the highly presumable difference of contour between a young sucking whale and a full-grown Platonian Leviathan; yet, even in the case of one of those young sucking whales hoisted to a ship's deck, such is then the outlandish, eel-like, limbered, varying shape of him, that his precise expression the devil himself could not catch.

But it may be fancied, that from the naked skeleton of the stranded whale, accurate hints may be derived touching his true form. Not at all. For it is one of the more curious things about this Leviathan, that his skeleton gives very little idea of his general shape. Though Jeremy Bentham's skeleton, which hangs for candelabra in the library of one of his executors, correctly conveys the idea of a burly-browed utilitarian old gentleman, with all Jeremy's other leading personal characteristics; yet nothing of this kind could be inferred from any leviathan's articulated bones. In fact, as the great Hunter says,[4] the mere skeleton of the whale bears the same relation to the fully invested and padded animal as the insect does to the chrysalis that so roundingly envelopes it. This peculiarity is strikingly evinced in the head, as in some part of this book will be incidentally shown. It is also very curiously displayed in the side fin, the bones of which almost exactly answer to the bones of the human hand, minus only the thumb. This fin has four regular bone-fingers, the index, middle, ring, and little finger. But all these are permanently lodged in their fleshy covering, as the human fingers in an artificial covering. "However recklessly the whale may sometimes serve us," said humorous Stubb one day, "he can never be truly said to handle us without mittens."

For all these reasons, then, any way you may look at it, you must needs conclude that the great Leviathan is that one creature in the world which must remain unpainted to the last. True, one portrait may hit the mark much nearer than another, but none can hit it with any very considerable degree of exactness. So there is no earthly way of finding out precisely what the whale really looks like. And the only mode in which you can derive even a tolerable idea of his living contour, is by going a whaling yourself; but by so doing, you run no small risk of being eternally stove and sunk by him. Wherefore, it seems to me you had best not be too fastidious in your curiosity touching this Leviathan.

---

4. Mansfield and Vincent show that despite Melville's air of familiarity, he had read Hunter only as quoted in Beale.

Chapter 56

OF THE LESS ERRONEOUS PICTURES OF WHALES, AND THE TRUE PICTURES OF WHALING SCENES

In connexion with the monstrous pictures of whales, I am strongly tempted here to enter upon those still more monstrous stories of them which are to be found in certain books, both ancient and modern, especially in Pliny, Purchas, Hackluyt, Harris, Cuvier, &c. But I pass that matter by.

I know of only four published outlines of the great Sperm Whale; Colnett's, Huggins's, Frederick Cuvier's, and Beale's. In the previous chapter Colnett and Cuvier have been referred to. Huggins's is far better than theirs; but, by great odds, Beale's is the best. All Beale's drawings of this whale are good, excepting the middle figure in the picture of three whales in various attitudes, capping his second chapter. His frontispiece, boats attacking Sperm Whales, though no doubt calculated to excite the civil scepticism of some parlor men, is admirably correct and life-like in its general effect. Some of the Sperm Whale drawings in J. Ross Browne are pretty correct in contour; but they are wretchedly engraved. That is not his fault though.

Of the Right Whale, the best outline pictures are in Scoresby; but they are drawn on too small a scale to convey a desirable impression. He has but one picture of whaling scenes, and this is a sad deficiency, because it is by such pictures only, when at all well done, that you can derive anything like a truthful idea of the living whale as seen by his living hunters.

But, taken for all in all, by far the finest, though in some details not the most correct, presentations of whales and whaling scenes to be anywhere found, are two large French engravings, well executed, and taken from paintings by one Garneray. Respectively, they represent attacks on the Sperm and Right Whale. In the first engraving a noble Sperm Whale is depicted in full majesty of might, just risen beneath the boat from the profundities of the ocean, and bearing high in the air upon his back the terrific wreck of the stoven planks. The prow of the boat is partially unbroken, and is drawn just balancing upon the monster's spine; and standing in that prow, for that one single incomputable flash of time, you behold an oarsman, half shrouded by the incensed boiling spout of the whale, and in the act of leaping, as if from a precipice. The action of the whole thing is wonderfully good and true. The half-emptied line-tub floats on the whitened sea; the wooden poles of the spilled harpoons obliquely bob in it; the heads of the swimming crew are scattered about the whale in contrasting expressions of affright; while in the black stormy distance the ship is bearing down upon the scene. Serious fault might be found with the anatomical details of this whale, but let that pass; since, for the life of me, I could not draw so good a one.

In the second engraving, the boat is in the act of drawing alongside the barnacled flank of a large running Right Whale, that rolls his black weedy bulk in the sea like some mossy rock-slide from the Patagonian cliffs. His jets are erect, full, and black like soot; so that from so abounding a smoke in the chimney, you would think there must be a brave supper cooking in the great bowels below. Sea fowls are pecking at the small crabs, shell-fish, and other sea candies and maccaroni, which the Right Whale sometimes carries on his pestilent back. And all the while the thick-lipped leviathan is rushing through the deep, leaving tons of tumultuous white curds in his wake, and causing the slight boat to rock in the swells like a skiff caught nigh the paddle-wheels of an ocean steamer. Thus, the fore-ground is all raging commotion; but behind, in admirable artistic contrast, is the glassy level of a sea becalmed, the drooping unstarched sails of the powerless ship, and the inert mass of a dead whale, a conquered fortress, with the flag of capture lazily hanging from the whale-pole inserted into his spout-hole.

Who Garneray the painter is, or was, I know not. But my life for it he was either practically conversant with his subject, or else marvellously tutored by some experienced whaleman. The French are the lads for painting action. Go and gaze upon all the paintings of Europe, and where will you find such a gallery of living and breathing commotion on canvas, as in that triumphal hall at Versailles; where the beholder fights his way, pell-mell, through the consecutive great battles of France; where every sword seems a flash of the Northern Lights, and the successive armed kings and Emperors dash by, like a charge of crowned centaurs? Not wholly unworthy of a place in that gallery, are these sea battle-pieces of Garneray.

The natural aptitude of the French for seizing the picturesqueness of things seems to be peculiarly evinced in what paintings and engravings they have of their whaling scenes. With not one tenth of England's experience in the fishery, and not the thousandth part of that of the Americans, they have nevertheless furnished both nations with the only finished sketches at all capable of conveying the real spirit of the whale hunt. For the most part, the English and American whale draughtsmen seem entirely content with presenting the mechanical outline of things, such as the vacant profile of the whale; which, so far as picturesqueness of effect is concerned, is about tantamount to sketching the profile of a pyramid. Even Scoresby, the justly renowned Right whaleman, after giving us a stiff full length of the Greenland whale, and three or four delicate miniatures of narwhales and porpoises, treats us to a series of classical engravings of boat hooks, chopping knives, and grapnels; and with the microscopic diligence of a Leuwenhoek submits to the inspection of a shivering world ninety-six fac-similes of magnified Arctic snow crystals. I mean no disparagement to the excellent voyager (I honor him for a veteran), but in so important a matter it was certainly an oversight not to have procured for every crystal a sworn affidavit taken before a Greenland Justice of the Peace.

In addition to those fine engravings from Garneray, there are two other French engravings worthy of note, by some one who subscribes himself "H. Durand." One of them, though not precisely adapted to our present purpose, nevertheless deserves mention on other accounts. It is a quiet noon-scene among the isles of the Pacific; a French whaler anchored, inshore, in a calm, and lazily taking water on board; the loosened sails of the ship, and the long leaves of the palms in the background, both drooping together in the breezeless air. The effect is very fine, when considered with reference to its presenting the hardy fishermen under one of their few aspects of oriental repose. The other engraving is quite a different affair: the ship hove-to upon the open sea, and in the very heart of the Leviathanic life, with a Right Whale alongside; the vessel (in the act of cutting-in) hove over to the monster as if to a quay; and a boat, hurriedly pushing off from this scene of activity, is about giving chase to whales in the distance. The harpoons and lances lie levelled for use; three oarsmen are just setting the mast in its hole; while from a sudden roll of the sea, the little craft stands half-erect out of the water, like a rearing horse. From the ship, the smoke of the torments of the boiling whale is going up like the smoke over a village of smithies; and to windward, a black cloud, rising up with earnest of squalls and rains, seems to quicken the activity of the excited seamen.

Chapter 57

OF WHALES IN PAINT; IN TEETH; IN WOOD; IN SHEET-IRON; IN STONE; IN MOUNTAINS; IN STARS

On Tower-hill, as you go down to the London docks, you may have seen a crippled beggar (or *kedger*, as the sailors say) holding a painted board before him, representing the tragic scene in which he lost his leg. There are three whales and three boats; and one of the boats (presumed to contain the missing leg in all its original integrity) is being crunched by the jaws of the foremost whale. Any time these ten years, they tell me, has that man held up that picture, and exhibited that stump to an incredulous world. But the time of his justification has now come. His three whales are as good whales as were ever published in Wapping, at any rate; and his stump as unquestionable a stump as any you will find in the western clearings. But, though for ever mounted on that stump, never a stump-speech does the poor whaleman make; but, with downcast eyes, stands ruefully contemplating his own amputation.

Throughout the Pacific, and also in Nantucket, and New Bedford, and Sag Harbor, you will come across lively sketches of whales and whaling-scenes, graven by the fishermen themselves on Sperm Whale-teeth, or ladies' busks wrought out of the Right Whale-bone, and other like skrimshander articles, as the whalemen call the numerous little ingenious contrivances they elaborrately carve out of the rough material, in their hours of ocean leisure. Some of them have little boxes of dentistical-looking implements, specially intended for the skrimshandering business. But, in general, they toil with their jack-knives alone; and, with that almost omnipotent tool of the sailor, they will turn you out anything you please, in the way of a mariner's fancy.

Long exile from Christendom and civilization inevitably restores a man to that condition in which God placed him, *i.e.* what is called savagery. Your true whale-hunter is as much a savage as an Iroquois. I myself am a savage, owning no allegiance but to the King of the Cannibals; and ready at any moment to rebel against him.

Now, one of the peculiar characteristics of the savage in his domestic hours, is his wonderful patience of industry. An ancient Hawaiian war-club or spear-paddle, in its full multiplicity and elaboration of carving, is as great a trophy of human perseverance as a Latin lexicon. For, with but a bit of broken sea-shell or a shark's tooth, that miraculous intricacy of wooden net-work has been achieved; and it has cost steady years of steady application.

As with the Hawaiian savage, so with the white sailor-savage. With the same marvellous patience, and with the same single shark's tooth, of his one poor jack-knife, he will carve you a bit of bone sculpture, not quite as workmanlike, but as close packed in its maziness of design, as the Greek savage, Achilles's shield; and full of barbaric spirit and suggestiveness, as the prints of that fine old German savage, Albert Dürer.

Wooden whales, or whales cut in profile out of the small dark slabs of the noble South Sea war-wood, are frequently met with in the forecastles of American whalers. Some of them are done with much accuracy.

At some old gable-roofed country houses you will see brass whales hung by the tail for knockers to the road-side door. When the porter is sleepy, the anvil-headed whale would be best. But these knocking whales are seldom remarkable as faithful essays. On the spires of some old-fashioned churches you will see sheet-iron whales placed there for weather-cocks; but they are so elevated, and besides that are to all intents and purposes so labelled with *"Hands off!"* you cannot examine them closely enough to decide upon their merit.

In bony, ribby regions of the earth, where at the base of high broken cliffs masses of rock lie strewn in fantastic groupings upon the plain, you will often discover images as of the petrified forms of the Leviathan partly merged in grass, which of a windy day breaks against them in a surf of green surges.

Then, again, in mountainous countries where the traveller is continually girdled by amphitheatrical heights; here and there from some lucky point of view you will catch passing glimpses of the profiles of whales defined along the undulating ridges. But you must be a thorough whaleman, to see these sights; and not only that, but if you wish to return to such a sight again, you must be sure and take the exact intersecting latitude and longitude of your first stand-point, else—so chance-like are such observations of the hills—your precise, previous stand-point would require a laborious re-discovery; like the Solomon islands, which still remain incognita, though once high-ruffed Mendaña trod them and old Figueroa chronicled them.

Nor when expandingly lifted by your subject, can you fail to trace out great whales in the starry heavens, and boats in pursuit of them; as when long filled with thoughts of war the Eastern nations saw armies locked in battle among the clouds. Thus at the North have I chased Leviathan round and round the Pole with the revolutions of the bright points that first defined him to me. And beneath the effulgent Antarctic skies I have boarded the Argo-Navis, and joined the chase against the starry Cetus far beyond the utmost stretch of Hydrus and the Flying Fish.

With a frigate's anchors for my bridle-bits and fasces of harpoons for spurs, would I could mount that whale and leap the topmost skies, to see whether the fabled heavens with all their countless tents really lie encamped beyond my mortal sight!

Chapter 58

BRIT

Steering north-eastward from the Crozets, we fell in with vast meadows of brit,[1] the minute, yellow substance, upon which the Right Whale largely feeds. For leagues and leagues it undulated round us, so that we seemed to be sailing through boundless fields of ripe and golden wheat.

On the second day, numbers of Right Whales were seen, who, secure from the attack of a Sperm Whaler like the Pequod, with open jaws sluggishly swam through the brit, which, adhering to the fringing fibres of that wondrous Venetian blind in their mouths, was in that manner separated from the water that escaped at the lip.

As morning mowers, who side by side slowly and seethingly advance their scythes through the long wet grass of marshy meads; even so these monsters swam, making a strange, grassy, cutting sound; and leaving behind them endless swaths of blue upon the yellow sea.*

But it was only the sound they made as they parted the brit which at all reminded one of mowers. Seen from the mast-heads, especially when they paused and were stationary for a while, their vast black forms looked more like lifeless masses of rock than anything else. And as in the great hunting countries of India, the stranger at a distance will sometimes pass on the plains recumbent elephants without knowing them to be such, taking them for bare, blackened elevations of the soil; even so, often, with him, who for the first time beholds this species of the leviathans of the sea. And even when recognised at last, their immense magnitude renders it very hard really to believe that such bulky masses of overgrowth can possibly be instinct, in all parts, with the same sort of life that lives in a dog or a horse.

Indeed, in other respects, you can hardly regard any creatures of the deep with the same feelings that you do those of the shore. For though some old naturalists have maintained that all creatures of the land are of their kind[2] in the sea; and though taking a broad general view of the thing, this may very well be; yet coming to specialities, where, for example, does the ocean furnish any fish that in disposition answers to the sagacious kindness of the

1. This "minute, yellow substance" is most likely composed of tiny crustaceans.
* That part of the sea known among whalemen as the "Brazil Banks" does not bear that name as the Banks of Newfoundland do, because of there being shallows and soundings there, but because of this remarkable meadow-like appearance, caused by the vast drifts of brit continually floating in those latitudes, where the Right Whale is often chased [Melville's note].
2. Have their counterparts.

dog? The accursed shark alone can in any generic respect be said to bear comparative analogy to him.

But though, to landsmen in general, the native inhabitants of the seas have ever been regarded with emotions unspeakably unsocial and repelling; though we know the sea to be an everlasting terra incognita, so that Columbus sailed over numberless unknown worlds to discover his one superficial western one; though, by vast odds, the most terrific of all mortal disasters have immemorially and indiscriminately befallen tens and hundreds of thousands of those who have gone upon the waters; though but a moment's consideration will teach, that however baby man may brag of his science and skill, and however much, in a flattering future, that science and skill may augment; yet for ever and for ever, to the crack of doom, the sea will insult and murder him, and pulverize the stateliest, stiffest frigate he can make; nevertheless, by the continual repetition of these very impressions, man has lost that sense of the full awfulness of the sea which aboriginally belongs to it.

The first boat we read of, floated on an ocean, that with Portuguese vengeance had whelmed a whole world without leaving so much as a widow. That same ocean rolls now; that same ocean destroyed the wrecked ships of last year. Yea, foolish mortals, Noah's flood is not yet subsided; two thirds of the fair world it yet covers.

Wherein differ the sea and the land, that a miracle upon one is not a miracle upon the other? Preternatural terrors rested upon the Hebrews, when under the feet of Korah and his company the live ground opened and swallowed them up for ever; yet not a modern sun ever sets, but in precisely the same manner the live sea swallows up ships and crews.

But not only is the sea such a foe to man who is an alien to it, but it is also a fiend to its own offspring; worse than the Persian host who murdered his own guests; sparing not the creatures which itself hath spawned. Like a savage tigress that tossing in the jungle overlays her own cubs, so the sea dashes even the mightiest whales against the rocks, and leaves them there side by side with the split wrecks of ships. No mercy, no power but its own controls it. Panting and snorting like a mad battle steed that has lost its rider, the masterless ocean overruns the globe.

Consider the subtleness of the sea; how its most dreaded creatures glide under water, unapparent for the most part, and treacherously hidden beneath the loveliest tints of azure. Consider also the devilish brilliance and beauty of many of its most remorseless tribes, as the dainty embellished shape of many species of sharks. Consider, once more, the universal cannibalism of the sea; all whose creatures prey upon each other, carrying on eternal war since the world began.

Consider all this; and then turn to this green, gentle, and most docile earth; consider them both, the sea and the land; and do you not find a strange analogy to something in yourself? For as this appalling ocean surrounds the verdant land, so in the soul of man there lies one insular Tahiti, full of peace and joy, but encompassed by all the horrors of the half known life. God keep thee! Push not off from that isle, thou canst never return!

Chapter 59

SQUID

Slowly wading through the meadows of brit, the Pequod still held on her way north-eastward towards the island of Java; a gentle air impelling her keel, so that in the surrounding serenity her three tall tapering masts mildly waved to that languid breeze, as three mild palms on a plain. And still, at wide intervals in the silvery night, the lonely, alluring jet would be seen.

But one transparent blue morning, when a stillness almost preternatural spread over the sea, however unattended with any stagnant calm; when the long burnished sun-glade on the waters seemed a golden finger laid across them, enjoining some secresy; when the slippered waves whispered together as they softly ran on; in this profound hush of the visible sphere a strange spectre was seen by Daggoo from the main-mast-head.

In the distance, a great white mass lazily rose, and rising higher and higher, and disentangling itself from the azure, at last gleamed before our prow like a snow-slide, new slid from the hills. Thus glistening for a moment, as slowly it subsided,[1] and sank. Then once more arose, and silently gleamed. It seemed not a whale; and yet is this Moby Dick? thought Daggoo. Again the phantom went down, but on re-appearing once more, with a stiletto-like cry that startled every man from his nod, the negro yelled out—"There! there again! there she breaches! right ahead! The White Whale, the White Whale!"

Upon this, the seamen rushed to the yard-arms, as in swarming-time the bees rush to the boughs. Bare-headed in the sultry sun, Ahab stood on the bowsprit, and with one hand pushed far behind in readiness to wave his orders to the helmsman, cast his eager glance in the direction indicated aloft by the outstretched motionless arm of Daggoo.

Whether the flitting attendance of the one still and solitary jet had gradually worked upon Ahab, so that he was now prepared to

1. That is, it subsided as slowly as it had risen.

connect the ideas of mildness and repose with the first sight of the particular whale he pursued; or whether his eagerness betrayed him; whichever way it might have been, no sooner did he distinctly perceive the white mass, than with a quick intensity he instantly gave orders for lowering.

The four boats were soon on the water; Ahab's in advance, and all swiftly pulling towards their prey. Soon it went down, and while, with oars suspended, we were awaiting its reappearance, lo! in the same spot where it sank, once more it slowly rose. Almost forgetting for the moment all thoughts of Moby Dick, we now gazed at the most wondrous phenomenon which the secret seas have hitherto revealed to mankind. A vast pulpy mass, furlongs in length and breadth, of a glancing cream-color, lay floating on the water, innumerable long arms radiating from its centre, and curling and twisting like a nest of anacondas, as if blindly to clutch at any hapless object within reach. No perceptible face or front did it have; no conceivable token of either sensation or instinct; but undulated there on the billows, an unearthly, formless, chance-like apparition of life.

As with a low sucking sound it slowly disappeared again, Starbuck still gazing at the agitated waters where it had sunk, with a wild voice exclaimed—"Almost rather had I seen Moby Dick and fought him, than to have seen thee, thou white ghost!"

"What was it, Sir?" said Flask.

"The great live squid, which, they say, few whale-ships ever beheld, and returned to their ports to tell of it."

But Ahab said nothing; turning his boat, he sailed back to the vessel; the rest as silently following.

Whatever superstitions the sperm whalemen in general have connected with the sight of this object, certain it is, that a glimpse of it being so very unusual, that circumstance has gone far to invest it with portentousness. So rarely is it beheld, that though one and all of them declare it to be the largest animated thing in the ocean, yet very few of them have any but the most vague ideas concerning its true nature and form; notwithstanding, they believe it to furnish to the sperm whale his only food. For though other species of whales find their food above water, and may be seen by man in the act of feeding, the spermaceti whale obtains his whole food in unknown zones below the surface; and only by inference is it that any one can tell of what, precisely, that food consists. At times, when closely pursued, he will disgorge what are supposed to be the detached arms of the squid; some of them thus exhibited exceeding twenty and thirty feet in length. They fancy that the monster to which these arms belonged ordinarily clings by them to the bed of the ocean;

and that the sperm whale, unlike other species, is supplied with teeth in order to attack and tear it.

There seems some ground to imagine that the great Kraken of Bishop Pontoppidan may ultimately resolve itself into Squid. The manner in which the Bishop describes it, as alternately rising and sinking, with some other particulars he narrates, in all this the two correspond. But much abatement is necessary with respect to the incredible bulk he assigns it.

By some naturalists who have vaguely heard rumors of the mysterious creature, here spoken of, it is included among the class of cuttle-fish, to which, indeed, in certain external respects it would seem to belong, but only as the Anak of the tribe.[2]

Chapter 60

THE LINE

With reference to the whaling scene shortly to be described, as well as for the better understanding of all similar scenes elsewhere presented, I have here to speak of the magical, sometimes horrible whale-line.

The line originally used in the fishery was of the best hemp, slightly vapored with tar, not impregnated with it, as in the case of ordinary ropes; for while tar, as ordinarily used, makes the hemp more pliable to the rope-maker, and also renders the rope itself more convenient to the sailor for common ship use; yet, not only would the ordinary quantity too much stiffen the whale-line for the close coiling to which it must be subjected; but as most seamen are beginning to learn, tar in general by no means adds to the rope's durability or strength, however much it may give it compactness and gloss.

Of late years the Manilla rope has in the American fishery almost entirely superseded hemp as a material for whale-lines; for, though not so durable as hemp, it is stronger, and far more soft and elastic; and I will add (since there is an æsthetics in all things), is much more handsome and becoming to the boat, than hemp. Hemp is a dusky, dark fellow, a sort of Indian; but Manilla is as a golden-haired Circassian to behold.

The whale line is only two thirds of an inch in thickness. At first sight, you would not think it so strong as it really is. By experiment its one and fifty yarns will each suspend a weight of one hundred and twenty pounds; so that the whole rope will bear a strain nearly equal to three tons. In length, the common sperm

2. ". . . and all the people that we saw in it are men of great stature. And there we saw the giants, the sons of Anak, which come of the giants: and we were in our own sight as grasshoppers. . . ." Numbers 14: 32–33

whale-line measures something over two hundred fathoms. Towards the stern of the boat it is spirally coiled away in the tub, not like the worm-pipe of a still though, but so as to form one round, cheese-shaped mass of densely bedded "sheaves," or layers of concentric spiralizations, without any hollow but the "heart," or minute vertical tube formed at the axis of the cheese. As the least tangle or kink in the coiling would, in running out, infallibly take somebody's arm, leg, or entire body off, the utmost precaution is used in stowing the line in its tub. Some harpooneers will consume almost an entire morning in this business, carrying the line high aloft and then reeving it downwards through a block towards the tub, so as in the act of coiling to free it from all possible wrinkles and twists.

In the English boats two tubs are used instead of one; the same line being continuously coiled in both tubs. There is some advantage in this; because these twin-tubs being so small they fit more readily into the boat, and do not strain it so much; whereas, the American tub, nearly three feet in diameter and of proportionate depth, makes a rather bulky freight for a craft whose planks are but one half-inch in thickness; for the bottom of the whale-boat is like critical ice, which will bear up a considerable distributed weight, but not very much of a concentrated one. When the painted canvas cover is clapped on the American line-tub, the boat looks as if it were pulling off with a prodigious great wedding-cake to present to the whales.

Both ends of the line are exposed; the lower end terminating in an eye-splice or loop coming up from the bottom against the side of the tub, and hanging over its edge completely disengaged from everything. This arrangement of the lower end is necessary on two accounts. First: In order to facilitate the fastening to it of an additional line from a neighboring boat, in case the stricken whale should sound so deep as to threaten to carry off the entire line originally attached to the harpoon. In these instances, the whale of course is shifted like a mug of ale, as it were, from the one boat to the other; though the first boat always hovers at hand to assist its consort. Second: This arrangement is indispensable for common safety's sake; for were the lower end of the line in any way attached to the boat, and were the whale then to run the line out to the end almost in a single, smoking minute as he sometimes does, he would not stop there, for the doomed boat would infallibly be dragged down after him into the profundity of the sea; and in that case no town-crier would ever find her again.

Before lowering the boat for the chase, the upper end of the line is taken aft from the tub, and passing round the loggerhead there, is again carried forward the entire length of the boat, resting crosswise upon the loom or handle of every man's oar, so that it jogs against his wrist in rowing; and also passing between the men, as they alternately sit at the opposite gunwales, to the leaded chocks or grooves in the extreme pointed prow of the boat, where a wooden pin or skewer the size of a common quill, prevents it from slipping out. From the chocks it hangs in a slight festoon over the bows, and is then passed inside the boat again; and some ten or twenty fathoms (called box-line) being coiled upon the box in the bows, it continues its way to the gunwale still a little further aft, and is then attached to the short-warp—the rope which is immediately connected with the harpoon; but previous to that connexion, the short-warp goes through sundry mystifications too tedious to detail.

Thus the whale-line folds the whole boat in its complicated coils, twisting and writhing around it in almost every direction. All the oarsmen are involved in its perilous contortions; so that to the timid eye of the landsman, they seem as Indian jugglers, with the deadliest snakes sportively festooning their limbs. Nor can any son of mortal woman, for the first time, seat himself amid those hempen intricacies, and while straining his utmost at the oar, bethink him that at any unknown instant the harpoon may be darted, and all these horrible contortions be put in play like ringed lightnings; he cannot be thus circumstanced without a shudder that makes the very marrow in his bones to quiver in him like a shaken jelly. Yet habit—strange thing! what cannot habit accomplish?—Gayer sallies, more merry mirth, better jokes, and brighter repartees, you never heard over your mahogany, than you will hear over the half-inch white cedar of the whale-boat, when thus hung in hangman's nooses; and, like the six burghers of Calais before King Edward, the six men composing the crew pull into the jaws of death, with a halter around every neck, as you may say.

Perhaps a very little thought will now enable you to account for those repeated whaling disasters—some few of which are casually chronicled—of this man or that man being taken out of the boat by the line, and lost. For, when the line is darting out, to be seated then in the boat, is like being seated in the midst of the manifold whizzings of a steam-engine in full play, when every flying beam, and shaft, and wheel, is grazing you. It is worse; for you cannot sit motionless in the heart of these perils, because the boat is rocking like a cradle, and you are pitched one way and the other, without the slightest warning; and only by a certain self-adjusting buoyancy and simultaneousness of volition and action, can you escape being made a Mazeppa [1] of, and run away with where the all-seeing sun himself could never pierce you out.

Again: as the profound calm which only apparently precedes and prophesies of the storm, is perhaps more awful than the storm itself; for, indeed, the calm is but the wrapper and envelope of the storm; and contains it in itself, as the seemingly harmless rifle holds the fatal powder, and the ball, and the explosion; so the graceful repose of the line, as it silently serpentines about the oarsmen before being brought into actual play—this is a thing which carries more of true terror than any other aspect of this dangerous affair. But why say more? All men live enveloped in whale-lines. All are born with halters round their necks; but it is only when caught in the swift, sudden turn of death, that mortals realize the silent, subtle, ever-present perils of life. And if you be a philosopher, though seated in the whale-boat, you would not at heart feel one whit more of terror, than though seated before your evening fire with a poker, and not a harpoon, by your side.

Chapter 61

STUBB KILLS A WHALE

If to Starbuck the apparition of the Squid was a thing of portents, to Queequeg it was quite a different object.

"When you see him 'quid," said the savage, honing his harpoon in the bow of his hoisted boat, "then you quick see him 'parm whale."

The next day was exceedingly still and sultry, and with nothing special to engage them, the Pequod's crew could hardly resist the spell of sleep induced by such a vacant sea. For this part of the Indian Ocean through which we then were voyaging is not what whalemen call a lively ground; that is, it affords fewer glimpses of porpoises, dolphins, flying-fish, and other vivacious denizens of more stirring waters, than those off the Rio de la Plata, or the in-shore ground off Peru.

It was my turn to stand at the foremast-head; and with my shoulders leaning against the slackened royal shrouds, to and fro I idly swayed in what seemed an enchanted air. No resolution could withstand it; in that dreamy mood losing all consciousness, at last my soul went out of my body; though my body still continued to sway as a pendulum will, long after the power which first moved it is withdrawn.

Ere forgetfulness altogether came over me, I had noticed that

1. In Byron's poem of that name, a jealous husband ties Mazeppa to a wild horse, then goads it.

the seamen at the main and mizen mast-heads were already drowsy. So that at last all three of us lifelessly swung from the spars, and for every swing that we made there was a nod from below from the slumbering helmsman. The waves, too, nodded their indolent crests; and across the wide trance of the sea, east nodded to west, and the sun over all.

Suddenly bubbles seemed bursting beneath my closed eyes; like vices my hands grasped the shrouds; some invisible, gracious agency preserved me; with a shock I came back to life. And lo! close under our lee, not forty fathoms off, a gigantic Sperm Whale lay rolling in the water like the capsized hull of a frigate, his broad, glossy back, of an Ethiopian hue, glistening in the sun's rays like a mirror. But lazily undulating in the trough of the sea, and ever and anon tranquilly spouting his vapory jet, the whale looked like a portly burgher smoking his pipe of a warm afternoon. But that pipe, poor whale, was thy last. As if struck by some enchanter's wand, the sleepy ship and every sleeper in it all at once started into wakefulness; and more than a score of voices from all parts of the vessel, simultaneously with the three notes from aloft, shouted forth the accustomed cry, as the great fish slowly and regularly spouted the sparkling brine into the air.

"Clear away the boats! Luff!" cried Ahab. And obeying his own order, he dashed the helm down before the helmsman could handle the spokes.

The sudden exclamations of the crew must have alarmed the whale; and ere the boats were down, majestically turning, he swam away to the leeward, but with such a steady tranquillity, and making so few ripples as he swam, that thinking after all he might not as yet be alarmed, Ahab gave orders that not an oar should be used, and no man must speak but in whispers. So seated like Ontario Indians on the gunwales of the boats, we swiftly but silently paddled along; the calm not admitting of the noiseless sails being set. Presently, as we thus glided in chase, the monster perpendicularly flitted his tail forty feet into the air, and then sank out of sight like a tower swallowed up.

"There go flukes!" was the cry, an announcement immediately followed by Stubb's producing his match and igniting his pipe, for now a respite was granted. After the full interval of his sounding had elapsed, the whale rose again, and being now in advance of the smoker's boat, and much nearer to it than to any of the others, Stubb counted upon the honor of the capture. It was obvious, now, that the whale had at length become aware of his pursuers. All silence of cautiousness was therefore no longer of use. Paddles were dropped, and oars came loudly into play. And still puffing at his pipe, Stubb cheered on his crew to the assault.

Yes, a mighty change had come over the fish. All alive to his jeopardy, he was going "head out;" that part obliquely projecting from the mad yeast which he brewed.*

"Start her, start her, my men! Don't hurry yourselves; take plenty of time—but start her; start her like thunder-claps, that's all," cried Stubb, spluttering out the smoke as he spoke. "Start her, now; give 'em the long and strong stroke, Tashtego. Start her, Tash, my boy—start her, all; but keep cool, keep cool—cucumbers is the word—easy, easy—only start her like grim death and grinning devils, and raise the buried dead perpendicular out of their graves, boys—that's all. Start her!"

"Woo-hoo! Wa-hee!" screamed the Gay-Header in reply, raising some old war-whoop to the skies; as every oarsman in the strained boat involuntarily bounced forward with the one tremendous leading stroke which the eager Indian gave.

But his wild screams were answered by others quite as wild. "Kee-hee! Kee-hee!" yelled Daggoo, straining forwards and backwards on his seat, like a pacing tiger in his cage.

"Ka-la! Koo-loo!" howled Queequeg, as if smacking his lips over a mouthful of Grenadier's steak. And thus with oars and yells the keels cut the sea. Meanwhile, Stubb retaining his place in the van, still encouraged his men to the onset, all the while puffing the smoke from his mouth. Like desperadoes they tugged and they strained, till the welcome cry was heard—"Stand up, Tashtego! —give it to him!" The harpoon was hurled. "Stern all!" The oarsmen backed water; the same moment something went hot and hissing along every one of their wrists. It was the magical line. An instant before, Stubb had swiftly caught two additional turns with it round the loggerhead, whence, by reason of its increased rapid circlings, a hempen blue smoke now jetted up and mingled with the steady fumes from his pipe. As the line passed round and round the loggerhead; so also, just before reaching that point, it blisteringly passed through and through both of Stubb's hands, from which the hand-cloths, or squares of quilted canvas sometimes worn at these times, had accidentally dropped. It was like holding an enemy's sharp two-edged sword by the blade, and that enemy all the time striving to wrest it out of your clutch.

"Wet the line! wet the line!" cried Stubb to the tub oarsman

---

* It will be seen in some other place of what a very light substance the entire interior of the sperm whale's enormous head consists. Though apparently the most massive, it is by far the most buoyant part about him. So that with ease he elevates it in the air, and invariably does so when going at his utmost speed. Besides, such is the breadth of the upper part of the front of his head, and such the tapering cutwater formation of the lower part, that by obliquely elevating his head, he thereby may be said to transform himself from a bluff-bowed sluggish galliot into a sharp-pointed New York pilot-boat [Melville's note].

(him seated by the tub) who, snatching off his hat, dashed the sea-water into it.* More turns were taken, so that the line began holding its place. The boat now flew through the boiling water like a shark all fins. Stubb and Tashtego here changed places—stem for stern—a staggering business truly in that rocking commotion.

From the vibrating line extending the entire length of the upper part of the boat, and from its now being more tight than a harpstring, you would have thought the craft had two keels —one cleaving the water, the other the air—as the boat churned on through both opposing elements at once. A continual cascade played at the bows; a ceaseless whirling eddy in her wake; and, at the slightest motion from within, even but of a little finger, the vibrating, cracking craft canted over her spasmodic gunwale into the sea. Thus they rushed; each man with might and main clinging to his seat, to prevent being tossed to the foam; and the tall form of Tashtego at the steering oar crouching almost double, in order to bring down his centre of gravity. Whole Atlantics and Pacifics seemed passed as they shot on their way, till at length the whale somewhat slackened his flight.

"Haul in—haul in!" cried Stubb to the bowsman; and, facing round towards the whale, all hands began pulling the boat up to him, while yet the boat was being towed on. Soon ranging up by his flank, Stubb, firmly planting his knee in the clumsy cleat, darted dart after dart into the flying fish; at the word of command, the boat alternately sterning out of the way of the whale's horrible wallow, and then ranging up for another fling.

The red tide now poured from all sides of the monster like brooks down a hill. His tormented body rolled not in brine but in blood, which bubbled and seethed for furlongs behind in their wake. The slanting sun playing upon this crimson pond in the sea, sent back its reflection into every face, so that they all glowed to each other like red men. And all the while, jet after jet of white smoke was agonizingly shot from the spiracle of the whale, and vehement puff after puff from the mouth of the excited heads-man; as at every dart, hauling in upon his crooked lance (by the line attached to it), Stubb straightened it again and again, by a few rapid blows against the gunwale, then again and again sent it into the whale.

"Pull up—pull up!" he now cried to the bowsman, as the waning whale relaxed in his wrath. "Pull up!—close to!" and the boat ranged along the fish's flank. When reaching far over the bow, Stubb slowly churned his long sharp lance into the fish, and kept

---

* Partly to show the indispensableness of this act, it may here be stated, that, in the old Dutch fishery, a mop was used to dash the running line with water; in many other ships, a wooden piggin, or bailer, is set apart for that purpose. Your hat, however, is the most convenient [Melville's note].

it there, carefully churning and churning, as if cautiously seeking to feel after some gold watch that the whale might have swallowed, and which he was fearful of breaking ere he could hook it out. But that gold watch he sought was the innermost life of the fish. And now it is struck; for, starting from his trance into that unspeakable thing called his "flurry," the monster horribly wallowed in his blood, overwrapped himself in impenetrable, mad, boiling spray, so that the imperilled craft, instantly dropping astern, had much ado blindly to struggle out from that phrensied twilight into the clear air of the day.

And now abating in his flurry, the whale once more rolled out into view; surging from side to side; spasmodically dilating and contracting his spout-hole, with sharp, cracking, agonized respirations. At last, gush after gush of clotted red gore, as if it had been the purple lees of red wine, shot into the frighted air; and falling back again, ran dripping down his motionless flanks into the sea. His heart had burst!

"He's dead, Mr. Stubb," said Tashtego.

"Yes; both pipes smoked out!" and withdrawing his own from his mouth, Stubb scattered the dead ashes over the water; and, for a moment, stood thoughtfully eyeing the vast corpse he had made.

Chapter 62

THE DART

A word concerning an incident in the last chapter.

According to the invariable usage of the fishery, the whaleboat pushes off from the ship, with the headsman or whale-killer as temporary steersman, and the harpooneer or whale-fastener pulling the foremost oar, the one known as the harpooneer-oar. Now it needs a strong, nervous arm to strike the first iron into the fish; for often, in what is called a long dart, the heavy implement has to be flung to the distance of twenty or thirty feet. But however prolonged and exhausting the chase, the harpooneer is expected to pull his oar meanwhile to the uttermost; indeed, he is expected to set an example of superhuman activity to the rest, not only by incredible rowing, but by repeated loud and intrepid exclamations; and what it is to keep shouting at the top of one's compass, while all the other muscles are strained and half started —what that is none know but those who have tried it. For one, I cannot bawl very heartily and work very recklessly at one and the same time. In this straining, bawling state, then, with his back to the fish, all at once the exhausted harpooneer hears the exciting cry—"Stand up, and give it to him!" He now has to drop and secure his oar, turn round on his centre half way, seize his harpoon from the crotch, and with what little strength may remain, he essays to pitch it somehow into the whale. No wonder, taking the whole fleet of whalemen in a body, that out of fifty fair chances for a dart, not five are successful; no wonder that so many hapless harpooneers are madly cursed and disrated; no wonder that some of them actually burst their blood-vessels in the boat; no wonder that some sperm whalemen are absent four years with four barrels; no wonder that to many ship owners, whaling is but a losing concern; for it is the harpooneer that makes the voyage, and if you take the breath out of his body how can you expect to find it there when most wanted!

Again, if the dart be successful, then at the second critical instant, that is, when the whale starts to run, the boat-header and harpooneer likewise start to running fore and aft, to the imminent jeopardy of themselves and every one else. It is then they change places; and the headsman, the chief officer of the little craft, takes his proper station in the bows of the boat.

Now, I care not who maintains the contrary, but all this is both foolish and unnecessary. The headsman should stay in the bows from first to last; he should both dart the harpoon and the lance, and no rowing whatever should be expected of him, except under circumstances obvious to any fisherman. I know that this would sometimes involve a slight loss of speed in the chase; but long experience in various whalemen of more than one nation has convinced me that in the vast majority of failures in the fishery, it has not by any means been so much the speed of the whale as the before described exhaustion of the harpooneer that has caused them.

To insure the greatest efficiency in the dart, the harpooneers of this world must start to their feet from out of idleness, and not from out of toil.

Chapter 63

THE CROTCH

Out of the trunk, the branches grow; out of them, the twigs. So, in productive subjects, grow the chapters.

The crotch alluded to on a previous page deserves independent mention. It is a notched stick of a peculiar form, some two feet in length, which is perpendicularly inserted into the starboard gunwale near the bow, for the purpose of furnishing a rest for the wooden extremity of the harpoon, whose other naked, barbed end slopingly projects from the prow. Thereby the weapon is instantly at hand to its hurler, who snatches it up as readily from its rest

as a backwoodsman swings his rifle from the wall. It is customary
to have two harpoons reposing in the crotch, respectively called
the first and second irons.

But these two harpoons, each by its own cord, are both connected with the line; the object being this: to dart them both,
if possible, one instantly after the other into the same whale; so
that if, in the coming drag, one should draw out, the other may
still retain a hold. It is a doubling of the chances. But it very
often happens that owing to the instantaneous, violent, convulsive
running of the whale upon receiving the first iron, it becomes
impossible for the harpooneer, however lightning-like in his movements, to pitch the second iron into him. Nevertheless, as the
second iron is already connected with the line, and the line is
running, hence that weapon must, at all events, be anticipatingly
tossed out of the boat, somehow and somewhere; else the most
terrible jeopardy would involve all hands. Tumbled into the water, it accordingly is in such cases; the spare coils of box line
(mentioned in a preceding chapter) making this feat, in most instances, prudently practicable. But this critical act is not always
unattended with the saddest and most fatal casualties.

Furthermore: you must know that when the second iron is
thrown overboard, it thenceforth becomes a dangling, sharp-edged
terror, skittishly curvetting about both boat and whale, entan-
gling the lines, or cutting them, and making a prodigious sensation in all directions. Nor, in general, is it possible to secure it
again until the whale is fairly captured and a corpse.

Consider, now, how it must be in the case of four boats all
engaging one unusually strong, active, and knowing whale; when
owing to these qualities in him, as well as to the thousand con-
curring accidents of such an audacious enterprise, eight or ten
loose second irons may be simultaneously dangling about him.
For, of course, each boat is supplied with several harpoons to bend
on to the line should the first one be ineffectually darted without
recovery. All these particulars are faithfully narrated here, as
they will not fail to elucidate several most important, however
intricate passages, in scenes hereafter to be painted.

Chapter 64

STUBB'S SUPPER

Stubb's whale had been killed some distance from the ship. It
was a calm; so, forming a tandem of three boats, we commenced
the slow business of towing the trophy to the Pequod. And now,
as we eighteen men with our thirty-six arms, and one hundred
and eighty thumbs and fingers, slowly toiled hour after hour

upon that inert, sluggish corpse in the sea; and it seemed hardly to budge at all, except at long intervals; good evidence was hereby furnished of the enormousness of the mass we moved. For, upon the great canal of Hang-Ho, or whatever they call it, in China, four or five laborers on the foot-path will draw a bulky freighted junk at the rate of a mile an hour; but this grand argosy we towed heavily forged along, as if laden with pig-lead in bulk.

Darkness came on; but three lights up and down in the Pequod's main-rigging dimly guided our way; till drawing nearer we saw Ahab dropping one of several more lanterns over the bulwarks. Vacantly eyeing the heaving whale for a moment, he issued the usual orders for securing it for the night, and then handing his lantern to a seaman, went his way into the cabin, and did not come forward again until morning.

Though, in overseeing the pursuit of this whale, Captain Ahab had evinced his customary activity, to call it so; yet now that the creature was dead, some vague dissatisfaction, or impatience, or despair, seemed working in him; as if the sight of that dead body reminded him that Moby Dick was yet to be slain; and though a thousand other whales were brought to his ship, all that would not one jot advance his grand, monomaniac object. Very soon you would have thought from the sound on the Pequod's decks, that all hands were preparing to cast anchor in the deep; for heavy chains are being dragged along the deck, and thrust rattling out of the port-holes. But by those clanking links, the vast corpse itself, not the ship, is to be moored. Tied by the head to the stern, and by the tail to the bows, the whale now lies with its black hull close to the vessel's, and seen through the darkness of the night, which obscured the spars and rigging aloft, the two—ship and whale, seemed yoked together like colossal bullocks, whereof one reclines while the other remains standing.*

If moody Ahab was now all quiescence, at least so far as could be known on deck, Stubb, his second mate, flushed with conquest, betrayed an unusual but still good-natured excitement. Such an unwonted bustle was he in that the staid Starbuck, his official superior, quietly resigned to him for the time the sole manage-

---

* A little item may as well be related here. The strongest and most reliable hold which the ship has upon the whale when moored alongside, is by the flukes or tail; and as from its greater density that part is relatively heavier than any other (excepting the side-fins), its flexibility even in death, causes it to sink low beneath the surface; so that with the hand you cannot get at it from the boat, in order to put the chain round it. But this difficulty is ingeniously overcome: a small, strong line is prepared with a wooden float at its outer end, and a weight in its middle, while the other end is secured to the ship. By adroit management the wooden float is made to rise on the other side of the mass, so that now having girdled the whale, the chain is readily made to follow suit; and being slipped along the body, is at last locked fast round the smallest part of the tail, at the point of junction with its broad flukes or lobes [Melville's note].

ment of affairs. One small, helping cause of all this liveliness in Stubb, was soon made strangely manifest. Stubb was a high liver; he was somewhat intemperately fond of the whale as a flavorish thing to his palate.

"A steak, a steak, ere I sleep! You, Daggoo! overboard you go, and cut me one from his small!"

Here be it known, that though these wild fishermen do not, as a general thing, and according to the great military maxim, make the enemy defray the current expenses of the war (at least before realizing the proceeds of the voyage), yet now and then you find some of these Nantucketers who have a genuine relish for that particular part of the Sperm Whale designated by Stubb; comprising the tapering extremity of the body.

About midnight that steak was cut and cooked; and lighted by two lanterns of sperm oil, Stubb stoutly stood up to his spermaceti supper at the capstan-head, as if that capstan were a sideboard. Nor was Stubb the only banqueter on whale's flesh that night. Mingling their mumblings with his own mastications, thousands on thousands of sharks, swarming round the dead leviathan, smackingly feasted on its fatness. The few sleepers below in their bunks were often startled by the sharp slapping of their tails against the hull, within a few inches of the sleepers' hearts. Peering over the side you could just see them (as before you heard them) wallowing in the sullen, black waters, and turning over on their backs as they scooped out huge globular pieces of the whale of the bigness of a human head. This particular feat of the shark seems all but miraculous. How, at such an apparently unassailable surface, they contrive to gouge out such symmetrical mouthfuls, remains a part of the universal problem of all things. The mark they thus leave on the whale, may best be likened to the hollow made by a carpenter in countersinking for a screw.

Though amid all the smoking horror and diabolism of a seafight, sharks will be seen longingly gazing up to the ship's decks, like hungry dogs round a table where red meat is being carved, ready to bolt down every killed man that is tossed to them; and though, while the valiant butchers over the deck-table are thus cannibally carving each other's live meat with carving-knives all gilded and tasselled, the sharks, also, with their jewel-hilted mouths, are quarrelsomely carving away under the table at the dead meat; and though, were you to turn the whole affair upside down, it would still be pretty much the same thing, that is to say, a shocking sharkish business enough for all parties; and though sharks also are the invariable outriders of all slave ships crossing the Atlantic, systematically trotting alongside, to be handy in case a parcel is to be carried anywhere, or a dead slave to be decently buried; and though one or two other like instances might be set down, touching the set terms, places, and occasions, when sharks do most socially congregate, and most hilariously feast; yet is there no conceivable time or occasion when you will find them in such countless numbers, and in gayer or more jovial spirits, than around a dead sperm whale, moored by night to a whale-ship at sea. If you have never seen that sight, then suspend your decision about the propriety of devil-worship, and the expediency of conciliating the devil.

But, as yet, Stubb heeded not the mumblings of the banquet that was going on so nigh him, no more than the sharks heeded the smacking of his own epicurean lips.

"Cook, cook!—where's that old Fleece?" he cried at length, widening his legs still further, as if to form a more secure base for his supper; and, at the same time, darting his fork into the dish, as if stabbing with his lance; "cook, you cook!—sail this way, cook!"

The old black, not in any very high glee at having been previously roused from his warm hammock at a most unseasonable hour, came shambling along from his galley, for, like many old blacks, there was something the matter with his knee-pans, which he did not keep well scoured like his other pans; this old Fleece, as they called him, came shuffling and limping along, assisting his step with his tongs, which, after a clumsy fashion, were made of straightened iron hoops; this old Ebony floundered along, and in obedience to the word of command, came to a dead stop on the opposite side of Stubb's sideboard; when, with both hands folded before him, and resting on his two-legged cane, he bowed his arched back still further over, at the same time sideways inclining his head, so as to bring his best ear into play.

"Cook," said Stubb, rapidly lifting a rather reddish morsel to his mouth, "don't you think this steak is rather overdone? You've been beating this steak too much, cook; it's too tender. Don't I always say that to be good, a whale-steak must be tough? There are those sharks now over the side, don't you see they prefer it tough and rare? What a shindy they are kicking up! Cook, go and talk to 'em; tell 'em they are welcome to help themselves civilly, and in moderation, but they must keep quiet. Blast me, if I can hear my own voice. Away, cook, and deliver my message. Here, take this lantern," snatching one from his sideboard; "now then, go and preach to 'em!"

Sullenly taking the offered lantern, old Fleece limped across the deck to the bulwarks; and then, with one hand dropping his light low over the sea, so as to get a good view of his congregation, with the other hand he solemnly flourished his tongs, and lean-

ing far over the side in a mumbling voice began addressing the
sharks, while Stubb, softly crawling behind, overheard all that
was said.

"Fellow-critters: I'se ordered here to say dat you must stop dat
dam noise dare. You hear? Stop dat dam smackin' ob de lip!
Massa Stubb say dat you can fill your dam bellies up to de hatch-
ings, but by Gor! you must stop dat dam racket!"

"Cook," here interposed Stubb, accompanying the word with a
sudden slap on the shoulder,—"Cook! why, damn your eyes, you
mustn't swear that way when you're preaching. That's no way
to convert sinners, Cook!"

"Who dat? Den preach to him yourself," sullenly turning to
go.

"No, Cook; go on, go on."

"Well, den, Belubed fellow-critters:"—

"Right!" exclaimed Stubb, approvingly, "coax 'em to it; try
that," and Fleece continued.

"Dough you is all sharks, and by natur wery woracious, yet I
zay to you, fellow-critters, dat dat woraciousness—'top dat dam
slappin' ob de tail! How you tink to hear, 'spose you keep up such
a dam slappin' and bitin' dare?"

"Cook," cried Stubb, collaring him, "I wont have that swearing.
Talk to 'em gentlemanly."

Once more the sermon proceeded.

"Your woraciousness, fellow-critters, I don't blame ye so much
for; dat is natur, and can't be helped; but to gobern dat wicked
natur, dat is de pint. You is sharks, sartin; but if you gobern de
shark in you, why den you be angel; for all angel is not'ing more
dan de shark well goberned. Now, look here, bred'ren, just try
wonst to be cibil, a helping yourselbs from dat whale. Don't be
tearin' de blubber out your neighbour's mout, I say. Is not one
shark dood right as toder to dat whale? And, by Gor, none on
you has de right to dat whale; dat whale belong to some one else.
I know some o' you has berry brig mout, brigger dan oders; but
den de brig mouts sometimes has de small bellies; so dat de
brigness ob de mout is not to swallar wid, but to bite off de
blubber for de small fry ob sharks, dat can't get into de scrouge
to help demselves."

"Well done, old Fleece!" cried Stubb, "that's Christianity; go
on."

"No use goin' on; de dam willains will keep a scrougin' and
slappin' each oder, Massa Stubb; dey don't hear one word; no use
a-preachin' to such dam g'uttons as you call 'em, till dare bellies is full, and dare bellies is bottomless; and when dey do get
'em full, dey wont hear you den; for den dey sink in de sea, go

fast to sleep on de coral, and can't hear not'ing at all, no more, for eber and eber."

"Upon my soul, I am about of the same opinion; so give the benediction, Fleece, and I'll away to my supper."

Upon this, Fleece, holding both hands over the fishy mob, raised his shrill voice, and cried—

"Cussed fellow-critters! Kick up de damndest row as ever you can; fill your dam' bellies till dey bust—and den die."

"Now, cook," said Stubb, resuming his supper at the capstan; "Stand just where you stood before, there, over against me, and pay particular attention."

"All 'dention," said Fleece, again stooping over upon his tongs in the desired position.

"Well," said Stubb, helping himself freely meanwhile; "I shall now go back to the subject of this steak. In the first place, how old are you, cook?"

"What dat do wid de 'teak," said the old black, testily.

"Silence! How old are you, cook?"

"'Bout ninety, dey say," he gloomily muttered.

"And have you lived in this world hard upon one hundred years, cook, and don't know yet how to cook a whale-steak?" rapidly bolting another mouthful at the last word, so that that morsel seemed a continuation of the question. "Where were you born, cook?"

"'Hind de hatchway, in ferry-boat, goin' ober de Roanoke."

"Born in a ferry-boat! That's queer, too. But I want to know what country you were born in, cook?"

"Didn't I say de Roanoke country?" he cried, sharply.

"No, you didn't, cook; but I'll tell you what I'm coming to, cook. You must go home and be born over again; you don't know how to cook a whale-steak yet."

"Bress my soul, if I cook 'noder one," he growled, angrily, turning round to depart.

"Come back, cook;—here, hand me those tongs;—now take that bit of steak there, and tell me if you think that steak cooked as it should be? Take it, I say"—holding the tongs towards him— "take it, and taste it."

Faintly smacking his withered lips over it for a moment, the old negro muttered, "Best cooked 'teak I eber taste; joosy, berry joosy."

"Cook," said Stubb, squaring himself once more; "do you belong to the church?"

"Passed one once in Cape-Down," said the old man sullenly.

"And you have once in your life passed a holy church in Cape-Town, where you doubtless overheard a holy parson addressing his hearers as his beloved fellow-creatures, have you, cook! And yet you come here, and tell me such a dreadful lie as you did just now, eh?" said Stubb. "Where do you expect to go to, cook?"

"Go to bed berry soon," he mumbled, half-turning as he spoke.

"Avast! heave to! I mean when you die, cook. It's an awful question. Now what's your answer?"

"When dis old brack man dies," said the negro slowly, changing his whole air and demeanor, "he hisself won't go nowhere; but some bressed angel will come and fetch him."

"Fetch him? How? In a coach and four, as they fetched Elijah?[1] And fetch him where?"

"Up dere," said Fleece, holding his tongs straight over his head, and keeping it there very solemnly.

"So, then, you expect to go up into our main-top, do you, cook, when you are dead? But don't you know the higher you climb, the colder it gets? Main-top eh?"

"Didn't say dat 'tall," said Fleece, again in the sulks.

"You said up there, didn't you? and now look yourself, and see where your tongs are pointing. But, perhaps you expect to get into heaven by crawling through the lubber's hole,[2] cook; but, no, no, cook, you don't get there, except you go the regular way, round by the rigging. It's a ticklish business, but must be done, or else it's no go. But none of us are in heaven yet. Drop your tongs, cook, and hear my orders. Do ye hear? Hold your hat in one hand, and clap t'other a'top of your heart, when I'm giving my orders, cook. What! that your heart, there?—that's your gizzard! Aloft! aloft!—that's it—now you have it. Hold it there now, and pay attention."

"All 'dention," said the old black, with both hands placed as desired, vainly wriggling his grizzled head, as if to get both ears in front at one and the same time.

"Well then, cook, you see this whale-steak of yours was so very bad, that I have put it out of sight as soon as possible; you see that, don't you? Well, for the future, when you cook another whale-steak for my private table here, the capstan, I'll tell you what to do so as not to spoil it by overdoing. Hold the steak in one hand, and show a live coal to it with the other; that done, dish it; d'ye hear? And now to-morrow, cook, when we are cutting in the fish, be sure you stand by to get the tips of his fins; have them put in pickle. As for the ends of the flukes, have them soused, cook. There, now ye may go."

But Fleece had hardly got three paces off, when he was re-

1. That is, in a chariot of fire drawn by horses of fire (see II Kings 2:11).
2. The hole in the maintop which only timorous lubbers crawled through to get to the top, whereas the real sailors boldly climbed over the outside edge.

called.

"Cook, give me cutlets for supper to-morrow night in the mid-watch. D'ye hear? away you sail, then.—Halloa! stop! make a bow before you go.—Avast heaving again! Whale-balls for break-fast—don't forget."

"Wish, by gor! whale eat him, 'stead of him eat whale. I'm bressed if he ain't more of shark dan Massa Shark hisself," muttered the old man, limping away; with which sage ejaculation he went to his hammock.

Chapter 65

THE WHALE AS A DISH

That mortal man should feed upon the creature that feeds his lamp, and, like Stubb, eat him by his own light, as you may say; this seems so outlandish a thing that one must needs go a little into the history and philosophy of it.

It is upon record, that three centuries ago the tongue of the Right Whale was esteemed a great delicacy in France, and commanded large prices there. Also, that in Henry VIIIth's time, a certain cook of the court obtained a handsome reward for inventing an admirable sauce to be eaten with barbacued porpoises, which, you remember, are a species of whale. Porpoises, indeed, are to this day considered fine eating. The meat is made into balls about the size of billiard balls, and being well seasoned and spiced might be taken for turtle-balls or veal balls. The old monks of Dunfermline were very fond of them. They had a great porpoise grant from the crown.

The fact is, that among his hunters at least, the whale would by all hands be considered a noble dish, were there not so much of him; but when you come to sit down before a meat-pie nearly one hundred feet long, it takes away your appetite. Only the most unprejudiced of men like Stubb, nowadays partake of cooked whales; but the Esquimaux are not so fastidious. We all know how they live upon whales, and have rare old vintages of prime old train oil. Zogranda,[1] one of their most famous doctors, recommends strips of blubber for infants, as being exceedingly juicy and nourishing. And this reminds me that certain Englishmen, who long ago were accidentally left in Greenland by a whaling vessel—that these men actually lived for several months on the mouldy scraps of whales which had been left ashore after trying out the blubber. Among the Dutch whalemen these scraps are called "fritters;" which, indeed, they greatly resemble, being brown and crisp, and smelling something like old Amsterdam

1. Another of Melville's private jokes at Scoresby's expense.

housewives' dough-nuts or oly-cooks, when fresh. They have such
an eatable look that the most self-denying stranger can hardly keep
his hands off.

But what further depreciates the whale as a civilized dish, is
his exceeding richness. He is the great prize ox of the sea, too fat
to be delicately good. Look at his hump, which would be as fine
eating as the buffalo's (which is esteemed a rare dish), were it not
such a solid pyramid of fat. But the spermaceti itself, how bland
and creamy that is; like the transparent, half-jellied, white meat of
a cocoanut in the third month of its growth, yet far too rich to
supply a substitute for butter. Nevertheless, many whalemen have
a method of absorbing it into some other substance, and then
partaking of it. In the long try watches of the night it is a common thing for the seamen to dip their ship-biscuit into the huge
oil-pots and let them fry there awhile. Many a good supper have I
thus made.

In the case of a small Sperm Whale the brains are accounted a
fine dish. The casket of the skull is broken into with an axe, and
the two plump, whitish lobes being withdrawn (precisely resembling two large puddings), they are then mixed with flour, and
cooked into a most delectable mess, in flavor somewhat resembling calves' head, which is quite a dish among some epicures;
and every one knows that some young bucks among the epicures,
by continually dining upon calves' brains, by and by get to have a
little brains of their own, so as to be able to tell a calf's head
from their own heads; which, indeed, requires uncommon discrimi-
nation. And that is the reason why a young buck with an intelligent looking calf's head before him, is somehow one of the
saddest sights you can see. The head looks a sort of reproachfully
at him, with an "Et tu Brute!" expression.

It is not, perhaps, entirely because the whale is so excessively
unctuous that landsmen seem to regard the eating of him with
abhorrence; that appears to result, in some way, from the consideration before mentioned: i.e. that a man should eat a
newly murdered thing of the sea, and eat it too by its own light.
But no doubt the first man that ever murdered an ox was regarded as a murderer; perhaps he was hung; and if he had been
put on his trial by oxen, he certainly would have been; and he
certainly deserved it if any murderer does. Go to the meat-market
of a Saturday night and see the crowds of live bipeds staring up
at the long rows of dead quadrupeds. Does not that sight take a
tooth out of the cannibal's jaw? Cannibals? who is not a cannibal?
I tell you it will be more tolerable for the Fejee that salted down
a lean missionary in his cellar against a coming famine; it will
be more tolerable for that provident Fejee, I say, in the day of

judgment, than for thee, civilized and enlightened gourmand, who nailest geese to the ground and feastest on their bloated livers in thy paté-de-foie-gras.

But Stubb, he eats the whale by its own light, does he? and that is adding insult to injury, is it? Look at your knife-handle, there, my civilized and enlightened gourmand dining off that roast beef, what is that handle made of?—what but the bones of the brother of the very ox you are eating? And what do you pick your teeth with, after devouring that fat goose? With a feather of the same fowl. And with what quill did the Secretary of the Society for the Suppression of Cruelty to Ganders formally indite his circulars? It is only within the last month or two that that society passed a resolution to patronize nothing but steel pens.

Chapter 66

THE SHARK MASSACRE

When in the Southern Fishery, a captured Sperm Whale, after long and weary toil, is brought alongside late at night, it is not, as a general thing at least, customary to proceed at once to the business of cutting him in. For that business is an exceedingly laborious one; is not very soon completed; and requires all hands to set about it. Therefore, the common usage is to take in all sail; lash the helm a'lee; and then send every one below to his hammock till daylight, with the reservation that, until that time, anchor-watches shall be kept; that is, two and two, for an hour each couple, the crew in rotation shall mount the deck to see that all goes well.

But sometimes, especially upon the Line in the Pacific, this plan will not answer at all; because such incalculable hosts of sharks gather round the moored carcase, that were he left so for six hours, say, on a stretch, little more than the skeleton would be visible by morning. In most other parts of the ocean, however, where these fish do not so largely abound, their wondrous voracity can be at times considerably diminished, by vigorously stirring them up with sharp whaling-spades, a procedure notwithstanding, which, in some instances, only seems to tickle them into still greater activity. But it was not thus in the present case with the Pequod's sharks; though, to be sure, any man unaccustomed to such sights, to have looked over her side that night, would have almost thought the whole round sea was one huge cheese, and those sharks the maggots in it.

Nevertheless, upon Stubb setting the anchor-watch after his supper was concluded; and when, accordingly, Queequeg and a forecastle seaman came on deck, no small excitement was created among the sharks; for immediately suspending the cutting stages over the side, and lowering three lanterns, so that they cast long gleams of light over the turbid sea, these two mariners, darting their long whaling-spades, kept up an incessant murdering of the sharks,* by striking the keen steel deep into their skulls, seemingly their only vital part. But in the foamy confusion of their mixed and struggling hosts, the marksmen could not always hit their mark; and this brought about new revelations of the incredible ferocity of the foe. They viciously snapped, not only at each other's disembowelments, but like flexible bows, bent round, and bit their own; till those entrails seemed swallowed over and over again by the same mouth, to be oppositely voided by the gaping wound. Nor was this all. It was unsafe to meddle with the corpses and ghosts of these creatures. A sort 'of generic or Pantheistic vitality seemed to lurk in their very joints and bones, after what might be called the individual life had departed. Killed and hoisted on deck for the sake of his skin, one of these sharks almost took poor Queequeg's hand off, when he tried to shut down the dead lid of his murderous jaw.

"Queequeg no care what god made him shark," said the savage, agonizingly lifting his hand up and down; "wedder Fejee god or Nantucket god; but de god wat made shark must be one dam Ingin."

Chapter 67

CUTTING IN

It was a Saturday night, and such a Sabbath as followed! Ex officio [1] professors of Sabbath breaking are all whalemen. The ivory Pequod was turned into what seemed a shamble; every sailor a butcher. You would have thought we were offering up ten thousand red oxen to the sea gods.

In the first place, the enormous cutting tackles, among other ponderous things comprising a cluster of blocks generally painted green, and which no single man can possibly lift—this vast bunch of grapes was swayed up to the main-top and firmly lashed to the lower mast-head, the strongest point anywhere above a ship's deck. The end of the hawser-like rope winding through these intricacies,

---

* The whaling-spade used for cutting-in is made of the very best steel; is about the bigness of a man's spread hand; and in general shape, corresponds to the garden implement after which it is named; only its sides are perfectly flat, and its upper end considerably narrower than the lower. This weapon is always kept as sharp as possible; and when being used is occasionally honed, just like a razor. In its socket, a stiff pole, from twenty to thirty feet long, is inserted for a handle [Melville's note].

1. By virtue of one's office or position.

was then conducted to the windlass, and the huge lower block of the tackles was swung over the whale; to this block the great blubber hook, weighing some one hundred pounds, was attached. And now suspended in stages over the side, Starbuck and Stubb, the mates, armed with their long spades, began cutting a hole in the body for the insertion of the hook just above the nearest of the two side-fins. This done, a broad, semicircular line is cut round the hole, the hook is inserted, and the main body of the crew striking up a wild chorus, now commence heaving in one dense crowd at the windlass. When instantly, the entire ship careens over on her side; every bolt in her starts like the nail-heads of an old house in frosty weather; she trembles, quivers, and nods her frighted mast-heads to the sky. More and more she leans over to the whale, while every gasping heave of the windlass is answered by a helping heave from the billows; till at last, a swift, startling snap is heard; with a great swash the ship rolls upwards and backwards from the whale, and the triumphant tackle rises into sight dragging after it the disengaged semicircular end of the first strip of blubber. Now as the blubber envelopes the whale precisely as the rind does an orange, so is it stripped off from the body precisely as an orange is sometimes stripped by spiraliz- ing it. For the strain constantly kept up by the windlass con- tinually keeps the whale rolling over and over in the water, and as the blubber in one strip uniformly peels off along the line called the "scarf," simultaneously cut by the spades of Starbuck and Stubb, the mates; and just as fast as it is thus peeled off, and in- deed by that very act itself, it is all the time being hoisted higher and higher aloft till its upper end grazes the main-top; the men at the windlass then cease heaving, and for a moment or two the prodigious blood-dripping mass sways to and fro as if let down from the sky, and every one present must take good heed to dodge it when it swings, else it may box his ears and pitch him headlong overboard.

One of the attending harpooneers now advances with a long, keen weapon called a boarding-sword, and watching his chance he dexterously slices out a considerable hole in the lower part of the swaying mass. Into this hole, the end of the second alternating great tackle is then hooked so as to retain a hold upon the blubber, in order to prepare for what follows. Whereupon, this accom- plished swordsman, warning all hands to stand off, once more makes a scientific dash at the mass, and with a few sidelong, desperate, lunging slicings, severs it completely in twain; so that while the short lower part is still fast, the long upper strip, called a blanket-piece, swings clear, and is all ready for lowering. The heavers forward now resume their song, and while the one tackle is peeling and hoisting a second strip from the whale, the other is slowly slackened away, and down goes the first strip through the main hatchway right beneath, into an unfurnished parlor called the blubber-room. Into this twilight apartment sundry nimble hands keep coiling away the long blanket-piece as if it were a great live mass of plaited serpents. And thus the work proceeds; the two tackles hoisting and lowering simultaneously; both whale and windlass heaving, the heavers singing, the blubber-room gentlemen coiling, the mates scarfing, the ship straining, and all hands swearing occasionally, by way of assuaging the general friction.

Chapter 68

THE BLANKET

I have given no small attention to that not unvexed subject, the skin of the whale. I have had controversies about it with experienced whalemen afloat, and learned naturalists ashore. My original opinion remains unchanged; but it is only an opinion.

The question is, what and where is the skin of the whale? Already you know what his blubber is. That blubber is something of the consistence of firm, close-grained beef, but tougher, more elastic and compact, and ranges from eight or ten to twelve and fifteen inches in thickness.

Now, however preposterous it may at first seem to talk of any creature's skin as being of that sort of consistence and thickness, yet in point of fact these are no arguments against such a presumption; because you cannot raise any other dense enveloping layer from the whale's body but that same blubber; and the outermost enveloping layer of any animal, if reasonably dense, what can that be but the skin? True, from the unmarred dead body of the whale, you may scrape off with your hand an infinitely thin, transparent substance, somewhat resembling the thinnest shreds of isinglass, only it is almost as flexible and soft as satin; that is, previous to being dried, when it not only contracts and thickens, but becomes rather hard and brittle. I have several such dried bits, which I use for marks in my whalebooks. It is transparent, as I said before; and being laid upon the printed page, I have sometimes pleased myself with fancying it exerted a magnifying influence. At any rate, it is pleasant to read about whales through their own spectacles, as you may say. But what I am driving at here is this. That same infinitely thin, isinglass substance, which, I admit, invests the entire body of the whale, is not so much to be regarded as the skin of the creature, as the skin of the skin, so to speak; for it were simply ridiculous to say, that the proper skin of the tremendous whale is thinner and more tender than the skin of a new-born child. But no more of this.

Assuming the blubber to be the skin of the whale; then, when this skin, as in the case of a very large Sperm Whale, will yield the bulk of one hundred barrels of oil; and, when it is considered that, in quantity, or rather weight, that oil, in its expressed state, is only three fourths, and not the entire substance of the coat; some idea may hence be had of the enormousness of that animated mass, a mere part of whose mere integument yields such a lake of liquid as that. Reckoning ten barrels to the ton, you have ten tons for the net weight of only three quarters of the stuff of the whale's skin.

In life, the visible surface of the Sperm Whale is not the least among the many marvels he presents. Almost invariably it is all over obliquely crossed and re-crossed with numberless straight marks in thick array, something like those in the finest Italian line engravings. But these marks do not seem to be impressed upon the isinglass substance above mentioned, but seem to be seen through it, as if they were engraved upon the body itself. Nor is this all. In some instances, to the quick, observant eye, those linear marks, as in a veritable engraving, but afford the ground for far other delineations. These are hieroglyphical; that is, if you call those mysterious cyphers on the walls of pyramids hieroglyphics, then that is the proper word to use in the present connexion. By my retentive memory of the hieroglyphics upon one Sperm Whale in particular, I was much struck with a plate representing the old Indian characters chiselled on the famous hieroglyphic palisades on the banks of the Upper Mississippi. Like those mystic rocks, too, the mystic-marked whale remains undecipherable. This allusion to the Indian rocks reminds me of another thing. Besides all the other phenomena which the exterior of the Sperm Whale presents, he not seldom displays the back, and more especially his flanks, effaced in great part of the regular linear appearance, by reason of numerous rude scratches, altogether of an irregular, random aspect. I should say that those New England rocks on the sea-coast, which Agassiz imagines to bear the marks of violent scraping contact with vast floating icebergs—I should say, that those rocks must not a little resemble the Sperm Whale in this particular. It also seems to me that such scratches in the whale are probably made by hostile contact with other whales; for I have most remarked them in the large, full-grown bulls of the species.

A word or two more concerning this matter of the skin or blubber of the whale. It has already been said, that it is stript from him in long pieces, called blanket-pieces. Like most sea-terms, this one is very happy and significant. For the whale is indeed wrapt up in his blubber as in a real blanket or counterpane; or, still better, an Indian poncho slipt over his head, and skirting his extremity. It is by reason of this cosy blanketing of his body, that the whale is enabled to keep himself comfortable in all weathers, in all seas, times, and tides. What would become of a Greenland whale, say, in those shuddering, icy seas of the North, if unsupplied with his cosy surtout? True, other fish are found exceedingly brisk in those Hyperborean waters; but these, be it observed, are your cold-blooded, lungless fish, whose very bellies are refrigerators; creatures, that warm themselves under the lee of an iceberg, as a traveller in winter would bask before an inn fire; whereas, like man, the whale has lungs and warm blood. Freeze his blood, and he dies. How wonderful is it then—except after explanation—that this great monster, to whom corporeal warmth is as indispensable as it is to man; how wonderful that he should be found at home, immersed to his lips for life in those Arctic waters! where, when seamen fall overboard, they are sometimes found, months afterwards, perpendicularly frozen into the hearts of fields of ice, as a fly is found glued in amber. But more surprising is it to know, as has been proved by experiment, that the blood of a Polar whale is warmer than that of a Borneo negro in summer.

It does seem to me, that herein we see the rare virtue of a strong individual vitality, and the rare virtue of thick walls, and the rare virtue of interior spaciousness. Oh, man! admire and model thyself after the whale! Do thou, too, remain warm among ice. Do thou, too, live in this world without being of it. Be cool at the equator; keep thy blood fluid at the Pole. Like the great dome of St. Peter's, and like the great whale, retain, O man! in all seasons a temperature of thine own.

But how easy and how hopeless to teach these fine things! Of erections, how few are domed like St. Peter's! of creatures, how few vast as the whale!

Chapter 69

THE FUNERAL

"Haul in the chains! Let the carcase go astern!"

The vast tackles have now done their duty. The peeled white body of the beheaded whale flashes like a marble sepulchre; though changed in hue, it has not perceptibly lost anything in bulk. It is still colossal. Slowly it floats more and more away, the water round it torn and splashed by the insatiate sharks, and the air above vexed with rapacious flights of screaming fowls, whose beaks are like so many insulting poniards in the whale. The vast white headless phantom floats further and further from the ship, and every rod that it so floats, what seem square roods of sharks and cubic roods of fowls, augment the murderous din. For hours and hours from the almost stationary ship that hideous sight is seen. Beneath the unclouded and mild azure sky, upon the fair face of the pleasant sea, wafted by the joyous breezes, that great mass of death floats on and on, till lost in infinite perspectives.

There's a most doleful and most mocking funeral! The sea-vultures all in pious mourning, the air-sharks all punctiliously in black or speckled. In life but few of them would have helped the whale, I ween, if peradventure he had needed it; but upon the banquet of his funeral they most piously do pounce. Oh, horrible vulturism of earth! from which not the mightiest whale is free.

Nor is this the end. Desecrated as the body is, a vengeful ghost survives and hovers over it to scare. Espied by some timid man-of-war or blundering discovery-vessel from afar, when the distance obscuring the swarming fowls, nevertheless still shows the white mass floating in the sun, and the white spray heaving high against it; straightway the whale's unharming corpse, with trembling fingers is set down in the log—*shoals, rocks, and breakers hereabouts: beware!* And for years afterwards, perhaps, ships shun the place; leaping over it as silly sheep leap over a vacuum, because their leader originally leaped there when a stick was held. There's your law of precedents; there's your utility of traditions; there's the story of your obstinate survival of old beliefs never bottomed on the earth, and now not even hovering in the air! There's orthodoxy!

Thus, while in life the great whale's body may have been a real terror to his foes, in his death his ghost becomes a powerless panic to a world.

Are you a believer in ghosts, my friend? There are other ghosts than the Cock-Lane one, and far deeper men than Doctor Johnson who believe in them.

Chapter 70

THE SPHYNX

It should not have been omitted that previous to completely stripping the body of the leviathan, he was beheaded. Now, the beheading of the Sperm Whale is a scientific anatomical feat, upon which experienced whale surgeons very much pride themselves: and not without reason.

Consider that the whale has nothing that can properly be called a neck; on the contrary, where his head and body seem to join, there, in that very place, is the thickest part of him. Remember, also, that the surgeon must operate from above, some eight or ten feet intervening between him and his subject, and that subject almost hidden in a discolored, rolling, and oftentimes tumultuous and bursting sea. Bear in mind, too, that under these untoward circumstances he has to cut many feet deep in the flesh; and in that subterraneous manner, without so much as getting one single peep into the ever-contracting gash thus made, he must skilfully steer clear of all adjacent, interdicted parts, and exactly divide the spine at a critical point hard by its insertion into the skull. Do you not marvel, then, at Stubb's boast, that he demanded but ten minutes to behead a sperm whale?

When first severed, the head is dropped astern and held there by a cable till the body is stripped. That done, if it belong to a small whale it is hoisted on deck to be deliberately disposed of. But, with a full grown leviathan this is impossible; for the sperm whale's head embraces nearly one third of his entire bulk, and completely to suspend such a burden as that, even by the immense tackles of a whaler, this were as vain a thing as to attempt weighing a Dutch barn in jewellers' scales.

The Pequod's whale being decapitated and the body stripped, the head was hoisted against the ship's side—about half way out of the sea, so that it might yet in great part be buoyed up by its native element. And there with the strained craft steeply leaning over to it, by reason of the enormous downward drag from the lower mast-head, and every yard-arm on that side projecting like a crane over the waves; there, that blood-dripping head hung to the Pequod's waist like the giant Holofernes's from the girdle of Judith.[1]

When this last task was accomplished it was noon, and the seamen went below to their dinner. Silence reigned over the before tumultuous but now deserted deck. An intense copper calm, like a universal yellow lotus, was more and more unfolding its noiseless measureless leaves upon the sea.

A short space elapsed, and up into this noiselessness came Ahab alone from his cabin. Taking a few turns on the quarterdeck, he paused to gaze over the side, then slowly getting into the main-chains he took Stubb's long spade—still remaining there after the whale's decapitation—and striking it into the lower part of the half-suspended mass, placed its other end crutch-wise under one arm, and so stood leaning over with eyes attentively

---

1. The Jewish heroine in the apocryphal Book of Judith, who saves her people by killing the Assyrian Holofernes.

fixed on this head.

It was a black and hooded head; and hanging there in the midst of so intense a calm, it seemed the Sphynx's in the desert. "Speak, thou vast and venerable head," muttered Ahab, "which, though ungarnished with a beard, yet here and there lookest hoary with mosses; speak, mighty head, and tell us the secret thing that is in thee. Of all divers, thou hast dived the deepest. That head upon which the upper sun now gleams, has moved amid this world's foundations. Where unrecorded names and navies rust, and untold hopes and anchors rot; where in her murderous hold this frigate earth is ballasted with bones of millions of the drowned; there, in that awful water-land, there was thy most familiar home. Thou hast been where bell or diver never went; hast slept by many a sailor's side, where sleepless mothers would give their lives to lay them down. Thou saw'st the locked lovers when leaping from their flaming ship; heart to heart they sank beneath the exulting wave; true to each other, when heaven seemed false to them. Thou saw'st the murdered mate when tossed by pirates from the midnight deck; for hours he fell into the deeper midnight of the insatiate maw; and his murderers still sailed on unharmed—while swift lightnings shivered the neighboring ship that would have borne a righteous husband to outstretched, longing arms. O head! thou hast seen enough to split the planets and make an infidel of Abraham, and not one syllable is thine!"

"Sail ho!" cried a triumphant voice from the main-mast-head.

"Aye? Well, now, that's cheering," cried Ahab, suddenly erecting himself, while whole thunder-clouds swept aside from his brow. "That lively cry upon this deadly calm might almost convert a better man.—Where away?"

"Three points on the starboard bow, sir, and bringing down her breeze to us!"

"Better and better, man. Would now St. Paul would come along that way, and to my breezelessness bring his breeze! O Nature, and O soul of man! how far beyond all utterance are your linked analogies! not the smallest atom stirs or lives in matter, but has its cunning duplicate in mind."

Chapter 71

THE JEROBOAM'S STORY

Hand in hand, ship and breeze blew on; but the breeze came faster than the ship, and soon the Pequod began to rock.

By and by, through the glass the stranger's boats and manned

mast-heads proved her a whale-ship. But as she was so far to windward, and shooting by, apparently making a passage to some
other ground, the Pequod could not hope to reach her. So the
signal was set to see what response would be made.

Here be it said, that like the vessels of military marines, the
ships of the American Whale Fleet have each a private signal; all
which signals being collected in a book with the names of the
respective vessels attached, every captain is provided with it.
Thereby, the whale commanders are enabled to recognise each
other upon the ocean, even at considerable distances, and with no
small facility.

The Pequod's signal was at last responded to by the stranger's
setting her own; which proved the ship to be the Jeroboam [1] of
Nantucket. Squaring her yards, she bore down, ranged abeam
under the Pequod's lee, and lowered a boat; it soon drew nigh;
but, as the side-ladder was being rigged by Starbuck's order to
accommodate the visiting captain, the stranger in question waved
his hand from his boat's stern in token of that proceeding being
entirely unnecessary. It turned out that the Jeroboam had a malignant epidemic on board, and that Mayhew, her captain, was
fearful of infecting the Pequod's company. For, though himself
and boat's crew remained untainted, and though his ship was half
a rifle-shot off, and an incorruptible sea and air rolling and flowing between; yet conscientiously adhering to the timid quarantine
of the land, he peremptorily refused to come into direct contact
with the Pequod.

But this did by no means prevent all communication. Preserving an interval of some few yards between itself and the ship, the
Jeroboam's boat by the occasional use of its oars contrived to keep
parallel to the Pequod, as she heavily forged through the sea (for
by this time it blew very fresh), with her main-top-sail aback;
though, indeed, at times by the sudden onset of a large rolling
wave, the boat would be pushed some way ahead; but would be
soon skilfully brought to her proper bearings again. Subject to
this, and other the like interruptions now and then, a conversation
was sustained between the two parties; but at intervals not without still another interruption of a very different sort.

Pulling an oar in the Jeroboam's boat, was a man of a singular
appearance, even in that wild whaling life where individual no-
tabilities make up all totalities. He was a small, short, youngish
man, sprinkled all over his face with freckles, and wearing redundant yellow hair. A long-skirted, cabalistically-cut coat of a
faded walnut tinge enveloped him; the overlapping sleeves of

1. Jeroboam was a wicked king of Israel. See I Kings 11–14.

which were rolled up on his wrists. A deep, settled, fanatic delirium was in his eyes.

So soon as this figure had been first descried, Stubb had exclaimed—"That's he! that's he!—the long-togged scaramouch the Town-Ho's company told us of!" Stubb here alluded to a strange story told of the Jeroboam, and a certain man among her crew, some time previous when the Pequod spoke the Town-Ho. According to this account and what was subsequently learned, it seemed that the scaramouch in question had gained a wonderful ascendency over almost everybody in the Jeroboam. His story was this:

He had been originally nurtured among the crazy society of Niskayuna [2] Shakers, where he had been a great prophet; in their cracked, secret meetings having several times descended from heaven by the way of a trap-door, announcing the speedy opening of the seventh vial,[3] which he carried in his vest-pocket; but, which, instead of containing gunpowder, was supposed to be charged with laudanum. A strange, apostolic whim having seized him, he had left Niskayuna for Nantucket, where, with that cunning peculiar to craziness, he assumed a steady, common sense exterior, and offered himself as a green-hand candidate for the Jeroboam's whaling voyage. They engaged him; but straightway upon the ship's getting out of sight of land, his insanity broke out in a freshet. He announced himself as the archangel Gabriel, and commanded the captain to jump overboard. He published his manifesto, whereby he set himself forth as the deliverer of the isles of the sea and vicar-general of all Oceanica. The unflinching earnestness with which he declared these things;—the dark, daring play of his sleepless, excited imagination, and all the preternatural terrors of real delirium, united to invest this Gabriel in the minds of the majority of the ignorant crew, with an atmosphere of sacredness. Moreover, they were afraid of him. As such a man, however, was not of much practical use in the ship, especially as he refused to work except when he pleased, the incredulous captain would fain have been rid of him; but apprised that that individual's intention was to land him in the first convenient port, the archangel forthwith opened all his seals and vials—devoting the ship and all hands to unconditional perdition, in case this intention was carried out. So strongly did he work upon his disciples among the crew, that at last in a body they went to the captain and told him if Gabriel was sent from the ship, not a man of them would remain. He was therefore forced to relinquish his plan. Nor would they permit Gabriel to be any way mal-

2. On the Hudson, near Albany.
3. In Revelation 16:17 the seventh vial is the last of the "vials of wrath" poured out by the angels.

treated, say or do what he would; so that it came to pass that Gabriel had the complete freedom of the ship. The consequence of all this was, that the archangel cared little or nothing for the captain and mates; and since the epidemic had broken out, he carried a higher hand than ever; declaring that the plague, as he called it, was at his sole command; nor should it be stayed but according to his good pleasure. The sailors, mostly poor devils, cringed, and some of them fawned before him; in obedience to his instructions, sometimes rendering him personal homage, as to a god. Such things may seem incredible; but, however wondrous, they are true. Nor is the history of fanatics half so striking in respect to the measureless self-deception of the fanatic himself, as his measureless power of deceiving and bedevilling so many others. But it is time to return to the Pequod.

"I fear not thy epidemic, man," said Ahab from the bulwarks, to Captain Mayhew, who stood in the boat's stern; "come on board."

But now Gabriel started to his feet.

"Think, think of the fevers, yellow and bilious! Beware of the horrible plague!"

"Gabriel, Gabriel!" cried Captain Mayhew; "thou must either—" But that instant a headlong wave shot the boat far ahead, and its seethings drowned all speech.

"Hast thou seen the White Whale?" demanded Ahab, when the boat drifted back.

"Think, think of thy whale-boat, stoven and sunk! Beware of the horrible tail!"

"I tell thee again, Gabriel, that—" But again the boat tore ahead as if dragged by fiends. Nothing was said for some moments, while a succession of riotous waves rolled by, which by one of those occasional caprices of the seas were tumbling, not heaving it. Meantime, the hoisted sperm whale's head jogged about very violently, and Gabriel was seen eyeing it with rather more apprehensiveness than his archangel nature seemed to warrant.

When this interlude was over, Captain Mayhew began a dark story concerning Moby Dick; not, however, without frequent interruptions from Gabriel, whenever his name was mentioned, and the crazy sea that seemed leagued with him.

It seemed that the Jeroboam had not long left home, when upon speaking a whale-ship, her people were reliably apprised of the existence of Moby Dick, and the havoc he had made. Greedily sucking in this intelligence, Gabriel solemnly warned the captain against attacking the White Whale, in case the monster should be seen; in his gibbering insanity, pronouncing the White Whale to be no less a being than the Shaker God incarnated; the Shakers receiving the Bible.[4] But when, some year or two afterwards, Moby Dick was fairly sighted from the mast-heads, Macey, the chief mate, burned with ardor to encounter him; and the captain himself being not unwilling to let him have the opportunity, despite all the archangel's denunciations and forewarnings, Macey succeeded in persuading five men to man his boat. With them he pushed off; and, after much weary pulling, and many perilous, unsuccessful onsets, he at last succeeded in getting one iron fast. Meantime, Gabriel, ascending to the main-royal mast-head, was tossing one arm in frantic gestures, and hurling forth prophecies of speedy doom to the sacrilegious assailants of his divinity. Now, while Macey, the mate, was standing up in his boat's bow, and with all the reckless energy of his tribe was venting his wild exclamations upon the whale, and essaying to get a fair chance for his poised lance, lo! a broad white shadow rose from the sea; by its quick, fanning motion, temporarily taking the breath out of the bodies of the oarsmen. Next instant, the luckless mate, so full of furious life, was smitten bodily into the air, and making a long arc in his descent, fell into the sea at the distance of about fifty yards. Not a chip of the boat was harmed, nor a hair of any oarsman's head; but the mate for ever sank.

(It is well to parenthesize here, that of the fatal accidents in the Sperm-Whale Fishery, this kind is perhaps almost as frequent as any. Sometimes, nothing is injured but the man who is thus annihilated; oftener the boat's bow is knocked off, or the thighboard, in which the headsman stands, is torn from its place and accompanies the body. But strangest of all is the circumstance, that in more instances than one, when the body has been recovered, not a single mark of violence is discernible; the man being stark dead.)

The whole calamity, with the falling form of Macey, was plainly descried from the ship. Raising a piercing shriek—"The vial! the vial!" Gabriel called off the terror-stricken crew from the further hunting of the whale. This terrible event clothed the archangel with added influence; because his credulous disciples believed that he had specifically fore-announced it, instead of only making a general prophecy, which any one might have done, and so have chanced to hit one of many marks in the wide margin allowed. He became a nameless terror to the ship.

Mayhew having concluded his narration, Ahab put such questions to him, that the stranger captain could not forbear inquiring

4. A crux, never satisfactorily explained. "Receiving" probably means accepting, or believing in. This phrase has been glossed in various ways, and may not be just what Melville wrote; it probably simply means that the Shakers accept the Bible literally.

whether he intended to hunt the White Whale, if opportunity should offer. To which Ahab answered—"Aye." Straightway, then, Gabriel once more started to his feet, glaring upon the old man, and vehemently exclaimed, with downward pointed finger— "Think, think of the blasphemer—dead, and down there!—beware of the blasphemer's end!"

Ahab stolidly turned aside; then said to Mayhew, "Captain, I have just bethought me of my letter-bag; there is a letter for one of thy officers, if I mistake not. Starbuck, look over the bag."

Every whale-ship takes out a goodly number of letters for various ships, whose delivery to the persons to whom they may be addressed, depends upon the mere chance of encountering them in the four oceans. Thus, most letters never reach their mark; and many are only received after attaining an age of two or three years or more.

Soon Starbuck returned with a letter in his hand. It was sorely tumbled, damp, and covered with a dull, spotted, green mould, in consequence of being kept in a dark locker of the cabin. Of such a letter, Death himself might well have been the post-boy.

"Can'st not read it?" cried Ahab. "Give it me, man. Aye, aye, it's but a dim scrawl;—what's this?" As he was studying it out, Starbuck took a long cutting-spade pole, and with his knife slightly split the end, to insert the letter there, and in that way, hand it to the boat, without its coming any closer to the ship.

Meantime, Ahab holding the letter, muttered, "Mr. Har—yes, Mr. Harry—(a woman's pinny hand,—the man's wife, I'll wager) —Aye—Mr. Harry Macey, Ship Jeroboam;—why it's Macey, and he's dead!"

"Poor fellow! poor fellow! and from his wife," sighed Mayhew; "but let me have it."

"Nay, keep it thyself," cried Gabriel to Ahab; "thou art soon going that way."

"Curses throttle thee!" yelled Ahab. "Captain Mayhew, stand by now to receive it;" and taking the fatal missive from Starbuck's hands, he caught it in the slit of the pole, and reached it over towards the boat. But as he did so, the oarsmen expectantly desisted from rowing; the boat drifted a little towards the ship's stern; so that, as if by magic, the letter suddenly ranged along with Gabriel's eager hand. He clutched it in an instant, seized the boat-knife, and impaling the letter on it, sent it thus loaded back into the ship. It fell at Ahab's feet. Then Gabriel shrieked out to his comrades to give way with their oars, and in that manner the mutinous boat rapidly shot away from the Pequod.

As, after this interlude, the seamen resumed their work upon the jacket of the whale, many strange things were hinted in reference to this wild affair.

Chapter 72

THE MONKEY-ROPE [1]

In the tumultuous business of cutting-in and attending to a whale, there is much running backwards and forwards among the crew. Now hands are wanted here, and then again hands are wanted there. There is no staying in any one place; for at one and the same time everything has to be done everywhere. It is much the same with him who endeavors the description of the scene. We must now retrace our way a little. It was mentioned that upon first breaking ground in the whale's back, the blubber-hook was inserted into the original hole there cut by the spades of the mates. But how did so clumsy and weighty a mass as that same hook get fixed in that hole? It was inserted there by my particular friend Queequeg, whose duty it was, as harpooneer, to descend upon the monster's back for the special purpose referred to. But in very many cases, circumstances require that the harpooneer shall remain on the whale till the whole flensing or stripping operation is concluded. The whale, be it observed, lies almost entirely submerged, excepting the immediate parts operated upon. So down there, some ten feet below the level of the deck, the poor harpooneer flounders about, half on the whale and half in the water, as the vast mass revolves like a tread-mill beneath him. On the occasion in question, Queequeg figured in the Highland costume—a shirt and socks—in which to my eyes, at least, he appeared to uncommon advantage; and no one had a better chance to observe him, as will presently be seen.

Being the savage's bowsman, that is, the person who pulled the bow-oar in his boat (the second one from forward), it was my cheerful duty to attend upon him while taking that hardscrabble scramble upon the dead whale's back. You have seen Italian organ-boys holding a dancing-ape by a long cord. Just so, from the ship's steep side, did I hold Queequeg down there in the sea, by what is technically called in the fishery a monkey-rope, attached to a strong strip of canvas belted round his waist.

It was a humorously perilous business for both of us. For, before we proceed further, it must be said that the monkey-rope was fast at both ends; fast to Queequeg's broad canvas belt, and fast to my narrow leather one. So that for better or for worse,

---

1. Mansfield and Vincent show that this chapter was suggested to Melville by Francis Allyn Olmsted's *Incidents of a Whaling Voyage* (New York, 1841).

we two, for the time, were wedded; and should poor Queequeg sink to rise no more, then both usage and honor demanded, that instead of cutting the cord, it should drag me down in his wake. So, then, an elongated Siamese ligature united us. Queequeg was my own inseparable twin brother; nor could I any way get rid of the dangerous liabilities which the hempen bond entailed.

So strongly and metaphysically did I conceive of my situation then, that while earnestly watching his motions, I seemed distinctly to perceive that my own individuality was now merged in a joint stock company of two: that my free will had received a mortal wound; and that another's mistake or misfortune might plunge innocent me into unmerited disaster and death. Therefore, I saw that here was a sort of interregnum in Providence; for its even-handed equity never could have sanctioned so gross an injustice. And yet still further pondering—while I jerked him now and then from between the whale and the ship, which would threaten to jam him—still further pondering, I say, I saw that this situation of mine was the precise situation of every mortal that breathes; only, in most cases, he, one way or other, has this Siamese connexion with a plurality of other mortals. If your banker breaks, you snap; if your apothecary by mistake sends you poison in your pills, you die. True, you may say that, by exceeding caution, you may possibly escape these and the multitudinous other evil chances of life. But handle Queequeg's monkey-rope heedfully as I would, sometimes he jerked it so, that I came very near sliding overboard. Nor could I possibly forget that, do what I would, I only had the management of one end of it.*

I have hinted that I would often jerk poor Queequeg from between the whale and the ship—where he would occasionally fall, from the incessant rolling and swaying of both. But this was not the only jamming jeopardy he was exposed to. Unappalled by the massacre made upon them during the night, the sharks now freshly and more keenly allured by the before pent blood which began to flow from the carcase—the rabid creatures swarmed round it like bees in a beehive.

And right in among those sharks was Queequeg; who often pushed them aside with his floundering feet. A thing altogether incredible were it not that attracted by such prey as a dead whale, the otherwise miscellaneously carnivorous shark will seldom touch a man.

---

* The monkey-rope is found in all whalers; but it was only in the Pequod that the monkey and his holder were ever tied together. This improvement upon the original usage was introduced by no less a man than Stubb, in order to afford to the imperilled harpooneer the strongest possible guarantee for the faithfulness and vigilance of his monkey-rope holder [Melville's note].

Nevertheless, it may well be believed that since they have such a ravenous finger in the pie, it is deemed but wise to look sharp to them. Accordingly, besides the monkey-rope, with which I now and then jerked the poor fellow from too close a vicinity to the maw of what seemed a peculiarly ferocious shark—he was provided with still another protection. Suspended over the side in one of the stages, Tashtego and Daggoo continually flourished over his head a couple of keen whale-spades, wherewith they slaughtered as many sharks as they could reach. This procedure of theirs, to be sure, was very disinterested and benevolent of them. They meant Queequeg's best happiness, I admit; but in their hasty zeal to befriend him, and from the circumstance that both he and the sharks were at times half hidden by the blood-mudded water, those indiscreet spades of theirs would come nearer amputating a leg than a tail. But poor Queequeg, I suppose, straining and gasping there with that great iron hook—poor Queequeg, I suppose, only prayed to his Yojo, and gave up his life into the hands of his gods.

Well, well, my dear comrade and twin-brother, thought I, as I drew in and then slacked off the rope to every swell of the sea—what matters it, after all? Are you not the precious image of each and all of us men in this whaling world? That unsounded ocean you gasp in, is Life; those sharks, your foes; those spades, your friends; and what between sharks and spades you are in a sad pickle and peril, poor lad.

But courage! there is good cheer in store for you, Queequeg. For now, as with blue lips and bloodshot eyes the exhausted savage at last climbs up the chains and stands all dripping and involuntarily trembling over the side; the steward advances, and with a benevolent, consolatory glance hands him—what? Some hot Cognac? No! hands him, ye gods! hands him a cup of tepid ginger and water!

"Ginger? Do I smell ginger?" suspiciously asked Stubb, coming near. "Yes, this must be ginger," peering into the as yet untasted cup. Then standing as if incredulous for a while, he calmly walked towards the astonished steward slowly saying, "Ginger? ginger? and will you have the goodness to tell me, Mr. Dough-Boy, where lies the virtue of ginger? Ginger! is ginger the sort of fuel you use, Dough-Boy, to kindle a fire in this shivering cannibal? Ginger!—what the devil is ginger?—sea-coal?—fire-wood?—lucifer matches?—tinder?—gunpowder?—what the devil is ginger, I say, that you offer this cup to our poor Queequeg here?"

"There is some sneaking Temperance Society movement about this business," he suddenly added, now approaching Starbuck, who had just come from forward. "Will you look at that kannakin, sir: smell of it, if you please." Then watching the mate's coun-tenance, he added: "The steward, Mr. Starbuck, had the face to offer that calomel and jalap to Queequeg, there, this instant off the whale. Is the steward an apothecary, sir? and may I ask whether this is the sort of bellows by which he blows back the breath into a half-drowned man?"

"I trust not," said Starbuck, "it is poor stuff enough."

"Aye, aye, steward," cried Stubb, "we'll teach you to drug a harpooneer; none of your apothecary's medicine here; you want to poison us, do ye? You have got out insurances on our lives and want to murder us all, and pocket the proceeds, do ye?"

"It was not me," cried Dough-Boy, "it was Aunt Charity that brought the ginger on board; and bade me never give the har-pooneers any spirits, but only this ginger-jub—so she called it."

"Ginger-jub! you gingerly rascal! take that! and run along with ye to the lockers, and get something better. I hope I do no wrong, Mr. Starbuck. It is the captain's orders—grog for the harpooneer on a whale."

"Enough," replied Starbuck, "only don't hit him again, but—"

"Oh, I never hurt when I hit, except when I hit a whale or something of that sort; and this fellow's a weazel. What were you about saying, sir?"

"Only this: go down with him, and get what thou wantest thy-self."

When Stubb reappeared, he came with a dark flask in one hand, and a sort of tea-caddy in the other. The first contained strong spirits, and was handed to Queequeg; the second was Aunt Charity's gift, and that was freely given to the waves.

Chapter 73

STUBB AND FLASK KILL A RIGHT WHALE; AND THEN HAVE A TALK OVER HIM

It must be borne in mind that all this time we have a Sperm Whale's prodigious head hanging to the Pequod's side. But we must let it continue hanging there a while till we can get a chance to attend to it. For the present other matters press, and the best we can do now for the head, is to pray heaven the tackles may hold.

Now, during the past night and forenoon, the Pequod had gradually drifted into a sea, which, by its occasional patches of yellow brit, gave unusual tokens of the vicinity of Right Whales, a species of the Leviathan that but few supposed to be at this particular time lurking anywhere near. And though all hands commonly disdained the capture of those inferior creatures; and though the Pequod was not commissioned to cruise for them at all, and though she had passed numbers of them near the Crozets without lowering a boat; yet now that a Sperm Whale had been brought alongside and beheaded, to the surprise of all, the announcement was made that a Right Whale should be captured that day, if opportunity offered.

Nor was this long wanting. Tall spouts were seen to leeward; and two boats, Stubb's and Flask's, were detached in pursuit. Pulling further and further away, they at last became almost invisible to the men at the mast-heads. But suddenly in the distance, they saw a great heap of tumultuous white water, and soon after news came from aloft that one or both the boats must be fast. An interval passed and the boats were in plain sight, in the act of being dragged right towards the ship by the towing whale. So close did the monster come to the hull, that at first it seemed as if he meant it malice; but suddenly going down in a maelstrom, within three rods of the planks, he wholly disappeared from view, as if diving under the keel. "Cut, cut!" was the cry from the ship to the boats, which, for one instant, seemed on the point of being brought with a deadly dash against the vessel's side. But having plenty of line yet in the tubs, and the whale not sounding very rapidly, they paid out abundance of rope, and at the same time pulled with all their might so as to get ahead of the ship. For a few minutes the struggle was intensely critical; for while they still slacked out the tightened line in one direction, and still plied their oars in another, the contending strain threatened to take them under. But it was only a few feet advance they sought to gain. And they stuck to it till they did gain it; when instantly, a swift tremor was felt running like lightning along the keel, as the strained line, scraping beneath the ship, suddenly rose to view under her bows, snapping and quivering; and so flinging off its drippings, that the drops fell like bits of broken glass on the water, while the whale beyond also rose to sight, and once more the boats were free to fly. But the fagged whale abated his speed, and blindly altering his course, went round the stern of the ship towing the two boats after him, so that they performed a complete circuit.

Meantime, they hauled more and more upon their lines, till close flanking him on both sides, Stubb answered Flask with lance for lance; and thus round and round the Pequod the battle went, while the multitudes of sharks that had before swum round the Sperm Whale's body, rushed to the fresh blood that was spilled, thirstily drinking at every new gash, as the eager Israelites did at the new bursting fountains that poured from the smitten rock.

At last his spout grew thick, and with a frightful roll and vomit, he turned upon his back a corpse.

While the two headsmen were engaged in making fast cords to his flukes, and in other ways getting the mass in readiness for towing, some conversation ensued between them.

"I wonder what the old man wants with this lump of foul lard," said Stubb, not without some disgust at the thought of having to do with so ignoble a leviathan.

"Wants with it?" said Flask, coiling some spare line in the boat's bow, "did you never hear that the ship which but once has a Sperm Whale's head hoisted on her starboard side, and at the same time a Right Whale's on the larboard; did you never hear, Stubb, that that ship can never afterwards capsize?"

"Why not?"

"I don't know, but I heard that gamboge ghost of a Fedallah saying so, and he seems to know all about ships' charms. But I sometimes think he'll charm the ship to no good at last. I don't half like that chap, Stubb. Did you ever notice how that tusk of his is a sort of carved into a snake's head, Stubb?"

"Sink him! I never look at him at all; but if ever I get a chance of a dark night, and he standing hard by the bulwarks, and no one by; look down there, Flask"—pointing into the sea with a peculiar motion of both hands—"Aye, will I! Flask, I take that Fedallah to be the devil in disguise. Do you believe that cock and bull story about his having been stowed away on board ship? He's the devil, I say. The reason why you don't see his tail, is because he tucks it up out of sight; he carries it coiled away in his pocket, I guess. Blast him! now that I think of it, he's always wanting oakum to stuff into the toes of his boots."

"He sleeps in his boots, don't he? He hasn't got any hammock; but I've seen him lay of nights in a coil of rigging."

"No doubt, and it's because of his cursed tail; he coils it down, do ye see, in the eye of the rigging."

"What's the old man have so much to do with him for?"

"Striking up a swap or a bargain, I suppose."

"Bargain?—about what?"

"Why, do ye see, the old man is hard bent after that White Whale, and the devil there is trying to come round him, and get him to swap away his silver watch, or his soul, or something of that sort, and then he'll surrender Moby Dick."

"Pooh! Stubb, you are skylarking; how can Fedallah do that?"

"I don't know, Flask, but the devil is a curious chap, and a wicked one, I tell ye. Why, they say[1] as how he went a sauntering into the old flag-ship once, switching his tail about devilish easy and gentlemanlike, and inquiring if the old governor was at home. Well, he was at home, and asked the devil what he wanted. The devil, switching his hoofs, up and says, 'I want John.' 'What for?' says the old governor. 'What business is that of yours,' says the devil, getting mad,—'I want to use him.' 'Take him,' says the governor—and by the Lord, Flask, if the devil didn't give John the Asiatic cholera before he got through with him, I'll eat this whale in one mouthful. But look sharp—aint you all ready there? Well, then, pull ahead, and let's get the whale alongside."

"I think I remember some such story as you were telling," said Flask, when at last the two boats were slowly advancing with their burden towards the ship, "but I can't remember where."

"Three Spaniards? [2] Adventures of those three bloody-minded soldadoes? Did ye read it there, Flask? I guess ye did?"

"No: never saw such a book; heard of it, though. But now, tell me, Stubb, do you suppose that that devil you was speaking of just now, was the same you say is now on board the Pequod?"

"Am I the same man that helped kill this whale? Doesn't the devil live for ever; who ever heard that the devil was dead? Did you ever see any parson a wearing mourning for the devil? And if the devil has a latch-key to get into the admiral's cabin, don't you suppose he can crawl into a port-hole? Tell me that, Mr. Flask?"

"How old do you suppose Fedallah is, Stubb?"

"Do you see that mainmast there?" pointing to the ship; "well, that's the figure one; now take all the hoops in the Pequod's hold, and string 'em along in a row with that mast, for oughts, do you see; well, that wouldn't begin to be Fedallah's age. Nor all the coopers in creation couldn't show hoops enough to make oughts enough."

"But see here, Stubb, I thought you a little boasted just now, that you meant to give Fedallah a sea-toss, if you got a good chance. Now, if he's so old as all those hoops of yours come to, and if he is going to live for ever, what good will it do to pitch him overboard—tell me that?"

"Give him a good ducking, anyhow."

"But he'd crawl back."

"Duck him again; and keep ducking him."

"Suppose he should take it into his head to duck you, though —yes, and drown you—what then?"

---

1. What follows is a travesty of the story of Job.

2. A reference to George Walker's melodramatic novel, *The Three Spaniards*.

"I should like to see him try it; I'd give him such a pair of black eyes that he wouldn't dare to show his face in the admiral's cabin again for a long while, let alone down in the orlop there, where he lives, and hereabouts on the upper decks where he sneaks so much. Damn the devil, Flask; do you suppose I'm afraid of the devil? Who's afraid of him, except the old governor who daresn't catch him and put him in double-darbies, as he deserves, but lets him go about kidnapping people; aye, and signed a bond with him, that all the people the devil kidnapped, he'd roast for him? There's a governor!"

"Do you suppose Fedallah wants to kidnap Captain Ahab?"

"Do I suppose it? You'll know it before long, Flask. But I am going now to keep a sharp look-out on him; and if I see anything very suspicious going on, I'll just take him by the nape of his neck, and say—Look here, Beelzebub, you don't do it; and if he makes any fuss, by the Lord I'll make a grab into his pocket for his tail, take it to the capstan, and give him such a wrenching and heaving, that his tail will come short off at the stump—do you see; and then, I rather guess when he finds himself docked in that queer fashion, he'll sneak off without the poor satisfaction of feeling his tail between his legs."

"And what will you do with the tail, Stubb?"

"Do with it? Sell it for an ox whip when we get home;—what else?"

"Now, do you mean what you say, and have been saying all along, Stubb?"

"Mean or not mean, here we are at the ship."

The boats were here hailed, to tow the whale on the larboard side, where fluke chains and other necessaries were already prepared for securing him.

"Didn't I tell you so?" said Flask; "yes, you'll soon see this right whale's head hoisted up opposite that parmacetti's."

In good time, Flask's saying proved true. As before, the Pequod steeply leaned over towards the sperm whale's head, now, by the counterpoise of both heads, she regained her even keel; though sorely strained, you may well believe. So, when on one side you hoist in Locke's head, you go over that way; but now, on the other side, hoist in Kant's and you come back again; but in very poor plight. Thus, some minds for ever keep trimming boat. Oh, ye foolish! throw all these thunderheads overboard, and then you will float light and right.

In disposing of the body of a right whale, when brought alongside the ship, the same preliminary proceedings commonly take place as in the case of a sperm whale; only, in the latter instance, the head is cut off whole, but in the former the lips and tongue are separately removed and hoisted on deck, with all the well known black bone attached to what is called the crown-piece. But nothing like this, in the present case, had been done. The carcases of both whales had dropped astern; and the head-laden ship not a little resembled a mule carrying a pair of overburdening panniers.

Meantime, Fedallah was calmly eyeing the right whale's head, and ever and anon glancing from the deep wrinkles there to the lines in his own hand. And Ahab chanced so to stand, that the Parsee occupied his shadow; while, if the Parsee's shadow was there at all it seemed only to blend with, and lengthen Ahab's. As the crew toiled on, Laplandish speculations were bandied among them, concerning all these passing things.

Chapter 74

THE SPERM WHALE'S HEAD—CONTRASTED VIEW

Here, now, are two great whales, laying their heads together; let us join them, and lay together our own.

Of the grand order of folio leviathans, the Sperm Whale and the Right Whale are by far the most noteworthy. They are the only whales regularly hunted by man. To the Nantucketer, they present the two extremes of all the known varieties of the whale. As the external difference between them is mainly observable in their heads; and as a head of each is this moment hanging from the Pequod's side; and as we may freely go from one to the other, by merely stepping across the deck:—where, I should like to know, will you obtain a better chance to study practical cetology than here?

In the first place, you are struck by the general contrast between these heads. Both are massive enough in all conscience; but there is a certain mathematical symmetry in the Sperm Whale's which the Right Whale's sadly lacks. There is more character in the Sperm Whale's head. As you behold it, you involuntarily yield the immense superiority to him, in point of pervading dignity. In the present instance, too, this dignity is heightened by the pepper and salt color of his head at the summit, giving token of advanced age and large experience. In short, he is what the fishermen technically call a "grey-headed whale."

Let us now note what is least dissimilar in these heads—namely, the two most important organs, the eye and the ear. Far back on the side of the head, and low down, near the angle of either whale's jaw, if you narrowly search, you will at last see a lashless eye, which you would fancy to be a young colt's eye; so out of all proportion is it to the magnitude of the head.

Now, from this peculiar sideway position of the whale's eyes, it is plain that he can never see an object which is exactly ahead, no more than he can one exactly astern. In a word, the position of the whale's eyes corresponds to that of a man's ears; and you may fancy, for yourself, how it would fare with you, did you sideways survey objects through your ears. You would find that you could only command some thirty degrees of vision in advance of the straight side-line of sight; and about thirty more behind it. If your bitterest foe were walking straight towards you, with dagger uplifted in broad day, you would not be able to see him, any more than if he were stealing upon you from behind. In a word, you would have two backs, so to speak; but, at the same time, also, two fronts (side fronts): for what is it that makes the front of a man—what, indeed, but his eyes?

Moreover, while in most other animals that I can now think of, the eyes are so planted as imperceptibly to blend their visual power, so as to produce one picture and not two to the brain; the peculiar position of the whale's eyes, effectually divided as they are by many cubic feet of solid head, which towers between them like a great mountain separating two lakes in valleys; this, of course, must wholly separate the impressions which each independent organ imparts. The whale, therefore, must see one distinct picture on this side, and another distinct picture on that side; while all between must be profound darkness and nothingness to him. Man may, in effect, be said to look out on the world from a sentry-box with two joined sashes for his window. But with the whale, these two sashes are separately inserted, making two distinct windows, but sadly impairing the view. This peculiarity of the whale's eyes is a thing always to be borne in mind in the fishery; and to be remembered by the reader in some subsequent scenes.

A curious and most puzzling question might be started concerning this visual matter as touching the Leviathan. But I must be content with a hint. So long as a man's eyes are open in the light, the act of seeing is involuntary; that is, he cannot then help mechanically seeing whatever objects are before him. Nevertheless, any one's experience will teach him, that though he can take in an undiscriminating sweep of things at one glance, it is quite impossible for him, attentively, and completely, to examine any two things—however large or however small—at one and the same instant of time; never mind if they lie side by side and touch each other. But if you now come to separate these two objects, and surround each by a circle of profound darkness; then, in order to see one of them, in such a manner as to bring your mind to bear on it, the other will be utterly excluded from your contemporary consciousness. How is it, then, with the whale? True, both his eyes, in themselves, must simultaneously act; but is his brain so much more comprehensive, combining, and subtle than man's, that he can at the same moment of time attentively examine two distinct prospects, one on one side of him, and the other in an exactly opposite direction? If he can, then is it as marvellous a thing in him, as if a man were able simultaneously to go through the demonstrations of two distinct problems in Euclid. Nor, strictly investigated, is there any incongruity in this comparison.

It may be but an idle whim, but it has always seemed to me, that the extraordinary vacillations of movement displayed by some whales when beset by three or four boats; the timidity and liability to queer frights, so common to such whales; I think that all this indirectly proceeds from the helpless perplexity of volition, in which their divided and diametrically opposite powers of vision must involve them.

But the ear of the whale is full as curious as the eye. If you are an entire stranger to their race, you might hunt over these two heads for hours, and never discover that organ. The ear has no external leaf whatever; and into the hole itself you can hardly insert a quill, so wondrously minute is it. It is lodged a little behind the eye. With respect to their ears, this important difference is to be observed between the sperm whale and the right. While the ear of the former has an external opening, that of the latter is entirely and evenly covered over with a membrane, so as to be quite imperceptible from without.

Is it not curious, that so vast a being as the whale should see the world through so small an eye, and hear the thunder through an ear which is smaller than a hare's? But if his eyes were broad as the lens of Herschel's great telescope; and his ears capacious as the porches of cathedrals; would that make him any longer of sight, or sharper of hearing? Not at all.—Why then do you try to "enlarge" your mind? Subtilize it.

Let us now with whatever levers and steam-engines we have at hand, cant over the sperm whale's head, so that it may lie bottom up; then, ascending by a ladder to the summit, have a peep down the mouth; and were it not that the body is now completely separated from it, with a lantern we might descend into the great Kentucky Mammoth Cave of his stomach. But let us hold on here by this tooth, and look about us where we are. What a really beautiful and chaste-looking mouth! from floor to ceiling, lined, or rather papered with a glistening white membrane, glossy as bridal satins.

But come out now, and look at this portentous lower jaw, which seems like the long narrow lid of an immense snuff-box, with the hinge at one end, instead of one side. If you pry it up, so as to get it overhead, and expose its rows of teeth, it seems a terrific portcullis; and such, alas! it proves to many a poor wight in the fishery, upon whom these spikes fall with impaling force. But far more terrible is it to behold, when fathoms down in the sea, you see some sulky whale, floating there suspended, with his prodigious jaw, some fifteen feet long, hanging straight down at right-angles with his body, for all the world like a ship's jib-boom. This whale is not dead; he is only dispirited; out of sorts, perhaps; hypochondriac; and so supine, that the hinges of his jaw have relaxed, leaving him there in that ungainly sort of plight, a reproach to all his tribe, who must, no doubt, imprecate lock-jaws upon him.

In most cases this lower jaw—being easily unhinged by a practised artist—is disengaged and hoisted on deck for the purpose of extracting the ivory teeth, and furnishing a supply of that hard white whalebone with which the fishermen fashion all sorts of curious articles, including canes, umbrella-stocks, and handles to riding-whips.

With a long, weary hoist the jaw is dragged on board, as if it were an anchor; and when the proper time comes—some few days after the other work—Queequeg, Daggoo, and Tashtego, being all accomplished dentists, are set to drawing teeth. With a keen cutting-spade, Queequeg lances the gums; then the jaw is lashed down to ringbolts, and a tackle being rigged from aloft, they drag out these teeth, as Michigan oxen drag stumps of old oaks out of wild wood-lands. There are generally forty-two teeth in all; in old whales, much worn down, but undecayed; nor filled after our artificial fashion. The jaw is afterwards sawn into slabs, and piled away like joists for building houses.

Chapter 75

THE RIGHT WHALE'S HEAD—CONTRASTED VIEW

Crossing the deck, let us now have a good long look at the Right Whale's head.

As in general shape the noble Sperm Whale's head may be compared to a Roman war-chariot (especially in front, where it is so broadly rounded); so, at a broad view, the Right Whale's head bears a rather inelegant resemblance to a gigantic galliot-toed shoe. Two hundred years ago an old Dutch voyager likened its shape to that of a shoemaker's last. And in this same last or shoe, that old woman of the nursery tale, with the swarming brood, might very comfortably be lodged, she and all her progeny.

But as you come nearer to this great head it begins to assume different aspects, according to your point of view. If you stand on its summit and look at these two ƒ-shaped spout-holes, you would take the whole head for an enormous bass-viol, and these spiracles, the apertures in its sounding-board. Then, again, if you fix your eye upon this strange, crested, comb-like incrustation on the top of the mass—this green, barnacled thing, which the Greenlanders call the "crown," and the Southern fishers the "bonnet" of the Right Whale; fixing your eyes solely on this, you would take the head for the trunk of some huge oak, with a bird's nest in its crotch. At any rate, when you watch those live crabs that nestle here on this bonnet, such an idea will be almost sure to occur to you; unless, indeed, your fancy has been fixed by the technical term "crown" also bestowed upon it; in which case you will take great interest in thinking how this mighty monster is actually a diademed king of the sea, whose green crown has been put together for him in this marvellous manner. But if this whale be a king, he is a very sulky looking fellow to grace a diadem. Look at that hanging lower lip! what a huge sulk and pout is there! a sulk and pout, by carpenter's measurement, about twenty feet long and five feet deep; a sulk and pout that will yield you some 500 gallons of oil and more.

A great pity, now, that this unfortunate whale should be hare-lipped. The fissure is about a foot across. Probably the mother during an important interval was sailing down the Peruvian coast, when earthquakes caused the beach to gape. Over this lip, as over a slippery threshold, we now slide into the mouth. Upon my word were I at Mackinaw, I should take this to be the inside of an Indian wigwam. Good Lord! is this the road that Jonah went? The roof is about twelve feet high, and runs to a pretty sharp angle, as if there were a regular ridge-pole there; while these ribbed, arched, hairy sides, present us with those wondrous, half vertical, scimitar-shaped slats of whalebone, say three hundred on a side, which depending from the upper part of the head or crown bone, form those Venetian blinds which have elsewhere been cursorily mentioned. The edges of these bones are fringed with hairy fibres, through which the Right Whale strains the water, and in whose intricacies he retains the small fish, when open-mouthed he goes through the seas of brit in feeding time. In the central blinds of bone, as they stand in their natural order, there are certain curious marks, curves, hollows, and ridges, whereby some whalemen calculate the creature's age, as the age of an oak by its circular rings. Though the certainty of this criterion is far from demonstrable, yet it has the savor of analogical probability. At any rate, if we yield to it, we must grant a far greater age to the Right Whale than at first glance will seem reasonable.

In old times, there seem to have prevailed the most curious fancies concerning these blinds. One voyager in Purchas calls them the wondrous "whiskers" inside of the whale's mouth;* another, "hogs' bristles;" a third old gentleman in Hackluyt uses the following elegant language: "There are about two hundred and fifty fins growing on each side of his upper *chop*, which arch over his tongue on each side of his mouth."

As every one knows, these same "hogs' bristles," "fins," "whiskers," "blinds," or whatever you please, furnish to the ladies their busks and other stiffening contrivances. But in this particular, the demand has long been on the decline. It was in Queen Anne's time that the bone was in its glory, the farthingale being then all the fashion. And as those ancient dames moved about gaily, though in the jaws of the whale, as you may say; even so, in a shower, with the like thoughtlessness, do we nowadays fly under the same jaws for protection; the umbrella being a tent spread over the same bone.

But now forget all about blinds and whiskers for a moment, and, standing in the Right Whale's mouth, look around you afresh. Seeing all these colonnades of bone so methodically ranged about, would you not think you were inside of the great Haarlem organ, and gazing upon its thousand pipes? For a carpet to the organ we have a rug of the softest Turkey—the tongue, which is glued, as it were, to the floor of the mouth. It is very fat and tender, and apt to tear in pieces in hoisting it on deck. This particular tongue now before us; at a passing glance I should say it was a six-barreler; that is, it will yield you about that amount of oil.

Ere this, you must have plainly seen the truth of what I started with—that the Sperm Whale and the Right Whale have almost entirely different heads. To sum up, then: in the Right Whale's there is no great well of sperm; no ivory teeth at all; no long, slender mandible of a lower jaw, like the Sperm Whale's. Nor in the Sperm Whale are there any of those blinds of bone; no huge lower lip; and scarcely anything of a tongue. Again, the Right Whale has two external spout-holes, the Sperm Whale only one.

Look your last, now, on these venerable hooded heads, while they yet lie together; for one will soon sink, unrecorded, in the sea; the other will not be very long in following.

Can you catch the expression of the Sperm Whale's there? It

---

* This reminds us that the Right Whale really has a sort of whisker, or rather a moustache, consisting of a few scattered white hairs on the upper part of the outer end of the lower jaw. Sometimes these tufts impart a rather brigandish expression to his otherwise solemn countenance [Melville's note].

is the same he died with, only some of the longer wrinkles in the forehead seem now faded away. I think his broad brow to be full of a prairie-like placidity, born of a speculative indifference as to death. But mark the other head's expression. See that amazing lower lip, pressed by accident against the vessel's side, so as firmly to embrace the jaw. Does not this whole head seem to speak of an enormous practical resolution in facing death? This Right Whale I take to have been a Stoic; the Sperm Whale, a Platonian, who might have taken up Spinoza in his latter years.

Chapter 76

THE BATTERING-RAM

Ere quitting, for the nonce, the Sperm Whale's head, I would have you, as a sensible physiologist, simply—particularly remark its front aspect, in all its compacted collectedness. I would have you investigate it now with the sole view of forming to yourself some unexaggerated, intelligent estimate of whatever battering-ram power may be lodged there. Here is a vital point; for you must either satisfactorily settle this matter with yourself, or for ever remain an infidel as to one of the most appalling, but not the less true events, perhaps anywhere to be found in all recorded history.

You observe that in the ordinary swimming position of the Sperm Whale, the front of his head presents an almost wholly vertical plane to the water; you observe that the lower part of that front slopes considerably backwards, so as to furnish more of a retreat for the long socket which receives the boom-like lower jaw; you observe that the mouth is entirely under the head, much in the same way, indeed, as though your own mouth were entirely under your chin. Moreover you observe that the whale has no external nose; and that what nose he has—his spout hole —is on the top of his head; you observe that his eyes and ears are at the sides of his head, nearly one third of his entire length from the front. Wherefore, you must now have perceived that the front of the Sperm Whale's head is a dead, blind wall, without a single organ or tender prominence of any sort whatsoever. Furthermore, you are now to consider that only in the extreme, lower, backward sloping part of the front of the head, is there the slightest vestige of bone; and not till you get near twenty feet from the forehead do you come to the full cranial development. So that this whole enormous boneless mass is as one wad. Finally, though, as will soon be revealed, its contents partly comprise the most delicate oil; yet, you are now to be apprised of the nature of the substance which so impregnably invests all that apparent effeminacy. In some previous place I have described to you how the blubber wraps the body of the whale, as the rind wraps an orange. Just so with the head; but with this difference: about the head this envelope, though not so thick, is of a boneless toughness, inestimable by any man who has not handled it. The severest pointed harpoon, the sharpest lance darted by the strongest human arm, impotently rebounds from it. It is as though the forehead of the Sperm Whale were paved with horses' hoofs. I do not think that any sensation lurks in it.

Bethink yourself also of another thing. When two large, loaded Indiamen chance to crowd and crush towards each other in the docks, what do the sailors do? They do not suspend between them, at the point of coming contact, any merely hard substance, like iron or wood. No, they hold there a large, round wad of tow and cork, enveloped in the thickest and toughest of ox-hide. That bravely and uninjured takes the jam which would have snapped all their oaken handspikes and iron crow-bars. By itself this sufficiently illustrates the obvious fact I drive at. But supplementary to this, it has hypothetically occurred to me, that as ordinary fish possess what is called a swimming bladder in them, capable, at will, of distension or contraction; and as the Sperm Whale, as far as I know, has no such provision in him; considering, too, the otherwise inexplicable manner in which he now depresses his head altogether beneath the surface, and anon swims with it high elevated out of the water; considering the unobstructed elasticity of its envelop; considering the unique interior of his head; it has hypothetically occurred to me, I say, that those mystical lung-celled honeycombs there may possibly have some hitherto unknown and unsuspected connexion with the outer air, so as to be susceptible to atmospheric distension and contraction. If this be so, fancy the irresistibleness of that might, to which the most impalpable and destructive of all elements contributes.

Now, mark. Unerringly impelling this dead, impregnable, uninjurable wall, and this most buoyant thing within; there swims behind it all a mass of tremendous life, only to be adequately estimated as piled wood is—by the cord; and all obedient to one volition, as the smallest insect. So that when I shall hereafter detail to you all the specialities and concentrations of potency everywhere lurking in this expansive monster; when I shall show you some of his more inconsiderable braining feats; I trust you will have renounced all ignorant incredulity, and be ready to abide by this; that though the Sperm Whale stove a passage through the Isthmus of Darien, and mixed the Atlantic with the Pacific, you would not elevate one hair of your eye-brow. For unless you own the whale, you are but a provincial and sentimentalist in Truth. But clear Truth is a thing for salamander giants only to encounter; how small the chances for the provincials then? What befel the weakling youth lifting the dread goddess's veil at Sais?

Chapter 77

THE GREAT HEIDELBERG TUN [1]

Now comes the Baling of the Case. But to comprehend it aright, you must know something of the curious internal structure of the thing operated upon.

Regarding the Sperm Whale's head as a solid oblong, you may, on an inclined plane, sideways divide it into two quoins,* whereof the lower is the bony structure, forming the cranium and jaws, and the upper and unctuous mass wholly free from bones; its broad forward end forming the expanded vertical apparent forehead of the whale. At the middle of the forehead horizontally subdivide this upper quoin, and then you have two almost equal parts, which before were naturally divided by an internal wall of a thick tendinous substance.

The lower subdivided part, called the junk, is one immense honeycomb of oil, formed by the crossing and re-crossing, into ten thousand infiltrated cells, of tough elastic white fibres throughout its whole extent. The upper part, known as the Case, may be regarded as the great Heidelberg Tun of the Sperm Whale. And as that famous great tierce is mystically carved in front, so the whale's vast plaited forehead forms innumerable strange devices for the emblematical adornment of his wondrous tun. Moreover, as that of Heidelberg was always replenished with the most excellent of the wines of the Rhenish valleys, so the tun of the whale contains by far the most precious of all his oily vintages; namely, the highly-prized spermaceti, in its absolutely pure, limpid, and odoriferous state. Nor is this precious substance found unalloyed in any other part of the creature. Though in life it remains perfectly fluid, yet, upon exposure to the air, after death, it soon begins to concrete; sending forth beautiful crystalline shoots, as when the first thin delicate ice is just forming in water. A large whale's case generally yields about five hundred gallons of sperm, though from unavoidable circumstances, considerable of it is spilled, leaks, and dribbles away, or is otherwise irrecoverably lost in the ticklish business of securing what you can.

1. A wine cask in Heidelberg with a capacity of 49,000 gallons.
* Quoin is not a Euclidean term. It belongs to the pure nautical mathematics. I know not that it has been defined before. A quoin is a solid which differs from a wedge in having its sharp end formed by the steep inclination of one side, instead of the mutual tapering of both sides [Melville's note].

I know not with what fine and costly material the Heidelberg Tun was coated within, but in superlative richness that coating could not possibly have compared with the silken pearl-colored membrane, like the lining of a fine pelisse, forming the inner surface of the Sperm Whale's case.

It will have been seen that the Heidelberg Tun of the Sperm Whale embraces the entire length of the entire top of the head; and since—as has been elsewhere set forth—the head embraces one third of the whole length of the creature, then setting that length down at eighty feet for a good sized whale, you have more than twenty-six feet for the depth of the tun, when it is length-wise hoisted up and down against a ship's side.

As in decapitating the whale, the operator's instrument is brought close to the spot where an entrance is subsequently forced into the spermaceti magazine; he has, therefore, to be uncommonly heedful, lest a careless, untimely stroke should invade the sanctuary and wastingly let out its invaluable contents. It is this decapitated end of the head, also, which is at last elevated out of the water, and retained in that position by the enormous cutting tackles, whose hempen combinations, on one side, make quite a wilderness of ropes in that quarter.

Thus much being said, attend now, I pray you, to that marvellous and—in this particular instance—almost fatal operation whereby the Sperm Whale's great Heidelberg Tun is tapped.

Chapter 78

CISTERN AND BUCKETS

Nimble as a cat, Tashtego mounts aloft; and without altering his erect posture, runs straight out upon the overhanging main-yard-arm, to the part where it exactly projects over the hoisted Tun. He has carried with him a light tackle called a whip, consisting of only two parts, travelling through a single-sheaved block. Securing this block, so that it hangs down from the yard-arm, he swings one end of the rope, till it is caught and firmly held by a hand on deck. Then, hand-over-hand, down the other part, the Indian drops through the air, till dexterously he lands on the summit of the head. There—still high elevated above the rest of the company, to whom he vivaciously cries—he seems some Turkish Muezzin calling the good people to prayers from the top of a tower. A short-handled sharp spade being sent up to him, he diligently searches for the proper place to begin breaking into the Tun. In this business he proceeds very heedfully, like a treasure-hunter in some old house, sounding the walls to find where the gold is masoned in. By the time this cautious search is over, a stout iron-bound bucket, precisely like a well-bucket, has been attached to one end of the whip; while the other end, being stretched across the deck, is there held by two or three alert hands. These last now hoist the bucket within grasp of the Indian, to whom another person has reached up a very long pole. Inserting this pole into the bucket, Tashtego downward guides the bucket into the Tun, till it entirely disappears; then giving the word to the seamen at the whip, up comes the bucket again, all bubbling like a dairy-maid's pail of new milk. Carefully lowered from its height, the full-freighted vessel is caught by an appointed hand, and quickly emptied into a large tub. Then remounting aloft, it again goes through the same round until the deep cistern will yield no more. Towards the end, Tashtego has to ram his long pole harder and harder, and deeper and deeper into the Tun, until some twenty feet of the pole have gone down.

Now, the people of the Pequod had been baling some time in this way; several tubs had been filled with the fragrant sperm; when all at once a queer accident happened. Whether it was that Tashtego, that wild Indian, was so heedless and reckless as to let go for a moment his one-handed hold on the great cabled tackles suspending the head; or whether the place where he stood was so treacherous and oozy; or whether the Evil One himself would have it to fall out so, without stating his particular reasons; how it was exactly, there is no telling now; but, on a sudden, as the eightieth or ninetieth bucket came suckingly up—my God! poor Tashtego—like the twin reciprocating bucket in a veritable well, dropped head-foremost down into this great Tun of Heidelberg, and with a horrible oily gurgling, went clean out of sight!

"Man overboard!" cried Daggoo, who amid the general consternation first came to his senses. "Swing the bucket this way!" and putting one foot into it, so as the better to secure his slippery hand-hold on the whip itself, the hoisters ran him high up to the top of the head, almost before Tashtego could have reached its interior bottom. Meantime, there was a terrible tumult. Looking over the side, they saw the before lifeless head throbbing and heaving just below the surface of the sea, as if that moment seized with some momentous idea; whereas it was only the poor Indian unconsciously revealing by those struggles the perilous depth to which he had sunk.

At this instant, while Daggoo, on the summit of the head, was clearing the whip—which had somehow got foul of the great cutting tackles—a sharp cracking noise was heard; and to the unspeakable horror of all, one of the two enormous hooks suspending the head tore out, and with a vast vibration the enormous mass sideways swung, till the drunk ship reeled and shook as if smitten by an iceberg. The one remaining hook, upon which the entire strain now depended, seemed every instant to be on the point of giving way; an event still more likely from the violent motions of the head.

"Come down, come down!" yelled the seamen to Daggoo, but with one hand holding on to the heavy tackles, so that if the head should drop, he would still remain suspended; the negro having cleared the foul line, rammed down the bucket into the now collapsed well, meaning that the buried harpooneer should grasp it, and so be hoisted out.

"In heaven's name, man," cried Stubb, "are you ramming home a cartridge there?—Avast! How will that help him; jamming that iron-bound bucket on top of his head? Avast, will ye!"

"Stand clear of the tackle!" cried a voice like the bursting of a rocket.

Almost in the same instant, with a thunder-boom, the enormous mass dropped into the sea, like Niagara's Table-Rock into the whirlpool; the suddenly relieved hull rolled away from it, to far down her glittering copper; and all caught their breath, as half swinging—now over the sailors' heads, and now over the water —Daggoo, through a thick mist of spray, was dimly beheld clinging to the pendulous tackles, while poor, buried-alive Tashtego was sinking utterly down to the bottom of the sea! But hardly had the blinding vapor cleared away, when a naked figure with a boarding-sword in its hand, was for one swift moment seen hovering over the bulwarks. The next, a loud splash announced that my brave Queequeg had dived to the rescue. One packed rush was made to the side, and every eye counted every ripple, as moment followed moment, and no sign of either the sinker or the diver could be seen. Some hands now jumped into a boat alongside, and pushed a little off from the ship.

"Ha! ha!" cried Daggoo, all at once, from his now quiet, swinging perch overhead; and looking further off from the side, we saw an arm thrust upright from the blue waves; a sight strange to see, as an arm thrust forth from the grass over a grave.

"Both! both!—it is both!"—cried Daggoo again with a joyful shout; and soon after, Queequeg was seen boldly striking out with one hand, and with the other clutching the long hair of the Indian. Drawn into the waiting boat, they were quickly brought to the deck; but Tashtego was long in coming to, and Queequeg did not look very brisk.

Now, how had this noble rescue been accomplished? Why, diving after the slowly descending head, Queequeg with his keen sword had made side lunges near its bottom, so as to scuttle a large hole there; then dropping his sword, had thrust his long arm far inwards and upwards, and so hauled out our poor Tash by the head. He averred, that upon first thrusting in for him, a leg was presented; but well knowing that that was not as it ought to be, and might occasion great trouble;—he had thrust back the leg, and by a dexterous heave and toss, had wrought a somerset upon the Indian; so that with the next trial, he came forth in the good old way—head foremost. As for the great head itself, that was doing as well as could be expected.

And thus, through the courage and great skill in obstetrics of Queequeg, the deliverance, or rather, delivery of Tashtego, was successfully accomplished, in the teeth, too, of the most untoward and apparently hopeless impediments; which is a lesson by no means to be forgotten. Midwifery should be taught in the same course with fencing and boxing, riding and rowing.

I know that this queer adventure of the Gay-Header's will be sure to seem incredible to some landsmen, though they themselves may have either seen or heard of some one's falling into a cistern ashore; an accident which not seldom happens, and with much less reason too than the Indian's, considering the exceeding slipperiness of the curb of the Sperm Whale's well.

But, peradventure, it may be sagaciously urged, how is this? We thought the tissued, infiltrated head of the Sperm Whale, was the lightest and most corky part about him; and yet thou makest it sink in an element of a far greater specific gravity than itself. We have thee there. Not at all, but I have ye; for at the time poor Tash fell in, the case had been nearly emptied of its lighter contents, leaving little but the dense tendinous wall of the well—a double welded, hammered substance, as I have before said, much heavier than the sea water, and a lump of which sinks in it like lead almost. But the tendency to rapid sinking in this substance was in the present instance materially counteracted by the other parts of the head remaining undetached from it, so that it sank very slowly and deliberately indeed, affording Queequeg a fair chance for performing his agile obstetrics on the run, as you may say. Yes, it was a running delivery, so it was.

Now, had Tashtego perished in that head, it had been a very precious perishing; smothered in the very whitest and daintiest of fragrant spermaceti; coffined, hearsed, and tombed in the secret inner chamber and sanctum sanctorum[1] of the whale. Only one sweeter end can readily be recalled—the delicious death of an Ohio honey-hunter, who seeking honey in the crotch of a hollow tree, found such exceeding store of it, that leaning too far over, it sucked him in, so that he died embalmed. How many, think ye, have likewise fallen into Plato's honey head, and sweetly perished there?

1. Holy of holies.

Chapter 79

THE PRAIRIE

To scan the lines of his face, or feel the bumps on the head of this Leviathan; this is a thing which no Physiognomist or Phrenologist has as yet undertaken. Such an enterprise would seem almost as hopeful as for Lavater[1] to have scrutinized the wrinkles on the Rock of Gibraltar, or for Gall to have mounted a ladder and manipulated the Dome of the Pantheon. Still, in that famous work of his, Lavater not only treats of the various faces of men, but also attentively studies the faces of horses, birds, serpents, and fish; and dwells in detail upon the modifications of expression discernible therein. Nor have Gall and his disciple Spurzheim failed to throw out some hints touching the phrenological characteristics of other beings than man. Therefore, though I am but ill qualified for a pioneer, in the application of these two semisciences to the whale, I will do my endeavor. I try all things; I achieve what I can.

Physiognomically regarded, the Sperm Whale is an anomalous creature. He has no proper nose. And since the nose is the central and most conspicuous of the features; and since it perhaps most modifies and finally controls their combined expression; hence it would seem that its entire absence, as an external appendage, must very largely affect the countenance of the whale. For as in landscape gardening, a spire, cupola, monument, or tower of some sort, is deemed almost indispensable to the completion of the scene; so no face can be physiognomically in keeping without the elevated open-work belfry of the nose. Dash the nose from Phidias's marble Jove, and what a sorry remainder! Nevertheless, Leviathan is of so mighty a magnitude, all his proportions are so stately, that the same deficiency which in the sculptured Jove were hideous, in him is no blemish at all. Nay, it is an added grandeur. A nose to the whale would have been impertinent. As on your physiognomical voyage you sail round his vast head in your jollyboat, your noble conceptions of him are never insulted by the reflection that he has a nose to be pulled. A pestilent conceit, which so often will insist upon obtruding even when beholding the mightiest royal beadle on his throne.

In some particulars, perhaps the most imposing physiognomical view to be had of the Sperm Whale, is that of the full front of his head. This aspect is sublime.

In thought, a fine human brow is like the East when troubled

---

1. An eighteenth-century Swiss physiognomist. He studied human character as revealed in the contours of the face, while the more recent phrenologists Gall and Spurzheim read the bumps on the skull (not including the face).

with the morning. In the repose of the pasture, the curled brow of the bull has a touch of the grand in it. Pushing heavy cannon up mountain defiles, the elephant's brow is majestic. Human or animal, the mystical brow is as that great golden seal affixed by the German emperors to their decrees. It signifies—"God: done this day by my hand." But in most creatures, nay in man himself, very often the brow is but a mere strip of alpine land lying along the snow line. Few are the foreheads which like Shakspeare's or Melancthon's rise so high, and descend so low, that the eyes themselves seem clear, eternal, tideless mountain lakes; and all above them in the forehead's wrinkles, you seem to track the antlered thoughts descending there to drink, as the Highland hunters track the snow prints of the deer. But in the great Sperm Whale, this high and mighty god-like dignity inherent in the brow is so immensely amplified, that gazing on it, in that full front view, you feel the Deity and the dread powers more forcibly than in beholding any other object in living nature. For you see no one point precisely; not one distinct feature is revealed; no nose, eyes, ears, or mouth; no face; he has none, proper; nothing but that one broad firmament of a forehead, pleated with riddles; dumbly lowering with the doom of boats, and ships, and men. Nor, in profile, does this wondrous brow diminish; though that way viewed, its grandeur does not domineer upon you so. In profile, you plainly perceive that horizontal, semi-crescentic depression in the forehead's middle, which, in man, is Lavater's mark of genius.

But how? Genius in the Sperm Whale? Has the Sperm Whale ever written a book, spoken a speech? No, his great genius is declared in his doing nothing particular to prove it. It is moreover declared in his pyramidical silence. And this reminds me that had the great Sperm Whale been known to the young Orient World, he would have been deified by their child-magian thoughts. They deified the crocodile of the Nile, because the crocodile is tongueless; and the Sperm Whale has no tongue, or at least it is so exceedingly small, as to be incapable of protrusion. If hereafter any highly cultured, poetical nation shall lure back to their birthright, the merry May-day gods of old; and livingly enthrone them again in the now egotistical sky; on the now unhaunted hill; then be sure, exalted to Jove's high seat, the great Sperm Whale shall lord it.

Champollion deciphered the wrinkled granite hieroglyphics. But there is no Champollion to decipher the Egypt of every man's and every being's face. Physiognomy, like every other human science, is but a passing fable. If then, Sir William Jones, who read in thirty languages, could not read the simplest peasant's face in its profounder and more subtle meanings, how may unlettered Ishmael hope to read the awful Chaldee of the Sperm Whale's brow? I but put that brow before you. Read it if you can.

Chapter 80

THE NUT

If the Sperm Whale be physiognomically a Sphinx, to the phrenologist his brain seems that geometrical circle which it is impossible to square.

In the full-grown creature the skull will measure at least twenty feet in length. Unhinge the lower jaw, and the side view of this skull is as the side view of a moderately inclined plane resting throughout on a level base. But in life—as we have elsewhere seen —this inclined plane is angularly filled up, and almost squared by the enormous superincumbent mass of the junk and sperm. At the high end the skull forms a crater to bed that part of the mass; while under the long floor of this crater—in another cavity seldom exceeding ten inches in length and as many in depth—reposes the mere handful of this monster's brain. The brain is at least twenty feet from his apparent forehead in life; it is hidden away behind its vast outworks, like the innermost citadel within the amplified fortifications of Quebec. So like a choice casket is it secreted in him, that I have known some whalemen who peremptorily deny that the Sperm Whale has any other brain than that palpable semblance of one formed by the cubic-yards of his sperm magazine. Lying in strange folds, courses, and convolutions, to their apprehensions, it seems more in keeping with the idea of his general might to regard that mystic part of him as the seat of his intelligence.

It is plain, then, that phrenologically the head of this Leviathan, in the creature's living intact state, is an entire delusion. As for his true brain, you can then see no indications of it, nor feel any. The whale, like all things that are mighty, wears a false brow to the common world.

If you unload his skull of its spermy heaps and then take a rear view of its rear end, which is the high end, you will be struck by its resemblance to the human skull, beheld in the same situation, and from the same point of view. Indeed, place this reversed skull (scaled down to the human magnitude) among a plate of men's skulls, and you would involuntarily confound it with them; and remarking the depressions on one part of its summit, in phrenological phrase you would say—This man had no self-esteem, and no veneration. And by those negations, considered along with the affirmative fact of his prodigious bulk and power, you can best form to yourself the truest, though not the most exhilarating conception of what the most exalted potency is.

But if from the comparative dimensions of the whale's proper brain, you deem it incapable of being adequately charted, then I have another idea for you. If you attentively regard almost any quadruped's spine, you will be struck with the resemblance of its vertebræ to a strung necklace of dwarfed skulls, all bearing rudimental resemblance to the skull proper. It is a German conceit, that the vertebræ are absolutely undeveloped skulls. But the curious external resemblance, I take it the Germans were not the first men to perceive. A foreign friend once pointed it out to me, in the skeleton of a foe he had slain, and with the vertebræ of which he was inlaying, in a sort of basso-relievo, the beaked prow of his canoe. Now, I consider that the phrenologists have omitted an important thing in not pushing their investigations from the cerebellum through the spinal canal. For I believe that much of a man's character will be found betokened in his backbone. I would rather feel your spine than your skull, whoever you are. A thin joist of a spine never yet upheld a full and noble soul. I rejoice in my spine, as in the firm audacious staff of that flag which I fling half out to the world.

Apply this spinal branch of phrenology to the Sperm Whale. His cranial cavity is continuous with the first neck-vertebra; and in that vertebra the bottom of the spinal canal will measure ten inches across, being eight in height, and of a triangular figure with the base downwards. As it passes through the remaining vertebræ the canal tapers in size, but for a considerable distance remains of large capacity. Now, of course, this canal is filled with much the same strangely fibrous substance—the spinal cord—as the brain; and directly communicates with the brain. And what is still more, for many feet after emerging from the brain's cavity, the spinal cord remains of an undecreasing girth, almost equal to that of the brain. Under all these circumstances, would it be unreasonable to survey and map out the whale's spine phrenologically? For, viewed in this light, the wonderful comparative smallness of his brain proper is more than compensated by the wonderful comparative magnitude of his spinal cord.

But leaving this hint to operate as it may with the phrenologists, I would merely assume the spinal theory for a moment, in reference to the Sperm Whale's hump. This august hump, if I mistake not, rises over one of the larger vertebræ, and is, therefore, in some sort, the outer convex mould of it. From its relative situation then, I should call this high hump the organ of firmness or indomitableness in the Sperm Whale. And that the great monster is indomitable, you will yet have reason to know.

Chapter 81

THE PEQUOD MEETS THE VIRGIN

The predestinated day arrived, and we duly met the ship Jung-frau, Derick De Deer, master, of Bremen.

At one time the greatest whaling people in the world, the Dutch and Germans are now among the least; but here and there at very wide intervals of latitude and longitude, you still occasionally meet with their flag in the Pacific.

For some reason, the Jungfrau seemed quite eager to pay her respects. While yet some distance from the Pequod, she rounded to, and dropping a boat, her captain was impelled towards us, impatiently standing in the bows instead of the stern.

"What has he in his hand there?" cried Starbuck, pointing to something wavingly held by the German. "Impossible!—a lamp-feeder!"

"Not that," said Stubb, "no, no, it's a coffee-pot, Mr. Starbuck; he's coming off to make us our coffee, is the Yarman; don't you see that big tin can there alongside of him?—that's his boiling water. Oh! he's all right, is the Yarman."

"Go along with you," cried Flask, "it's a lamp-feeder and an oil-can. He's out of oil, and has come a-begging."

However curious it may seem for an oil-ship to be borrowing oil on the whale-ground, and however much it may invertedly contradict the old proverb about carrying coals to Newcastle, yet sometimes such a thing really happens; and in the present case Captain Derick De Deer did indubitably conduct a lamp-feeder as Flask did declare.

As he mounted the deck, Ahab abruptly accosted him, without at all heeding what he had in his hand; but in his broken lingo, the German soon evinced his complete ignorance of the White Whale; immediately turning the conversation to his lamp-feeder and oil can, with some remarks touching his having to turn into his hammock at night in profound darkness—his last drop of Bremen oil being gone, and not a single flying-fish yet captured to supply the deficiency; concluding by hinting that his ship was indeed what in the Fishery is technically called a *clean* one (that is, an empty one), well deserving the name of Jungfrau or the Virgin.

His necessities supplied, Derick departed; but he had not gained his ship's side, when whales were almost simultaneously raised from the mast-heads of both vessels; and so eager for the chase was Derick, that without pausing to put his oil-can and lamp-feeder aboard, he slewed round his boat and made after the leviathan lamp-feeders.

Now, the game having risen to leeward, he and the other three German boats that soon followed him, had considerably the start of the Pequod's keels. There were eight whales, an average pod. Aware of their danger, they were going all abreast with great speed straight before the wind, rubbing their flanks as closely as so many spans of horses in harness. They left a great, wide wake, as though continually unrolling a great wide parchment upon the sea.

Full in this rapid wake, and many fathoms in the rear, swam a huge, humped old bull, which by his comparatively slow progress, as well as by the unusual yellowish incrustations over-growing him, seemed afflicted with the jaundice, or some other infirmity. Whether this whale belonged to the pod in advance, seemed questionable; for it is not customary for such venerable leviathans to be at all social. Nevertheless, he stuck to their wake, though indeed their back water must have retarded him, because the white-bone or swell at his broad muzzle was a dashed one, like the swell formed when two hostile currents meet. His spout was short, slow, and laborious; coming forth with a choking sort of gush, and spending itself in torn shreds, followed by strange subterranean commotions in him, which seemed to have egress at his other buried extremity, causing the waters behind him to upbubble.

"Who's got some paregoric?" said Stubb, "he has the stomach-ache, I'm afraid. Lord, think of having half an acre of stomach-ache! Adverse winds are holding mad Christmas in him, boys. It's the first foul wind I ever knew to blow from astern; but look, did ever whale yaw so before? it must be, he's lost his tiller."

As an overladen Indiaman bearing down the Hindostan coast with a deck load of frightened horses, careens, buries, rolls, and wallows on her way; so did this old whale heave his aged bulk, and now and then partly turning over on his cumbrous rib-ends, expose the cause of his devious wake in the unnatural stump of his starboard fin. Whether he had lost that fin in battle, or had been born without it, it were hard to say.

"Only wait a bit, old chap, and I'll give ye a sling for that wounded arm," cried cruel Flask, pointing to the whale-line near him.

"Mind he don't sling thee with it," cried Starbuck. "Give way, or the German will have him."

With one intent all the combined rival boats were pointed for this one fish, because not only was he the largest, and therefore the most valuable whale, but he was nearest to them, and the other whales were going with such great velocity, moreover, as almost to defy pursuit for the time. At this juncture, the Pequod's keels had shot by the three German boats last lowered; but from the great start he had had, Derick's boat still led the chase, though every moment neared by his foreign rivals. The only thing they feared, was, that from being already so nigh to his mark, he would be enabled to dart his iron before they could completely overtake and pass him. As for Derick, he seemed quite confident that this would be the case, and occasionally with a deriding gesture shook his lamp-feeder at the other boats.

"The ungracious and ungrateful dog!" cried Starbuck; "he mocks and dares me with the very poor-box I filled for him not five minutes ago!"—then in his old intense whisper—"give way, greyhounds! Dog to it!"

"I tell ye what it is, men"—cried Stubb to his crew—"It's against my religion to get mad; but I'd like to eat that villanous Yarman—Pull—wont ye? Are ye going to let that rascal beat ye? Do ye love brandy? A hogshead of brandy, then, to the best man. Come, why don't some of ye burst a blood-vessel? Who's that been dropping an anchor overboard—we don't budge an inch—we're becalmed. Halloo, here's grass growing in the boat's bottom—and by the Lord, the mast there's budding. This won't do, boys. Look at that Yarman! The short and long of it is, men, will ye spit fire or not?"

"Oh! see the suds he makes!" cried Flask, dancing up and down—"What a hump—Oh, *do* pile on the beef—lays like a log! Oh! my lads, *do* spring—slap-jacks and quohogs for supper, you know, my lads—baked clams and muffins—oh, *do, do,* spring—he's a hundred barreler—don't lose him now—don't, oh, *don't!*—see that Yarman—Oh! won't ye pull for your duff, my lads—such a sog! such a sogger![1] Don't ye love sperm? There goes three thousand dollars, men!—a bank!—a whole bank! The bank of England!—Oh, *do, do, do!*—What's that Yarman about now?"

At this moment Derick was in the act of pitching his lamp-feeder at the advancing boats, and also his oil-can; perhaps with the double view of retarding his rivals' way, and at the same time economically accelerating his own by the momentary impetus of the backward toss.

"The unmannerly Dutch dogger!" cried Stubb. "Pull now, men, like fifty thousand line-of-battle-ship loads of red-haired devils. What d'ye say, Tashtego; are you the man to snap your spine in two-and-twenty pieces for the honor of old Gay-head? What d'ye say?"

"I say, pull like god-dam,"—cried the Indian.

---

1. A sog is "a large whale" (*Dictionary of American English*, citing Cheever, *The Whale and his Captors*); a sogger is "anything large and heavy" (Wright, *English Dialect Dictionary*).

Fiercely but evenly, incited by the taunts of the German, the Pequod's three boats now began ranging almost abreast; and, so disposed, momentarily neared him. In that fine, loose, chivalrous attitude of the headsman when drawing near to his prey, the three mates stood up proudly, occasionally backing the after oarsman with an exhilarating cry of, "There she slides, now! Hurrah for the white-ash breeze! Down with the Yarman! Sail over him!"

But so decided an original start had Derick had, that spite of all their gallantry, he would have proved the victor in this race, had not a righteous judgment descended upon him in a crab[2] which caught the blade of his midship oarsman. While this clumsy lubber was striving to free his white-ash, and while, in consequence, Derick's boat was nigh to capsizing, and he thundering away at his men in a mighty rage;—that was a good time for Starbuck, Stubb, and Flask. With a shout, they took a mortal start forwards, and slantingly ranged up on the German's quarter. An instant more, and all four boats were diagonally in the whale's immediate wake, while stretching from them, on both sides, was the foaming swell that he made.

It was a terrific, most pitiable, and maddening sight. The whale was now going head out, and sending his spout before him in a continual tormented jet; while his one poor fin beat his side in an agony of fright. Now to this hand, now to that, he yawed in his faltering flight, and still at every billow that he broke, he spasmodically sank in the sea, or sideways rolled towards the sky his one beating fin. So have I seen a bird with clipped wing, making affrighted broken circles in the air, vainly striving to escape the piratical hawks. But the bird has a voice, and with plaintive cries will make known her fear; but the fear of this vast dumb brute of the sea, was chained up and enchanted in him; he had no voice, save that choking respiration through his spiracle, and this made the sight of him unspeakably pitiable; while still, in his amazing bulk, portcullis jaw, and omnipotent tail, there was enough to appal the stoutest man who so pitied.

Seeing now that but a very few moments more would give the Pequod's boats the advantage, and rather than be thus foiled of his game, Derick chose to hazard what to him must have seemed a most unusually long dart, ere the last chance would for ever escape.

But no sooner did his harpooneer stand up for the stroke, than all three tigers—Queequeg, Tashtego, Daggoo—instinctively sprang to their feet, and standing in a diagonal row, simultaneously

---

2. To "catch (or be caught by) a crab" in rowing is to manage the oar so clumsily that it gets caught in the water, as by a wave on the backstroke.

pointed their barbs; and, darted over the head of the German harpooneer, their three Nantucket irons entered the whale. Blinding vapors of foam and white-fire! The three boats, in the first fury of the whale's headlong rush, bumped the German's aside with such force, that both Derick and his baffled harpooneer were spilled out, and sailed over by the three flying keels.

"Don't be afraid, my butter-boxes," cried Stubb, casting a passing glance upon them as he shot by; "ye'll be picked up presently—all right—I saw some sharks astern—St. Bernard's dogs, you know—relieve distressed travellers. Hurrah! this is the way to sail now. Every keel a sun-beam! Hurrah!—Here we go like three tin kettles at the tail of a mad cougar! This puts me in mind of fastening to an elephant in a tilbury on a plain—makes the wheel-spokes fly, boys, when you fasten to him that way; and there's danger of being pitched out too, when you strike a hill. Hurrah! this is the way a fellow feels when he's going to Davy Jones—all a rush down an endless inclined plane! Hurrah! this whale carries the everlasting mail!"

But the monster's run was a brief one. Giving a sudden gasp, he tumultuously sounded. With a grating rush, the three lines flew round the loggerheads with such a force as to gouge deep grooves in them; while so fearful were the harpooneers that this rapid sounding would soon exhaust the lines, that using all their dexterous might, they caught repeated smoking turns with the rope to hold on; till at last—owing to the perpendicular strain from the lead-lined chocks of the boats, whence the three ropes went straight down into the blue—the gunwales of the bows were almost even with the water, while the three sterns tilted high in the air. And the whale soon ceasing to sound, for some time they remained in that attitude, fearful of expending more line, though the position was a little ticklish. But though boats have been taken down and lost in this way, yet it is this "holding on," as it is called; this hooking up by the sharp barbs of his live flesh from the back; this it is that often torments the Leviathan into soon rising again to meet the sharp lance of his foes. Yet not to speak of the peril of the thing, it is to be doubted whether this course is always the best; for it is but reasonable to presume, that the longer the stricken whale stays under water, the more he is exhausted. Because, owing to the enormous surface of him—in a full grown sperm whale something less than 2000 square feet—the pressure of the water is immense. We all know what an astonishing atmospheric weight we ourselves stand up under; even here, above-ground, in the air; how vast, then, the burden of a whale, bearing on his back a column of two hundred fathoms of ocean! It must at least equal the weight of fifty atmospheres. One whaleman has estimated it at the weight of twenty line-of-battle ships, with all their guns, and stores, and men on board.

As the three boats lay there on that gently rolling sea, gazing down into its eternal blue noon; and as not a single groan or cry of any sort, nay, not so much as a ripple or a bubble came up from its depths; what landsman would have thought, that beneath all that silence and placidity, the utmost monster of the seas was writhing and wrenching in agony! Not eight inches of perpendicular rope were visible at the bows. Seems it credible that by three such thin threads the great Leviathan was suspended like the big weight to an eight day clock. Suspended? and to what? To three bits of board. Is this the creature of whom it was once so triumphantly said—"Canst thou fill his skin with barbed irons? or his head with fish-spears? The sword of him that layeth at him cannot hold, the spear, the dart, nor the habergeon: he esteemeth iron as straw; the arrow cannot make him flee; darts are counted as stubble; he laugheth at the shaking of a spear!" [3] This the creature? this he? Oh! that unfulfilments should follow the prophets. For with the strength of a thousand thighs in his tail, Leviathan had run his head under the mountains of the sea, to hide him from the Pequod's fish-spears!

In that sloping afternoon sunlight, the shadows that the three boats sent down beneath the surface, must have been long enough and broad enough to shade half Xerxes' army. Who can tell how appalling to the wounded whale must have been such huge phantoms flitting over his head!

"Stand by, men; he stirs," cried Starbuck, as the three lines suddenly vibrated in the water, distinctly conducting upwards to them, as by magnetic wires, the life and death throbs of the whale, so that every oarsman felt them in his seat. The next moment, relieved in great part from the downward strain at the bows, the boats gave a sudden bounce upwards, as a small ice-field will, when a dense herd of white bears are scared from it into the sea.

"Haul in! Haul in!" cried Starbuck again; "he's rising."

The lines, of which, hardly an instant before, not one hand's breadth could have been gained, were now in long quick coils flung back all dripping into the boats, and soon the whale broke water within two ship's lengths of the hunters.

His motions plainly denoted his extreme exhaustion. In most land animals there are certain valves or flood-gates in many of their veins, whereby when wounded, the blood is in some degree at least instantly shut off in certain directions. Not so with the

3. Job 41: 7, 26–29.

whale; one of whose peculiarities it is, to have an entire non-valvular structure of the blood-vessels, so that when pierced even by so small a point as a harpoon, a deadly drain is at once begun upon his whole arterial system; and when this is heightened by the extraordinary pressure of water at a great distance below the surface, his life may be said to pour from him in incessant streams. Yet so vast is the quantity of blood in him, and so distant and numerous its interior fountains, that he will keep thus bleeding and bleeding for a considerable period; even as in a drought a river will flow, whose source is in the well-springs of far-off and undiscernible hills. Even now, when the boats pulled upon this whale, and perilously drew over his swaying flukes, and the lances were darted into him, they were followed by steady jets from the new made wound, which kept continually playing, while the natural spout-hole in his head was only at intervals, however rapid, sending its affrighted moisture into the air. From this last vent no blood yet came, because no vital part of him had thus far been struck. His life, as they significantly call it, was untouched.

As the boats now more closely surrounded him, the whole upper part of his form, with much of it that is ordinarily submerged, was plainly revealed. His eyes, or rather the places where his eyes had been, were beheld. As strange misgrown masses gather in the knot-holes of the noblest oaks when prostrate, so from the points which the whale's eyes had once occupied, now protruded blind bulbs, horribly pitiable to see. But pity there was none. For all his old age, and his one arm, and his blind eyes, he must die the death and be murdered, in order to light the gay bridals and other merry-makings of men, and also to illuminate the solemn churches that preach unconditional inoffensiveness by all to all. Still rolling in his blood, at last he partially disclosed a strangely discolored bunch or protuberance, the size of a bushel, low down on the flank.

"A nice spot," cried Flask; "just let me prick him there once."

"Avast!" cried Starbuck, "there's no need of that!"

But humane Starbuck was too late. At the instant of the dart an ulcerous jet shot from this cruel wound, and goaded by it into more than sufferable anguish, the whale now spouting thick blood, with swift fury blindly darted at the craft, bespattering them and their glorying crews all over with showers of gore, capsizing Flask's boat and marring the bows. It was his death stroke. For, by this time, so spent was he by loss of blood, that he helplessly rolled away from the wreck he had made; lay panting on his side, impotently flapped with his stumped fin, then over and over slowly revolved like a waning world; turned up the white secrets of his belly; lay like a log, and died. It was most piteous, that last ex-

piring spout. As when by unseen hands the water is gradually
drawn off from some mighty fountain, and with half-stifled melancholy gurglings the spray-column lowers and lowers to the ground
—so the last long dying spout of the whale.

Soon, while the crews were awaiting the arrival of the ship,
the body showed symptoms of sinking with all its treasures un-
rifled. Immediately, by Starbuck's orders, lines were secured to it
at different points, so that ere long every boat was a buoy; the
sunken whale being suspended a few inches beneath them by the
cords. By very heedful management, when the ship drew nigh, the
whale was transferred to her side, and was strongly secured there
by the stiffest fluke-chains, for it was plain that unless artificially
upheld, the body would at once sink to the bottom.

It so chanced that almost upon first cutting into him with the
spade, the entire length of a corroded harpoon was found imbedded in his flesh, on the lower part of the bunch before described. But as the stumps of harpoons are frequently found in
the dead bodies of captured whales, with the flesh perfectly healed
around them, and no prominence of any kind to denote their
place; therefore, there must needs have been some other unknown
reason in the present case fully to account for the ulceration
alluded to. But still more curious was the fact of a lance-head of
stone being found in him, not far from the buried iron, the flesh
perfectly firm about it. Who had darted that stone lance? And
when? It might have been darted by some Nor' West Indian long
before America was discovered.

What other marvels might have been rummaged out of this
monstrous cabinet there is no telling. But a sudden stop was put
to further discoveries, by the ship's being unprecedentedly dragged
over sideways to the sea, owing to the body's immensely increasing
tendency to sink. However, Starbuck, who had the ordering of
affairs, hung on to it to the last; hung on to it so resolutely, indeed, that when at length the ship would have been capsized, if
still persisting in locking arms with the body; then, when the
command was given to break clear from it, such was the immovable
strain upon the timber-heads to which the fluke-chains and cables
were fastened, that it was impossible to cast them off. Meantime
everything in the Pequod was aslant. To cross to the other side
of the deck was like walking up the steep gabled roof of a house.
The ship groaned and gasped. Many of the ivory inlayings of her
bulwarks and cabins were started from their places, by the unnatural dislocation. In vain handspikes and crows were brought to
bear upon the immovable fluke-chains, to pry them adrift from the
timber-heads; and so low had the whale now settled that the
submerged ends could not be at all approached, while every

moment whole tons of ponderosity seemed added to the sinking bulk, and the ship seemed on the point of going over.

"Hold on, hold on, won't ye?" cried Stubb to the body, "don't be in such a devil of a hurry to sink! By thunder, men, we must do something or go for it. No use prying there; avast, I say with your handspikes, and run one of ye for a prayer book and a penknife, and cut the big chains."

"Knife? Aye, aye," cried Queequeg, and seizing the carpenter's heavy hatchet, he leaned out of a porthole, and steel to iron, began slashing at the largest fluke-chains. But a few strokes, full of sparks, were given, when the exceeding strain effected the rest. With a terrific snap, every fastening went adrift; the ship righted, the carcase sank.

Now, this occasional inevitable sinking of the recently killed Sperm Whale is a very curious thing; nor has any fisherman yet adequately accounted for it. Usually the dead Sperm Whale floats with great buoyancy, with its side or belly considerably elevated above the surface. If the only whales that thus sank were old, meagre, and broken-hearted creatures, their pads of lard diminished and all their bones heavy and rheumatic; then you might with some reason assert that this sinking is caused by an uncommon specific gravity in the fish so sinking, consequent upon this absence of buoyant matter in him. But it is not so. For young whales, in the highest health, and swelling with noble aspirations, prematurely cut off in the warm flush and May of life, with all their panting lard about them; even these brawny, buoyant heroes do sometimes sink.

Be it said, however, that the Sperm Whale is far less liable to this accident than any other species. Where one of that sort goes down, twenty Right Whales do. This difference in the species is no doubt imputable in no small degree to the greater quantity of bone in the Right Whale; his Venetian blinds alone sometimes weighing more than a ton; from this incumbrance the Sperm Whale is wholly free. But there are instances where, after the lapse of many hours or several days, the sunken whale again rises, more buoyant than in life. But the reason of this is obvious. Gases are generated in him; he swells to a prodigious magnitude; becomes a sort of animal balloon. A line-of-battle ship could hardly keep him under then. In the Shore Whaling, on soundings, among the Bays of New Zealand, when a Right Whale gives token of sinking, they fasten buoys to him, with plenty of rope; so that when the body has gone down, they know where to look for it when it shall have ascended again.

It was not long after the sinking of the body that a cry was heard from the Pequod's mast-heads, announcing that the Jungfrau was again lowering her boats; though the only spout in sight was that of a Fin-Back, belonging to the species of uncapturable whales, because of its incredible power of swimming. Nevertheless, the Fin-Back's spout is so similar to the Sperm Whale's, that by unskilful fishermen it is often mistaken for it. And consequently Derick and all his host were now in valiant chase of this unnearable brute. The Virgin crowding all sail, made after her four young keels, and thus they all disappeared far to leeward, still in bold, hopeful chase.

Oh! many are the Fin-Backs, and many are the Dericks, my friend.

Chapter 82

THE HONOR AND GLORY OF WHALING [1]

There are some enterprises in which a careful disorderliness is the true method.

The more I dive into this matter of whaling, and push my researches up to the very spring-head of it, so much the more am I impressed with its great honorableness and antiquity; and especially when I find so many great demi-gods and heroes, prophets of all sorts, who one way or other have shed distinction upon it, I am transported with the reflection that I myself belong, though but subordinately, to so emblazoned a fraternity.

The gallant Perseus, a son of Jupiter, was the first whaleman; and to the eternal honor of our calling be it said, that the first whale attacked by our brotherhood was not killed with any sordid intent. Those were the knightly days of our profession, when we only bore arms to succor the distressed, and not to fill men's lamp-feeders. Every one knows the fine story of Perseus and Andromeda; how the lovely Andromeda, the daughter of a king, was tied to a rock on the sea-coast, and as Leviathan was in the very act of carrying her off, Perseus, the prince of whalemen, intrepidly advancing, harpooned the monster, and delivered and married the maid. It was an admirable artistic exploit, rarely achieved by the best harpooneers of the present day; inasmuch as this Leviathan was slain at the very first dart. And let no man doubt this Arkite story; for in the ancient Joppa, now Jaffa, on the Syrian coast, in one of the Pagan temples, there stood for many ages the vast skeleton of a whale, which the city's legends and all the inhabitants asserted to be the identical bones of the monster

1. "Most of this chapter and the next came from the article on 'Jonas' in Pierre Bayle, *An Historical and Critical Dictionary* . . . Vol. 3, pp. 577–580; the articles on 'Jonah' and 'Whale' in John Kitto, ed., *Cyclopedia of Biblical Literature*, Vol. 2; and various passages from Sir Thomas Browne. . . . Kitto seems to have been freshest in Melville's mind" (Mansfield-Vincent).

that Perseus slew. When the Romans took Joppa, the same skeleton was carried to Italy in triumph. What seems most singular and suggestively important in this story, is this: it was from Joppa that Jonah set sail.

Akin to the adventure of Perseus and Andromeda—indeed, by some supposed to be indirectly derived from it—is that famous story of St. George and the Dragon; which dragon I maintain to have been a whale; for in many old chronicles whales and dragons are strangely jumbled together, and often stand for each other. "Thou art as a lion of the waters, and as a dragon of the sea," saith Ezekiel; hereby, plainly meaning a whale; in truth, some versions of the Bible use that word itself. Besides, it would much subtract from the glory of the exploit had St. George but encountered a crawling reptile of the land, instead of doing battle with the great monster of the deep. Any man may kill a snake, but only a Perseus, a St. George, a Coffin, have the heart in them to march boldly up to a whale.

Let not the modern paintings of this scene mislead us; for though the creature encountered by that valiant whaleman of old is vaguely represented of a griffin-like shape, and though the battle is depicted on land and the saint on horseback, yet considering the great ignorance of those times, when the true form of the whale was unknown to artists; and considering that as in Perseus' case, St. George's whale might have crawled up out of the sea on the beach; and considering that the animal ridden by St. George might have been only a large seal, or sea-horse; bearing all this in mind, it will not appear altogether incompatible with the sacred legend and the ancientest draughts of the scene, to hold this so-called dragon no other than the great Leviathan himself. In fact, placed before the strict and piercing truth, this whole story will fare like that fish, flesh, and fowl idol of the Philistines, Dagon by name; who being planted before the ark of Israel, his horse's head and both the palms of his hands fell off from him, and only the stump or fishy part of him remained. Thus, then, one of our own noble stamp, even a whaleman, is the tutelary guardian of England; and by good rights, we harpooneers of Nantucket should be enrolled in the most noble order of St. George. And therefore, let not the knights of that honorable company (none of whom, I venture to say, have ever had to do with a whale like their great patron), let them never eye a Nantucketer with disdain, since even in our woollen frocks and tarred trowsers we are much better entitled to St. George's decoration than they.

Whether to admit Hercules among us or not, concerning this I long remained dubious: for though according to the Greek my-

2. Ezekiel 32:2.   3. I Samuel 5: 2–4.

thologies, that antique Crockett and Kit Carson—that brawny doer of rejoicing good deeds, was swallowed down and thrown up by a whale; still, whether that strictly makes a whaleman of him, that might be mooted. It nowhere appears that he ever actually harpooned his fish, unless, indeed, from the inside. Nevertheless, he may be deemed a sort of involuntary whaleman; at any rate the whale caught him, if he did not the whale. I claim him for one of our clan.

But, by the best contradictory authorities, this Grecian story of Hercules and the whale is considered to be derived from the still more ancient Hebrew story of Jonah and the whale; and vice versa; certainly they are very similar. If I claim the demi-god then, why not the prophet?

Nor do heroes, saints, demigods, and prophets alone comprise the whole roll of our order. Our grand master is still to be named; for like royal kings of old times, we find the head-waters of our fraternity in nothing short of the great gods themselves. That wondrous oriental story is now to be rehearsed from the Shaster, which gives us the dread Vishnoo, one of the three persons in the godhead of the Hindoos; gives us this divine Vishnoo himself for our Lord;—Vishnoo, who, by the first of his ten earthly incarnations, has for ever set apart and sanctified the whale. When Brahma, or the God of Gods, saith the Shaster, resolved to recreate the world after one of its periodical dissolutions, he gave birth to Vishnoo, to preside over the work; but the Vedas, or mystical books, whose perusal would seem to have been indispensable to Vishnoo before beginning the creation, and which therefore must have contained something in the shape of practical hints to young architects, these Vedas were lying at the bottom of the waters; so Vishnoo became incarnate in a whale, and sounding down in him to the uttermost depths, rescued the sacred volumes. Was not this Vishnoo a whaleman, then? even as a man who rides a horse is called a horseman?

Perseus, St. George, Hercules, Jonah, and Vishnoo! there's a member-roll for you! What club but the whaleman's can head off like that?

Chapter 83

JONAH HISTORICALLY REGARDED

Reference was made to the historical story of Jonah and the whale in the preceding chapter. Now some Nantucketers rather distrust this historical story of Jonah and the whale. But then there were some sceptical Greeks and Romans, who, standing out from the orthodox pagans of their times, equally doubted the story of Hercules and the whale, and Arion and the dolphin; and yet their doubting those traditions did not make those traditions one whit the less facts, for all that.

One old Sag-Harbor whaleman's chief reason for questioning the Hebrew story was this:—He had one of those quaint old-fashioned Bibles, embellished with curious, unscientific plates; one of which represented Jonah's whale with two spouts in his head—a peculiarity only true with respect to a species of the Leviathan (the Right Whale, and the varieties of that order), concerning which the fishermen have this saying, "A penny roll would choke him;" his swallow is so very small. But, to this, Bishop Jebb's anticipative answer is ready. It is not necessary, hints the Bishop, that we consider Jonah as tombed in the whale's belly, but as temporarily lodged in some part of his mouth. And this seems reasonable enough in the good Bishop. For truly, the Right Whale's mouth would accommodate a couple of whist-tables, and comfortably seat all the players. Possibly, too, Jonah might have ensconced himself in a hollow tooth; but, on second thoughts, the Right Whale is toothless.

Another reason which Sag-Harbor (he went by that name) urged for his want of faith in this matter of the prophet, was something obscurely in reference to his incarcerated body and the whale's gastric juices. But this objection likewise falls to the ground, because a German exegetist supposes that Jonah must have taken refuge in the floating body of a *dead* whale—even as the French soldiers in the Russian campaign turned their dead horses into tents, and crawled into them. Besides, it has been divined by other continental commentators, that when Jonah was thrown overboard from the Joppa ship, he straightway effected his escape to another vessel near by, some vessel with a whale for a figure-head; and, I would add, possibly called "The Whale," as some craft are nowadays christened the "Shark," the "Gull," the "Eagle." Nor have there been wanting learned exegetists who have opined that the whale mentioned in the book of Jonah merely meant a life-preserver—an inflated bag of wind—which the endangered prophet swam to, and so was saved from a watery doom. Poor Sag-Harbor, therefore, seems worsted all round. But he had still another reason for his want of faith. It was this, if I remember right: Jonah was swallowed by the whale in the Mediterranean Sea, and after three days he was vomited up somewhere within three days' journey of Nineveh, a city on the Tigris, very much more than three days' journey across from the nearest point of the Mediterranean coast. How is that?

But was there no other way for the whale to land the prophet within that short distance of Nineveh? Yes. He might have carried him round by the way of the Cape of Good Hope. But not to speak of the passage through the whole length of the Mediterranean, and another passage up the Persian Gulf and Red Sea, such a supposition would involve the complete circumnavigation of all Africa in three days, not to speak of the Tigris waters, near the site of Nineveh, being too shallow for any whale to swim in. Besides, this idea of Jonah's weathering the Cape of Good Hope at so early a day would wrest the honor of the discovery of that great headland from Bartholomew Diaz, its reputed discoverer, and so make modern history a liar.

But all these foolish arguments of old Sag-Harbor only evinced his foolish pride of reason—a thing still more reprehensible in him, seeing that he had but little learning except what he had picked up from the sun and the sea. I say it only shows his foolish, impious pride, and abominable, devilish rebellion against the reverend clergy. For by a Portuguese Catholic priest, this very idea of Jonah's going to Nineveh via the Cape of Good Hope was advanced as a signal magnification of the general miracle. And so it was. Besides, to this day, the highly enlightened Turks devoutly believe in the historical story of Jonah. And some three centuries ago, an English traveller in old Harris's Voyages, speaks of a Turkish Mosque built in honor of Jonah, in which mosque was a miraculous lamp that burnt without any oil.

Chapter 84

PITCHPOLING

To make them run easily and swiftly, the axles of carriages are anointed; and for much the same purpose, some whalers perform an analogous operation upon their boat; they grease the bottom. Nor is it to be doubted that as such a procedure can do no harm, it may possibly be of no contemptible advantage; considering that oil and water are hostile; that oil is a sliding thing, and that the object in view is to make the boat slide bravely. Queequeg believed strongly in anointing his boat, and one morning not long after the German ship Jungfrau disappeared, took more than customary pains in that occupation; crawling under its bottom, where it hung over the side, and rubbing in the unctuousness as though diligently seeking to insure a crop of hair from the craft's bald keel. He seemed to be working in obedience to some particular presentiment. Nor did it remain unwarranted by the event.

Towards noon whales were raised; but so soon as the ship sailed down to them, they turned and fled with swift precipitancy; a disordered flight, as of Cleopatra's barges from Actium.

Nevertheless, the boats pursued, and Stubb's was foremost. By great exertion, Tashtego at last succeeded in planting one iron; but the stricken whale, without at all sounding, still continued his horizontal flight, with added fleetness. Such unintermitted strainings upon the planted iron must sooner or later inevitably extract it. It became imperative to lance the flying whale, or be content to lose him. But to haul the boat up to his flank was impossible, he swam so fast and furious. What then remained?

Of all the wondrous devices and dexterities, the sleights of hand and countless subtleties, to which the veteran whaleman is so often forced, none exceed that fine manœuvre with the lance called pitchpoling. Small sword, or broad sword, in all its exercises boasts nothing like it. It is only indispensable with an inveterate running whale; its grand fact and feature is the wonderful distance to which the long lance is accurately darted from a violently rocking, jerking boat, under extreme headway. Steel and wood included, the entire spear is some ten or twelve feet in length; the staff is much slighter than that of the harpoon, and also of a lighter material—pine. It is furnished with a small rope called a warp, of considerable length, by which it can be hauled back to the hand after darting.

But before going further, it is important to mention here, that though the harpoon may be pitchpoled in the same way with the lance, yet it is seldom done; and when done, is still less frequently successful, on account of the greater weight and inferior length of the harpoon as compared with the lance, which in effect become serious drawbacks. As a general thing, therefore, you must first get fast to a whale, before any pitchpoling comes into play.

Look now at Stubb; a man who from his humorous, deliberate coolness and equanimity in the direst emergencies, was specially qualified to excel in pitchpoling. Look at him; he stands upright in the tossed bow of the flying boat; wrapt in fleecy foam, the towing whale is forty feet ahead. Handling the long lance lightly, glancing twice or thrice along its length to see if it be exactly straight, Stubb whistlingly gathers up the coil of the warp in one hand, so as to secure its free end in his grasp, leaving the rest unobstructed. Then holding the lance full before his waistband's middle, he levels it at the whale; when, covering him with it, he steadily depresses the butt-end in his hand, thereby elevating the point till the weapon stands fairly balanced upon his palm, fifteen feet in the air. He minds you somewhat of a juggler, balancing a long staff on his chin. Next moment with a rapid, nameless impulse, in a superb lofty arch the bright steel spans the foaming distance, and quivers in the life spot of the whale. Instead of sparkling water, he now spouts red blood.

"That drove the spigot out of him!" cries Stubb. " 'Tis July's immortal Fourth; all fountains must run wine to-day! Would now, it were old Orleans whiskey, or old Ohio, or unspeakable old Monongahela! Then, Tashtego, lad, I'd have ye hold a canakin to the jet, and we'd drink round it! Yea, verily, hearts alive, we'd brew choice punch in the spread of his spout-hole there, and from that live punch-bowl quaff the living stuff!"

Again and again to such gamesome talk, the dexterous dart is repeated, the spear returning to its master like a greyhound held in skilful leash. The agonized whale goes into his flurry; the tow-line is slackened, and the pitchpoler dropping astern, folds his hands, and mutely watches the monster die.

Chapter 85

THE FOUNTAIN

That for six thousand years—and no one knows how many millions of ages before—the great whales should have been spouting all over the sea, and sprinkling and mistifying the gardens of the deep, as with so many sprinkling or mistifying pots; and that for some centuries back, thousands of hunters should have been close by the fountain of the whale, watching these sprinklings and spoutings—that all this should be, and yet, that down to this blessed minute (fifteen and a quarter minutes past one o'clock P.M. of this sixteenth day of December, A.D. 1850), it should still remain a problem, whether these spoutings are, after all, really water, or nothing but vapor—this is surely a noteworthy thing.

Let us, then, look at this matter, along with some interesting items contingent. Every one knows that by the peculiar cunning of their gills, the finny tribes in general breathe the air which at all times is combined with the element in which they swim; hence, a herring or a cod might live a century, and never once raise its head above the surface. But owing to his marked internal structure which gives him regular lungs, like a human being's, the whale can only live by inhaling the disengaged air in the open atmosphere. Wherefore the necessity for his periodical visits to the upper world. But he cannot in any degree breathe through his mouth, for, in his ordinary attitude, the Sperm Whale's mouth is buried at least eight feet beneath the surface; and what is still more, his windpipe has no connexion with his mouth. No, he breathes through his spiracle alone; and this is on the top of his head.

If I say, that in any creature breathing is only a function indispensable to vitality, inasmuch as it withdraws from the air a certain element, which being subsequently brought into contact with the blood imparts to the blood its vivifying principle, I do not think I shall err; though I may possibly use some superfluous scientific words. Assume it, and it follows that if all the blood in a man could be aerated with one breath, he might then seal up his nostrils and not fetch another for a considerable time. That is to say, he would then live without breathing. Anomalous as it may seem, this is precisely the case with the whale, who systematically lives, by intervals, his full hour and more (when at the bottom) without drawing a single breath, or so much as in any way inhaling a particle of air; for, remember, he has no gills. How is this? Between his ribs and on each side of his spine he is supplied with a remarkable involved Cretan labyrinth of vermicelli-like vessels, which vessels, when he quits the surface, are completely distended with oxygenated blood. So that for an hour or more, a thousand fathoms in the sea, he carries a surplus stock of vitality in him, just as the camel crossing the waterless desert carries a surplus supply of drink for future use in its four supplementary stomachs. The anatomical fact of this labyrinth is indisputable; and that the supposition founded upon it is reasonable and true, seems the more cogent to me, when I consider the otherwise inexplicable obstinacy of that leviathan in *having his spoutings out*, as the fishermen phrase it. This is what I mean. If unmolested, upon rising to the surface, the Sperm Whale will continue there for a period of time exactly uniform with all his other unmolested risings. Say he stays eleven minutes, and jets seventy times, that is, respires seventy breaths; then whenever he rises again, he will be sure to have his seventy breaths over again, to a minute. Now, if after he fetches a few breaths you alarm him, so that he sounds, he will be always dodging up again to make good his regular allowance of air. And not till those seventy breaths are told, will he finally go down to stay out his full term below. Remark, however, that in different individuals these rates are different; but in any one they are alike. Now, why should the whale thus insist upon having his spoutings out, unless it be to replenish his reservoir of air, ere descending for good? How obvious is it, too, that this necessity for the whale's rising exposes him to all the fatal hazards of the chase. For not by hook or by net could this vast leviathan be caught, when sailing a thousand fathoms beneath the sunlight. Not so much thy skill, then, O hunter, as the great necessities, that strike the victory to thee!

In man, breathing is incessantly going on—one breath only serving for two or three pulsations; so that whatever other business he has to attend to, waking or sleeping, breathe he must, or die he will. But the Sperm Whale only breathes about one seventh or Sunday of his time.

It has been said that the whale only breathes through his spout-hole; if it could truthfully be added that his spouts are mixed with water, then I opine we should be furnished with the reason why his sense of smell seems obliterated in him; for the only thing about him that at all answers to his nose is that identical spout-hole; and being so clogged with two elements, it could not be expected to have the power of smelling. But owing to the mystery of the spout—whether it be water or whether it be vapor—no absolute certainty can as yet be arrived at on this head. Sure it is, nevertheless, that the Sperm Whale has no proper olfactories. But what does he want of them? No roses, no violets, no Cologne-water in the sea.

Furthermore, as his windpipe solely opens into the tube of his spouting canal, and as that long canal—like the grand Erie Canal —is furnished with a sort of locks (that open and shut) for the downward retention of air or the upward exclusion of water, therefore the whale has no voice; unless you insult him by saying, that when he so strangely rumbles, he talks through his nose. But then again, what has the whale to say? Seldom have I known any profound being that had anything to say to this world, unless forced to stammer out something by way of getting a living. Oh! happy that the world is such an excellent listener!

Now, the spouting canal of the Sperm Whale, chiefly intended as it is for the conveyance of air, and for several feet laid along, horizontally, just beneath the upper surface of his head, and a little to one side; this curious canal is very much like a gas-pipe laid down in a city on one side of a street. But the question returns whether this gas-pipe is also a water-pipe; in other words, whether the spout of the Sperm Whale is the mere vapor of the exhaled breath, or whether that exhaled breath is mixed with water taken in at the mouth, and discharged through the spiracle. It is certain that the mouth indirectly communicates with the spouting canal; but it cannot be proved that this is for the purpose of discharging water through the spiracle. Because the greatest necessity for so doing would seem to be, when in feeding he accidentally takes in water. But the Sperm Whale's food is far beneath the surface, and there he cannot spout even if he would. Besides, if you regard him very closely, and time him with your watch, you will find that when unmolested, there is an undeviating rhyme between the periods of his jets and the ordinary periods of respiration.

But why pester one with all this reasoning on the subject? Speak out! You have seen him spout; then declare what the spout is; can you not tell water from air? My dear sir, in this world it is not so easy to settle these plain things. I have ever found your plain things the knottiest of all. And as for this whale spout, you might almost stand in it, and yet be undecided as to what it is precisely.

The central body of it is hidden in the snowy sparkling mist enveloping it; and how can you certainly tell whether any water falls from it, when, always, when you are close enough to a whale to get a close view of his spout, he is in a prodigious commotion, the water cascading all around him. And if at such times you should think that you really perceived drops of moisture in the spout, how do you know that they are not merely condensed from its vapor; or how do you know that they are not those identical drops superficially lodged in the spout-hole fissure, which is countersunk into the summit of the whale's head? For even when tranquilly swimming through the mid-day sea in a calm, with his elevated hump sun-dried as a dromedary's in the desert; even then, the whale always carries a small basin of water on his head, as under a blazing sun you will sometimes see a cavity in a rock filled up with rain.

Nor is it at all prudent for the hunter to be over curious touching the precise nature of the whale spout. It will not do for him to be peering into it, and putting his face in it. You cannot go with your pitcher to this fountain and fill it, and bring it away. For even when coming into slight contact with the outer, vapory shreds of the jet, which will often happen, your skin will feverishly smart, from the acridness of the thing so touching it. And I know one, who coming into still closer contact with the spout, whether with some scientific object in view, or otherwise, I cannot say, the skin peeled off from his cheek and arm. Wherefore, among whalemen, the spout is deemed poisonous; they try to evade it. Another thing; I have heard it said, and I do not much doubt it, that if the jet is fairly spouted into your eyes, it will blind you. The wisest thing the investigator can do then, it seems to me, is to let this deadly spout alone.

Still, we can hypothesize, even if we cannot prove and establish. My hypothesis is this: that the spout is nothing but mist. And besides other reasons, to this conclusion I am impelled, by considerations touching the great inherent dignity and sublimity of the Sperm Whale; I account him no common, shallow being, inasmuch as it is an undisputed fact that he is never found on soundings, or near shores; all other whales sometimes are. He is both ponderous and profound. And I am convinced that from the heads of all ponderous profound beings, such as Plato, Pyrrho, the Devil, Jupiter, Dante, and so on, there always goes up a certain semi-visible steam, while in the act of thinking deep thoughts. While composing a little treatise on Eternity, I had the curiosity to place a mirror before me; and ere long saw reflected there, a curious involved worming and undulation in the atmosphere over my head. The invariable moisture of my hair, while plunged in deep thought, after six cups of hot tea in my thin shingled attic, of an August noon; this seems an additional argument for the above supposition.

And how nobly it raises our conceit of the mighty, misty monster, to behold him solemnly sailing through a calm tropical sea; his vast, mild head overhung by a canopy of vapor, engendered by his incommunicable contemplations, and that vapor—as you will sometimes see it—glorified by a rainbow, as if Heaven itself had put its seal upon his thoughts. For, d'ye see, rainbows do not visit the clear air; they only irradiate vapor. And so, through all the thick mists of the dim doubts in my mind, divine intuitions now and then shoot, enkindling my fog with a heavenly ray. And for this I thank God; for all have doubts; many deny; but doubts or denials, few along with them, have intuitions. Doubts of all things earthly, and intuitions of some things heavenly; this combination makes neither believer nor infidel, but makes a man who regards them both with equal eye.

Chapter 86

THE TAIL

Other poets have warbled the praises of the soft eye of the antelope, and the lovely plumage of the bird that never alights; less celestial, I celebrate a tail.

Reckoning the largest sized Sperm Whale's tail to begin at that point of the trunk where it tapers to about the girth of a man, it comprises upon its upper surface alone, an area of at least fifty square feet. The compact round body of its root expands into two broad, firm, flat palms or flukes, gradually shoaling away to less than an inch in thickness. At the crotch or junction, these flukes slightly overlap, then sideways recede from each other like wings, leaving a wide vacancy between. In no living thing are the lines of beauty more exquisitely defined than in the crescentic borders of these flukes. At its utmost expansion in the full grown whale, the tail will considerably exceed twenty feet across.

The entire member seems a dense webbed bed of welded sinews; but cut into it, and you find that three distinct strata compose it:—upper, middle, and lower. The fibres in the upper and lower layers, are long and horizontal; those of the middle one, very short, and running crosswise between the outside layers. This triune structure, as much as anything else, imparts power to the tail. To the student of old Roman walls, the middle layer will furnish a curious parallel to the thin course of tiles always alternating with the stone in those wonderful relics of the antique, and which undoubtedly contribute so much to the great strength of the masonry.

But as if this vast local power in the tendinous tail were not enough, the whole bulk of the leviathan is knit over with a warp and woof of muscular fibres and filaments, which passing on either side the loins and running down into the flukes, insensibly blend with them, and largely contribute to their might; so that in the tail the confluent measureless force of the whole whale seems concentrated to a point. Could annihilation occur to matter, this were the thing to do it.

Nor does this—its amazing strength, at all tend to cripple the graceful flexion of its motions; where infantileness of ease undulates through a Titanism of power. On the contrary, those motions derive their most appalling beauty from it. Real strength never impairs beauty or harmony, but it often bestows it; and in everything imposingly beautiful, strength has much to do with the magic. Take away the tied tendons that all over seem bursting from the marble in the carved Hercules, and its charm would be gone. As devout Eckermann lifted the linen sheet from the naked corpse of Goethe, he was overwhelmed with the massive chest of the man, that seemed as a Roman triumphal arch. When Angelo paints even God the Father in human form, mark what robustness is there. And whatever they may reveal of the divine love in the Son, the soft, curled, hermaphroditical Italian pictures, in which his idea has been most successfully embodied; these pictures, so destitute as they are of all brawniness, hint nothing of any power, but the mere negative, feminine one of submission and endurance, which on all hands it is conceded, form the peculiar practical virtues of his teachings.

Such is the subtle elasticity of the organ I treat of, that whether wielded in sport, or in earnest, or in anger, whatever be the mood it be in, its flexions are invariably marked by exceeding grace. Therein no fairy's arm can transcend it.

Five great motions are peculiar to it. First, when used as a fin for progression; Second, when used as a mace in battle; Third, in sweeping; Fourth, in lobtailing; Fifth, in peaking flukes.

First: Being horizontal in its position, the Leviathan's tail acts in a different manner from the tails of all other sea creatures. It never wriggles. In man or fish, wriggling is a sign of inferiority. To the whale, his tail is the sole means of propulsion. Scroll-wise coiled forwards beneath the body, and then rapidly sprung backwards, it is this which gives that singular darting, leaping motion to the monster when furiously swimming. His side-fins only serve to steer by.

Second: It is a little significant, that while one sperm whale only fights another sperm whale with his head and jaw, nevertheless, in his conflicts with man, he chiefly and contemptuously uses his tail. In striking at a boat, he swiftly curves away his flukes from it, and the blow is only inflicted by the recoil. If it be made in the unobstructed air, especially if it descend to its mark, the stroke is then simply irresistible. No ribs of man or boat can withstand it. Your only salvation lies in eluding it; but if it comes sideways through the opposing water, then partly owing to the light buoyancy of the whaleboat, and the elasticity of its materials, a cracked rib or a dashed plank or two, a sort of stitch in the side, is generally the most serious result. These submerged side blows are so often received in the fishery, that they are accounted mere child's play. Some one strips off a frock, and the hole is stopped.

Third: I cannot demonstrate it, but it seems to me, that in the whale the sense of touch is concentrated in the tail; for in this respect there is a delicacy in it only equalled by the daintiness of the elephant's trunk. This delicacy is chiefly evinced in the action of sweeping, when in maidenly gentleness the whale with a certain soft slowness moves his immense flukes from side to side upon the surface of the sea; and if he feel but a sailor's whisker, woe to that sailor, whiskers and all. What tenderness there is in that preliminary touch! Had this tail any prehensile power, I should straightway bethink me of Darmonodes' elephant that so frequented the flower-market, and with low salutations presented nosegays to damsels, and then caressed their zones. On more accounts than one, a pity it is that the whale does not possess this prehensile virtue in his tail; for I have heard of yet another elephant, that when wounded in the fight, curved round his trunk and extracted the dart.

Fourth: Stealing unawares upon the whale in the fancied security of the middle of solitary seas, you find him unbent from the vast corpulence of his dignity, and kitten-like, he plays on the ocean as if it were a hearth. But still you see his power in his play. The broad palms of his tail are flirted high into the air; then smiting the surface, the thunderous concussion resounds for miles. You would almost think a great gun had been discharged; and if you noticed the light wreath of vapor from the spiracle at his other extremity, you would think that that was the smoke from the touch-hole.

Fifth: As in the ordinary floating posture of the leviathan the flukes lie considerably below the level of his back, they are then completely out of sight beneath the surface; but when he is about to plunge into the deeps, his entire flukes with at least thirty feet of his body are tossed erect in the air, and so remain vibrating a moment, till they downwards shoot out of view. Excepting the sublime *breach*—somewhere else to be described—this peaking of the whale's flukes is perhaps the grandest sight to be seen in all animated nature. Out of the bottomless profundities the gigantic tail seems spasmodically snatching at the highest heaven. So in dreams, have I seen majestic Satan thrusting forth his tormented colossal claw from the flame Baltic of Hell. But in gazing at such scenes, it is all in all what mood you are in; if in the Dantean, the devils will occur to you; if in that of Isaiah, the archangels. Standing at the mast-head of my ship during a sunrise that crimsoned sky and sea, I once saw a large herd of whales in the east, all heading towards the sun, and for a moment vibrating in concert with peaked flukes. As it seemed to me at the time, such a grand embodiment of adoration of the gods was never beheld, even in Persia, the home of the fire worshippers. As Ptolemy Philopater testified of the African elephant, I then testified of the whale, pronouncing him the most devout of all beings. For according to King Juba, the military elephants of antiquity often hailed the morning with their trunks uplifted in the profoundest silence.

The chance comparison in this chapter, between the whale and the elephant, so far as some aspects of the tail of the one and the trunk of the other are concerned, should not tend to place those two opposite organs on an equality, much less the creatures to which they respectively belong. For as the mightiest elephant is but a terrier to Leviathan, so, compared with Leviathan's tail, his trunk is but the stalk of a lily. The most direful blow from the elephant's trunk were as the playful tap of a fan, compared with the measureless crush and crash of the sperm whale's ponderous flukes, which in repeated instances have one after the other hurled entire boats with all their oars and crews into the air, very much as an Indian juggler tosses his balls.*

The more I consider this mighty tail, the more do I deplore my inability to express it. At times there are gestures in it, which, though they would well grace the hand of man, remain wholly inexplicable. In an extensive herd, so remarkable, occasionally, are these mystic gestures, that I have heard hunters who have declared them akin to Free-Mason signs and symbols; that the whale, indeed, by these methods intelligently conversed with the world. Nor are there wanting other motions of the whale in his general

* Though all comparison in the way of general bulk between the whale and the elephant is preposterous, inasmuch as in that particular the elephant stands in much the same respect to the whale that a dog does to the elephant; nevertheless, there are not wanting some points of curious similitude; among these is the spout. It is well known that the elephant will often draw up water or dust in his trunk, and then elevating it, jet it forth in a stream [Melville's note].

body, full of strangeness, and unaccountable to his most experienced assailant. Dissect him how I may, then, I but go skin deep; I know him not, and never will. But if I know not even the tail of this whale, how understand his head? much more, how comprehend his face, when face he has none? Thou shalt see my back parts, my tail, he seems to say, but my face shall not be seen. But I cannot completely make out his back parts; and hint what he will about his face, I say again he has no face.

Chapter 87

THE GRAND ARMADA

The long and narrow peninsula of Malacca, extending southeastward from the territories of Birmah, forms the most southerly point of all Asia. In a continuous line from that peninsula stretch the long islands of Sumatra, Java, Bally, and Timor; which, with many others, form a vast mole, or rampart, lengthwise connecting Asia with Australia, and dividing the long unbroken Indian ocean from the thickly studded oriental archipelagoes. This rampart is pierced by several sally-ports for the convenience of ships and whales; conspicuous among which are the straits of Sunda and Malacca. By the straits of Sunda, chiefly, vessels bound to China from the west, emerge into the China seas.

Those narrow straits of Sunda divide Sumatra from Java; and standing midway in that vast rampart of islands, buttressed by that bold green promontory, known to seamen as Java Head; they not a little correspond to the central gateway opening into some vast walled empire: and considering the inexhaustible wealth of spices, and silks, and jewels, and gold, and ivory, with which the thousand islands of that oriental sea are enriched, it seems a significant provision of nature, that such treasures, by the very formation of the land, should at least bear the appearance, however ineffectual, of being guarded from the all-grasping western world. The shores of the Straits of Sunda are unsupplied with those domineering fortresses which guard the entrances to the Mediterranean, the Baltic, and the Propontis. Unlike the Danes, these Orientals do not demand the obsequious homage of lowered top-sails from the endless procession of ships before the wind, which for centuries past, by night and by day, have passed between the islands of Sumatra and Java, freighted with the costliest cargoes of the east. But while they freely waive a ceremonial like this, they do by no means renounce their claim to more solid tribute.

Time out of mind the piratical proas of the Malays, lurking among the low-shaded coves and islets of Sumatra, have sallied out upon the vessels sailing through the straits, fiercely demanding tribute at the point of their spears. Though by the repeated bloody chastisements they have received at the hands of European cruisers, the audacity of these corsairs has of late been somewhat repressed; yet, even at the present day, we occasionally hear of English and American vessels, which, in those waters, have been remorselessly boarded and pillaged.

With a fair, fresh wind, the Pequod was now drawing nigh to these straits; Ahab purposing to pass through them into the Javan sea, and thence, cruising northwards, over waters known to be frequented here and there by the Sperm Whale, sweep inshore by the Philippine Islands, and gain the far coast of Japan, in time for the great whaling season there. By these means, the circumnavigating Pequod would sweep almost all the known Sperm Whale cruising grounds of the world, previous to descending upon the Line in the Pacific; where Ahab, though everywhere else foiled in his pursuit, firmly counted upon giving battle to Moby Dick, in the sea he was most known to frequent; and at a season when he might most reasonably be presumed to be haunting it.

But how now? in this zoned quest, does Ahab touch no land? does his crew drink air? Surely, he will stop for water. Nay. For a long time, now, the circus-running sun has raced within his fiery ring, and needs no sustenance but what's in himself. So Ahab. Mark this, too, in the whaler. While other hulls are loaded down with alien stuff, to be transferred to foreign wharves; the world-wandering whale-ship carries no cargo but herself and crew, their weapons and their wants. She has a whole lake's contents bottled in her ample hold. She is ballasted with utilities; not altogether with unusable pig-lead and kentledge. She carries years' water in her. Clear old prime Nantucket water; which, when three years afloat, the Nantucketer, in the Pacific, prefers to drink before the brackish fluid, but yesterday rafted off in casks, from the Peruvian or Indian streams. Hence it is, that, while other ships may have gone to China from New York, and back again, touching at a score of ports, the whale-ship, in all that interval, may not have sighted one grain of soil; her crew having seen no man but floating seamen like themselves. So that did you carry them the news that another flood had come; they would only answer— "Well, boys, here's the ark!"

Now, as many Sperm Whales had been captured off the western coast of Java, in the near vicinity of the Straits of Sunda; indeed, as most of the ground, roundabout, was generally recognised by the fishermen as an excellent spot for cruising; therefore, as the Pequod gained more and more upon Java Head, the lookouts were repeatedly hailed, and admonished to keep wide awake.

But though the green palmy cliffs of the land soon loomed on the starboard bow, and with delighted nostrils the fresh cinnamon was snuffed in the air, yet not a single jet was descried. Almost renouncing all thought of falling in with any game hereabouts, the ship had well nigh entered the straits, when the customary cheering cry was heard from aloft, and ere long a spectacle of singular magnificence saluted us.

But here be it premised, that owing to the unwearied activity with which of late they have been hunted over all four oceans, the Sperm Whales, instead of almost invariably sailing in small detached companies, as in former times, are now frequently met with in extensive herds, sometimes embracing so great a multitude, that it would almost seem as if numerous nations of them had sworn solemn league and covenant for mutual assistance and protection. To this aggregation of the Sperm Whale into such immense caravans, may be imputed the circumstance that even in the best cruising grounds, you may now sometimes sail for weeks and months together, without being greeted by a single spout; and then be suddenly saluted by what sometimes seems thousands on thousands.

Broad on both bows, at the distance of some two or three miles, and forming a great semicircle, embracing one half of the level horizon, a continuous chain of whale-jets were up-playing and sparkling in the noon-day air. Unlike the straight perpendicular twin-jets of the Right Whale, which, dividing at top, fall over in two branches, like the cleft drooping boughs of a willow, the single forward-slanting spout of the Sperm Whale presents a thick curled bush of white mist, continually rising and falling away to leeward.

Seen from the Pequod's deck, then, as she would rise on a high hill of the sea, this host of vapory spouts, individually curling up into the air, and beheld through a blending atmosphere of bluish haze, showed like the thousand cheerful chimneys of some dense metropolis, descried of a balmy autumnal morning, by some horseman on a height.

As marching armies approaching an unfriendly defile in the mountains, accelerate their march, all eagerness to place that perilous passage in their rear, and once more expand in comparative security upon the plain; even so did this vast fleet of whales now seem hurrying forward through the straits; gradually contracting the wings of their semicircle, and swimming on, in one solid, but still crescentic centre.

Crowding all sail the Pequod pressed after them; the harpooneers handling their weapons, and loudly cheering from the heads of their yet suspended boats. If the wind only held, little doubt had they, that chased through these Straits of Sunda, the vast host would only deploy into the Oriental seas to witness the capture of not a few of their number. And who could tell whether, in that congregated caravan, Moby Dick himself might not temporarily be swimming, like the worshipped white-elephant in the coronation procession of the Siamese! So with stun-sail piled on stun-sail, we sailed along, driving these leviathans before us; when, of a sudden, the voice of Tashtego was heard, loudly directing attention to something in our wake.

Corresponding to the crescent in our van, we beheld another in our rear. It seemed formed of detached white vapors, rising and falling something like the spouts of the whales; only they did not so completely come and go; for they constantly hovered, without finally disappearing. Levelling his glass at this sight, Ahab quickly revolved in his pivot-hole, crying, "Aloft there, and rig whips and buckets to wet the sails;—Malays, sir, and after us!"

As if too long lurking behind the headlands, till the Pequod should fairly have entered the straits, these rascally Asiatics were now in hot pursuit, to make up for their over-cautious delay. But when the swift Pequod, with a fresh leading wind, was herself in hot chase; how very kind of these tawny philanthropists to assist in speeding her on to her own chosen pursuit,—mere riding-whips and rowels to her, that they were. As with glass under arm, Ahab to-and-fro paced the deck; in his forward turn beholding the monsters he chased, and in the after one the bloodthirsty pirates chasing *him*; some such fancy as the above seemed his. And when he glanced upon the green walls of the watery defile in which the ship was then sailing, and bethought him that through that gate lay the route to his vengeance, and beheld, how that through that same gate he was now both chasing and being chased to his deadly end; and not only that, but a herd of remorseless wild pirates and inhuman atheistical devils were infernally cheering him on with their curses;—when all these conceits had passed through his brain, Ahab's brow was left gaunt and ribbed, like the black sand beach after some stormy tide has been gnawing it, without being able to drag the firm thing from its place.

But thoughts like these troubled very few of the reckless crew; and when, after steadily dropping and dropping the pirates astern, the Pequod at last shot by the vivid green Cockatoo Point on the Sumatra side, emerging at last upon the broad waters beyond; then, the harpooneers seemed more to grieve that the swift whales had been gaining upon the ship, than to rejoice that the ship had so victoriously gained upon the Malays. But still driving on in the wake of the whales, at length they seemed abating their speed; gradually the ship neared them; and the wind now dying away, word was passed to spring to the boats. But no sooner did the herd, by some presumed wonderful instinct of the Sperm Whale, become notified of the three keels that were after them, —though as yet a mile in their rear,—than they rallied again, and forming in close ranks and battalions, so that their spouts all looked like flashing lines of stacked bayonets, moved on with redoubled velocity.

Stripped to our shirts and drawers, we sprang to the white-ash, and after several hours' pulling were almost disposed to renounce the chase, when a general pausing commotion among the whales gave animating token that they were now at last under the influence of that strange perplexity of inert irresolution, which, when the fishermen perceive it in the whale, they say he is *gallied*.* The compact martial columns in which they had been hitherto rapidly and steadily swimming, were now broken up in one measureless rout; and like King Porus' elephants in the Indian battle with Alexander, they seemed going mad with consternation. In all directions expanding in vast irregular circles, and aimlessly swimming hither and thither, by their short thick spoutings, they plainly betrayed their distraction of panic. This was still more strangely evinced by those of their number, who, completely paralysed as it were, helplessly floated like water-logged dismantled ships on the sea. Had these leviathans been but a flock of simple sheep, pursued over the pasture by three fierce wolves, they could not possibly have evinced such excessive dismay. But this occasional timidity is characteristic of almost all herding creatures. Though banding together in tens of thousands, the lion-maned buffaloes of the West have fled before a solitary horseman. Witness, too, all human beings, how when herded together in the sheep-fold of a theatre's pit, they will, at the slightest alarm of fire, rush helter-skelter for the outlets, crowding, trampling, jamming, and remorselessly dashing each other to death. Best, therefore, withhold any amazement at the strangely gallied whales before us, for there is no folly of the beasts of the earth which is not infinitely outdone by the madness of men.

Though many of the whales, as has been said, were in violent motion, yet it is to be observed that as a whole the herd neither

---

* To *gally*, or *gallow*, is to frighten excessively,—to confound with fright. It is an old Saxon word. It occurs once in Shakspere:—

"The wrathful skies
Gallow the very wanderers of the dark,
And make them keep their caves."
        Lear, Act iii. sc. ll.

To common land usages, the word is now completely obsolete. When the polite landsman first hears it from the gaunt Nantucketer, he is apt to set it down as one of the whaleman's self-derived savageries. Much the same is it with many other sinewy Saxonisms of this sort, which emigrated to the New-England rocks with the noble brawn of the old English emigrants in the time of the Commonwealth. Thus, some of the best and furthest-descended English words—the etymological Howards and Percys—are now democratised, nay, plebeianised—so to speak—in the New World [Melville's note].

advanced nor retreated, but collectively remained in one place. As is customary in those cases, the boats at once separated, each making for some one lone whale on the outskirts of the shoal. In about three minutes' time, Queequeg's harpoon was flung; the stricken fish darted blinding spray in our faces, and then running away with us like light, steered straight for the heart of the herd. Though such a movement on the part of the whale struck under such circumstances, is in no wise unprecedented; and indeed is almost always more or less anticipated; yet does it present one of the more perilous vicissitudes of the fishery. For as the swift monster drags you deeper and deeper into the frantic shoal, you bid adieu to circumspect life and only exist in a delirious throb.

As, blind and deaf, the whale plunged forward, as if by sheer power of speed to rid himself of the iron leech that had fastened to him; as we thus tore a white gash in the sea, on all sides menaced as we flew, by the crazed creatures to and fro rushing about us; our beset boat was like a ship mobbed by ice-isles in a tempest, and striving to steer through their complicated channels and straits, knowing not at what moment it may be locked in and crushed.

But not a bit daunted, Queequeg steered us manfully; now sheering off from this monster directly across our route in advance; now edging away from that, whose colossal flukes were suspended overhead, while all the time, Starbuck stood up in the bows, lance in hand, pricking out of our way whatever whales he could reach by short darts, for there was no time to make long ones. Nor were the oarsmen quite idle, though their wonted duty was now altogether dispensed with. They chiefly attended to the shouting part of the business. "Out of the way, Commodore!" cried one, to a great dromedary that of a sudden rose bodily to the surface, and for an instant threatened to swamp us. "Hard down with your tail, there!" cried a second to another, which, close to our gunwale, seemed calmly cooling himself with his own fan-like extremity.

All whaleboats carry certain curious contrivances, originally invented by the Nantucket Indians, called druggs. Two thick squares of wood of equal size are stoutly clenched together, so that they cross each other's grain at right angles; a line of considerable length is then attached to the middle of this block, and the other end of the line being looped, it can in a moment be fastened to a harpoon. It is chiefly among gallied whales that this drugg is used. For then, more whales are close round you than you can possibly chase at one time. But sperm whales are not every day encountered; while you may, then, you must kill all you can. And if you cannot kill them all at once, you must wing them, so that they can be afterwards killed at your leisure. Hence it is, that at times like these the drugg comes into requisition. Our boat was furnished with three of them. The first and second were successfully darted, and we saw the whales staggeringly running off, fettered by the enormous sidelong resistance of the towing drugg. They were cramped like malefactors with the chain and ball. But upon flinging the third, in the act of tossing overboard the clumsy wooden block, it caught under one of the seats of the boat, and in an instant tore it out and carried it away, dropping the oarsman in the boat's bottom as the seat slid from under him. On both sides the sea came in at the wounded planks, but we stuffed two or three drawers and shirts in, and so stopped the leaks for the time.

It had been next to impossible to dart these drugged-harpoons, were it not that as we advanced into the herd, our whale's way greatly diminished; moreover, that as we went still further and further from the circumference of commotion, the direful disorders seemed waning. So that when at last the jerking harpoon drew out, and the towing whale sideways vanished; then, with the tapering force of his parting momentum, we glided between two whales into the innermost heart of the shoal, as if from some mountain torrent we had slid into a serene valley lake. Here the storms in the roaring glens between the outermost whales, were heard but not felt. In this central expanse the sea presented that smooth satin-like surface, called a sleek, produced by the subtle moisture thrown off by the whale in his more quiet moods. Yes, we were now in that enchanted calm which they say lurks at the heart of every commotion. And still in the distracted distance we beheld the tumults of the outer concentric circles, and saw successive pods of whales, eight or ten in each, swiftly going round and round, like multiplied spans of horses in a ring; and so closely shoulder to shoulder, that a Titanic circus-rider might easily have over-arched the middle ones, and so have gone round on their backs. Owing to the density of the crowd of reposing whales, more immediately surrounding the embayed axis of the herd, no possible chance of escape was at present afforded us. We must watch for a breach in the living wall that hemmed us in; the wall that had only admitted us in order to shut us up. Keeping at the centre of the lake, we were occasionally visited by small tame cows and calves; the women and children of this routed host.

Now, inclusive of the occasional wide intervals between the revolving outer circles, and inclusive of the spaces between the various pods in any one of those circles, the entire area at this juncture, embraced by the whole multitude, must have contained at least two or three square miles. At any rate—though indeed such a test at such a time might be deceptive—spoutings might be discovered from our low boat that seemed playing up almost from the rim of the horizon. I mention this circumstance, because, as if the cows and calves had been purposely locked up in this innermost fold; and as if the wide extent of the herd had hitherto prevented them from learning the precise cause of its stopping; or, possibly, being so young, unsophisticated, and every way innocent and inexperienced; however it may have been, these smaller whales—now and then visiting our becalmed boat from the margin of the lake—evinced a wondrous fearlessness and confidence, or else a still, becharmed panic which it was impossible not to marvel at. Like household dogs they came snuffling round us, right up to our gunwales, and touching them; till it almost seemed that some spell had suddenly domesticated them. Queequeg patted their foreheads; Starbuck scratched their backs with his lance; but fearful of the consequences, for the time refrained from darting it.

But far beneath this wondrous world upon the surface, another and still stranger world met our eyes as we gazed over the side. For, suspended in those watery vaults, floated the forms of the nursing mothers of the whales, and those that by their enormous girth seemed shortly to become mothers. The lake, as I have hinted, was to a considerable depth exceedingly transparent; and as human infants while suckling will calmly and fixedly gaze away from the breast, as if leading two different lives at the time; and while yet drawing mortal nourishment, be still spiritually feasting upon some unearthly reminiscence;—even so did the young of these whales seem looking up towards us, but not at us, as if we were but a bit of Gulf-weed in their new-born sight. Floating on their sides, the mothers also seemed quietly eyeing us. One of these little infants, that from certain queer tokens seemed hardly a day old, might have measured some fourteen feet in length, and some six feet in girth. He was a little frisky; though as yet his body seemed scarce yet recovered from that irksome position it had so lately occupied in the maternal reticule; where, tail to head, and all ready for the final spring, the unborn whale lies bent like a Tartar's bow. The delicate side-fins, and the palms of his flukes, still freshly retained the plaited crumpled appearance of a baby's ears newly arrived from foreign parts.

"Line! line!" cried Queequeg, looking over the gunwale; "him fast! him fast!—Who line him! Who struck?—Two whale; one big, one little!"

"What ails ye, man?" cried Starbuck.

"Look-e here," said Queequeg pointing down.

As when the stricken whale, that from the tub has reeled out hundreds of fathoms of rope; as, after, deep sounding, he floats up again, and shows the slackened curling line buoyantly rising and spiralling towards the air; so now, Starbuck saw long coils of the umbilical cord of Madame Leviathan, by which the young cub seemed still tethered to its dam. Not seldom in the rapid vicissitudes of the chase, this natural line, with the maternal end loose, becomes entangled with the hempen one, so that the cub is thereby trapped. Some of the subtlest secrets of the seas seemed divulged to us in this enchanted pond. We saw young Leviathan amours in the deep.*

And thus, though surrounded by circle upon circle of consternations and affrights, did these inscrutable creatures at the centre freely and fearlessly indulge in all peaceful concernments; yea, serenely revelled in dalliance and delight. But even so, amid the tornadoed Atlantic of my being, do I myself still for ever centrally disport in mute calm; and while ponderous planets of unwaning woe revolve round me, deep down and deep inland there I still bathe me in eternal mildness of joy.

Meanwhile, as we thus lay entranced, the occasional sudden frantic spectacles in the distance evinced the activity of the other boats, still engaged in drugging the whales on the frontier of the host; or possibly carrying on the war within the first circle, where abundance of room and some convenient retreats were afforded them. But the sight of the enraged drugged whales now and then blindly darting to and fro across the circles, was nothing to what at last met our eyes. It is sometimes the custom when fast to a whale more than commonly powerful and alert, to seek to hamstring him, as it were, by sundering or maiming his gigantic tail-tendon. It is done by darting a short-handled cutting-spade, to which is attached a rope for hauling it back again. A whale wounded (as we afterwards learned) in this part, but not effectually, as it seemed, had broken away from the boat, carrying along with him half of the harpoon line; and in the extraordinary agony of the wound, he was now dashing among the revolving circles like the lone mounted desperado Arnold, at the battle of Saratoga, carrying dismay wherever he went.

But agonizing as was the wound of this whale, and an appalling

---

* The sperm whale, as with all other species of the Leviathan, but unlike most other fish, breeds indifferently at all seasons; after a gestation which may probably be set down at nine months, producing but one at a time; though in some few known instances giving birth to an Esau and Jacob:—a contingency provided for in suckling by two teats, curiously situated, one on each side of the anus; but the breasts themselves extend upwards from that. When by chance these precious parts in a nursing whale are cut by the hunter's lance, the mother's pouring milk and blood rivallingly discolor the sea for rods. The milk is very sweet and rich; it has been tasted by man; it might do well with strawberries. When overflowing with mutual esteem, the whales salute *more hominum* [Melville's note]. *More hominum:* in the manner of man, i.e., they copulate.

spectacle enough, any way; yet the peculiar horror with which he seemed to inspire the rest of the herd, was owing to a cause which at first the intervening distance obscured from us. But at length we perceived that by one of the unimaginable accidents of the fishery, this whale had become entangled in the harpoon-line that he towed; he had also run away with the cutting-spade in him; and while the free end of the rope attached to that weapon, had permanently caught in the coils of the harpoon-line round his tail, the cutting-spade itself had worked loose from his flesh. So that tormented to madness, he was now churning through the water, violently flailing with his flexible tail, and tossing the keen spade about him, wounding and murdering his own comrades.

This terrific object seemed to recall the whole herd from their stationary fright. First, the whales forming the margin of our lake began to crowd a little, and tumble against each other, as if lifted by half spent billows from afar; then the lake itself began faintly to heave and swell; the submarine bridal-chambers and nurseries vanished; in more and more contracting orbits the whales in the more central circles began to swim in thickening clusters. Yes, the long calm was departing. A low advancing hum was soon heard; and then like to the tumultuous masses of block-ice when the great river Hudson breaks up in Spring, the entire host of whales came tumbling upon their inner centre, as if to pile themselves up in one common mountain. Instantly Starbuck and Queequeg changed places; Starbuck taking the stern.

"Oars! Oars!" he intensely whispered, seizing the helm— "gripe your oars, and clutch your souls, now! My God, men, stand by! Shove him off, you Queequeg—the whale there!—prick him! —hit him! Stand up—stand up, and stay so! Spring, men—pull, men; never mind their backs—scrape them!—scrape away!"

The boat was now all but jammed between two vast black bulks, leaving a narrow Dardanelles between their long lengths. But by desperate endeavor we at last shot into a temporary opening; then giving way rapidly, and at the same time earnestly watching for another outlet. After many similar hair-breadth escapes, we at last swiftly glided into what had just been one of the outer circles, but now crossed by random whales, all violently making for one centre. This lucky salvation was cheaply purchased by the loss of Queequeg's hat, who, while standing in the bows to prick the fugitive whales, had his hat taken clean from his head by the air-eddy made by the sudden tossing of a pair of broad flukes close by.

Riotous and disordered as the universal commotion now was, it soon resolved itself into what seemed a systematic movement; for having clumped together at last in one dense body, they then renewed their onward flight with augmented fleetness. Further pursuit was useless; but the boats still lingered in their wake to pick up what drugged whales might be dropped astern, and likewise to secure one which Flask had killed and waifed. The waif is a pennoned pole, two or three of which are carried by every boat; and which, when additional game is at hand, are inserted upright into the floating body of a dead whale, both to mark its place on the sea, and also as token of prior possession, should the boats of any other ship draw near.

The result of this lowering was somewhat illustrative of that sagacious saying in the Fishery,—the more whales the less fish. Of all the drugged whales only one was captured. The rest contrived to escape for the time, but only to be taken, as will hereafter be seen, by some other craft than the Pequod.

Chapter 88

SCHOOLS AND SCHOOLMASTERS

The previous chapter gave account of an immense body or herd of Sperm Whales, and there was also then given the probable cause inducing those vast aggregations.

Now, though such great bodies are at times encountered, yet, as must have been seen, even at the present day, small detached bands are occasionally observed, embracing from twenty to fifty individuals each. Such bands are known as schools. They generally are of two sorts; those composed almost entirely of females, and those mustering none but young vigorous males, or bulls, as they are familiarly designated.

In cavalier attendance upon the school of females, you invariably see a male of full grown magnitude, but not old; who, upon any alarm, evinces his gallantry by falling in the rear and covering the flight of his ladies. In truth, this gentleman is a luxurious Ottoman, swimming about over the watery world, surroundingly accompanied by all the solaces and endearments of the harem. The contrast between this Ottoman and his concubines is striking; because, while he is always of the largest leviathanic proportions, the ladies, even at full growth, are not more than one third of the bulk of an average-sized male. They are comparatively delicate, indeed; I dare say, not to exceed half a dozen yards round the waist. Nevertheless, it cannot be denied, that upon the whole they are hereditarily entitled to *en bon point*.

It is very curious to watch this harem and its lord in their indolent ramblings. Like fashionables, they are for ever on the move in leisurely search of variety. You meet them on the Line in time for the full flower of the Equatorial feeding season, having just returned, perhaps, from spending the summer in the Northern seas, and so cheating summer of all unpleasant weariness and warmth. By the time they have lounged up and down the promenade of the Equator awhile, they start for the Oriental waters in anticipation of the cool season there, and so evade the other excessive temperature of the year.

When serenely advancing on one of these journeys, if any strange suspicious sights are seen, my lord whale keeps a wary eye on his interesting family. Should any unwarrantably pert young Leviathan coming that way, presume to draw confidentially close to one of the ladies, with what prodigious fury the Bashaw assails him, and chases him away! High times, indeed, if unprincipled young rakes like him are to be permitted to invade the sanctity of domestic bliss; though do what the Bashaw will, he cannot keep the most notorious Lothario out of his bed; for, alas! all fish bed in common. As ashore, the ladies often cause the most terrible duels among their rival admirers; just so with the whales, who sometimes come to deadly battle, and all for love. They fence with their long lower jaws, sometimes locking them together, and so striving for the supremacy like elks that warringly interweave their antlers. Not a few are captured having the deep scars of these encounters,—furrowed heads, broken teeth, scolloped fins; and in some instances, wrenched and dislocated mouths.

But supposing the invader of domestic bliss to betake himself away at the first rush of the harem's lord, then is it very diverting to watch that lord. Gently he insinuates his vast bulk among them again and revels there awhile, still in tantalizing vicinity to young Lothario, like pious Solomon devoutly worshipping among his thousand concubines. Granting other whales to be in sight, the fishermen will seldom give chase to one of these Grand Turks; for these Grand Turks are too lavish of their strength, and hence their unctuousness is small. As for the sons and the daughters they beget, why, those sons and daughters must take care of themselves; at least, with only the maternal help. For like certain other omnivorous roving lovers that might be named, my Lord Whale has no taste for the nursery, however much for the bower; and so, being a great traveller, he leaves his anonymous babies all over the world; every baby an exotic. In good time, nevertheless, as the ardor of youth declines; as years and dumps increase; as reflection lends her solemn pauses; in short, as a general lassitude overtakes the sated Turk; then a love of ease and virtue supplants the love for maidens; our Ottoman enters upon the impotent, repentant, admonitory stage of life, forswears, disbands the harem, and grown to an exemplary, sulky old soul, goes about all alone among the meridians and parallels saying his prayers, and warning each young Leviathan from his amorous errors.

Now, as the harem of whales is called by the fishermen a school, so is the lord and master of that school technically known as the schoolmaster. It is therefore not in strict character, however admirably satirical, that after going to school himself, he should then go abroad inculcating not what he learned there, but the folly of it. His title, schoolmaster, would very naturally seem derived from the name bestowed upon the harem itself, but some have surmised that the man who first thus entitled this sort of Ottoman whale, must have read the memoirs of Vidocq, and informed himself what sort of a country-schoolmaster [1] that famous Frenchman was in his younger days, and what was the nature of those occult lessons he inculcated into some of his pupils.

The same secludedness and isolation to which the schoolmaster whale betakes himself in his advancing years, is true of all aged Sperm Whales. Almost universally, a lone whale—as a solitary Leviathan is called—proves an ancient one. Like venerable moss-bearded Daniel Boone, he will have no one near him but Nature herself; and her he takes to wife in the wilderness of waters, and the best of wives she is, though she keeps so many moody secrets.

The schools composing none but young and vigorous males, previously mentioned, offer a strong contrast to the harem schools. For while those female whales are characteristically timid, the young males, or forty-barrel-bulls, as they call them, are by far the most pugnacious of all Leviathans, and proverbially the most dangerous to encounter; excepting those wondrous grey-headed, grizzled whales, sometimes met, and these will fight you like grim fiends exasperated by a penal gout.

The Forty-barrel-bull schools are larger than the harem schools. Like a mob of young collegians, they are full of fight, fun, and wickedness, tumbling round the world at such a reckless, rollicking rate, that no prudent underwriter would insure them any more than he would a riotous lad at Yale or Harvard. They soon relinquish this turbulence though, and when about three fourths grown, break up, and separately go about in quest of settlements, that is, harems.

Another point of difference between the male and female schools is still more characteristic of the sexes. Say you strike a Forty-barrel-bull—poor devil! all his comrades quit him. But strike a member of the harem school, and her companions swim around her with every token of concern, sometimes lingering so near her and so long, as themselves to fall a prey.

1. The sort who would seduce the young girls in his charge.

Chapter 89

FAST-FISH AND LOOSE-FISH

The allusion to the waifs and waif-poles in the last chapter but one, necessitates some account of the laws and regulations of the whale fishery, of which the waif may be deemed the grand symbol and badge.

It frequently happens that when several ships are cruising in company, a whale may be struck by one vessel, then escape, and be finally killed and captured by another vessel; and herein are indirectly comprised many minor contingencies, all partaking of this one grand feature. For example,—after a weary and perilous chase and capture of a whale, the body may get loose from the ship by reason of a violent storm; and drifting far away to leeward, be retaken by a second whaler, who, in a calm, snugly tows it alongside, without risk of life or line. Thus the most vexatious and violent disputes would often arise between the fishermen, were there not some written or unwritten, universal, undisputed law applicable to all cases.

Perhaps the only formal whaling code authorized by legislative enactment, was that of Holland. It was decreed by the States-General in A.D. 1695. But though no other nation has ever had any written whaling law, yet the American fishermen have been their own legislators and lawyers in this matter. They have provided a system which for terse comprehensiveness surpasses Justinian's Pandects and the By-laws of the Chinese Society for the Suppression of Meddling with other People's Business. Yes; these laws might be engraven on a Queen Anne's farthing,[1] or the barb of a harpoon, and worn round the neck, so small are they.

I. A Fast-Fish belongs to the party fast to it.

II. A Loose-Fish is fair game for anybody who can soonest catch it.

But what plays the mischief with this masterly code is the admirable brevity of it, which necessitates a vast volume of commentaries to expound it.

First: What is a Fast-Fish? Alive or dead a fish is technically fast, when it is connected with an occupied ship or boat, by any medium at all controllable by the occupant or occupants,—a mast, an oar, a nine-inch cable, a telegraph wire, or a strand of cobweb, it is all the same. Likewise a fish is technically fast when it bears a waif, or any other recognised symbol of possession; so long as

---

1. Queen Anne's farthings are commonly—and erroneously—thought to be extremely rare; one story insists that only three were minted. Perhaps Melville had scarcity confused with smallness: some commemorative farthings, though not Queen Anne's farthings, are much smaller than an American dime.

the party waifing it plainly evince their ability at any time to take it alongside, as well as their intention so to do.

These are scientific commentaries; but the commentaries of the whalemen themselves sometimes consist in hard words and harder knocks—the Coke-upon-Littleton [2] of the fist. True, among the more upright and honorable whalemen allowances are always made for peculiar cases, where it would be an outrageous moral injustice for one party to claim possession of a whale previously chased or killed by another party. But others are by no means so scrupulous.

Some fifty years ago there was a curious case of whale-trover litigated in England, wherein the plaintiffs set forth that after a hard chase of a whale in the northern seas, they (the plaintiffs) had succeeded in harpooning the fish; but at last, through peril of their lives, were obliged to forsake, not only their lines, but their boat itself,—Furthermore: ultimately the defendants (the crew of another ship) came up with the whale; struck, killed, seized, and finally appropriated it before the very eyes of the plaintiffs;—Yet again:—and when those defendants were remonstrated with, their captain snapped his fingers in the plaintiffs' teeth, and assured them that by way of doxology to the deed he had done, he would now retain their line, harpoons, and boat, all of which had remained attached to the whale at the time of the seizure. Wherefore, the plaintiffs now sued for the recovery of the value of their whale, line, harpoons, and boat.

Mr. Erskine was counsel for the defendants; Lord Ellenborough was the judge. In the course of the defence, the witty Erskine went on to illustrate his position, by alluding to a recent crim. con. case,[3] wherein a gentleman, after in vain trying to bridle his wife's viciousness, had at last abandoned her upon the seas of life; but in the course of years, repenting of that step, he instituted an action to recover possession of her. He then proceeded to say that, though the gentleman had originally harpooned the lady, and had once had her fast, and only by reason of the great stress of her plunging viciousness, had at last abandoned her; yet abandon her he did, so that she became a loose-fish; and therefore when a subsequent gentleman re-harpooned her, the lady then became that subsequent gentleman's property, along with whatever harpoon might have been found sticking in her.

Now in the present case Erskine contended that the examples of the whale and the lady were reciprocally illustrative of each other.

2. Sir Edward Coke's early seventeenth-century commentary upon a fifteenth-century work on real property by Sir Thomas Littleton.
3. A case of "criminal conversation"—that is, adultery.

These pleadings, and the counter pleadings, being duly heard, the very learned judge in set terms decided, to wit:—That as for the boat, he awarded it to the plaintiffs, because they had merely abandoned it to save their lives; but that with regard to the controverted whale, harpoons, and line, they belonged to the defendants; the whale, because it was a Loose-Fish at the time of the final capture; and the harpoons and line because when the fish made off with them, it (the fish) acquired a property in those articles; and hence anybody who afterwards took the fish had a right to them. Now, the defendants afterwards took the fish; ergo, the aforesaid articles were theirs.

A common man looking at this decision of the very learned Judge, might possibly object to it. But ploughed up to the primary rock of the matter, the two great principles laid down in the twin whaling laws previously quoted, and applied and elucidated by Lord Ellenborough in the above cited case; these two laws touching Fast-Fish and Loose-Fish, I say, will, on reflection, be found the fundamentals of all human jurisprudence; for notwithstanding its complicated tracery of sculpture, the Temple of the Law, like the Temple of the Philistines, has but two props to stand on.

Is it not a saying in every one's mouth, Possession is half of the law: that is, regardless of how the thing came into possession? But often possession is the whole of the law. What are the sinews and souls of Russian serfs and Republican slaves [4] but Fast-Fish, whereof possession is the whole of the law? What to the rapacious landlord is the widow's last mite but a Fast-Fish? What is yonder undetected villain's marble mansion with a door-plate for a waif; what is that but a Fast-Fish? What is the ruinous discount [5] which Mordecai,[6] the broker, gets from poor Woebegone, the bankrupt, on a loan to keep Woebegone's family from starvation; what is that ruinous discount but a Fast-Fish? What is the Archbishop of Savesoul's income of £100,000 seized from the scant bread and cheese of hundreds of thousands of broken-backed laborers (all sure of heaven without any of Savesoul's help) what is that globular 100,000 but a Fast-Fish? What are the Duke of Dunder's hereditary towns and hamlets but Fast-Fish? What to that redoubted harpooneer, John Bull, is poor Ireland, but a Fast-Fish? What to that apostolic lancer, Brother Jonathan, is Texas but a Fast-Fish? And concerning all these, is not Possession the whole of the law?

But if the doctrine of Fast-Fish be pretty generally applicable,

4. Slaves in a republic, like the United States.
5. Interest deducted in advance from the loan itself.
6. Generic name for a Jew.

the kindred doctrine of Loose-Fish is still more widely so. That is internationally and universally applicable.

What was America in 1492 but a Loose-Fish, in which Columbus struck the Spanish standard by way of waifing it for his royal master and mistress? What was Poland to the Czar? What Greece to the Turk? What India to England? What at last will Mexico be to the United States? All Loose-Fish.

What are the Rights of Man and the Liberties of the World but Loose-Fish? What all men's minds and opinions but Loose-Fish? What is the principle of religious belief in them but a Loose-Fish? What to the ostentatious smuggling verbalists are the thoughts of thinkers but Loose-Fish? What is the great globe itself but a Loose-Fish? And what are you, reader, but a Loose-Fish and a Fast-Fish, too?

Chapter 90

HEADS OR TAILS

"De balena vero sufficit, si rex habeat caput, et regina caudam." [1]
Bracton, l. 3, c. 3.

Latin from the books of the Laws of England, which taken along with the context, means, that of all whales captured by anybody on the coast of that land, the King, as Honorary Grand Harpooneer, must have the head, and the Queen be respectfully presented with the tail. A division which, in the whale, is much like halving an apple; there is no intermediate remainder. Now as this law, under a modified form, is to this day in force in England; and as it offers in various respects a strange anomaly touching the general law of Fast and Loose-Fish, it is here treated of in a separate chapter, on the same courteous principle that prompts the English railways to be at the expense of a separate car, specially reserved for the accommodation of royalty. In the first place, in curious proof of the fact that the above-mentioned law is still in force, I proceed to lay before you a circumstance that happened within the last two years.

It seems that some honest mariners of Dover, or Sandwich, or some one of the Cinque Ports, had after a hard chase succeeded in killing and beaching a fine whale which they had originally descried afar off from the shore. Now the Cinque Ports are partially or somehow under the jurisdiction of a sort of policeman or beadle, called a Lord Warden. Holding the office directly from the crown, I believe, all the royal emoluments incident to the Cinque Port territories become by assignment his. By some writers

---

1. "Concerning the whale, truly it suffices, if the king have the head, and the queen the tail."

this office is called a sinecure. But not so. Because the Lord Warden is busily employed at times in fobbing [2] his perquisites; which
are his chiefly by virtue of that same fobbing of them.

Now when these poor sun-burnt mariners, bare-footed, and with
their trowsers rolled high up on their eely legs, had wearily hauled
their fat fish high and dry, promising themselves a good £150
from the precious oil and bone; and in fantasy sipping rare tea
with their wives, and good ale with their cronies, upon the
strength of their respective shares; up steps a very learned and most
Christian and charitable gentleman, with a copy of Blackstone
under his arm; and laying it upon the whale's head, he says—
"Hands off! this fish, my masters, is a Fast-Fish. I seize it as the
Lord Warden's." Upon this the poor mariners in their respectful
consternation—so truly English—knowing not what to say, fall to
vigorously scratching their heads all round; meanwhile ruefully
glancing from the whale to the stranger. But that did in nowise
mend the matter, or at all soften the hard heart of the learned
gentleman with the copy of Blackstone. At length one of them,
after long scratching about for his ideas, made bold to speak.

"Please, sir, who is the Lord Warden?"

"The Duke."

"But the duke had nothing to do with taking this fish?"

"It is his."

"We have been at great trouble, and peril, and some expense,
and is all that to go to the Duke's benefit; we getting nothing
at all for our pains but our blisters?"

"It is his."

"Is the Duke so very poor as to be forced to this desperate
mode of getting a livelihood?"

"It is his."

"I thought to relieve my old bed-ridden mother by part of my
share of this whale."

"It is his."

"Won't the Duke be content with a quarter or a half?"

"It is his."

In a word, the whale was seized and sold, and his Grace the
Duke of Wellington received the money. Thinking that viewed
in some particular lights, the case might by a bare possibility in
some small degree be deemed, under the circumstances, a rather
hard one, an honest clergyman of the town respectfully addressed
a note to his Grace, begging him to take the case of those unfortunate mariners into full consideration. To which my Lord
Duke in substance replied (both letters were published) that he
had already done so, and received the money, and would be

2. Pocketing.

obliged to the reverend gentleman if for the future he (the reverend gentleman) would decline meddling with other people's business. Is this the still militant old man, standing at the corners of the three kingdoms, on all hands coercing alms of beggars?

It will readily be seen that in this case the alleged right of the Duke to the whale was a delegated one from the Sovereign. We must needs inquire then on what principle the Sovereign is originally invested with that right. The law itself has already been set forth. But Plowdon gives us the reason for it. Says Plowdon, the whale so caught belongs to the King and Queen, "because of its superior excellence." And by the soundest commentators this has ever been held a cogent argument in such matters.

But why should the King have the head, and the Queen the tail? A reason for that, ye lawyers!

In his treatise on "Queen-Gold," or Queen-pinmoney, an old King's Bench author, one William Prynne, thus discourseth: "Ye tail is ye Queen's, that ye Queen's wardrobe may be supplied with ye whalebone." Now this was written at a time when the black limber bone of the Greenland or Right whale was largely used in ladies' bodices. But this same bone is not in the tail; it is in the head, which is a sad mistake for a sagacious lawyer like Prynne. But is the Queen a mermaid, to be presented with a tail? An allegorical meaning may lurk here.

There are two royal fish so styled by the English law writers —the whale and the sturgeon; both royal property under certain limitations, and nominally supplying the tenth branch of the crown's ordinary revenue. I know not that any other author has hinted of the matter; but by inference it seems to me that the sturgeon must be divided in the same way as the whale, the King receiving the highly dense and elastic head peculiar to that fish, which, symbolically regarded, may possibly be humorously grounded upon some presumed congeniality. And thus there seems a reason in all things, even in law.

Chapter 91

THE PEQUOD MEETS THE ROSE-BUD

"In vain it was to rake for Ambergriese in the paunch of this Leviathan, insufferable fetor denying that inquiry."

Sir T. Browne, V. E.

It was a week or two after the last whaling scene recounted, and when we were slowly sailing over a sleepy, vapory, mid-day sea, that the many noses on the Pequod's deck proved more vigilant discoverers than the three pairs of eyes aloft. A peculiar and not very pleasant smell was smelt in the sea.

"I will bet something now," said Stubb, "that somewhere here-abouts are some of those drugged whales we tickled the other day. I thought they would keel up before long."

Presently, the vapors in advance slid aside; and there in the distance lay a ship, whose furled sails betokened that some sort of whale must be alongside. As we glided nearer, the stranger showed French colors from his peak; and by the eddying cloud of vulture sea-fowl that circled, and hovered, and swooped around him, it was plain that the whale alongside must be what the fishermen call a blasted whale, that is, a whale that has died unmolested on the sea, and so floated an unappropriated corpse. It may well be conceived, what an unsavory odor such a mass must exhale; worse than an Assyrian city in the plague, when the living are incompetent to bury the departed. So intolerable indeed is it regarded by some, that no cupidity could persuade them to moor alongside of it. Yet are there those who will still do it; not-withstanding the fact that the oil obtained from such subjects is of a very inferior quality, and by no means of the nature of attar-of-rose.

Coming still nearer with the expiring breeze, we saw that the Frenchman had a second whale alongside; and this second whale seemed even more of a nosegay than the first. In truth, it turned out to be one of those problematical whales that seem to dry up and die with a sort of prodigious dyspepsia, or indigestion; leaving their defunct bodies almost entirely bankrupt of anything like oil. Nevertheless, in the proper place we shall see that no knowing fisherman will ever turn up his nose at such a whale as this, however much he may shun blasted whales in general.

The Pequod had now swept so nigh to the stranger, that Stubb vowed he recognised his cutting spade-pole entangled in the lines that were knotted round the tail of one of these whales.

"There's a pretty fellow, now," he banteringly laughed, standing in the ship's bows, "there's a jackal for ye! I well know that these Crappoes [1] of Frenchmen are but poor devils in the fishery; some-times lowering their boats for breakers, mistaking them for Sperm Whale spouts; yes, and sometimes sailing from their port with their hold full of boxes of tallow candles, and cases of snuffers, foreseeing that all the oil they will get won't be enough to dip the Captain's wick into; aye, we all know these things; but look ye, here's a Crappo that is content with our leavings, the drugged whale there, I mean; aye, and is content too with scraping the dry bones of that other precious fish he has there. Poor devil! I say, pass round a hat, some one, and let's make him a present of a little oil for dear charity's sake. For what oil he'll get from

1. From the French *crapauds*, toads.

that drugged whale there, wouldn't be fit to burn in a jail; no, not in a condemned cell. And as for the other whale, why, I'll agree to get more oil by chopping up and trying out these three masts of ours, than he'll get from that bundle of bones; though, now that I think of it, it may contain something worth a good deal more than oil; yes, ambergris. I wonder now if our old man has thought of that. It's worth trying. Yes, I'm in for it;" and so saying he started for the quarter-deck.

By this time the faint air had become a complete calm; so that whether or no, the Pequod was now fairly entrapped in the smell, with no hope of escaping except by its breezing up again. Issuing from the cabin, Stubb now called his boat's crew, and pulled off for the stranger. Drawing across her bow, he perceived that in accordance with the fanciful French taste, the upper part of her stem-piece was carved in the likeness of a huge drooping stalk, was painted green, and for thorns had copper spikes projecting from it here and there; the whole terminating in a symmetrical folded bulb of a bright red color. Upon her head boards, in large gilt letters, he read "Bouton de Rose,"—Rose-button, or Rose-bud; and this was the romantic name of this aromatic ship.

Though Stubb did not understand the *Bouton* part of the inscription, yet the word *rose*, and the bulbous figure-head put together, sufficiently explained the whole to him.

"A wooden rose-bud, eh?" he cried with his hand to his nose, "that will do very well; but how like all creation it smells!"

Now in order to hold direct communication with the people on deck, he had to pull round the bows to the starboard side, and thus come close to the blasted whale; and so talk over it.

Arrived then at this spot, with one hand still to his nose, he bawled—"Bouton-de-Rose, ahoy! are there any of you Bouton-de-Roses that speak English?"

"Yes," rejoined a Guernsey-man from the bulwarks, who turned out to be the chief-mate.

"Well, then, my Bouton-de-Rose-bud, have you seen the White Whale?"

"*What* whale?"

"The *White* Whale—a Sperm Whale—Moby Dick, have ye seen him?"

"Never heard of such a whale. Cachalot Blanche! White Whale—no."

"Very good, then; good bye now, and I'll call again in a minute."

Then rapidly pulling back towards the Pequod, and seeing Ahab leaning over the quarter-deck rail awaiting his report, he moulded his two hands into a trumpet and shouted—"No, Sir!

No!" Upon which Ahab retired, and Stubb returned to the Frenchman.

He now perceived that the Guernsey-man, who had just got into the chains, and was using a cutting-spade, had slung his nose in a sort of bag.

"What's the matter with your nose, there?" said Stubb. "Broke it?"

"I wish it was broken, or that I didn't have any nose at all!" answered the Guernsey-man, who did not seem to relish the job he was at very much. "But what are you holding *yours* for?"

"Oh, nothing! It's a wax nose; I have to hold it on. Fine day, aint it? Air rather gardenny, I should say; throw us a bunch of posies, will ye, Bouton-de-Rose?"

"What in the devil's name do you want here?" roared the Guernsey-man, flying into a sudden passion.

"Oh! keep cool—cool? yes, that's the word; why don't you pack those whales in ice while you're working at 'em? But joking aside, though; do you know, Rose-bud, that it's all nonsense trying to get any oil out of such whales? As for that dried up one, there, he hasn't a gill in his whole carcase."

"I know that well enough; but, d'ye see, the Captain here won't believe it; this is his first voyage; he was a Cologne manufacturer before. But come aboard, and mayhap he'll believe you, if he won't me; and so I'll get out of this dirty scrape."

"Anything to oblige ye, my sweet and pleasant fellow," rejoined Stubb, and with that he soon mounted to the deck. There a queer scene presented itself. The sailors, in tasselled caps of red worsted, were getting the heavy tackles in readiness for the whales. But they worked rather slow and talked very fast, and seemed in anything but a good humor. All their noses upwardly projected from their faces like so many jib-booms. Now and then pairs of them would drop their work, and run up to the masthead to get some fresh air. Some thinking they would catch the plague, dipped oakum in coal-tar, and at intervals held it to their nostrils. Others having broken the stems of their pipes almost short off at the bowl, were vigorously puffing tobacco-smoke, so that it constantly filled their olfactories.

Stubb was struck by a shower of outcries and anathemas proceeding from the Captain's round-house [2] abaft; and looking in that direction saw a fiery face thrust from behind the door, which was held ajar from within. This was the tormented surgeon, who, after in vain remonstrating against the proceedings of the day, had betaken himself to the Captain's round-house (*cabinet* he

2. The Captain's privy. As Bernard Mosher explains, the surgeon prefers the odor of the *"cabinet"* to that of the blasted whale.

called it) to avoid the pest; but still, could not help yelling out his entreaties and indignations at times.

Marking all this, Stubb augured well for his scheme, and turning to the Guernsey-man had a little chat with him, during which the stranger mate expressed his detestation of his Captain as a conceited ignoramus, who had brought them all into so unsavory and unprofitable a pickle. Sounding him carefully, Stubb further perceived that the Guernsey-man had not the slightest suspicion concerning the ambergris. He therefore held his peace on that head, but otherwise was quite frank and confidential with him, so that the two quickly concocted a little plan for both circumventing and satirizing the Captain, without his at all dreaming of distrusting their sincerity. According to this little plan of theirs, the Guernsey-man, under cover of an interpreter's office, was to tell the Captain what he pleased, but as coming from Stubb; and as for Stubb, he was to utter any nonsense that should come uppermost in him during the interview.

By this time their destined victim appeared from his cabin. He was a small and dark, but rather delicate looking man for a sea-captain, with large whiskers and moustache, however; and wore a red cotton velvet vest with watch-seals at his side. To this gentleman, Stubb was now politely introduced by the Guernsey-man, who at once ostentatiously put on the aspect of interpreting between them.

"What shall I say to him first?" said he.

"Why," said Stubb, eyeing the velvet vest and the watch and seals, "you may as well begin by telling him that he looks a sort of babyish to me, though I don't pretend to be a judge."

"He says, Monsieur," said the Guernsey-man, in French, turning to his captain, "that only yesterday his ship spoke a vessel, whose captain and chief-mate, with six sailors, had all died of a fever caught from a blasted whale they had brought alongside."

Upon this the captain started, and eagerly desired to know more.

"What now?" said the Guernsey-man to Stubb.

"Why, since he takes it so easy, tell him that now I have eyed him carefully, I'm quite certain that he's no more fit to command a whale-ship than a St. Jago monkey. In fact, tell him from me he's a baboon."

"He vows and declares, Monsieur, that the other whale, the dried one, is far more deadly than the blasted one; in fine, Monsieur, he conjures us, as we value our lives, to cut loose from these fish."

Instantly the captain ran forward, and in a loud voice commanded his crew to desist from hoisting the cutting-tackles, and at once cast loose the cables and chains confining the whales to the ship.

"What now?" said the Guernsey-man, when the captain had returned to them.

"Why, let me see; yes, you may as well tell him now that—that—in fact, tell him I've diddled him, and (aside to himself) perhaps somebody else."

"He says, Monsieur, that he's very happy to have been of any service to us."

Hearing this, the captain vowed that they were the grateful parties (meaning himself and mate) and concluded by inviting Stubb down into his cabin to drink a bottle of Bordeaux.

"He wants you to take a glass of wine with him," said the interpreter.

"Thank him heartily; but tell him it's against my principles to drink with the man I've diddled. In fact, tell him I must go."

"He says, Monsieur, that his principles won't admit of his drinking; but that if Monsieur wants to live another day to drink, then Monsieur had best drop all four boats, and pull the ship away from these whales, for it's so calm they won't drift."

By this time Stubb was over the side, and getting into his boat, hailed the Guernsey-man to this effect,—that having a long tow-line in his boat, he would do what he could to help them, by pulling out the lighter whale of the two from the ship's side. While the Frenchman's boats, then, were engaged in towing the ship one way, Stubb benevolently towed away at his whale the other way, ostentatiously slacking out a most unusually long tow-line.

Presently a breeze sprang up; Stubb feigned to cast off from the whale; hoisting his boats, the Frenchman soon increased his distance, while the Pequod slid in between him and Stubb's whale. Whereupon Stubb quickly pulled to the floating body, and hailing the Pequod to give notice of his intentions, at once proceeded to reap the fruit of his unrighteous cunning. Seizing his sharp boat-spade, he commenced an excavation in the body, a little behind the side fin. You would almost have thought he was digging a cellar there in the sea; and when at length his spade struck against the gaunt ribs, it was like turning up old Roman tiles and pottery buried in fat English loam. His boat's crew were all in high excitement, eagerly helping their chief, and looking as anxious as gold-hunters.

And all the time numberless fowls were diving, and ducking, and screaming, and yelling, and fighting around them. Stubb was beginning to look disappointed, especially as the horrible nosegay increased, when suddenly from out the very heart of this plague, there stole a faint stream of perfume, which flowed through the tide of bad smells without being absorbed by it, as one river will flow into and then along with another, without at all blending with it for a time.

"I have it, I have it," cried Stubb, with delight, striking something in the subterranean regions, "a purse! a purse!"

Dropping his spade, he thrust both hands in, and drew out handfuls of something that looked like ripe Windsor soap, or rich mottled old cheese; very unctuous and savory withal. You might easily dent it with your thumb; it is of a hue between yellow and ash color. And this, good friends, is ambergris, worth a gold guinea an ounce to any druggist. Some six handfuls were obtained; but more was unavoidably lost in the sea, and still more, perhaps, might have been secured were it not for impatient Ahab's loud command to Stubb to desist, and come on board, else the ship would bid them good bye.

Chapter 92

AMBERGRIS [1]

Now this ambergris is a very curious substance, and so important as an article of commerce, that in 1791 a certain Nantucket-born Captain Coffin was examined at the bar of the English House of Commons on that subject. For at that time, and indeed until a comparatively late day, the precise origin of ambergris remained, like amber itself, a problem to the learned. Though the word ambergris is but the French compound for grey amber, yet the two substances are quite distinct. For amber, though at times found on the sea-coast, is also dug up in some far inland soils, whereas ambergris is never found except upon the sea. Besides, amber is a hard, transparent, brittle, odorless substance, used for mouth-pieces to pipes, for beads and ornaments; but ambergris is soft, waxy, and so highly fragrant and spicy, that it is largely used in perfumery, in pastilles, precious candles, hair-powders, and pomatum. The Turks use it in cooking, and also carry it to Mecca, for the same purpose that frankincense is carried to St. Peter's in Rome. Some wine merchants drop a few grains into claret, to flavor it.

Who would think, then, that such fine ladies and gentlemen should regale themselves with an essence found in the inglorious bowels of a sick whale! Yet so it is. By some, ambergris is supposed to be the cause, and by others the effect, of the dyspepsia

1. Mansfield and Vincent cite Beale as Melville's source for many details in this chapter.

in the whale. How to cure such a dyspepsia it were hard to say, unless by administering three or four boat loads of Brandreth's pills,[2] and then running out of harm's way, as laborers do in blasting rocks.

I have forgotten to say that there were found in this ambergris, certain hard, round, bony plates, which at first Stubb thought might be sailors' trousers buttons; but it afterwards turned out that they were nothing more than pieces of small squid bones embalmed in that manner.

Now that the incorruption of this most fragrant ambergris should be found in the heart of such decay; is this nothing? Bethink thee of that saying of St. Paul in Corinthians, about corruption and incorruption; how that we are sown in dishonor, but raised in glory. And likewise call to mind that saying of Paracelsus about what it is that maketh the best musk.[3] Also forget not the strange fact that of all things of ill-savor, Cologne-water, in its rudimental manufacturing stages, is the worst.

I should like to conclude the chapter with the above appeal, but cannot, owing to my anxiety to repel a charge often made against whalemen, and which, in the estimation of some already biased minds, might be considered as indirectly substantiated by what has been said of the Frenchman's two whales. Elsewhere in this volume the slanderous aspersion has been disproved, that the vocation of whaling is throughout a slatternly, untidy business. But there is another thing to rebut. They hint that all whales always smell bad. Now how did this odious stigma originate?

I opine, that it is plainly traceable to the first arrival of the Greenland whaling ships in London, more than two centuries ago. Because those whalemen did not then, and do not now, try out their oil at sea as the Southern ships have always done; but cutting up the fresh blubber in small bits, thrust it through the bung holes of large casks, and carry it home in that manner; the shortness of the season in those Icy Seas, and the sudden and violent storms to which they are exposed, forbidding any other course. The consequence is, that upon breaking into the hold, and unloading one of these whale cemeteries, in the Greenland dock, a savor is given forth somewhat similar to that arising from excavating an old city grave-yard, for the foundations of a Lying-in Hospital.

I partly surmise also, that this wicked charge against whalers may be likewise imputed to the existence on the coast of Greenland, in former times, of a Dutch village called Schmerenburgh or Smeerenberg, which latter name is the one used by the

2. A laxative.   3. "What it is" is excrement.

learned Fogo Von Slack,[4] in his great work on Smells, a textbook on that subject. As its name imports (smeer, fat; berg, to put up), this village was founded in order to afford a place for the blubber of the Dutch whale fleet to be tried out, without being taken home to Holland for that purpose. It was a collection of furnaces, fat-kettles, and oil sheds; and when the works were in full operation certainly gave forth no very pleasant savor. But all this is quite different with a South Sea Sperm Whaler; which in a voyage of four years perhaps, after completely filling her hold with oil, does not, perhaps, consume fifty days in the business of boiling out; and in the state that it is casked, the oil is nearly scentless. The truth is, that living or dead, if but decently treated, whales as a species are by no means creatures of ill odor; nor can whalemen be recognised, as the people of the middle ages affected to detect a Jew in the company, by the nose. Nor indeed can the whale possibly be otherwise than fragrant, when, as a general thing, he enjoys such high health; taking abundance of exercise; always out of doors; though, it is true, seldom in the open air. I say, that the motion of a Sperm Whale's flukes above water dispenses a perfume, as when a musk-scented lady rustles her dress in a warm parlor. What then shall I liken the Sperm Whale to for fragrance, considering his magnitude? Must it not be to that famous elephant, with jewelled tusks, and redolent with myrrh, which was led out of an Indian town to do honor to Alexander the Great?

Chapter 93

THE CASTAWAY

It was but some few days after encountering the Frenchman, that a most significant event befell the most insignificant of the Pequod's crew; an event most lamentable; and which ended in providing the sometimes madly merry and predestinated craft with a living and ever accompanying prophecy of whatever shattered sequel might prove her own.

Now, in the whale ship, it is not every one that goes in the boats. Some few hands are reserved called ship-keepers, whose province it is to work the vessel while the boats are pursuing the whale. As a general thing, these ship-keepers are as hardy fellows as the men comprising the boats' crews. But if there happen to be an unduly slender, clumsy, or timorous wight in the ship, that wight is certain to be made a ship-keeper. It was so in the Pequod with the little negro Pippin by nick-name, Pip by abbreviation. Poor Pip! ye have heard of him before; ye must remember his

4. Another of Melville's comic names for Scoresby.

tambourine on that dramatic midnight, so gloomy-jolly.

In outer aspect, Pip and Dough-Boy made a match, like a black pony and a white one, of equal developments, though of dissimilar color, driven in one eccentric span. But while hapless Dough-Boy was by nature dull and torpid in his intellects, Pip, though over tender-hearted, was at bottom very bright, with that pleasant, genial, jolly brightness peculiar to his tribe; a tribe, which ever enjoy all holidays and festivities with finer, freer relish than any other race. For blacks, the year's calendar should show naught but three hundred and sixty-five Fourth of Julys and New Year's Days. Nor smile so, while I write that this little black was brilliant, for even blackness has its brilliancy; behold yon lustrous ebony, panelled in kings' cabinets. But Pip loved life, and all life's peaceable securities; so that the panic-striking business in which he had somehow unaccountably become entrapped, had most sadly blurred his brightness; though, as ere long will be seen, what was thus temporarily subdued in him, in the end was destined to be luridly illumined by strange wild fires, that fictitiously showed him off to ten times the natural lustre with which in his native Tolland County in Connecticut, he had once enlivened many a fiddler's frolic on the green; and at melodious even-tide, with his gay ha-ha! had turned the round horizon into one star-belled tambourine. So, though in the clear air of day, suspended against a blue-veined neck, the pure-watered diamond drop will healthful glow; yet, when the cunning jeweller would show you the diamond in its most impressive lustre, he lays it against a gloomy ground, and then lights it up, not by the sun, but by some unnatural gases. Then come out those fiery effulgences, infernally superb; then the evil-blazing diamond, once the divinest symbol of the crystal skies, looks like some crownjewel stolen from the King of Hell. But let us to the story.

It came to pass, that in the ambergris affair Stubb's afteroarsman chanced so to sprain his hand, as for a time to become quite maimed; and, temporarily, Pip was put into his place.

The first time Stubb lowered with him, Pip evinced much nervousness; but happily, for that time, escaped close contact with the whale; and therefore came off not altogether discreditably; though Stubb observing him, took care, afterwards, to exhort him to cherish his courageousness to the utmost, for he might often find it needful.

Now upon the second lowering, the boat paddled upon the whale; and as the fish received the darted iron, it gave its customary rap, which happened, in this instance, to be right under poor Pip's seat. The involuntary consternation of the moment caused him to leap, paddle in hand, out of the boat; and in such a way, that part of the slack whale line coming against his chest, he breasted it overboard with him, so as to become entangled in it, when at last plumping into the water. That instant the stricken whale started on a fierce run, the line swiftly straightened; and presto! poor Pip came all foaming up to the chocks of the boat, remorselessly dragged there by the line, which had taken several turns around his chest and neck.

Tashtego stood in the bows. He was full of the fire of the hunt. He hated Pip for a poltroon. Snatching the boat-knife from its sheath, he suspended its sharp edge over the line, and turning towards Stubb, exclaimed interrogatively, "Cut?" Meantime Pip's blue, choked face plainly looked, Do, for God's sake! All passed in a flash. In less than half a minute, this entire thing happened.

"Damn him, cut!" roared Stubb; and so the whale was lost and Pip was saved.

So soon as he recovered himself, the poor little negro was assailed by yells and execrations from the crew. Tranquilly permitting these irregular cursings to evaporate, Stubb then in a plain, business-like, but still half humorous manner, cursed Pip officially; and that done, unofficially gave him much wholesome advice. The substance was, Never jump from a boat, Pip, except—but all the rest was indefinite, as the soundest advice ever is. Now, in general, *Stick to the boat*, is your true motto in whaling; but cases will sometimes happen when *Leap from the boat*, is still better. Moreover, as if perceiving at last that if he should give undiluted conscientious advice to Pip, he would be leaving him too wide a margin to jump in for the future; Stubb suddenly dropped all advice, and concluded with a peremptory command, "Stick to the boat, Pip, or by the Lord, I wont pick you up if you jump; mind that. We can't afford to lose whales by the likes of you; a whale would sell for thirty times what you would, Pip, in Alabama. Bear that in mind, and don't jump any more." Hereby perhaps Stubb indirectly hinted, that though man loves his fellow, yet man is a money-making animal, which propensity too often interferes with his benevolence.

But we are all in the hands of the Gods; and Pip jumped again. It was under very similar circumstances to the first performance; but this time he did not breast out the line; and hence, when the whale started to run, Pip was left behind on the sea, like a hurried traveller's trunk. Alas! Stubb was but too true to his word. It was a beautiful, bounteous, blue day; the spangled sea calm and cool, and flatly stretching away, all round, to the horizon, like gold-beater's skin [1] hammered out to the extremest. Bobbing up and down in that sea, Pip's ebon head showed like a

1. Membrane of an ox's intestine, used to separate sheets of gold while they are   beaten into gold leaf.

head of cloves. No boat-knife was lifted when he fell so rapidly astern. Stubb's inexorable back was turned upon him; and the whale was winged. In three minutes, a whole mile of shoreless ocean was between Pip and Stubb. Out from the centre of the sea, poor Pip turned his crisp, curling, black head to the sun, another lonely castaway, though the loftiest and the brightest.

Now, in calm weather, to swim in the open ocean is as easy to the practised swimmer as to ride in a spring-carriage ashore. But the awful lonesomeness is intolerable. The intense concentration of self in the middle of such a heartless immensity, my God! who can tell it? Mark, how when sailors in a dead calm bathe in the open sea—mark how closely they hug their ship and only coast along her sides.

But had Stubb really abandoned the poor little negro to his fate? No; he did not mean to, at least. Because there were two boats in his wake, and he supposed, no doubt, that they would of course come up to Pip very quickly, and pick him up; though, indeed, such considerateness towards oarsmen jeopardized through their own timidity, is not always manifested by the hunters in all similar instances; and such instances not unfrequently occur; almost invariably in the fishery, a coward, so called, is marked with the same ruthless detestation peculiar to military navies and armies.

But it so happened, that those boats, without seeing Pip, suddenly spying whales close to them on one side, turned, and gave chase; and Stubb's boat was now so far away, and he and all his crew so intent upon his fish, that Pip's ringed horizon began to expand around him miserably. By the merest chance the ship itself at last rescued him; but from that hour the little negro went about the deck an idiot; such, at least, they said he was. The sea had jeeringly kept his finite body up, but drowned the infinite of his soul. Not drowned entirely, though. Rather carried down alive to wondrous depths, where strange shapes of the unwarped primal world glided to and fro before his passive eyes; and the miser-merman, Wisdom, revealed his hoarded heaps; and among the joyous, heartless, ever-juvenile eternities, Pip saw the multitudinous, God-omnipresent, coral insects, that out of the firmament of waters heaved the colossal orbs. He saw God's foot upon the treadle of the loom, and spoke it; and therefore his shipmates called him mad. So man's insanity is heaven's sense; and wandering from all mortal reason, man comes at last to that celestial thought, which, to reason, is absurd and frantic; and weal or woe, feels then uncompromised, indifferent as his God.

For the rest, blame not Stubb too hardly. The thing is common in that fishery; and in the sequel of the narrative, it will then be seen what like abandonment befell myself.

Chapter 94

A SQUEEZE OF THE HAND

That whale of Stubb's, so dearly purchased, was duly brought to the Pequod's side, where all those cutting and hoisting operations previously detailed, were regularly gone through, even to the baling of the Heidelberg Tun, or Case.

While some were occupied with this latter duty, others were employed in dragging away the larger tubs, so soon as filled with the sperm; and when the proper time arrived, this same sperm was carefully manipulated ere going to the try-works, of which anon.

It had cooled and crystallized to such a degree, that when, with several others, I sat down before a large Constantine's bath of it, I found it strangely concreted into lumps, here and there rolling about in the liquid part. It was our business to squeeze these lumps back into fluid. A sweet and unctuous duty! No wonder that in old times this sperm was such a favorite cosmetic. Such a clearer! such a sweetener! such a softener! such a delicious mollifier! After having my hands in it for only a few minutes, my fingers felt like eels, and began, as it were, to serpentine and spiralize.

As I sat there at my ease, cross-legged on the deck; after the bitter exertion at the windlass; under a blue tranquil sky; the ship under indolent sail, and gliding so serenely along; as I bathed my hands among those soft, gentle globules of infiltrated tissues, woven almost within the hour; as they richly broke to my fingers, and discharged all their opulence, like fully ripe grapes their wine; as I snuffed up that uncontaminated aroma,—literally and truly, like the smell of spring violets; I declare to you, that for the time I lived as in a musky meadow; I forgot all about our horrible oath; in that inexpressible sperm, I washed my hands and my heart of it; I almost began to credit the old Paracelsan superstition that sperm is of rare virtue in allaying the heat of anger: while bathing in that bath, I felt divinely free from all ill-will, or petulance, or malice, of any sort whatsoever.

Squeeze! squeeze! squeeze! all the morning long; I squeezed that sperm till I myself almost melted into it; I squeezed that sperm till a strange sort of insanity came over me; and I found myself unwittingly squeezing my co-laborers' hands in it, mistaking their hands for the gentle globules. Such an abounding, affectionate, friendly, loving feeling did this avocation beget; that at last I was continually squeezing their hands, and looking up into their eyes sentimentally; as much as to say,—Oh! my dear fellow beings, why should we longer cherish any social acerbities, or know the slightest ill-humor or envy! Come; let us squeeze hands all round; nay, let us all squeeze ourselves into each other; let us squeeze ourselves universally into the very milk and sperm of kindness.

Would that I could keep squeezing that sperm for ever! For now, since by many prolonged, repeated experiences, I have perceived that in all cases man must eventually lower, or at least shift, his conceit of attainable felicity; not placing it anywhere in the intellect or the fancy; but in the wife, the heart, the bed, the table, the saddle, the fire-side, the country; now that I have perceived all this, I am ready to squeeze case eternally. In visions of the night, I saw long rows of angels in paradise, each with his hands in a jar of spermaceti.

*   *   *   *   *   *   *   *   *

Now, while discoursing of sperm, it behooves to speak of other things akin to it, in the business of preparing the sperm whale for the try-works.

First comes white-horse, so called, which is obtained from the tapering part of the fish, and also from the thicker portions of his flukes. It is tough with congealed tendons—a wad of muscle— but still contains some oil. After being severed from the whale, the white-horse is first cut into portable oblongs ere going to the mincer. They look much like blocks of Berkshire marble.

Plum-pudding is the term bestowed upon certain fragmentary parts of the whale's flesh, here and there adhering to the blanket of blubber, and often participating to a considerable degree in its unctuousness. It is a most refreshing, convivial, beautiful object to behold. As its name imports, it is of an exceedingly rich, mottled tint, with a bestreaked snowy and golden ground, dotted with spots of the deepest crimson and purple. It is plums of rubies, in pictures of citron. Spite of reason, it is hard to keep yourself from eating it. I confess, that once I stole behind the foremast to try it. It tasted something as I should conceive a royal cutlet from the thigh of Louis le Gros might have tasted, supposing him to have been killed the first day after the venison season, and that particular venison season contemporary with an unusually fine vintage of the vineyards of Champagne.

There is another substance, and a very singular one, which turns up in the course of this business, but which I feel it to be very puzzling adequately to describe. It is called slobgollion; an appellation original with the whalemen, and even so is the nature of the substance. It is an ineffably oozy, stringy affair, most frequently found in the tubs of sperm, after a prolonged squeezing, and subsequent decanting. I hold it to be the wondrously thin, ruptured membranes of the case, coalescing.

Gurry, so called, is a term properly belonging to right whalemen, but sometimes incidentally used by the sperm fishermen. It designates the dark, glutinous substance which is scraped off the back of the Greenland or right whale, and much of which covers the decks of those inferior souls who hunt that ignoble Leviathan.

Nippers. Strictly this word is not indigenous to the whale's vocabulary. But as applied by whalemen, it becomes so. A whaleman's nipper is a short firm strip of tendinous stuff cut from the tapering part of Leviathan's tail: it averages an inch in thickness, and for the rest, is about the size of the iron part of a hoe. Edgewise moved along the oily deck, it operates like a leathern squilgee; and by nameless blandishments, as of magic, allures along with it all impurities.

But to learn all about these recondite matters, your best way is at once to descend into the blubber-room, and have a long talk with its inmates. This place has previously been mentioned as the receptacle for the blanket-pieces, when stript and hoisted from the whale. When the proper time arrives for cutting up its contents, this apartment is a scene of terror to all tyros, especially by night. On one side, lit by a dull lantern, a space has been left clear for the workmen. They generally go in pairs,—a pike-and-gaff-man and a spade-man. The whaling-pike is similar to a frigate's boarding-weapon of the same name. The gaff is something like a boat-hook. With his gaff, the gaffman hooks on to a sheet of blubber, and strives to hold it from slipping, as the ship pitches and lurches about. Meanwhile, the spade-man stands on the sheet itself, perpendicularly chopping it into the portable horse-pieces. This spade is sharp as hone can make it; the spade-man's feet are shoeless; the thing he stands on will sometimes irresistibly slide away from him, like a sledge. If he cuts off one of his own toes, or one of his assistant's, would you be very much astonished? Toes are scarce among veteran blubber-room men.

Chapter 95

THE CASSOCK

Had you stepped on board the Pequod at a certain juncture of this post-mortemizing of the whale; and had you strolled forward nigh the windlass, pretty sure am I that you would have scanned with no small curiosity a very strange, enigmatical object,[1] which you would have seen there, lying along lengthwise in the lee scuppers. Not the wondrous cistern in the whale's huge head; not the prodigy of his unhinged lower jaw; not the miracle of his sym-

1. The whale's penis.

metrical tail; none of these would so surprise you, as half a glimpse of that unaccountable cone,—longer than a Kentuckian is tall, nigh a foot in diameter at the base, and jet-black as Yojo, the ebony idol of Queequeg. And an idol, indeed, it is; or, rather, in old times, its likeness was. Such an idol as that found in the secret groves of Queen Maachah in Judea; and for worshipping which, King Asa, her son, did depose her, and destroyed the idol, and burnt it for an abomination at the brook Kedron, as darkly [2] set forth in the 15th chapter of the first book of Kings.

Look at the sailor, called the mincer, who now comes along, and assisted by two allies, heavily backs the grandissimus, as the mariners call it, and with bowed shoulders, staggers off with it as if he were a grenadier carrying a dead comrade from the field. Extending it upon the forecastle deck, he now proceeds cylindrically to remove its dark pelt, as an African hunter the pelt of a boa. This done he turns the pelt inside out, like a pantaloon leg; gives it a good stretching, so as almost to double its diameter; and at last hangs it, well spread, in the rigging, to dry. Ere long, it is taken down; when removing some three feet of it, towards the pointed extremity, and then cutting two slits for arm-holes at the other end, he lengthwise slips himself bodily into it. The mincer now stands before you invested in the full canonicals of his calling. Immemorial to all his order, this investiture alone will adequately protect him, while employed in the peculiar functions of his office.

That office consists in mincing the horse-pieces of blubber for the pots; an operation which is conducted at a curious wooden horse, planted endwise against the bulwarks, and with a capacious tub beneath it, into which the minced pieces drop, fast as the sheets from a rapt orator's desk. Arrayed in decent black; occupying a conspicuous pulpit; intent on bible leaves; what a candidate for an archbishoprick,[3] what a lad for a Pope were this mincer! *

Chapter 96

THE TRY-WORKS

Besides her hoisted boats, an American whaler is outwardly distinguished by her try-works. She presents the curious anomaly of the most solid masonry joining with oak and hemp in con-

2. In the sense of "obscurely," as in "through a glass, darkly" (I Corinthians 13: 12).
3. The unusual archaic spelling with final *k* emphasizes the phallic pun.
* Bible leaves! Bible leaves! This is the invariable cry from the mates to the mincer. It enjoins him to be careful, and cut his work into as thin slices as possible, inasmuch as by so doing the business of boiling out the oil is much accelerated, and its quantity considerably increased, besides perhaps improving it in quality [Melville's note].

stituting the completed ship. It is as if from the open field a brick-kiln were transported to her planks.

The try-works are planted between the foremast and main-mast, the most roomy part of the deck. The timbers beneath are of a peculiar strength, fitted to sustain the weight of an almost solid mass of brick and mortar, some ten feet by eight square, and five in height. The foundation does not penetrate the deck, but the masonry is firmly secured to the surface by ponderous knees of iron bracing it on all sides, and screwing it down to the timbers. On the flanks it is cased with wood, and at top completely covered by a large, sloping, battened hatchway. Removing this hatch we expose the great try-pots, two in number, and each of several barrels' capacity. When not in use, they are kept remarkably clean. Sometimes they are polished with soapstone and sand, till they shine within like silver punch-bowls. During the night-watches some cynical old sailors will crawl into them and coil themselves away there for a nap. While employed in polishing them—one man in each pot, side by side—many confidential communications are carried on, over the iron lips. It is a place also for profound mathematical meditation. It was in the left hand try-pot of the Pequod, with the soapstone diligently circling round me, that I was first indirectly struck by the remarkable fact, that in geometry all bodies gliding along the cycloid, my soapstone for example, will descend from any point in precisely the same time.

Removing the fire-board from the front of the try-works, the bare masonry of that side is exposed, penetrated by the two iron mouths of the furnaces, directly underneath the pots. These mouths are fitted with heavy doors of iron. The intense heat of the fire is prevented from communicating itself to the deck, by means of a shallow reservoir extending under the entire inclosed surface of the works. By a tunnel inserted at the rear, this reservoir is kept replenished with water as fast as it evaporates. There are no external chimneys; they open direct from the rear wall. And here let us go back for a moment.

It was about nine o'clock at night that the Pequod's try-works were first started on this present voyage. It belonged to Stubb to oversee the business.

"All ready there? Off hatch, then, and start her. You cook, fire the works." This was an easy thing, for the carpenter had been thrusting his shavings into the furnace throughout the passage. Here be it said that in a whaling voyage the first fire in the try-works has to be fed for a time with wood. After that no wood is used, except as a means of quick ignition to the staple fuel. In a word, after being tried out, the crisp, shrivelled blubber, now called scraps or fritters, still contains considerable of its unctuous properties. These fritters feed the flames. Like a plethoric burning martyr, or a self-consuming misanthrope, once ignited, the whale supplies his own fuel and burns by his own body. Would that he consumed his own smoke! for his smoke is horrible to inhale, and inhale it you must, and not only that, but you must live in it for the time. It has an unspeakable, wild, Hindoo odor about it, such as may lurk in the vicinity of funereal pyres. It smells like the left wing of the day of judgment; it is an argument for the pit.

By midnight the works were in full operation. We were clear from the carcase; sail had been made; the wind was freshening; the wild ocean darkness was intense. But that darkness was licked up by the fierce flames, which at intervals forked forth from the sooty flues, and illuminated every lofty rope in the rigging, as with the famed Greek fire. The burning ship drove on, as if remorselessly commissioned to some vengeful deed. So the pitch and sulphur-freighted brigs of the bold Hydriote, Canaris,[1] issuing from their midnight harbors, with broad sheets of flame for sails, bore down upon the Turkish frigates, and folded them in conflagrations.

The hatch, removed from the top of the works, now afforded a wide hearth in front of them. Standing on this were the Tartarean shapes of the pagan harpooneers, always the whale-ship's stokers. With huge pronged poles they pitched hissing masses of blubber into the scalding pots, or stirred up the fires beneath, till the snaky flames darted, curling, out of the doors to catch them by the feet. The smoke rolled away in sullen heaps. To every pitch of the ship there was a pitch of the boiling oil, which seemed all eagerness to leap into their faces. Opposite the mouth of the works, on the further side of the wide wooden hearth, was the windlass. This served for a sea-sofa. Here lounged the watch, when not otherwise employed, looking into the red heat of the fire, till their eyes felt scorched in their heads. Their tawny features, now all begrimed with smoke and sweat, their matted beards, and the contrasting barbaric brilliancy of their teeth, all these were strangely revealed in the capricious emblazonings of the works. As they narrated to each other their unholy adventures, their tales of terror told in words of mirth; as their uncivilized laughter forked upwards out of them, like the flames from the furnace; as to and fro, in their front, the harpooneers wildly gesticulated with their huge pronged forks and dippers; as the wind howled on, and the sea leaped, and the ship groaned and dived, and yet steadfastly shot her red hell further and further into the blackness of the sea and the night, and scornfully champed the white bone in her mouth, and

1. The Greek hero who developed this fire-ship strategy in 1822, during the Greek war for independence.

viciously spat round her on all sides; then the rushing Pequod, freighted with savages, and laden with fire, and burning a corpse, and plunging into that blackness of darkness, seemed the material counterpart of her monomaniac commander's soul. —*Ahab's Obsessive soul*

So seemed it to me, as I stood at her helm, and for long hours silently guided the way of this fire-ship on the sea. Wrapped, for that interval, in darkness myself, I but the better saw the redness, the madness, the ghastliness of others. The continual sight of the fiend shapes before me, capering half in smoke and half in fire, these at last begat kindred visions in my soul, so soon as I began to yield to that unaccountable drowsiness which ever would come over me at a midnight helm.

But that night, in particular, a strange (and ever since inexplicable) thing occurred to me. Starting from a brief standing sleep, I was horribly conscious of something fatally wrong. The jaw-bone tiller smote my side, which leaned against it; in my ears was the low hum of sails, just beginning to shake in the wind; I thought my eyes were open; I was half conscious of putting my fingers to the lids and mechanically stretching them still further apart. But, spite of all this, I could see no compass before me to steer by; though it seemed but a minute since I had been watching the card, by the steady binnacle lamp illuminating it. Nothing seemed before me but a jet gloom, now and then made ghastly by flashes of redness. Uppermost was the impression, that whatever swift, rushing thing I stood on was not so much bound to any haven ahead as rushing from all havens astern. A stark, bewildered feeling, as of death, came over me. Convulsively my hands grasped the tiller, but with the crazy conceit that the tiller was, somehow, in some enchanted way, inverted. My God! what is the matter with me? thought I. Lo! in my brief sleep I had turned myself about, and was fronting the ship's stern, with my back to her prow and the compass. In an instant I faced back, just in time to prevent the vessel from flying up into the wind, and very probably capsizing her. How glad and how grateful the relief from this unnatural hallucination of the night, and the fatal contingency of being brought by the lee!

Look not too long in the face of the fire, O man! Never dream with thy hand on the helm! Turn not thy back to the compass; accept the first hint of the hitching tiller; believe not the artificial fire, when its redness makes all things look ghastly. To-morrow, in the natural sun, the skies will be bright; those who glared like devils in the forking flames, the morn will show in far other, at least gentler, relief; the glorious, golden, glad sun, the only true lamp—all others but liars!

Nevertheless the sun hides not Virginia's Dismal Swamp, nor

Rome's accursed Campagna, nor wide Sahara, nor all the millions of miles of deserts and of griefs beneath the moon. The sun hides not the ocean, which is the dark side of this earth, and which is two thirds of this earth. So, therefore, that mortal man who hath more of joy than sorrow in him, that mortal man cannot be true—not true, or undeveloped. With books the same. The truest of all men was the Man of Sorrows, and the truest of all books is Solomon's, and Ecclesiastes is the fine hammered steel of woe. "All is vanity." ALL. This wilful world hath not got hold of unchristian Solomon's wisdom yet. But he who dodges hospitals and jails, and walks fast crossing grave-yards, and would rather talk of operas than hell; calls Cowper, Young, Pascal, Rousseau, poor devils all of sick men; and throughout a care-free lifetime swears by Rabelais as passing wise, and therefore jolly;—not that man is fitted to sit down on tomb-stones, and break the green damp mould with unfathomably wondrous Solomon.

But even Solomon, he says, "the man that wandereth out of the way of understanding shall remain" (*i. e.* even while living) "in the congregation of the dead." [2] Give not thyself up, then, to fire, lest it invert thee, deaden thee; as for the time it did me. There is a wisdom that is woe; but there is a woe that is madness. And there is a Catskill eagle in some souls that can alike dive down into the blackest gorges, and soar out of them again and become invisible in the sunny spaces. And even if he for ever flies within the gorge, that gorge is in the mountains; so that even in his lowest swoop the mountain eagle is still higher than other birds upon the plain, even though they soar.

Chapter 97

THE LAMP

Had you descended from the Pequod's try-works to the Pequod's forecastle, where the off duty watch were sleeping, for one single moment you would have almost thought you were standing in some illuminated shrine of canonized kings and counsellors. There they lay in their triangular oaken vaults, each mariner a chiselled muteness; a score of lamps flashing upon his hooded eyes.

In merchantmen, oil for the sailor is more scarce than the milk of queens. To dress in the dark, and eat in the dark, and stumble in darkness to his pallet, this is his usual lot. But the whaleman, as he seeks the food of light, so he lives in light. He makes his berth an Aladdin's lamp, and lays him down in it; so that in the pitchiest night the ship's black hull still houses an illumination.

2. Proverbs 21:16.

See with what entire freedom the whaleman takes his handful of lamps—often but old bottles and vials, though—to the copper cooler at the try-works, and replenishes them there, as mugs of ale at a vat. He burns, too, the purest of oil, in its unmanufactured, and, therefore, unvitiated state; a fluid unknown to solar, lunar, or astral contrivances ashore. It is sweet as early grass butter in April. He goes and hunts for his oil, so as to be sure of its freshness and genuineness, even as the traveller on the prairie hunts up his own supper of game.

Chapter 98

STOWING DOWN AND CLEARING UP

Already has it been related how the great leviathan is afar off descried from the mast-head; how he is chased over the watery moors, and slaughtered in the valleys of the deep; how he is then towed alongside and beheaded; and how (on the principle which entitled the headsman of old to the garments in which the beheaded was killed) his great padded surtout becomes the property of his executioner; how, in due time, he is condemned to the pots, and, like Shadrach, Meshach, and Abednego, his spermaceti, oil, and bone pass unscathed through the fire;—but now it remains to conclude the last chapter of this part of the description by rehearsing—singing, if I may—the romantic proceeding of decanting off his oil into the casks and striking them down into the hold, where once again leviathan returns to his native profundities, sliding along beneath the surface as before; but, alas! never more to rise and blow.

While still warm, the oil, like hot punch, is received into the six-barrel casks; and while, perhaps, the ship is pitching and rolling this way and that in the midnight sea, the enormous casks are slewed round and headed over, end for end, and sometimes perilously scoot across the slippery deck, like so many land slides, till at last man-handled and stayed in their course; and all round the hoops, rap, rap, go as many hammers as can play upon them, for now, *ex officio*, every sailor is a cooper.

At length, when the last pint is casked, and all is cool, then the great hatchways are unsealed, the bowels of the ship are thrown open, and down go the casks to their final rest in the sea. This done, the hatches are replaced, and hermetically closed, like a closet walled up.

In the sperm fishery, this is perhaps one of the most remarkable incidents in all the business of whaling. One day the planks stream with freshets of blood and oil; on the sacred quarter-deck enormous masses of the whale's head are profanely piled;

great rusty casks lie about, as in a brewery yard; the smoke from the try-works has besooted all the bulwarks; the mariners go about suffused with unctuousness; the entire ship seems great leviathan himself; while on all hands the din is deafening.

But a day or two after, you look about you, and prick your ears in this self-same ship; and were it not for the tell-tale boats and try-works, you would all but swear you trod some silent merchant vessel, with a most scrupulously neat commander. The unmanufactured sperm oil possesses a singularly cleansing virtue. This is the reason why the decks never look so white as just after what they call an affair of oil. Besides, from the ashes of the burned scraps of the whale, a potent ley is readily made; and whenever any adhesiveness from the back of the whale remains clinging to the side, that ley quickly exterminates it. Hands go diligently along the bulwarks, and with buckets of water and rags restore them to their full tidiness. The soot is brushed from the lower rigging. All the numerous implements which have been in use are likewise faithfully cleansed and put away. The great hatch is scrubbed and placed upon the try-works, completely hiding the pots; every cask is out of sight; all tackles are coiled in unseen nooks; and when by the combined and simultaneous industry of almost the entire ship's company, the whole of this conscientious duty is at last concluded, then the crew themselves proceed to their own ablutions; shift themselves from top to toe; and finally issue to the immaculate deck, fresh and all aglow, as bridegrooms new-leaped from out the daintiest Holland.

Now, with elated step, they pace the planks in twos and threes, and humorously discourse of parlors, sofas, carpets, and fine cambrics; propose to mat the deck; think of having hangings to the top; object not to taking tea by moonlight on the piazza of the forecastle. To hint to such musked mariners of oil, and bone, and blubber, were little short of audacity. They know not the thing you distantly allude to. Away, and bring us napkins!

But mark: aloft there, at the three mast heads, stand three men intent on spying out more whales, which, if caught, infallibly will again soil the old oaken furniture, and drop at least one small grease-spot somewhere. Yes; and many is the time, when, after the severest uninterrupted labors, which know no night; continuing straight through for ninety-six hours; when from the boat, where they have swelled their wrists with all day rowing on the Line,— they only step to the deck to carry vast chains, and heave the heavy windlass, and cut and slash, yea, and in their very sweatings to be smoked and burned anew by the combined fires of the equatorial sun and the equatorial try-works; when, on the heel of all this, they have finally bestirred themselves to cleanse the ship, and make a spotless dairy room of it; many is the time the poor fellows, just buttoning the necks of their clean frocks, are startled by the cry of "There she blows!" and away they fly to fight another whale, and go through the whole weary thing again. Oh! my friends, but this is man-killing! Yet this is life. For hardly have we mortals by long toilings extracted from this world's vast bulk its small but valuable sperm; and then, with weary patience, cleansed ourselves from its defilements, and learned to live here in clean tabernacles of the soul; hardly is this done, when— *There she blows!*—the ghost is spouted up, and away we sail to fight some other world, and go through young life's old routine again.

Oh! the metempsychosis! Oh! Pythagoras, that in bright Greece, two thousand years ago, did die, so good, so wise, so mild; I sailed with thee along the Peruvian coast last voyage —and, foolish as I am, taught thee, a green simple boy, how to splice a rope!

Chapter 99

THE DOUBLOON

Ere now it has been related how Ahab was wont to pace his quarter-deck, taking regular turns at either limit, the binnacle and mainmast; but in the multiplicity of other things requiring narration it has not been added how that sometimes in these walks, when most plunged in his mood, he was wont to pause in turn at each spot, and stand there strangely eyeing the particular object before him. When he halted before the binnacle, with his glance fastened on the pointed needle in the compass, that glance shot like a javelin with the pointed intensity of his purpose; and when resuming his walk he again paused before the mainmast, then, as the same riveted glance fastened upon the riveted gold coin there, he still wore the same aspect of nailed firmness, only dashed with a certain wild longing, if not hopefulness.

But one morning, turning to pass the doubloon, he seemed to be newly attracted by the strange figures and inscriptions stamped on it, as though now for the first time beginning to interpret for himself in some monomaniac way whatever significance might lurk in them. And some certain significance lurks in all things, else all things are little worth, and the round world itself but an empty cipher, except to sell by the cartload, as they do hills about Boston, to fill up some morass in the Milky Way.

Now this doubloon was of purest, virgin gold, raked somewhere out of the heart of gorgeous hills, whence, east and west, over golden sands, the head-waters of many a Pactolus flow. And though now nailed amidst all the rustiness of iron bolts and the verdigris of copper spikes, yet, untouchable and immaculate to any foulness, it still preserved its Quito glow. Nor, though placed amongst a ruthless crew and every hour passed by ruthless hands, and through the livelong nights shrouded with thick darkness which might cover any pilfering approach, nevertheless every sunrise found the doubloon where the sunset left it last. For it was set apart and sanctified to one awe-striking end; and however wanton in their sailor ways, one and all, the mariners revered it as the white whale's talisman. Sometimes they talked it over in the weary watch by night, wondering whose it was to be at last, and whether he would ever live to spend it.

Now those noble golden coins of South America are as medals of the sun and tropic token-pieces. Here palms, alpacas, and volcanoes; sun's disks and stars; ecliptics, horns-of-plenty, and rich banners waving, are in luxuriant profusion stamped; so that the precious gold seems almost to derive an added preciousness and enhancing glories, by passing through those fancy mints, so Spanishly poetic.

It so chanced that the doubloon of the Pequod was a most wealthy example of these things. On its round border it bore the letters, REPUBLICA DEL ECUADOR: QUITO. So this bright coin came from a country planted in the middle of the world, and beneath the great equator, and named after it; and it had been cast midway up the Andes, in the unwaning clime that knows no autumn. Zoned by those letters you saw the likeness of three Andes' summits; from one a flame; a tower on another; on the third a crowing cock; while arching over all was a segment of the partitioned zodiac, the signs all marked with their usual cabalistics, and the keystone sun entering the equinoctial point at Libra.

Before this equatorial coin, Ahab, not unobserved by others, was now pausing.

"There's something ever egotistical in mountain-tops and towers, and all other grand and lofty things; look here,—three peaks as proud as Lucifer. The firm tower, that is Ahab; the volcano, that is Ahab; the courageous, the undaunted, and victorious fowl, that, too, is Ahab; all are Ahab; and this round gold is but the image of the rounder globe, which, like a magician's glass, to each and every man in turn but mirrors back his own mysterious self. Great pains, small gains for those who ask the world to solve them; it cannot solve itself. Methinks now this coined sun wears a ruddy face; but see! aye, he enters the sign of storms, the equinox! and but six months before he wheeled out of a former equinox at Aries! From storm to storm! So be it, then.

Born in throes, 'tis fit that man should live in pains and die in pangs! So be it, then! Here's stout stuff for woe to work on. So be it, then."

"No fairy fingers can have pressed the gold, but devil's claws must have left their mouldings there since yesterday," murmured Starbuck to himself, leaning against the bulwarks. "The old man seems to read Belshazzar's awful writing.[1] I have never marked the coin inspectingly. He goes below; let me read. A dark valley between three mighty, heaven-abiding peaks, that almost seem the Trinity, in some faint earthly symbol. So in this vale of Death, God girds us round; and over all our gloom, the sun of Righteousness still shines a beacon and a hope. If we bend down our eyes, the dark vale shows her mouldy soil; but if we lift them, the bright sun meets our glance half way, to cheer. Yet, oh, the great sun is no fixture; and if, at midnight, we would fain snatch some sweet solace from him, we gaze for him in vain! This coin speaks wisely, mildly, truly, but still sadly to me. I will quit it, lest Truth shake me falsely."

"There now's the old Mogul," soliloquized Stubb by the try-works, "he's been twigging it; and there goes Starbuck from the same, and both with faces which I should say might be somewhere within nine fathoms long. And all from looking at a piece of gold, which did I have it now on Negro Hill or in Corlaer's Hook, I'd not look at it very long ere spending it. Humph! in my poor, insignificant opinion, I regard this as queer. I have seen doubloons before now in my voyagings; your doubloons of old Spain, your doubloons of Peru, your doubloons of Chili, your doubloons of Bolivia, your doubloons of Popayan; with plenty of gold moidores and pistoles, and joes, and half joes, and quarter joes. What then should there be in this doubloon of the Equator that is so killing wonderful? By Golconda! let me read it once. Halloa! here's signs and wonders truly! That, now, is what old Bowditch in his Epitome calls the zodiac, and what my almanack below calls ditto. I'll get the almanack; and as I have heard devils can be raised with Daboll's arithmetic, I'll try my hand at raising a meaning out of these queer curvicues here with the Massachusetts calendar. Here's the book. Let's see now. Signs and wonders; and the sun, he's always among 'em. Hem, hem, hem; here they are—here they go—all alive:—Aries, or the Ram; Taurus, or the Bull;—and Jimimi! here's Gemini himself, or the Twins. Well; the sun he wheels among 'em. Aye, here on the coin he's just crossing the threshold between two of twelve sitting-rooms all in a ring. Book! you lie there; the fact is, you books must know your places. You'll do to give us the bare words and facts, but we

1. Daniel 5.

come in to supply the thoughts. That's my small experience, so far as the Massachusetts calendar, and Bowditch's navigator, and Daboll's arithmetic go. Signs and wonders, eh? Pity if there is nothing wonderful in signs, and significant in wonders! There's a clue somewhere; wait a bit; hist—hark! By Jove, I have it! Look you, Doubloon, your zodiac here is the life of man in one round chapter; and now I'll read it off, straight out of the book. Come, Almanack! To begin: there's Aries, or the Ram—lecherous dog, he begets us; then, Taurus, or the Bull—he bumps us the first thing; then Gemini, or the Twins—that is, Virtue and Vice; we try to reach Virtue, when lo! comes Cancer the Crab, and drags us back; and here, going from Virtue, Leo, a roaring Lion, lies in the path—he gives a few fierce bites and surly dabs with his paw; we escape, and hail Virgo, the Virgin! that's our first love; we marry and think to be happy for aye, when pop comes Libra, or the Scales—happiness weighed and found wanting; and while we are very sad about that, Lord! how we suddenly jump, as Scorpio, or the Scorpion, stings us in rear; we are curing the wound, when whang come the arrows all round; Sagittarius, or the Archer, is amusing himself. As we pluck out the shafts, stand aside! here's the battering-ram, Capricornus, or the Goat; full tilt, he comes rushing, and headlong we are tossed; when Aquarius, or the Water-bearer, pours out his whole deluge and drowns us; and, to wind up, with Pisces, or the Fishes, we sleep. There's a sermon now, writ in high heaven, and the sun goes through it every year, and yet comes out of it all alive and hearty. Jollily he, aloft there, wheels through toil and trouble; and so, alow here, does jolly Stubb. Oh, jolly's the word for aye! Adieu, Doubloon! But stop; here comes little King-Post; dodge round the try-works, now, and let's hear what he'll have to say. There; he's before it; he'll out with something presently. So, so; he's beginning."

"I see nothing here, but a round thing made of gold, and whoever raises a certain whale, this round thing belongs to him. So, what's all this staring been about? It is worth sixteen dollars, that's true; and at two cents the cigar, that's nine hundred and sixty cigars.[2] I wont smoke dirty pipes like Stubb, but I like cigars, and here's nine hundred and sixty of them; so here goes Flask aloft to spy 'em out."

"Shall I call that wise or foolish, now; if it be really wise it has a foolish look to it; yet, if it be really foolish, then has it a sort of wiseish look to it. But, avast; here comes our old Manxman—the old hearse-driver, he must have been, that is, before he took to the sea. He luffs up before the doubloon; halloa, and goes

2. The arithmetic seems in error. Perhaps it involves some sales custom such as the "baker's dozen."

round on the other side of the mast; why, there's a horse-shoe nailed on that side; and now he's back again; what does that mean? Hark! he's muttering—voice like an old worn-out coffee-mill. Prick ears, and listen!"

"If the White Whale be raised, it must be in a month and a day, when the sun stands in some one of these signs. I've studied signs, and know their marks; they were taught me two score years ago, by the old witch in Copenhagen. Now, in what sign will the sun then be? The horse-shoe sign; for there it is, right opposite the gold. And what's the horse-shoe sign? The lion is the horse-shoe sign—the roaring and devouring lion. Ship, old ship! my old head shakes to think of thee."

"There's another rendering now; but still one text. All sorts of men in one kind of world, you see. Dodge again! here comes Quee-queg—all tattooing—looks like the signs of the Zodiac himself. What says the Cannibal? As I live he's comparing notes; looking at his thigh bone; thinks the sun is in the thigh, or in the calf, or in the bowels, I suppose, as the old women talk Sur-geon's Astronomy in the back country. And by Jove, he's found something there in the vicinity of his thigh—I guess it's Sagittarius, or the Archer. No: he don't know what to make of the doubloon; he takes it for an old button off some king's trowsers. But, aside again! here comes that ghost-devil, Fedallah; tail coiled out of sight as usual, oakum in the toes of his pumps as usual. What does he say, with that look of his? Ah, only makes a sign to the sign and bows himself; there is a sun on the coin—fire worshipper, depend upon it. Ho! more and more. This way comes Pip—poor boy! would he had died, or I; he's half horrible to me. He too has been watching all of these interpreters—myself included—and look now, he comes to read, with that unearthly idiot face. Stand away again and hear him. Hark!"

"I look, you look, he looks; we look, ye look, they look."

"Upon my soul, he's been studying Murray's Grammar! Improv-ing his mind, poor fellow! But what's that he says now—hist!"

"I look, you look, he looks; we look, ye look, they look."

"Why, he's getting it by heart—hist! again."

"I look, you look, he looks; we look, ye look, they look."

"Well, that's funny."

"And I, you, and he; and we, ye, and they, are all bats; and I'm a crow, especially when I stand a'top of this pine tree here. Caw! caw! caw! caw! caw! caw! Ain't I a crow? And where's the scare-crow? There he stands; two bones stuck into a pair of old trowsers, and two more poked into the sleeves of an old jacket."

"Wonder if he means me?—complimentary!—poor lad!—I could go hang myself. Any way, for the present, I'll quit Pip's vicinity. I can stand the rest, for they have plain wits; but he's too crazy-witty for my sanity. So, so, I leave him muttering."

"Here's the ship's navel, this doubloon here, and they are all on fire to unscrew it. But, unscrew your navel, and what's the consequence? ³ Then again, if it stays here, that is ugly, too, for when aught's nailed to the mast it's a sign that things grow desperate. Ha, ha! old Ahab! the White Whale; he'll nail ye! This is a pine tree. My father, in old Tolland county, cut down a pine tree once, and found a silver ring grown over in it; some old darkey's wedding ring. How did it get there? And so they'll say in the resurrection, when they come to fish up this old mast, and find a doubloon lodged in it, with bedded oysters for the shaggy bark. Oh, the gold! the precious, precious gold!—the green miser 'll hoard ye soon! Hish! hish! God goes 'mong the worlds blackberrying. Cook! ho, cook! and cook us! Jenny! hey, hey, hey, hey, hey, Jenny, Jenny! and get your hoe-cake done!"

Chapter 100

LEG AND ARM

THE PEQUOD, OF NANTUCKET, MEETS THE SAMUEL ENDERBY, OF LONDON.

"Ship, ahoy! Hast seen the White Whale?"

So cried Ahab, once more hailing a ship showing English colors, bearing down under the stern. Trumpet to mouth, the old man was standing in his hoisted quarter-boat, his ivory leg plainly revealed to the stranger captain, who was carelessly reclining in his own boat's bow. He was a darkly-tanned, burly, good-natured, fine-looking man, of sixty or thereabouts, dressed in a spacious roundabout, that hung round him in festoons of blue pilot-cloth; and one empty arm of this jacket streamed behind him like the broidered arm of a huzzar's surcoat.

"Hast seen the White Whale?"

"See you this?" and withdrawing it from the folds that had hidden it, he held up a white arm of sperm whale bone, terminating in a wooden head like a mallet.

"Man my boat!" cried Ahab, impetuously, and tossing about the oars near him—"Stand by to lower!"

In less than a minute, without quitting his little craft, he and his crew were dropped to the water, and were soon alongside of the stranger. But here a curious difficulty presented itself. In the excitement of the moment, Ahab had forgotten that since the loss of his leg he had never once stepped on board of any vessel at sea but his own, and then it was always by an ingenious and

3. The consequence, according to folklore, is that one's backside falls off.

very handy mechanical contrivance peculiar to the Pequod, and a thing not to be rigged and shipped in any other vessel at a moment's warning. Now, it is no very easy matter for anybody —except those who are almost hourly used to it, like whalemen —to clamber up a ship's side from a boat on the open sea; for the great swells now lift the boat high up towards the bulwarks, and then instantaneously drop it half way down to the kelson. So, deprived of one leg, and the strange ship of course being altogether unsupplied with the kindly invention, Ahab now found himself abjectly reduced to a clumsy landsman again; hopelessly eyeing the uncertain changeful height he could hardly hope to attain.

It has before been hinted, perhaps, that every little untoward circumstance that befel him, and which indirectly sprang from his luckless mishap, almost invariably irritated or exasperated Ahab. And in the present instance, all this was heightened by the sight of the two officers of the strange ship, leaning over the side, by the perpendicular ladder of nailed cleets there, and swinging towards him a pair of tastefully-ornamented man-ropes; for at first they did not seem to bethink them that a one-legged man must be too much of a cripple to use their sea bannisters. But this awkwardness only lasted a minute, because the strange captain, observing at a glance how affairs stood, cried out, "I see, I see!—avast heaving there! Jump, boys, and swing over the cutting-tackle."

As good luck would have it, they had had a whale alongside a day or two previous, and the great tackles were still aloft, and the massive curved blubber-hook, now clean and dry, was still attached to the end. This was quickly lowered to Ahab, who at once comprehending it all, slid his solitary thigh into the curve of the hook (it was like sitting in the fluke of an anchor, or the crotch of an apple tree), and then giving the word, held himself fast, and at the same time also helped to hoist his own weight, by pulling hand-over-hand upon one of the running parts of the tackle. Soon he was carefully swung inside the high bulwarks, and gently landed upon the capstan head. With his ivory arm frankly thrust forth in welcome, the other captain advanced, and Ahab, putting out his ivory leg, and crossing the ivory arm (like two sword-fish blades) cried out in his walrus way, "Aye, aye, hearty! let us shake bones together!—an arm and a leg!—an arm that never can shrink, d'ye see; and a leg that never can run. Where did'st thou see the White Whale?—how long ago?"

"The White Whale," said the Englishman, pointing his ivory arm towards the East, and taking a rueful sight along it, as if it had been a telescope; "There I saw him, on the Line, last season."

"And he took that arm off, did he?" asked Ahab, now sliding down from the capstan, and resting on the Englishman's shoulder, as he did so.

"Aye, he was the cause of it, at least; and that leg, too?"

"Spin me the yarn," said Ahab; "how was it?"

"It was the first time in my life that I ever cruised on the Line," began the Englishman. "I was ignorant of the White Whale at that time. Well, one day we lowered for a pod of four or five whales, and my boat fastened to one of them; a regular circus horse he was, too, that went milling and milling round so, that my boat's crew could only trim dish, by sitting all their sterns on the outer gunwale. Presently up breaches from the bottom of the sea a bouncing great whale, with a milky-white head and hump, all crows' feet and wrinkles."

"It was he, it was he!" cried Ahab, suddenly letting out his suspended breath.

"And harpoons sticking in near his starboard fin."

"Aye, aye—they were mine—*my* irons," cried Ahab, exultingly —"but on!"

"Give me a chance, then," said the Englishman, good-humoredly. "Well, this old great-grandfather, with the white head and hump, runs all afoam into the pod, and goes to snapping furiously at my fast-line."

"Aye, I see!—wanted to part it; free the fast-fish—an old trick —I know him."

"How it was exactly," continued the one-armed commander, "I do not know; but in biting the line, it got foul of his teeth, caught there somehow; but we didn't know it then; so that when we afterwards pulled on the line, bounce we came plump on to his hump! instead of the other whale's that went off to windward, all fluking. Seeing how matters stood, and what a noble great whale it was—the noblest and biggest I ever saw, sir, in my life—I resolved to capture him, spite of the boiling rage he seemed to be in. And thinking the hap-hazard line would get loose, or the tooth it was tangled to might draw (for I have a devil of a boat's crew for a pull on a whale-line); seeing all this, I say, I jumped into my first mate's boat—Mr. Mounttop's here (by the way, Captain—Mounttop; Mounttop—the captain);—as I was saying, I jumped into Mounttop's boat, which, d'ye see, was gunwale and gunwale with mine, then; and snatching the first harpoon, let this old great-grandfather have it. But, Lord, look you, sir—hearts and souls alive, man—the next instant, in a jiff, I was blind as a bat— both eyes out—all befogged and bedeadened with black foam— the whale's tail looming straight up out of it, perpendicular in the air, like a marble steeple. No use sterning all, then; but as I was groping at midday, with a blinding sun, all crown-jewels; as I was groping, I say, after the second iron, to toss it overboard—down comes the tail like a Lima tower, cutting my boat in two, leaving each half in splinters; and, flukes first, the white hump backed through the wreck, as though it was all chips. We all struck out. To escape his terrible flailings, I seized hold of my harpoon-pole sticking in him, and for a moment clung to that like a sucking fish. But a combing sea dashed me off, and at the same instant, the fish, taking one good dart forwards, went down like a flash; and the barb of that cursed second iron towing along near me caught me here" (clapping his hand just below his shoulder); "yes, caught me just here, I say, and bore me down to Hell's flames, I was thinking; when, when, all of a sudden, thank the good God, the barb ript its way along the flesh—clear along the whole length of my arm—came out nigh my wrist, and up I floated;—and that gentleman there will tell you the rest (by the way, captain—Dr. Bunger, ship's surgeon: Bunger, my lad,—the captain). Now, Bunger boy, spin your part of the yarn."

The professional gentleman thus familiarly pointed out, had been all the time standing near them, with nothing specific visible, to denote his gentlemanly rank on board. His face was an exceedingly round but sober one; he was dressed in a faded blue woollen frock or shirt, and patched trowsers; and had thus far been dividing his attention between a marlingspike he held in one hand, and a pill-box held in the other, occasionally casting a critical glance at the ivory limbs of the two crippled captains. But, at his superior's introduction of him to Ahab, he politely bowed, and straightway went on to do his captain's bidding.

"It was a shocking bad wound," began the whale-surgeon; "and, taking my advice, Captain Boomer here, stood our old Sammy—"

"Samuel Enderby is the name of my ship," interrupted the one-armed captain, addressing Ahab; "go on, boy."

"Stood our old Sammy off to the northward, to get out of the blazing hot weather there on the Line. But it was no use—I did all I could; sat up with him nights; was very severe with him in the matter of diet—"

"Oh, very severe!" chimed in the patient himself; then suddenly altering his voice, "Drinking hot rum toddies with me every night, till he couldn't see to put on the bandages; and sending me to bed, half seas over, about three o'clock in the morning. Oh, ye stars! he sat up with me indeed, and was very severe in my diet. Oh! a great watcher, and very dietetically severe, is Dr. Bunger. (Bunger, you dog, laugh out! why don't ye? You know you're a precious jolly rascal.) But, heave ahead, boy, I'd rather be killed by you than kept alive by any other man."

"My captain, you must have ere this perceived, respected sir"
—said the imperturbable godly-looking Bunger, slightly bowing to
Ahab—"is apt to be facetious at times; he spins us many clever
things of that sort. But I may as well say—en passant, as the
French remark—that I myself—that is to say, Jack Bunger, late
of the reverend clergy—am a strict total abstinence man; I never
drink—"

"Water!" cried the captain; "he never drinks it; it's a sort of
fits to him; fresh water throws him into the hydrophobia; but go
on—go on with the arm story."

"Yes, I may as well," said the surgeon, coolly. "I was about
observing, sir, before Captain Boomer's facetious interruption,
that spite of my best and severest endeavors, the wound kept
getting worse and worse; the truth was, sir, it was as ugly gaping
wound as surgeon ever saw; more than two feet and several inches
long. I measured it with the lead line. In short, it grew black;
I knew what was threatened, and off it came. But I had no hand
in shipping that ivory arm there; that thing is against all rule"—
pointing at it with the marlingspike—"that is the captain's work,
not mine; he ordered the carpenter to make it; he had that club-
hammer there put to the end, to knock some one's brains out
with, I suppose, as he tried mine once. He flies into diabolical passions sometimes. Do ye see this dent, sir"—removing his hat, and
brushing aside his hair, and exposing a bowl-like cavity in his
skull, but which bore not the slightest scarry trace, or any token
of ever having been a wound—"Well, the captain there will tell
you how that came here; he knows."

"No, I don't," said the captain, "but his mother did; he was
born with it. Oh, you solemn rogue, you—you Bunger! was there
ever such another Bunger in the watery world? Bunger, when you
die, you ought to die in pickle, you dog; you should be preserved
to future ages, you rascal."

"What became of the White Whale?" now cried Ahab, who
thus far had been impatiently listening to this bye-play between
the two Englishmen.

"Oh!" cried the one-armed captain, "Oh, yes! Well; after he
sounded, we didn't see him again for some time; in fact, as I
before hinted, I didn't then know what whale it was that had
served me such a trick, till some time afterwards, when coming
back to the Line, we heard about Moby Dick—as some call him
—and then I knew it was he."

"Did'st thou cross his wake again?"

"Twice."

"But could not fasten?"

"Didn't want to try to: ain't one limb enough? What should

I do without this other arm? And I'm thinking Moby Dick doesn't bite so much as he swallows."

"Well, then," interrupted Bunger, "give him your left arm for bait to get the right. Do you know, gentlemen"—very gravely and mathematically bowing to each Captain in succession—"Do you know, gentlemen, that the digestive organs of the whale are so inscrutably constructed by Divine Providence, that it is quite impossible for him to completely digest even a man's arm? And he knows it too. So that what you take for the White Whale's malice is only his awkwardness. For he never means to swallow a single limb; he only thinks to terrify by feints. But sometimes he is like the old juggling fellow, formerly a patient of mine in Ceylon, that making believe swallow jack-knives, once upon a time let one drop into him in good earnest, and there it stayed for a twelve-month or more; when I gave him an emetic, and he heaved it up in small tacks, d'ye see. No possible way for him to digest that jack-knife, and fully incorporate it into his general bodily system. Yes, Captain Boomer, if you are quick enough about it, and have a mind to pawn one arm for the sake of the privilege of giving decent burial to the other, why in that case the arm is yours; only let the whale have another chance at you shortly, that's all."

"No, thank ye, Bunger," said the English Captain, "he's welcome to the arm he has, since I can't help it, and didn't know him then; but not to another one. No more White Whales for me; I've lowered for him once, and that has satisfied me. There would be great glory in killing him, I know that; and there is a ship-load of precious sperm in him, but, hark ye, he's best let alone; don't you think so, Captain?"—glancing at the ivory leg.

"He is. But he will still be hunted, for all that. What is best let alone, that accursed thing is not always what least allures. He's all a magnet! How long since thou saw'st him last? Which way heading?"

"Bless my soul, and curse the foul fiend's," cried Bunger, stoopingly walking round Ahab, and like a dog, strangely snuffing; "this man's blood—bring the thermometer!—it's at the boiling point!—his pulse makes these planks beat!—sir!"—taking a lancet from his pocket, and drawing near to Ahab's arm.

"Avast!" roared Ahab, dashing him against the bulwarks—"Man the boat! Which way heading?"

"Good God!" cried the English Captain, to whom the question was put. "What's the matter? He was heading east, I think.—Is your Captain crazy?" whispering Fedallah.

But Fedallah, putting a finger on his lip, slid over the bulwarks to take the boat's steering oar, and Ahab, swinging the cutting-tackle towards him, commanded the ship's sailors to stand by to lower.

In a moment he was standing in the boat's stern, and the Manilla men were springing to their oars. In vain the English Captain hailed him. With back to the stranger ship, and face set like a flint to his own, Ahab stood upright till alongside of the Pequod.

Chapter 101

THE DECANTER

Ere the English ship fades from sight, be it set down here, that she hailed from London, and was named after the late Samuel Enderby, merchant of that city, the original of the famous whaling house of Enderby & Sons [1]; a house which in my poor whaleman's opinion, comes not far behind the united royal houses of the Tudors and Bourbons, in point of real historical interest. How long, prior to the year of our Lord 1775, this great whaling house was in existence, my numerous fish-documents do not make plain; but in that year (1775) it fitted out the first English ships that ever regularly hunted the Sperm Whale; though for some score of years previous (ever since 1726) our valiant Coffins and Maceys of Nantucket and the Vineyard had in large fleets pursued that Leviathan, but only in the North and South Atlantic: not elsewhere. Be it distinctly recorded here, that the Nantucketers were the first among mankind to harpoon with civilized steel the great Sperm Whale; and that for half a century they were the only people of the whole globe who so harpooned him.

In 1778, a fine ship, the Amelia, fitted out for the express purpose, and at the sole charge of the vigorous Enderbys, boldly rounded Cape Horn, and was the first among the nations to lower a whale-boat of any sort in the great South Sea. The voyage was a skilful and lucky one; and returning to her berth with her hold full of the precious sperm, the Amelia's example was soon followed by other ships, English and American, and thus the vast Sperm Whale grounds of the Pacific were thrown open. But not content with this good deed, the indefatigable house again bestirred itself: Samuel and all his Sons—how many, their mother only knows—and under their immediate auspices, and partly, I think, at their expense, the British government was induced to send the sloop-of-war Rattler on a whaling voyage of discovery into the South Sea. Commanded by a naval Post-Captain, the Rattler made a rattling voyage of it, and did some service; how much does not appear. But this is not all. In 1819, the same house fitted out

1. Mansfield and Vincent show that Melville learned most of these details about the Enderby family from Beale.

a discovery whale ship of their own, to go on a testing cruise to the remote waters of Japan. That ship—well called the "Syren"—made a noble experimental cruise; and it was thus that the great Japanese Whaling Ground first became generally known. The Syren in this famous voyage was commanded by a Captain Coffin, a Nantucketer.

All honor to the Enderbys, therefore, whose house, I think, exists to the present day; though doubtless the original Samuel must long ago have slipped his cable for the great South Sea of the other world.

The ship named after him was worthy of the honor, being a very fast sailer and a noble craft every way. I boarded her once at midnight somewhere off the Patagonian coast, and drank good flip down in the forecastle. It was a fine gam we had, and they were all trumps—every soul on board. A short life to them, and a jolly death. And that fine gam I had—long, very long after old Ahab touched her planks with his ivory heel—it minds me of the noble, solid, Saxon hospitality of that ship; and may my parson forget me, and the devil remember me, if I ever lose sight of it. Flip? Did I say we had flip? Yes, and we flipped it at the rate of ten gallons the hour; and when the squall came (for it's squally off there by Patagonia), and all hands—visitors and all—were called to reef topsails, we were so top-heavy that we had to swing each other aloft in bowlines; and we ignorantly furled the skirts of our jackets into the sails, so that we hung there, reefed fast in the howling gale, a warning example to all drunken tars. However, the masts did not go overboard; and by and bye we scrambled down, so sober, that we had to pass the flip again, though the savage salt spray bursting down the forecastle scuttle, rather too much diluted and pickled it to my taste.

The beef was fine—tough, but with body in it. They said it was bull-beef; others, that it was dromedary beef; but I do not know, for certain, how that was. They had dumplings too; small, but substantial, symmetrically globular, and indestructible dumplings. I fancied that you could feel them, and roll them about in you after they were swallowed. If you stooped over too far forward, you risked their pitching out of you like billiard-balls. The bread—but that couldn't be helped; besides, it was an anti-scorbutic; in short, the bread contained the only fresh fare they had.[2] But the forecastle was not very light, and it was very easy to step over into a dark corner when you ate it. But all in all, taking her from truck to helm, considering the dimensions of the cook's boilers, including his own live parchment boilers; fore and aft, I say, the Samuel Enderby was a jolly ship; of good fare and

2. The fresh fare was maggots or weevils.

plenty; fine flip and strong; crack fellows all, and capital from boot heels to hat-band.

But why was it, think ye, that the Samuel Enderby, and some other English whalers I know of—not all though—were such famous, hospitable ships; that passed round the beef, and the bread, and the can, and the joke; and were not soon weary of eating, and drinking, and laughing? I will tell you. The abounding good cheer of these English whalers is matter for historical research. Nor have I been at all sparing of historical whale research, when it has seemed needed.

The English were preceded in the whale fishery by the Hollanders, Zealanders, and Danes; from whom they derived many terms still extant in the fishery; and what is yet more, their fat old fashions, touching plenty to eat and drink. For, as a general thing, the English merchant-ship scrimps her crew; but not so the English whaler. Hence, in the English, this thing of whaling good cheer is not normal and natural, but incidental and particular; and, therefore, must have some special origin, which is here pointed out, and will be still further elucidated.

During my researches in the Leviathanic histories, I stumbled upon an ancient Dutch volume,[3] which, by the musty whaling smell of it, I knew must be about whalers. The title was, "Dan Coopman," wherefore I concluded that this must be the invaluable memoirs of some Amsterdam cooper in the fishery, as every whale ship must carry its cooper. I was reinforced in this opinion by seeing that it was the production of one "Fitz Swackhammer." But my friend Dr. Snodhead, a very learned man, professor of Low Dutch and High German in the college of Santa Claus and St. Pott's, to whom I handed the work for translation, giving him a box of sperm candles for his trouble—this same Dr. Snodhead, so soon as he spied the book, assured me that "Dan Coopman" did not mean "The Cooper," but "The Merchant." In short, this ancient and learned Low Dutch book treated of the commerce of Holland; and, among other subjects, contained a very interesting account of its whale fishery. And in this chapter it was, headed "Smeer," or "Fat," that I found a long detailed list of the outfits for the larders and cellars of 180 sail of Dutch whalemen; from which list, as translated by Dr. Snodhead, I transcribe the following:

> 400,000 lbs. of beef.
> 60,000 lbs. Friesland pork.
> 150,000 lbs. of stock fish.

3. "This long passage with all its statistics was Melville's parody of a a similar one, heavy with detail and pedantic, in Scoresby" (Mansfield-Vincent).

550,000 lbs. of biscuit.
 72,000 lbs. of soft bread.
  2,800 firkins of butter.
 20,000 lbs. Texel & Leyden cheese.
144,000 lbs. cheese (probably an inferior article).
   550 ankers of Geneva.
 10,800 barrels of beer.

Most statistical tables are parchingly dry in the reading; not so in the present case, however, where the reader is flooded with whole pipes, barrels, quarts, and gills of good gin and good cheer.

At the time, I devoted three days to the studious digesting of all this beer, beef, and bread, during which many profound thoughts were incidentally suggested to me, capable of a transcendental and Platonic application; and, furthermore, I compiled supplementary tables of my own, touching the probable quantity of stock-fish, &c., consumed by every Low Dutch harpooneer in that ancient Greenland and Spitzbergen whale fishery. In the first place, the amount of butter, and Texel and Leyden cheese consumed, seems amazing. I impute it, though, to their naturally unctuous natures, being rendered still more unctuous by the nature of their vocation, and especially by their pursuing their game in those frigid Polar Seas, on the very coasts of that Esquimaux country where the convivial natives pledge each other in bumpers of train oil.

The quantity of beer, too, is very large, 10,800 barrels. Now, as those polar fisheries could only be prosecuted in the short summer of that climate, so that the whole cruise of one of these Dutch whalemen, including the short voyage to and from the Spitzbergen sea, did not much exceed three months, say, and reckoning 30 men to each of their fleet of 180 sail, we have 5,400 Low Dutch seamen in all; therefore, I say, we have precisely two barrels of beer per man, for a twelve weeks' allowance, exclusive of his fair proportion of that 550 ankers of gin. Now, whether these gin and beer harpooneers, so fuddled as one might fancy them to have been, were the right sort of men to stand up in a boat's head, and take good aim at flying whales; this would seem somewhat improbable. Yet they did aim at them, and hit them too. But this was very far North, be it remembered, where beer agrees well with the constitution; upon the Equator, in our southern fishery, beer would be apt to make the harpooneer sleepy at the mast-head and boozy in his boat; and grievous loss might ensue to Nantucket and New Bedford.

. But no more; enough has been said to show that the old Dutch whalers of two or three centuries ago were high livers; and that the English whalers have not neglected so excellent an example.

For, say they, when cruising in an empty ship, if you can get nothing better out of the world, get a good dinner out of it, at least. And this empties the decanter.

Chapter 102

A BOWER IN THE ARSACIDES

Hitherto, in descriptively treating of the Sperm Whale, I have chiefly dwelt upon the marvels of his outer aspect; or separately and in detail upon some few interior structural features. But to a large and thorough sweeping comprehension of him, it behoves me now to unbutton him still further, and untrussing the points of his hose, unbuckling his garters, and casting loose the hooks and the eyes of the joints of his innermost bones, set him before you in his ultimatum; that is to say, in his unconditional skeleton.

But how now, Ishmael? How is it, that you, a mere oarsman in the fishery, pretend to know aught about the subterranean parts of the whale? Did erudite Stubb, mounted upon your capstan, deliver lectures on the anatomy of the Cetacea; and by help of the windlass, hold up a specimen rib for exhibition? Explain thyself, Ishmael. Can you land a full-grown whale on your deck for examination, as a cook dishes a roast-pig? Surely not. A veritable witness have you hitherto been, Ishmael; but have a care how you seize the privilege of Jonah alone; the privilege of discoursing upon the joists and beams; the rafters, ridge-pole, sleepers, and under-pinnings, making up the frame-work of leviathan; and belike of the tallow-vats, dairy-rooms, butteries, and cheeseries in his bowels.

I confess, that since Jonah, few whalemen have penetrated very far beneath the skin of the adult whale; nevertheless, I have been blessed with an opportunity to dissect him in miniature. In a ship I belonged to, a small cub Sperm Whale was once bodily hoisted to the deck for his poke or bag, to make sheaths for the barbs of the harpoons, and for the heads of the lances. Think you I let that chance go, without using my boat-hatchet and jack-knife, and breaking the seal and reading all the contents of that young cub?

And as for my exact knowledge of the bones of the leviathan in their gigantic, full grown development, for that rare knowledge I am indebted to my late royal friend Tranquo, king of Tranque, one of the Arsacides. For being at Tranque, years ago, when attached to the trading-ship Dey of Algiers, I was invited to spend part of the Arsacidean holidays with the lord of Tranque, at his retired palm villa at Pupella; a sea-side glen not very far distant from what our sailors called Bamboo-Town, his capital.

Among many other fine qualities, my royal friend Tranquo,

being gifted with a devout love for all matters of barbaric virtu,[1] had brought together in Pupella whatever rare things the more ingenious of his people could invent; chiefly carved woods of wonderful devices, chiselled shells, inlaid spears, costly paddles, aromatic canoes; and all these distributed among whatever natural wonders, the wonder-freighted, tribute-rendering waves had cast upon his shores.

Chief among these latter was a great Sperm Whale, which, after an unusually long raging gale, had been found dead and stranded, with his head against a cocoa-nut tree, whose plumage-like, tufted droopings seemed his verdant jet. When the vast body had at last been stripped of its fathom-deep enfoldings, and the bones become dust dry in the sun, then the skeleton was carefully transported up the Pupella glen, where a grand temple of lordly palms now sheltered it.

The ribs were hung with trophies; the vertebræ were carved with Arsacidean annals, in strange hieroglyphics; in the skull, the priests kept up an unextinguished aromatic flame, so that the mystic head again sent forth its vapory spout; while, suspended from a bough, the terrific lower jaw vibrated over all the devotees, like the hair-hung sword that so affrighted Damocles.

It was a wondrous sight. The wood was green as mosses of the Icy Glen;[2] the trees stood high and haughty, feeling their living sap; the industrious earth beneath was as a weaver's loom, with a gorgeous carpet on it, whereof the ground-vine tendrils formed the warp and woof, and the living flowers the figures. All the trees, with all their laden branches; all the shrubs, and ferns, and grasses; the message-carrying air; all these unceasingly were active. Through the lacings of the leaves, the great sun seemed a flying shuttle weaving the unwearied verdure. Oh, busy weaver! unseen weaver!—pause!—one word!—whither flows the fabric? what palace may it deck? wherefore all these ceaseless toilings? Speak, weaver!—stay thy hand!—but one single word with thee! Nay— the shuttle flies—the figures float from forth the loom; the freshet-rushing carpet for ever slides away. The weaver-god, he weaves; and by that weaving is he deafened, that he hears no mortal voice; and by that humming, we, too, who look on the loom are deafened; and only when we escape it shall we hear the thousand voices that speak through it. For even so it is in all material factories. The spoken words that are inaudible among the flying spindles; those same words are plainly heard without the walls, bursting from the opened casements. Thereby have villanies been detected. Ah, mortal! then, be heedful; for so, in all this

1. Curios and antiques, or any strange and rare objects of art.

2. Near Stockbridge, Massachusetts, and not far from Melville's residence.

din of the great world's loom, thy subtlest thinkings may be over-heard afar.

Now, amid the green, life-restless loom of that Arsacidean wood, the great, white, worshipped skeleton lay lounging—a gigantic idler! Yet, as the ever-woven verdant warp and woof intermixed and hummed around him, the mightly idler seemed the cunning weaver; himself all woven over with the vines; every month assuming greener, fresher verdure; but himself a skeleton. Life folded Death; Death trellised Life; the grim god wived with youthful Life, and begat him curly-headed glories.

Now, when with royal Tranquo I visited this wondrous whale, and saw the skull and altar, and the artificial smoke ascending from where the real jet had issued, I marvelled that the king should regard a chapel as an object of virtù. He laughed. But more I marvelled that the priests should swear that smoky jet of his was genuine. To and fro I paced before this skeleton—brushed the vines aside—broke through the ribs—and with a ball of Arsacidean twine,[3] wandered, eddied long amid its many winding, shaded colonnades and arbors. But soon my line was out; and following it back, I emerged from the opening where I entered. I saw no living thing within; naught was there but bones.

Cutting me a green measuring-rod, I once more dived within the skeleton. From their arrow-slit in the skull, the priests perceived me taking the altitude of the final rib. "How now!" they shouted; "Dar'st thou measure this our god! That's for us." "Aye, priests—well, how long do ye make him, then?" But hereupon a fierce contest rose among them, concerning feet and inches; they cracked each other's sconces with their yard-sticks—the great skull echoed—and seizing that lucky chance, I quickly concluded my own admeasurements.

These admeasurements I now propose to set before you. But first, be it recorded, that, in this matter, I am not free to utter any fancied measurement I please. Because there are skeleton authorities you can refer to, to test my accuracy. There is a Leviathanic Museum, they tell me, in Hull, England, one of the whaling ports of that country, where they have some fine specimens of fin-backs and other whales. Likewise, I have heard that in the museum of Manchester, in New Hampshire, they have what the proprietors call "the only perfect specimen of a Greenland or River Whale in the United States." Moreover, at a place in Yorkshire, England, Burton Constable by name, a certain Sir Clifford Constable has in his possession the skeleton of a Sperm Whale, but of moderate size, by no means of the full-grown magnitude of

3. A recollection of the way Theseus found his way back out of the Cretan labyrinth after killing the Minotaur.

my friend King Tranquo's.

In both cases, the stranded whales to which these two skeletons belonged, were originally claimed by their proprietors upon similar grounds. King Tranquo seizing his because he wanted it; and Sir Clifford, because he was lord of the seignories of those parts. Sir Clifford's whale has been articulated throughout; so that, like a great chest of drawers, you can open and shut him, in all his bony cavities—spread out his ribs like a gigantic fan—and swing all day upon his lower jaw. Locks are to be put upon some of his trap-doors and shutters; and a footman will show round future visitors with a bunch of keys at his side. Sir Clifford thinks of charging twopence for a peep at the whispering gallery in the spinal column; threepence to hear the echo in the hollow of his cerebellum; and sixpence for the unrivalled view from his forehead.

The skeleton dimensions I shall now proceed to set down are copied verbatim from my right arm, where I had them tattooed; as in my wild wanderings at that period, there was no other secure way of preserving such valuable statistics. But as I was crowded for space, and wished the other parts of my body to remain a blank page for a poem I was then composing—at least, what untattooed parts might remain—I did not trouble myself with the odd inches; nor, indeed, should inches at all enter into a congenial admeasurement of the whale.

Chapter 103

MEASUREMENT OF THE WHALE'S SKELETON

In the first place, I wish to lay before you a particular, plain statement, touching the living bulk of this leviathan, whose skeleton we are briefly to exhibit. Such a statement may prove useful here.

According to a careful calculation I have made, and which I partly base upon Captain Scoresby's estimate, of seventy tons for the largest sized Greenland whale of sixty feet in length; according to my careful calculation, I say, a Sperm Whale of the largest magnitude, between eighty-five and ninety feet in length, and something less than forty feet in its fullest circumference, such a whale will weigh at least ninety tons; so that, reckoning thirteen men to a ton, he would considerably outweigh the combined population of a whole village of one thousand one hundred inhabitants.

Think you not then that brains, like yoked cattle, should be put to this leviathan, to make him at all budge to any landsman's imagination?

Having already in various ways put before you his skull, spout-hole, jaw, teeth, tail, forehead, fins, and divers other parts, I shall now simply point out what is most interesting in the general bulk of his unobstructed bones. But as the colossal skull embraces so very large a proportion of the entire extent of the skeleton; as it is by far the most complicated part; and as nothing is to be repeated concerning it in this chapter, you must not fail to carry it in your mind, or under your arm, as we proceed, otherwise you will not gain a complete notion of the general structure we are about to view.

In length, the Sperm Whale's skeleton at Tranque measured seventy-two feet; so that when fully invested and extended in life, he must have been ninety feet long; for in the whale, the skeleton loses about one fifth in length compared with the living body. Of this seventy-two feet, his skull and jaw comprised some twenty feet, leaving some fifty feet of plain back-bone. Attached to this back-bone, for something less than a third of its length, was the mighty circular basket of ribs which once enclosed his vitals.

To me this vast ivory-ribbed chest, with the long, unrelieved spine, extending far away from it in a straight line, not a little resembled the embryo hull of a great ship new-laid upon the stocks, when only some twenty of her naked bow-ribs are inserted, and the keel is otherwise, for the time, but a long, disconnected timber.

The ribs were ten on a side. The first, to begin from the neck, was nearly six feet long; the second, third, and fourth were each successively longer, till you came to the climax of the fifth, or one of the middle ribs, which measured eight feet and some inches. From that part, the remaining ribs diminished, till the tenth and last only spanned five feet and some inches. In general thickness, they all bore a seemly correspondence to their length. The middle ribs were the most arched. In some of the Arsacides they are used for beams whereon to lay foot-path bridges over small streams.

In considering these ribs, I could not but be struck anew with the circumstance, so variously repeated in this book, that the skeleton of the whale is by no means the mould of his invested form. The largest of the Tranque ribs, one of the middle ones, occupied that part of the fish which, in life, is greatest in depth. Now, the greatest depth of the invested body of this particular whale must have been at least sixteen feet; whereas, the corresponding rib measured but little more than eight feet. So that this rib only conveyed half of the true notion of the living magnitude of that part. Besides, for some way, where I now saw but a naked spine, all that had been once wrapped round with tons of added bulk in flesh, muscle, blood, and bowels. Still more, for the ample fins, I here saw but a few disordered joints; and in place of the weighty and majestic, but boneless flukes, an utter blank!

How vain and foolish, then, thought I, for timid untravelled man to try to comprehend aright this wondrous whale, by merely poring over his dead attenuated skeleton, stretched in this peaceful wood. No. Only in the heart of quickest perils; only when within the eddyings of his angry flukes; only on the profound unbounded sea, can the fully invested whale be truly and livingly found out.

But the spine. For that, the best way we can consider it is, with a crane, to pile its bones high up on end. No speedy enterprise. But now it's done, it looks much like Pompey's Pillar.

There are forty and odd vertebræ in all, which in the skeleton are not locked together. They mostly lie like the great knobbed blocks on a Gothic spire, forming solid courses of heavy masonry. The largest, a middle one, is in width something less than three feet, and in depth more than four. The smallest, where the spine tapers away into the tail, is only two inches in width, and looks something like a white billiard-ball. I was told that there were still smaller ones, but they had been lost by some little cannibal urchins, the priest's children, who had stolen them to play marbles with. Thus we see how that the spine of even the hugest of living things tapers off at last into simple child's play.

Chapter 104

THE FOSSIL WHALE

From his mighty bulk the whale affords a most congenial theme whereon to enlarge, amplify, and generally expatiate. Would you, you could not compress him. By good rights he should only be treated of in imperial folio. Not to tell over again his furlongs from spiracle to tail, and the yards he measures about the waist; only think of the gigantic involutions of his intestines, where they lie in him like great cables and hausers coiled away in the subterranean orlop-deck of a line-of-battle-ship.

Since I have undertaken to manhandle this Leviathan, it behoves me to approve myself omnisciently exhaustive in the enterprise; not overlooking the minutest seminal germs of his blood, and spinning him out to the uttermost coil of his bowels. Having already described him in most of his present habitatory and anatomical peculiarities, it now remains to magnify him in an archæological, fossiliferous, and antediluvian point of view. Applied to any other creature than the Leviathan—to an ant or a flea—such portly terms might justly be deemed unwarrantably grandiloquent. But when Leviathan is the text, the case is altered. Fain am I to stagger to this emprise under the weightiest words of the dictionary. And here be it said, that whenever it has been convenient to consult one in the course of these dissertations, I have invariably used a huge quarto edition of Johnson, expressly purchased for that purpose; because that famous lexicographer's uncommon personal bulk more fitted him to compile a lexicon to be used by a whale author like me.

One often hears of writers that rise and swell with their subject, though it may seem but an ordinary one. How, then, with me, writing of this Leviathan? Unconsciously my chirography expands into placard capitals. Give me a condor's quill! Give me Vesuvius' crater for an inkstand! Friends, hold my arms! For in the mere act of penning my thoughts of this Leviathan, they weary me, and make me faint with their outreaching comprehensiveness of sweep, as if to include the whole circle of the sciences, and all the generations of whales, and men, and mastodons, past, present, and to come, with all the revolving panoramas of empire on earth, and throughout the whole universe, not excluding its suburbs. Such, and so magnifying, is the virtue of a large and liberal theme! We expand to its bulk. To produce a mighty book, you must choose a mighty theme. No great and enduring volume can ever be written on the flea, though many there be who have tried it.

Ere entering upon the subject of Fossil Whales, I present my credentials as a geologist, by stating that in my miscellaneous time I have been a stone-mason, and also a great digger of ditches, canals and wells, wine-vaults, cellars, and cisterns of all sorts. Likewise, by way of preliminary, I desire to remind the reader, that while in the earlier geological strata there are found the fossils of monsters now almost completely extinct; the subsequent relics discovered in what are called the Tertiary formations seem the connecting, or at any rate intercepted links, between the ante-chronical creatures, and those whose remote posterity are said to have entered the Ark; all the Fossil Whales hitherto discovered belong to the Tertiary period, which is the last preceding the superficial formations. And though none of them precisely answer to any known species of the present time, they are yet sufficiently akin to them in general respects, to justify their taking rank as Cetacean fossils.

Detached broken fossils of pre-adamite whales, fragments of their bones and skeletons, have within thirty years past, at various intervals, been found at the base of the Alps, in Lombardy, in France, in England, in Scotland, and in the States of Louisiana, Mississippi, and Alabama. Among the more curious of such

1. Creatures existing before time ("for time began with man," as Ishmael says three paragraphs later).

remains is part of a skull, which in the year 1779 was disinterred in the Rue Dauphine in Paris, a short street opening almost directly upon the palace of the Tuileries; and bones disinterred in excavating the great docks of Antwerp, in Napoleon's time. Cuvier pronounced these fragments to have belonged to some utterly unknown Leviathanic species.

But by far the most wonderful of all cetacean relics was the almost complete vast skeleton of an extinct monster, found in the year 1842, on the plantation of Judge Creagh, in Alabama. The awe-stricken credulous slaves in the vicinity took it for the bones of one of the fallen angels. The Alabama doctors declared it a huge reptile, and bestowed upon it the name of Basilosaurus. But some specimen bones of it being taken across the sea to Owen, the English anatomist, it turned out that this alleged reptile was a whale, though of a departed species. A significant illustration of the fact, again and again repeated in this book, that the skeleton of the whale furnishes but little clue to the shape of his fully invested body. So Owen re-christened the monster Zeuglodon; and in his paper read before the London Geological Society, pronounced it, in substance, one of the most extraordinary creatures which the mutations of the globe have blotted out of existence.

When I stand among these mighty Leviathan skeletons, skulls, tusks, jaws, ribs, and vertebræ, all characterized by partial resemblances to the existing breeds of sea-monsters; but at the same time bearing on the other hand similar affinities to the annihilated ante-chronical Leviathans, their incalculable seniors; I am, by a flood, borne back to that wondrous period, ere time itself can be said to have begun; for time began with man. Here Saturn's grey chaos [2] rolls over me, and I obtain dim, shuddering glimpses into those Polar eternities; when wedged bastions of ice pressed hard upon what are now the Tropics; and in all the 25,000 miles of this world's circumference, not an inhabitable hand's breadth of land was visible. Then the whole world was the whale's; and, king of creation, he left his wake along the present lines of the Andes and the Himmalehs. Who can show a pedigree like Leviathan? Ahab's harpoon had shed older blood than the Pharaohs'. Methuselah seems a schoolboy. I look round to shake hands with Shem. I am horror-struck at this antemosaic, unsourced existence of the unspeakable terrors of the whale, which, having been before all time, must needs exist after all humane ages are over.

But not alone has this Leviathan left his pre-adamite traces in the stereotype plates of nature, and in limestone and marl bequeathed his ancient bust; but upon Egyptian tablets, whose

2. Saturn was chief of the Titans, the pre-Olympian gods of Greek mythology.

antiquity seems to claim for them an almost fossiliferous character, we find the unmistakable print of his fin. In an apartment of the great temple of Denderah, some fifty years ago, there was discovered upon the granite ceiling a sculptured and painted planisphere, abounding in centaurs, griffins, and dolphins, similar to the grotesque figures on the celestial globe of the moderns. Gliding among them, old Leviathan swam as of yore; was there swimming in that planisphere, centuries before Solomon was cradled.

Nor must there be omitted another strange attestation of the antiquity of the whale, in his own osseous post-diluvian reality, as set down by the venerable John Leo, the old Barbary traveller.

"Not far from the Sea-side, they have a Temple, the Rafters and Beams of which are made of Whale-Bones; for Whales of a monstrous size are oftentimes cast up dead upon that shore. The Common People imagine, that by a secret Power bestowed by God upon the Temple, no Whale can pass it without immediate death. But the truth of the Matter is, that on either side of the Temple, there are Rocks that shoot two Miles into the Sea, and wound the Whales when they light upon 'em. They keep a Whale's Rib of an incredible length for a Miracle, which lying upon the Ground with its convex part uppermost, makes an Arch, the Head of which cannot be reached by a Man upon a Camel's Back. This Rib" (says John Leo) "is said to have layn there a hundred Years before I saw it. Their Historians affirm, that a Prophet who prophesy'd of Mahomet, came from this Temple, and some do not stand to assert, that the Prophet Jonas was cast forth by the Whale at the Base of the Temple."

In this Afric Temple of the Whale I leave you, reader, and if you be a Nantucketer, and a whaleman, you will silently worship there.

Chapter 105

DOES THE WHALE'S MAGNITUDE DIMINISH?—WILL HE PERISH?

Inasmuch, then, as this Leviathan comes floundering down upon us from the head-waters of the Eternities, it may be fitly inquired, whether, in the long course of his generations, he has not degenerated from the original bulk of his sires.

But upon investigation we find, that not only are the whales of the present day superior in magnitude to those whose fossil remains are found in the Tertiary system (embracing a distinct geological period prior to man), but of the whales found in that Tertiary system, those belonging to its latter formations exceed in size those of its earlier ones.

Of all the pre-adamite whales yet exhumed, by far the largest is the Alabama one mentioned in the last chapter, and that was less than seventy feet in length in the skeleton. Whereas, we have already seen, that the tape-measure gives seventy-two feet for the skeleton of a large sized modern whale. And I have heard, on whalemen's authority, that Sperm Whales have been captured near a hundred feet long at the time of capture.

But may it not be, that while the whales of the present hour are an advance in magnitude upon those of all previous geological periods; may it not be, that since Adam's time they have degenerated?

Assuredly, we must conclude so, if we are to credit the accounts of such gentlemen as Pliny, and the ancient naturalists generally. For Pliny tells us of whales that embraced acres of living bulk, and Aldrovandus of others which measured eight hundred feet in length—Rope Walks and Thames Tunnels of Whales! And even in the days of Banks and Solander. Cook's naturalists, we find a Danish member of the Academy of Sciences setting down certain Iceland Whales (reydan-siskur, or Wrinkled Bellies) at one hundred and twenty yards; that is, three hundred and sixty feet. And Lacépède, the French naturalist, in his elaborate history of whales, in the very beginning of his work (page 3), sets down the Right Whale at one hundred metres, three hundred and twenty-eight feet. And this work was published so late as A. D. 1825.

But will any whaleman believe these stories? No. The whale of to-day is as big as his ancestors in Pliny's time. And if ever I go where Pliny is, I, a whaleman (more than he was), will make bold to tell him so. Because I cannot understand how it is, that while the Egyptian mummies that were buried thousands of years before even Pliny was born, do not measure so much in their coffins as a modern Kentuckian in his socks; and while the cattle and other animals sculptured on the oldest Egyptian and Nineveh tablets, by the relative proportions in which they are drawn, just as plainly prove that the high-bred, stall-fed, prize cattle of Smithfield, not only equal, but far exceed in magnitude the fattest of Pharaoh's fat kine; in the face of all this, I will not admit that of all animals the whale alone should have degenerated.

But still another inquiry remains; one often agitated by the more recondite Nantucketers. Whether owing to the almost omniscient look-outs at the mast-heads of the whale-ships, now penetrating even through Behring's straits, and into the remotest secret drawers and lockers of the world; and the thousand harpoons and lances darted along all continental coasts; the moot point is, whether Leviathan can long endure so wide a chase, and so remorseless a havoc; whether he must not at last be exterminated from the waters, and the last whale, like the last man, smoke his last pipe, and then himself evaporate in the final puff.

Comparing the humped herds of whales with the humped herds of buffalo, which, not forty years ago, overspread by tens of thousands the prairies of Illinois and Missouri, and shook their iron manes and scowled with their thunder-clotted brows upon the sites of populous river-capitals, where now the polite broker sells you land at a dollar an inch; in such a comparison an irresistible argument would seem furnished, to show that the hunted whale cannot now escape speedy extinction.

But you must look at this matter in every light. Though so short a period ago—not a good life-time—the census of the buffalo in Illinois exceeded the census of men now in London, and though at the present day not one horn or hoof of them remains in all that region; and though the cause of this wondrous extermination was the spear of man; yet the far different nature of the whale-hunt peremptorily forbids so inglorious an end to the Leviathan. Forty men in one ship hunting the Sperm Whale for forty-eight months think they have done extremely well, and thank God, if at last they carry home the oil of forty fish. Whereas, in the days of the old Canadian and Indian hunters and trappers of the West, when the far west (in whose sunset suns still rise) was a wilderness and a virgin, the same number of moccasined men, for the same number of months, mounted on horse instead of sailing in ships, would have slain not forty, but forty thousand and more buffaloes; a fact that, if need were, could be statistically stated.

Nor, considered aright, does it seem any argument in favor of the gradual extinction of the Sperm Whale, for example, that in former years (the latter part of the last century, say) these Leviathans, in small pods, were encountered much oftener than at present, and, in consequence, the voyages were not so prolonged, and were also much more remunerative. Because, as has been elsewhere noticed, those whales, influenced by some views to safety, now swim the seas in immense caravans, so that to a large degree the scattered solitaries, yokes, and pods, and schools of other days are now aggregated into vast but widely separated, unfrequent armies. That is all. And equally fallacious seems the conceit, that because the so-called whale-bone whales no longer haunt many grounds in former years abounding with them, hence that species also is declining. For they are only being driven from promontory to cape; and if one coast is no longer enlivened with their jets, then, be sure, some other and remoter strand has been very recently startled by the unfamiliar spectacle.

Furthermore: concerning these last mentioned Leviathans, they have two firm fortresses, which, in all human probability, will for ever remain impregnable. And as upon the invasion of their valleys, the frosty Swiss have retreated to their mountains; so, hunted from the savannas and glades of the middle seas, the whale-bone whales can at last resort to their Polar citadels, and diving under the ultimate glassy barriers and walls there, come up among icy fields and floes; and in a charmed circle of everlasting December, bid defiance to all pursuit from man.

But as perhaps fifty of these whale-bone whales are harpooned for one cachalot, some philosophers of the forecastle have concluded that this positive havoc has already very seriously diminished their battalions. But though for some time past a number of these whales, not less than 13,000, have been annually slain on the nor' west coast by the Americans alone; yet there are considerations which render even this circumstance of little or no account as an opposing argument in this matter.

Natural as it is to be somewhat incredulous concerning the populousness of the more enormous creatures of the globe, yet what shall we say to Horto, the historian of Goa, when he tells us that at one hunting the King of Siam took 4000 elephants; that in those regions elephants are numerous as droves of cattle in the temperate climes. And there seems no reason to doubt that if these elephants, which have now been hunted for thousands of years, by Semiramis, by Porus, by Hannibal, and by all the successive monarchs of the East—if they still survive there in great numbers, much more may the great whale outlast all hunting, since he has a pasture to expatiate in, which is precisely twice as large as all Asia, both Americas, Europe and Africa, New Holland, and all the Isles of the sea combined.

Moreover: we are to consider, that from the presumed great longevity of whales, their probably attaining the age of a century and more, therefore at any one period of time, several distinct adult generations must be contemporary. And what that is, we may soon gain some idea of, by imagining all the grave-yards, cemeteries, and family vaults of creation yielding up the live bodies of all the men, women, and children who were alive seventy-five years ago; and adding this countless host to the present human population of the globe.

Wherefore, for all these things, we account the whale immortal in his species, however perishable in his individuality. He swam the seas before the continents broke water; he once swam over the site of the Tuileries, and Windsor Castle, and the Kremlin. In

Noah's flood he despised Noah's Ark; and if ever the world is to be again flooded, like the Netherlands, to kill off its rats, then the eternal whale will still survive, and rearing upon the topmost crest of the equatorial flood, spout his frothed defiance to the skies.

Chapter 106

AHAB'S LEG

The precipitating manner in which Captain Ahab had quitted the Samuel Enderby of London, had not been unattended with some small violence to his own person. He had lighted with such energy upon a thwart of his boat that his ivory leg had received a half-splintering shock. And when after gaining his own deck, and his own pivot-hole there, he so vehemently wheeled round with an urgent command to the steersman (it was, as ever, something about his not steering inflexibly enough); then, the already shaken ivory received such an additional twist and wrench, that though it still remained entire, and to all appearances lusty, yet Ahab did not deem it entirely trustworthy.

And, indeed, it seemed small matter for wonder, that for all his pervading, mad recklessness, Ahab did at times give careful heed to the condition of that dead bone upon which he partly stood. For it had not been very long prior to the Pequod's sailing from Nantucket, that he had been found one night lying prone upon the ground, and insensible; by some unknown, and seemingly inexplicable, unimaginable casualty, his ivory limb having been so violently displaced, that it had stake-wise smitten, and all but pierced his groin; nor was it without extreme difficulty that the agonizing wound was entirely cured.

Nor, at the time, had it failed to enter his monomaniac mind, that all the anguish of that then present suffering was but the direct issue of a former woe; and he too plainly seemed to see, that as the most poisonous reptile of the marsh perpetuates his kind as inevitably as the sweetest songster of the grove; so, equally with every felicity, all miserable events do naturally beget their like. Yea, more than equally, thought Ahab; since both the ancestry and posterity of Grief go further than the ancestry and posterity of Joy. For, not to hint of this: that it is an inference from certain canonic teachings, that while some natural enjoyments here shall have no children born to them for the other world, but, on the contrary, shall be followed by the joy-childlessness of all hell's despair; whereas, some guilty mortal miseries shall still fertilely beget to themselves an eternally progressive progeny of griefs beyond the grave; not at all to hint of this, there still seems an inequality in the deeper analysis of the thing. For, thought Ahab, while even the highest earthly felicities ever have a certain unsignifying pettiness lurking in them, but, at bottom, all heart-woes, a mystic significance, and, in some men, an arch-angelic grandeur; so do their diligent tracings-out not belie the obvious deduction. To trail the genealogies of these high mortal miseries, carries us at last among the sourceless primogenitures of the gods; so that, in the face of all the glad, hay-making suns, and soft-cymballing, round harvest-moons, we must needs give in to this: that the gods themselves are not for ever glad. The ineffaceable, sad birth-mark in the brow of man, is but the stamp of sorrow in the signers.

Unwittingly here a secret has been divulged, which perhaps might more properly, in set way, have been disclosed before. With many other particulars concerning Ahab, always had it remained a mystery to some, why it was, that for a certain period, both before and after the sailing of the Pequod, he had hidden himself away with such Grand-Lama-like exclusiveness; and, for that one interval, sought speechless refuge, as it were, among the marble senate of the dead. Captain Peleg's bruited reason for this thing appeared by no means adequate; though, indeed, as touching all Ahab's deeper part, every revelation partook more of significant darkness than of explanatory light. But, in the end, it all came out; this one matter did, at least. That direful mishap was at the bottom of his temporary recluseness. And not only this, but to that ever-contracting, dropping circle ashore, who, for any reason, possessed the privilege of a less banned approach to him; to that timid circle the above hinted casualty—remaining, as it did, moodily unaccounted for by Ahab—invested itself with terrors, not entirely underived from the land of spirits and of wails. So that, through their zeal for him, they had all conspired, so far as in them lay, to muffle up the knowledge of this thing from others; and hence it was, that not till a considerable interval had elapsed, did it transpire upon the Pequod's decks.

But be all this as it may; let the unseen, ambiguous synod in the air, or the vindictive princes and potentates of fire, have to do or not with earthly Ahab, yet, in this present matter of his leg, he took plain practical procedures;—he called the carpenter.

And when that functionary appeared before him, he bade him without delay set about making a new leg, and directed the mates to see him supplied with all the studs and joists of jaw-ivory (Sperm Whale) which had thus far been accumulated on the voyage, in order that a careful selection of the stoutest, clearest-grained stuff might be secured. This done, the carpenter received orders to have the leg completed that night; and to provide all the fittings for it, independent of those pertaining to the distrusted one in use. Moreover, the ship's forge was ordered to be hoisted out of its temporary idleness in the hold; and, to accelerate the affair, the blacksmith was commanded to proceed at once to the forging of whatever iron contrivances might be needed.

Chapter 107

THE CARPENTER

Seat thyself sultanically among the moons of Saturn, and take high abstracted man alone; and he seems a wonder, a grandeur, and a woe. But from the same point, take mankind in mass, and for the most part, they seem a mob of unnecessary duplicates, both contemporary and hereditary. But most humble though he was, and far from furnishing an example of the high, humane abstraction; the Pequod's carpenter was no duplicate; hence, he now comes in person on this stage.

Like all sea-going ship carpenters, and more especially those belonging to whaling vessels, he was, to a certain off-handed, practical extent, alike experienced in numerous trades and callings collateral to his own; the carpenter's pursuit being the ancient and outbranching trunk of all those numerous handicrafts which more or less have to do with wood as an auxiliary material. But, besides the application to him of the generic remark above, this carpenter of the Pequod was singularly efficient in those thousand nameless mechanical emergencies continually recurring in a large ship, upon a three or four years' voyage, in uncivilized and far-distant seas. For not to speak of his readiness in ordinary duties: —repairing stove boats, sprung spars, reforming the shape of clumsy-bladed oars, inserting bull's eyes in the deck, or new tree-nails in the side planks, and other miscellaneous matters more directly pertaining to his special business; he was moreover unhesitatingly expert in all manner of conflicting aptitudes, both useful and capricious.

The one grand stage where he enacted all his various parts so manifold, was his vice-bench; a long rude ponderous table furnished with several vices, of different sizes, and both of iron and of wood. At all times except when whales were alongside, this bench was securely lashed athwartships against the rear of the Try-works.

A belaying pin is found too large to be easily inserted into its hole: the carpenter claps it into one of his ever-ready vices, and straightway files it smaller. A lost land-bird of strange plumage strays on board, and is made a captive: out of clean shaved rods of right-whale bone, and cross-beams of sperm whale ivory, the carpenter makes a pagoda-looking cage for it. An oarsman sprains his wrist: the carpenter concocts a soothing lotion. Stubb longs for vermillion stars to be painted upon the blade of his every oar: screwing each oar in his big vice of wood, the carpenter symmetrically supplies the constellation. A sailor takes a fancy to wear shark-bone ear-rings: the carpenter drills his ears. Another has the toothache: the carpenter out pincers, and clapping one hand upon his bench bids him be seated there; but the poor fellow unmanageably winces under the unconcluded operation; whirling round the handle of his wooden vice, the carpenter signs him to clap his jaw in that, if he would have him draw the tooth.

Thus, this carpenter was prepared at all points, and alike indifferent and without respect in all. Teeth he accounted bits of ivory; heads he deemed but top-blocks; men themselves he lightly held for capstans. But while now upon so wide a field thus variously accomplished, and with such liveliness of expertness in him, too; all this would seem to argue some uncommon vivacity of intelligence. But not precisely so. For nothing was this man more remarkable, than for a certain impersonal stolidity as it were; impersonal, I say; for it so shaded off into the surrounding infinite of things, that it seemed one with the general stolidity discernible in the whole visible world; which while pauselessly active in uncounted modes, still eternally holds its peace, and ignores you, though you dig foundations for cathedrals. Yet was this half-horrible stolidity in him, involving, too, as it appeared, an all-ramifying heartlessness;—yet was it oddly dashed at times, with an old, crutch-like, antediluvian, wheezing humorousness, not unstreaked now and then with a certain grizzled wittiness; such as might have served to pass the time during the midnight watch on the bearded forecastle of Noah's ark. Was it that this old carpenter had been a life-long wanderer, whose much rolling, to and fro, not only had gathered no moss; but what is more, had rubbed off whatever small outward clingings might have originally pertained to him? He was a stript abstract; an unfractioned integral; uncompromised as a new-born babe; living without premeditated reference to this world or the next. You might almost say, that this strange uncompromisedness in him involved a sort of unintelligence; for in his numerous trades, he did not seem to work so much by reason or by instinct, or simply because he had been tutored to it, or by any intermixture of all these, even or uneven; but merely by a kind of deaf and dumb, spontaneous literal process. He was a pure manipulator; his brain, if he had ever had one, must have early oozed along into the muscles of his fingers. He was like one of those unreasoning but still highly useful, *multum in parvo*,[1] Sheffield contrivances, assuming the exterior

---

1. *multum in parvo:* much in little.

—though a little swelled—of a common pocket knife; but containing, not only blades of various sizes, but also screw-drivers, cork-screws, tweezers, awls, pens, rulers, nail-filers, countersinkers. So, if his superiors wanted to use the carpenter for a screw-driver, all they had to do was to open that part of him, and the screw was fast: or if for tweezers, take him up by the legs, and there they were.

Yet, as previously hinted, this omnitooled, open-and-shut carpenter, was, after all, no mere machine of an automaton. If he did not have a common soul in him, he had a subtle something that somehow anomalously did its duty. What that was, whether essence of quicksilver, or a few drops of hartshorn, there is no telling. But there it was; and there it had abided for now some sixty years or more. And this it was, this same unaccountable, cunning life-principle in him; this it was, that kept him a great part of the time soliloquizing; but only like an unreasoning wheel, which also hummingly soliloquizes; or rather, his body was a sentry-box and this soliloquizer on guard there, and talking all the time to keep himself awake.

Chapter 108

AHAB AND THE CARPENTER

THE DECK—FIRST NIGHT WATCH

(*Carpenter standing before his vice-bench, and by the light of two lanterns busily filing the ivory joist for the leg, which joist is firmly fixed in the vice. Slabs of ivory, leather straps, pads, screws, and various tools of all sorts lying about the bench. Forward, the red flame of the forge is seen, where the blacksmith is at work.*)

Drat the file, and drat the bone! That is hard which should be soft, and that is soft which should be hard. So we go, who file old jaws and shinbones. Let's try another. Aye, now, this works better (*sneezes*). Halloa, this bone dust is (*sneezes*)—why it's (*sneezes*)—yes it's (*sneezes*)—bless my soul, it won't let me speak! This is what an old fellow gets now for working in dead lumber. Saw a live tree, and you don't get this dust; amputate a live bone, and you don't get it (*sneezes*). Come, come, you old Smut, there, bear a hand, and let's have that ferule and buckle-screw; I'll be ready for them presently. Lucky now (*sneezes*) there's no knee-joint to make; that might puzzle a little; but a mere shinbone—why it's easy as making hop-poles; only I should like to put a good finish on. Time, time; if I but only had the time, I could turn him out as neat a leg now as ever (*sneezes*) scraped to a lady in a parlor. Those buckskin legs and calves of legs I've seen in shop windows wouldn't compare at all. They soak water, they do; and of course get rheumatic, and have to be doctored (*sneezes*) with washes and lotions, just like live legs. There; before I saw it off, now, I must call his old Mogulship, and see whether the length will be all right; too short, if anything, I guess. Ha! that's the heel; we are in luck; here he comes, or it's somebody else, that's certain.

AHAB (advancing).

(During the ensuing scene, the carpenter continues sneezing at times.)

Well, manmaker!

Just in time, sir. If the captain pleases, I will now mark the length. Let me measure, sir.

Measured for a leg! good. Well, it's not the first time. About it! There; keep thy finger on it. This is a cogent vice thou hast here, carpenter; let me feel its grip once. So, so; it does pinch some.

Oh, sir, it will break bones—beware, beware!

No fear; I like a good grip; I like to feel something in this slippery world that can hold, man. What's Prometheus about there?—the blacksmith, I mean—what's he about?

He must be forging the buckle-screw, sir, now.

Right. It's a partnership; he supplies the muscle part. He makes a fierce red flame there!

Aye, sir; he must have the white heat for this kind of fine work.

Um-m. So he must. I do deem it now a most meaning thing, that that old Greek, Prometheus, who made men, they say, should have been a blacksmith, and animated them with fire; for what's made in fire must properly belong to fire; and so hell's probable. How the soot flies! This must be the remainder the Greek made the Africans of. Carpenter, when he's through with that buckle, tell him to forge a pair of steel shoulder-blades; there's a pedlar aboard with a crushing pack.

Sir?

Hold; while Prometheus is about it, I'll order a complete man after a desirable pattern. Imprimis, fifty feet high in his socks; then, chest modelled after the Thames Tunnel; then, legs with roots to 'em, to stay in one place; then, arms three feet through the wrist; no heart at all, brass forehead, and about a quarter of an acre of fine brains; and let me see—shall I order eyes to see outwards? No, but put a sky-light on top of his head to illuminate inwards. There, take the order, and away.

Now, what's he speaking about, and who's he speaking to, I should like to know? Shall I keep standing here? (*aside.*)

'Tis but indifferent architecture to make a blind dome; here's one. No, no, no; I must have a lantern.

Ho, ho! That's it, hey? Here are two, sir; one will serve my turn. What art thou thrusting that thief-catcher into my face for, man? Thrusted light is worse than presented pistols.

I thought, sir, that you spoke to carpenter.

Carpenter? why that's—but no;—a very tidy, and, I may say, an extremely gentlemanlike sort of business thou art in here, carpenter;—or would'st thou rather work in clay?

Sir?—Clay? clay, sir? That's mud; we leave clay to ditchers, sir.

The fellow's impious! What art thou sneezing about?

Bone is rather dusty, sir.

Take the hint, then; and when thou art dead, never bury thyself under living people's noses.

Sir?—oh! ah!—I guess so;—yes—oh, dear!

Look ye, carpenter, I dare say thou callest thyself a right good workmanlike workman, eh? Well, then, will it speak thoroughly well for thy work, if, when I come to mount this leg thou makest, I shall nevertheless feel another leg in the same identical place with it; that is, carpenter, my old lost leg; the flesh and blood one, I mean. Canst thou not drive that old Adam away?

Truly, sir, I begin to understand somewhat now. Yes, I have heard something curious on that score, sir; how that a dismasted man never entirely loses the feeling of his old spar, but it will be still pricking him at times. May I humbly ask if it be really so, sir?

It is, man. Look, put thy live leg here in the place where mine once was; so, now, here is only one distinct leg to the eye yet two to the soul. Where thou feelest tingling life; there, exactly there, there to a hair, do I. Is't a riddle?

I should humbly call it a poser, sir.

Hist, then. How dost thou know that some entire, living, thinking thing may not be invisibly and uninterpenetratingly standing precisely where thou now standest; aye, and standing there in thy spite? In thy most solitary hours, then, dost thou not fear eavesdroppers? Hold, don't speak! And if I still feel the smart of my crushed leg, though it be now so long dissolved; then, why mayst not thou, carpenter, feel the fiery pains of hell for ever, and without a body? Hah!

Good Lord! Truly, sir, if it comes to that, I must calculate over again; I think I didn't carry a small figure, sir.

Look ye, pudding-heads should never grant premises.—How long before the leg is done?

Perhaps an hour, sir.

Bungle away at it then, and bring it to me (*turns to go*). Oh, Life! Here I am, proud as a Greek god, and yet standing debtor to this blockhead for a bone to stand on! Cursed be that mortal inter-indebtedness which will not do away with ledgers. I would be free as air; and I'm down in the whole world's books. I am so rich, I could have given bid for bid with the wealthiest Præ-torians at the auction of the Roman empire (which was the world's); and yet I owe for the flesh in the tongue I brag with. By heavens! I'll get a crucible, and into it, and dissolve myself down to one small, compendious vertebra. So.

CARPENTER (*resuming his work*).

Well, well, well! Stubb knows him best of all, and Stubb al-ways says he's queer; says nothing but that one sufficient little word queer; he's queer, says Stubb; he's queer—queer, queer; and keeps dinning it into Mr. Starbuck all the time—queer, sir—queer, queer, very queer. And here's his leg! Yes, now that I think of it, here's his bedfellow! has a stick of whale's jaw-bone for a wife! And this is his leg; he'll stand on this. What was that now about one leg standing in three places, and all three places standing in one hell—how was that? Oh! I don't wonder he looked so scornful at me! I'm a sort of strange-thoughted some-times, they say; but that's only hap-hazard-like. Then, a short, little old body like me, should never undertake to wade out into deep waters with tall, heron-built captains; the water chucks you under the chin pretty quick, and there's a great cry for life-boats. And here's the heron's leg! long and slim, sure enough! Now, for most folks one pair of legs lasts a lifetime, and that must be because they use them mercifully, as a tender-hearted old lady uses her roly-poly old coach-horses. But Ahab; oh he's a hard driver. Look, driven one leg to death, and spavined the other for life, and now wears out bone legs by the cord. Halloa, there, you Smut! bear a hand there with those screws, and let's finish it before the resur-rection fellow comes a-calling with his horn for all legs, true or false, as brewery-men go round collecting old beer barrels, to fill 'em up again. What a leg this is! It looks like a real live leg, filed down to nothing but the core; he'll be standing on this to-morrow; he'll be taking altitudes on it. Halloa! I almost forgot the little oval slate, smoothed ivory, where he figures up the latitude. So, so; chisel, file, and sand-paper, now!

Chapter 109

AHAB AND STARBUCK IN THE CABIN

According to usage they were pumping the ship next morning; and lo! no inconsiderable oil came up with the water; the casks below must have sprung a bad leak. Much concern was shown; and Starbuck went down into the cabin to report this unfavorable affair.*

Now, from the South and West the Pequod was drawing nigh to Formosa and the Bashee Isles, between which lies one of the tropical outlets from the China waters into the Pacific. And so Starbuck found Ahab with a general chart of the oriental archipelagoes spread before him; and another separate one representing the long eastern coasts of the Japanese islands—Niphon, Matsmai, and Sikoke. With his snow-white new ivory leg braced against the screwed leg of his table, and with a long pruning-hook of a jack-knife in his hand, the wondrous old man, with his back to the gangway door, was wrinkling his brow, and tracing his old courses again.

"Who's there?" hearing the footstep at the door, but not turning round to it. "On deck! Begone!"

"Captain Ahab mistakes; it is I. The oil in the hold is leaking, sir. We must up Burtons and break out."

"Up Burtons and break out? Now that we are nearing Japan; heave-to here for a week to tinker a parcel of old hoops?"

"Either do that, sir, or waste in one day more oil than we may make good in a year. What we come twenty thousand miles to get is worth saving, sir."

"So it is, so it is; if we get it."

"I was speaking of the oil in the hold, sir."

"And I was not speaking or thinking of that at all. Begone! Let it leak! I'm all aleak myself. Aye! leaks in leaks! not only full of leaky casks, but those leaky casks are in a leaky ship; and that's a far worse plight than the Pequod's, man. Yet I don't stop to plug my leak; for who can find it in the deep-loaded hull; or how hope to plug it, even if found, in this life's howling gale? Starbuck! I'll not have the Burtons hoisted."

"What will the owners say, sir?"

"Let the owners stand on Nantucket beach and outyell the Typhoons. What cares Ahab? Owners, owners? Thou art always prating to me, Starbuck, about those miserly owners, as if the owners were my conscience. But look ye, the only real owner of anything is its commander; and hark ye, my conscience is in this ship's keel.—On deck!"

"Captain Ahab," said the reddening mate, moving further into the cabin, with a daring so strangely respectful and cautious that it almost seemed not only every way seeking to avoid the slightest outward manifestation of itself, but within also seemed more than

* In Sperm-whalemen with any considerable quantity of oil on board, it is a regular semi-weekly duty to conduct a hose into the hold, and drench the casks with sea-water; which afterwards, at varying intervals, is removed by the ship's pumps. Hereby the casks are sought to be kept damply tight; while by the changed character of the withdrawn water, the mariners readily detect any serious leakage in the precious cargo [Melville's note].

half distrustful of itself; "A better man than I might well pass over in thee what he would quickly enough resent in a younger man; aye, and in a happier, Captain Ahab."

"Devils! Dost thou then so much as dare to critically think of me?—On deck!"

"Nay, sir, not yet; I do entreat. And I do dare, sir—to be forbearing! Shall we not understand each other better than hitherto, Captain Ahab?"

Ahab seized a loaded musket from the rack (forming part of most South-Sea-men's cabin furniture), and pointing it towards Starbuck, exclaimed: "There is one God that is Lord over the earth, and one Captain that is lord over the Pequod.—On deck!"

For an instant in the flashing eyes of the mate, and his fiery cheeks, you would have almost thought that he had really received the blaze of the levelled tube. But, mastering his emotion, he half calmly rose, and as he quitted the cabin, paused for an instant and said: "Thou hast outraged, not insulted me, sir; but for that I ask thee not to beware of Starbuck; thou wouldst but laugh; but let Ahab beware of Ahab; beware of thyself, old man."

"He waxes brave, but nevertheless obeys; most careful bravery that!" murmured Ahab, as Starbuck disappeared. "What's that he said—Ahab beware of Ahab—there's something there!" Then unconsciously using the musket for a staff, with an iron brow he paced to and fro in the little cabin; but presently the thick plaits of his forehead relaxed, and returning the gun to the rack, he went to the deck.

"Thou art but too good a fellow, Starbuck," he said lowly to the mate; then raising his voice to the crew: "Furl the t'gallant-sails, and close-reef the top-sails, fore and aft; back the main-yard; up Burtons, and break out in the main-hold."

It were perhaps vain to surmise exactly why it was, that as respecting Starbuck, Ahab thus acted. It may have been a flash of honesty in him; or mere prudential policy which, under the circumstances, imperiously forbade the slightest symptom of open disaffection, however transient, in the important chief officer of his ship. However it was, his orders were executed; and the Burtons were hoisted.

Chapter 110

QUEEQUEG IN HIS COFFIN

Upon searching, it was found that the casks last struck into the hold were perfectly sound, and that the leak must be further off. So, it being calm weather, they broke out deeper and deeper, disturbing the slumbers of the huge ground-tier butts; and from that black midnight sending those gigantic moles into the daylight above. So deep did they go; and so ancient, and corroded, and weedy the aspect of the lowermost puncheons, that you almost looked next for some mouldy corner-stone cask containing coins of Captain Noah, with copies of the posted placards, vainly warning the infatuated old world from the flood. Tierce after tierce, too, of water, and bread, and beef, and shooks of staves, and iron bundles of hoops, were hoisted out, till at last the piled decks were hard to get about; and the hollow hull echoed under foot, as if you were treading over empty catacombs, and reeled and rolled in the sea like an air-freighted demijohn. Top-heavy was the ship as a dinnerless student with all Aristotle in his head. Well was it that the Typhoons did not visit them then.

Now, at this time it was that my poor pagan companion, and fast bosom-friend, Queequeg, was seized with a fever, which brought him nigh to his endless end.

Be it said, that in this vocation of whaling, sinecures are unknown; dignity and danger go hand in hand; till you get to be Captain, the higher you rise the harder you toil. So with poor Queequeg, who, as harpooneer, must not only face all the rage of the living whale, but—as we have elsewhere seen—mount his dead back in a rolling sea; and finally descend into the gloom of the hold, and bitterly sweating all day in that subterraneous confinement, resolutely manhandle the clumsiest casks and see to their stowage. To be short, among whalemen, the harpooneers are the holders, so called.

Poor Queequeg! when the ship was about half disembowelled, you should have stooped over the hatchway, and peered down upon him there; where, stripped to his woollen drawers, the tattooed savage was crawling about amid that dampness and slime, like a green spotted lizard at the bottom of a well. And a well, or an ice-house, it somehow proved to him, poor pagan; where, strange to say, for all the heat of his sweatings, he caught a terrible chill which lapsed into a fever; and at last, after some days' suffering, laid him in his hammock, close to the very sill of the door of death. How he wasted and wasted away in those few long-lingering days, till there seemed but little left of him but his frame and tattooing. But as all else in him thinned, and his cheekbones grew sharper, his eyes, nevertheless, seemed growing fuller and fuller; they became of a strange softness of lustre; and mildly but deeply looked out at you there from his sickness, a wondrous testimony to that immortal health in him which could not die, or be weakened. And like circles on the water, which, as they grow fainter, expand; so his eyes seemed rounding and rounding, like the rings of Eternity. An awe that cannot be named would steal over you as you sat by the side of this waning savage, and saw as strange things in his face, as any beheld who were by-standers when Zoroaster died. For whatever is truly wondrous and fearful in man, never yet was put into words or books. And the drawing near of Death, which alike levels all, alike impresses all with a last revelation, which only an author from the dead could adequately tell. So that—let us say it again—no dying Chaldee or Greek had higher and holier thoughts than those, whose mys-terious shades you saw creeping over the face of poor Queequeg, as he quietly lay in his swaying hammock, and the rolling sea seemed gently rocking him to his final rest, and the ocean's in-visible flood-tide lifted him higher and higher towards his destined heaven.

Not a man of the crew but gave him up; and, as for Queequeg himself, what he thought of his case was forcibly shown by a curious favor he asked. He called one to him in the grey morning watch, when the day was just breaking, and taking his hand, said that while in Nantucket he had chanced to see certain little canoes of dark wood, like the rich war-wood of his native isle; and upon inquiry, he had learned that all whalemen who died in Nantucket, were laid in those same dark canoes, and that the fancy of being so laid had much pleased him; for it was not unlike the custom of his own race, who, after embalming a dead warrior, stretched him out in his canoe, and so left him to be floated away to the starry archipelagoes; for not only do they believe that the stars are isles, but that far beyond all visible horizons, their own mild, uncontinented seas, interflow with the blue heavens; and so form the white breakers of the milky way—after saying this he added, that he shuddered at the thought of being buried in his hammock, according to the usual sea-custom, tossed like something vile to the death-devouring sharks. No: he desired a canoe like those of Nantucket, all the more congenial to him, being a whaleman, that like a whale-boat these coffin-canoes were without a keel; though that involved but uncertain steering, and much lee-way adown the dim ages.

Now, when this strange circumstance was made known aft, the carpenter was at once commanded to do Queequeg's bidding, whatever it might include. There was some heathenish, coffin-colored old lumber aboard, which, upon a long previous voyage, had been cut from the aboriginal groves of the Lackaday islands, and from these dark planks the coffin was recommended to be made. No sooner was the carpenter apprised of the order, than taking his rule, he forthwith with all the indifferent promptitude of his character, proceeded into the forecastle and took Quee-queg's measure with great accuracy, regularly chalking Queequeg's person as he shifted the rule.

"Ah! poor fellow! he'll have to die now," ejaculated the Long Island sailor.

Going to his vice-bench, the carpenter for convenience' sake and general reference, now transferringly measured on it the exact length the coffin was to be, and then made the transfer permanent by cutting two notches at its extremities. This done, he marshalled the planks and his tools, and to work.

When the last nail was driven, and the lid duly planed and fitted, he lightly shouldered the coffin and went forward with it, inquiring whether they were ready for it yet in that direction.

Overhearing the indignant but half-humorous cries with which the people on deck began to drive the coffin away, Queequeg, to every one's consternation, commanded that the thing should be instantly brought to him, nor was there any denying him; seeing that, of all mortals, some dying men are the most tyrannical; and certainly, since they will shortly trouble us so little for evermore, the poor fellows ought to be indulged.

Leaning over in his hammock, Queequeg long regarded the coffin with an attentive eye. He then called for his harpoon, had the wooden stock drawn from it, and then had the iron part placed in the coffin along with one of the paddles of his boat. All by his own request, also, biscuits were then ranged round the sides within: a flask of fresh water was placed at the head, and a small bag of woody earth scraped up in the hold at the foot; and a piece of sail-cloth being rolled up for a pillow, Queequeg now entreated to be lifted into his final bed, that he might make trial of its comforts, if any it had. He lay without moving a few minutes, then told one to go to his bag and bring out his little god, Yojo. Then crossing his arms on his breast with Yojo between, he called for the coffin lid (hatch he called it) to be placed over him. The head part turned over with a leather hinge, and there lay Queequeg in his coffin with little but his composed countenance in view. "Rarmai" (it will do; it is easy), he murmured at last, and signed to be replaced in his hammock.

But ere this was done, Pip, who had been slily hovering near by all this while, drew nigh to him where he lay, and with soft sobbings, took him by the hand; in the other, holding his tambourine.

"Poor rover! will ye never have done with all this weary roving? where go ye now? But if the currents carry ye to those sweet Antilles where the beaches are only beat with water-lilies, will ye do one little errand for me? Seek out one Pip, who's now been missing long: I think he's in those far Antilles. If ye find him, then comfort him; for he must be very sad; for look! he's left his tambourine behind;—I found it. Rig-a-dig, dig, dig! Now, Queequeg, die; and I'll beat ye your dying march."

"I have heard," murmured Starbuck, gazing down the scuttle, "that in violent fevers, men, all ignorance, have talked in ancient tongues; and that when the mystery is probed, it turns out always that in their wholly forgotten childhood those ancient tongues had been really spoken in their hearing by some lofty scholars. So, to my fond faith, poor Pip, in this strange sweetness of his lunacy, brings heavenly vouchers of all our heavenly homes. Where learned he that, but there?—Hark! he speaks again: but more wildly now."

"Form two and two! Let's make a General of him! Ho, where's his harpoon? Lay it across here.—Rig-a-dig, dig, dig! huzza! Oh for a game cock now to sit upon his head and crow! Queequeg dies game!—mind ye that; Queequeg dies game!—take ye good heed of that; Queequeg dies game! I say; game, game, game! but base little Pip, he died a coward; died all a'shiver;—out upon Pip! Hark ye; if ye find Pip, tell all the Antilles he's a runaway; a coward, a coward, a coward! Tell them he jumped from a whale-boat! I'd never beat my tambourine over base Pip, and hail him General, if he were once more dying here. No, no! shame upon all cowards—shame upon them! Let 'em go drown like Pip, that jumped from a whale-boat. Shame! shame!"

During all this, Queequeg lay with closed eyes, as if in a dream. Pip was led away, and the sick man was replaced in his hammock.

But now that he had apparently made every preparation for death; now that his coffin was proved a good fit, Queequeg suddenly rallied; soon there seemed no need of the carpenter's box: and thereupon, when some expressed their delighted surprise, he, in substance, said, that the cause of his sudden convalescence was this;—at a critical moment, he had just recalled a little duty ashore, which he was leaving undone; and therefore had changed his mind about dying: he could not die yet, he averred. They asked him, then, whether to live or die was a matter of his own sovereign will and pleasure. He answered, certainly. In a word, it was Queequeg's conceit, that if a man made up his mind to live, mere sickness could not kill him: nothing but a whale, or a gale, or some violent, ungovernable, unintelligent destroyer of that sort.

Now, there is this noteworthy difference between savage and civilized; that while a sick, civilized man may be six months convalescing, generally speaking, a sick savage is almost half-well again in a day. So, in good time my Queequeg gained strength; and at length after sitting on the windlass for a few indolent days (but eating with a vigorous appetite) he suddenly leaped to his feet, threw out arms and legs, gave himself a good stretching, yawned a little bit, and then springing into the head of his hoisted boat, and poising a harpoon, pronounced himself fit for a fight.

With a wild whimsiness, he now used his coffin for a sea-chest; and emptying into it his canvas bag of clothes, set them in order there. Many spare hours he spent, in carving the lid with all manner of grotesque figures and drawings; and it seemed that hereby he was striving, in his rude way, to copy parts of the twisted tattooing on his body. And this tattooing, had been the work of a departed prophet and seer of his island, who, by those hieroglyphic marks, had written out on his body a complete theory of the heavens and the earth, and a mystical treatise on the art of attaining truth; so that Queequeg in his own proper person was a riddle to unfold; a wondrous work in one volume; but whose mysteries not even himself could read, though his own live heart beat against them; and these mysteries were therefore destined in the end to moulder away with the living parchment whereon they were inscribed, and so be unsolved to the last. And this thought it must have been which suggested to Ahab that wild ex-clamation of his, when one morning turning away from surveying poor Queequeg—"Oh, devilish tantalization of the gods!"

Chapter 111

THE PACIFIC

When gliding by the Bashee isles we emerged at last upon the great South Sea; were it not for other things, I could have greeted my dear Pacific with uncounted thanks, for now the long sup-plication of my youth was answered; that serene ocean rolled eastwards from me a thousand leagues of blue.

There is, one knows not what sweet mystery about this sea, whose gently awful stirrings seem to speak of some hidden soul beneath; like those fabled undulations of the Ephesian sod over the buried Evangelist St. John. And meet it is, that over these sea-pastures, wide-rolling watery prairies and Potters' Fields of all four continents, the waves should rise and fall, and ebb and flow unceasingly; for here, millions of mixed shades and shadows, drowned dreams, somnambulisms, reveries; all that we call lives and souls, lie dreaming, dreaming, still; tossing like slumberers in their beds; the ever-rolling waves but made so by their rest-lessness.

To any meditative Magian rover, this serene Pacific, once be-held, must ever after be the sea of his adoption. It rolls the mid-most waters of the world, the Indian ocean and Atlantic being but its arms. The same waves wash the moles of the new-built Californian towns, but yesterday planted by the recentest race of men, and lave the faded but still gorgeous skirts of Asiatic lands, older than Abraham; while all between float milky-ways of coral isles, and low-lying, endless, unknown Archipelagoes, and impenetrable Japans. Thus this mysterious, divine Pacific zones the world's whole bulk about; makes all coasts one bay to it; seems the tide-beating heart of earth. Lifted by those eternal swells, you needs must own the seductive god, bowing your head to Pan.

But few thoughts of Pan stirred Ahab's brain, as standing like an iron statue at his accustomed place beside the mizen rigging, with one nostril he unthinkingly snuffed the sugary musk from the Bashee isles (in whose sweet woods mild lovers must be walking), and with the other consciously inhaled the salt breath of the new found sea; that sea in which the hated White Whale must even then be swimming. Launched at length upon these almost final waters, and gliding towards the Japanese cruising-ground, the old man's purpose intensified itself. His firm lips met like the lips of a vice; the Delta of his forehead's veins swelled like overladen brooks; in his very sleep, his ringing cry ran through the vaulted hull, "Stern all! the White Whale spouts thick blood!"

Chapter 112

THE BLACKSMITH

Availing himself of the mild, summer-cool weather that now reigned in these latitudes, and in preparation for the peculiarly active pursuits shortly to be anticipated, Perth, the begrimed, blistered old blacksmith, had not removed his portable forge to the hold again, after concluding his contributory work for Ahab's leg, but still retained it on deck, fast lashed to ringbolts by the foremast; being now almost incessantly invoked by the headsmen, and harpooneers, and bowsmen to do some little job for them; altering, or repairing, or new shaping their various weapons and boat furniture. Often he would be surrounded by an eager circle, all waiting to be served; holding boat-spades, pike-heads, harpoons, and lances, and jealously watching his every sooty movement, as he toiled. Nevertheless, this old man's was a patient hammer wielded by a patient arm. No murmur, no impatience, no petulance did come from him. Silent, slow, and solemn; bowing over still further his chronically broken back, he toiled away, as if toil were life itself, and the heavy beating of his hammer the heavy beating of his heart. And so it was.—Most miserable!

A peculiar walk in this old man, a certain slight but painful appearing yawing in his gait, had at an early period of the voyage excited the curiosity of the mariners. And to the importunity of their persisted questionings he had finally given in; and so it came to pass that every one now knew the shameful story of his wretched fate.

Belated, and not innocently, one bitter winter's midnight, on the road running between two country towns, the blacksmith half-stupidly felt the deadly numbness stealing over him, and sought refuge in a leaning, dilapidated barn. The issue was, the loss of the extremities of both feet. Out of this revelation, part by part, at last came out the four acts of the gladness, and the one long, and as yet uncatastrophied fifth act of the grief of his life's drama.

He was an old man, who, at the age of nearly sixty, had postponedly encountered that thing in sorrow's technicals called ruin. He had been an artisan of famed excellence, and with plenty to do; owned a house and garden; embraced a youthful, daughter-like, loving wife, and three blithe, ruddy children; every Sunday went to a cheerful-looking church, planted in a grove. But one night, under cover of darkness, and further concealed in a most cunning disguisement, a desperate burglar slid into his happy home, and robbed them all of everything. And darker yet to tell, the blacksmith himself did ignorantly conduct this burglar into his family's heart. It was the Bottle Conjuror! Upon the opening of that fatal cork, forth flew the fiend, and shrivelled up his home. Now, for prudent, most wise, and economic reasons, the blacksmith's shop was in the basement of his dwelling, but with a separate entrance to it; so that always had the young and loving healthy wife listened with no unhappy nervousness, but with vigorous pleasure, to the stout ringing of her young-armed old husband's hammer; whose reverberations, muffled by passing through the floors and walls, came up to her, not unsweetly, in her nursery; and so, to stout Labor's iron lullaby, the blacksmith's infants were rocked to slumber.

Oh, woe on woe! Oh, Death, why canst thou not sometimes be timely? Hadst thou taken this old blacksmith to thyself ere his full ruin came upon him, then had the young widow had a delicious grief, and her orphans a truly venerable, legendary sire to dream of in their after years; and all of them a care-killing competency. But Death plucked down some virtuous elder brother, on whose whistling daily toil solely hung the responsibilities of some other family, and left the worse than useless old man standing, till the hideous rot of life should make him easier to harvest.

Why tell the whole? The blows of the basement hammer every day grew more and more between; and each blow every day grew fainter than the last; the wife sat frozen at the window, with tearless eyes, glitteringly gazing into the weeping faces of her children;

the bellows fell; the forge choked up with cinders; the house was sold; the mother dived down into the long church-yard grass; her children twice followed her thither; and the houseless, familyless old man staggered off a vagabond in crape; his every woe un-reverenced; his grey head a scorn to flaxen curls!

Death seems the only desirable sequel for a career like this; but Death is only a launching into the region of the strange Untried; it is but the first salutation to the possibilities of the immense Re-mote, the Wild, the Watery, the Unshored; therefore, to the death-longing eyes of such men, who still have left in them some interior compunctions against suicide, does the all-contributed and all-receptive ocean alluringly spread forth his whole plain of un-imaginable, taking terrors, and wonderful, new-life adventures; and from the hearts of infinite Pacifics, the thousand mermaids sing to them—"Come hither, broken-hearted; here is another life without the guilt of intermediate death; here are wonders super-natural, without dying for them. Come hither! bury thyself in a life which, to your now equally abhorred and abhorring, landed world, is more oblivious than death. Come hither! put up *thy* grave-stone, too, within the churchyard, and come hither, till we marry thee!"

Hearkening to these voices, East and West, by early sun-rise, and by fall of eve, the blacksmith's soul responded, Aye, I come! And so Perth went a-whaling.

Chapter 113

THE FORGE

With matted beard, and swathed in a bristling shark-skin apron, about mid-day, Perth was standing between his forge and anvil, the latter placed upon an iron-wood log, with one hand holding a pike-head in the coals, and with the other at his forge's lungs, when Captain Ahab came along, carrying in his hand a small rusty-looking leathern bag. While yet a little distance from the forge, moody Ahab paused; till at last, Perth, withdrawing his iron from the fire, began hammering it upon the anvil—the red mass sending off the sparks in thick hovering flights, some of which flew close to Ahab.

"Are these thy Mother Carey's chickens, Perth? they are al-ways flying in thy wake; birds of good omen, too, but not to all; —look here, they burn; but thou—thou liv'st among them without a scorch."

"Because I am scorched all over, Captain Ahab," answered Perth, resting for a moment on his hammer; "I am past scorching;

not easily can'st thou scorch a scar."

"Well, well; no more. Thy shrunk voice sounds too calmly, sanely woful to me. In no Paradise myself, I am impatient of all misery in others that is not mad. Thou should'st go mad, blacksmith; say, why dost thou not go mad? How can'st thou endure without being mad? Do the heavens yet hate thee, that thou can'st not go mad?—What wert thou making there?"

"Welding an old pike-head, sir; there were seams and dents in it."

"And can'st thou make it all smooth again, blacksmith, after such hard usage as it had?"

"I think so, sir."

"And I suppose thou can'st smooth almost any seams and dents; never mind how hard the metal, blacksmith?"

"Aye, sir, I think I can; all seams and dents but one."

"Look ye here, then," cried Ahab, passionately advancing, and leaning with both hands on Perth's shoulders; "look ye here— *here*—can ye smooth out a seam like this, blacksmith," sweeping one hand across his ribbed brow; "if thou could'st, blacksmith, glad enough would I lay my head upon thy anvil, and feel thy heaviest hammer between my eyes. Answer! Can'st thou smooth this seam?"

"Oh! that is the one, sir! Said I not all seams and dents but one?"

"Aye, blacksmith, it is the one; aye, man, it is unsmoothable; for though thou only see'st it here in my flesh, it has worked down into the bone of my skull—*that* is all wrinkles! But, away with child's play; no more gaffs and pikes to-day. Look ye here!" jingling the leathern bag, as if it were full of gold coins. "I, too, want a harpoon made; one that a thousand yoke of fiends could not part, Perth; something that will stick in a whale like his own fin-bone. There's the stuff," flinging the pouch upon the anvil. "Look ye, blacksmith, these are the gathered nail-stubs of the steel shoes of racing horses."

"Horse-shoe stubs, sir? Why, Captain Ahab, thou hast here, then, the best and stubbornest stuff we blacksmiths ever work."

"I know it, old man; these stubs will weld together like glue from the melted bones of murderers. Quick! forge me the harpoon. And forge me first, twelve rods for its shank; then wind, and twist, and hammer these twelve together like the yarns and strands of a tow-line. Quick! I'll blow the fire."

When at last the twelve rods were made, Ahab tried them, one by one, by spiralling them, with his own hand, round a long, heavy iron bolt. "A flaw!" rejecting the last one. "Work that over again, Perth."

This done, Perth was about to begin welding the twelve into one, when Ahab stayed his hand, and said he would weld his own iron. As, then, with regular, gasping hems, he hammered on the anvil, Perth passing to him the glowing rods, one after the other, and the hard pressed forge shooting up its intense straight flame, the Parsee passed silently, and bowing over his head towards the fire, seemed invoking some curse or some blessing on the toil. But, as Ahab looked up, he slid aside.

"What's that bunch of lucifers dodging about there for?" muttered Stubb, looking on from the forecastle. "That Parsee smells fire like a fusee; and smells of it himself, like a hot musket's powder-pan."

At last the shank, in one complete rod, received its final heat; and as Perth, to temper it, plunged it all hissing into the cask of water near by, the scalding steam shot up into Ahab's bent face.

"Would'st thou brand me, Perth?" wincing for a moment with the pain; "have I been but forging my own branding-iron, then?"

"Pray God, not that; yet I fear something, Captain Ahab. Is not this harpoon for the White Whale?"

"For the white fiend! But now for the barbs; thou must make them thyself, man. Here are my razors—the best of steel; here, and make the barbs sharp as the needle-sleet of the Icy Sea."

For a moment, the old blacksmith eyed the razors as though he would fain not use them.

"Take them, man, I have no need for them; for I now neither shave, sup, nor pray till——but here—to work!"

Fashioned at last into an arrowy shape, and welded by Perth to the shank, the steel soon pointed the end of the iron; and as the blacksmith was about giving the barbs their final heat, prior to tempering them, he cried to Ahab to place the water-cask near.

"No, no—no water for that; I want it of the true death-temper. Ahoy, there! Tashtego, Queequeg, Daggoo! What say ye, pagans! Will ye give me as much blood as will cover this barb?" holding it high up. A cluster of dark nods replied, Yes. Three punctures were made in the heathen flesh, and the White Whale's barbs were then tempered.

"Ego non baptizo te in nomine patris, sed in nomine diaboli!" [1] deliriously howled Ahab, as the malignant iron scorchingly devoured the baptismal blood.

Now, mustering the spare poles from below, and selecting one of hickory, with the bark still investing it, Ahab fitted the end to the socket of the iron. A coil of new tow-line was then unwound, and some fathoms of it taken to the windlass, and stretched to a

1. ". . . *sed in nomine diaboli!*" "I do   father, but in the name of the devil."
not baptize you in the name of the

great tension. Pressing his foot upon it, till the rope hummed like a harp-string, then eagerly bending over it, and seeing no strandings, Ahab exclaimed, "Good! and now for the seizings."

At one extremity the rope was unstranded, and the separate spread yarns were all braided and woven round the socket of the harpoon; the pole was then driven hard up into the socket; from the lower end the rope was traced half way along the pole's length, and firmly secured so, with intertwistings of twine. This done, pole, iron, and rope—like the Three Fates—remained inseparable, and Ahab moodily stalked away with the weapon; the sound of his ivory leg, and the sound of the hickory pole, both hollowly ringing along every plank. But ere he entered his cabin, a light, unnatural, half-bantering, yet most piteous sound was heard. Oh, Pip! thy wretched laugh, thy idle but unresting eye; all thy strange mummeries not unmeaningly blended with the black tragedy of the melancholy ship, and mocked it!

Chapter 114

THE GILDER

Penetrating further and further into the heart of the Japanese cruising ground, the Pequod was soon all astir in the fishery. Often, in mild, pleasant weather, for twelve, fifteen, eighteen, and twenty hours on the stretch, they were engaged in the boats, steadily pulling, or sailing, or paddling after the whales, or for an interlude of sixty or seventy minutes calmly awaiting their uprising; though with but small success for their pains.

At such times, under an abated sun; afloat all day upon smooth, slow heaving swells; seated in his boat, light as a birch canoe; and so sociably mixing with the soft waves themselves, that like hearth-stone cats they purr against the gunwale; these are the times of dreamy quietude, when beholding the tranquil beauty and brilliancy of the ocean's skin, one forgets the tiger heart that pants beneath it; and would not willingly remember, that this velvet paw but conceals a remorseless fang.

These are the times, when in his whale-boat the rover softly feels a certain filial, confident, land-like feeling towards the sea; that he regards it as so much flowery earth; and the distant ship revealing only the tops of her masts, seems struggling forward, not through high rolling waves, but through the tall grass of a rolling prairie: as when the western emigrants' horses only show their erected ears, while their hidden bodies widely wade through the amazing verdure.

The long-drawn virgin vales; the mild blue hill-sides; as over these there steals the hush, the hum; you almost swear that play-wearied children lie sleeping in these solitudes, in some glad May-time, when the flowers of the woods are plucked. And all this mixes with your most mystic mood; so that fact and fancy, half-way meeting, interpenetrate, and form one seamless whole.

Nor did such soothing scenes, however temporary, fail of at least as temporary an effect on Ahab. But if these secret golden keys did seem to open in him his own secret golden treasuries, yet did his breath upon them prove but tarnishing.

Oh, grassy glades! oh, ever vernal endless landscapes in the soul; in ye,—though long parched by the dead drought of the earthy life,—in ye, men yet may roll, like young horses in new morning clover; and for some few fleeting moments, feel the cool dew of the life immortal on them. Would to God these blessed calms would last. But the mingled, mingling threads of life are woven by warp and woof: calms crossed by storms, a storm for every calm. There is no steady unretracing progress in this life; we do not advance through fixed gradations, and at the last one pause:—through infancy's unconscious spell, boyhood's thoughtless faith, adolescence' doubt (the common doom), then scepticism, then disbelief, resting at last in manhood's pondering repose of If. But once gone through, we trace the round again; and are infants, boys, and men, and Ifs eternally. Where lies the final harbor, whence we unmoor no more? In what rapt ether sails the world, of which the weariest will never weary? Where is the foundling's father hidden? Our souls are like those orphans whose unwedded mothers die in bearing them: the secret of our paternity lies in their grave, and we must there to learn it.

And that same day, too, gazing far down from his boat's side into that same golden sea, Starbuck lowly murmured:—

"Loveliness unfathomable, as ever lover saw in his young bride's eye!—Tell me not of thy teeth-tiered sharks, and thy kidnapping cannibal ways. Let faith oust fact; let fancy oust memory; I look deep down and do believe."

And Stubb, fish-like, with sparkling scales, leaped up in that same golden light:—

"I am Stubb, and Stubb has his history; but here Stubb takes oaths that he has always been jolly!"

Chapter 115

THE PEQUOD MEETS THE BACHELOR

And jolly enough were the sights and the sounds that came bearing down before the wind, some few weeks after Ahab's harpoon had been welded.

It was a Nantucket ship, the Bachelor, which had just wedged in her last cask of oil, and bolted down her bursting hatches; and now, in glad holiday apparel, was joyously, though somewhat vain-gloriously, sailing round among the widely-separated ships on the ground, previous to pointing her prow for home.

The three men at her mast-heads wore long streamers of narrow red bunting at their hats; from the stern, a whale-boat was suspended, bottom down; and hanging captive from the bowsprit was seen the long lower jaw of the last whale they had slain. Signals, ensigns, and jacks of all colors were flying from her rigging, on every side. Sideways lashed in each of her three basketed tops were two barrels of sperm; above which, in her top-mast cross-trees, you saw slender breakers of the same precious fluid; and nailed to her main truck was a brazen lamp.

As was afterwards learned, the Bachelor had met with the most surprising success; all the more wonderful, for that while cruising in the same seas numerous other vessels had gone entire months without securing a single fish. Not only had barrels of beef and bread been given away to make room for the far more valuable sperm, but additional supplemental casks had been bartered for, from the ships she had met; and these were stowed along the deck, and in the captain's and officers' state-rooms. Even the cabin table itself had been knocked into kindling-wood; and the cabin mess dined off the broad head of an oil-butt, lashed down to the floor for a centrepiece. In the forecastle, the sailors had actually caulked and pitched their chests, and filled them; it was humorously added, that the cook had clapped a head on his largest boiler, and filled it; that the steward had plugged his spare coffee-pot and filled it; that the harpooneers had headed the sockets of their irons and filled them; that indeed everything was filled with sperm, except the captain's pantaloons pockets, and those he reserved to thrust his hands into, in self-complacent testimony of his entire satisfaction.

As this glad ship of good luck bore down upon the moody Pequod, the barbarian sound of enormous drums came from her forecastle; and drawing still nearer, a crowd of her men were seen standing round her huge try-pots, which, covered with the parchment-like *poke* or stomach skin of the black fish, gave forth a loud roar to every stroke of the clenched hands of the crew. On the quarter-deck, the mates and harpooneers were dancing with the olive-hued girls who had eloped with them from the Polynesian Isles; while suspended in an ornamented boat, firmly secured aloft between the foremast and mainmast, three Long Island negroes, with glittering fiddle-bows of whale ivory, were presiding over the hilarious jig. Meanwhile, others of the ship's company were tumultuously busy at the masonry of the try-works, from which the huge pots had been removed. You would have almost thought they were pulling down the cursed Bastille, such wild cries they raised, as the now useless brick and mortar were being hurled into the sea.

Lord and master over all this scene, the captain stood erect on the ship's elevated quarter-deck, so that the whole rejoicing drama was full before him, and seemed merely contrived for his own individual diversion.

And Ahab, he too was standing on his quarter-deck, shaggy and black, with a stubborn gloom; and as the two ships crossed each other's wakes—one all jubilations for things passed, the other all forebodings as to things to come—their two captains in themselves impersonated the whole striking contrast of the scene.

"Come aboard, come aboard!" cried the gay Bachelor's commander, lifting a glass and a bottle in the air.

"Hast seen the White Whale?" gritted Ahab in reply.

"No; only heard of him; but don't believe in him at all," said the other good-humoredly. "Come aboard!"

"Thou art too damned jolly. Sail on. Hast lost any men?"

"Not enough to speak of—two islanders, that's all;—but come aboard, old hearty, come along. I'll soon take that black from your brow. Come along, will ye (merry's the play); a full ship and homeward-bound."

"How wondrous familiar is a fool!" muttered Ahab; then aloud, "Thou art a full ship and homeward bound, thou sayst; well, then, call me an empty ship, and outward-bound. So go thy ways, and I will mine. Forward there! Set all sail, and keep her to the wind!"

And thus, while the one ship went cheerily before the breeze, the other stubbornly fought against it; and so the two vessels parted; the crew of the Pequod looking with grave, lingering glances towards the receding Bachelor; but the Bachelor's men never heeding their gaze for the lively revelry they were in. And as Ahab, leaning over the taffrail, eyed the homeward-bound craft, he took from his pocket a small vial of sand, and then looking from the ship to the vial, seemed thereby bringing two remote associations together, for that vial was filled with Nantucket soundings.

Chapter 116

THE DYING WHALE

Not seldom in this life, when, on the right side, fortune's favorites sail close by us, we, though all adroop before, catch somewhat of the rushing breeze, and joyfully feel our bagging sails fill out. So seemed it with the Pequod. For next day after encountering the gay Bachelor, whales were seen and four were slain; and one of them by Ahab.

It was far down the afternoon; and when all the spearings of the crimson fight were done: and floating in the lovely sunset sea and sky, sun and whale both stilly died together; then, such a sweetness and such plaintiveness, such inwreathing orisons curled up in that rosy air, that it almost seemed as if far over from the deep green convent valleys of the Manilla isles, the Spanish land-breeze, wantonly turned sailor, had gone to sea, freighted with these vesper hymns.

Soothed again, but only soothed to deeper gloom, Ahab, who had sterned off from the whale, sat intently watching his final wanings from the now tranquil boat. For that strange spectacle observable in all sperm whales dying—the turning sunwards of the head, and so expiring—that strange spectacle, beheld of such a placid evening, somehow to Ahab conveyed a wondrousness unknown before.

"He turns and turns him to it,—how slowly, but how steadfastly, his homage-rendering and invoking brow, with his last dying motions. He too worships fire; most faithful, broad, baronial vassal of the sun!—Oh that these too-favoring eyes should see these too-favoring sights. Look! here, far water-locked; beyond all hum of human weal or woe; in these most candid and impartial seas; where to traditions no rocks furnish tablets; where for long Chinese ages, the billows have still rolled on speechless and unspoken to, as stars that shine upon the Niger's unknown source; here, too, life dies sunwards full of faith; but see! no sooner dead, than death whirls round the corpse, and it heads some other way.—

"Oh, thou dark Hindoo half of nature, who of drowned bones hast builded thy separate throne somewhere in the heart of these unverdured seas; thou art an infidel, thou queen, and too truly speakest to me in the wide-slaughtering Typhoon, and the hushed burial of its after calm. Nor has this thy whale sunwards turned his dying head, and then gone round again, without a lesson to me.

"Oh, trebly hooped and welded hip of power! Oh, high aspiring, rainbowed jet!—that one striveth, this one jetteth all in vain! In vain, oh whale, dost thou seek intercedings with yon all-quickening sun, that only calls forth life, but gives it not again. Yet dost thou, darker half, rock me with a prouder, if a darker faith. All thy unnamable imminglings float beneath me here; I am buoyed by breaths of once living things, exhaled as air, but water now.

"Then hail, for ever hail, O sea, in whose eternal tossings the wild fowl finds his only rest. Born of earth, yet suckled by the sea; though hill and valley mothered me, ye billows are my foster-brothers!"

Chapter 117

THE WHALE WATCH

The four whales slain that evening had died wide apart; one, far to windward; one, less distant, to leeward; one ahead; one astern. These last three were brought alongside ere nightfall; but the windward one could not be reached till morning; and the boat that had killed it lay by its side all night; and that boat was Ahab's.

The waif-pole was thrust upright into the dead whale's spout-hole; and the lantern hanging from its top, cast a troubled flickering glare upon the black, glossy back, and far out upon the midnight waves, which gently chafed the whale's broad flank, like soft surf upon a beach.

Ahab and all his boat's crew seemed asleep but the Parsee; who crouching in the bow, sat watching the sharks, that spectrally played round the whale, and tapped the light cedar planks with their tails. A sound like the moaning in squadrons over Asphaltites of unforgiven ghosts of Gomorrah, ran shuddering through the air.

Started from his slumbers, Ahab, face to face, saw the Parsee; and hooped round by the gloom of the night they seemed the last men in a flooded world. "I have dreamed it again," said he.

"Of the hearses? Have I not said, old man, that neither hearse nor coffin can be thine?"

"And who are hearsed that die on the sea?"

"But I said, old man, that ere thou couldst die on this voyage, two hearses must verily be seen by thee on the sea; the first not made by mortal hands; and the visible wood of the last one must be grown in America."

"Aye, aye! a strange sight that, Parsee:—a hearse and its plumes floating over the ocean with the waves for the pall-bearers. Ha! Such a sight we shall not soon see."

"Believe it or not, thou canst not die till it be seen, old man."

"And what was that saying about thyself?"

"Though it come to the last, I shall still go before thee thy pilot."

"And when thou art so gone before—if that ever befall—then ere I can follow, thou must still appear to me, to pilot me still?— Was it not so? Well, then, did I believe all ye say, oh my pilot! I have here two pledges that I shall yet slay Moby Dick and survive it."

"Take another pledge, old man," said the Parsee, as his eyes lighted up like fire-flies in the gloom—"Hemp only can kill thee."

"The gallows, ye mean.—I am immortal then, on land and on sea," cried Ahab, with a laugh of derision;—"Immortal on land and on sea!"

Both were silent again, as one man. The grey dawn came on, and the slumbering crew arose from the boat's bottom, and ere noon the dead whale was brought to the ship.

Chapter 118

THE QUADRANT

The season for the Line at length drew near; and every day when Ahab, coming from his cabin, cast his eyes aloft, the vigilant helmsman would ostentatiously handle his spokes, and the eager mariners quickly run to the braces, and would stand there with all their eyes centrally fixed on the nailed doubloon; impatient for the order to point the ship's prow for the equator. In good time the order came. It was hard upon high noon; and Ahab, seated in the bows of his high-hoisted boat, was about taking his wonted daily observation of the sun to determine his latitude.

Now, sometimes, in that Japanese sea, the days in summer are as freshets of effulgences. That unblinkingly vivid Japanese sun seems the blazing focus of the glassy ocean's immeasurable burning-glass. The sky looks lacquered; clouds there are none; the horizon floats; and this nakedness of unrelieved radiance is as the insufferable splendors of God's throne. Well that Ahab's quadrant was furnished with colored glasses, through which to take sight of that solar fire. So, swinging his seated form to the roll of the ship, and with his astrological-looking instrument placed to his eye, he remained in that posture for some moments to catch the precise instant when the sun should gain its precise meridian. Meantime while his whole attention was absorbed, the Parsee was kneeling beneath him on the ship's deck, and with face thrown up like Ahab's, was eyeing the same sun with him; only the lids of his eyes half hooded their orbs, and his wild face was subdued to an unearthly passionlessness. At length the desired observation was taken; and with his pencil upon his ivory leg, Ahab soon calculated what his latitude must be at that precise instant. Then falling into a moment's revery, he again looked up towards the sun and murmured to himself: "Thou sea-mark! thou high and mighty Pilot! thou tellest me truly where I *am*—but canst thou cast the least hint where I *shall* be? Or canst thou tell where some other thing besides me is this moment living? Where is Moby Dick?

This instant thou must be eyeing him. These eyes of mine look into the very eye that is even now beholding him; aye, and into the eye that is even now equally beholding the objects on the unknown, thither side of thee, thou sun!"

Then gazing at his quadrant, and handling, one after the other, its numerous cabalistical contrivances, he pondered again, and muttered: "Foolish toy! babies' plaything of haughty Admirals, and Commodores, and Captains; the world brags of thee, of thy cunning and might; but what after all canst thou do, but tell the poor, pitiful point, where thou thyself happenest to be on this wide planet, and the hand that holds thee: no! not one jot more! Thou canst not tell where one drop of water or one grain of sand will be to-morrow noon; and yet with thy impotence thou insultest the sun! Science! Curse thee, thou vain toy; and cursed be all the things that cast man's eyes aloft to that heaven, whose live vividness but scorches him, as these old eyes are even now scorched with thy light, O sun! Level by nature to this earth's horizon are the glances of man's eyes; not shot from the crown of his head, as if God had meant him to gaze on his firmament. Curse thee, thou quadrant!" dashing it to the deck, "no longer will I guide my earthly way by thee; the level ship's compass, and the level dead-reckoning, by log and by line; *these* shall conduct me, and show me my place on the sea. Aye," lighting from the boat to the deck, "thus I trample on thee, thou paltry thing that feebly pointest on high; thus I split and destroy thee!"

As the frantic old man thus spoke and thus trampled with his live and dead feet, a sneering triumph that seemed meant for Ahab, and a fatalistic despair that seemed meant for himself —these passed over the mute, motionless Parsee's face. Unobserved he rose and glided away; while, awestruck by the aspect of their commander, the seamen clustered together on the forecastle, till Ahab, troubledly pacing the deck, shouted out—"To the braces! Up helm!—square in!"

In an instant the yards swung round; and as the ship half-wheeled upon her heel, her three firm-seated graceful masts erectly poised upon her long, ribbed hull, seemed as the three Horatii pirouetting on one sufficient steed.

Standing between the knight-heads, Starbuck watched the Pequod's tumultuous way, and Ahab's also, as he went lurching along the deck.

"I have sat before the dense coal fire and watched it all aglow, full of its tormented flaming life; and I have seen it wane at last, down, down, to dumbest dust. Old man of oceans! of all this fiery life of thine, what will at length remain but one little heap of ashes!"

"Aye," cried Stubb, "but sea-coal ashes—mind ye that, Mr. Starbuck—sea-coal, not your common charcoal. Well, well; I heard Ahab mutter, 'Here some one thrusts these cards into these old hands of mine; swears that I must play them, and no others.' And damn me, Ahab, but thou actest right; live in the game, and die in it!"

Chapter 119

THE CANDLES

Warmest climes but nurse the cruellest fangs: the tiger of Bengal crouches in spiced groves of ceaseless verdure. Skies the most effulgent but basket the deadliest thunders: gorgeous Cuba knows tornadoes that never swept tame northern lands. So, too, it is, that in these resplendent Japanese seas the mariner encounters the direst of all storms, the Typhoon. It will sometimes burst from out that cloudless sky, like an exploding bomb upon a dazed and sleepy town.

Towards evening of that day, the Pequod was torn of her canvas, and bare-poled was left to fight a Typhoon which had struck her directly ahead. When darkness came on, sky and sea roared and split with the thunder, and blazed with the lightning, that showed the disabled masts fluttering here and there with the rags which the first fury of the tempest had left for its after sport.

Holding by a shroud, Starbuck was standing on the quarter-deck; at every flash of the lightning glancing aloft, to see what additional disaster might have befallen the intricate hamper there; while Stubb and Flask were directing the men in the higher hoisting and firmer lashing of the boats. But all their pains seemed naught. Though lifted to the very top of the cranes, the windward quarter boat (Ahab's) did not escape. A great rolling sea, dashing high up against the reeling ship's high tetering side, stove in the boat's bottom at the stern, and left it again, all dripping through like a sieve.

"Bad work, bad work! Mr. Starbuck," said Stubb, regarding the wreck, "but the sea will have its way. Stubb, for one, can't fight it. You see, Mr. Starbuck, a wave has such a great long start before it leaps, all round the world it runs, and then comes the spring! But as for me, all the start I have to meet it, is just across the deck here. But never mind; it's all in fun: so the old song says;"—(*sings.*)

> Oh! jolly is the gale,
> And a joker is the whale,
> A' flourishin' his tail,—
> Such a funny, sporty, gamy, jesty, joky, hoky-poky lad,
> is the Ocean, oh!

> The scud all a flyin',
> That's his flip only foamin';
> When he stirs in the spicin',—
> Such a funny, sporty, gamy, jesty, joky, hoky-poky lad,
>   is the Ocean, oh!
>
> Thunder splits the ships,
> But he only smacks his lips,
> A tastin' of this flip,—
> Such a funny, sporty, gamy, jesty, joky, hoky-poky lad,
>   is the Ocean, oh!

"Avast Stubb," cried Starbuck, "let the Typhoon sing, and strike his harp here in our rigging; but if thou art a brave man thou wilt hold thy peace."

"But I am not a brave man; never said I was a brave man; I am a coward; and I sing to keep up my spirits. And I tell you what it is, Mr. Starbuck, there's no way to stop my singing in this world but to cut my throat. And when that's done, ten to one I sing ye the doxology for a wind-up."

"Madman! look through my eyes if thou hast none of thine own."

"What! how can you see better of a dark night than anybody else, never mind how foolish?"

"Here!" cried Starbuck, seizing Stubb by the shoulder, and pointing his hand towards the weather bow, "markest thou not that the gale comes from the eastward, the very course Ahab is to run for Moby Dick? the very course he swung to this day noon? now mark his boat there; where is that stove? In the stern-sheets, man; where he is wont to stand—his stand-point is stove, man! Now jump overboard, and sing away, if thou must!"

"I don't half understand ye: what's in the wind?"

"Yes, yes, round the Cape of Good Hope is the shortest way to Nantucket," soliloquized Starbuck suddenly, heedless of Stubb's question. "The gale that now hammers at us to stave us, we can turn it into a fair wind that will drive us towards home. Yonder, to windward, all is blackness of doom; but to leeward, homeward—I see it lightens up there; but not with the lightning."

At that moment in one of the intervals of profound darkness, following the flashes, a voice was heard at his side; and almost at the same instant a volley of thunder peals rolled overhead.

"Who's there?"

"Old Thunder!" said Ahab, groping his way along the bulwarks to his pivot-hole; but suddenly finding his path made plain to him by elbowed lances of fire.

Now, as the lightning rod to a spire on shore is intended to carry off the perilous fluid into the soil; so the kindred rod which at sea some ships carry to each mast, is intended to conduct it into the water. But as this conductor must descend to considerable depth, that its end may avoid all contact with the hull; and as moreover, if kept constantly towing there, it would be liable to many mishaps, besides interfering not a little with some of the rigging, and more or less impeding the vessel's way in the water; because of all this, the lower parts of a ship's lightning-rods are not always overboard; but are generally made in long slender links, so as to be the more readily hauled up into the chains outside, or thrown down into the sea, as occasion may require.

"The rods! the rods!" cried Starbuck to the crew, suddenly admonished to vigilance by the vivid lightning that had just been darting flambeaux, to light Ahab to his post. "Are they overboard? drop them over, fore and aft. Quick!"

"Avast!" cried Ahab; "let's have fair play here, though we be the weaker side. Yet I'll contribute to raise rods on the Himmalehs and Andes, that all the world may be secured; but out on privileges! Let them be, sir."

"Look aloft!" cried Starbuck. "The corpusants! the corpusants!"

All the yard-arms were tipped with a pallid fire; and touched at each tri-pointed lightning-rod-end with three tapering white flames, each of the three tall masts was silently burning in that sulphurous air, like three gigantic wax tapers before an altar.

"Blast the boat! let it go!" cried Stubb at this instant, as a swashing sea heaved up under his own little craft, so that its gunwale violently jammed his hand, as he was passing a lashing. "Blast it!"—but slipping backward on the deck, his uplifted eyes caught the flames; and immediately shifting his tone, he cried— "The corpusants have mercy on us all!"

To sailors, oaths are household words; they will swear in the trance of the calm, and in the teeth of the tempest; they will imprecate curses from the topsail-yard-arms, when most they teter over to a seething sea; but in all my voyagings, seldom have I heard a common oath when God's burning finger has been laid on the ship; when His "Mene, Mene, Tekel, Upharsin" [1] has been woven into the shrouds and the cordage.

While this pallidness was burning aloft, few words were heard from the enchanted crew; who in one thick cluster stood on the forecastle, all their eyes gleaming in that pale phosphorescence, like a far away constellation of stars. Relieved against the ghostly light, the gigantic jet negro, Daggoo, loomed up to thrice his real stature, and seemed the black cloud from which the thunder

---

1. Cryptic words written on the wall of Belshazzar's banquet hall by disembodied "fingers of a man's hand." Daniel interprets the words as God's judgment against Belshazzar. Daniel 5:5, 25–28.

had come. The parted mouth of Tashtego revealed his shark-white teeth, which strangely gleamed as if they too had been tipped by corpusants; while lit up by the preternatural light, Queequeg's tattooing burned like Satanic blue flames on his body.

The tableau all waned at last with the pallidness aloft; and once more the Pequod and every soul on her decks were wrapped in a pall. A moment or two passed, when Starbuck, going forward, pushed against some one. It was Stubb. "What thinkest thou now, man; I heard thy cry; it was not the same in the song."

"No, no, it wasn't; I said the corpusants have mercy on us all; and I hope they will, still. But do they only have mercy on long faces?—have they no bowels for a laugh? And look ye, Mr. Starbuck—but it's too dark to look. Hear me, then: I take that masthead flame we saw for a sign of good luck; for those masts are rooted in a hold that is going to be chock a' block with sperm-oil, d'ye see; and so, all that sperm will work up into the masts, like sap in a tree. Yes, our three masts will yet be as three spermaceti candles—that's the good promise we saw."

At that moment Starbuck caught sight of Stubb's face slowly beginning to glimmer into sight. Glancing upwards, he cried: "See! see!" and once more the high tapering flames were beheld with what seemed redoubled supernaturalness in their pallor.

"The corpusants have mercy on us all," cried Stubb, again.

At the base of the mainmast, full beneath the doubloon and the flame, the Parsee was kneeling in Ahab's front, but with his head bowed away from him; while near by, from the arched and overhanging rigging, where they had just been engaged securing a spar, a number of the seamen, arrested by the glare, now cohered together, and hung pendulous, like a knot of numbed wasps from a drooping, orchard twig. In various enchanted attitudes, like the standing, or stepping, or running skeletons in Herculaneum, others remained rooted to the deck; but all their eyes upcast.

"Aye, aye, men!" cried Ahab. "Look up at it; mark it well; the white flame but lights the way to the White Whale! Hand me those main-mast links there; I would fain feel this pulse, and let mine beat against it; blood against fire! So."

Then turning—the last link held fast in his left hand, he put his foot upon the Parsee; and with fixed upward eye, and high-flung right arm, he stood erect before the lofty tri-pointed trinity of flames.

"Oh! thou clear spirit of clear fire, whom on these seas I as Persian once did worship, till in the sacramental act so burned by thee, that to this hour I bear the scar; I now know thee, thou clear spirit, and I now know that thy right worship is defiance. To neither love nor reverence wilt thou be kind; and e'en for hate thou canst but kill; and all are killed. No fearless fool now fronts thee. I own thy speechless, placeless power; but to the last gasp of my earthquake life will dispute its unconditional, unintegral mastery in me. In the midst of the personified impersonal, a personality stands here. Though but a point at best; whencesoe'er I came; wheresoe'er I go; yet while I earthly live, the queenly personality lives in me, and feels her royal rights. But war is pain, and hate is woe. Come in thy lowest form of love, and I will kneel and kiss thee; but at thy highest, come as mere supernal power; and though thou launchest navies of full-freighted worlds, there's that in here that still remains indifferent. Oh, thou clear spirit, of thy fire thou madest me, and like a true child of fire, I breathe it back to thee."

[*Sudden, repeated flashes of lightning; the nine flames leap lengthwise to thrice their previous height; Ahab, with the rest, closes his eyes, his right hand pressed hard upon them.*]

"I own thy speechless, placeless power; said I not so? Nor was it wrung from me; nor do I now drop these links. Thou canst blind; but I can then grope. Thou canst consume; but I can then be ashes. Take the homage of these poor eyes, and shutter-hands. I would not take it. The lightning flashes through my skull; mine eye-balls ache and ache; my whole beaten brain seems as beheaded, and rolling on some stunning ground. Oh, oh! Yet blindfold, yet will I talk to thee. Light though thou be, thou leapest out of darkness; but I am darkness leaping out of light, leaping out of thee! The javelins cease; open eyes; see, or not? There burn the flames! Oh, thou magnanimous! now I do glory in my genealogy. But thou art but my fiery father; my sweet mother, I know not. Oh, cruel! what hast thou done with her? There lies my puzzle; but thine is greater. Thou knowest not how came ye, hence callest thyself unbegotten; certainly knowest not thy beginning, hence callest thyself unbegun. I know that of me, which thou knowest not of thyself, oh, thou omnipotent. There is some unsuffusing thing beyond thee, thou clear spirit, to whom all thy eternity is but time, all thy creativeness mechanical. Through thee, thy flaming self, my scorched eyes do dimly see it. Oh, thou foundling fire, thou hermit immemorial, thou too hast thy incommunicable riddle, thy unparticipated grief. Here again with haughty agony, I read my sire. Leap! leap up, and lick the sky! I leap with thee; I burn with thee; would fain be welded with thee; defyingly I worship thee!"

"The boat! the boat!" cried Starbuck, "look at thy boat, old man!"

Ahab's harpoon, the one forged at Perth's fire, remained firmly lashed in its conspicuous crotch, so that it projected beyond his whale-boat's bow; but the sea that had stove its bottom had caused the loose leather sheath to drop off; and from the keen steel barb there now came a levelled flame of pale, forked fire. As the silent harpoon burned there like a serpent's tongue, Starbuck grasped Ahab by the arm—"God, God is against thee, old man; forbear! 'tis an ill voyage! ill begun, ill continued; let me square the yards, while we may, old man, and make a fair wind of it homewards, to go on a better voyage than this."

Overhearing Starbuck, the panic-stricken crew instantly ran to the braces—though not a sail was left aloft. For the moment all the aghast mate's thoughts seemed theirs; they raised a half mutinous cry. But dashing the rattling lightning links to the deck, and snatching the burning harpoon, Ahab waved it like a torch among them; swearing to transfix with it the first sailor that but cast loose a rope's end. Petrified by his aspect, and still more shrinking from the fiery dart that he held, the men fell back in dismay, and Ahab again spoke:—

"All your oaths to hunt the White Whale are as binding as mine; and heart, soul, and body, lungs and life, old Ahab is bound. And that ye may know to what tune this heart beats; look ye here; thus I blow out the last fear!" And with one blast of his breath he extinguished the flame.

As in the hurricane that sweeps the plain, men fly the neighborhood of some lone, gigantic elm, whose very height and strength but render it so much the more unsafe, because so much the more a mark for thunderbolts; so at those last words of Ahab's many of the mariners did run from him in a terror of dismay.

Chapter 120

THE DECK TOWARDS THE END OF THE FIRST NIGHT WATCH

Ahab standing by the helm. Starbuck approaching him.

"We must send down the main-top-sail yard, sir. The band is working loose, and the lee lift is half-stranded. Shall I strike it, sir?"

"Strike nothing; lash it. If I had sky-sail poles, I'd sway them up now."

"Sir?—in God's name!—sir?"

"Well."

"The anchors are working, sir. Shall I get them inboard?"

"Strike nothing, and stir nothing, but lash everything. The wind rises, but it has not got up to my table-lands yet. Quick, and see to it.—By masts and keels! he takes me for the hunchbacked skipper of some coasting smack. Send down my main-top-sail yard! Ho, gluepots! Loftiest trucks were made for wildest winds, and this brain-truck of mine now sails amid the cloud-scud. Shall I strike that? Oh, none but cowards send down their brain-trucks in tempest time. What a hooroosh aloft there! I would e'en take it for sublime, did I not know that the colic is a noisy malady. Oh, take medicine, take medicine!"

Chapter 121

MIDNIGHT.—THE FORECASTLE BULWARKS

Stubb and Flask mounted on them, and passing additional lashings over the anchors there hanging.

"No, Stubb; you may pound that knot there as much as you please, but you will never pound into me what you were just now saying. And how long ago is it since you said the very contrary? Didn't you once say that whatever ship Ahab sails in, that ship should pay something extra on its insurance policy, just as though it were loaded with powder barrels aft and boxes of lucifers forward? Stop, now; didn't you say so?"

"Well, suppose I did? What then? I've part changed my flesh since that time, why not my mind? Besides, supposing we *are* loaded with powder barrels aft and lucifers forward; how the devil could the lucifers get afire in this drenching spray here? Why, my little man, you have pretty red hair, but you couldn't get afire now. Shake yourself; you're Aquarius, or the water-bearer, Flask; might fill pitchers at your coat collar. Don't you see, then, that for these extra risks the Marine Insurance companies have extra guarantees? Here are hydrants, Flask. But hark, again, and I'll answer ye the other thing. First take your leg off from the crown of the anchor here, though, so I can pass the rope; now listen. What's the mighty difference between holding a mast's lightning-rod in the storm, and standing close by a mast that hasn't got any lightning-rod at all in a storm? Don't you see, you timber-head, that no harm can come to the holder of the rod, unless the mast is first struck? What are you talking about, then? Not one ship in a hundred carries rods, and Ahab,—aye, man, and all of us,—were in no more danger then, in my poor opinion, than all the crews in ten thousand ships now sailing the seas. Why, you King-Post, you, I suppose you would have every man in the world go about with a small lightning-rod running up the corner of his hat, like a militia officer's skewered feather, and trailing behind like his sash. Why don't ye be sensible, Flask? it's easy to be sensible; why don't ye, then? any man with half an eye can be sensible."

"I don't know that, Stubb. You sometimes find it rather hard."

"Yes, when a fellow's soaked through, it's hard to be sensible, that's a fact. And I am about drenched with this spray. Never mind; catch the turn there, and pass it. Seems to me we are lashing down these anchors now as if they were never going to be used again. Tying these two anchors here, Flask, seems like tying a man's hands behind him. And what big generous hands they are, to be sure. These are your iron fists, hey? What a hold they have, too! I wonder, Flask, whether the world is anchored anywhere; if she is, she swings with an uncommon long cable, though. There, hammer that knot down, and we've done. So; next to touching land, lighting on deck is the most satisfactory. I say, just wring out my jacket skirts, will ye? Thank ye. They laugh at long-togs so, Flask; but seems to me, a long tailed coat ought always to be worn in all storms afloat. The tails tapering down that way, serve to carry off the water, d'ye see. Same with cocked hats; the cocks form gable-end eave-troughs, Flask. No more monkey-jackets and tarpaulins for me; I must mount a swallow-tail, and drive down a beaver; so. Halloa! whew! there goes my tarpaulin overboard; Lord, Lord, that the winds that come from heaven should be so unmannerly! This is a nasty night, lad."

Chapter 122

MIDNIGHT ALOFT.—THUNDER AND LIGHTNING

The Main-top-sail yard.—Tashtego passing new lashings around it.

"Um, um, um. Stop that thunder! Plenty too much thunder up here. What's the use of thunder? Um, um, um. We don't want thunder; we want rum; give us a glass of rum. Um, um, um!"

Chapter 123

THE MUSKET

During the most violent shocks of the Typhoon, the man at the Pequod's jaw-bone tiller had several times been reelingly hurled to the deck by its spasmodic motions, even though preventer tackles had been attached to it—for they were slack—because some play to the tiller was indispensable.

In a severe gale like this, while the ship is but a tossed shuttle-cock to the blast, it is by no means uncommon to see the needles in the compasses, at intervals, go round and round. It was thus with the Pequod's; at almost every shock the helmsman had not failed to notice the whirling velocity with which they revolved upon the cards; it is a sight that hardly any one can behold without some sort of unwonted emotion.

Some hours after midnight, the Typhoon abated so much, that through the strenuous exertions of Starbuck and Stubb—

one engaged forward and the other aft—the shivered remnants of
the jib and fore and main-top-sails were cut adrift from the spars,
and went eddying away to leeward, like the feathers of an albatross, which sometimes are cast to the winds when that storm-
tossed bird is on the wing.

The three corresponding new sails were now bent and reefed,
and a storm-trysail was set further aft; so that the ship soon
went through the water with some precision again; and the course
—for the present, East-south-east—which he was to steer, if
practicable, was once more given to the helmsman. For during the
violence of the gale, he had only steered according to its
vicissitudes. But as he was now bringing the ship as near her
course as possible, watching the compass meanwhile, lo! a good
sign! the wind seemed coming round astern; aye, the foul breeze
became fair!

Instantly the yards were squared, to the lively song of *"Ho!
the fair wind! oh-he-yo, cheerly, men!"* the crew singing for joy,
that so promising an event should so soon have falsified the evil
portents preceding it.

In compliance with the standing order of his commander—to
report immediately, and at any one of the twenty-four hours, any
decided change in the affairs of the deck,—Starbuck had no sooner
trimmed the yards to the breeze—however reluctantly and gloomily,—than he mechanically went below to apprise Captain Ahab
of the circumstance.

Ere knocking at his state-room, he involuntarily paused before
it a moment. The cabin lamp—taking long swings this way and
that—was burning fitfully, and casting fitful shadows upon the
old man's bolted door,—a thin one, with fixed blinds inserted, in
place of upper panels. The isolated subterraneousness of the
cabin made a certain humming silence to reign there, though it
was hooped round by all the roar of the elements. The loaded
muskets in the rack were shiningly revealed, as they stood upright against the forward bulkhead. Starbuck was an honest,
upright man; but out of Starbuck's heart, at that instant when
he saw the muskets, there strangely evolved an evil thought; but
so blent with its neutral or good accompaniments that for the instant he hardly knew it for itself.

"He would have shot me once," he murmured, "yes, there's the
very musket that he pointed at me;—that one with the studded
stock; let me touch it—lift it. Strange, that I, who have handled so
many deadly lances, strange, that I should shake so now. Loaded?
I must see. Aye, aye; and powder in the pan;—that's not good.
Best spill it?—wait. I'll cure myself of this. I'll hold the musket
boldly while I think.—I come to report a fair wind to him. But

how fair? Fair for death and doom,—*that's* fair for Moby Dick. It's a fair wind that's only fair for that accursed fish.—The very tube he pointed at me!—the very one; *this* one—I hold it here; he would have killed me with the very thing I handle now.—Aye and he would fain kill all his crew. Does he not say he will not strike his spars to any gale? Has he not dashed his heavenly quadrant? and in these same perilous seas, gropes he not his way by mere dead reckoning of the error-abounding log? and in this very Typhoon, did he not swear that he would have no lightning-rods? But shall this crazed old man be tamely suffered to drag a whole ship's company down to doom with him?—Yes, it would make him the wilful murderer of thirty men and more, if this ship come to any deadly harm; and come to deadly harm, my soul swears this ship will, if Ahab have his way. If, then, he were this instant—put aside, that crime would not be his. Ha! is he muttering in his sleep? Yes, just there,—in there, he's sleeping. Sleeping? aye, but still alive, and soon awake again. I can't withstand thee, then, old man. Not reasoning; not remonstrance; not entreaty wilt thou hearken to; all this thou scornest. Flat obedience to thy own flat commands, this is all thou breathest. Aye, and say'st the men have vow'd thy vow; say'st all of us are Ahabs. Great God forbid!—But is there no other way? no lawful way?—Make him a prisoner to be taken home? What! hope to wrest this old man's living power from his own living hands? Only a fool would try it. Say he were pinioned even; knotted all over with ropes and hawsers; chained down to ring-bolts on this cabin floor; he would be more hideous than a caged tiger, then. I could not endure the sight; could not possibly fly his howlings; all comfort, sleep itself, inestimable reason would leave me on the long intolerable voyage. What, then, remains? The land is hundreds of leagues away, and locked Japan the nearest. I stand alone here upon an open sea, with two oceans and a whole continent between me and law.—Aye, aye, 'tis so.—Is heaven a murderer when its lightning strikes a would-be murderer in his bed, tindering sheets and skin together?—And would I be a murderer, then, if——"and slowly, stealthily, and half sideways looking, he placed the loaded musket's end against the door.

"On this level, Ahab's hammock swings within; his head this way. A touch, and Starbuck may survive to hug his wife and child again.—Oh Mary! Mary!—boy! boy! boy!—But if I wake thee not to death, old man, who can tell to what unsounded deeps Starbuck's body this day week may sink, with all the crew! Great God, where art thou? Shall I? shall I?——The wind has gone down and shifted, sir; the fore and main topsails are reefed and set; she heads her course."

"Stern all! Oh Moby Dick, I clutch thy heart at last!"

Such were the sounds that now came hurtling from out the old man's tormented sleep, as if Starbuck's voice had caused the long dumb dream to speak.

The yet levelled musket shook like a drunkard's arm against the panel; Starbuck seemed wrestling with an angel; but turning from the door, he placed the death-tube in its rack, and left the place.

"He's too sound asleep, Mr. Stubb; go thou down, and wake him, and tell him. I must see to the deck here. Thou know'st what to say."

Chapter 124

THE NEEDLE[1]

Next morning the not-yet-subsided sea rolled in long slow billows of mighty bulk, and striving in the Pequod's gurgling track, pushed her on like giants' palms outspread. The strong, unstaggering breeze abounded so, that sky and air seemed vast outbellying sails; the whole world boomed before the wind. Muffled in the full morning light, the invisible sun was only known by the spread intensity of his place; where his bayonet rays moved on in stacks. Emblazonings, as of crowned Babylonian kings and queens, reigned over everything. The sea was as a crucible of molten gold, that bubblingly leaps with light and heat.

Long maintaining an enchanted silence, Ahab stood apart; and every time the tetering ship loweringly pitched down her bowsprit, he turned to eye the bright sun's rays produced ahead; and when she profoundly settled by the stern, he turned behind, and saw the sun's rearward place, and how the same yellow rays were blending with his undeviating wake.

"Ha, ha, my ship! thou mightest well be taken now for the sea-chariot of the sun. Ho, ho! all ye nations before my prow, I bring the sun to ye! Yoke on the further billows; hallo! a tandem, I drive the sea!"

But suddenly reined back by some counter thought, he hurried towards the helm, huskily demanding how the ship was heading.

"East-sou-east, sir," said the frightened steersman.

"Thou liest!" smiting him with his clenched fist. "Heading East at this hour in the morning, and the sun astern?"

Upon this every soul was confounded; for the phenomenon just then observed by Ahab had unaccountably escaped every one else;

1. Mansfield and Vincent find that Melville "built up" this chapter from information in Scoresby's *Journal of a* *Voyage to the Northern Whale-Fishery* (Edinburgh, 1823).

but its very blinding palpableness must have been the cause.

Thrusting his head half way into the binnacle, Ahab caught one glimpse of the compasses; his uplifted arm slowly fell; for a moment he almost seemed to stagger. Standing behind him Starbuck looked, and lo! the two compasses pointed East, and the Pequod was as infallibly going West.

But ere the first wild alarm could get out abroad among the crew, the old man with a rigid laugh exclaimed, "I have it! It has happened before. Mr. Starbuck, last night's thunder turned our compasses—that's all. Thou hast before now heard of such a thing, I take it."

"Aye; but never before has it happened to me, sir," said the pale mate, gloomily.

Here, it must needs be said, that accidents like this have in more than one case occurred to ships in violent storms. The magnetic energy, as developed in the mariner's needle, is, as all know, essentially one with the electricity beheld in heaven; hence it is not to be much marvelled at, that such things should be. In instances where the lightning has actually struck the vessel, so as to smite down some of the spars and rigging, the effect upon the needle has at times been still more fatal; all its loadstone virtue being annihilated, so that the before magnetic steel was of no more use than an old wife's knitting needle. But in either case, the needle never again, of itself, recovers the original virtue thus marred or lost; and if the binnacle compasses be affected, the same fate reaches all the others that may be in the ship; even were the lowermost one inserted into the kelson.

Deliberately standing before the binnacle, and eyeing the trans-pointed compasses, the old man, with the sharp of his extended hand, now took the precise bearing of the sun, and satisfied that the needles were exactly inverted, shouted out his orders for the ship's course to be changed accordingly. The yards were braced hard up; and once more the Pequod thrust her undaunted bows into the opposing wind, for the supposed fair one had only been juggling her.

Meanwhile, whatever were his own secret thoughts, Starbuck said nothing, but quietly he issued all requisite orders; while Stubb and Flask—who in some small degree seemed then to be sharing his feelings—likewise unmurmuringly acquiesced. As for the men, though some of them lowly rumbled, their fear of Ahab was greater than their fear of Fate. But as ever before, the pagan harpooneers remained almost wholly unimpressed; or if impressed, it was only with a certain magnetism shot into their congenial hearts from inflexible Ahab's.

For a space the old man walked the deck in rolling reveries. But chancing to slip with his ivory heel, he saw the crushed copper sight-tubes of the quadrant he had the day before dashed to the deck.

"Thou poor, proud heaven-gazer and sun's pilot! yesterday I wrecked thee, and to-day the compasses would fain have wrecked me. So, so. But Ahab is lord over the level loadstone yet. Mr. Starbuck—a lance without the pole; a top-maul, and the smallest of the sail-maker's needles. Quick!"

Accessory, perhaps, to the impulse dictating the thing he was now about to do, were certain prudential motives, whose object might have been to revive the spirits of his crew by a stroke of his subtile skill, in a matter so wondrous as that of the inverted compasses. Besides, the old man well knew that to steer by transpointed needles, though clumsily practicable, was not a thing to be passed over by superstitious sailors, without some shudderings and evil portents.

"Men," said he, steadily turning upon the crew, as the mate handed him the things he had demanded, "my men, the thunder turned old Ahab's needles; but out of this bit of steel Ahab can make one of his own, that will point as true as any."

Abashed glances of servile wonder were exchanged by the sailors, as this was said; and with fascinated eyes they awaited whatever magic might follow. But Starbuck looked away.

With a blow from the top-maul Ahab knocked off the steel head of the lance, and then handing to the mate the long iron rod remaining, bade him hold it upright, without its touching the deck. Then, with the maul, after repeatedly smiting the upper end of this iron rod, he placed the blunted needle endwise on the top of it, and less strongly hammered that, several times, the mate still holding the rod as before. Then going through some small strange motions with it—whether indispensable to the magnetizing of the steel, or merely intended to augment the awe of the crew, is uncertain—he called for linen thread; and moving to the binnacle, slipped out the two reversed needles there, and horizontally suspended the sail-needle by its middle, over one of the compasscards. At first, the steel went round and round, quivering and vibrating at either end; but at last it settled to its place, when Ahab, who had been intently watching for this result, stepped frankly back from the binnacle, and pointing his stretched arm towards it, exclaimed,—"Look ye, for yourselves, if Ahab be not lord of the level loadstone! The sun is East, and that compass swears it!"

One after another they peered in, for nothing but their own eyes could persuade such ignorance as theirs, and one after another they slunk away.

In his fiery eyes of scorn and triumph, you then saw Ahab in all his fatal pride.

Chapter 125

THE LOG AND LINE

While now the fated Pequod had been so long afloat this voyage, the log and line had but very seldom been in use. Owing to a confident reliance upon other means of determining the vessel's place, some merchantmen, and many whalemen, especially when cruising, wholly neglect to heave the log; though at the same time, and frequently more for form's sake than anything else, regularly putting down upon the customary slate the course steered by the ship, as well as the presumed average rate of progression every hour. It had been thus with the Pequod. The wooden reel and angular log attached hung, long untouched, just beneath the railing of the after bulwarks. Rains and spray had damped it; sun and wind had warped it; all the elements had combined to rot a thing that hung so idly. But heedless of all this, his mood seized Ahab, as he happened to glance upon the reel, not many hours after the magnet scene, and he remembered how his quadrant was no more, and recalled his frantic oath about the level log and line. The ship was sailing plungingly; astern the billows rolled in riots.

"Forward, there! Heave the log!"

Two seamen came. The golden-hued Tahitian and the grizzly Manxman. "Take the reel, one of ye, I'll heave."

They went towards the extreme stern, on the ship's lee side, where the deck, with the oblique energy of the wind, was now almost dipping into the creamy, sidelong-rushing sea.

The Manxman took the reel, and holding it high up, by the projecting handle-ends of the spindle, round which the spool of line revolved, so stood with the angular log hanging downwards, till Ahab advanced to him.

Ahab stood before him, and was lightly unwinding some thirty or forty turns to form a preliminary hand-coil to toss overboard, when the old Manxman, who was intently eyeing both him and the line, made bold to speak.

"Sir, I mistrust it; this line looks far gone, long heat and wet have spoiled it."

"'Twill hold, old gentleman. Long heat and wet, have they spoiled thee? Thou seem'st to hold. Or, truer perhaps, life holds thee; not thou it."

"I hold the spool, sir. But just as my captain says. With these grey hairs of mine 'tis not worth while disputing, 'specially with a superior, who'll ne'er confess."

"What's that? There now's a patched professor in Queen

Nature's granite-founded College; but methinks he's too subservient. Where wert thou born?"

"In the little rocky Isle of Man, sir."

"Excellent! Thou'st hit the world by that."

"I know not, sir, but I was born there."

"In the Isle of Man, hey? Well, the other way, it's good. Here's a man from Man; a man born in once independent Man, and now unmanned of Man; which is sucked in—by what? Up with the reel! The dead, blind wall butts all inquiring heads at last. Up with it! So."

The log was heaved. The loose coils rapidly straightened out in a long dragging line astern, and then, instantly, the reel began to whirl. In turn, jerkily raised and lowered by the rolling billows, the towing resistance of the log caused the old reelman to stagger strangely.

"Hold hard!"

Snap! the overstrained line sagged down in one long festoon; the tugging log was gone.

"I crush the quadrant, the thunder turns the needles, and now the mad sea parts the log-line. But Ahab can mend all. Haul in here, Tahitian; reel up, Manxman. And look ye, let the carpenter make another log, and mend thou the line. See to it."

"There he goes now; to him nothing's happened; but to me, the skewer seems loosening out of the middle of the world. Haul in, haul in, Tahitian! These lines run whole, and whirling out: come in broken, and dragging slow. Ha, Pip? come to help; eh, Pip?"

"Pip? whom call ye Pip? Pip jumped from the whaleboat. Pip's missing. Let's see now if ye haven't fished him up here, fisherman. It drags hard; I guess he's holding on. Jerk him, Tahiti! Jerk him off; we haul in no cowards here. Ho! there's his arm just breaking water. A hatchet! a hatchet! cut it off—we haul in no cowards here. Captain Ahab! sir, sir! here's Pip, trying to get on board again."

"Peace, thou crazy loon," cried the Manxman, seizing him by the arm. "Away from the quarter-deck!"

"The greater idiot ever scolds the lesser," muttered Ahab, advancing. "Hands off from that holiness! Where sayest thou Pip was, boy?"

"Astern there, sir, astern! Lo, lo!"

"And who art thou, boy? I see not my reflection in the vacant pupils of thy eyes. Oh God! that man should be a thing for immortal souls to sieve through! Who art thou, boy?"

"Bell-boy, sir; ship's-crier; ding, dong, ding! Pip! Pip! Pip! One hundred pounds of clay reward for Pip; five feet high—looks cowardly—quickest known by that! Ding, dong, ding! Who's seen Pip the coward?"

"There can be no hearts above the snow-line. Oh, ye frozen heavens! look down here. Ye did beget this luckless child, and have abandoned him, ye creative libertines. Here, boy; Ahab's cabin shall be Pip's home henceforth, while Ahab lives. Thou touchest my inmost centre, boy; thou art tied to me by cords woven of my heart-strings. Come, let's down."

"What's this? here's velvet shark-skin," intently gazing at Ahab's hand, and feeling it. "Ah, now, had poor Pip but felt so kind a thing as this, perhaps he had ne'er been lost! This seems to me, sir, as a man-rope; something that weak souls may hold by. Oh, sir, let old Perth now come and rivet these two hands together; the black one with the white, for I will not let this go."

"Oh, boy, nor will I thee, unless I should thereby drag thee to worse horrors than are here. Come, then, to my cabin. Lo! ye believers in gods all goodness, and in man all ill, lo you! see the omniscient gods oblivious of suffering man; and man, though idiotic, and knowing not what he does, yet full of the sweet things of love and gratitude. Come! I feel prouder leading thee by thy black hand, than though I grasped an Emperor's!"

"There go two daft ones now," muttered the old Manxman. "One daft with strength, the other daft with weakness. But here's the end of the rotten line—all dripping, too. Mend it, eh? I think we had best have a new line altogether. I'll see Mr. Stubb about it."

Chapter 126

THE LIFE-BUOY

Steering now south-eastward by Ahab's levelled steel, and her progress solely determined by Ahab's level log and line; the Pequod held on her path towards the Equator. Making so long a passage through such unfrequented waters, descrying no ships, and ere long, sideways impelled by unvarying trade winds, over waves monotonously mild; all these seemed the strange calm things preluding some riotous and desperate scene.

At last, when the ship drew near to the outskirts, as it were, of the Equatorial fishing-ground, and in the deep darkness that goes before the dawn, was sailing by a cluster of rocky islets; the watch —then headed by Flask—was startled by a cry so plaintively wild and unearthly—like half-articulated wailings of the ghosts of all Herod's murdered Innocents [1]—that one and all, they started

1. The male children two years old or younger whom King Herod slew "in Bethlehem and in all the coasts thereof" in his attempt to kill the young Jesus, Matthew 2, Mansfield and Vincent point out that the "episode of the seal

from their reveries, and for the space of some moments stood, or sat, or leaned all transfixedly listening, like the carved Roman slave, while that wild cry remained within hearing. The Christian or civilized part of the crew said it was mermaids, and shuddered; but the pagan harpooneers remained unappalled. Yet the grey Manxman—the oldest mariner of all—declared that the wild thrilling sounds that were heard, were the voices of newly drowned men in the sea.

Below in his hammock, Ahab did not hear of this till grey dawn, when he came to the deck; it was then recounted to him by Flask, not unaccompanied with hinted dark meanings. He hollowly laughed, and thus explained the wonder.

Those rocky islands the ship had passed were the resort of great numbers of seals, and some young seals that had lost their dams, or some dams that had lost their cubs, must have risen nigh the ship and kept company with her, crying and sobbing with their human sort of wail. But this only the more affected some of them, because most mariners cherish a very superstitious feeling about seals, arising not only from their peculiar tones when in distress, but also from the human look of their round heads and semi-intelligent faces, seen peeringly uprising from the water alongside. In the sea, under certain circumstances, seals have more than once been mistaken for men.

But the bodings of the crew were destined to receive a most plausible confirmation in the fate of one of their number that morning. At sun-rise this man went from his hammock to his mast-head at the fore; and whether it was that he was not yet half waked from his sleep (for sailors sometimes go aloft in a transition state), whether it was thus with the man, there is now no telling; but, be that as it may, he had not been long at his perch, when a cry was heard—a cry and a rushing—and looking up, they saw a falling phantom in the air; and looking down, a little tossed heap of white bubbles in the blue of the sea.

The life-buoy—a long slender cask—was dropped from the stern, where it always hung obedient to a cunning spring; but no hand rose to seize it, and the sun having long beat upon this cask it had shrunken, so that it slowly filled, and the parched wood also filled at its every pore; and the studded iron-bound cask followed the sailor to the bottom, as if to yield him his pillow, though in sooth but a hard one.

And thus the first man of the Pequod that mounted the mast to look out for the White Whale, on the White Whale's own peculiar ground; that man was swallowed up in the deep. But few,

cry" was developed from Captain James Colnett's *A Voyage to the South Atlantic and Round Cape Horn . . . for the Purpose of Extending the Spermaceti Whale Fisheries* (London, 1798).

perhaps, thought of that at the time. Indeed, in some sort, they were not grieved at this event, at least as a portent; for they regarded it, not as a foreshadowing of evil in the future, but as the fulfilment of an evil already presaged. They declared that now they knew the reason of those wild shrieks they had heard the night before. But again the old Manxman said nay.

The lost life-buoy was now to be replaced; Starbuck was directed to see to it; but as no cask of sufficient lightness could be found, and as in the feverish eagerness of what seemed the approaching crisis of the voyage, all hands were impatient of any toil but what was directly connected with its final end, whatever that might prove to be; therefore, they were going to leave the ship's stern unprovided with a buoy, when by certain strange signs and innuendoes Queequeg hinted a hint concerning his coffin.

"A life-buoy of a coffin!" cried Starbuck, starting.

"Rather queer, that, I should say," said Stubb.

"It will make a good enough one," said Flask, "the carpenter here can arrange it easily."

"Bring it up; there's nothing else for it," said Starbuck, after a melancholy pause. "Rig it, carpenter; do not look at me so—the coffin, I mean. Dost thou hear me? Rig it."

"And shall I nail down the lid, sir?" moving his hand as with a hammer.

"Aye."

"And shall I caulk the seams, sir?" moving his hand as with a caulking-iron.

"Aye."

"And shall I then pay over the same with pitch, sir?" moving his hand as with a pitch-pot.

"Away! what possesses thee to this? Make a life-buoy of the coffin, and no more.—Mr. Stubb, Mr. Flask, come forward with me."

"He goes off in a huff. The whole he can endure; at the parts he baulks. Now I don't like this. I make a leg for Captain Ahab, and he wears it like a gentleman; but I make a bandbox for Queequeg, and he wont put his head into it. Are all my pains to go for nothing with that coffin? And now I'm ordered to make a life-buoy of it. It's like turning an old coat; going to bring the flesh on the other side now. I don't like this cobbling sort of business—I don't like it at all; it's undignified; it's not my place. Let tinkers' brats do tinkerings; we are their betters. I like to take in hand none but clean, virgin, fair-and-square mathematical jobs, something that regularly begins at the beginning, and is at the middle when midway, and comes to an end at the conclusion; not a cobbler's job, that's at an end in the middle, and at the beginning at the end. It's the old woman's tricks to be giving cobbling jobs. Lord! what an affection all old women have for tinkers. I know an old woman of sixty-five who ran away with a bald-headed young tinker once. And that's the reason I never would work for lonely widow old women ashore, when I kept my job-shop in the Vineyard; they might have taken it into their lonely old heads to run off with me. But heigh-ho! there are no caps at sea but snow-caps. Let me see. Nail down the lid; caulk the seams; pay over the same with pitch; batten them down tight, and hang it with the snap-spring over the ship's stern. Were ever such things done before with a coffin? Some superstitious old carpenters, now, would be tied up in the rigging, ere they would do the job. But I'm made of knotty Aroostook hemlock; I don't budge. Cruppered with a coffin! Sailing about with a grave-yard tray! But never mind. We workers in woods make bridal-bedsteads and card-tables, as well as coffins and hearses. We work by the month, or by the job, or by the profit; not for us to ask the why and wherefore of our work, unless it be too confounded cobbling, and then we stash it if we can. Hem! I'll do the job, now, tenderly. I'll have me—let's see—how many in the ship's company, all told? But I've forgotten. Any way, I'll have me thirty separate, Turk's-headed life-lines, each three feet long hanging all round to the coffin. Then, if the hull go down, there'll be thirty lively fellows all fighting for one coffin, a sight not seen very often beneath the sun! Come hammer, calking-iron, pitch-pot, and marling-spike! Let's to it."

Chapter 127

THE DECK

The coffin laid upon two line-tubs, between the vice-bench and the open hatchway; the Carpenter calking its seams; the string of twisted oakum slowly unwinding from a large roll of it placed in the bosom of his frock.—Ahab comes slowly from the cabin-gangway, and hears Pip following him.

"Back, lad; I will be with ye again presently. He goes! Not this hand complies with my humor more genially than that boy.— Middle aisle of a church! What's here?"

"Life-buoy, sir. Mr. Starbuck's orders. Oh, look, sir! Beware the hatchway!"

"Thank ye, man. Thy coffin lies handy to the vault."

"Sir? The hatchway? oh! So it does, sir, so it does."

"Art not thou the leg-maker? Look, did not this stump come from thy shop?"

"I believe it did, sir; does the ferrule stand, sir?"

"Well enough. But art thou not also the undertaker?"

"Aye, sir; I patched up this thing here as a coffin for Queequeg; but they've set me now to turning it into something else."

"Then tell me; art thou not an arrant, all-grasping, inter-meddling, monopolizing, heathenish old scamp, to be one day making legs, and the next day coffins to clap them in, and yet again life-buoys out of those same coffins? Thou art as unprincipled as the gods, and as much of a jack-of-all-trades."

"But I do not mean anything, sir. I do as I do."

"The gods again. Hark ye, dost thou not ever sing working about a coffin? The Titans, they say, hummed snatches when chipping out the craters for volcanoes; and the grave-digger in the play sings, spade in hand. Dost thou never?"

"Sing, sir? Do I sing? Oh, I'm indifferent enough, sir, for that; but the reason why the grave-digger made music must have been because there was none in his spade, sir. But the calking mallet is full of it. Hark to it."

"Aye, and that's because the lid there's a sounding-board; and what in all things makes the sounding-board is this—there's naught beneath. And yet, a coffin with a body in it rings pretty much the same, Carpenter. Hast thou ever helped carry a bier, and heard the coffin knock against the church-yard gate, going in?"

"Faith, sir, I've——"

"Faith? What's that?"

"Why, faith, sir, it's only a sort of exclamation-like—that's all, sir."

"Um, um; go on."

"I was about to say, sir, that——"

"Art thou a silk-worm? Dost thou spin thy own shroud out of thyself? Look at thy bosom! Despatch! and get 'these traps out of my sight."

"He goes aft. That was sudden, now; but squalls come sudden in hot latitudes. I've heard that the Isle of Albemarle, one of the Gallipagos, is cut by the Equator right in the middle. Seems to me some sort of Equator cuts yon old man, too, right in his middle. He's always under the Line—fiery hot, I tell ye! He's looking this way—come, oakum; quick. Here we go again. This wooden mallet is the cork, and I'm the professor of musical glasses—tap, tap!"

(Ahab to himself.)

"There's a sight! There's a sound! The greyheaded wood-pecker tapping the hollow tree! Blind and dumb might well be envied now. See! that thing rests on two line-tubs, full of tow-lines. A most malicious wag, that fellow. Rat-tat! So man's seconds tick! Oh! how immaterial are all materials! What things real are there, but imponderable thoughts? Here now's the very dreaded symbol of grim death, by a mere hap, made the expressive sign of the help and hope of most endangered life. A life-buoy of a coffin! Does it go further? Can it be that in some spiritual sense the coffin is, after all, but an immortality-preserver! I'll think of that. But no. So far gone am I in the dark side of earth, that its other side, the theoretic bright one, seems but uncertain twilight to me. Will ye never have done, Carpenter, with that accursed sound? I go below; let me not see that thing here when I return again. Now, then, Pip, we'll talk this over; I do suck most wondrous philosophies from thee! Some unknown conduits from the unknown worlds must empty into thee!"

Chapter 128

THE PEQUOD MEETS THE RACHEL

Next day, a large ship, the Rachel, was descried, bearing directly down upon the Pequod, all her spars thickly clustering with men. At the time the Pequod was making good speed through the water; but as the broad-winged windward stranger shot nigh to her, the boastful sails all fell together as blank bladders that are burst, and all life fled from the smitten hull.

"Bad news; she brings bad news," muttered the old Manxman. But ere her commander, who, with trumpet to mouth, stood up in his boat; ere he could hopefully hail, Ahab's voice was heard.

"Hast seen the White Whale?"

"Aye, yesterday. Have ye seen a whale-boat adrift?"

Throttling his joy, Ahab negatively answered this unexpected question; and would then have fain boarded the stranger, when the stranger captain himself, having stopped his vessel's way, was seen descending her side. A few keen pulls, and his boat-hook soon clinched the Pequod's main-chains, and he sprang to the deck. Immediately he was recognised by Ahab for a Nantucketer he knew. But no formal salutation was exchanged.

"Where was he?—not killed!—not killed!" cried Ahab, closely advancing. "How was it?"

It seemed that somewhat late on the afternoon of the day previous, while three of the stranger's boats were engaged with a shoal of whales, which had led them some four or five miles from the ship; and while they were yet in swift chase to windward, the white hump and head of Moby Dick had suddenly loomed up out of the blue water, not very far to leeward; whereupon, the fourth rigged boat—a reserved one—had been instantly lowered in chase. After a keen sail before the wind, this fourth boat—the swiftest keeled of all—seemed to have succeeded in fastening—at least, as well as the man at the mast-head could tell anything about it. In the distance he saw the diminished dotted boat; and then a swift gleam of bubbling white water; and after that nothing more; whence it was concluded that the stricken whale must have indefinitely run away with his pursuers, as often happens. There was some apprehension, but no positive alarm, as yet. The recall signals were placed in the rigging; darkness came on; and forced to pick up her three far to windward boats—ere going in quest of the fourth one in the precisely opposite direction—the ship had not only been necessitated to leave that boat to its fate till near midnight, but, for the time, to increase her distance from it. But the rest of her crew being at last safe aboard, she crowded all sail— stunsail on stunsail—after the missing boat; kindling a fire in her try-pots for a beacon; and every other man aloft on the look-out. But though when she had thus sailed a sufficient distance to gain the presumed place of the absent ones when last seen; though she then paused to lower her spare boats to pull all around her; and not finding anything, had again dashed on; again paused, and lowered her boats; and though she had thus continued doing till day light; yet not the least glimpse of the missing keel had been seen.

The story told, the stranger Captain immediately went on to reveal his object in boarding the Pequod. He desired that ship to unite with his own in the search; by sailing over the sea some four or five miles apart, on parallel lines, and so sweeping a double horizon, as it were.

"I will wager something now," whispered Stubb to Flask, "that some one in that missing boat wore off that Captain's best coat; mayhap, his watch—he's so cursed anxious to get it back. Who ever heard of two pious whale-ships cruising after one missing whale-boat in the height of the whaling season? See, Flask, only see how pale he looks—pale in the very buttons of his eyes—look —it wasn't the coat—it must have been the—"

"My boy, my own boy is among them. For God's sake—I beg, I conjure"—here exclaimed the stranger Captain to Ahab, who thus far had but icily received his petition. "For eight-and-forty hours let me charter your ship—I will gladly pay for it, and roundly pay for it—if there be no other way—for eight-and-forty hours only— only that—you must, oh, you must, and you *shall* do this thing."

"His son!" cried Stubb, "oh, it's his son he's lost! I take back the coat and watch—what says Ahab? We must save that boy."

"He's drowned with the rest on 'em, last night," said the old Manx sailor standing behind them; "I heard; all of ye heard their spirits."

Now, as it shortly turned out, what made this incident of the

Rachel's the more melancholy, was the circumstance, that not only was one of the Captain's sons among the number of the missing boat's crew; but among the number of the other boats' crews, at the same time, but on the other hand, separated from the ship during the dark vicissitudes of the chase, there had been still another son; as that for a time, the wretched father was plunged to the bottom of the cruellest perplexity; which was only solved for him by his chief mate's instinctively adopting the ordinary procedure of a whale-ship in such emergencies, that is, when placed between jeopardized but divided boats, always to pick up the majority first. But the captain, for some unknown constitutional reason, had refrained from mentioning all this, and not till forced to it by Ahab's iciness did he allude to his one yet missing boy; a little lad, but twelve years old, whose father with the earnest but unmisgiving hardihood of a Nantucketer's paternal love, had thus early sought to initiate him in the perils and wonders of a vocation almost immemorially the destiny of all his race. Nor does it unfrequently occur, that Nantucket captains will send a son of such tender age away from them, for a protracted three or four years' voyage in some other ship than their own; so that their first knowledge of a whaleman's career shall be unenervated by any chance display of a father's natural but untimely partiality, or undue apprehensiveness and concern.

Meantime, now the stranger was still beseeching his poor boon of Ahab; and Ahab still stood like an anvil, receiving every shock, but without the least quivering of his own.

"I will not go," said the stranger, "till you say *aye* to me. Do to me as you would have me do to you in the like case. For *you* too have a boy, Captain Ahab—though but a child, and nestling safely at home now—a child of your old age too—Yes, yes, you relent; I see it—run, run, men, now, and stand by to square in the yards."

"Avast," cried Ahab—"touch not a rope-yarn;" then in a voice that prolongingly moulded every word—"Captain Gardiner, I will not do it. Even now I lose time. Good bye, good bye. God bless ye, man, and may I forgive myself, but I must go. Mr. Starbuck, look at the binnacle watch, and in three minutes from this present instant warn off all strangers: then brace forward again, and let the ship sail as before."

Hurriedly turning, with averted face, he descended into his cabin, leaving the strange captain transfixed at this unconditional and utter rejection of his so earnest suit. But starting from his enchantment, Gardiner silently hurried to the side; more fell than stepped into his boat, and returned to his ship.

Soon the two ships diverged their wakes; and long as the

436 · Moby-Dick

strange vessel was in view, she was seen to yaw hither and thither
at every dark spot, however small, on the sea. This way and that
her yards were swung round; starboard and larboard, she continued
to tack; now she beat against a head sea; and again it pushed her
before it; while all the while, her masts and yards were thickly
clustered with men, as three tall cherry trees, when the boys are
cherrying among the boughs.

But by her still halting course and winding, woful way, you
plainly saw that this ship that so wept with spray, still remained
without comfort. She was Rachel, weeping for her children,[1] because they were not.

Chapter 129

THE CABIN

*(Ahab moving to go on deck; Pip catches him by the hand to
follow.)*

"Lad, lad, I tell thee thou must not follow Ahab now. The hour
is coming when Ahab would not scare thee from him, yet would
not have thee by him. There is that in thee, poor lad, which I
feel too curing to my malady. Like cures like; and for this hunt, my
malady becomes my most desired health. Do thou abide below
here, where they shall serve thee, as if thou wert the captain. Aye,
lad, thou shalt sit here in my own screwed chair; another screw
to it, thou must be."

"No, no, no! ye have not a whole body, sir; do ye but use
poor me for your one lost leg; only tread upon me, sir; I ask no
more, so I remain a part of ye."

"Oh! spite of million villains, this makes me a bigot[2] in the
fadeless fidelity of man!—and a black! and crazy!—but methinks
like-cures-like applies to him too; he grows so sane again."

"They tell me, sir, that Stubb did once desert poor little Pip,
whose drowned bones now show white, for all the blackness of his
living skin. But I will never desert ye, sir, as Stubb did him. Sir, I
must go with ye."

"If thou speakest thus to me much more, Ahab's purpose keels
up in him. I tell thee no; it cannot be."

"Oh good master, master, master!"

"Weep so, and I will murder thee! have a care, for Ahab too
is mad. Listen, and thou wilt often hear my ivory foot upon
the deck, and still know that I am there. And now I quit thee.
Thy hand!—Met! True art thou, lad, as the circumference to its
centre. So: God for ever bless thee; and if it come to that,—God

1. Not literally Rachel, the beautiful
wife of Jacob, but Rachel the mother
of the Jewish people. See Jeremiah
31:15 and Matthew 2:18.
2. An unshakable believer.

for ever save thee, let what will befall."

(*Ahab goes; Pip steps one step forward.*)

"Here he this instant stood; I stand in his air,—but I'm alone. Now were even poor Pip here I could endure it, but he's missing. Pip! Pip! Ding, dong, ding! Who's seen Pip? He must be up here; let's try the door. What? neither lock, nor bolt, nor bar; and yet there's no opening it. It must be the spell; he told me to stay here: Aye, and told me this screwed chair was mine. Here, then, I'll seat me, against the transom, in the ship's full middle, all her keel and her three masts before me. Here, our old sailors say, in their black seventy-fours great admirals sometimes sit at table, and lord it over rows of captains and lieutenants. Ha! what's this? epaulets! epaulets! the epaulets all come crowding! Pass round the decanters; glad to see ye; fill up, monsieurs! What an odd feeling, now, when a black boy's host to white men with gold lace upon their coats!—Monsieurs, have ye seen one Pip?— a little negro lad, five feet high, hang-dog look, and cowardly! Jumped from a whale-boat once;—seen him? No! Well then, fill up again, captains, and let's drink shame upon all cowards! I name no names. Shame upon them! Put one foot upon the table. Shame upon all cowards.—Hist! above there, I hear ivory—Oh, master! master! I am indeed downhearted when you walk over me. But here I'll stay, though this stern strikes rocks; and they bulge through; and oysters come to join me."

Chapter 130

THE HAT

And now that at the proper time and place, after so long and wide a preliminary cruise, Ahab,—all other whaling waters swept —seemed to have chased his foe into an ocean-fold, to slay him the more securely there; now, that he found himself hard by the very latitude and longitude where his tormenting wound had been inflicted; now that a vessel had been spoken which on the very day preceding had actually encountered Moby Dick;—and now that all his successive meetings with various ships contrastingly concurred to show the demoniac indifference with which the white whale tore his hunters, whether sinning or sinned against; now it was that there lurked a something in the old man's eyes, which it was hardly sufferable for feeble souls to see. As the unsetting polar star, which through the livelong, arctic, six months' night sustains its piercing, steady, central gaze; so Ahab's purpose now fixedly gleamed down upon the constant midnight of the gloomy crew. It domineered above them so, that all their bodings, doubts, misgivings, fears, were fain to hide beneath their souls, and not sprout forth a single spear or leaf.

In this foreshadowing interval too, all humor, forced or natural, vanished. Stubb no more strove to raise a smile; Starbuck no more strove to check one. Alike, joy and sorrow, hope and fear, seemed ground to finest dust, and powdered, for the time, in the clamped mortar of Ahab's iron soul. Like machines, they dumbly moved about the deck, ever conscious that the old man's despot eye was on them.

But did you deeply scan him in his more secret confidential hours; when he thought no glance but one was on him; then you would have seen that even as Ahab's eyes so awed the crew's, the inscrutable Parsee's glance awed his; or somehow, at least, in some wild way, at times affected it. Such an added, gliding strangeness began to invest the thin Fedallah now; such ceaseless shudderings shook him; that the men looked dubious at him; half uncertain, as it seemed, whether indeed he were a mortal substance, or else a tremulous shadow cast upon the deck by some unseen being's body. And that shadow was always hovering there. For not by night, even, had Fedallah ever certainly been known to slumber, or go below. He would stand still for hours: but never sat or leaned; his wan but wondrous eyes did plainly say—We two watchmen never rest.

Nor, at any time, by night or day could the mariners now step upon the deck, unless Ahab was before them; either standing in his pivot-hole, or exactly pacing the planks between two undeviating limits,—the main-mast and the mizen; or else they saw him standing in the cabin-scuttle,—his living foot advanced upon the deck, as if to step; his hat slouched heavily over his eyes; so that however motionless he stood, however the days and nights were added on, that he had not swung in his hammock; yet hidden beneath that slouching hat, they could never tell unerringly whether, for all this, his eyes were really closed at times: or whether he was still intently scanning them; no matter, though he stood so in the scuttle for a whole hour on the stretch, and the unheeded night-damp gathered in beads of dew upon that stone-carved coat and hat. The clothes that the night had wet, the next day's sunshine dried upon him; and so, day after day, and night after night; he went no more beneath the planks; whatever he wanted from the cabin that thing he sent for.

He ate in the same open air; that is, his two only meals,—breakfast and dinner: supper he never touched; nor reaped his beard; which darkly grew all gnarled, as unearthed roots of trees blown over, which still grow idly on at naked base, though perished in the upper verdure. But though his whole life was now become one watch on deck; and though the Parsee's mystic watch was without intermission as his own; yet these two never seemed to speak—one man to the other—unless at long intervals some passing unmomentous matter made it necessary. Though such a potent spell seemed secretly to join the twain; openly, and to the awe-struck crew, they seemed pole-like asunder. If by day they chanced to speak one word; by night, dumb men were both, so far as concerned the slightest verbal interchange. At times, for longest hours, without a single hail, they stood far parted in the starlight; Ahab in his scuttle, the Parsee by the mainmast; but still fixedly gazing upon each other; as if in the Parsee Ahab saw his forethrown shadow, in Ahab the Parsee his abandoned substance.

And yet, somehow, did Ahab—in his own proper self, as daily, hourly, and every instant, commandingly revealed to his subordinates,—Ahab seemed an independent lord; the Parsee but his slave. Still again both seemed yoked together, and an unseen tyrant driving them; the lean shade siding the solid rib. For be this Parsee what he may, all rib and keel was solid Ahab.

At the first faintest glimmering of the dawn, his iron voice was heard from aft—"Man the mast-heads!"—and all through the day, till after sunset and after twilight, the same voice every hour, at the striking of the helmsman's bell, was heard—"What d'ye see? —sharp! sharp!"

But when three or four days had slided by, after meeting the children-seeking Rachel; and no spout had yet been seen; the monomaniac old man seemed distrustful of his crew's fidelity; at least, of nearly all except the Pagan harpooneers; he seemed to doubt, even, whether Stubb and Flask might not willingly overlook the sight he sought. But if these suspicions were really his, he sagaciously refrained from verbally expressing them, however his actions might seem to hint them.

"I will have the first sight of the whale myself,"—he said. "Aye! Ahab must have the doubloon!" and with his own hands he rigged a nest of basketed bowlines; and sending a hand aloft, with a single sheaved block, to secure to the main-mast head, he received the two ends of the downward-reeved rope; and attaching one to his basket prepared a pin for the other end, in order to fasten it at the rail. This done, with that end yet in his hand and standing beside the pin, he looked round upon his crew, sweeping from one to the other; pausing his glance long upon Daggoo, Queequeg, Tashtego; but shunning Fedallah; and then settling his firm relying eye upon the chief mate, said,—"Take the rope, sir —I give it into thy hands, Starbuck." Then arranging his person in the basket, he gave the word for them to hoist him to his perch, Starbuck being the one who secured the rope at last; and afterwards stood near it. And thus, with one hand clinging round the royal mast, Ahab gazed abroad upon the sea for miles and miles,—ahead, astern, this side, and that,—within the wide expanded circle commanded at so great a height.

When in working with his hands at some lofty almost isolated place in the rigging, which chances to afford no foothold, the sailor at sea is hoisted up to that spot, and sustained there by the rope; under these circumstances, its fastened end on deck is always given in strict charge to some one man who has the special watch of it. Because in such a wilderness of running rigging, whose various different relations aloft cannot always be infallibly discerned by what is seen of them at the deck; and when the deck-ends of these ropes are being every few minutes cast down from the fastenings, it would be but a natural fatality, if, unprovided with a constant watchman, the hoisted sailor should by some carelessness of the crew be cast adrift and fall all swooping to the sea. So Ahab's proceedings in this matter were not unusual; the only strange thing about them seemed to be, that Starbuck, almost the one only man who had ever ventured to oppose him with anything in the slightest degree approaching to decision—one of those too, whose faithfulness on the look-out he had seemed to doubt somewhat;—it was strange, that this was the very man he should select for his watchman; freely giving his whole life into such an otherwise distrusted person's hands.

Now, the first time Ahab was perched aloft; ere he had been there ten minutes; one of those red-billed savage sea-hawks which so often fly incommodiously close round the manned mast-heads of whalemen in these latitudes; one of these birds came wheeling and screaming round his head in a maze of untrackably swift circlings. Then it darted a thousand feet straight up into the air; then spiralized downwards, and went eddying again round his head.

But with his gaze fixed upon the dim and distant horizon, Ahab seemed not to mark this wild bird; nor, indeed, would any one else have marked it much, it being no uncommon circumstance; only now almost the least heedful eye seemed to see some sort of cunning meaning in almost every sight.

"Your hat, your hat, sir!" suddenly cried the Sicilian seaman, who being posted at the mizen-mast-head, stood directly behind Ahab, though somewhat lower than his level, and with a deep gulf of air dividing them.

But already the sable wing was before the old man's eyes; the long hooked bill at his head: with a scream, the black hawk darted away with his prize.

An eagle flew thrice round Tarquin's head, removing his cap to replace it, and thereupon Tanaquil, his wife, declared that Tarquin would be king of Rome. But only by the replacing of the cap was that omen accounted good. Ahab's hat was never restored; the wild hawk flew on and on with it; far in advance of the prow: and at last disappeared; while from the point of that disappearance, a minute black spot was dimly discerned, falling from that vast height into the sea.

Chapter 131

THE PEQUOD MEETS THE DELIGHT

The intense Pequod sailed on; the rolling waves and days went by; the life-buoy-coffin still lightly swung; and another ship, most miserably misnamed the Delight, was descried. As she drew nigh, all eyes were fixed upon her broad beams, called shears, which, in some whaling-ships, cross the quarter-deck at the height of eight or nine feet; serving to carry the spare, unrigged, or disabled boats.

Upon the stranger's shears were beheld the shattered, white ribs, and some few splintered planks, of what had once been a whale-boat; but you now saw through this wreck, as plainly as you see through the peeled, half-unhinged, and bleaching skeleton of a horse.

"Hast seen the White Whale?"

"Look!" replied the hollow-cheeked captain from his taffrail; and with his trumpet he pointed to the wreck.

"Hast killed him?"

"The harpoon is not yet forged that will ever do that," answered the other, sadly glancing upon a rounded hammock on the deck, whose gathered sides some noiseless sailors were busy in sewing together.

"Not forged!" and snatching Perth's levelled iron from the crotch, Ahab held it out, exclaiming—"Look ye, Nantucketer; here in this hand I hold his death! Tempered in blood, and tempered by lightning are these barbs; and I swear to temper them triply in that hot place behind the fin, where the White Whale most feels his accursed life!"

"Then God keep thee, old man—see'st thou that"—pointing to the hammock—"I bury but one of five stout men, who were alive only yesterday; but were dead ere night. Only *that* one I bury; the rest were buried before they died; you sail upon their tomb." Then turning to his crew—"Are ye ready there? place the plank then on the rail, and lift the body; so, then—Oh! God"—advancing towards the hammock with uplifted hands—"may the resurrection and the life——"

"Brace forward! Up helm!" cried Ahab like lightning to his men.

But the suddenly started Pequod was not quick enough to escape the sound of the splash that the corpse soon made as it struck the sea; not so quick, indeed, but that some of the flying bubbles might have sprinkled her hull with their ghostly baptism.

As Ahab now glided from the dejected Delight, the strange life-buoy hanging at the Pequod's stern came into conspicuous relief.

"Ha! yonder! look yonder, men!" cried a foreboding voice in her wake. "In vain, oh, ye strangers, ye fly our sad burial; ye but turn us your taffrail to show us your coffin!"

Chapter 132

THE SYMPHONY

It was a clear steel-blue day. The firmaments of air and sea were hardly separable in that all-pervading azure; only, the pensive air was transparently pure and soft, with a woman's look, and the robust and man-like sea heaved with long, strong, lingering swells, as Samson's chest in his sleep.

Hither, and thither, on high, glided the snow-white wings of small, unspeckled birds; these were the gentle thoughts of the feminine air; but to and fro in the deeps, far down in the bottomless blue, rushed mighty leviathans, sword-fish, and sharks; and these were the strong, troubled, murderous thinkings of the masculine sea.

But though thus contrasting within, the contrast was only in shades and shadows without; those two seemed one; it was only the sex, as it were, that distinguished them.

Aloft, like a royal czar and king, the sun seemed giving this gentle air to this bold and rolling sea; even as bride to groom. And at the girdling line of the horizon, a soft and tremulous motion—most seen here at the equator—denoted the fond, throbbing trust, the loving alarms, with which the poor bride gave her bosom away.

Tied up and twisted; gnarled and knotted with wrinkles; haggardly firm and unyielding; his eyes glowing like coals, that still glow in the ashes of ruin; untottering Ahab stood forth in the clearness of the morn; lifting his splintered helmet of a brow to the fair girl's forehead of heaven.

Oh, immortal infancy, and innocency of the azure! Invisible winged creatures that frolic all round us! Sweet childhood of air and sky! how oblivious were ye of old Ahab's close-coiled woe! But so have I seen little Miriam and Martha, laughing-eyed elves, heedlessly gambol around their old sire; sporting with the circle of singed locks which grew on the marge of that burnt-out crater of his brain.

Slowly crossing the deck from the scuttle, Ahab leaned over the side, and watched how his shadow in the water sank and sank to his gaze, the more and the more that he strove to pierce the profundity. But the lovely aromas in that enchanted air did at last seem to dispel, for a moment, the cankerous thing in his soul. That glad, happy air, that winsome sky, did at last stroke and caress him; the step-mother world, so long cruel—forbidding—now threw affectionate arms round his stubborn neck, and did seem to joyously sob over him, as if over one, that however wilful and erring, she could yet find it in her heart to save and to bless. From beneath his slouched hat Ahab dropped a tear into the sea; nor did all the Pacific contain such wealth as that one wee drop.

Starbuck saw the old man; saw him, how he heavily leaned over the side; and he seemed to hear in his own true heart the measureless sobbing that stole out of the centre of the serenity around. Careful not to touch him, or be noticed by him, he yet drew near to him, and stood there.

Ahab turned.

"Starbuck!"

"Sir."

"Oh, Starbuck! it is a mild, mild wind, and a mild looking sky. On such a day—very much such a sweetness as this—I struck my first whale—a boy-harpooneer of eighteen! Forty—forty—forty years ago!—ago! Forty years of continual whaling! forty years of privation, and peril, and storm-time! forty years on the pitiless sea! for forty years has Ahab forsaken the peaceful land, for forty years to make war on the horrors of the deep! Aye and yes, Starbuck, out of those forty years I have not spent three ashore. When I think of this life I have led; the desolation of solitude it has been; the masoned, walled-town of a Captain's exclusiveness, which admits but small entrance to any sympathy from the green country without—oh, weariness! heaviness! Guinea-coast slavery of solitary command!—when I think of all this; only half-suspected, not so keenly known to me before—and how for forty years I have fed upon dry salted fare—fit emblem of the dry nourishment of my soul!—when the poorest landsman has had fresh fruit to his daily hand, and broken the world's fresh bread, to my mouldy crusts—away, whole oceans away, from that young girl-wife I wedded past fifty, and sailed for Cape Horn the next day, leaving but one dent in my marriage pillow—wife? wife?—rather a widow with her husband alive! Aye, I widowed that poor girl when I married her, Starbuck; and then, the madness, the frenzy, the boiling blood and the smoking brow, with which, for a thousand lowerings old Ahab has furiously, foamingly chased his prey—more a demon than a man!—aye, aye! what a forty years' fool—fool—old fool, has old Ahab been! Why this strife of the chase? why weary, and palsy the arm at the oar, and the iron, and the lance? how the richer or better is Ahab now? Behold. Oh, Starbuck! is it not hard, that with this weary load I bear, one poor leg should have been snatched from under me? Here, brush this old hair aside; it blinds me, that I seem to weep. Locks so grey did never grow but from out some ashes! But do I look very old, so very, very old, Starbuck? I feel deadly faint, bowed, and humped, as though I were Adam, staggering beneath the piled centuries since Paradise. God! God! God!—crack my heart!—stave my brain!—mockery! mockery! bitter, biting mockery of grey hairs, have I lived enough joy to wear ye; and seem and feel thus intolerably old? Close! stand close to me, Starbuck; let me look into a human eye; it is better than to gaze into sea or sky; better than to gaze upon God. By the green land; by the bright hearth-stone! this is the magic glass, man; I see my wife and my child in thine eye. No, no; stay on board, on board!—lower not when I do; when branded Ahab gives chase to Moby Dick. That hazard shall not be thine. No, no! not with the far away home I see in that eye!"

"Oh, my Captain! my Captain! noble soul! grand old heart, after all! why should any one give chase to that hated fish! Away with me! let us fly these deadly waters! let us home! Wife and child, too, are Starbuck's—wife and child of his brotherly, sisterly, play-fellow youth; even as thine, sir, are the wife and child of thy loving, longing, paternal old age! Away! let us away!—this instant let me alter the course! How cheerily, how hilariously, O my Captain, would we bowl on our way to see old Nantucket again! I think, sir, they have some such mild blue days, even as this, in Nantucket."

"They have, they have. I have seen them—some summer days in the morning. About this time—yes, it is his noon nap now—the boy vivaciously wakes; sits up in bed; and his mother tells him of me, of cannibal old me; how I am abroad upon the deep, but will yet come back to dance him again."

"'Tis my Mary, my Mary herself! She promised that my boy, every morning, should be carried to the hill to catch the first glimpse of his father's sail! Yes, yes! no more! it is done! we head for Nantucket! Come, my Captain, study out the course, and let us away! See, see! the boy's face from the window! the boy's hand on the hill!"

But Ahab's glance was averted; like a blighted fruit tree he shook, and cast his last, cindered apple to the soil.

"What is it, what nameless, inscrutable, unearthly thing is it;

what cozening, hidden lord and master, and cruel, remorseless emperor commands me; that against all natural lovings and longings, I so keep pushing, and crowding, and jamming myself on all the time; recklessly making me ready to do what in my own proper, natural heart, I durst not so much as dare? Is Ahab, Ahab? Is it I, God, or who, that lifts this arm? But if the great sun move not of himself; but is as an errand-boy in heaven; nor one single star can revolve, but by some invisible power; how then can this one small heart beat; this one small brain think thoughts; unless God does that beating, does that thinking, does that living, and not I. By heaven, man, we are turned round and round in this world, like yonder windlass, and Fate is the handspike. And all the time, lo! that smiling sky, and this unsounded sea! Look! see yon Albicore! who put it into him to chase and fang that flying-fish? Where do murderers go, man! Who's to doom, when the judge himself is dragged to the bar? But it is a mild, mild wind, and a mild looking sky; and the air smells now, as if it blew from a far-away meadow; they have been making hay somewhere under the slopes of the Andes, Starbuck, and the mowers are sleeping among the new-mown hay. Sleeping? Aye, toil we how we may, we all sleep at last on the field. Sleep? Aye, and rust amid greenness; as last year's scythes flung down, and left in the half-cut swaths—Starbuck!"

But blanched to a corpse's hue with despair, the mate had stolen away.

Ahab crossed the deck to gaze over on the other side; but started at two reflected, fixed eyes in the water there. Fedallah was motionlessly leaning over the same rail.

Chapter 133

THE CHASE—FIRST DAY

That night, in the mid-watch, when the old man—as his wont at intervals—stepped forth from the scuttle in which he leaned, and went to his pivot-hole, he suddenly thrust out his face fiercely, snuffing up the sea air as a sagacious ship's dog will, in drawing nigh to some barbarous isle. He declared that a whale must be near. Soon that peculiar odor, sometimes to a great distance given forth by the living sperm whale, was palpable to all the watch; nor was any mariner surprised when, after inspecting the compass, and then the dog-vane, and then ascertaining the precise bearing of the odor as nearly as possible, Ahab rapidly ordered the ship's course to be slightly altered, and the sail to be shortened.

The acute policy dictating these movements was sufficiently vindicated at daybreak, by the sight of a long sleek on the sea directly and lengthwise ahead, smooth as oil, and resembling in the pleated watery wrinkles bordering it, the polished metallic-like marks of some swift tide-rip, at the mouth of a deep, rapid stream.

"Man the mast-heads! Call all hands!"

Thundering with the butts of three clubbed handspikes on the forecastle deck, Daggoo roused the sleepers with such judgment claps that they seemed to exhale from the scuttle, so instantaneously did they appear with their clothes in their hands.

"What d'ye see?" cried Ahab, flattening his face to the sky.

"Nothing, nothing, sir!" was the sound hailing down in reply.

"T'gallant sails!—stunsails! alow and aloft, and on both sides!"

All sail being set, he now cast loose the life-line, reserved for swaying him to the main royal-mast head; and in a few moments they were hoisting him thither, when, while but two thirds of the way aloft, and while peering ahead through the horizontal vacancy between the main-top-sail and top-gallant-sail, he raised a gull-like cry in the air, "There she blows!—there she blows! A hump like a snow-hill! It is Moby Dick!"

Fired by the cry which seemed simultaneously taken up by the three look-outs, the men on deck rushed to the rigging to behold the famous whale they had so long been pursuing. Ahab had now gained his final perch, some feet above the other look-outs, Tashtego standing just beneath him on the cap of the top-gallant-mast, so that the Indian's head was almost on a level with Ahab's heel. From this height the whale was now seen some mile or so ahead, at every roll of the sea revealing his high sparkling hump, and regularly jetting his silent spout into the air. To the credulous mariners it seemed the same silent spout they had so long ago beheld in the moonlit Atlantic and Indian Oceans.

"And did none of ye see it before?" cried Ahab, hailing the perched men all around him.

"I saw him almost that same instant, sir, that Captain Ahab did, and I cried out," said Tashtego.

"Not the same instant; not the same—no, the doubloon is mine, Fate reserved the doubloon for me. *I* only; none of ye could have raised the White Whale first. There she blows! there she blows!—there she blows! There again!—there again!" he cried, in long-drawn, lingering, methodic tones, attuned to the gradual prolongings of the whale's visible jets. "He's going to sound! In stunsails! Down top-gallant-sails! Stand by three boats. Mr. Starbuck, remember, stay on board, and keep the ship. Helm there! Luff, luff a point! So; steady, man, steady! There go flukes! No, no; only black water! All ready the boats there? Stand by, stand by! Lower me, Mr. Starbuck; lower, lower,—quick, quicker!" and he slid through the air to the deck.

"He is heading straight to leeward, sir," cried Stubb, "right away from us; cannot have seen the ship yet."

"Be dumb, man! Stand by the braces! Hard down the helm!—brace up! Shiver her!—shiver her! So; well that! Boats, boats!"

Soon all the boats but Starbuck's were dropped; all the boat-sails set—all the paddles plying; with rippling swiftness, shooting to leeward; and Ahab heading the onset. A pale, death-glimmer lit up Fedallah's sunken eyes; a hideous motion gnawed his mouth.

Like noiseless nautilus shells, their light prows sped through the sea; but only slowly they neared the foe. As they neared him, the ocean grew still more smooth; seemed drawing a carpet over its waves; seemed a noon-meadow, so serenely it spread. At length the breathless hunter came so nigh his seemingly unsuspecting prey, that his entire dazzling hump was distinctly visible, sliding along the sea as if an isolated thing, and continually set in a revolving ring of finest, fleecy, greenish foam. He saw the vast, involved wrinkles of the slightly projecting head beyond. Before it, far out on the soft Turkish-rugged waters, went the glistening white shadow from his broad, milky forehead, a musical rippling play-fully accompanying the shade; and behind, the blue waters inter-changeably flowed over into the moving valley of his steady wake; and on either hand bright bubbles arose and danced by his side. But these were broken again by the light toes of hundreds of gay fowl softly feathering the sea, alternate with their fitful flight; and like to some flag-staff rising from the painted hull of an argosy, the tall but shattered pole of a recent lance projected from the white whale's back; and at intervals one of the cloud of soft-toed fowls hovering, and to and fro skimming like a canopy over the fish, silently perched and rocked on this pole, the long tail feathers streaming like pennons.

A gentle joyousness—a mighty mildness of repose in swiftness, invested the gliding whale. Not the white bull Jupiter swimming away with ravished Europa clinging to his graceful horns; his lovely, leering eyes sideways intent upon the maid; with smooth bewitch-ing fleetness, rippling straight for the nuptial bower in Crete; not Jove, not that great majesty Supreme! did surpass the glorified White Whale as he so divinely swam.

On each soft side—coincident with the parted swell, that but once laving him, then flowed so wide away—on each bright side, the whale shed off enticings. No wonder there had been some among the hunters who namelessly transported and allured by all that serenity, had ventured to assail it; but had fatally found that quietude but the vesture of tornadoes. Yet calm, enticing calm, oh, whale! thou glidest on, to all who for the first time eye thee, no matter how many in that same way thou may'st have bejuggled and destroyed before.

And thus, through the serene tranquillities of the tropical sea, among waves whose hand-clappings were suspended by exceeding rapture, Moby Dick moved on, still withholding from sight the full terrors of his submerged trunk, entirely hiding the wrenched hideousness of his jaw. But soon the fore part of him slowly rose from the water; for an instant his whole marbleized body formed a high arch, like Virginia's Natural Bridge, and warningly waving his bannered flukes in the air, the grand god revealed himself, sounded, and went out of sight. Hoveringly halting, and dipping on the wing, the white sea-fowls longingly lingered over the agitated pool that he left.

With oars apeak, and paddles down, the sheets of their sails adrift, the three boats now stilly floated, awaiting Moby Dick's reappearance.

"An hour," said Ahab, standing rooted in his boat's stern; and he gazed beyond the whale's place, towards the dim blue spaces and wide wooing vacancies to leeward. It was only an instant; for again his eyes seemed whirling round in his head as he swept the watery circle. The breeze now freshened; the sea began to swell.

"The birds!—the birds!" cried Tashtego.

In long Indian file, as when herons take wing, the white birds were now all flying towards Ahab's boat; and when within a few yards began fluttering over the water there, wheeling round and round, with joyous, expectant cries. Their vision was keener than man's; Ahab could perceive no sign in the sea. But suddenly as he peered down and down into its depths, he profoundly saw a white living spot no bigger than a white weasel, with wonderful celerity uprising, and magnifying as it rose, till it turned, and then there were plainly revealed two long crooked rows of white, glistening teeth, floating up from the undiscoverable bottom. It was Moby Dick's open mouth and scrolled jaw; his vast, shadowed bulk still half blending with the blue of the sea. The glittering mouth yawned beneath the boat like an open-doored marble tomb; and giving one sidelong sweep with his steering oar, Ahab whirled the craft aside from this tremendous apparition. Then, calling upon Fedallah to change places with him, went forward to the bows, and seizing Perth's harpoon, commanded his crew to grasp their oars and stand by to stern.

Now, by reason of this timely spinning round the boat upon its axis, its bow, by anticipation, was made to face the whale's head while yet under water. But as if perceiving this stratagem, Moby Dick, with that malicious intelligence ascribed to him, sidelingly transplanted himself, as it were, in an instant, shooting his pleated head lengthwise beneath the boat.

Through and through; through every plank and each rib, it thrilled for an instant, the whale obliquely lying on his back, in the manner of a biting shark, slowly and feelingly taking its bows full within his mouth, so that the long, narrow, scrolled lower jaw curled high up into the open air, and one of the teeth caught in a row-lock. The bluish pearl-white of the inside of the jaw was within six inches of Ahab's head, and reached higher than that. In this attitude the White Whale now shook the slight cedar as a mildly cruel cat her mouse. With unastonished eyes Fedallah gazed, and crossed his arms; but the tiger-yellow crew were tumbling over each other's heads to gain the uttermost stern.

And now, while both elastic gunwales were springing in and out, as the whale dallied with the doomed craft in this devilish way; and from his body being submerged beneath the boat, he could not be darted at from the bows, for the bows were almost inside of him, as it were; and while the other boats involuntarily paused, as before a quick crisis impossible to withstand, then it was that monomaniac Ahab, furious with this tantalizing vicinity of his foe, which placed him all alive and helpless in the very jaws he hated; frenzied with all this, he seized the long bone with his naked hands, and wildly strove to wrench it from its gripe. As now he thus vainly strove, the jaw slipped from him; the frail gunwales bent in, collapsed, and snapped, as both jaws, like an enormous shears, sliding further aft, bit the craft completely in twain, and locked themselves fast again in the sea, midway between the two floating wrecks. These floated aside, the broken ends drooping, the crew at the stern-wreck clinging to the gunwales, and striving to hold fast to the oars to lash them across.

At that preluding moment, ere the boat was yet snapped, Ahab, the first to perceive the whale's intent, by the crafty uprising of his head, a movement that loosed his hold for the time; at that moment his hand had made one final effort to push the boat out of the bite. But only slipping further into the whale's mouth, and tilting over sideways as it slipped, the boat had shaken off his hold on the jaw; spilled him out of it, as he leaned to the push; and so he fell flat-faced upon the sea.

Ripplingly withdrawing from his prey, Moby Dick now lay at a little distance, vertically thrusting his oblong white head up and down in the billows; and at the same time slowly revolving his whole spindled body; so that when his vast wrinkled forehead rose—some twenty or more feet out of the water—the now rising swells, with all their confluent waves, dazzlingly broke against it;

vindictively tossing their shivered spray still higher into the air.* So, in a gale, the but half baffled Channel billows only recoil from the base of the Eddystone, triumphantly to overleap its summit with their scud.

But soon resuming his horizontal attitude, Moby Dick swam swiftly round and round the wrecked crew; sideways churning the water in his vengeful wake, as if lashing himself up to still another and more deadly assault. The sight of the splintered boat seemed to madden him, as the blood of grapes and mulberries cast before Antiochus's elephants in the book of Maccabees.[1] Meanwhile Ahab half smothered in the foam of the whale's insolent tail, and too much of a cripple to swim,—though he could still keep afloat, even in the heart of such a whirlpool as that; helpless Ahab's head was seen, like a tossed bubble which the least chance shock might burst. From the boat's fragmentary stern, Fedallah incuriously and mildly eyed him; the clinging crew, at the other drifting end, could not succor him; more than enough was it for them to look to themselves. For so revolvingly appalling was the White Whale's aspect, and so planetarily swift the ever-contracting circles he made, that he seemed horizontally swooping upon them. And though the other boats, unharmed, still hovered hard by; still they dared not pull into the eddy to strike, lest that should be the signal for the instant destruction of the jeopardized castaways, Ahab and all; nor in that case could they themselves hope to escape. With straining eyes, then, they remained on the outer edge of the direful zone, whose centre had now become the old man's head.

Meantime, from the beginning all this had been descried from the ship's mast heads; and squaring her yards, she had borne down upon the scene; and was now so nigh, that Ahab in the water hailed her;—"Sail on the"—but that moment a breaking sea dashed on him from Moby Dick, and whelmed him for the time. But struggling out of it again, and chancing to rise on a towering crest, he shouted,—"Sail on the whale!—Drive him off!"

The Pequod's prow was pointed; and breaking up the charmed circle, she effectually parted the white whale from his victim. As he sullenly swam off, the boats flew to the rescue.

Dragged into Stubb's boat with blood-shot, blinded eyes, the white brine caking in his wrinkles; the long tension of Ahab's bodily strength did crack, and helplessly he yielded to his body's doom: for a time, lying all crushed in the bottom of Stubb's boat,

* This motion is peculiar to the sperm whale. It receives its designation (pitchpoling) from its being likened to that preliminary up-and-down poise of the whale-lance, in the exercise called pitchpoling, previously described. By this motion the whale must best and most comprehensively view whatever objects may be encircling him [Melville's note].

1. I Maccabees 6:34, in the Apocrypha.

like one trodden under foot of herds of elephants. Far inland, nameless wails came from him, as desolate sounds from out ravines.

But this intensity of his physical prostration did but so much the more abbreviate it. In an instant's compass, great hearts sometimes condense to one deep pang, the sum total of those shallow pains kindly diffused through feebler men's whole lives. And so, such hearts, though summary in each one suffering; still, if the gods decree it, in their life-time aggregate a whole age of woe, wholly made up of instantaneous intensities; for even in their pointless centres, those noble natures contain the entire circumferences of inferior souls.

"The harpoon," said Ahab, half way rising, and draggingly leaning on one bended arm—"is it safe?"

"Aye, sir, for it was not darted; this is it," said Stubb, showing it.

"Lay it before me;—any missing men?"

"One, two, three, four, five;—there were five oars, sir, and here are five men."

"That's good.—Help me, man; I wish to stand. So, so, I see him! there! there! going to leeward still; what a leaping spout!— Hands off from me! The eternal sap runs up in Ahab's bones again! Set the sail; out oars; the helm!"

It is often the case that when a boat is stove, its crew, being picked up by another boat, help to work that second boat; and the chase is thus continued with what is called double-banked oars. It was thus now. But the added power of the boat did not equal the added power of the whale, for he seemed to have treble-banked his every fin; swimming with a velocity which plainly showed, that if now, under these circumstances, pushed on, the chase would prove an indefinitely prolonged, if not a hopeless one; nor could any crew endure for so long a period, such an unintermitted, intense straining at the oar; a thing barely tolerable only in some one brief vicissitude. The ship itself, then, as it sometimes happens, offered the most promising intermediate means of overtaking the chase. Accordingly, the boats now made for her, and were soon swayed up to their cranes—the two parts of the wrecked boat having been previously secured by her—and then hoisting everything to her side, and stacking her canvas high up, and sideways outstretching it with stun-sails, like the double-jointed wings of an albatross; the Pequod bore down in the leeward wake of Moby-Dick. At the well known, methodic intervals, the whale's glittering spout was regularly announced from the manned mast-heads; and when he would be reported as just gone down, Ahab would take the time, and then pacing the deck, binnacle-watch in hand, so soon as the last second of the allotted hour expired, his voice was heard.—"Whose is the doubloon now? D'ye see him?" and if the reply was, No, sir! straightway he commanded them to lift him to his perch. In this way the day wore on; Ahab, now aloft and motionless; anon, unrestingly pacing the planks.

As he was thus walking, uttering no sound, except to hail the men aloft, or to bid them hoist a sail still higher, or to spread one to a still greater breadth—thus to and fro pacing, beneath his slouched hat, at every turn he passed his own wrecked boat, which had been dropped upon the quarter-deck, and lay there reversed; broken bow to shattered stern. At last he paused before it; and as in an already over-clouded sky fresh troops of clouds will sometimes sail across, so over the old man's face there now stole some such added gloom as this.

Stubb saw him pause; and perhaps intending, not vainly, though, to evince his own unabated fortitude, and thus keep up a valiant place in his Captain's mind, he advanced, and eyeing the wreck exclaimed—"The thistle the ass refused; it pricked his mouth too keenly, sir; ha! ha!"

"What soulless thing is this that laughs before a wreck? Man, man! did I not know thee brave as fearless fire (and as mechanical) I could swear thou wert a poltroon. Groan nor laugh should be heard before a wreck."

"Aye, sir," said Starbuck drawing near, "'tis a solemn sight; an omen, and an ill one."

"Omen? omen?—the dictionary! If the gods think to speak outright to man, they will honorably speak outright; not shake their heads, and give an old wives' darkling hint.—Begone! Ye two are the opposite poles of one thing; Starbuck is Stubb reversed, and Stubb is Starbuck; and ye two are all mankind; and Ahab stands alone among the millions of the peopled earth, nor gods nor men his neighbors! Cold, cold—I shiver!—How now? Aloft there! D'ye see him? Sing out for every spout, though he spout ten times a second!"

The day was nearly done; only the hem of his golden robe was rustling. Soon, it was almost dark, but the look-out men still remained unset.

"Can't see the spout now, sir;—too dark"—cried a voice from the air.

"How heading when last seen?"

"As before, sir,—straight to leeward."

"Good! he will travel slower now 'tis night. Down royals and top-gallant stun-sails, Mr. Starbuck. We must not run over him before morning; he's making a passage now, and may heave-to a while. Helm there! keep her full before the wind!—Aloft! come down!—Mr. Stubb, send a fresh hand to the fore-mast head, and see it manned till morning."—Then advancing towards the doubloon in the main-mast—"Men, this gold is mine, for I earned it; but I shall let it abide here till the White Whale is dead; and then, whosoever of ye first raises him, upon the day he shall be killed, this gold is that man's; and if on that day I shall again raise him, then, ten times its sum shall be divided among all of ye! Away now!—the deck is thine, sir."

And so saying, he placed himself half way within the scuttle, and slouching his hat, stood there till dawn, except when at intervals rousing himself to see how the night wore on.

Chapter 134

THE CHASE—SECOND DAY

At day-break, the three mast-heads were punctually manned afresh.

"D'ye see him?" cried Ahab, after allowing a little space for the light to spread.

"See nothing, sir."

"Turn up all hands and make sail! he travels faster than I thought for;—the top-gallant sails!—aye, they should have been kept on her all night. But no matter—'tis but resting for the rush."

Here be it said, that this pertinacious pursuit of one particular whale, continued through day into night, and through night into day, is a thing by no means unprecedented in the South sea fishery. For such is the wonderful skill, prescience of experience, and invincible confidence acquired by some great natural geniuses among the Nantucket commanders; that from the simple observation of a whale when last descried, they will, under certain given circumstances, pretty accurately foretell both the direction in which he will continue to swim for a time, while out of sight, as well as his probable rate of progression during that period. And, in these cases, somewhat as a pilot, when about losing sight of a coast, whose general trending he well knows, and which he desires shortly to return to again, but at some further point; like as this pilot stands by his compass, and takes the precise bearing of the cape at present visible, in order the more certainly to hit aright the remote, unseen headland, eventually to be visited: so does the fisherman, at his compass, with the whale; for after being chased, and diligently marked, through several hours of daylight, then, when night obscures the fish, the creature's future wake through the darkness is almost as established to the sagacious mind of the hunter, as the pilot's coast is to him. So that to this hunter's wondrous skill, the proverbial evanescence of a thing writ in water, a wake, is to all desired purposes well nigh as reliable as the steadfast land. And as the mighty iron Leviathan of the modern railway is so familiarly known in its every pace, that, with watches in their hands, men time his rate as doctors that of a baby's pulse; and lightly say of it, the up train or the down train will reach such or such a spot, at such or such an hour; even so, almost, there are occasions when these Nantucketers time that other Leviathan of the deep, according to the observed humor of his speed; and say to themselves, so many hours hence this whale will have gone two hundred miles, will have about reached this or that degree of latitude or longitude. But to render this acuteness at all successful in the end, the wind and the sea must be the whaleman's allies; for of what present avail to the becalmed or windbound mariner is the skill that assures him he is exactly ninety-three leagues and a quarter from his port? Inferable from these statements, are many collateral subtile matters touching the chase of whales.

The ship tore on; leaving such a furrow in the sea as when a cannon-ball, missent, becomes a plough-share and turns up the level field.

"By salt and hemp!" cried Stubb, "but this swift motion of the deck creeps up one's legs and tingles at the heart. This ship and I are two brave fellows!—Ha! ha! Some one take me up, and launch me, spine-wise, on the sea,—for by live-oaks! my spine's a keel. Ha, ha! we go the gait that leaves no dust behind!"

"There she blows—she blows!—she blows!—right ahead!" was now the mast-head cry.

"Aye, aye!" cried Stubb, "I knew it—ye can't escape—blow on and split your spout, O whale! the mad fiend himself is after ye! blow your trump—blister your lungs!—Ahab will dam off your blood, as a miller shuts his water-gate upon the stream!"

And Stubb did but speak out for well nigh all that crew. The frenzies of the chase had by this time worked them bubblingly up, like old wine worked anew. Whatever pale fears and forebodings some of them might have felt before; these were not only now kept out of sight through the growing awe of Ahab, but they were broken up, and on all sides routed, as timid prairie hares that scatter before the bounding bison. The hand of Fate had snatched all their souls; and by the stirring perils of the previous day; the rack of the past night's suspense; the fixed, unfearing, blind, reckless way in which their wild craft went plunging towards its flying mark; by all these things, their hearts were bowled along. The wind that made great bellies of their sails, and rushed the vessel on by arms invisible as irresistible; this seemed the symbol of that unseen agency which so enslaved them to the race.

They were one man, not thirty. For as the one ship that held them all; though it was put together of all contrasting things—

oak, and maple, and pine wood; iron, and pitch, and hemp—yet all these ran into each other in the one concrete hull, which shot on its way, both balanced and directed by the long central keel; even so, all the individualities of the crew, this man's valor, that man's fear; guilt and guiltlessness, all varieties were welded into oneness, and were all directed to that fatal goal which Ahab their one lord and keel did point to.

The rigging lived. The mast-heads, like the tops of tall palms, were outspreadingly tufted with arms and legs. Clinging to a spar with one hand, some reached forth the other with impatient wavings; others, shading their eyes from the vivid sunlight, sat far out on the rocking yards; all the spars in full bearing of mortals, ready and ripe for their fate. Ah! how they still strove through that infinite blueness to seek out the thing that might destroy them!

"Why sing ye not out for him, if ye see him?" cried Ahab, when, after the lapse of some minutes since the first cry, no more had been heard. "Sway me up, men; ye have been deceived; not Moby Dick casts one odd jet that way, and then disappears."

It was even so; in their headlong eagerness, the men had mistaken some other thing for the whale-spout, as the event itself soon proved; for hardly had Ahab reached his perch; hardly was the rope belayed to its pin on deck, when he struck the key-note to an orchestra, that made the air vibrate as with the combined discharges of rifles. The triumphant halloo of thirty buckskin lungs was heard, as—much nearer to the ship than the place of the imaginary jet, less than a mile ahead—Moby Dick bodily burst into view! For not by any calm and indolent spoutings; not by the peaceable gush of that mystic fountain in his head, did the White Whale now reveal his vicinity; but by the far more wondrous phenomenon of breaching. Rising with his utmost velocity from the furthest depths, the Sperm Whale thus booms his entire bulk into the pure element of air, and piling up a mountain of dazzling foam, shows his place to the distance of seven miles and more. In those moments, the torn, enraged waves he shakes off, seem his mane; in some cases, this breaching is his act of defiance.

"There she breaches! there she breaches!" was the cry, as in his immeasurable bravadoes the White Whale tossed himself salmon-like to Heaven. So suddenly seen in the blue plain of the sea, and relieved against the still bluer margin of the sky, the spray that he raised, for the moment, intolerably glittered and glared like a glacier; and stood there gradually fading and fading away from its first sparkling intensity, to the dim mistiness of an advancing shower in a vale.

"Aye, breach your last to the sun, Moby Dick!" cried Ahab,

"thy hour and thy harpoon are at hand!—Down! down all of ye, but one man at the fore. The boats!—stand by!"

Unmindful of the tedious rope-ladders of the shrouds, the men, like shooting stars, slid to the deck, by the isolated backstays and halyards; while Ahab, less dartingly, but still rapidly was dropped from his perch.

"Lower away," he cried, so soon as he had reached his boat—a spare one, rigged the afternoon previous. "Mr. Starbuck, the ship is thine—keep away from the boats, but keep near them. Lower, all!"

As if to strike a quick terror into them, by this time being the first assailant himself, Moby Dick had turned, and was now coming for the three crews. Ahab's boat was central; and cheering his men, he told them he would take the whale head-and-head,—that is, pull straight up to his forehead,—a not uncommon thing; for when within a certain limit, such a course excludes the coming onset from the whale's sidelong vision. But ere that close limit was gained, and while yet all three boats were plain as the ship's three masts to his eye; the White Whale churning himself into furious speed, almost in an instant as it were, rushing among the boats with open jaws, and a lashing tail, offered appalling battle on every side; and heedless of the irons darted at him from every boat, seemed only intent on annihilating each separate plank of which those boats were made. But skilfully manœuvred, incessantly wheeling like trained chargers in the field; the boats for a while eluded him; though, at times, but by a plank's breadth; while all the time, Ahab's unearthly slogan tore every other cry but his to shreds.

But at last in his untraceable evolutions, the White Whale so crossed and recrossed, and in a thousand ways entangled the slack of the three lines now fast to him, that they foreshortened, and, of themselves, warped the devoted boats towards the planted irons in him; though now for a moment the whale drew aside a little, as if to rally for a more tremendous charge. Seizing that opportunity, Ahab first paid out more line: and then was rapidly hauling and jerking in upon it again—hoping that way to disencumber it of some snarls—when lo!—a sight more savage than the embattled teeth of sharks!

Caught and twisted—corkscrewed in the mazes of the line, loose harpoons and lances, with all their bristling barbs and points, came flashing and dripping up to the chocks in the bows of Ahab's boat. Only one thing could be done. Seizing the boat-knife, he critically reached within—through—and then, without—the rays of steel; dragged in the line beyond, passed it, inboard, to the bowsman, and then, twice sundering the rope near the chocks—dropped the intercepted fagot of steel into the sea; and was all fast again. That instant, the White Whale made a sudden rush among the remaining tangles of the other lines; by so doing, irresistibly dragged the more involved boats of Stubb and Flask towards his flukes; dashed them together like two rolling husks on a surf-beaten beach, and then, diving down into the sea, disappeared in a boiling maelstrom, in which, for a space, the odorous cedar chips of the wrecks danced round and round, like the grated nutmeg in a swiftly stirred bowl of punch.

While the two crews were yet circling in the waters, reaching out after the revolving line-tubs, oars, and other floating furniture, while aslope little Flask bobbed up and down like an empty vial, twitching his legs upwards to escape the dreaded jaws of sharks; and Stubb was lustily singing out for some one to ladle him up; and while the old man's line—now parting—admitted of his pulling into the creamy pool to rescue whom he could;—in that wild simultaneousness of a thousand concreted perils,—Ahab's yet unstricken boat seemed drawn up towards Heaven by invisible wires, —as, arrow-like, shooting perpendicularly from the sea, the White Whale dashed his broad forehead against its bottom, and sent it, turning over and over, into the air; till it fell again—gunwale downwards—and Ahab and his men struggled out from under it, like seals from a sea-side cave.

The first uprising momentum of the whale—modifying its direction as he struck the surface—involuntarily launched him along it, to a little distance from the centre of the destruction he had made; and with his back to it, he now lay for a moment slowly feeling with his flukes from side to side; and whenever a stray oar, bit of plank, the least chip or crumb of the boats touched his skin, his tail swiftly drew back, and came sideways smiting the sea. But soon, as if satisfied that his work for that time was done, he pushed his pleated forehead through the ocean, and trailing after him the intertangled lines, continued his leeward way at a traveller's methodic pace.

As before, the attentive ship having descried the whole fight, again came bearing down to the rescue, and dropping a boat, picked up the floating mariners, tubs, oars, and whatever else could be caught at, and safely landed them on her decks. Some sprained shoulders, wrists, and ankles; livid contusions; wrenched harpoons and lances; inextricable intricacies of rope; shattered oars and planks; all these were there; but no fatal or even serious ill seemed to have befallen any one. As with Fedallah the day before, so Ahab was now found grimly clinging to his boat's broken half, which afforded a comparatively easy float; nor did it so exhaust him as the previous day's mishap.

But when he was helped to the deck, all eyes were fastened upon him; as instead of standing by himself he still half-hung upon the shoulder of Starbuck, who had thus far been the foremost to assist him. His ivory leg had been snapped off, leaving but one short sharp splinter.

"Aye aye, Starbuck, 'tis sweet to lean sometimes, be the leaner who he will; and would old Ahab had leaned oftener than he has."

"The ferrule has not stood, sir," said the carpenter, now coming up; "I put good work into that leg."

"But no bones broken, sir, I hope," said Stubb with true concern.

"Aye! and all splintered to pieces, Stubb!—d'ye see it.—But even with a broken bone, old Ahab is untouched; and I account no living bone of mine one jot more me, than this dead one that's lost. Nor white whale, nor man, nor fiend, can so much as graze old Ahab in his own proper and inaccessible being. Can any lead touch yonder floor, any mast scrape yonder roof?—Aloft there! which way?"

"Dead to leeward, sir."

"Up helm, then; pile on the sail again, ship keepers! down the rest of the spare boats and rig them—Mr. Starbuck away, and muster the boats' crews."

"Let me first help thee towards the bulwarks, sir."

"Oh, oh, oh! how this splinter gores me now! Accursed fate! that the unconquerable captain in the soul should have such a craven mate!"

"Sir?"

"My body, man, not thee. Give me something for a cane—there, that shivered lance will do. Muster the men. Surely I have not seen him yet. By heaven it cannot be!—missing?—quick! call them all."

The old man's hinted thought was true. Upon mustering the company, the Parsee was not there.

"The Parsee!" cried Stubb—"he must have been caught in——"

"The black vomit wrench thee!—run all of ye above, alow, cabin, forecastle—find him—not gone—not gone!"

But quickly they returned to him with the tidings that the Parsee was nowhere to be found.

"Aye, sir," said Stubb—"caught among the tangles of your line—I thought I saw him dragging under."

"*My* line! *my* line? Gone?—gone? What means that little word? —What death-knell rings in it, that old Ahab shakes as if he were the belfry. The harpoon, too!—toss over the litter there,—d'ye see it?—the forged iron, men, the white whale's—no, no, no,— blistered fool! this hand did dart it!—'tis in the fish!—Aloft there! Keep him nailed—Quick!—all hands to the rigging of the boats—

collect the oars—harpooneers! the irons, the irons!—hoist the royals higher—a pull on all the sheets!—helm there! steady, steady for your life! I'll ten times girdle the unmeasured globe; yea and dive straight through it, but I'll slay him yet!"

"Great God! but for one single instant show thyself," cried Starbuck; "never, never wilt thou capture him, old man—In Jesus' name no more of this, that's worse than devil's madness. Two days chased; twice stove to splinters; thy very leg once more snatched from under thee; thy evil shadow gone—all good angels mobbing thee with warnings:—what more wouldst thou have?— Shall we keep chasing this murderous fish till he swamps the last man? Shall we be dragged by him to the bottom of the sea? Shall we be towed by him to the infernal world? Oh, oh,—Impiety and blasphemy to hunt him more!"

"Starbuck, of late I've felt strangely moved to thee; ever since that hour we both saw—thou know'st what, in one another's eyes. But in this matter of the whale, be the front of thy face to me as the palm of this hand—a lipless, unfeatured blank. Ahab is for ever Ahab, man. This whole act's immutably decreed. 'Twas rehearsed by thee and me a billion years before this ocean rolled. Fool! I am the Fates' lieutenant; I act under orders. Look thou, underling! that thou obeyest mine.—Stand round me, men. Ye see an old man cut down to the stump; leaning on a shivered lance; propped up on a lonely foot. 'Tis Ahab—his body's part; but Ahab's soul's a centipede, that moves upon a hundred legs. I feel strained, half stranded, as ropes that tow dismasted frigates in a gale; and I may look so. But ere I break, ye'll hear me crack; and till ye hear *that*, know that Ahab's hawser tows his purpose yet. Believe ye, men, in the things called omens? Then laugh aloud, and cry encore! For ere they drown, drowning things will twice rise to the surface; then rise again, to sink for evermore. So with Moby Dick—two days he's floated—to-morrow will be the third. Aye, men, he'll rise once more,—but only to spout his last! D'ye feel brave, men, brave?"

"As fearless fire," cried Stubb.

"And as mechanical," muttered Ahab. Then as the men went forward, he muttered on:—"The things called omens! And yesterday I talked the same to Starbuck there, concerning my broken boat. Oh! how valiantly I seek to drive out of others' hearts what's clinched so fast in mine!—The Parsee—the Parsee!—gone, gone? and he was to go before:—but still was to be seen again ere I could perish—How's that?—There's a riddle now might baffle all the lawyers backed by the ghosts of the whole line of judges:— like a hawk's beak it pecks my brain. *I'll, I'll* solve it, though!"

When dusk descended, the whale was still in sight to leeward.

So once more the sail was shortened, and everything passed nearly as on the previous night; only, the sound of hammers, and the hum of the grindstone was heard till nearly daylight, as the men toiled by lanterns in the complete and careful rigging of the spare boats and sharpening their fresh weapons for the morrow. Meantime, of the broken keel of Ahab's wrecked craft the carpenter made him another leg; while still as on the night before, slouched Ahab stood fixed within his scuttle; his hid, heliotrope glance anticipatingly gone backward on its dial; set due eastward for the earliest sun.

Chapter 135

THE CHASE.—THIRD DAY

The morning of the third day dawned fair and fresh, and once more the solitary night-man at the fore-mast-head was relieved by crowds of the daylight look-outs, who dotted every mast and almost every spar.

"D'ye see him?" cried Ahab; but the whale was not yet in sight.

"In his infallible wake, though; but follow that wake, that's all. Helm there; steady, as thou goest, and hast been going. What a lovely day again! were it a new-made world, and made for a summer-house to the angels, and this morning the first of its throwing open to them, a fairer day could not dawn upon that world. Here's food for thought, had Ahab time to think; but Ahab never thinks; he only feels, feels, feels; *that's* tingling enough for mortal man! to think's audacity. God only has that right and privilege. Thinking is, or ought to be, a coolness and a calmness; and our poor hearts throb, and our poor brains beat too much for that. And yet, I've sometimes thought my brain was very calm—frozen calm, this old skull cracks so, like a glass in which the contents turn to ice, and shiver it. And still this hair is growing now; this moment growing, and heat must breed it; but no, it's like that sort of common grass that will grow anywhere, between the earthy clefts of Greenland ice or in Vesuvius' lava. How the wild winds blow it; they whip it about me as the torn shreds of split sails lash the tossed ship they cling to. A vile wind that has no doubt blown ere this through prison corridors and cells, and wards of hospitals, and ventilated them, and now comes blowing hither as innocent as fleeces. Out upon it!—it's tainted. Were I the wind, I'd blow no more on such a wicked, miserable world. I'd crawl somewhere to a cave, and slink there. And yet, 'tis a noble and heroic thing, the wind! who ever conquered it? In every fight it has the last and bitterest blow. Run tilting at it, and you but run through it. Ha! a coward wind that strikes stark naked men, but will not stand to receive a single blow. Even Ahab is a braver thing—a nobler thing than *that*. Would now the wind but had a body; but all the things that most exasperate and outrage mortal man, all these things are bodiless, but only bodiless as objects, not as agents. There's a most special, a most cunning, oh, a most malicious difference! And yet, I say again, and swear it now, that there's something all glorious and gracious in the wind. These warm Trade Winds, at least, that in the clear heavens blow straight on, in strong and steadfast, vigorous mildness; and veer not from their mark, however the baser currents of the sea may turn and tack, and mightiest Mississippies of the land shift and swerve about, uncertain where to go at last. And by the eternal Poles! these same Trades that so directly blow my good ship on; these Trades, or something like them—something so unchangeable, and full as strong, blow my keeled soul along! To it! Aloft there! What d'ye see?"

"Nothing, sir."

"Nothing! and noon at hand! The doubloon goes a-begging! See the sun! Aye, aye, it must be so. I've oversailed him. How, got the start? Aye, he's chasing *me* now; not I, *him*—that's bad; I might have known it, too. Fool! the lines—the harpoons he's towing. Aye, aye, I have run him by last night. About! about! Come down, all of ye, but the regular look outs! Man the braces!"

Steering as she had done, the wind had been somewhat on the Pequod's quarter, so that now being pointed in the reverse direction, the braced ship sailed hard upon the breeze as she rechurned the cream in her own white wake.

"Against the wind he now steers for the open jaw," murmured Starbuck to himself, as he coiled the new-hauled main-brace upon the rail. "God keep us, but already my bones feel damp within me, and from the inside wet my flesh. I misdoubt me that I disobey my God in obeying him!"

"Stand by to sway me up!" cried Ahab, advancing to the hempen basket. "We should meet him soon."

"Aye, aye, sir," and straightway Starbuck did Ahab's bidding, and once more Ahab swung on high.

A whole hour now passed; gold-beaten out to ages. Time itself now held long breaths with keen suspense. But at last, some three points off the weather bow, Ahab descried the spout again, and instantly from the three mast-heads three shrieks went up as if the tongues of fire had voiced it.

"Forehead to forehead I meet thee, this third time, Moby Dick! On deck there!—brace sharper up; crowd her into the wind's eye. He's too far off to lower yet, Mr. Starbuck. The sails shake! Stand over that helmsman with a top-maul! So, so; he travels fast,

and I must down. But let me have one more good round look
aloft here at the sea; there's time for that. An old, old sight, and
yet somehow so young; aye, and not changed a wink since I first
saw it, a boy, from the sand-hills of Nantucket! The same!—the
same!—the same to Noah as to me. There's a soft shower to leeward. Such lovely leewardings! They must lead somewhere—to
something else than common land, more palmy than the palms.
Leeward! the white whale goes that way; look to windward, then;
the better if the bitterer quarter. But good bye, good bye, old
mast-head! What's this?—green? aye, tiny mosses in these warped
cracks. No such green weather stains on Ahab's head! There's the
difference now between man's old age and matter's. But aye, old
mast, we both grow old together; sound in our hulls, though, are
we not, my ship? Aye, minus a leg, that's all. By heaven this dead
wood has the better of my live flesh every way. I can't compare
with it; and I've known some ships made of dead trees outlast the
lives of men made of the most vital stuff of vital fathers. What's
that he said? he should still go before me, my pilot; and yet to be
seen again? But where? Will I have eyes at the bottom of the sea,
supposing I descend those endless stairs? and all night I've been
sailing from him, wherever he did sink to. Aye, aye, like many
more thou told'st direful truth as touching thyself, O Parsee;
but, Ahab, there thy shot fell short. Good by, mast-head—keep a
good eye upon the whale, the while I'm gone. We'll talk to-morrow, nay, to-night, when the white whale lies down there, tied by
head and tail."

He gave the word; and still gazing round him, was steadily lowered through the cloven blue air to the deck.

In due time the boats were lowered; but as standing in his shal-
lop's stern, Ahab just hovered upon the point of the descent,
he waved to the mate,—who held one of the tackle-ropes on deck
—and bade him pause.

"Starbuck!"

"Sir?"

"For the third time my soul's ship starts upon this voyage, Starbuck."

"Aye, sir, thou wilt have it so."

"Some ships sail from their ports, and ever afterwards are missing, Starbuck!"

"Truth, sir: saddest truth."

"Some men die at ebb tide; some at low water; some at the full
of the flood;—and I feel now like a billow that's all one crested
comb, Starbuck. I am old;—shake hands with me, man."

Their hands met; their eyes fastened; Starbuck's tears the glue.

"Oh, my captain, my captain!—noble heart—go not—go not!—

see, it's a brave man that weeps; how great the agony of the persuasion then!"

"Lower away!"—cried Ahab, tossing the mate's arm from him. "Stand by the crew!"

In an instant the boat was pulling round close under the stern.

"The sharks! the sharks!" cried a voice from the low cabin-window there; "O master, my master, come back!"

But Ahab heard nothing; for his own voice was high-lifted then; and the boat leaped on.

Yet the voice spake true; for scarce had he pushed from the ship, when numbers of sharks, seemingly rising from out the dark waters beneath the hull, maliciously snapped at the blades of the oars, every time they dipped in the water; and in this way accompanied the boat with their bites. It is a thing not uncommonly happening to the whale-boats in those swarming seas; the sharks at times apparently following them in the same prescient way that vultures hover over the banners of marching regiments in the east. But these were the first sharks that had been observed by the Pequod since the White Whale had been first descried; and whether it was that Ahab's crew were all such tiger-yellow barbarians, and therefore their flesh more musky to the senses of the sharks—a matter sometimes well known to affect them,—however it was, they seemed to follow that one boat without molesting the others.

"Heart of wrought steel!" murmured Starbuck gazing over the side, and following with his eyes the receding boat—"canst thou yet ring boldly to that sight?—lowering thy keel among ravening sharks, and followed by them, open-mouthed to the chase; and this the critical third day?—For when three days flow together in one continuous intense pursuit; be sure the first is the morning, the second the noon, and the third the evening and the end of that thing—be that end what it may. Oh! my God! what is this that shoots through me, and leaves me so deadly calm, yet expectant,—fixed at the top of a shudder! Future things swim before me, as in empty outlines and skeletons; all the past is somehow grown dim. Mary, girl! thou fadest in pale glories behind me; boy! I seem to see but thy eyes grown wondrous blue. Strangest problems of life seem clearing; but clouds sweep between—Is my journey's end coming? My legs feel faint; like his who has footed it all day. Feel thy heart,—beats it yet?—Stir thyself, Starbuck!—stave it off—move, move! speak aloud!—Mast-head there! See ye my boy's hand on the hill?—Crazed;—aloft there!—keep thy keenest eye upon the boats:—mark well the whale!—Ho! again! —drive off that hawk! see! he pecks—he tears the vane"—pointing to the red flag flying at the main-truck—"Ha! he soars away with it!—Where's the old man now? sees't thou that sight, oh Ahab!—

shudder, shudder!"

The boats had not gone very far, when by a signal from the mast-heads—a downward pointed arm, Ahab knew that the whale had sounded; but intending to be near him at the next rising, he held on his way a little sideways from the vessel; the becharmed crew maintaining the profoundest silence, as the head-beat waves hammered and hammered against the opposing bow.

"Drive, drive in your nails, oh ye waves! to their uttermost heads drive them in! ye but strike a thing without a lid; and no coffin and no hearse can be mine:—and hemp only can kill me! Ha! ha!"

Suddenly the waters around them slowly swelled in broad circles; then quickly upheaved, as if sideways sliding from a submerged berg of ice, swiftly rising to the surface. A low rumbling sound was heard; a subterraneous hum; and then all held their breaths; as bedraggled with trailing ropes, and harpoons, and lances, a vast form shot lengthwise, but obliquely from the sea. Shrouded in a thin drooping veil of mist, it hovered for a moment in the rainbowed air; and then fell swamping back into the deep. Crushed thirty feet upwards, the waters flashed for an instant like heaps of fountains, then brokenly sank in a shower of flakes, leaving the circling surface creamed like new milk round the marble trunk of the whale.

"Give way!" cried Ahab to the oarsmen, and the boats darted forward to the attack; but maddened by yesterday's fresh irons that corroded in him, Moby Dick seemed combinedly possessed by all the angels that fell from heaven. The wide tiers of welded tendons overspreading his broad white forehead, beneath the transparent skin, looked knitted together; as head on, he came churning his tail among the boats; and once more flailed them apart; spilling out the irons and lances from the two mates' boats, and dashing in one side of the upper part of their bows, but leaving Ahab's almost without a scar.

While Daggoo and Queequeg were stopping the strained planks; and as the whale swimming out from them, turned, and showed one entire flank as he shot by them again; at that moment a quick cry went up. Lashed round and round to the fish's back; pinioned in the turns upon turns in which, during the past night, the whale had reeled the involutions of the lines around him, the half torn body of the Parsee was seen; his sable raiment frayed to shreds; his distended eyes turned full upon old Ahab.

The harpoon dropped from his hand.

"Befooled, befooled!"—drawing in a long lean breath—"Aye, Parsee! I see thee again.—Aye, and thou goest before; and this, *this* then is the hearse that thou didst promise. But I hold thee to the last letter of thy word. Where is the second hearse? Away, mates, to the ship! those boats are useless now; repair them if ye can in time, and return to me; if not, Ahab is enough to die— Down, men! the first thing that but offers to jump from this boat I stand in, that thing I harpoon. Ye are not other men, but my arms and my legs; and so obey me.—Where's the whale? gone down again?"

But he looked too nigh the boat; for as if bent upon escaping with the corpse he bore, and as if the particular place of the last encounter had been but a stage in his leeward voyage, Moby Dick was now again steadily swimming forward; and had almost passed the ship,—which thus far had been sailing in the contrary direction to him, though for the present her headway had been stopped. He seemed swimming with his utmost velocity, and now only intent upon pursuing his own straight path in the sea.

"Oh! Ahab," cried Starbuck, "not too late is it, even now, the third day, to desist. See! Moby Dick seeks thee not. It is thou, thou, that madly seekest him!"

Setting sail to the rising wind, the lonely boat was swiftly impelled to leeward, by both oars and canvas. And at last when Ahab was sliding by the vessel, so near as plainly to distinguish Starbuck's face as he leaned over the rail, he hailed him to turn the vessel about, and follow him, not too swiftly, at a judicious interval. Glancing upwards, he saw Tashtego, Queequeg, and Daggoo, eagerly mounting to the three mast-heads; while the oarsmen were rocking in the two staved boats which had but just been hoisted to the side, and were busily at work in repairing them. One after the other, through the port-holes, as he sped, he also caught flying glimpses of Stubb and Flask, busying themselves on deck among bundles of new irons and lances. As he saw all this; as he heard the hammers in the broken boats; far other hammers seemed driving a nail into his heart. But he rallied. And now marking that the vane or flag was gone from the main-mast-head, he shouted to Tashtego, who had just gained that perch, to descend again for another flag, and a hammer and nails, and so nail it to the mast.

Whether fagged by the three days' running chase, and the resistance to his swimming in the knotted hamper he bore; or whether it was some latent deceitfulness and malice in him: whichever was true, the White Whale's way now began to abate, as it seemed, from the boat so rapidly nearing him once more; though indeed the whale's last start had not been so long a one as before. And still as Ahab glided over the waves the unpitying sharks accompanied him; and so pertinaciously stuck to the boat; and so continually bit at the plying oars, that the blades became jagged and crunched, and left small splinters in the sea, at almost every dip.

"Heed them not! those teeth but give new rowlocks to your oars. Pull on! 'tis the better rest, the shark's jaw than the yielding water."

"But at every bite, sir, the thin blades grow smaller and smaller!"

"They will last long enough! pull on!—But who can tell"—he muttered—"whether these sharks swim to feast on the whale or on Ahab?—But pull on! Aye, all alive, now—we near him. The helm! take the helm; let me pass,"—and so saying, two of the oarsmen helped him forward to the bows of the still flying boat.

At length as the craft was cast to one side, and ran ranging along with the White Whale's flank, he seemed strangely oblivious of its advance—as the whale sometimes will—and Ahab was fairly within the smoky mountain mist, which, thrown off from the whale's spout, curled round his great, Monadnock hump; he was even thus close to him; when, with body arched back, and both arms lengthwise high-lifted to the poise, he darted his fierce iron, and his far fiercer curse into the hated whale. As both steel and curse sank to the socket, as if sucked into a morass, Moby Dick sideways writhed; spasmodically rolled his nigh flank against the bow, and, without staving a hole in it, so suddenly canted the boat over, that had it not been for the elevated part of the gunwale to which he then clung, Ahab would once more have been tossed into the sea. As it was, three of the oarsmen—who foreknew not the precise instant of the dart, and were therefore unprepared for its effects—these were flung out; but so fell, that, in an instant two of them clutched the gunwale again, and rising to its level on a combing wave, hurled themselves bodily inboard again; the third man helplessly dropping astern, but still afloat and swimming.

Almost simultaneously, with a mighty volition of ungraduated, instantaneous swiftness, the White Whale darted through the weltering sea. But when Ahab cried out to the steersman to take new turns with the line, and hold it so; and commanded the crew to turn round on their seats, and tow the boat up to the mark; the moment the treacherous line felt that double strain and tug, it snapped in the empty air!

"What breaks in me? Some sinew cracks!—'tis whole again; oars! oars! Burst in upon him!"

Hearing the tremendous rush of the sea-crashing boat, the whale wheeled round to present his blank forehead at bay; but in that evolution, catching sight of the nearing black hull of the ship; seemingly seeing in it the source of all his persecutions; bethinking it—it may be—a larger and nobler foe; of a sudden, he bore down upon its advancing prow, smiting his jaws amid fiery showers of foam.

Ahab staggered; his hand smote his forehead. "I grow blind; hands! stretch out before me that I may yet grope my way. Is't night?"

"The whale! The ship!" cried the cringing oarsmen.

"Oars! oars! Slope downwards to thy depths, O sea, that ere it be for ever too late, Ahab may slide this last, last time upon his mark! I see: the ship! the ship! Dash on, my men! Will ye not save my ship?"

But as the oarsmen violently forced their boat through the sledge-hammering seas, the before whale-smitten bow-ends of two planks burst through, and in an instant almost, the temporarily disabled boat lay nearly level with the waves; its half-wading, splashing crew, trying hard to stop the gap and bale out the pouring water.

Meantime, for that one beholding instant, Tashtego's mast-head hammer remained suspended in his hand; and the red flag, half-wrapping him as with a plaid, then streamed itself straight out from him, as his own forward-flowing heart; while Starbuck and Stubb, standing upon the bowsprit beneath, caught sight of the down-coming monster just as soon as he.

"The whale, the whale! Up helm, up helm! Oh, all ye sweet powers of air, now hug me close! Let not Starbuck die, if die he must, in a woman's fainting fit. Up helm, I say—ye fools, the jaw! the jaw! Is this the end of all my bursting prayers? all my life-long fidelities? Oh, Ahab, Ahab, lo, thy work. Steady! helmsman, steady. Nay, nay! Up helm again! He turns to meet us! Oh, his unappeasable brow drives on towards one, whose duty tells him he cannot depart. My God, stand by me now!"

"Stand not by me, but stand under me, whoever you are that will now help Stubb; for Stubb, too, sticks here. I grin at thee, thou grinning whale! Who ever helped Stubb, or kept Stubb awake, but Stubb's own unwinking eye? And now poor Stubb goes to bed upon a mattrass that is all too soft; would it were stuffed with brushwood! I grin at thee, thou grinning whale! Look ye, sun, moon, and stars! I call ye assassins of as good a fellow as ever spouted up his ghost. For all that, I would yet ring glasses with ye, would ye but hand the cup! Oh, oh! oh, oh! thou grinning whale, but there'll be plenty of gulping soon! Why fly ye not, O Ahab! For me, off shoes and jacket to it; let Stubb die in his drawers! A most mouldy and over salted death, though;—cherries! cherries! cherries! Oh, Flask, for one red cherry ere we die!"

"Cherries? I only wish that we were where they grow. Oh, Stubb, I hope my poor mother's drawn my part-pay ere this; if not, few coppers will now come to her, for the voyage is up."

From the ship's bows, nearly all the seamen now hung inactive; hammers, bits of plank, lances, and harpoons, mechanically retained in their hands, just as they had darted from their various employments; all their enchanted eyes intent upon the whale, which from side to side strangely vibrating his predestinating head, sent a broad band of overspreading semicircular foam before him as he rushed. Retribution, swift vengeance, eternal malice were in his whole aspect, and spite of all that mortal man could do, the solid white buttress of his forehead smote the ship's starboard bow, till men and timbers reeled. Some fell flat upon their faces. Like dislodged trucks, the heads of the harpooneers aloft shook on their bull-like necks. Through the breach, they heard the waters pour, as mountain torrents down a flume.

"The ship! The hearse!—the second hearse!" cried Ahab from the boat; "its wood could only be American!"

Diving beneath the settling ship, the whale ran quivering along its keel; but turning under water, swiftly shot to the surface again, far off the other bow, but within a few yards of Ahab's boat, where, for a time, he lay quiescent.

"I turn my body from the sun. What ho, Tashtego! let me hear thy hammer. Oh! ye three unsurrendered spires of mine; thou uncracked keel; and only god-bullied hull; thou firm deck, and haughty helm, and Pole-pointed prow,—death-glorious ship! must ye then perish, and without me? Am I cut off from the last fond pride of meanest shipwrecked captains? Oh, lonely death on lonely life! Oh, now I feel my topmost greatness lies in my topmost grief. Ho, ho! from all your furthest bounds, pour ye now in, ye bold billows of my whole foregone life, and top this one piled comber of my death! Towards thee I roll, thou all-destroying but unconquering whale; to the last I grapple with thee; from hell's heart I stab at thee; for hate's sake I spit my last breath at thee. Sink all coffins and all hearses to one common pool! and since neither can be mine, let me then tow to pieces, while still chasing thee, though tied to thee, thou damned whale! *Thus*, I give up the spear!"

The harpoon was darted; the stricken whale flew forward; with igniting velocity the line ran through the groove;—ran foul. Ahab stooped to clear it; he did clear it; but the flying turn caught him round the neck, and voicelessly as Turkish mutes bowstring their victim, he was shot out of the boat, ere the crew knew he was gone. Next instant, the heavy eye-splice in the rope's final end flew out of the stark-empty tub, knocked down an oarsman, and smiting the sea, disappeared in its depths.

For an instant, the tranced boat's crew stood still; then turned.

"The ship? Great God, where is the ship?" Soon they through dim, bewildering mediums saw her sidelong fading phantom, as in the gaseous Fata Morgana; only the uppermost masts out of water; while fixed by infatuation, or fidelity, or fate, to their once lofty perches, the pagan harpooneers still maintained their sinking look-outs on the sea. And now, concentric circles seized the lone boat itself, and all its crew, and each floating oar, and every lance-pole, and spinning, animate and inanimate, all round and round in one vortex, carried the smallest chip of the Pequod out of sight.

But as the last whelmings intermixingly poured themselves over the sunken head of the Indian at the mainmast, leaving a few inches of the erect spar yet visible, together with long streaming yards of the flag, which calmly undulated, with ironical coincid-ings, over the destroying billows they almost touched;—at that instant, a red arm and a hammer hovered backwardly uplifted in the open air, in the act of nailing the flag faster and yet faster to the subsiding spar. A sky-hawk that tauntingly had fol-lowed the main-truck downwards from its natural home among the stars, pecking at the flag, and incommoding Tashtego there; this bird now chanced to intercept its broad fluttering wing be-tween the hammer and the wood; and simultaneously feeling that etherial thrill, the submerged savage beneath, in his death-grasp, kept his hammer frozen there; and so the bird of heaven, with archangelic shrieks, and his imperial beak thrust upwards, and his whole captive form folded in the flag of Ahab, went down with his ship, which, like Satan, would not sink to hell till she had dragged a living part of heaven along with her, and helmeted her-self with it.

Now small fowls flew screaming over the yet yawning gulf; a sullen white surf beat against its steep sides; then all collapsed, and the great shroud of the sea rolled on as it rolled five thousand years ago.[1]

---

1. At the time of the Flood, according to a Biblical chronology.

EPILOGUE

"AND I ONLY AM ESCAPED ALONE TO TELL THEE." [1]

Job.

The drama's done. Why then here does any one step forth?— Because one did survive the wreck.

It so chanced, that after the Parsee's disappearance, I was he whom the Fates ordained to take the place of Ahab's bowsman, when that bowsman assumed the vacant post; the same, who, when on the last day the three men were tossed from out the rocking boat, was dropped astern. So, floating on the margin of the ensuing scene, and in full sight of it, when the half-spent suction of the sunk ship reached me, I was then, but slowly, drawn towards the closing vortex. When I reached it, it had subsided to a creamy pool. Round and round, then, and ever contracting towards the button-like black bubble at the axis of that slowly wheeling circle, like another Ixion I did revolve. Till, gaining that vital centre, the black bubble upward burst; and now, liberated by reason of its cunning spring, and, owing to its great buoyancy, rising with great force, the coffin life-buoy shot lengthwise from the sea, fell over, and floated by my side. Buoyed up by that coffin, for almost one whole day and night, I floated on a soft and dirge-like main. The unharming sharks, they glided by as if with padlocks on their mouths; the savage sea-hawks sailed with sheathed beaks. On the second day, a sail drew near, nearer, and picked me up at last. It was the devious-cruising Rachel, that in her retracing search after her missing children, only found another orphan.

FINIS

---

1. The formula with which each of four messengers concludes his story of the death and destruction of Job's family and possessions (Job 1: 14–19).

The Text: History, Variants, and Emendations

1. TEXTUAL PROBLEMS OF *MOBY-DICK*

The textual problems of *Moby-Dick* arise out of the complex circumstances under which the book was written, copied, transmitted to the compositors, proofread, and then, after plating, corrected and revised on the proof sheets which were sent to be reset in England, where the publisher and his typesetters made further changes.

The circumstances of composition are responsible for the important textual problem of "incomplete revisions." These are of two kinds: first, those vestiges that evidently result from incomplete recasting of certain sections of the book; and second (the ones we are more concerned with here), the words and phrases that Melville meant to mark for deletion but that somehow remain in the text along with the words or phrases meant to replace them. Given the circumstances of composition, the wonder is that there are not more of these evidences of incomplete revision than we have noted. For, with interruptions, the composition took nearly two years, from early 1850 till the late summer of 1851.[1] Melville began the book in New York City, progressing so rapidly that on the first of May 1850 he described himself as "half way in the work," and by the end of June he offered it to his English publisher, saying it would be ready by "the latter part of the coming autumn." The summer of 1850 Melville spent in the Berkshires of western Massachusetts, where a work routine was hard to establish, though he felt he was "mostly done" in August, the same month that he—and perhaps his book—was profoundly affected by meeting Hawthorne and reading his *Mosses*. In September he bought a farm near Pittsfield, and returned to New York City only long enough to get his family moved. It was late fall before he was again working regularly on the book that had seemed half finished at the first of May and "mostly done" in August. Even then he worked under bad conditions, for years later his wife made this brief note about his habits during the winter of 1850–1851 and the spring of 1851:

1. Our references to dates and events can be readily verified in Jay Leyda's *The Melville Log*, which is arranged chronologically. We footnote only references to documents or information which are not in the *Log*. Letters, including some not in the *Log*, will be found in the Davis-Gilman edition cited in the Bibliography.

Wrote White Whale or Moby Dick under unfavorable circumstances—
would sit at his desk all day not eating any thing till four or five o'clock—
then ride to the village after dark [sic] would be up early and out walking
before breakfast—sometimes splitting wood for exercise.

The writing of the book continued into the summer of 1851, while it
was already (as shown below) "going through the press," and was not
completed until about the first of August. Thus the composition was protracted, and the completion delayed, for a full year after the book had
seemed "mostly done" in August of 1850. From this fact, indicated by the
allusions quoted above and by others quoted below, scholars have inferred
that Melville at first planned, and between February and August 1850
largely wrote, a book which he radically altered and reworked between the
fall of 1850 and August 1851 into *Moby-Dick* as it was finally published.[2]
Several theories of just what Melville was doing with his manuscript have
been offered. Whether he actually was writing "two *Moby-Dicks*" (as that
hypothesis has come popularly to be stated) or only "elaborating" and
perfecting his one "idea that impelled the book" remains open to conjecture. In any case, the prolonged process that produced so complex a book
as *Moby-Dick* almost certainly eventuated in a manuscript bearing many
revisions, insertions, and deletions of the sort we see in the manuscript of
his essay on Hawthorne's *Mosses*, which he wrote for the *Literary World*
in August 1850, during the composition of *Moby-Dick*. The bulky pile of
pages cannot have been an ideal fair copy, clear, consistent, and easy for the
compositor to follow accurately. Its "chirographical incoherencies," like
those of Pierre's manuscripts in Melville's next book, must have induced
many of the textual errors and cruxes we encounter in the printed work.

Even more than the protracted and interrupted composition, the circumstances of copying the manuscript are responsible for textual corruption. By
the time he wrote his third book, *Mardi*, in 1847 and 1848, Melville had
become enough of a professional writer to know that he could not inflict his
handwriting and his misspellings upon a publisher. His wife, and later one
or probably more of his sisters, took on the task of copying his manuscripts.
The procedures that were followed may be deduced from the manuscript of
his essay on Hawthorne. After his wife had copied a manuscript, he would
correct such errors as he noticed. Often enough his wife could not read his
writing, and would either guess at a reading, or leave a blank space to fill in
after consulting him or for him to fill in himself; sometimes, to complicate
matters still more, he did not notice the misreadings or see that she had
left a blank. Besides corrections, he would make final revisions on her fair
copy before submitting it to the American publisher. When he did not
notice errors, or when he simply forgot what he had first written and overlooked them in proofreading, his copyist's misreadings or omissions became
part of the printed work.

The essay on Hawthorne, the longest surviving manuscript of this period,
is in his wife's hand, in ink, with numerous marginal pencil x-marks to direct

2. For discussions of the "two *Moby-
Dick*s" theory see the section from Leon
Howard's biography printed in this edition, Howard P. Vincent's *The Trying-*
Out of MOBY-DICK, pp. 22–49, and the
article by George R. Stewart (for full
citations see the Bibliography).

his attention to words she was doubtful about, some of which were later corrected in her hand, some in his.[3] In addition, Melville supplied and corrected words and made numerous revisions. There are many words he altered which are obviously her mistakes for manuscript readings—and some mistakes he did not see when he checked her fair copy.

Nor was Melville a patient corrector of the proofs he received from his publishers. A famous passage in his *Pierre* (1852), written immediately after *Moby-Dick*, indirectly provides some insights into Melville's irritation at the need for minutely accurate proofreading after the moment of creation had passed and when his mind was already occupied with new creative thoughts. It also suggests another source of error: to spare his eyes (tender and sorely overstrained, like Pierre's) sometimes he may have had proofs read aloud to him.

> As every evening, after his [Pierre's] day's writing was done, the proofs of the beginning of his work came home for correction, Isabel would read them to him. They were replete with errors; but preoccupied by the thronging and undiluted, pure imaginings of things, he became impatient of such minute, gnat-like torments; he randomly corrected the worst, and let the rest go; jeering with himself at the rich harvest thus furnished to the entomological critics. [*Pierre*, Book XXV, Ch. III.]

Melville himself during the composition and publication of *Moby-Dick* was less contemptuous than Pierre about the gross errors that appeared in printed texts of his work. He wrote his friend Evert A. Duyckinck, the editor of the *Literary World*, about the first installment of the Hawthorne essay: "Under the circumstances the printing is far more correct, than I expected; but there are one or two ugly errors. However, no one sees them, I suppose, but myself.—Send me the other proof, if you can; but don't, if it will be the least inconvenience." To Hawthorne and his wife, after they had learned he was the anonymous author of the *Literary World* essay, Melville was evidently more honest about his chagrin at these errors. Sophia Hawthorne wrote her mother: "He told me that the Review was too carelessly written—that he dashed it off in great haste & did not see the proof sheets, & that there was one provoking mistake in it. Instead of 'the same madness of [vital] truth' it should be 'the *sane* madness of [vital] truth' " (bracketed words supplied).[4] Just such errors abound in the first American—and even in the first English—edition of *Moby-Dick*, and have been perpetuated in subsequent reprints. Melville the professional writer would have wanted them corrected, and as editors we have done so.

The circumstances under which *Moby-Dick* went to and through the press are not yet altogether clear, but clear enough to show that they are also partly responsible for the many corruptions in the text. It has always been assumed that the press was that of the Harpers, Melville's regular

3. The significance of these pencil x-marks has previously been unrecognized. Our footnotes to the *Mosses* essay (pp. 535–551) indicate typical revisions.
4. This important letter was not known to Leyda or Howard and does not appear in Leyda's *Log;* it was first printed in Eleanor Melville Metcalf's *Herman Melville: Cycle and Epicycle*, p. 91 (see below, p. 542, line 4).

American publisher, but that may not have been so.[5] What follows is a summary of the evidence so far at hand. Melville's account was so much in debt to the Harpers that on April 29, 1851, they refused him an advance on the book that he was then calling "The Whale." Thereupon, on May 1, Melville borrowed $2050 from one "T.D.S." in Pittsfield. Perhaps this enabled him to pay for stereotyping the book himself. At any rate, a month later he wrote Hawthorne:

> In a week or so, I go to New York, to bury myself in a third-story room, and work & slave on my "Whale" while it is driving thro' the press. *That* is the only way I can finish it now,—I am so pulled hither & thither by circumstances.

He wrote many of the last chapters (and made late revisions) under particularly difficult conditions: working in the discomfort of a New York summer, and perhaps without a copyist to prepare his new pages for the compositors. On June 29 he wrote Hawthorne from Pittsfield:

> The "Whale" is only half thro' the press; for, wearied with the long delays of the printers, and disgusted with the heat & dust of the Babylonish brick-kiln of New York, I came back to the country to feel the grass, and end the book reclining on it, if I may.

On July 20 Melville wrote his English publisher Richard Bentley:

> I am now passing thro' the press, the closing sheets of my new work; so that I shall be able to forward it to you in the course of two or three weeks—perhaps a little longer.

He waited until July 29 to mail this letter; then he accompanied it with a signed and witnessed agreement with Bentley for the London publication of a book called *The Whale*. Melville evidently did his remaining proof-reading for the American text at Pittsfield. Without having returned to New York, so far as is known, he told a Pittsfield neighbor early in September: "It is off my hands, but must cross the sea before publication here." [6] (Such a delay of the American publication was a regular stratagem for assuring—or trying to assure—British copyright privileges.)

The anomalous fact is that as late as the first week of August the book, though complete in proofs, was not *finally* committed to any American publisher, for Evert A. Duyckinck wrote his wife from Pittsfield on August 7, 1851, that although he had urged Melville to let Redfield publish it, the decision to let Harper's do so "appears to have been concluded." Not until September 12 did Allan Melville, acting as his brother's attorney, sign an agreement with "the said Harper and Brothers" whereby they "agreed to publish and sell and keep for sale a certain work entitled 'The Whale' whereof the said Herman Melville is the author." The agreement provided

---

5. In Melville's letter to his English publisher, Richard Bentley, on June 27, 1850, he alludes as a settled matter to his whaling book's passing through the Harpers' press before he mails it to Bentley. At this early stage he clearly assumed the Harpers would print the book.

6. Davis and Gilman give the date of this letter as "12 [?] September 1851."

for the publication of the book from "the plates in the possession of R. Craighead." [7]

The problem is why Craighead should have had the plates. He was a stereotyper (he had stereotyped *Typee*) and apparently only a minor publisher. A possible explanation may be that Melville, when Harper's refused him an advance in April, had used some of the borrowed $2050 to have his book set and stereotyped by Craighead at his own expense—perhaps in order to be able to bargain for a better price from a publisher, perhaps to control the text and own its plates, as some authors did. Duyckinck's even bothering to argue for Redfield makes unlikely the possible explanation that Harper's, without a contract, had been the prospective publisher all along but had arranged and authorized the stereotyping by Craighead.

In any case, the textual significance of all this is that Melville saw the book through the press under more than usual difficulties, perhaps even without such help as working with his regular publisher would have afforded him, and hence both the words and the accidentals of the first American edition of *Moby-Dick* are less certainly what he wanted than in any of his other works except possibly *Typee*.

By late July 1851, to repeat, Melville was passing the "closing sheets" of his book through the press, but the proofs were not mailed to England until September 10. This interval gave Melville several weeks to spend making final revisions on the proofs. Since he knew the book would be entirely reset for the English edition, Melville was free to make whatever corrections and revisions he wanted and had time to make. He was not equally free to make revisions for the American edition, since the book was already plated and he would have to pay for any changes himself. In any event, our collations of the first American edition with the first English edition have revealed that Melville in fact availed himself of the month or six weeks between the time he had the final proofs and the time his brother mailed them to England: he made corrections and minor revisions all through the book, although hardly systematically and seldom throughout a lengthy passage.

But with *Moby-Dick* a major textual complication is the fact that (as scholars have known since the 1920's) the English publisher, Bentley—or his agent or agents—made extensive unauthorized changes where he, or they, found Americanisms, blasphemy, obscenity, or even jokes at the expense of royalty; and the English compositors introduced minor changes of their own, many inadvertently, some probably deliberately. Lacking the marked proof sheets Melville sent to England, no edition of *Moby-Dick* can ever isolate all the changes Melville made on them from the further changes made by the English publisher and printer. Isolating all his corrections of "accidentals" (such matters as punctuation, spelling, capitalization) is hopeless, although there are frequent instances where the English punctuation makes noticeably better sense, and there are some changes of accidentals that only an author could or would have made. With substantive changes—changes of words—we can be much surer when it was Melville

7. Melville's copy of the contract is in the Melville Collection of the Harvard College Library; the clause about Craighead is not in the *Log*.

himself who made a given change and when it was not. To use Fredson Bowers's apt figure, the "odds shift."

The resulting textual situation for *Moby-Dick* is this: both the first American edition (A) and the first English edition (E) have textual authority, not just the first American edition, as all previous editors have assumed. (However, some editors have inconsistently adopted a few readings from E, including a long footnote too obviously Melville's to be disregarded.) An editor may now, therefore, follow one of two basic courses (unless he chooses to print a facsimile text). He may still choose to follow the policy adopted by Thorp, Mansfield-Vincent, and Feidelson (to name the best previous editors) before the authority of E was recognized to be what we have discovered. He will reproduce A as his copy-text, with a minimum of emendations (only obvious typographical or factual errors); perhaps he will call attention to obviously better variant readings in E without incorporating them. The second course open to an editor is to construct—conflate—a text by using A as his copy-text and emending into it (a) such readings from E as appear to be Melville's own corrections, (b) corrections of errors of various sorts that appear in both editions, and (c) as much regularization as seems advisable or feasible. This second course is the policy adopted in the present edition.

An editor of *Moby-Dick* must face one major problem even after identifying and adopting the readings from E that are surely Melville's: many other E readings are not Melville's but those of an expurgating and sophisticating editor, or of "improving" and regularizing compositors. Many of the bowdlerizations and sophistications of the first English edition are attributable to the publisher, Richard Bentley, or the sort of man in his employ whom in 1852 (writing to Melville about the excisions *Pierre* required if it were to be "properly appreciated here") Bentley called "a judicious literary friend." Others—and the line is impossible to draw surely—may be inadvertent, or even deliberate, compositorial "corrections." And perhaps in being so cautious about adopting English readings that smack of the schoolmaster we have rejected a few of Melville's own corrections. At least we have the defense in these instances that in following the first American edition we are printing words he certainly once wrote.

The Melville Edition Project will study Melville's manuscript and proofstage revisions in his other writings to discover any patterns in them. Already patterns certain to be helpful in further treatment of the *Moby-Dick* text are discernible in his essay on Hawthorne's *Mosses*, in *The Piazza Tales*, and in *The Confidence-Man*. The Project's collations have revealed extensive, hitherto unnoticed, revisions and additions in some passages of the first English edition of *White-Jacket*, and these changes are certainly Melville's own; he probably made them on the American proof sheets which he took to London to arrange publication of the English edition. (The changes, it seems clear, led to alterations in the American plates after his return to New York, before publication of the first American edition.) Further study of these and other such changes may lead to the adoption of more classes of English readings than we have now adopted; one likely group might be such qualifying words as "hardly" and "scarcely," which E occasionally substitutes for a more assertive A reading. For the present, we have judged it better to risk not incorporating a few that may be Melville's than to risk adopting changes that may not be his.

Several problems besides Melville's habits of revision require further study. Mainly they are technical bibliographical problems. One is the question of the exact full title Melville finally intended, and whether the main title should or should not be hyphenated (*Moby-Dick* or *Moby Dick*). Another concerns the formal inconsistencies among chapter titles and verbal variations between some chapter titles as they appear at the chapter heads and in the table of contents—as well as inconsistencies between American and English chapter titles. An interrelated set of problems arises from differences between the American and the English edition. Why did the English edition omit the Epilogue? Why did it place the Extracts at the end of the book (in Vol. III) instead of at the beginning, before Ch. 1? When did Melville add the dedication to Hawthorne, and did he intend to retain it? The Melville Edition Project will study these and similar problems that bear on establishment of a definitive text.

Thus, to repeat, our policy in this Norton text has been conservative; even so, our recognition of Melville's revisions in the English text and of corruptions in both texts has required us to make many emendations. The lists in the following pages are meant not only to serve as a record of every change we have made in the text of the first American edition but also to stimulate further close study of the text. To anyone interested in Melville's way of writing, they are particularly valuable because so few of his actual manuscripts survive.

2A. SUBSTANTIVE VARIANTS BETWEEN *MOBY-DICK* AND *THE WHALE*

The following list reports all the substantive variants (*i.e.*, differences in wording) between the first American edition and the first English edition, as revealed by multiple collations of the American and English editions. (Collations of the 1851 and 1853 English issues revealed no substantive differences except a reset 1853 title page without the *Paradise Lost* quotation.) This list also reports the results of collations with the chapter "The Town-Ho's Story" in the October 1851 issue of *Harper's New Monthly Magazine*. It does not include spelling variants (*e.g.*, honor/honour) or the English substitution of "G – d" for "God," "d – – n for "damn," etc. In this list those English readings which we have adopted are marked by an asterisk before the *E* (*E*) and are listed before the American readings they replace. American readings are indicated by *A*; those from Harper's New Monthly Magazine by *H*. A collation of the English and American tables of contents is not included. The "Etymology" and "Extracts" appear in *The Whale* not in Vol. I but in an "Appendix" in Vol. III, 313–328. Boldface type identifies the Norton reading (*N*) at the page and line specified.

xiii.5-10 * E (*title page*) "There Leviathan, / Hugest of living creatures, in the deep / Stretch'd like a promontory sleeps or swims, / And seems a moving land; and at his gills / Draws in, and at his breath spouts out a sea." / PARADISE LOST. A (*Not included.*)

1.9 * E (*omitted*) A ETYMOLOGY. (A *reduplicated heading on a separate line at the top of a new page in A, preceding the Hackluyt quotation.*)

3.34 * E a boiling pan A boiling pan

4.25 * E Holy War A *Pilgrim's Progress*

5.8 A Voyages into Asia E *Voyages to Asia*

5.10 A huge E large

6.4 * E Tho' stiff A Tho' stuffed

6.10 * E Goldsmith's Nat. Hist. A *Goldsmith, Nat. His.*

10.29 * E her mere A her near

11.16 A as upon turning E as turning

12.28 A of a dreamy E on a dreamy

13.11 * E in the needles A of the needles

14.2 * E and make him the own brother A and own brother

14.34 A about some E about

15.6–8 A Do you think the archangel Gabriel thinks anything the less of me, because I promptly and respectfully obey that old hunks in that particular instance? E (*Omitted.*)

15.8 A aint E is not

15.14 A other's E others'

15.20–22 A The act of paying is perhaps the most uncomfortable infliction that the two orchard thieves entailed upon us. But *being paid*,—what will compare with it? E (*Omitted.*)

15.41–16.3 A And, doubtless, my going on this whaling voyage, formed part of the grand programme of Providence that was drawn up a long time ago. It came in as a sort of brief interlude and solo between more extensive performances. E (*Omitted.*)

16.3–4 A the bill must E the bill, of those three mysterious ladies, must

16.37 * E midmost A mid most

18.27 * E of out- / hanging light A of light

19.3 A poor Paul's E St. Paul's

19.16–23 A The universe is finished; the copestone is on, and the chips were carted off a million years ago. Poor Lazarus there, chattering his teeth against the curbstone for his pillow, and shaking off his tatters with his shiverings, he might plug up both ears with rags, and put a corn-cob into his mouth, and yet that would not keep out the tempestuous Euroclydon. Euroclydon! says old Dives, in his red silken wrapper—(he had a redder one afterwards) pooh, pooh! E (*Omitted.*)

19.28—20.3 A But what . . . may be. E (*Three paragraphs omitted.*)

21.25 A of such a E on such a

21.35–36 A like another cursed Jonah (by which name indeed they called him), E (*Omitted.*)

22.2 * E gulp A gulph

22.23 A he E she

23.17 A old Jonah E old fellow

23.19 A Jonah E the old fellow

23.22 A or whether E whether

23.34 A He stood E (*New Paragraph:*) He stood

24.22–25 A It was fair to presume that being a harpooneer, his linen or woollen, as the case might be, would not be of the tidiest, certainly none of the finest. I began to twitch all over. Besides, E (*Omitted, and next word capitalized:* It)

24.25 * A any decent A my decent

24.32 A feeling of E feeling

25.16 A tell but what E tell but that

27.45 * E the same as in A as you see the same in

28.6 A of a rainy day E on a rainy day

28.7–8 A I never saw such a sight in my life. I E (*Omitted.*)

30.44 A so long been E been so long

32.30 A my mother E my stepmother

32.38 A hope for a resurrection E hope to get out of bed again

33.2 A going down in E going in

33.33 A his bridegroom clasp E his clasp

33.44 A in that matrimonial sort E in that sort

37.39 * E they come A they came

38.18–19 A as howling condition E as howling a condition

38.32–33 A Can Herr Alexander perform a feat like that? E (*Omitted.*)

39.2–3 A upon the barren refuse rocks thrown aside at creation's final day. E upon these barren refuse rocks.

41.11 A a universal E an universal

41.22 A wherefore but the rumor E wherefore the rumour

41.42 A it is not me E it is not myself.

41.43–44 A for stave my soul, Jove himself cannot. E for stave my soul, who can do this?

42.31 A without a stairs E without stairs

44.1–2 A the storm of God's quick wrath E that the storm's quick wrath

44.3 A it is the E it is that the

44.27 * E And left me A And lift me

44.28 * E the open maw A the opening maw

48.8 A clattering overboard E tumbling overboard

49.2 * E become A became

49.10 A lay hold of E lay hold upon

49.41–42 A communing with God and himself. E communing with his God.

52.23 A the night previous E the previous night

53.29 A And then we sat E And there we sat

54.13–16 A thought I. Do you suppose now, Ishmael, that the magnanimous God of heaven and earth—pagans and all included—can possibly be jealous of an insignificant bit of black wood? Impossible! But E thought I—But

54.32 *A* Thus, then, in our hearts' honeymoon, lay I and Queequeg *E* Thus, then, lay I and Queequeg

54.37–39 *A* and Queequeg now and then affectionately throwing his brown tattooed legs over mine, and then drawing them back; so entirely sociable and free and easy were we; *E (Omitted.)*

56.15 * *E* While yet *A* When

57.6 *A* like Czar Peter *E* like the Czar Peter,

57.8 * *E* might haply gain *A* might happily gain

58.15–17 *A* stories about him had previously so much alarmed me concerning the very person whom I now companied with. *E* stories had previously so much alarmed me about him.

60.8 * *E* dived her bows *A* dived her brows

62.16 *A* extravaganzas *E* extravagances

62.24–25 *A* and there they found *E* and there found

63.12 *A* a Noah's flood would not interrupt *E* a Noah's flood would scarcely interrupt

65.6 *A* fishing *E* fishy

65.16 *A* if this here has *E* if this has

65.16 *A* on the head *E* upon the head

65.25 * *E* vertebræ *A* vertebra

65.43 * *E* a-night *A* at night

66.2 *A* herring *E* herrings

66.14 *A* Yojo purposed *E* Yojo proposed

66.37 *A* his liturgies and XXXIX Articles *E* his religion

67.38 *A* travelled over sheaves *E* travelled through sheaves

68.1 *A* its jaw *E* his jaw

69.37 *A* by his energy *E* about his energy

71.34 *A* he have *E* he has

72.7 * *E* worthy Captain Bildad *A* worthy Captain Peleg

74.11 *A* know but what *E* know but that

74.12 *A* might have a mighty deal *E* might have a deal

76.2 *A* wants to ship *E* wants a ship

76.21 *A* shore intervals *E* short intervals

76.22 *A* if the captain have *E* if the captain has

78.3 *A* Ramadan, or Fasting and Humiliation, was *E* Ramadan was

80.9 * *E* knob *A* knot

80.13 *A* on top *E* on the top

80.29 * *E* all I could do *A* all he could do

81.37—82.6 *A* that all these Lents . . . nurtured by Ramadans. *E (Omitted.)* that all fasts, voluntary or otherwise, were excessively bad for the digestion.

82.40 * *E* CHAPTER XVIII *A* CHAPTER XVII *(An error.)*

83.13–41 *A* Church." Here . . . all join hands." *E (Most of eight paragraphs omitted and replaced thus:)* Church;" and I entered upon a long rigmarole story, touching the conversion of Queequeg, and concluded by saying

that in the grand belief we all joined hands.

84.9 *A* his harpoon *E* the harpoon

89.31 * *E* stowage *A* storage

90.18 * *E* came running *A* came hobbling

91.22 *A* we had *E* he had

92.5 *A* slumber slept upon him. *E* slumber was upon him.

92.9 *A* would *E* should

96.45—97.1 *A* If ye touch at the islands, Mr. Flask, beware of fornication. *E (Omitted.)*

97.41 *A* indefinite as God *E* indefinite as the Almighty

99.20–21 *A* the ships worth *E* the ships' worth

100.17 *A* those colonies *E* these colonies

101.14 *A* that somehow whaling *E* that whaling

101.27–28 *A* the very heavens attest *E* the heavens attest

101.39 *A* more properly *E* more probably

101.43 *A* * See *(Footnote is keyed by asterisks to two points above: after royal fish." * and after procession.*) E (Footnote is keyed only to the first of these.)*

102.1–28 *A* CHAPTER XXV . . . stuff! *E (Whole chapter omitted. Consequently all subsequent chapters in Volume 1 of E are numbered one lower than those in A.)*

102.33 *A* on an icy coast *E* on icy coast

103.29 * *E* courage is *A* courage was

103.36 *A* any other whale hunter *E any* whale-hunter

103.39 *A* all mortally practical occasions *E* all practical occasions

104.38–39 *A* The great God absolute! The centre and circumference of all democracy! His omnipresence, our divine equality! *E (Omitted.)*

105.3–4 *A* thou great democratic God! *E* thou great God!

105.18 *A* crisis *E* crises

106.40 *A* universal prescription *E* universal consent

108.30 * *E* he never did! Poor Alabama boy! *A* he never did—oh, no! he went before. Poor Alabama boy! *(N follows E in omitting the clause, presuming it to be Melville's own correction of a misstatement of fact: as Leon Howard points out in his Herman Melville, p. 166, Pip goes mad but does not precede anybody before the heavenly throne, and most likely the passage omitted was vestigial from an earlier plan for Pip's death.)*

109.39 *A* fore- / noon watch *E* afternoon watch

110.4 *A* cast Perseus. *E* cast of Perseus.

111.7 *A* with a crucifixion in his face *E* with an apparently eternal anguish in his face

111.9 *A* visit in the air *E* visit into the air

115.40 *A* **eating of his own gums** *E* eating his own gums

116.23 * *E* **never speak quick to him,** *A* never speak to him

118.28–29 *A* **to much of any description. My object here is simply to project the draught of a systematization of cetology.** *E* to much of any systematization of cetology.

118.38 *A* swam *E* swum

122.3 *A* man-haters *E* men-haters

122.24 *A* **to afford the basis** *E* to afforded the bases

122.32 *A* **each of these has** *E* each has

122.38 *A* has *E* have

123.29 * *E* **the Tartarean tiles** *A* the Tartarian tiles

124.43 *A* **and bill-fish** *E* and the bill-fish

125.19 *A* **his bold ship** *E* his old ship

125.23 *A* **hung in the** *E* hung at the

126.5–6 *A* **in the lawless seas** *E* in lawless seas

128.1 *A* **God keep me** *E* Heaven keep me

128.33 * *E* **Now, one of the grand distinctions** *A* Now, the grand distinction

129.35 *A* **highest honors** *E* highest honour

130.2 * *E* **direst swing** *A* direct swing

130.10 *A* **in the deep** *E* in the deeps

131.26 *A* **Over his** *E* Over this

131.28 *A* **proper turn** *E* proper tune

132.39 *A* **in order to obtain** *E* in order obtain

133.1 *A* **hurried order** *E* hurried method

133.31 *A* **of its door** *E* of his door

134.8 * *E* **the whetstones** *A* the whetstone

134.28 *A* **anybody else is** *E* anybody is

134.34 *A* **lose much hereby** *E* lose much thereby

136.6 *A* **Louis the Devil.** *E* Louis Napoleon.

136.10 * *E* **even when most** *A* ever when most

136.32 *A* **The three mast-heads** *E* The three masts

137.25 * *E* **coolish weather** *A* cold weather

137.37 *A* crow's-nests *E* crows'-nests

138.5 *A* **ridiculous false delicacy** *E* ridiculously false delicacy

139.6 *E* **we Southern fishers** *A* we South fishers

139.24 *A* **before they can be killed** *E* before they are killed

139.25 *A* **sunken-eyed young Platonist** *E* sunken-eyed Platonist

140.1 *A* **a harpooneer** *E* an harpooneer

140.16 * *E* **Wickliff's** *A* Cranmer's

140.16 *A* **sprinkled Pantheistic ashes** *E* sprinkled ashes

141.43 *A* **while the mariners** *E* when the mariners

142.9 * *E* **men,—a doubloon.** *A* men.

142.37 *A* **"Do ye know** *E* "Do you know

143.9 *A* **with Stubb** *E* with Stubbs

143.17 *A* **animal sob** *E* animal shout

144.19 *A* **blasphemy, man** *E* blasphemy, men

144.29–30 *A* **unrecking** *E* unreeking

144.40 *A* **silence, then,** *that* *E* silence, that—*that*

144.43 *A* **oppose me now,** *E* oppose me,

145.35 *A* **a noble custom** *E* an old custom

145.38 * *E* **wert not thou** *A* wer't not thou

146.1 *A* **shocked into them** *E* shocked them into

146.11 *A* **yon three** *E* you three

147.1 *A* **goblet's** *E* goblets

147.3 *A* **slow dived** *E* long dived

147.9–11 *A* **metal; aye, steel skull, mine; the sort that needs no helmet in the most brain-battering fight!** *E* metal. (*Rest omitted.*)

147.28 *A* **prophesy** *E* prophecy

147.40 *A* **unsounded gorges** *E* unsound gorges

148.33 *A* **'tis not me!** *E* 'tis not I!

148.41 *A* **Ha! ha! ha! ha!** *E* Ha! ha! ha!

149.21 *A* **through with this job** *E* through this job

150.14–16 *A* **Tell 'em it's the resurrection; they must kiss their last, and come to judgment.** *E* (*Omitted.*)

151.17 *A* **break the jinglers!** *E* break the jigglers!

151.19 *A* **Jinglers** *E* Jigglers

151.35 *A* **O Christ!** *E* O Lord!

151.36 * *E* **one ball** *A* a ball

152.1 * *E* **your scholars** *A* you scholars

152.23 *A* **not taste, observe ye, else come satiety.** *E* (*Omitted.*)

152.28 * *E* **low-valed, high-palmed Tahiti!** *A* low veiled, high palmed Tahiti!

153.33 *A* **his one case** *E* his own case

154.19–20 *A* **No? Why then, God, mad'st thou the ring?** *E* No! (*Rest omitted.*)

154.28 *A* **Blang-whang! God! Duck** lower *E* Blang-whang! Duck lower

158.21 * *E* **and also a thing** *A* and as well a thing

158.41 *A* **for immortality** *E* for mortality

159.31 *A* **infernal aforethought** *E* infernal forethought

160.12–13 *A* **to whose dominion even the modern Christians ascribe one-half of the worlds;** *E* (*Omitted.*)

160.30 *A* **probably but felt** *E* probably felt

161.17 *A* **concentred cannon** *E* concentrated cannon

161.25 *A* **ye nobler, sadder souls** *E* ye nobler, and sadder souls

162.12 *A* **scorched without** *E* sore without

162.21 *A* **the one only** *E* the only

162.22 * *E* **Had any of** *A* Had any one of

162.30 *A* **a crew, too, chiefly** *E* a crew, too, that chiefly

164.62 *A* **whence** *Requiem* *E* hence *Requiem*

165.14 *A* **revived the glories** *E* have revived the glories

165.34 *A* **vast archangel wings** *E* vast wings

165.41 *A* **secrets which took hold of God.** *E* secrets not below the heavens.

165.61 *A* **upon our deck** *E* upon the deck

165.83–87 *A* **But I doubt not, that leathern tally, meant for man, was taken off in Heaven, when the white fowl flew to join the wing-folding, the invoking, and adoring cherubim!** *E* (*Omitted.*)

166.27–28 * *E* **as much the badge** *A* as much like the badge

169.12 *A* **of distant Oregon?** *E* of the distant Oregon?

169.14 *A* **demonism in the world** *E* demonism of the world

170.3–5 *A* **so that all deified Nature absolutely paints like the harlot, whose allurements cover nothing but the charnel-house within;** *E* (*Omitted.*)

170.39 *A* **ye eat for supper** *E* ye ate for supper

172.34 *A* **grounds he could, by his art, so place** *E* grounds, by his art, so place

173.19 * *E* **time and place** *A* time or place

173.44 * *E* **been covertly selected** *A* been correctly selected

174.41 *A* **weakness, or fright** *E* weakness, of fright

175.13 *A* **unbidden and unfathered birth** *E* unbidden and unfeathered birth

175.28 *A* **but the leading** *E* the leading

176.24 *A* **three years previous** *E* three years previously

177.20 * *E* **New Zealand Jack** *A* New Zealand Tom

178.13 *A* **three that had** *E* three had

178.17 *A* **People ashore** *E* People on shore

178.30 *A* **First: In the year** *E* In the year

178.30–31 *A* **of Nantucket** *E* of the Nantucket

178.38 *A* **has been seen since** *E* has ever been seen since

179.24–25 *A* **Was not Saul of Tarsus converted from unbelief by a similar fright?** *E* (*Omitted.*)

179.46–47 *A* **just before entered** *E* just entered

183.17 * *E* **stands** *A* stand

185.12 *A* **for the shuttle** *E* for a shuttle

185.38 * *E* **modified by free will** *A* directed by free will

186.33 *A* **swiftly swims** *E* swims swiftly

187.15 *A* **A rumpled Chinese jacket** *E* A rumbled Chinese jacket

187.16 * *E* **wide trowsers** *A* wide black trowsers

188.9 * *E* **back!—Never heed** *A* back!" (*New paragraph*) "Never heed

188.11 *A* **in the hold** *E* in hold

188.29 *A* **ye pull** *E* you pull

189.37 *A* **some time previous** *E* some time previously

190.21 *A* **The whales** *E* The whale

190.25 * *E* **along his oar!"** *A* along his oars!"

190.44 *A* **full of a large** *E* full of large

191.1–2 *A* **let me on to that** *E* let me go on to that

191.36 *A* **as his wont** *E* as is wont

192.21 *A* **startlingly** *E* startingly

192.37 *A* **hearts-alive** *E* heart's-alive

193.23 *A* **of the headsmen** *E* of the headsman

194.6 *A* **sprang** *E* sprung

195.36 *A* **worryings, prospects** *E* worrying prospects

197.7–8 *A* **would be as good as the days that Lazarus lived after his resurrection; a supplementary clean gain** *E* would be a supplementary clean gain

197.38 *A* **comprises a peril** *E* compromises a peril

197.39 *A* **enter a whale- / boat** *E* enter the whale-boat

198.24 *A* **for bracing the knee against in darting** *E* for bracing the knee against it in darting

198.26 *A* **in the cleat** *E* of the cleat

198.28 *A* **straightened it a little** *E* straightened a little

198.36 *A* **soon waned away** *E* soon went away

198.41 *A* **on planks, bits of wreck** *E* on plank, bits of wrecks

199.19 *A* **and asked of** *E* and ask of

199.38 *A* **For of these moonlight nights** *E* for on these moonlight nights

200.10 *A* **Had the trump of judgment blown, they could not have quivered more** *E* Had the trump of judgment blown, they could hardly have quivered more

200.22 *A* **to drive yawingly** *E* to drive yawningly

202.5 *A* **its accustomed hole** *E* its customary hole

206.12 *A* **straightway** *E* straitway

206.34 *A* **down the columns** *E* down columns

208.16 *A* **own particular accompaniments** *E* own peculiar accompaniments

210.23 *A* **yet was he** *E* still was he

213.23 *A* **could but ill brook** *E* could ill brook

213.28 *A* **"Steelkilt rose** *E* "Steelkilt arose

214.17 *A* **tell ye** *E* tell you

214.21 *A* **most thriving villages** *E* thriving villages

214.23–24 *A* **through the holy-of-holies of great forests** *E* through great forests

215.8 *A* **openly toying with his red-cheeked Cleopatra, ripening his apricot thigh upon the sunny deck** *E* openly toying with his red-cheeked Cleopatra upon the sunny deck

215.21 *A* **scarce any race** *E* scarcely any race

216.27 * *E and H* **boys' business** *A* boy's business

216.31 *A* **Captain, by God, look** *E* Captain, look

217.34 *A* **united perhaps to** *E* united to

217.38 *A* **three others of** *E* three other of

218.38 * *H* But all three *A and E* But all these

220.5 *A* for salvation. *E* for security.

220.11 *A* her leak *E* her leek

222.11 *A* topmost *E* topmast

223.3 *A* cannon *E* cannons

224.4 *A* you, tell *E* you to tell

224.20–22 *A* " 'Excuse me for running after you, Don Sebastian; but may I also beg that you will be particular in procuring the largest sized Evangelists you can.' *E* (*Omitted.*)

224.32 *A* I have seen *E* and I have seen

227.8 *A* systemized *E* systematized

228.13–14 *A* Jeremy Bentham's skeleton, which hangs for candelabra *E* Jeremy Bentham's skeleton, which is preserved

230.30 *A* consecutive great battles *E* consecutive battles

232.44 * *E* German savage *A* Dutch savage

233.26–27 * *E* else—so chance-like are such observations of the hills—your precise *A* else so chance-like are such observations of the hills, that your precise

234.11 *A* fringing *E* fringy

235.7 *A* his one superficial *E* his own superficial

235.10 *A* waters *E* water

237.8 *A* were awaiting *E* were waiting

240.23 * *E* horrible contortions *A* horrible contortion

241.4 *A* prophesies *E* prophecies

241.29 *A* we then were *E* we were then

242.18 *A* all at once *E* at once

244.5 *A* that rocking *E* that rocky

244.39 *A* bowsman *E* bowman

245.34 *A* to the uttermost *E* to the utmost

250.8–9 *A* the propriety of devil-worship, and the expediency of conciliating the devil *E* the propriety and expediency of conciliating the devil

250.38 *A* Blast me *E* Hang me

251.9 *A* why, damn your eyes, you mustn't swear *E* why you mustn't swear

251.18 * *E* "Dough you is *A* "Do you is

251.39 *A* "that's Christianity *E* "that's the right sort

252.3–4 *A* so give the benediction *E* so give them a blessing

253.10–13 *A* "Fetch him? How? In a coach and four, as they fetched Elijah? And fetch him where?" *E* "Fetch him —and fetch him where?"

253.15–16 *A* But don't you know the higher you climb, the colder it gets? Main-top eh?" *E* (*Omitted.*)

253.19–23 *A* But, perhaps you expect to get into heaven by crawling through the lubber's hole, cook; but, no, no, cook, you don't get there, except you go the regular way, round by the rigging. It's a ticklish business, but must be done, or else it's no go. But none of us are in heaven yet. *E* (*Omitted.*)

253.41 *A* now ye may *E* now you may

254.7 *A* more of shark *E* more a shark

255.12 *A* substance *E* substances

255.36 *A* the first man *E* the first man man

255.43–256.3 *A* I tell you it will be more tolerable for the Fejee that salted down a lean missionary in his cellar against a coming famine; it will be more tolerable for that provident Fejee, I say, in the day of judgment, than for thee, civilized and enlightened gourmand, who nailest geese to the ground and feastest on their bloated livers in thy paté-de-foie-gras. *E* (*Omitted.*)

256.38 *A* over her side *E* over side

257.8 *A* the marksmen *E* the marksman

257.21–24 *A* "Queequeg no care what god made him shark," said the savage, agonizingly lifting his hand up and down; "wedder Fejee god or Nantucket god; but de god wat made shark must be one dam Ingin." *E* (*Omitted.*)

257.44 *A* end considerably *E* end is considerably

258.42 *A* slicings *E* slices

262.28–29 *A* There's orthodoxy! *E* (*Omitted.*)

262.31 *A* a powerless panic *E* a powerful panic

264.23–25 *A* arms. O head! thou hast seen enough to split the planets and make an infidel of Abraham, and not one syllable is thine!" *E* arms!" (*Rest omitted.*)

264.36 * *E* lives in matter *A* lives on matter

264.42 * *E* stranger's *A* strangers'

265.33 *A* some way ahead; *E* away ahead,

266.15 *A* by the way *E* by way

266.37 *A* the archangel forthwith *E* the maniac forthwith

266.43 *A* to be any way *E* to be in any way

267.3 *A* the archangel cared *E* he cared

267.34 *A* his archangel nature *E* his self-styled archangel nature

268.34 *A* This terrible event *E* This event

270.1 *A* upon the jacket *E* on the jacket

271.27 *A* Nor could I *E* How could I

272.22 *A* all of us men in *E* all of us in

272.28–29 *A* and involuntarily trembling *E* and trembling

273.5–6 * *E* the sort of bellows by which he blows back the breath *A* the sort of bitters by which he blows back the life

273.19 *A* hit him *E* strike him

274.36 *A* the fagged whale *E* the flagged whale

275.31 *A* Blast him! *E* D——n him!

275.41–42 *A* and get him *E* and to get him

276.21 *A* helped kill *E* helped to kill

277.8 * *E* lets *A* let's

277.12 *A* "Do I suppose it? *E* "Do I suppose?

277.14 *A* nape of his neck *E* nape of the neck

277.19 *A* and then *E* an then

278.2 *A* black bone *E* back-bone

278.7 *A* Meantime, Fedallah *E* Meanwhile, Fedallah

279.3 *A* he can one *E* he can see one

280.4 *A* at the same moment of time *E* at the same time

281.30 *A* sawn into slabs *E* sawn in slabs

282.42 *A* by its circular rings *E* by circular rings

283.7 *A* arch over *E* reach over

284.28 *A* as though your own mouth were *E* as though your own mouth was

286.38 * *E* irrecoverably lost *A* irrevocably lost

287.36 *A* high elevated *E* highly elevated

288.20 *A* cabled tackles *E* cable tackles

288.23 *A* it to fall *E* it fall

289.13 *A* on top of his head? *E* on the top of his head?

290.9 *A* skill in obstetrics of Queequeg *E* skill of Queequeg

290.13–14 *A* Midwifery should be taught in the same course with fencing and boxing, riding and rowing. *E* (*Omitted.*)

290.32 *A* remaining undetached *E* remaining detached

290.34 *A* agile obstetrics *E* agile dexterities

290.35 *A* Yes, it was a running delivery, so it was. *E* (*Omitted.*)

291.37 *A* royal beadle *E* royalty

292.14 *A* mighty god-like *E* mighty and god-like

295.18 *A* can there alongside *E* can alongside

296.19 *A* of gush *E* of a gush

296.27 *A* did ever whale yaw so *E* did ever whale yawn so

297.12 *A* tell ye *E* tell you

297.20 *A* The short and long *E* The short and the long

298.18 * *E* diagonally *A* diagonically

298.24 *A* he yawed *E* he yawled

299.5 *A* harpooneer *E* harpooneers

299.26 *A* lead-lined *E* lead-line

299.33 *A* sharp barbs *E* keen barbs,

300.19–20 *A* Oh! that unfulfilments should follow the prophets. For with *E* Why, with (*Rest omitted.*)

300.21 *A* had run *E* has run

300.40 *A* ship's *E* ships'

301.13–14 *A* new made wound *E* newly-made wound

303.29 * *E* of that sort goes down *A* one of that sort go down

306.17 *A* fraternity *E* paternity

306.19 *A* in the godhead *E* of the godhead

307.39 *A* by the whale *E* by a whale

308.29 *A* that as such *E* that such

309.41 *A* He minds you *E* He reminds you

310.3–4 *A* unspeakable old Monongahela! *E* unspeakable Monongahela!

310.10 *A* his flurry *E* its flurry

310.23 * *E* 1850 *A* 1851

313.8 *A* perceived *E* perceive

313.42 *A* the Devil, *E* (*Omitted.*)

315.25 *A* the soft, curled, hermaphroditical Italian pictures *E* the soft, curled, Italian pictures

316.6 *A* if it descend *E* if it descends

316.9 *A* water *E* waters

316.32 *A* of solitary *E* of the solitary

316.37 *A* would almost think *E* would think

317.6 *A* heaven *E* heavens

317.10 *A* of my ship *E* (*Omitted.*)

318.2 *A* I but go *E* I go but

318.3 *A* will *E* shall

318.5–8 *A* Thou shalt see my back parts, my tail, he seems to say, but my face shall not be seen. But I cannot completely make out his back parts; and hint what he will about his face, I say again he has no face. *E* (*Omitted.*)

318.27 *A* spices, and silks, and jewels *E* spices, and jewels

319.17 *A* in his pursuit *E* in the pursuit

321.1 *A* these Straits *E* the Straits

321.10 *A* Corresponding to the *E* Corresponding to to the

321.33 *A* conceits had passed *E* conceits has passed

322.6 *A* flashing lines *E* fishing lines

322.31 *A* for the outlets *E* from the outlets

322.38–49 * *E* (The whole footnote to the word *gallied* did not appear in A.)

324.7 *A* tossing overboard *E* tossing over

325.12 *A* snuffling *E* snuffing

325.34 *A* scarce yet recovered *E* scarce recovered

326.9–10 *A* pond. We saw young Leviathan amours in the deep.* *E* pond. * (*Rest omitted.*)

326.55–58 *A* man; it might do well with strawberries. When over- / flowing with mutual esteem, the whales salute *more hominum*. *E* man. (*Rest omitted.*)

329.13 *A* times *E* time

329.15–17 *A* he cannot keep the most notorious Lothario out of his bed; for, alas! all fish bed in common. *E* he cannot always frustrate the most notorious Lothario; for, alas! all fish have very vague ideas of the connubial tie.

329.29–30 *A* Lothario, like pious Solomon devoutly worshipping among his thousand concubines. *E* Lothario. (*Rest omitted.*)

329.32–33 *A* Turks; for these Grand Turks are too lavish of their strength, and hence their unctuousness is small. *E* Turks. (*Rest omitted.*)

329.43 *A* the impotent, repentant *E* the repentant

330.3 *A* amorous errors *E* own juvenile errors

330.4　*A* by the fishermen　*E* by the fisherman

331.22　*A* American fishermen　*E* American fisherman

332.13–16　* *E* northern seas, they (the plaintiffs) had succeeded in harpooning the fish; but at last, through peril of their lives, were obliged to forsake, not only their lines, but their boat itself,—Furthermore: ultimately　*A* Northern seas; and when indeed they (the plaintiffs) had succeeded in harpooning the fish; they were at last, through peril of their lives, obliged to forsake not only their lines, but their boat itself. Ultimately

332.19　* *E* plaintiffs;—Yet again:—and when　*A* plaintiffs. And when

332.20　*A* plaintiffs'　*E* plaintiff's

332.21　*A* by way　*E* by the way

332.22–23　* *E* and boat, all of which　*A* and boat, which

332.32–33　* *E* possession of her. He then proceeded to say that,　*A* possession of her. Erskine was on the other side; and he then supported it by saying, that

333.10　* *E* the defendants afterwards took　*A* the plaintiffs afterwards took

333.35　*A* laborers (all sure of heaven without any of Savesoul's help) what　*E* labourers; what (*Rest omitted.*)

333.36　*A* 100,000　*E* 100,000*l*.

334.10　*A* religious belief in them　*E* religious belief in many of us

336.3–4　*A* Is this the still militant old man, standing at the corners of the three kingdoms, on all hands coercing alms of beggars?　*E* (*Omitted.*)

336.28　*A* hinted of　*E* hinted at

336.37　* *E* denying that　*A* denying not

336.40　*A* vapory　*E* vapour

339.30　*A* a good humor　*E* good humour

341.20　*A* for it's so　*E* for its so

343.18　*A* the chapter　*E* this chapter

344.7　*A* gave forth no　*E* gave no

344.38　*A* boats'　*E* boat's

344.42　*A* heard of him　*E* head him

346.33–35　* *N* loves . . . interferes　*A* loved . . . interferes　*E* loved . . . interfered

347.18　* *E* such considerateness towards　*A* such considerations towards

347.43　*A* uncompromised, indifferent as his God.　*E* uncompromised. (*Rest omitted.*)

348.28　*A* I snuffed up　*E* I sniffed up

349.39　*A* and a very　*E* a very

349.44　*A* in the tubs　*E* in tubs

350.29　*A* This spade　*E* The spade

351.49　*A* boiling out　*E* boiling

352.3　*A* foremast and main- / mast　*E* fore- / and mainmast

353.2–3　*A* Like a plethoric burning martyr, or a self-consuming misanthrope　*E* Like a self-consuming misanthrope (*Rest omitted.*)

353.5　*A* he consumed　*E* he had consumed

353.8–9　*A* It smells like the left wing of the day of judgment; it is an argument

for the pit.　*E* (*Omitted.*)

353.11　*A* the carcase　*E* the case

353.19　*A* conflagrations　*E* conflagration

354.20　*A* But, spite of all this　*E* But, in spite of all this

356.19　*A* and, like Shadrach, Meshach, and Abednego, his　*E* and how his (*Rest omitted.*)

357.25–26　*A* aglow, as bridegrooms new- / leaped from out the daintiest Holland.　*E* aglow. (*Rest omitted.*)

358.43　* *E* flow.　*A* flows.

359.27　*A* on the third　*E* on a third

360.34　*A* I have　*E* I've

361.8　*A* lecherous dog,　*E* (*Omitted.*)

361.18　*A* in rear　*E* in the rear

362.9　*A* there it is　*E* there is it

362.23　*A* that ghost-devil　*E* that old ghost-devil

363.11　*A* say in the resurrection　*E* say one day

363.14–16　*A* soon! Hish! hish! God goes 'mong the worlds blackberrying. Cook! ho, cook! and cook us! Jenny! hey, hey, hey, hey, hey, Jenny, Jenny! and get your hoe-cake done!"　*E* soon!" (*Rest omitted.*)

364.28　*A* blubber-hook　*E* blubber-book

365.12　*A* from the bottom　*E* from bottom

365.18　*A* they were mine　*E* they are mine

365.29　*A* on to his hump!　*E* on his hump!

366.13　*A* when, when,　*E* when,

366.43　*A* You know you're　*E* You know you are

367.14–15　*A* as ugly gaping wound　*E* as ugly gaping a wound

367.23　*A* Do ye see　*E* Do you see

368.13　*A* making believe swallow　*E* making believe to swallow

368.31　*A* thou saw'st　*E* ye saw

369.29　*A* a whale-boat　*E* a a whale-boat

369.35–36　*A* all his Sons—how many, their mother only knows—and under　*E* all his Sons, and under (*Rest omitted.*)

371.6　*A* eating, and drinking　*E* eating, drinking

373.10　* *E* untrussing the points of his hose　*A* untagging the points of his hose

373.23　*A* upon the joists　*E* upon joists

373.35　*A* And as for　*E* As for

374.21　*A* hair-hung sword　*E* air-hung sword

374.27　*A* with all their　*E* with their

374.36　*A* is he deafened　*E* he is deafened

376.3　*A* upon similar grounds　*E* on similar grounds

376.11–14　*A* Sir Clifford thinks of charging twopence for a peep at the whispering gallery in the spinal column; threepence to hear the echo in the hollow of his cerebellum; and sixpence for the unrivalled view from his forehead.　*E* (*Omitted.*)

376.19　*A* wished the　*E* wished all the

377.20 * E the embryo hull A the hull
378.1 A weighty E mighty
378.12 A knobbed blocks E knobbled blocks
378.19 A cannibal urchins, the priest's children, who E cannibal urchins, who (*Rest omitted.*)
379.3 A a huge quarto edition of Johnson E a huge quarto of Johnson
379.17–18 A the whole universe, not excluding its suburbs. E the whole universe. (*Rest omitted.*)
379.31–32 * E ante-chronical A antichronical
380.17 A skeleton of the whale furnishes E skeleton furnishes
380.27 * E ante-chronical A antichronical
380.36 A like Leviathan? E like the Leviathan?
380.37 * E Pharaohs' A Pharaoh's
380.41 A all humane ages E all human ages
381.24 A This Rib" (says John Leo) "is said E This Rib is said
382.27 A these stories E the stories
383.28 A mounted on horse E mounted on horses,
385.38 A canonic teachings E canonical teachings
386.12 A signers E singers
389.5 A had to do was E had was
389.10 A he did not have a E he had not a
391.45 * E proud as a Greek god A proud as Greek god
392.8 A vertebra E vertebræ
392.30–33 A let's finish it before the resurrection fellow comes a-calling with his horn for all legs, true or false, as brewery-men go round collecting old beer barrels, to fill 'em up again. E let's finish it. (*Rest omitted.*)
392.43 A down into the E down in the
395.37 A but little left of him but E little left of him but
396.5 A alike levels all, alike impresses all E alike levels all, impresses all
396.28–29 * E milky way—after saying this he added A milky way. He added
397.6 A to be E to be made
397.36 A hovering near by E hovering by
398.20 A were once more dying E were dying
398.21 A them E 'em
398.21 A drown E down
399.28 A gently awful E gentle awful
399.31 A watery prairies and Potters' Fields of E water prairies of
400.5 A whole bulk E own bulk
400.41 A painful E painfully
401.31 A iron lullaby E lullaby
404.34 A dark nods E dark nobs
407.21 A officers' E officer's
407.30 A pantaloons pockets E pantaloon pockets
407.35 A still nearer E still near
408.2 A cursed Bastile E accursed Bastile

409.42 A unnamable imminglings E nameless imminglings
411.14 A the eager mariners E eager mariners
411.21 * E Now, sometimes, in A Now, in
411.31 A its precise E the precise
411.36 * E unearthly passionlessness A earthly passionlessness
412.12 A drop of water E drop water
413.30 A reeling ship's E reelish ship's
413.30 A tetering side E tottering side
414.6–7 A ships . . . lips E ship . . . lip
415.2 A to considerable depth E to a considerable depth
415.30 * E To sailors, oaths A To sailors' oaths
416.17 A will yet be E will be
416.40–41 A tri-pointed trinity of flames E try-pointed flames
417.16 A leap lengthwise to E leap to
417.34 A thou omnipotent. E thou omniscient!
418.6 * N 'tis A t' is E It's
418.9 A instantly ran E instantly run
420.10 A jacket skirts E jacket shirts
420.20 A THUNDER AND LIGHTNING E LIGHTNING AND THUNDER
420.36 A Pequod's E Pequod
421.1 A shivered remnants E shivering remnants
421.17 A oh-he-yo E ho-he-ho
421.20 A order E orders
422.12 A if this ship come E if this ship comes
422.35 A stealthily E steadily
424.32 * E were braced hard up A were hard up
424.37 A quietly he issued E quietly issued
424.44 A from inflexible Ahab's E from the inflexible Ahab's
427.6 A Man, hey? E Man, eh?
427.23 A nothing's happened E nothing happened
427.31 A A hatchet! a hatchet! cut E A hatchet! cut
428.6 A my inmost E mine inmost
428.8 A "What's this E "Who's this
428.8 * E intently A intenting
429.11 A He hollowly E He then hollowly
429.36 A having long beat E having beaten
431.8 A from the cabin-gangway E from cabin-gangway
431.34 A I will E I'll
432.21 A helped carry E helped to carry
432.31 * E out of my sight." A out of sight."
433.6 A of earth E of the earth
433.39 A loomed up out E loomed out
433.41 A instantly lowered in chase E instantly in chase
436.1 A to yaw E to yawl
436.5 A while all E yet all
436.32 A his living skin E his skin

437.33 *A* **day preceding had** *E* day preceding that had

438.21 *A* **did plainly say—** *E* plainly said,

438.40 *A* **two only** *E* only two

439.16 *A* **seemed yoked** *E* seemed yoked

439.25 *A* **had yet been seen;** *E* had been seen,

439.42 *A* **mate, said,—** *E* mate, he said,

440.27 *A* **incommodiously close round** *E* incommodiously round

440.30 *A* **Then it darted** *E* Now it darted

440.45—441.7 *A* **An eagle flew . . . into the sea.** *E* (*Whole paragraph omitted.*)

441.40 *A* **ye** *E* you

442.28–33 *A* **Aloft, like a royal czar . . . gave her bosom away.** *E* (*Whole paragraph omitted.*)

442.37 *A* **of the morn;** *E* of the moon,

442.39—443.2 *A* **Oh, immortal infancy . . . of his brain.** *E* (*Whole paragraph omitted.*)

443.11 *A* **however wilful and erring** *E* however erring

443.25 *A* **Forty—forty—forty** *E* Forty—forty

443.34 *A* **country without—** *E* country throughout—

444.10 *A* **as though** *E* and as though

444.16 *A* **into sea** *E* into the sea

444.16 *A* **to gaze upon God** *E* to look upon God

444.26 *A* **wife and child** *E* wife and children

445.5 *A* **Is Ahab, Ahab?** *E* Is it Ahab, Ahab?

445.17 * *E* **air** *A* airs

447.22 *A* **of his steady** *E* off his steady

447.37 *A* **not Jove, not that great majesty Supreme!** *E* not Jove, (*Rest omitted.*)

447.40 * *E* **once laving him** *A* once leaving him

447.43 * *E* **that serenity** *A* this serenity

448.6 *A* **wrenched hideousness** *E* wretched hideousness

448.27 * *E* **could perceive** *A* could discover

449.23 *A* **from its gripe** *E* from his gripe

449.36 *A* **tilting over** *E* tilting it over

450.34 * *E* **prow was pointed** *A* prows were pointed

450.39 *A* **strength did crack,** *E* strength cracked,

451.10 *A* **circumferences** *E* circumference

452.19 *A* **this that laughs** *E* that that laughs

452.27 *A* **old wives' darkling** *E* old wife's darkling

454.22 *A* **my spine's** *E* my spin's

455.7 *A* **did point to** *E* pointed to

456.24 *A* **those boats** *E* these boats

456.44 *A* **the rope** *E* the ropes

457.42 *A* **found grimly clinging** *E* found clinging

458.7 *A* **not stood** *E* not not stood

458.21 * *E* **boats'** *A* boat's

459.43 *A* **of the whole** *E* of all the whole

460.9 * *E* **set** *A* sat

460.29 * *E* **turn to ice** *A* turned to ice

461.2 *A* **wind but had** *E* wind had but

461.11 * *E* **shift and swerve** *A* swift and swerve

462.19 *A* **Will I have** *E* Shall I have

463.37 *A* **clouds sweep** *E* clouds step

464.12 *A* **Suddenly the waters** *E* Suddenly the waves

465.15 *A* **his own straight** *E* his straight

466.29 *A* **inboard again;** *E* inboard,

466.32 *A* **Almost simultaneously,** *E* Almost instantaneously,

467.5 *A* **Is't night?"** *E* Is't nigh?"

467.38 *A* **with ye,** *E* with thee,

467.39 *A* **oh, oh!** *E* oh, ho!

468.23 *A* **and only god-bullied hull;** *E* (*Omitted.*)

469.10 *A* **intermixingly poured** *E* intermixedly poured

469.22 * *E* **in his death- / grasp,** *A* in his death-gasp,

469.24 *A* **archangelic shrieks** *E* unearthly shrieks

470.1–27 *A* **EPILOGUE . . . FINIS.** *E* (*Whole Epilogue omitted.*)

2B. ENGLISH READINGS ADOPTED

This table reports all the substantive emendations (changes in *wording*) which we have adopted from *E*, the first English edition, judging that they are Melville's own alterations of the A text. Some, it is true, were so obviously called for that they may have been made in the English publishing house after Melville had overlooked them just as both he and the English revisers missed some equally obvious ones; in any case, since our object is to recover Melville's *intention*, no harm is done by including such necessary corrections among those which must be Melville's own.

These readings which we adopt from the first English edition fall into several categories. Most important are his *additions* and his *revisions* for meaning or for style. Of the additions, the long footnote on "gallied" in Ch. 87 is by itself proof enough of Melville's intervention in the English text—it has been recognized as his and adopted by Mansfield-Vincent and by Feidelson. Some single added words are as clearly authorial. No one but Melville would have expanded "the hull" to "the embryo hull" and "of light" to "of out-hanging light." As for revisions, the long one in Ch. 89 has to be Melville's, though some English bowdlerizing also enters near the end of the chapter.

A second important category is Melville's corrections (in *E*) of his own or his copyist's manuscript lapses which the American compositors had set as they found them. In some of these he caught and rectified his wrong assignments of identity: from *Pilgrim's Progress*" to "*Holy War*"; "Peleg" to "Bildad"; "Cranmer's" to "Wickliff's"; "New Zealand Tom" to "New Zealand Jack"; "plaintiffs" to "defendants." In two or three others he cut away awkward or redundant vestiges of his revisions that had passed from his manuscript into print: he cut "as you see the same in" to "the same as in" and "as much like the badge" to "as much the badge." Most interesting among these tidying-up cuts was his excision of the clause on Pip's death in the passage at the end of Ch. 27 about not many of the crew ever coming back: "Black Little Pip—he never did—oh, no! he went before. Poor Alabama boy!" From this sentence Melville cut out the clause "oh, no! he went before." Very likely it had survived from a stage of composition when Melville intended to have Pip somehow "go" (*i.e.*, die) before the end; Leon Howard (p. 714) and George Stewart (see Bibliography) in theorizing about the earlier stages both commented on this vestigial detail.

A closely related third category is the correction of lapses in such matters as spacing, the placing of apostrophes, and spelling—minor lapses which because they affect the intended meaning may be considered "substantive," not merely "accidental." For some of these lapses the compositors of the American edition were to blame, but that others were Melville's own or his copyist-wife's, no one will doubt who looks at the spelling in his letters and his *Mosses* essay (535–568). In the English edition the spacing of "mid most of them all" is corrected to read "midmost of them all." Apostrophes are shifted to change the sense from singular to plural and vice versa: "boy's business" to "boys' business" and "strangers' " to "stranger's." "To sailors' oaths" is corrected to "To sailors, oaths" and "wer't not thou" becomes "wert not thou." The most striking correction of a spelling blunder alters in two places the American reading "anti-chronical" to what the context plainly demands, "ante-chronical." Another shifts the rendering of "though" in Old Fleece's Negro dialect from "Do" to "Dough." "Gulph" is corrected to "gulp," "low veiled" to "low-valed," the anomalous "diagonically" to ordinary "diagonally."

In an intermediate fourth category, minor compositional omissions from the American text are supplied in the English: "boiling pan" becomes "a boiling pan"; "and own brother" is filled out to "and make him the own brother"; the quite misleading advice "never speak to him" becomes the idiom "never speak quick to him"; "we South fishers" becomes "we Southern fishers"; "proud as Greek god" fills out to "proud as a Greek god"; and sails which were "hard up" were, in the correction, "braced hard up."

An important fifth category is Melville's correction of misreadings. In these instances either his copyist had misread his hand in the original manuscript or the American compositors had misread the copyist's—or Melville's —hand in the printer's copy-text. (There are repeated instances of such misreadings in his *Mosses* essay, as we point out in our notes to it, pp. 535–551.) In all but one or two cases ("intenting" for "intently"; "knot" for "knob") the American compositorial readings made sense, but the English versions so clearly make better sense that they must be attributed not to English compositors sophisticating the American proof sheets they were setting from but to Melville's own corrections on those proof sheets. Salient instances establish the case. Only Melville would have restored the right word in two quoted passages: correcting the plausible misreading "her near appearance" to "her mere appearance" as it is in the original passage quoted by J. Ross Browne, from whom his "extract" is taken, and likewise correcting "denying not inquiry" to "denying that inquiry" as in Sir Thomas Browne's original. And surely only the author, Melville himself, detected the American text's misreading that let his sense leak away in the phrase "correctly selected" which the English text restores to "covertly selected." An even more striking restoration of sense occurs in a sentence near the end of Ch. 22; here the American edition reads: "Nor, will the tragic dramatist who would depict mortal indomitableness in its fullest sweep and *direct* swing, ever forget a hint, incidentally so important in his art, as the one now alluded to" (our italics). Only Melville can have changed the adjective "direct" (which has evidently never troubled another reader) to what he must have originally written: "direst" —"its fullest sweep and *direst* swing."

Among the more routine copyist's or compositor's misreadings which were corrected in the English edition, few could have been noticed by anyone but the author. In almost every case Melville's handwriting was evidently to blame. In several cases its lack of clarity had led to wrong conjectural readings: to "my decent," which he restored to "any decent"; "happily" for his "haply"; "considerations" for his "considerateness"; "leaving" for his "laving"; and "swift" for his "shift." Other misreadings rose from habitual peculiarities in his formation of letters (see the discussion of these by Davis and Gilman, *Letters*, pp. xxi ff). His indeterminate a/o led to these readings: "came" for his "come" and "became" for his "become"; his *r* caused trouble, inducing the following American misreadings, corrected in the English edition: "brows" for his "bows"; "even" for his "ever"; "you" for his "your"; "death-gasp" for his "death-grasp." Likewise his indistinct final *s* gave trouble: on the one hand "whetstone" for his "whetstones," "stand" for his "stands," "contortion" for his "contortions"—and on the other hand "oars" for his "oar" and "flows" for his "flow." The difficulty in distinguishing his "in" from his "on" led to one misreading he noticed and corrected: "lives on matter" to "lives in matter." (We believe he overlooked further instances of this as of other misreadings; see the ensuing list of emendations we make that were not made in *E.*)

The reader impressed by such Melville readings recovered from the

English text—or perhaps not convinced that all are indeed his—is invited to apply his own critical judgment to the complete collation of the two first editions in section 2A. That table includes both the English changes, listed here, which we adopt as Melville's, and many others we have not yet judged to be his, though some may be so.

xiii.5-10 *E and N* "There . . . LOST. *A* (*Not present.*)

1.9 *E and N* (*Omitted.*) *A* ETYMOLOGY.

3.34 *E and N* **a boiling pan** *A* boiling pan

4.25 *E and N* **Holy War.** *A* Pilgrim's Progress.

6.4 *E and N* **Tho' stiff** *A* Tho' stuffed

6.10 *E and N* **Goldsmith's Nat. Hist.** *A* Goldsmith, Nat. His.

10.29 *E and N* **her mere** *A* her near

13.11 *E and N* **in the needles** *A* of the needles

14.2 *E and N* **and make him the own brother** *A* and own brother

18.27 *E and N* **of out- / hanging light** *A* of light

22.2 *E and N* **gulp** *A* gulph

24.25 *E and N* **any decent** *A* my decent

27.45 *E and N* **the same as in** *A* as you see the same in

37.39 *E and N* **they come** *A* they came

44.27 *E and N* **And left me** *A* And lift me

44.28 *E and N* **the open maw** *A* the opening maw

49.2 *E and N* **become** *A* became

56.15 *E and N* **While yet** *A* When

57.8 *E and N* **might haply gain** *A* might happily gain

60.8 *E and N* **dived her bows** *A* dived her brows

72.7 *E and N* **worthy Captain Bildad** *A* worthy Captain Peleg

80.9 *E and N* **knob** *A* knot

80.29 *E and N* **all I could do** *A* all he could do

89.31 *E and N* **stowage** *A* storage

90.18 *E and N* **came running** *A* came hobbling

103.29 *E and N* **courage is** *A* courage was

108.30 *E and N* **he never did! Poor Alabama boy!** *A* he never did—oh, no! he went before. Poor Alabama boy!

116.23 *E and N* **never speak quick to him** *A* never speak to him

123.29 *E and N* **the Tartarean tiles** *A* the Tartarian tiles

128.33 *E and N* **Now, one of the grand distinctions** *A* Now, the grand distinction

130.2 *E and N* **direst swing** *A* direct swing

134.8 *E and N* **the whetstones** *A* the whetstone

136.10 *E and N* **even when most** *A* ever when most

137.25 *E and N* **coolish weather** *A* cold weather

139.6 *E and N* **we Southern fishers** *A* we South fishers

140.16 *E and N* **Wickliff's** *A* Cranmer's

142.9 *E and N* **men,—a doubloon.** *A* men.

145.38 *E and N* **wert not thou** *A* wer't not thou

151.36 *E and N* **one ball** *A* a ball

152.1 *E and N* **your scholars** *A* you scholars

152.28 *E and N* **low-valed, high-palmed Tahiti!** *A* low veiled, high palmed Tahiti!

158.21 *E and N* **and also a thing** *A* and as well a thing

162.22 *E and N* **Had any of** *A* Had any one of

166.27-28 *E and N* **as much the badge** *A* as much like the badge

173.19 *E and N* **time and place** *A* time or place

173.44 *E and N* **been covertly selected** *A* been correctly selected

177.20 *E and N* **New Zealand Jack** *A* New Zealand Tom

183.17 *E and N* **stands** *A* stand

185.38 *E and N* **modified by free will** *A* directed by free will

187.16 *E and N* **wide trowsers** *A* wide black trowsers

188.9 *E and N* **back!—Never heed** *A* back!" (*New paragraph*) "Never heed

190.25 *E and N* **along his oar!"** *A* along his oars!"

216.27 *E and N* **boys' business** (Harper's Magazine *agrees with* E.) *A* boy's business

218.38 *H and N* **But all three** (E *agrees with* A, *but we adopt this reading from* Harper's Magazine.) *A* But all these

232.44 *E and N* **German savage** *A* Dutch savage

233.26-27 *E and N* **else—so chance-like are such observations of the hills—your precise** *A* else so chance-like are such observations of the hills, that your precise

240.23 *E and N* **horrible contortions** *A* horrible contortion

251.18 *E and N* **"Dough you is** *A* "Do you is

264.36 *E and N* **lives in matter** *A* lives on matter

264.42 *E and N* **stranger's** *A* strangers'

273.5-6 *E and N* **the sort of bellows by which he blows back the breath** *A* the sort of bitters by which he blows back the life

277.8 *E and N* **lets** *A* let's

286.38 *E and N* **irrecoverably lost** *A* irrevocably lost

298.18 *E and N* **diagonally** *A* diagonically

303.29 *E and N* **one of that sort goes down** *A* one of that sort go down

310.23 *E and N* **1850** *A* 1851

322.38–49 *E and N* (*The whole footnote to the word* **gallied** *did not appear in* A.) *A* (*Not present.*)

332.13–16 *E and N* **northern seas, they (the plaintiffs) had succeeded in harpooning the fish; but at last, through peril of their lives, were obliged to forsake, not only their lines, but their boat itself,—Furthermore: ultimately** *A* Northern seas; and when indeed they (the plaintiffs) had succeeded in harpooning the fish; they were at last, through peril of their lives, obliged to forsake not only their lines, but their boat itself. Ultimately

332.19 *E and N* **plaintiffs;—Yet again:— and when** *A* plaintiffs. And when

332.22–23 *E and N* **and boat, all of which** *A* and boat, which

332.32–33 *E and N* **possession of her. He then proceeded to say that,** *A* possession of her. Erskine was on the other side; and he then supported it by saying, that

333.10 *E and N* **the defendants afterwards took** *A* the plaintiffs afterwards took

336.37 *E and N* **denying that** *A* denying not

347.18 *E and N* **such considerateness towards** *A* such considerations towards

358.43 *E and N* **flow.** *A* flows.

373.10 *E and N* **untrussing the points of his hose** *A* untagging the points of his hose

377.20 *E and N* **the embryo hull** *A* the hull

379.30–31 *E and N* **ante-chronical** *A* antichronical

380.27 *E and N* **ante-chronical** *A* antichronical

380.37 *E and N* **Pharaohs'** *A* Pharaoh's

391.45 *E and N* **proud as a Greek god** *A* proud as Greek god

396.28–29 *E and N* **milky way—after saying this he added** *A* milky way. He added

411.21 *E and N* **Now, sometimes, in** *A* Now, in

411.36 *E and N* **unearthly passionlessness** *A* earthly passionlessness

415.30 *E and N* **To sailors, oaths** *A* to sailors' oaths

424.32–33 *E and N* **were braced hard up** *A* were hard up

428.8 *E and N* **intently** *A* intenting

432.31 *E and N* **out of my sight."** *A* out of sight."

445.17 *E and N* **air** *A* airs

447.40 *E and N* **once laving him** *A* once leaving him

447.43 *E and N* **that serenity** *A* this serenity

448.27 *E and N* **could perceive** *A* could discover

450.34 *E and N* **prow was pointed** *A* prows were pointed

458.21 *E and N* **boats'** *A* boat's

460.9 *E and N* **set due eastward** *A* sat due eastward

460.29 *E and N* **turn to ice,** *A* turned to ice,

461.11 *E and N* **shift and swerve** *A* swift and swerve

469.22 *E and N* **in his death- / grasp,** *A* in his death-gasp,

2c. ENGLISH READINGS CONSIDERED

This table consists of English readings which we considered adopting or at least felt might be authorial. Many of these readings are attractive, and a few of them, we think, are almost certainly what Melville meant to write, but miswrote, or what he wrote only to have someone miscopy. One striking possible emendation is the *E* reading of "Is it Ahab, Ahab?" for "Is Ahab, Ahab?" (Ch. 132). Once the Melvillean who has long understood Ahab to be questioning his own identity recovers from his surprise, he may decide that the parallel construction in the sentences which precede and follow this one supports the English reading. (The sentence which follows is: "Is it I, God, or who, that lifts this arm?") But the American reading makes adequate sense, and we have retained it in this edition.

There are several items in this list which will challenge anyone interested in Melville's stylistic revisions. At the beginning of Ch. 13, in A, Ishmael says:

The grinning landlord, as well as the boarders, seemed amazingly tickled at the sudden friendship which had sprung up between me and Queequeg —especially as Peter Coffin's cock and bull stories about him had previously so much alarmed me concerning the very person whom I now companied with.

The English version concludes instead with these words:

. . . stories had previously so much alarmed me about him.

At first glance, the English reading seems altogether less awkward. But it may well be that the American reading was *meant* to be somewhat complex, as part of Ishmael's characterization. Other characters more than once have to ask him to "twist that smaller," to say things more simply. Possibly Melville himself made the change that appears in E; if he did, he may after a year or more have forgotten why the language as he had written it was especially appropriate to Ishmael. This is speculation, but many of the E changes require a good deal of casting about for explanations. The temptation we share with earlier editors is to defend A readings against the English readings, not only against any changes that expurgate or anglicize the American text, but revisions that look merely "schoolmasterish." Yet Melville and, if you will, Ishmael were both former schoolmasters, and some of the schoolmasterish changes we have not adopted may be Melville's. Again, the curious reader should examine the full collation in section 2A.

Within this table is a tiny special class of expurgations or modifications in E that are so good—and so "Melvillean"—as to suggest that Melville made them; he was given to "second thoughts," and under the threat of censorship he may have been making anticipatory expurgations which would at least be his own if not what he had first wanted. The reading "an apparently eternal anguish in his face" is really not a bad replacement, as the publisher's or copy editor's replacements go in E. It is inferior to A's "a crucifixion in his face," but it is better than the perfunctory and unconvincing "and I entered upon a long rigmarole story" which E puts into Ishmael's mouth to mask the deletion of a whole page of A at the beginning of Ch. 18. Still, even if Melville did make, say, the "Lothario" revision in Ch. 88 (and the E reading is funnier, though more genteel), the Bentley publishing house thought it necessary to further expurgate the same passage.

In short, this table provides the reader with very real problems of textual criticism.

15.41—16.4 *A and N* **And, doubtless, my going on this whaling voyage, formed part of the grand programme of Providence that was drawn up a long time ago. It came as a sort of brief interlude and solo between more extensive performances. I take it that this part of the bill must have** *E* I take it that this part of the bill, of those three mysterious ladies, must have

48.8 *A and N* **clattering overboard** *E* tumbling overboard

58.15–17 *A and N* **stories about him had** previously so much alarmed me concerning the very person whom I now companied with. *E* stories had previously so much alarmed me about him.

111.7 *A and N* **a crucifixion in his face** *E* an apparently eternal anguish in his face

118.28–29 *A and N* **to much of any description. My object here is simply to project the draught of a systematization of cetology.** *E* to much of any systematization of cetology.

147.3 *A and N* **slow dived** *E* long dived

160.30 *A and N* **probably but felt** *E* probably felt
170.39 *A and N* **ye eat for supper** *E* ye ate for supper
208.16 *A and N* **own particular accompaniments** *E* own peculiar accompaniments
210.23 *A and N* **yet was he** *E* still was he
254.7 *A and N* **more of shark** *E* more a shark
262.31 *A and N* **a powerless panic** *E* a powerful panic
266.15 *A and N* **by the way** *E* by way
329.15–17 *A and N* **he cannot keep the most notorious Lothario out of his bed; for, alas! all fish bed in common** *E* he cannot always frustrate the most notorious Lothario; for, alas! all fish have very vague ideas of the connubial tie.
330.3 *A and N* **amorous errors** *E* own juvenile errors
361.18 *A and N* **in rear** *E* in the rear

378.1 *A and N* **weighty** *E* mighty
383.28 *A and N* **mounted on horse** *E* mounted on horses,
395.37 *A and N* **but little left of him** but *E* little left of him but
398.21 *A and N* **shame upon them!** *E* shame upon 'em!
411.14 *A and N* **the eager mariners** *E* eager mariners
411.31 *A and N* **its precise** *E* the precise
414.6–7 *A and N* **ships . . . lips** *E* ship . . . lip
415.2 *A and N* **to considerable depth** *E* to a considerable depth
422.12 *A and N* **if this ship come** *E* if this ship comes
428.6 *A and N* **my inmost** *E* mine inmost
440.30 *A and N* **Then it darted** *E* Now it darted
445.5 *A and N* **Is Ahab, Ahab?** *E* Is it Ahab, Ahab?

2D. HAYFORD-PARKER READINGS ADOPTED

In the following list are substantive emendations we have introduced into the Norton text even though the American and English first edition readings agree. We have no documentary authority for them, but we are convinced by the sense required within their contexts that they are the readings Melville intended. (It is not quite accurate to label the list "Hayford-Parker Substantive Emendations," since some eight or ten of the three dozen have been suggested, and a few of them have been adopted, by other scholars, chiefly Mansfield and Vincent. But this label makes clear our responsibility for bringing all these readings into the text itself, not just into textual notes or footnotes.) We believe that most of these emendations will immediately strike the reader as right and necessary, even though a few of them occur in very familiar passages. Our "at last *came*" replaces "at last *come*" in the first paragraph of Ch. 3, the description of the oil painting in the Spouter-Inn. (The context clearly calls for "came," and so, since Melville's o's and a's were often not distinguishable, we have assumed that a copyist misread his handwriting and that he did not catch the mistake when proofreading.) In Ch. 18 all editions make Peleg retreat toward the cabin gangway. Our addition of the one word, "to," makes Bildad do the retreating (our "to" is bracketed here):

"Quick, Bildad," said Peleg, [to] his partner, who, aghast at the close vicinity of the flying harpoon, had retreated towards the cabin gangway. "Quick, I say, you Bildad, and get the ship's papers. . . ."

In Ch. 91 Stubb in our edition is not "*arguing* well for his scheme"—he is *auguring* well for it; "arguing" was an easy mistake for a copyist or compositor to make, even assuming that Melville spelled "auguring" right in the first place.

Our reasoning with other instances will be apparent from the contexts, but one more change perhaps needs explanation. When we change "In thoughts of the visions of the night" to "In visions of the night" we are assuming that Melville first wrote "In thoughts of" and then changed it to "In visions of" without adequately marking the first phrase for deletion. Our hope is that this list will encourage closer attention to the words of *Moby-Dick* and the meaning of its sentences.

2.30 *N* (Omitted.) *A and E* EXTRACTS. (*A reduplicated heading on a separate line at the top of a new page in A, preceding the quotation from Genesis; see the* 2A. *list at* 1.9.)

20.19 *N* **at last came** *A and E* at last come

34.13 *N* **having the whole** *A and E* leaving the whole

60.36 *N* **bery** *A and E* bevy

75.42–43 *N* **Thank ye; thank ye** *A and E* That's he; thank ye

84.18 *N* **Peleg, to his partner** *A and E* Peleg, his partner

85.29 *N* **off Japan** *A and E* on Japan

93.29 *N* **gifts** *A and E* gift

108.29 *N* **came back** *A and E* come back

152.13 *N* **the waves'—the snow-caps'** *A and E* the waves—the snow's caps

174.16 *N* **No.** *A and E* Yes.

191.33 *N* **the second mate** *A and E* the third mate

192.12 *N* **bade fair** *A and E* bade far

198.10 *N* **Until Archy's** *A and E* Until Cabaco's

209.3 *N* **sail westward** *A and E* sail eastward

210.13 *N* **birch canoe** *A and E* beech canoe

212.10 *N* **sailor's talk** *A and E* sailors' talk

220.33 *N* **down beneath** *A and E* down between

237.2 *N* **or** *A and E* however this was, or

245.18 *N* **said Tashtego.** *A and E* said Daggoo.

274.11 *N* **mast-heads.** *A and E* mast-head.

286.4 *N* **Sais?** *A and E* Lais?

292.38 *N* **on the now** *A and E* in the now

293.32 *N* **false brow** *A and E* false bow

340.3 *N* **Stubb augured** *A and E* Stubb argued

346.33 *N* **man loves** *A and E* man loved

349.12–13 *N* **In visions of the night** *A and E* In thoughts of the visions of the night,

350.32 *N* **assistant's** *A and E* assistants'

370.1 *N* **testing cruise** *A and E* tasting cruise

388.1 *N* **Stubb longs** *A and E* Stubb longed

394.34 *N* **the circumstances** *A and E* the circumstance,

407.5 *N* **her mast-heads** *A and E* her mast-head

409.38 *N* **striveth, this one jetteth** *A and E* strivest, this one jettest

413.6 *N* **die in it** *A and E* die it

435.3 *N* **boats' crews** *A and E* boat's crews

455.5 *N* **guiltlessness** *A and E* guiltiness

2E. HAYFORD-PARKER READINGS CONSIDERED

This table differs from the one in 2c. in that it contains readings which we considered introducing although the American and English editions agreed. Again, we suspect many of these readings are what Melville meant to write, but miswrote, or what he really wrote though it was miscopied by his copyist or compositor. One item needs explanation: the suggestion that the American "hobbling" and the English "running" should be "roaring" is based on a paleographic argument. Melville's *r*'s were frequently looped so as to resemble *h*'s, and his *n*'s could be peaked so as to resemble *b*'s. Our assumption is that he wrote "roaring" (note the parallel repetition of "roaring" in the sentence) only to have it misread by his copyist or American compositor as "hobbling," and then corrected it to "roaring" on the proof sheets only to have the English compositor misread the word as "running." Peleg, after all, is characterized as active of limb and should not be hobbling in this one passage.

Most of the other items fit into classes already discussed under 2B., 2C., and 2D. Again, the reader may well feel we have sometimes been too conservative, as when we exclude so appealing a reading as "formerly" for "formally" at the end of Ch. 65, but as long as the American and English readings make sense, we have followed them.

33.21 *A and E* **I knew not how** *H-P* I know not how
56.14 *A and E* **in any map** *H-P* on any map
62.2 *A and E* **and elbow of sand** *H-P* an elbow of sand
71.30–31 *A and E* **to learn a bold and nervous** *H-P* learning a bold and nervous
79.28 *A and E* **the vinegar-cruet** *H-P* the mustard-pot
90.18 *E* **running** *A* hobbling *H-P* roaring
143.42 *A and E* **measurer** *H-P* measure
144.21 *A and E* **jealousy** *H-P* jealously
167.1 *A and E* **but, nevertheless,** *H-P* nevertheless.
209.28 *A and E* **a Vineyarder,** *H-P* a Nantucketer,

223.5 *A and E* **not to approach the ship at their peril** *H-P* to approach the ship at their peril
241.16 *A and E* **than though seated** *H-P* than seated
251.31 *A and E* **Is not one shark** *H-P* Has not one shark
256.11 *A and E* **formally indite his circulars?** *H-P* formerly indite his circulars?
406.9–27 *A and E* **Oh, grassy . . . learn it.** *H-P* "Oh, grassy . . . learn it." *(making Ahab speak the ¶)*
407.7 *A and E* **bottom down** *H-P* bottom up
408.11 *A and E* **things passed,** *H-P* things past,
431.5 *A and E* **lonely widow old women** *H-P* lonely old widow women

3. TREATMENT OF ACCIDENTALS

The first American edition of *Moby-Dick* has proved intelligible to its readers despite the many mistakes, omissions, and inconsistencies in spelling, capitalization, hyphenation, and punctuation that make it an editorial mare's nest. Editing it, we became especially aware that by any standards, of Melville's own time or ours, the first American edition is confusingly punctuated. It frequently pairs a dash with some other mark of punctuation when two dashes are required by the meaning (Ch. 54: "Now, as you well know, it is not seldom the case in this conventional world of ours—watery or otherwise; that when a person . . . ."). Less often, it uses a pair of dashes when only one is needed (Ch. 54: "In good time, the Town-Ho reached her port—a savage, solitary place—where no civilized creature resided."). It is clogged with semicolons which frequently disguise the meaning, at least for the reader who uses pointing as a guide to the sense. In page-long "Though . . . though . . . though . . . though . . . though . . . yet . . ." constructions, semicolons may separate not only five or six parallel elements but also one or more parts of one or more of these parallel elements; see the third paragraph in Ch. 42. Many times quotation marks occur on what now seems the wrong side of an exclamation point or a question mark. Frequently enough an absolutely necessary comma is not there. Most of the long chapter "The Town-Ho's Story" is improperly punctuated as to quotation marks, with double and single quotes around the speeches of the company at the Golden Inn instead of merely double quotes—except when an occasional error in the punctuation accidentally makes it right!

Faced with the vast number of pages swarming like Pierre's proofs (in Melville's next book, *Pierre*) with "such minute, gnat-like torments," the temptation is to "randomly" correct "the worst, and let the rest go." But an editor can scarcely adopt this policy, for his improving the punctuation of one sentence may leave him with no consistent grounds for not "improving" hundreds of similar sentences. An editor who seeks a consistent policy finally must choose between one of three courses: presenting (a) a diplomatic text (with all errors of substantives and accidentals intact); (b) a greatly "improved" or modernized text in which the spelling, capitalization, hyphenation, and punctuation are "brought into conformity with modern usage," and no attempt is made to list all the hundreds of changes; (c) a somewhat improved text in which all outright errors and all accidentals very likely to make a reader misinterpret a passage are corrected, and all editorial departures from the copy-text are listed.

In accordance with our general conservatism in this critical edition, we have chosen the third course. For example, Melville certainly meant Ahab to say, "D'ye feel brave, men, brave?" not "D'ye feel brave men, brave?" as the American text says. For another example, in our text by our emendation, the smaller whales evince "a still, becharmed panic," not "a still becharmed panic," as in both first editions. (The reader should note especially the comma changes we have made, since several of them do impose one meaning on a possibly ambiguous sentence in the first edition; see the "bravery chiefly visible" entry for such an example.) But punctuation not absolutely misleading has been left untouched, and variant spellings appearing in any one of several contemporary dictionaries have been retained (we print such forms as "envelop," "ley," "villanous," and retain "calk/caulk" and "cleat/cleet" variants). We have adopted many of E's corrections of errors in accidentals, especially of words misspelled in A, since such corrections may be, and frequently certainly *are*, Melville's own. But even when A and E agree we have changed what we consider to be either erroneous or likely to mislead. But to repeat: with the exception noted in the following paragraph, *we have listed all our changes of accidentals*, just as we listed all substantive emendations we introduced into the text.

The only exception to a complete listing of changes is that we have corrected the use of double and single quotation marks in "The Town-Ho's Story" without listing each correction. In all three of the printings of the chapter which have separate authority (*Harper's Magazine* [October 1851], A, and E), both double and single quotes are used *erroneously* to enclose the speeches of Ishmael and the young dons at the Golden Inn, and are also used *properly* to enclose the speeches of the men on the ship *Town-Ho*. (As we said above, occasionally all three of the early authoritative texts of this story are inconsistent with themselves in this matter, and at least in the case of Ishmael and the dons, an error sometimes results accidentally in correct punctuation.) We have felt that no scholarly purpose would be served by our listing all of our corrections of quotation marks in this chapter, and that any such list would create new confusion. We do want to call attention to one passage where by moving a quotation mark we have adopted the *Harper's* and English indication of speaker instead of that of the American edition. The first American edition has:

> "It was just between daybreak and sunrise of the morning of the second day, when they were washing down the decks, that a stupid Teneriffe man, drawing water in the main-chains, all at once shouted out, 'There she rolls! there she rolls!' Jesu, what a whale! It was Moby Dick.
> " 'Moby Dick!' cried Don Sebastian; 'St. Dominic! Sir sailor, but do whales have christenings? Whom call you Moby Dick?'

Following *H* and *E* for indication of speakers, and *H* for the exclamation point after the word "Jesu," but making necessary corrections, we print:

> "It was just between daybreak and sunrise of the morning of the second day, when they were washing down the decks, that a stupid Teneriffe man, drawing water in the main-chains, all at once shouted out, 'There she rolls! there she rolls! Jesu! what a whale!' It was Moby Dick."
> "Moby Dick!" cried Don Sebastian; "St. Dominic! Sir sailor, but do whales have christenings? Whom call you Moby Dick?"

This passage is the only one that calls for special mention; to repeat, throughout the chapter we have put the conversations at the Golden Inn in double quotes, and the conversations on the *Town-Ho* in double and single quotes, to indicate that Ishmael is quoting their speeches.

SPELLING CHANGES ADOPTED FROM E

xvii.3 *E and N* **Prairie** *A* Praire
9.33 *E and N* **Cruise** *A* Cruize
25.32 *E and N* **airley** *A* early
37.31 *E and N* **Tongatabooans** *A* Tongatabooarrs
54.24 *E and N* **salaamed** *A* salamed
59.6 *E and N* **Kokovoko** *A* Rokovoko
59.10 *E and N* **Kokovoko** *A* Rokovoko
62.32 *E and N* **Behring's** *A* Bhering's
65.25 *E and N* **vertebræ** *A* vertebra
65.40 *E and N* **ony** *A* only
65.43 *E and N* **a-night** *A* at night
67.21 *E and N* **Becket** *A* Beckett
68.45 *E and N* **Marchant** *A* Merchant
73.35 *E and N* **net** *A* nett
85.9 *E and N* **Bel** *A* Bell
95.11 *E and N* **Quohog** *A* Quohag
100.1 *E and N* **Cooks** *A* Cookes
100.3 *E and N* **Cook** *A* Cooke
100.6 *E and N* **Cook** *A* Cooke
109.17 *E and N* **warranty** *A* warrantry
114.12 *E and N* **plaguy** *A* plaguey
121.10 *E and N* **Baleine** *A* Baliene
134.19 *E and N* **scimitars** *A* scimetars
136.3 *E and N* **Vendôme** *A* Vendome

148.23 *E and N* **demogorgon** *A* demigorgon
165.3 *E and N* **Prairies** *A* Praries
233.40 *E and N* **bridle-bits** *A* bridlebitts
251.30 *E and N* **yourselbs** *A* yoursebls
262.15 *E and N* **vulturism** *A* vultureism
272.31 *E and N* **Cognac** *A* Cogniac
291.2 *E and N* **PRAIRIE** *A* PRAIRE
326.6 *E and N* **vicissitudes** *A* vicisitudes
348.35 *E and N* **petulance** *A* petulence
360.40 *E and N* **Jimini** *A* Jimimi
374.1 *E and N* **virtù** *A* vertú
375.14 *E and N* **virtù** *A* vertú
370.7 *E and N* **Enderbys** *A* Enderbies
382.18 *E and N* **Cook's** *A* Cooke's
400.36-37 *E and N* **petulance** *A* petulence
403.13 *E and N* **smooth** *A* smoothe
403.18 *E and N* **smooth** *A* smoothe
403.21 *E and N* **smooth** *A* smoothe
425.4 *E and N* **fain** *A* feign
447.28 *E and N* **fowls** *A* fowels

OTHER SPELLING CHANGES MADE IN N

xvii.1 *N* **Heidelberg** *A* Heidelburgh
4.11 *N* **Hofmannus** *A* Hosmannus
8.19 *N* **Chase** *A* Chace
8.24 *N* **Chase** *A* Chace
23.41 *N* **Alleghanian** *A* Alleganian
25.36 *N* **bamboozling** *A* bamboozingly
26.39 *N* **onions** *A* inions
27.7 *N* **Sal** *A* Sall

60.36 *N* **bery** *A* bevy
65.39 *N* **unfort'nate** *A* unfort'nt
69.10 *N* **innuendoes** *A* inuendoes
117.26 *N* **Olmsted** *A* Olmstead
120.16 *N* **Pottfisch** *A* Pottsfich
121.11 *N* **Gröndlands Valfisk** *A* Growlands Walfish
144.33 *N* **Chilean** *A* Chilian

151.6	*N* comes	*A* come's	
157.20	*N* Olafsen	*A* Olassen	
157.20	*N* Povelsen	*A* Povelson	
157.31	*N* Povelsen	*A* Povelson	
177.15	*N* Chilean	*A* Chilian	
178.45	*N* Chase	*A* Chace	
179.31	*N* Chase's	*A* Chace's	
180.39	*N* Fernandez	*A* Fernandes	
201.31–32	*N* Tormentoso	*A* Tormen-toto	
202.36	*N* Crozets	*A* Crozetts	
214.36	*H and N* plaza	*A* plazza	
229.30	*N* Garneray	*A* Garnery	
230.23	*N* Garneray	*A* Garnery	
230.34	*N* Garneray	*A* Garnery	
231.7	*N* Leuwenhoek	*A* Leuwenhoeck	
231.13	*N* Garneray	*A* Garnery	
232.44	*N* Dürer	*A* Durer	
233.28	*N* Solomon	*A* Soloma	
233.29	*N* Mendaña	*A* Mendanna	
233.30	*N* Figueroa	*A* Figuera	
234.3	*N* Crozets	*A* Crozetts	
238.4	*N* Pontoppidan	*A* Pontoppodan	

266.13	*N* Niskayuna	*A* Neskyeuna	
266.19	*N* Niskayuna	*A* Neskyeuna	
274.4	*N* Crozets	*A* Crozetts	
282.33	*N* scimitar	*A* scimetar	
286.6	*N* HEIDELBERG	*A* HEIDEL-BURGH	
286.23	*N* Heidelberg	*A* Heidelburgh	
286.27	*N* Heidelberg	*A* Heidelburgh	
287.1	*N* Heidelberg	*A* Heidelburgh	
287.6	*N* Heidelberg	*A* Heidelburgh	
287.24	*N* Heidelberg	*A* Heidelburgh	
288.27	*N* Heidelberg	*A* Heidelburgh	
306.11	*N* versa	*A* versâ	
308.17	*N* via	*A* viâ	
315.20	*N* Eckermann	*A* Eckerman	
342.32	*N* pastilles	*A* pastiles	
348.6	*N* Heidelberg	*A* Heidelburgh	
380.2	*N* Dauphine	*A* Dauphiné	
384.22	*N* Horto	*A* Harto	
408.2	*N* Bastille	*A* Bastile	
430.13–14	*N* innuendoes	*A* inuendoes	
430.40	*N* it's	*A* its	
445.1	*N* cozening	*A* cozzening	

COMMA CHANGES ADOPTED FROM E

27.16	*E and N* exclaimed, *A* exclaimed
71.29	*E and N* virgin, voluntary, *A* virgin voluntary
77.1	*E and N* that, *A* that
91.28	*E and N* saying, *A* saying
92.28	*E and N* him, in his broken fashion *A* him in his broken fashion,
163.29	*E and N* Cæsarian *A* Cæsarian,
191.27	*E and N* Though, *A* Though
191.27	*E and N* truly, *A* truly
221.33	*E and N* Now, *A* Now.

224.29	*E and N* honor, *A* honor
250.16	*E and N* time, *A* time
256.24	*E and N* two and two, *A* two and two
256.24	*E and N* hour *A* hour,
332.24	*E and N* Wherefore, *A* Wherefore
333.10	*E and N* Now, *A* Now
415.35	*E and N* Tekel, *A* Tekel
459.34	*E and N* brave, *A* brave

OTHER COMMA CHANGES MADE IN N

38.22	*N* Canaan, *A* Canaan;
51.20	*N* remained, *A* remained
104.14	*N* bravery, chiefly *A* bravery chiefly,
105.9	*N* mighty *A* mighty,
136.16	*N* however, *A* however
178.11	*N* others, *A* others
192.17	*N* eyes, *A* eyes

298.1	*N* Fiercely but evenly, *A* Fiercely, but evenly
299.1	*N* and, *A* and
311.40	*N* necessities, *A* necessities
325.11	*N* still, *A* still
361.23–24	*N* and, to wind up, *A* and to wind up
443.39	*N* bread, *A* bread

QUOTATION MARK CHANGES ADOPTED FROM E

45.5–6	*E and N* 'And . . . Jonah.' *A* "And . . . Jonah."
46.29	*E and N* " 'Who's *A* 'Who's
46.45	*E and N* "Now *A* Now
49.11	*E and N* "And *A* And
88.5	*E and N* will you?" *A* will you?

118.36–37	*E and N* he" (the leviathan) "make *A* he (the leviathan) make
188.10	*E and N* sir," *A* sir,'
414.31	*E and N* "Yes *A* Yes
422.35	*E and N* if—" *A* if"—

OTHER QUOTATION MARK CHANGES MADE IN N

8.24	*N* Ocean." *A* Ocean.
9.37	*N* Mutiny," *A* Mutiny,
74.19–20	*N* " 'Lay . . . moth—' " *A* "Lay . . . moth—"
74.40–41	*N* " 'for . . . also.' " *A* "for . . . also."

186.24	*N* steward!" *A* steward!
362.31	*N* Hark!" *A* Hark!
381.24	*N* Rib" (says John Leo) "is *A* Rib (says John Leo) is

APOSTROPHE CHANGES ADOPTED FROM E

116.1	*E and N* 'Halloa,' *A* 'Halloa,
251.45	*E and N* 'em *A* em
252.12	*E and N* 'dention *A* dention
252.32	*E and N* 'noder *A* noder

397.4	*E and N* convenience' *A* convenience
444.37	*E and N* " 'Tis *A* "Tis
460.33	*E and N* Vesuvius' *A* Vesuvius

OTHER APOSTROPHE CHANGES MADE IN N

115.30 *N* 'Slid *A* Slid
141.9 *N* 'Twill *A* T'will
252.8 *N* till *A* 'till
253.17 *N* 'tall *A* t'all

345.13 *N* kings' *A* king's
418.6 *N* 'tis *A* t'is
435.3 *N* boats' *A* boat's

CAPITALIZATION CHANGES ADOPTED FROM E

12.24 *E and N* **Battery** *A* battery
83.12 *E and N* **First** *A* first
87.1 *E and N* **Captain** *A* captain
154.10 *E and N* **gods** *A* Gods

179.17 *E and N* **Commodore** *A* commodore
351.7 *E and N* **King Asa** *A* king Asa
445.24 *E and N* **mate** *A* Mate

OTHER CAPITALIZATION CHANGES MADE IN N

83.11 *N* **Christian** *A* christian

380.14 *N* **anatomist** *A* Anatomist

MISCELLANEOUS CHANGES ADOPTED FROM E

1.4 *E and N* **[The** *A* The
1.8 *E and N* **mortality.]** *A* mortality.
2.3 *E and N* **[It** *A* It
2.29 *N* **glasses!]** *E* glasses.] *A* glasses!
38.25 *E and N* **houses,** *A* houses;
71.18-19 *E and N* **thee and thou** *A* thee and thou
76.6 *E and N* **does he want** *A* does he want
80.33 *E and N* **island?** *A* island.
87.15 *E and N* **prophecy?** *A* prophecy.
110.14 *E and N* **say.** *A* say,
126.17 *E and N* **i.e.** *A* i.e
136.35 *E and N* **pleasant—** *A* pleasant
148.42 *E and N* **ha-ha's** *A* ha, ha's
149.29 *E and N* **commanded—** *A* commanded.—

164.31 *E and N* **albatross:** *A* albatross,
167.39 *E and N* **seas;** *A* seas:
210.18 *E and N* **(*New Paragraph*) Thus** *A* Thus
244.20 *E and N* **bowsman;** *A* bowsman!
268.22 *E and N* **(It** *A* It
268.30 *E and N* **dead.)** *A* dead.
322.13 *E and N* **gallied *** *A* gallied
336.17 *E and N* **is yᵉ** *A* is ye
336.18 *E and N* **y ᵉ** *A* ye
360.34 *E and N* **almanack;** *A* almanack
360.40 *E and N* **the Bull;—** *A* the Bull
458.15 *E and N* **being.** *A* being
467.25 *E and N* **fit.** *A* fit

OTHER MISCELLANEOUS CHANGES MADE IN N

19.23 *N* **wrapper** *A* wrapper—
19.23 *N* **afterwards)—** *A* afterwards)
58.20 *N* **the "Moss,"** *A* "the Moss,"
168.28 *N* **me"?** *A* me?"
189.19 *N* **boys!)"** *A* boys!")
218.6 *N* **run amuck** *A* run a muck
221.22-23 *N* **there she rolls! Jesu! what a whale!' It was Moby Dick."** (Harper's

reading, *except the final double quote.*)
A there she rolls!' Jesu, what a whale! It was Moby Dick.
318.43 *N* **low-shaded** *A* low shaded
336.16 *N* **Yᵉ** *A* Ye
336.17 *N* **that yᵉ** *A* that ye
388.2 *N* **oar!** *A* oar;
409.37 *N* **power!** *A* power?

TYPOGRAPHICAL ERRORS CORRECTED

92.15 *N* **then,** *A* hen,
103.36 *N* **Stubb,** *A* Stbub,
143.15 *N* **that** *A* tha
157.2 *N* **fearfully** *A* fearfnlly
172.33 *N* **in crossing** *A* incrossing
221.32 *N* **up** *A* up up
254.32 *N* **fastidious** *A* fastidions

311.22 *N* **fishermen** *A* fishermon
336.17 *N* **wardrobe** *A* warbrobe
345.29 *N* **effulgences** *A* effulgenees
416.13 *N* **to** *A* too
419.31 *N* **the holder** *A* theh older
441.13 *N* **upon** *A* upom
464.34 *N* **While** *A* Whilc

Features of the *design* of *A* are extra-textual and not necessarily followed in *N*. Thus, while in wording our running heads follow *A*, (even when they differ from the chapter title, as on p. 233), they are not in small capitals, as those in *A* are. And for convenience we have changed the chapter numbers from roman to arabic numerals. When compound words were hyphenated at the ends of lines in *A*, we had to decide whether to print them as single word compounds without hyphens or as hyphenated compounds (except when they were accidentally hyphenated at the ends of lines in *N* also). Our decisions were based on a survey of the occurrences of the same and analogous words elsewhere in *A*; where evidence was inconclusive, we retained the hyphens. It has seemed inappropriate to print here a complete list of line-end hyphens in *A* and a list of the forms in *A* of compounds which happen to be hyphenated at the line-ends in *N*.

Glossary of Nautical Terms

To preserve something of the tang of nautical idioms contemporary with Melville, and to avoid introducing anachronistic definitions, we have drawn on nineteenth-century dictionaries of sea terms in compiling this glossary, mainly Richard Henry Dana's *The Seaman's Friend* (Boston, 1856, 8th Edition), W. H. Smyth's *Sailor's Word-Book* (London, 1867), and W. Clark Russell's *Sailor's Language* (London, 1883). We have not included every nautical term in *Moby-Dick* (notably those like "pitchpoling" and "waif pole" that Melville defines himself), and we have defined a few words *not* in *Moby-Dick,* because they occur in definitions of other words. Not all the meanings given here are exactly those carried by the terms in *Moby-Dick*: Melville uses some of these words, like "grapnels" or "slip the cable," metaphorically; and he sometimes invests the *Pequod* with unusual properties, such as a tiller made not of wood or metal but of bone.

abaft Toward the stern of a vessel; behind (Anything behind another thing is called *abaft* it. Russell).

abeam In a line at right angles to the vessel's length. Smyth.

aft Toward the hinder part of a ship (the stern).

a-lee the helm So place the helm that the rudder is brought on the weather side of the stern-post. Smyth.

alow A term sometimes but very rarely used for *below,* and then perhaps only for the sake of alliteration, as "She had studding-sails aloft and alow." Russell.

articles A ship's articles are the document in which are recorded the names and signatures of the crew, their wages, the food to be given, etc. Russell.

athwart Across.

athwartships Across the ship, or across anything; opposed to fore-and-aft.

avast An order to stop hauling or heaving, or to stop doing anything.

avast heaving The cry to arrest the capstan when any impediment occurs in heaving the cable, not infrequently when a hand, foot, or finger, is jammed;—stop! Smyth.

azimuth compass An instrument for finding the magnetic azimuth or amplitude of a heavenly object. Russell.

back (to back a sail) To brace its yard so that the wind may blow directly on the front of the sail, and thus retard the ship's course. Smyth.

backstay A rope to support a mast and leading down abaft it to the side of the vessel. Russell.

499

ballast Heavy material, as iron, lead, or stone, placed in the bottom of the hold, to keep a vessel from upsetting. Dana.

bank A seat.

batten down The hatches [hatchways] are said to be *battened down* when they are covered up with gratings or hatches, and tarpaulins which are secured by battens [pieces of wood or iron] to prevent them from being washed away. Russell.

battering-ram A large piece of timber, armed at each end with iron caps and fitted with ropes. It is used for removing the angular blocks when a docked ship is sitting on them. Russell.

before the mast Living in the forecastle, serving as a "common sailor." Russell.

belay To make a rope fast by taking a turn with it over a belaying-pin. Russell.

belaying pins Iron, brass, or wooden bars tapered, placed in holes in rails, hoops, etc., to make the running gear [running ropes] fast to. Russell.

bells The denoting of time on board ship [by striking a bell every half hour]. Eight bells signify noon or midnight, eight or four o'clock; half-past twelve, one bell; one o'clock, two bells; half-past one, three bells, and so on to eight bells. [To make eight bells a single bell is sounded eight times with a pause after each two strikes.] Russell.

bend To attach. To *bend a sail* is to attach it to the yard. Russell.

binnacle A stand or box of brass or wood in which a compass is placed. Russell.

binnacle lamp A lamp to throw light upon the compass-card. From Smyth.

block A piece of wood with sheaves, or wheels, in it, through which the running rigging passes, to add to the purchase. Dana.

bluff A term applied to a ship's bows, and meaning full and square. Russell.

boat hook A pole furnished with an iron hook and spike for shoving off or holding on to an object when in a boat. Russell.

boom A long spar run out to extend or boom out the foot of a particular sail. A ship is said to come booming forwards when she comes with all the sail she can make. Smyth.

bow The rounded part of a vessel, forward. Dana. [The *bows* of the ship are the sides at the stem, and for some way back.]

bowline A rope leading forward from the leech [the vertical edge] of a square sail, to keep the leech well out when sailing close-hauled. Dana.

bowman (also bowsman) The headmost rower in a boat. Russell.

bowsprit A large spar projecting over the bows.

brace sharp up To *brace up*, or *brace sharp up*, [is] to lay the yards more obliquely fore and aft, by easing off the weather-braces and hauling in the lee ones, which enables a ship to lie as close to the wind as possible. Smyth.

braces The braces are ropes belonging to all the yards of a ship. Smyth. [Their function is to position the yards in the horizontal plane.]

breakers Small barrels for containing water or other liquids. Also, those billows which break violently over reefs, rocks, or shallows, lying immediately at, or under, the surface of the sea. Smyth.

breaking out The act of extricating casks or other objects from the hold-stowage. Smyth.

bring by the lee To incline so rapidly to leeward that the lee-side is unexpectedly brought to windward, and by laying the sails all aback exposes her to the danger of oversetting. Smyth.

bulkhead The bulkhead, afore, is the partition between the forecastle and gratings in the head. [Gratings are open wood-work of cross battens, forming the cover for the hatchways, and permitting light to enter the lower decks.] From Smyth.

bull's-eye A sort of block without a sheave, for a rope to reeve through. Also, a hemispherical piece of ground glass of great thickness, inserted into small openings in the decks and scuttle-hatches, for admission of light below. Smyth.

bulwarks The protection around a vessel's weather deck, consisting of solid planking fixed to stanchions. Russell.

burton A kind of tackle. From Dana.

capstan A barrel of wood or iron revolved by bars [used for lifting great weights]. Russell.

capstan-head The flat, circular top of the capstan, with square holes around its edge. From Smyth.

carlines (carlings) Pieces of timber about five inches square, lying fore and aft, along from one beam to another. On and athwart these the ledges rest, whereon the planks of the deck and other portions of carpentry are made fast. Smyth.

chocks Wooden supports for the bottom of a boat to rest on while not in use. From Russell.

chronometer A timepiece to indicate Greenwich mean time for the purpose of finding the longitude. Russell.

cleat (or cleet) A piece of wood used in different parts of a vessel to belay ropes to. Dana.

clumsy-cleat A knee-brace in the bow of a whale-boat. Russell.

close-haul A vessel is close-hauled when she is sailing with her yards braced up so as to get as much as possible to windward; *full and by* is the same as close-hauled. From Dana.

close-reefed When all the reefs of the top-sails are taken in. From Smyth.

companion-way The staircase to the cabin. Smyth.

compass-card The circular card attached to the needles of a mariner's compass on which are marked 32 points of the compass and the 360 degrees of the circle.

copper-bottomed Said of a wooden ship whose bottom is sheathed with copper. Russell.

cross-trees Cross-pieces of timber on top of the trestletrees [fore-and-aft pieces on each side of a mast]. From Russell.

crowd To *crowd sail* is to set all sail. Russell.

crown That part of an anchor where the shank and arms meet. Russell.

cutting stages Platforms hung over the side for men to stand on while cutting in.

darbies Handcuffs.

dog-vane A small flag or streamer at the mast-head or at the side to indicate the direction of the wind. Russell.

double banked A boat is double banked when two oars, one opposite the other, are pulled by men seated on the same thwart. Dana.

douse To lower or slacken down suddenly; expressed of a sail in a squall of wind, an extended hawser, etc. Smyth.

drawing water The number of feet from the waterline to the lowermost part of the keel.

fiddle-head The head of a ship that has no figure, but is decorated with a scroll shaped like a fiddle. Russell.

fore The forward part of a vessel; opposed to aft.

forecastle deck The deck over the forecastle [the compartment where sailors live, in the bows of a ship]. From Russell.

fore-mast The lower mast nearest the bows of a ship. Russell.

fore-scuttle A hatchway by which the forecastle is entered.

furl To roll up and bind a sail neatly on its respective yard or boom. Smyth.

gaff An instrument like a boat-hook used in the blubber-room of whalers; also, a spar used to extend the heads of fore-and-aft sails which are not set on stays. From Russell.

galliots A Dutch or Flemish vessel for cargoes, with very rounded ribs and flattish bottom, with a mizenmast stept far aft, carrying a square-mainsail and main-topsail. Smyth.

gangway A part of the vessel's side, nearly amidships, by which people enter and leave a ship. Russell.

give way! An order to men who are rowing to pull with more force. Russell.

grapnel A sort of small anchor for boats, having a ring at one end, and four palmed claws at the other. Smyth.

gunwale The gunwale [pronounced gun'l] of a boat is a piece of timber going round the upper sheer-strake as a binder for its top-work. Smyth. [The sheer-strake is the line of plank on a vessel's side, running fore-and-aft under the gunwale. Dana.]

halyards (often halliards) The ropes or tackles used to hoist or lower sail. From Smyth.

handspike A lever of wood used in heaving round a windlass [a large barrel, revolved by handles, on the forecastle, and used in getting up the anchor]. Russell.

hard a-lee "Hard a-lee!" means hard over—put the rudder as far as it will go to windward. Russell.

hatches Openings in the deck for admission into the interior of a ship. Also, the open wood-work of cross battens and ledges forming cover for the hatchways.

hatchway A square or oblong opening in the middle of the deck of a ship, of which there are generally three—the fore, main, and after—affording passages up and down from one deck to another, and again descending into the hold. The hatches of a smaller kind are distinguished by the name of *scuttles*. Smyth.

hawser A large rope used for towing, etc. Russell.

head The fore end of a ship.

head-wind A breeze blowing from the direction of the ship's intended course. Smyth.

headway A vessel's direct passage through the water. Russell.

heave down To drag one side of a ship down with tackles affixed to the mast-heads, in order to repair an injury which is below the water line on the other side. From Smyth and Russell.

heave to To put a vessel in the position of *lying-to,* by adjusting her sails so as to counteract each other, and thereby check her way, or keep her perfectly still. In a gale, it implies to set merely enough sail to steady the ship. Smyth.

helm A term for all the steering arrangements of a ship. Russell.

helmsman Steersman.

hold The interior of a vessel, where the cargo is stored. Dana.

jib A large triangular sail, set on a stay, forward. Smyth.

jib-stay A stay is a rope that supports a mast by leading forward; a jib-stay is the stay on which the jib is set.

jury-mast A temporary mast to replace one that has been lost. Russell.

keel The lowest and principal timber of a vessel, running fore-and-aft its whole length, and supporting the whole frame. It is composed of several pieces, placed lengthwise, and scarfed and bolted together. Dana.

kelson (often keelson) An internal keel, laid upon the middle of the floor-timbers, immediately over the keel, and serving to bind all together by means of long bolts driven from without, and clinched on the upper side of the keelson. Smyth.

kentledge Pieces of iron for ballast, usually laid over the kelson-plates. From Russell and Smyth.

knight-heads Timbers next to the stem [the foremost piece uniting the bows of a ship], the ends of which come up through the deck and form a support for the bowsprit. From Russell and Smyth.

lanyards Ropes rove through dead-eyes (holes in wooden discs) for setting up rigging. Also, a rope made fast to anything to secure it, or as a handle. Dana.

larboard The left side of a vessel, looking forward. Same as port.

lead line A line attached to a leaden weight and used for ascertaining the depth of water. Russell.

league Three nautical miles, or 3041 fathoms. From Smyth.

lee (or leeward) The side opposite to that from which the wind is blowing. *Lee-shore* means the wind is blowing toward the shore, which is on the lee side of the ship. From Smyth.

lee-beam On the lee side of the ship, at right angles with the keel. Smyth.

lee way What a vessel loses by drifting to leeward in her course. Smyth.

lifts Ropes which reach from each mast-head to their respective yard-arms to steady and suspend the ends. Smyth.

line-of-battle ships Before the days of ironclads, ships of seventy-four guns and upwards. Russell.

log-line A line wound on a reel. At the end of the line is a piece of wood with a peg in it called a [log or] logship. On the logship being thrown overboard the velocity with which the vessel leaves it astern is measured by a sand glass which runs a certain number of seconds. From Russell.

loggerhead A sort of post fitted to a whaling-boat's bottom and rising about two feet above the level of the stern platform. Russell.

lubber An awkward unseamanlike fellow. Smyth.

lubber's hole An aperture in the tops so called because raw hands [being timid climbers] prefer to creep through it to going over the shroud. Russell.

luff To luff is to bring a ship closer to the wind. Russell. [A ship is close to the wind when her head is just so near the wind as to fill the sails without shaking them. From Smyth.]

lugger A small vessel with four-cornered cut sails, set fore-and-aft. Smyth.

main brace A purchase attached to the main-yard for trimming it to the wind. Smyth.

main-royal mast The mast above the main-topgallant mast. Russell.

main-yard The lowest yard on the main-mast. Russell.

make To make is to descry. From Russell.

marline A kind of small line, composed of two strands very little twisted. Smyth.

marlingspike An iron pin, sharpened at one end, and having a hole in the other for a lanyard. Dana.

mast-head The portion of the mast above the top of the rigging. From Russell.

midships The middle part of the vessel, either with regard to her length or breadth. Smyth.

muffled oars Oars are muffled by putting mats or canvass round their looms in the row-locks. (The loom is the part of the oar between the handle or grip and the blade.) From Dana.

mincing knives Knives for mincing the horse-pieces of blubber for the try-pots. From Russell.

mizen-mast The mizen (mizzen) mast is the aftermost mast of a ship. Smyth.

offing Distance from the shore. Russell.

orlop The lowest deck, consisting of a platform laid over the beams in the hold, whereon the cables [are] usually coiled. Smyth.

perch A pole stuck up on a shoal as a beacon; or a spar erected on or projected from a cliff whence to watch fish. Smyth.

pike A long, slender, round staff, armed at the end with iron. Smyth.

piled up A vessel is piled up when all sails are set.

plug-hole A hole in the bottom of a boat to let water drain out. Russell.

point of the compass The 32nd part of the circumference, or $11°15'$. Smyth.

poop The aftermost and highest part of a large ship's hull. Smyth.

port-hole An aperture in a ship's side to point a gun through. A window for a cabin. Russell.

post-captain A [Royal Navy] captain of three years' standing. Smyth.

preventer A rope used as an additional support for masts, booms, etc. Russell.

proas [prahu, Malay for boat] The larger war-vessels among the Malays, ranging from 55 to 156 feet in length and carrying 76 to 96 rowers, with about 40 to 60 fighting men. From Smyth.

prow The projecting front part of a ship; the bow.

purchase A mechanical power which increases the force applied. Dana.

quarter (on the quarter) 45° abaft the beam. Smyth.

quarter-boat A boat suspended on davits [curved iron bars affixed to a ship's sides] near the quarters [the after sides of a ship]. Russell.

quarter-deck That part of the upper deck which is abaft the main-mast. Smyth.

range Range alongside, to draw abreast. Russell.

razeed A ship is razeed when one entire deck is cut down. From Russell.

reef To diminish the expanse of a sail by knotting the reef points in it upon the yard, or at the foot. Russell. A certain portion of a sail comprehended between the head of a sail and any of the reef-bands. The intention of each reef is to reduce the sail in proportion to the increase of the wind. Reef is also a group or continuous chain of rocks, sufficiently near the surface of the water to occasion its breaking over them. Smyth.

riggers Men who fit the standing ["permanent"] and running ["temporary"] rigging, or dismantle them. From Smyth.

rigging Standing rigging consists of all those ropes which are fixed, such as shrouds, backstays, etc., running rigging of all those ropes which can be pulled upon, such as halliards, clew-lines, etc. Russell.

ring-bolt An iron bolt with an eye at one end, wherein is fitted a circular ring. Smyth.

round-house A cabin built on deck roofed by the poop. Russell.

rowlocks (rollocks) Places cut in the gunwale of a boat for the oar to rest in while pulling. Dana.

royal masthead The upper end of the topmost mast of a ship, unless skysail masts are carried.

royal yard The yard above the topgallant yard to which the royal sail is bent [to bend a sail is to attach it to a yard]. Russell.

run The hollow curving in a vessel's bottom that rises and narrows under the quarters. From Dana.

scud To drive before a gale, with no sail, or only enough to keep the vessel ahead of the wind. Also, low, thin clouds that fly swiftly before the wind. Dana.

scuppers The gutter of a ship's decks; the water-ways. Russell.

scuttle A small hole or port cut either in the deck or side of a ship, generally for ventilation. That in the deck is a small hatch-way. Smyth.

scuttle-butt A cask on deck in which fresh water is kept. Russell.

seas Waves (as in "three seas off").

seize To seize is to make a thing fast, by securing it to a place; as to seize a flag in the rigging. Russell.

seizings The seizings are lines with which anything is made fast.

sheave The wheel inside a block which revolves with the rope that is hauled through it. Russell.

sheet home To extend the sheets [the ropes fastened to one or both the lower corners of a sail] to the outer extremities of the yards. From Smyth.

shiver   To shiver a ship is to trim a ship's yards so that the wind strikes on the edges of the sails, making them flutter in the wind. The same effect may be intentionally produced by means of the helm. Smyth.

shorten sail   To reduce [take in some of, or reef some of] the sails that are set. From Smyth.

shrouds   A set of ropes reaching from the mast-heads to the vessel's sides, to support the masts. Dana.

sky-larking   Horse-play. Russell.

skysail   A small square sail set above a royal sail.

skysail-pole   A mast on which the sky-sail yard travels. It is a continuation of the royal mast. Russell.

slip the cable   To *slip*, is to let go the cable with a buoy on the end, and quit the position, from any sudden requirement, instead of weighing the anchor. Smyth.

soundings   To be off soundings is to be in water whose bottom cannot be reached by the [line and] lead. [Or, to be within soundings is to be in water shallow enough for the depth to be measured thus; hence, to know where the ship is.] From Russell.

spar   Any kind of mast, boom, etc. Russell.

sprung spar   A spar is *sprung* when the fibres of the wood are injured by straining. Russell.

spile   A small wooden pin. Smyth.

splice   To join two untwisted ends of rope together.

square yards   Literally, when the yards lie fair upon the masts exactly athwartships, but the term is also applied to very long yards. Russell.

stand by!   The order to be prepared to do something. From Smyth.

stand by the braces!   The order to take hold of the braces (preparatory to executing some further order). From Smyth.

starboard   The right-hand side of a vessel (as one faces toward the bow).

star-bolins (or star-boleens)   The old familiar term for the men of the starboard watch. Smyth.

stay   A supporting rope that leads forward from the upper end of the mast (the shrouds extend not forward but on each side). Russell.

stem-piece   The foremost timber fastening together the bows of a ship.

storm-trysail   A fore-and-aft sail, hoisted by a gaff, but having no boom at its foot, and used only in foul weather. Smyth.

strike   To strike is to lower anything.

strike down   To lower casks, etc., into the hold. Smyth.

stun' sails   Fine-weather sails set outside the squaresails. Smyth.

sway up   To apply a strain on a mast-rope in order to lift the spar upwards, so that the fid may be taken out, previous to lowering the mast. [A fid is a square bar of wood or iron, with a shoulder at one end, used to support the weight of the topmast when erected at the head of the lower mast.] Smyth.

tackle   (Pronounced tay-cle.) A purchase, formed by a rope rove through one or more blocks. Dana.

taffrail The upper part of a ship's stern, a curved railing, the ends of which unite to the quarter-pieces. Smyth.

tell-tale A compass hanging face downwards from the beams in the cabin, showing the position of the vessel's head. Smyth.

thole-pins Pins in the gunwale of a boat serving to retain the oars in position when pulling. Smyth.

thwart A rower's seat in an open boat—so called because the thwart lies athwart, or across, the boat.

tierce A cask of beef. Russell.

tiller A piece of timber or metal fitted upon the rudder-head fore-and-aft and used for steering. Russell.

timber heads The heads of the timbers that rise above the decks and are used for belaying hawsers, large ropes, etc. Smyth.

top-blocks Large single iron-bound blocks used for sending top-masts up or down. Russell.

topgallant-mast The third mast above the deck; the uppermost before the days of royals and flying kites. Smyth.

top-gallant sails The third sails above the decks. Smyth.

top-maul A large hammer used by riggers. Russell.

top-sails The second sails above the decks. Smyth.

transom Timbers bolted to a ship's stern-post for receiving the ends of deck planks; a crossbeam attached to the stern-post and used as a seat.

tree-nails Long cylindrical oak pins driven through the planks and timbers of a vessel to connect her various parts. Smyth.

trim dish To adjust a vessel's posture properly. From Russell.

trysail A fore-and-aft sail, set with a boom and gaff, and hoisted on a small mast abaft the lower mast, called a *trysail-mast.* Dana.

trucks Circular [wooden] caps on the upper mastheads. Smyth.

turn to To go to work. To fall to. Russell.

under weight A ship is *under weight* when she has weighed [heaved up] her anchor; a ship *under way* is beginning to move under her canvas after her anchor is weighed. From Smyth.

waist The deck between the main deck and the forecastle. Russell.

weather The opposite of lee—the windward side of a ship. From Smyth.

weather-sheets Those fast to the weather-clues of the sails. [Clues are the lower corners of a square sail.] From Smyth.

whip A single rope rove through a single block to hoist in light articles. Smyth.

windlass A large barrel, revolved by handles, on the forecastle, and used in getting up the anchor. Russell.

windlass-bitts The bitts [perpendicular pieces of timber going through the deck] which support the ends or spindles of the windlass. Smyth.

work A ship is said *to work* when she strains in a tempestuous sea, so as to loosen her joints. Smyth.

yard A long cylindrical timber suspended upon the mast of a vessel to spread a sail. Smyth.

yaw The motion of a vessel when she goes off from her course. Dana.

JOHN B. PUTNAM

Whaling and Whalecraft: A Pictorial Account

From its beginning, when Captain John Smith hunted whales along the New England coast under a crown permit in 1614, to its end, with the wreck of the bark *Wanderer* off Cuttyhunk in 1924, the American whale fishery was basically a struggle between men in wooden ships and boats against the world's largest mammals, inhabitants of an inhospitable ocean. The Cape Cod or Nantucket whaleman of the seventeenth century would have felt very much at home on the New Bedford barks of the early twentieth, for neither the sailing ship nor the craft of whaling had changed much during the intervening centuries.

Elevation and Plan View of a Typical Whaleship

There were, to be sure, modifications and refinements in ship design, whaleboat construction, and whaling weaponry, as the industry became increasingly standardized toward the end of the nineteenth century. In the 1840's, when Melville sailed in the *Acushnet*, American whaling was in its most striking period of transition: the Industrial Revolution made possible greater quantities of better harpoons, lances, whaleline, and the like; and the growing scarcity of skilled carpenters willing to go to sea made it necessary for whalers to carry better built boats, and more of them, against the inevitable destruction attendant upon the rigors of a whaling voyage. Accordingly, the following brief discussion of whaling and whalecraft will concentrate on whaling as Melville knew it and wrote of it; where possible, we shall refer to appropriate chapters in *Moby-Dick* for further detail.

Whaling bark under sail

The American whaleship, in the days when Ishmael embarked in the *Pequod*, was generally built especially for its task, but it was not uncommon to find vessels of exceptionally sturdy construction that had been converted from merchantman to whaler. The whaler, owing to the heavy stresses she was subjected to in "cutting-in" a whale and to the long periods she would spend at sea without opportunity for overhaul, had to be especially heavy-timbered and stoutly built. Both modern and contemporary writers have tended to regard the whaler as lubberly in appearance and design (see Melville's comments in Chapter 16), but it was generally the longevity and durability of these sturdy vessels that caused them to compare so unfavorably with the more modern—but shorter-lived—men of war and merchantmen with which they shared the seas.

The whaler's cluttered superstructure and sparse spread of canvas also contributed to her awkward appearance. In order to allow more space below for barrels of oil, a deckhouse aft provided quarters for the mates, the harpooneers, the carpenter, the cooper, and the smith. Forward of this was a high decked-over framework, called the "gallows," for spare whaleboats. Just abaft the foremast stood the tryworks (Chapter 96), which had its own shelter. Finally, along the entire port side and aft on the starboard side were the towering davits from which were slung the whaleboats and the cranes which supported the keels of these lightly-built craft. There would generally be three boats on the port side and one on the starboard. Occasionally a large whaler would carry a fifth boat forward on the starboard side, and very rarely another might be carried on "tail-feathers," or stern davits, across the transom.

Davits

Cranes

Whaleboat slung from davits

A whaler seldom carried as much sail as a merchantman of equal tonnage, for a variety of reasons: first of all, it was necessary to keep the rig short and simple in order that it might be handled safely and quickly by the small force of shipkeepers—usually no more than six men—left aboard when the boats were away on the chase. Then too, sails were costly and subject to considerable wear during a three- or four-year voyage, and owners and officers alike were reluctant to spend hard-earned cash on the luxury of unnecessary canvas. Finally, since there was no pressure on a whaler to get anywhere in a great hurry, only sufficient sail was carried to maintain steerageway and to run down to faraway boats after a long chase to leeward. On a passage to or from the whaling grounds, a whaler might carry royals or skysails to save time, but while cruising on the grounds and seeking whales, these upper sails were unbent and the spars unrigged, and the whaler would loaf along under top sails and topgallantsails.

Four features in particular were unique to the rigging of the whaler. The most conspicuous of these were the masthead hoops in which the lookouts stood during the daylight hours to watch for whales (see Chapter 35). Then there was the cutting-in tackle, consisting of four large double blocks assembled in two falls, and the attached blubber hooks. This assembly was suspended below the maintop, just forward of the main yard; it was used in stripping the blubber from a whale's carcass while cutting-in alongside. Less noticeable were the preventer pin rails, mounted in the standing rigging several feet above deck level. The running rigging (lines used in setting sails and squaring yards), usually secured to belaying pins inside the main bulwarks, was belayed to these preventer rails while cutting-in a whale to prevent its becoming fouled by the unwieldy blanket piece of blubber as it was hauled inboard by the cutting-in tackle. Finally, although most whaling vessels were

bark-rigged—with no square yards on the mizzen mast—there was a short spar just below the mizzen top platform, called a crojack (originally crossjack), to which were led the main braces, which on vessels other than whalers were led to the deck aft. This peculiarity, like the preventer pin rails, was designed to keep the braces clear of the deck area and superstructure.

The American whaleboat was perhaps the most nearly perfect sea-going small craft ever developed. Combining the lightness and streamlining of the Indian canoe, on which it was patterned, with the strength and durability of the wooden boat, it was unequalled in speed and seaworthiness. Its lines have survived essentially intact in the whaleboats and motor whaleboats used by the seamen of a nuclear age.

During Melville's years at sea, the whaleboat was undergoing a transition; although essentially unchanged in size and hull form, the whaleboat of the second half of the nineteenth century differed from that of the first in having a centerboard and in being carvel-built, as opposed to clinker-built (see drawing). Minor changes included the substitution of metal oarlocks for the older tholepins, and more sophisticated means of stepping, or raising, the mast.

The boat was built of cedar planking on a temporary form, and light steam-bent ribs of oak or ash were sprung in to give the hull transverse strength. The thwarts and their "knees" added strength also. Since the hull was still relatively limber, however, special supports called "cranes" cradled the keel when the boat was slung from the davits, and the heavy line tubs were stowed on deck until the boat had been lowered away. Color schemes varied somewhat, but boats were typically painted white outside with black sheer strakes. Interiors were painted gray, blue, or buff. The oars were

Plan View and Elevation of a Typical Whaleboat ~ For the sake of clarity, the location of only a portion of the whalecraft, or equipment, is shown in the elevation below. The rest is shown in the plan view.

of unequal length, owing to the fact that the oarsmen sat at varying distances from their respective tholepins; the steering sweep or oar was longest of all, some twenty-two feet in length. It was used while rowing or being towed by a whale; under sail, the boatsteerer used a removable rudder.

Drugs" (tied to whale-line cast overboard, to tire a running whale)

Fresh water firkin

Grapnel (for retrieving whaleline)

Buckets (2)

Bailing piggin

Boat hook

Line tubs

Boat spade

Waif (for marking dead whales cast adrift)

In "going on the whale," as the approach was called, the boat was rowed or sailed to within a hundred yards or so of the quarry; the oars were then peaked—their handles thrust into peaking cleats fastened to the side of the boat opposite the tholepins; then the crew used paddles to close the distance to the whale, in order to avoid gallying or frightening him with the rumble of the oars against the tholepins.

In "getting fast," the harpooneer used a one- or two-flued iron (the better-known toggle iron was not yet in wide use in Melville's day), which he attempted to embed in the tough knot of muscles at the sperm whale's hump. The struck whale would at once run, breach, or sound, towing the boat along

Whaleboat under sail

Cross section of whaleboat amidships, showing oar in peaked position at a violent clip on a "Nantucket sleighride." Meanwhile, the boatsteerer, usually one of the ship's officers, and the harpooneer would change places—not a simple maneuver under the circumstances. All hands would keep as low in the boats as possible to prevent its capsizing; the peaked oars helped in this as well. Meanwhile, the whaleline was sizzling the length of the boat and out through the bow chocks. For a description of how the whaleline was stowed and rigged refer to Chapter 60

Two-flued iron

Lance

Single-flued iron

Socket
(Same on all three)

and the sketch (p.514). Note that while Melville mentions that American boats carry only one line tub, and English boats two, our sketch shows two. This development took place during Melville's time, and was owing partly to the introduction of the centerboard and partly to greater ease in handling.

As the whale began to tire, the crew would laboriously haul in on the line until abeam of the animal. The mate would now lance the exhausted beast, repeatedly thrusting the sharp, long-shafted lance into the lungs and churning it about. Here again, we must turn to Melville (Chapters 60 through 63) for the best possible description of the chase and kill. When at last the whale had gone through his flurry and turned fin-out, he was marked by a waif and set adrift, or towed to the ship for cutting-in.

The whale's carcass was now hauled alongside the starboard side of the whaler and made fast with chains around the flukes. The cutting-stage was lowered away, and the jaw cut loose and hoisted aboard for the extraction of the ivory in the case of a sperm whale, or the baleen in the case of a right or bowhead whale. The junk and case of the sperm whale were also cut loose and raised on deck at this point. Melville's description of the cutting-in (Chapter 67) is, once again, far better than any we can give here.

The trying-out was a hot, messy, malodorous process that could stretch into days if a whaler made a number of kills from a single "pod," or group of whales. The tryworks sat just abaft the foremast in a low square enclosure called the "goosepen." This wooden-sided trough was floored with bricks checkerboard fashion to allow water to be poured in and to flow freely beneath the firebox, in order to prevent the wooden deck beneath from igniting. On this base was built a square structure of bricks and mortar, into which were set the trypots, twin round cauldrons of about 250 gallons capacity each. The whole business was covered either by a removable cover such as Melville describes in Chapter 66, or more often by a structure similar to the gallows further aft.

When the tryworks were first lit off, firewood was used in the fireboxes. Thereafter, however, the scrap from the tried-out blubber

One whaleman pitches "bible leaves" into the trypot as another ladles hot oil into the cooling tank. Barrels await cooled oil.

Whalemen man windlass, taking a strain on cutting tackle, which in turn hauls in blanket piece.

Smith sharpens spades and knives.

Fluke chains hold carcass.

The case of a small sperm whale has been cut from the head and hoisted aboard. A whaleman bails the spermaceti through a slit cut in the case.

Men on cutting stage strip blanket piece from carcass with cutting spades as mate stands by with boarding knife.

Blanket pieces are cut into "horse pieces," which in turn are sliced into "books," or "bible leaves."

was fished from the bubbling oil and pitched into the firebox to sustain the fires. The hot oil was ladled from the trypots with large long-handled dippers and poured into cooling tanks before being stored in barrels below. The greasy smoke from the tryworks blackened sails, rigging, topsides, and whalemen with a sticky black soot that was the hallmark of a successful whaler.

Melville's description of bailing the case (Chapter 78) gives an excellent idea of the hazards to be endured once the whale was killed and secure alongside. Whaling was always a business of long handles, sharp edges, and sudden deaths for the clumsy or unwary. The rolling of the ship, the slippery footing in blood and blubber, the frenzied tearing of sharks at the whale's carcass inches below the cutting stage, the perilous swoop of tons of blubber across the foredeck as the blanket-piece was severed—all combined to make the whale fishery amongst the most arduous and dangerous of livings.

Mincing knife

for cutting "horse pieces" into "books" or "bible leaves"

"Save-all," for scooping up stray bits of blubber and spermaceti adrift on deck

"Pricker" or blubber fork for pitching bible leaves into trypots and scrap into fire boxes

Strainer for removing scraps of tried-out blubber from trypots

Bailer for removing boiling oil from trypots

Contemporary Engravings

"THERE SHE BLOWS!"
A fairly accurate rendition of the spreaders at the head of one of the top-masts of a squarerigger. It should be noted, however, that the lookouts on a whaler routinely stood their watches in hoops at the head of the topgallant mast—a full mast higher than shown here—where they could command a more far-reaching view.

STRUCK ON A BREACH.
This view gives an excellent idea of the shape and location of the sperm whale's lower jaw. A whale "breaches" when he leaps clear of the water. Normally, the boat-steerer (at left, in stern of boat) would be facing forward, toward the whale. Note the whaleboat at right, under sail.

LANCING.
In this picture, the boats' crews have hauled in on the whaleline until abreast of the exhausted prey, and the boatheaders are using the long-handled, barbless lances to complete the kill. See Chapter 61: "Stubb Kills a Whale."

BOAT DESTROYED BY A WHALE.
The flukes, spanning a dozen feet or more, could reduce a whaleboat to splinters with a single blow; the sort of mishap shown here was an all-too-frequent occurrence in the whale fishery. The boats shown here, incidentally, are atypical, in being manned by ten rather than six men, and in being square-sterned rather than double-ended.

IN THE WHALE'S JAW.
A peculiarity of the sperm whale is its habit of rolling over on its side or back to snap at a tormentor with its strong lower jaw. There are no teeth in the upper jaw, but rather sockets for the teeth of the lower jaw.

BAILING THE "CASE."
A shark's-eye view of the case, or upper portion of the head, of a sperm whale, held up on the whaleship's starboard by the cutting tackle. To the left of the whaleman in the picture is the case-bucket, which was used to remove the spermaceti through a small hole cut atop the case. The bucket was tapered toward both ends, barrel fashion, to prevent its becoming jammed inside the case.

"CUTTING-IN."
One of the cutting falls with its blubber hook taking in the blanket piece. Normally, the two planks shown here were connected by another at their outboard ends to form the cutting stage. Note the fluke chain leading from the bow of the ship; it was passed around the root of the flukes to allow the carcass to revolve as the blanket piece was stripped.

TRYING OUT.
A view of the tryworks from the foremast. This picture shows three trypots, but the use of only two was virtually universal in the American fishery. The pitchfork-like implement held by the whaleman is a "pricker" or blubber-fork, used to put the blubber into the pots, and to fish out the tried-out scraps to feed the fires.

"THERE SHE BLOWS!"

STRUCK ON A BREACH.

LANCING.

BOAT DESTROYED BY A WHALE.

IN A WHALE'S JAW.

BAILING THE "CASE."

"CUTTING-IN."

TRYING OUT.

Reviews and Letters by Melville

From The Literary World †

March 6, 1847

Etchings of a Whaling Cruise, with Notes of a Sojourn on the Island of Zanzibar. To which is appended, a Brief History of the Whale Fishery; its Past and Present Condition. By J. Ross Browne. Illustrated with numerous Engravings on Steel and Wood. Harper & Brothers: 1846. 8vo.

Sailors' Life and Sailors' Yarns. By Captain Ringbolt. New York: C. S. Francis & Co. 1847. 12mo.

From time immemorial many fine things have been said and sung of the sea. The days have been, when sailors were considered veritable mermen; [1] and the ocean itself, as the peculiar theatre of the romantic and wonderful. But of late years there have been revealed so many plain, matter-of-fact details connected with nautical life that at the present day the poetry of salt water is very much on the wane. The perusal of Dana's "Two Years before the Mast," for instance, somewhat impairs the relish with which we read Byron's spiritual "Address to the Ocean." And when the noble poet raves about laying his hands upon the ocean's mane (in other words manipulating the crest of a wave), the most vivid image suggested is that of a valetudinarian bather at Rockaway, spluttering and choking in the surf, with his mouth full of brine.

Mr. J. Ross Browne's narrative tends still further to impair the charm with which poesy and fiction have invested the sea. [2] It is a book of unvarnished facts; and with some allowances for the general application of an individual example unquestionably presents a faithful picture of the life led by the twenty thousand seamen employed in the seven hundred whaling vessels which pursue their game under the American flag. [3] Indeed, what Mr.

† The manuscript of this two-in-one review is in the Duyckinck Collection in the New York Public Library. It is in Melville's own hand and is unusually legible, especially in the first pages. We print a slightly normalized reading text. The punctuation is that of the manuscript rather than the comma-ridden *Literary World* text, but we have adopted the *Literary World* (hereafter cited as *LW*) expansions of abbreviations and corrections of spelling errors (Melville wrote "Brown", not "Browne"). Our footnotes call attention to Melville's revisions and to points where we restore for the first time the manuscript reading. The only previous modern reprinting followed the *LW* text and included the misreadings.

1. Melville first wrote "veritable mermen; ships, floating prodigies; & the ocean itself. * * * " Then in the same ink he deleted "ships, floating prodigies;"—one of the few revisions in this fair copy manuscript.

2. We restore the manuscript reading "poesy" instead of the *LW* "poetry".

3. Melville wrote "which now pursue their mighty game under the American flag", then deleted "now" and "mighty"; *LW* carelessly restored "now" but not "mighty"; both should be deleted.

Dana has so admirably done in describing the vicissitudes of the merchant sailor's life, Mr. Browne has very creditably achieved with respect to that of the hardy whaleman's. And the book which possesses this merit deserves much in the way of commendation. The personal narrative interwoven with it, also, cannot fail to enlist our sympathies for the adventurous author himself. The scenes presented are always graphically and truthfully sketched, and hence fastidious objections may be made to some of them, on the score of their being too coarsely or harshly drawn. But we take it, that as true, unreserved descriptions they are in no respect faulty—and, doubtless, the author never dreamed of softening down or withholding anything with a view of rendering his sketches the more attractive and pretty. The book is eminently a practical one; and written with the set purpose of accomplishing good by revealing the simple truth. When the brutal tyranny of the Captain of the "Styx" is painted without apology or palliation, it holds up the outrageous abuse to which seamen in our whaling marine are actually subjected, a matter which demands legislation.[4] Mr. Browne himself, it seems, was to some extent, the victim of the tyranny of which he complains, and, upon this ground, the personal bitterness in which he at times indulges may be deemed excusable.

As the book professes to embrace a detailed account of all that is interesting in the business of whaling, and, essentially, possesses this merit, one or two curious errors into which the author has unaccountably fallen may, without captiousness, be pointed out.——We are told, for example, of a whale's *roaring* when wounded by the harpoon. We can imagine the veteran Coffins, and Colemans, and Maceys of old Nantucket elevating their brows at the bare announcement of such a thing. Now the creature in question is as dumb as a shad, or any other of the finny tribes. And no doubt, if Jonah himself could be summoned to the stand, he would cheerfully testify to his not having heard a single syllable, growl, grunt, or bellow engendered in the ventricle cells of the leviathan during the irksome period of his incarceration therein.

That in some encounters with the sperm whale a low indistinct sound *apparently* issues from the monster is true enough. But all Nantucket and New Bedford are divided as to the causes which produce the phenomenon.[5] Many suppose, however, that it is produced——not by the creature itself——but by the peculiar motion in the water of the line which is attached to the harpoon.

4. The *LW* reading makes no sense: "are actually subjected, or rather, which demands legislation"; the manuscript clearly reads "a matter" instead of "or rather".

5. The *LW* text quite destroys the sense of this passage by printing "decided" instead of "divided". Melville's "v" was more than once miscopied as "c"; in *Typee* what the first English edition printed as "traces" was all but surely "leaves" in the manuscript.

For, if upon being struck, the whale "sounds" (descends) as is usually the case, and remains below the surface for any length of time, the rope frequently becomes as stiff as the cord of a harp, and the struggles of the animal keep it continually vibrating.

Considering the disenchanting nature of the revelations of sea life with which we are presented in Mr. Browne's book, we are inclined to believe that the shipping agents employed in our various cities by the merchants of New Bedford will have to present additional inducements to "enterprising and industrious young Americans of good moral character," in order to persuade them to embark in the fishery. In particular, the benevolent old gentleman in Front street (one of the shipping agents of whom our author discourseth) who so politely accosted Browne and his comrade, upon their entering his office for the purpose of seeking further information touching the rate of promotion in the whaling service—this old gentleman, we say, must hereafter infuse into his address still more of the *suaviter in modo*.

As unaffectedly described by Browne, the scene alluded to is irresistibly comic. The agent's business, be it understood, consists in decoying "green hands" to send on to the different whaling ports. A conspicuous placard without the office announces to the anxious world, that a few choice vacancies remain to be filled in certain crews of whalemen about to sail upon the most delightful voyages imaginable (only four years long).——To secure a place, of course, instant application should be made.

Our author and his friend attracted by the placard, hurry up a ladder to a dark loft above, where the old man lurks like a spider in the midst of his toils.——But a single glance at the gentlemanly dress and white hands of his visitors impresses the wily agent with the idea that notwithstanding their calling upon him, they may very possibly have heard disagreeable accounts of the nature of whaling. So, after making a bow, and offering a few legs of a chair, he proceeds to disabuse their minds of any unfavorable impressions. Succeeding in this, he then becomes charmingly facetious and complimentary; assures the youths that they need not be concerned because of their slender waists and silken muscles, for those who employed him were not so particular about weight as beauty. In short the captains of whaling vessels preferred handsome young fellows who dressed well and conversed genteelly—in short, those who would reflect credit upon the business of tarring down rigging, and cutting up blubber. Delighted with the agreeable address of the old gentleman, and with many pleasant anticipations of sea life the visitors listen with increased attention. Whereupon the agent waxes eloquent, and enlarges upon his animating theme in the style parliamentary. "A whaler, gentlemen," he observes, "is the home of the unfortunate—the asylum of the oppressed," &c., &c., &c.

Duped Browne! Hapless H——! In the end, they enter into an engagement with the old gentleman, who subsequently sends them on to New Bedford consigned to a mercantile house there. From New Bedford the adventurers at length sail in a small whaling barque bound to the Indian Ocean. While yet half dead with sea sickness, the unfortunate H—— is sent by the brutal captain to the masthead, to stand there his allotted two hours on the look out for whale-spouts. He receives a stroke of the sun, which, for a time, takes away his reason and endangers his life. He raves of home and friends, and poor Browne watching by his side, upbraids himself for having been concerned in bringing his companion to such a state.——Ere long the vessel touches at the Azores, where H—— being altogether unfit for duty is left to be sent home by the American consul.

He never recovered from the effects of his hardships; for in the sequel Browne relates that after reaching home himself, he visited his old friend in Ohio, and found him still liable to temporary prostrations directly referable to his sufferings at sea.

With a heavy heart our author after leaving the Azores weathers the Cape of Good Hope and enters upon the Indian Ocean. The ship's company——composed mostly of ignorant, half-civilized Portuguese from the Western Islands——are incessantly quarrelling and fighting; the provisions are of the most wretched kind; ——their success in the fishery is small; and to crown all, the captain himself is the very incarnation of all that is dastardly, mean, and heartless.

We cannot follow Browne through all his adventures. Suffice it to say, that heartily disgusted with his situation he at length, with great difficulty, succeeds in leaving the vessel on the coast of Zanzibar. There he tarries for some months, and his residence in this remote region (the Eastern coast of Africa, near Madagascar) enables him to make sundry curious observations upon men and things, of which the reader of his work has the benefit. From Zanzibar he ultimately sails for home in a merchant brig; and at last arrives in Boston thoroughly out of conceit of the ocean.

Give ear, now, all ye shore-disdaining, ocean-enamored youth, who labor under the lamentable delusion, that the sea—the "glorious sea" is always and in reality "the blue, the fresh, the ever free!" Give ear to Mr. J. Ross Browne, and hearken unto what that experienced young gentleman has to say about the manner in which Barry Cornwall has been humbugging the rising generation on this subject.——Alas! Hereafter we shall never look upon an unsophisticated stripling in flowing "duck" trousers and a bright blue jacket,[6] loitering away the interval which elapses before sailing on his maiden cruise, without mourning over the hard fate in store for him.——In a ship's forecastle, alas, he will find no Psyche glass in which to survey his picturesque attire. And the business of making his toilet will be comprised in trying to keep as dry and comfortable as the utter absence of umbrellas; wet decks, and leaky forecastles will admit of. We shudder at all realities of the career they will be entering upon. The long, dark, cold night-watches which, month after month, they must battle out the best way they can;——the ship pitching and thumping against the bullying waves—every plank dripping—every jacket soaked—and the captain not at all bland in issuing his order for the poor fellows to mount aloft in the icy sleet and howling tempest. "Bless me, Captain, go away up there this excessively disagreeable night?" "Aye, up with you, you lubber—*bare*, I say, or look out for squalls"—a figurative expression, conveying a remote allusion to the hasty application of a sea-bludgeon to the head.

Then the whaling part of the business.—My young friends, just fancy yourselves, for the first time in an open boat (so slight that three men might walk off with it) some twelve or fifteen miles from your ship, and about a hundred times as far from the nearest land, giving chase to one of the oleaginous monsters. "Pull, pull, you lubberly *hay makers!*" cries the boat-header jumping up and down in the stern-sheets in a frenzy of professional excitement, while the gasping admirers of Captain Marryatt and the sea, tug with might and main at the truckling oars—"Pull, pull, I say; break your lazy backs!" Presently the whale is within "darting distance," and you hear the roar of the waters in his wake.——How palpitating the hearts of the frightened oarsmen at this interesting juncture! My young friends, just turn round and snatch a look at that whale——. There he goes, surging through the brine, which ripples about his vast head, as if it were the bow of a ship. Believe me, it's quite as terrible as going into battle to a raw recruit.

"Stand up and give it to him!" shrieks the boat-header at the steering oar to the harpooner in the bow. The latter drops his oar, and snatches his "iron." It flies from his hands—and where are we then, my lovelies?——It's all a mist, a crash,—a horrible blending of sounds and sights, as the agonized whale lashes the water around him into suds and vapor—dashes the boat aside, and at last rushes, madly, through the water, towing after him the

6. The manuscript clearly reads "bright", not "light", as the *LW* text prints it. Mrs. Melville made the same error in copying his essay on Hawthorne, but it was caught in the fair copy and was printed correctly.

half-filled craft which rocks from side to side while the disordered
crew, clutch at the gunwale to avoid being tossed out. Meanwhile
all sorts of horrific edged tools—lances, harpoons, and spades
——are slipping about; and the imminent line itself—smoking
round the logger-head and passing along the entire length of
the boat—is almost death to handle, though it grazes your
person.

But all this is nothing to what follows. As yet you have but
simply *fastened* to the whale: he must be fought and killed. But
let imagination supply the rest——the monster staving the
boat with a single sweep of his ponderous flukes;——taking its
bows between his jaws (as is frequently the case) and playing with
it as a cat with a mouse. Sometimes he bites it in twain; sometimes crunches it into chips, and strews the sea with them.——

But we forbear. Enough has been said to convince the uniniti-
ated what sort of a vocation whaling in truth is. If further information is desired, Mr. Browne's book is purchasable in which they
will find the whole matter described in all its interesting details.

After reading the "Etchings of a Whaling Cruise" a perusal of
"Sailors' Life and Sailors' Yarns" is, in one respect at least, like
hearing "the other side of the question." For, while Browne's is
a "Voice from the Forecastle" Captain Ringbolt hails us from
the quarter deck, the other end of the ship. Browne gives us a
sailor's version of sailors' wrongs, and is not altogether free from
prejudices acquired during his little experience on ship board;
Captain Ringbolt almost denies that the sailor has any wrongs,
and more than insinuates that sea-captains are not only the best
natured fellows in the world, but that they have been sorely
maligned. Indeed, he explicitly charges Mr. Dana and Mr.
Browne with having presented a decidedly one sided view of the
matter. And he manfully exclaims that the Captain of the
Pilgrim—poor fellow!—died too soon to vindicate his character
from unjust aspersions. Now as a class ship owners are seldom disposed partially to judge the captains in their employ. And
yet we know of a verity, that at least one of the owners of the
Pilgrim,——an esteemed citizen of the good old town of Boston,
will never venture to dispute that to the extent of his knowledge
at least Mr. Dana's captain was a most "strict and harsh discipli-
narian" which words so applied by a ship owner, mean that the
man in question was nothing less than what Mr. Dana describes
him to have been.——But where is Browne's captain? He is alive
and hearty we presume. Let him come forward then and show why
he ought not to be regarded in the decidedly unfavorable light in
which he is held up to us in the narrative we have noticed. Now for
aught we know to the contrary this same captain of the Styx,

who was such a heartless, domineering tyrant at sea, may be quite a different character ashore. In truth we think this very probable. For the god Janus never had two more decidedly different faces than your sea captain. Ashore his Nautical Highness has nothing to ruffle him,——friends grasp him by the hand, and are overjoyed to see him after his long absence——he is invited out, relates his adventures pleasantly, and everybody thinks what lucky dogs his sailors must have been to have sailed with such a capital fellow.——But let poor Jack have a word to say. Why, sir, he will tell you that when they embarked, his Nautical Highness left behind him all his "quips and cranks and wreathed smiles." Very far indeed is the Captain from cracking any of his jokes with his crew—that would be altogether too condescending. But then there is no reason why he should bestow a curse every time he gives an order—there is no reason why he should never say a word of sympathy to his men.[7] True in this respect all sea captains are not alike; but still——there is enough truth in both Mr. Dana's and Mr. Browne's statements to justify nearly to the full, the general conclusions to be drawn from what they have said on this subject.—— [8]

But Captain Ringbolt's book is very far from being a mere plea for the class to which he belongs.——What he has to say upon the matter is chiefly contained in one brief sketch under the head of "Sailor's Rights and Sailor's Wrongs."——The rest of the book is made up of little stories of the sea, simply and pleasantly told and withal entertaining.

Hawthorne and His Mosses

By a *Virginian Spending July in Vermont* †

From The Literary World, August 17 and 24, 1850

A papered chamber in a fine old farm-house—a mile from any other dwelling, and dipped to the eaves in foliage—surrounded

7. In the manuscript there is a space between "of" and "sympathy" which is partly filled by what appears to be "h n"; there is at least a chance that Melville meant to write "of human sympathy" and simply did not notice that his pen did not work properly. By this point in the manuscript Melville's handwriting has greatly deteriorated.

8. The *LW* reads "there is enough of truth", with the word "of" erroneously interpolated.

† This is a slightly normalized reading text. The punctuation is that of the manuscript (except for necessary corrections such as insertion of close quotes, which we adopt from the *Literary World* text). From the *Literary World* (hereafter cited as *LW*) we also adopt such expansions as "and" for the manuscript "&" and "through" for the manuscript "thro'", and corrections of manuscript misspellings such as "perrenial", "warrantry", "offerred", "subltest", "heigth", "recieve", "discernable", "noisless", and "immitations". The manuscript is in the Duyckinck Collection in the New York Public Library. Our footnotes report Mrs. Melville's scribal procedures and some of Melville's corrections and revisions, as evidence of how certain errors got into the first American edition of *Moby-Dick*.

by mountains, old woods, and Indian ponds,—this, surely, is the place to write of Hawthorne. Some charm is in this northern air, for love and duty seem both impelling to the task. A man of a deep and noble nature has seized me in this seclusion. His wild, witch voice rings through me; or, in softer cadences, I seem to hear it in the songs of the hill-side birds, that sing in the larch trees at my window.

Would that all excellent books were foundlings, without father or mother, that so it might be, we could glorify them, without including their ostensible authors. Nor would any true man take exception to this;—least of all, he who writes,—"When the Artist rises high enough to achieve the Beautiful, the symbol by which he makes it perceptible to mortal senses becomes of little value in his eyes, while his spirit possesses itself in the enjoyment of the reality."

But more than this. I know not what would be the right name to put on the title-page of an excellent book, but this I feel, that the names of all fine authors are fictitious ones, far more so than that of Junius,—simply standing, as they do, for the mystical, ever-eluding Spirit of all Beauty, which ubiquitously possesses men of genius. Purely imaginative as this fancy may appear, it nevertheless seems to receive some warranty from the fact, that on a personal interview no great author has ever come up to the idea of his reader. But that dust of which our bodies are composed, how can it fitly express the nobler intelligences among us? With reverence be it spoken, that not even in the case of one deemed more than man, not even in our Saviour, did his visible frame betoken anything of the augustness of the nature within. Else, how could those Jewish eyewitnesses fail to see heaven in his glance.

It is curious, how a man may travel along a country road, and yet miss the grandest, or sweetest of prospects, by reason of an intervening hedge, so like all other hedges, as in no way to hint of the wide landscape beyond. So has it been with me concerning the enchanting landscape in the soul of this Hawthorne, this most excellent Man of Mosses. His "Old Manse" has been written now four years, but I never read it till a day or two since. I had seen it in the book-stores—heard of it often—even had it recommended to me by a tasteful friend, as a rare, quiet book, perhaps too deserving of popularity to be popular. But there are so many books called "excellent," and so much unpopular merit, that amid the thick stir of other things, the hint of my tasteful friend was disregarded; and for four years the Mosses on the Old Manse never refreshed me with their perennial green. It may be, however, that all this while, the book, like wine, was only improving in flavor and body. At any rate, it so chanced that this long procrastination eventuated in a happy result. At breakfast the other day, a mountain girl, a cousin of mine, who for the last two weeks has every morning helped me to strawberries and raspberries,—which, like the roses and pearls in the fairy-tale, seemed to fall into the saucer from those strawberry-beds her cheeks,—this delightful creature, this charming Cherry says to me—"I see you spend your mornings in the hay-mow; and yesterday I found there 'Dwight's Travels in New England'. Now I have something far better than that,—something more congenial to our summer on these hills. Take these raspberries, and then I will give you some moss."—"Moss!" said I.—"Yes, and you must take it to the barn with you, and good-bye to 'Dwight.' "

With that she left me, and soon returned with a volume, verdantly bound, and garnished with a curious frontispiece in green,—nothing less, than a fragment of real moss cunningly pressed to a fly-leaf.—"Why this," said I, spilling my raspberries, "this is the 'Mosses from an Old Manse'." "Yes," said cousin Cherry, "yes, it is that flowery Hawthorne."—"Hawthorne and Mosses," said I, "no more: it is morning: it is July in the country: and I am off for the barn."

Stretched on that new mown clover,[1] the hill-side breeze blowing over me through the wide barn door, and soothed by the hum of the bees in the meadows around, how magically stole over me this Mossy Man! And how amply, how bountifully, did he redeem that delicious promise to his guests in the Old Manse, of whom it is written—"Others could give them pleasure, or amusement, or instruction—these could be picked up anywhere —but it was for me to give them rest. Rest, in a life of trouble! What better could be done for weary and world-worn spirits? what better could be done for anybody, who came within our magic circle, than to throw the spell of a magic spirit over him?" —So all that day, half-buried in the new clover, I watched this Hawthorne's "Assyrian dawn, and Paphian sunset and moonrise, from the summit of our Eastern Hill."

The soft ravishments of the man spun me round about in a web

---

1. During the composition of *Mardi* (see *Log*, 276), Mrs. Melville in a letter to her stepmother apologized for perhaps having left out punctuation marks, explaining that as Herman's copyist she was in the habit of leaving all the punctuation for him to supply. This passage (4.2–4.8 in the manuscript) is clear proof that in 1850 she was still omitting punctuation. In Melville's hand, in different ink, are the following additions and changes: he added the comma after "clover"; he altered "with the hill side breeze blowing over me from the wide barn door" to "the hill-side breeze blowing over me thro' the wide barn door," (Melville's comma after "door"); he added a comma after "around"; he mended the "m's" in "mossy man" to capitals; he added an exclamation point after "Man" and commas after "amply" and "bountifully"; and he changed "old manse" to "Old Manse". Presumably the extraordinary absence of hundreds of necessary periods and quotation marks in the first American edition of *Mardi* is due to Melville's failure to add the punctuation, and certain unusual absences of commas in *Moby-Dick* may be due to the same cause.

of dreams, and when the book was closed, when the spell was over, this wizard "dismissed me with but misty reminiscences, as if I had been dreaming of him."

What a wild moonlight of contemplative humor bathes that Old Manse!—the rich and rare distilment of a spicy and slowly-oozing heart. No rollicking rudeness, no gross fun fed on fat dinners, and bred in the lees of wine,—but a humor so spiritually gentle, so high, so deep, and yet so richly relishable, that it were hardly inappropriate in an angel. It is the very religion of mirth; for nothing so human but it may be advanced to that. The orchard of the Old Manse seems the visible type of the fine mind that has described it. Those twisted, and contorted old trees, "that stretch out their crooked branches, and take such hold of the imagination, that we remember them as humorists and odd-fellows." And then, as surrounded by these grotesque forms, and hushed in the noon-day repose of this Hawthorne's spell, how aptly might the still fall of his ruddy thoughts into your soul be symbolized by "the thump of a great apple, in the stillest afternoon, falling without a breath of wind, from the mere necessity of perfect ripeness"! For no less ripe than ruddy are the apples of the thoughts and fancies in this sweet Man of Mosses.

"Buds and Bird-Voices"—What a delicious thing is that!—"Will the world ever be so decayed, that Spring may not renew its greenness?"—And the "Fire-Worship." Was ever the hearth so glorified into an altar before? The mere title of that piece is better than any common work in fifty folio volumes. How exquisite is this:—"Nor did it lessen the charm of his soft, familiar courtesy and helpfulness, that the mighty spirit, were opportunity offered him, would run riot through the peaceful house, wrap its inmates in his terrible embrace, and leave nothing of them save their whitened bones. This possibility of mad destruction only made his domestic kindness the more beautiful and touching. It was so sweet of him, being endowed with such power, to dwell, day after day, and one long, lonesome night after another, on the dusky hearth, only now and then betraying his wild nature, by thrusting his red tongue out of the chimney-top! True, he had done much mischief in the world, and was pretty certain to do more, but his warm heart atoned for all. He was kindly to the race of man."

But he has still other apples, not quite so ruddy, though full as ripe:—apples, that have been left to wither on the tree, after the pleasant autumn gathering is past. The sketch of "The Old Apple Dealer" is conceived in the subtlest spirit of sadness; he whose "subdued and nerveless boyhood prefigured his abortive prime, which, likewise, contained within itself the prophecy and image of his lean and torpid age." Such touches as are in this piece can not proceed from any common heart.[2] They argue such a depth of tenderness, such a boundless sympathy with all forms of being, such an omnipresent love, that we must needs say, that this Hawthorne is here almost alone in his generation,—at least, in the artistic manifestation of these things. Still more. Such touches as these,—and many, very many similar ones, all through his chapters—furnish clews, whereby we enter a little way into the intricate, profound heart where they originated. And we see, that suffering, some time or other and in some shape or other, —this only can enable any man to depict it in others. All over him, Hawthorne's melancholy rests like an Indian Summer, which, though bathing a whole country in one softness, still reveals the distinctive hue of every towering hill, and each far-winding vale.

But it is the least part of genius that attracts admiration. Where Hawthorne is known, he seems to be deemed a pleasant writer, with a pleasant style,—a sequestered, harmless man, from whom any deep and weighty thing would hardly be anticipated:—a man who means no meanings. But there is no man, in whom humor and love, like mountain peaks, soar to such a rapt height, as to receive the irradiations of the upper skies;—there is no man in whom humor and love are developed in that high form called genius; no such man can exist without also possessing, as the indispensable complement of these, a great, deep intellect, which drops down into the universe like a plummet.[3] Or, love and humor are only the eyes, through which such an intellect views this world. The great beauty in such a mind is but the product of its strength. What, to all readers, can be more charming than the piece entitled "Monsieur du Miroir"; and to a reader at all capable of fully fathoming it, what, at the same time, can possess more mystical depth of meaning?—Yes, there he sits, and looks at me,— this "shape of mystery," this "identical Monsieur du Miroir."—

2. The first part of this sentence occurs on 6.22 of the manuscript. In the left margin is a small penciled "x"—erased, but still visible. An examination of the whole manuscript reveals that such marginal "x's" were Mrs. Melville's way of reminding herself that she was uncertain about what she had copied and that she would have to ask her husband for the correct reading. After she had checked with him, she would erase the "x"—but lightly enough so that most are still readily visible. Here she first copied "Such tones as are in this piece", and later inserted the correct word, "touches", above "tones". Often enough in the manuscript inserted words are simply revisions of Melville's, but frequently, as here, the reading Mrs. Melville first copied can never have been what Melville wrote.

3. At 7.21 in the manuscript Mrs. Melville copied "into the universe like a planet"; she later marked out "planet" and inserted the correct "plummet" above it. Here no "x" is visible in the margin, perhaps an indication that she had not questioned her reading. It is not clear why the correction is in her hand instead of Melville's: perhaps she simply caught the error herself later, and corrected it, as she did at other points; perhaps she was reading her copy aloud to him to spare his eyes and making the changes herself; perhaps he was proofreading with her nearby to enter any corrections.

"Methinks I should tremble now, were his wizard power of gliding through all impediments in search of me, to place him suddenly before my eyes."

How profound, nay appalling, is the moral evolved by the "Earth's Holocaust"; where—beginning with the hollow follies and affectations of the world,—all vanities and empty theories and forms, are, one after another, and by an admirably graduated, growing comprehensiveness, thrown into the allegorical fire, till, at length, nothing is left but the all-engendering heart of man; which remaining still unconsumed, the great conflagration is naught.

Of a piece with this, is the "Intelligence Office," a wondrous symbolizing of the secret workings in men's souls.[4] There are other sketches, still more charged with ponderous import.

"The Christmas Banquet," and "The Bosom Serpent" would be fine subjects for a curious and elaborate analysis, touching the conjectural parts of the mind that produced them. For spite of all the Indian-summer sunlight on the hither side of Hawthorne's soul,[5] the other side—like the dark half of the physical sphere —is shrouded in a blackness, ten times black. But this darkness but gives more effect to the evermoving dawn, that forever advances through it, and circumnavigates his world.[6] Whether Hawthorne has simply availed himself of this mystical blackness as a means to the wondrous effects he makes it to produce in his lights and shades; or whether there really lurks in him, perhaps unknown to himself, a touch of Puritanic gloom,—this, I cannot altogether tell. Certain it is, however, that this great power of blackness in him derives its force from its appeals to that Calvinistic sense of Innate Depravity and Original Sin, from whose visitations, in some shape or other, no deeply thinking mind is always and wholly free. For, in certain moods, no man can weigh

4. In the manuscript 8.14 reads "of secret workings in this world. There are" (in Mrs. Melville's hand); in Melville's hand "the" is inserted before "secret", and "this world" is altered to "men's souls". Mrs. Melville evidently did not suspect she had miscopied, for no "x" is visible in the margin.

5. In this sentence at 8.20 in the manuscript is a clear instance of Mrs. Melville's misreading Melville's "on" as "in". She copied the passage as "sunlight in the hither side of Hawthorne's soul", and Melville mended the "in" to "on", which must have been the original reading. She made the same "in/on" error in copying *Moby-Dick:* see our lists of emendations adopted or suggested for adoption.

6. At 8.25 in the manuscript Mrs. Melville left two blanks: "that forever   through it, and   "; then she put *two* "x's" in the margin. Later, presumably after consulting her husband, she added "advances" in the first space, and "circumnavigates" in the second. It is almost always easy to detect which words have been added later by the unusual spacing and the anomalous slanting of the added word. In *Moby-Dick* there are instances of Melville's adding words in the English edition that seem likely to have been in his manuscript, though they do not appear in the first American edition. It may be that sometimes the blanks Mrs. Melville left simply never got detected and filled in, despite her habit of putting cautionary "x's" in the margin.

this world, without throwing in something, somehow like Original Sin, to strike the uneven balance. At all events, perhaps no writer has ever wielded this terrific thought with greater terror than this same harmless Hawthorne. Still more: this black conceit pervades him, through and through. You may be witched by his sunlight,—transported by the bright gildings in the skies he builds over you;—but there is the blackness of darkness beyond; and even his bright gildings but fringe, and play upon the edges of thunder-clouds.—In one word, the world is mistaken in this Nathaniel Hawthorne. He himself must often have smiled at its absurd misconception of him. He is immeasurably deeper than the plummet of the mere critic. For it is not the brain that can test such a man; it is only the heart.[7] You cannot come to know greatness by inspecting it; there is no glimpse to be caught of it, except by intuition; you need not ring it, you but touch it, and you find it is gold.[8]

Now it is that blackness in Hawthorne, of which I have spoken, that so fixes and fascinates me. It may be, nevertheless, that it is too largely developed in him. Perhaps he does not give us a ray of his light for every shade of his dark. But however this may be, this blackness it is that furnishes the infinite obscure of his background,—that background, against which Shakespeare plays his grandest conceits, the things that have made for Shakespeare his loftiest, but most circumscribed renown, as the profoundest of thinkers. For by philosophers Shakespeare is not adored as the great man of tragedy and comedy.—"Off with his head! so much for Buckingham!"[9] this sort of rant, interlined by another hand, brings down the house,—those mistaken souls, who dream of Shakespeare as a mere man of Richard-the-Third humps, and Macbeth daggers. But it is those deep far-away things in him; those occasional flashings-forth of the intuitive Truth in him; those short, quick probings at the very axis of reality:—these are the things that make Shakespeare, Shakespeare. Through the mouths of the dark characters of Hamlet, Timon, Lear, and Iago, he craftily says, or sometimes insinuates the things, which we feel to be so

7. At 9.23 in the manuscript a word clearly baffled Mrs. Melville. She put an "x" in the margin, and left a blank, in which she later inserted the word "brain".
8. At 9.27 in the manuscript is a clear instance of Mrs. Melville's omitting words which Melville restored as he proofread her copy. She copied "you ring it you but touch it and you find"; he later inserted "need not" before "ring", and added a comma after both the first and the second "it".
9. At 10.12–13 in the manuscript Mrs.

Melville copied "Buckingham" [these close quotes are in the manuscript] this sort of rant introduced by some other hand bring down the house those". Melville crowded in an exclamation point between "Buckingham" and the following double quotes, added a comma after "rant", inserted "interlined" in place of "introduced", marked out "some" and altered "other" to "another", added a comma after "hand", added (or traced over) the "s" in "brings", and added a comma-dash after "house", but no separating punctuation before "this".

terrifically true, that it were all but madness for any good man, in his own proper character, to utter, or even hint of them.[1] Tormented into desperation, Lear the frantic King tears off the mask, and speaks the sane madness of vital truth.[2] But, as I before said, it is the least part of genius that attracts admiration. And so, much of the blind, unbridled admiration that has been heaped upon Shakespeare, has been lavished upon the least part of him. And few of his endless commentators and critics seem to have remembered, or even perceived, that the immediate products of a great mind are not so great, as that undeveloped, (and sometimes undevelopable) yet dimly-discernible greatness, to which these immediate products are but the infallible indices.[3] In Shakespeare's tomb lies infinitely more than Shakespeare ever wrote. And if I magnify Shakespeare, it is not so much for what he did do, as for what he did not do, or refrained from doing. For in this world of lies, Truth is forced to fly like a scared white doe in the woodlands; and only by cunning glimpses will she reveal herself, as in Shakespeare and other masters of the great Art of Telling the Truth,—even though it be covertly, and by snatches.[4]

But if this view of the all-popular Shakespeare be seldom taken by his readers, and if very few who extol him, have ever read him deeply, or, perhaps, only have seen him on the tricky stage, (which alone made, and is still making him his mere mob renown)—if few men have time, or patience, or palate, for the spiritual truth as it is in that great genius;—it is, then, no matter of surprise that in a contemporaneous age, Nathaniel Hawthorne is a man, as yet, almost utterly mistaken among men. Here and there, in some quiet arm-chair in the noisy town, or some deep nook among the noiseless mountains, he may be appreciated for something of what he is. But unlike Shakespeare, who was forced to the contrary course by circumstances, Hawthorne (either from simple disinclination, or else from inaptitude) refrains from all the popularizing noise and show of broad farce, and blood-besmeared tragedy; content with the still, rich utterances of a great intellect in repose, and which sends few thoughts into circula-

1. At 10.21 in the manuscript Mrs. Melville copied "Through the issues of the dark characters"—an impossible reading. In Melville's hand "issues" is marked out and replaced with "mouths"; no "x" is visible in the margin.
2. *LW* read "same". See p. 473.
3. At 11.7 in the manuscript Mrs. Melville copied "divinely" then at once realized her error, marked out "divinely" and on the same line added "dimly-discerned" (which Melville later altered to "dimly-discernable"—a misspelling corrected in *LW*).
4. At 11.12 in the manuscript Mrs.

Melville copied "Truth is found", and recorded her doubt with an "x" in the margin. Later she marked out "found" and inserted "forced". Melville himself, still later, added a comma after "herself" (line 11.15) and altered the impossible reading "other writers" to "other masters" (there is no "x" at this point to indicate Mrs. Melville was uncertain about what she copied). In 11.16 Melville altered "art" to "Art", and inserted a comma-dash after Truth. In the next line he inserted a comma after "covertly", even though it had to be crowded in.

tion, except they be arterialized at his large warm lungs, and expanded in his honest heart.

Nor need you fix upon that blackness in him, if it suit you not. Nor, indeed, will all readers discern it, for it is, mostly, insinuated to those who may best understand it, and account for it; it is not obtruded upon every one alike.

Some may start to read of Shakespeare and Hawthorne on the same page. They may say, that if an illustration were needed, a lesser light might have sufficed to elucidate this Hawthorne, this small man of yesterday. But I am not, willingly, one of those, who, as touching Shakespeare at least, exemplify the maxim of Rochefoucauld, that "we exalt the reputation of some, in order to depress that of others";—who, to teach all noble-souled aspirants that there is no hope for them, pronounce Shakespeare absolutely unapproachable. But Shakespeare has been approached. There are minds that have gone as far as Shakespeare into the universe. And hardly a mortal man, who, at some time or other, has not felt as great thoughts in him as any you will find in Hamlet. We must not inferentially malign mankind for the sake of any one man, whoever he may be. This is too cheap a purchase of contentment for conscious mediocrity to make. Besides, this absolute and unconditional adoration of Shakespeare has grown to be a part of our Anglo Saxon superstitions. The Thirty-Nine Articles are now Forty. Intolerance has come to exist in this matter. You must believe in Shakespeare's unapproachability, or quit the country. But what sort of a belief is this for an American, a man who is bound to carry republican progressiveness into Literature, as well as into Life? Believe me, my friends, that men not very much inferior to Shakespeare, are this day being born on the banks of the Ohio. And the day will come, when you shall say who reads a book by an Englishman that is a modern? The great mistake seems to be, that even with those Americans who look forward to the coming of a great literary genius among us, they somehow fancy he will come in the costume of Queen Elizabeth's day,—be a writer of dramas founded upon old English history, or the tales of Boccaccio. Whereas, great geniuses are parts of the times; they themselves are the times; and possess a correspondent coloring. It is of a piece with the Jews, who while their Shiloh was meekly walking in their streets, were still praying for his magnificent coming; looking for him in a chariot, who was already among them on an ass. Nor must we forget, that, in his own life-time, Shakespeare was not Shakespeare, but only Master William Shakespeare of the shrewd, thriving business firm of Condell, Shakespeare & Co., proprietors of the Globe Theatre in London; and by a courtly author, of the name of Chettle, was hooted

at, as an "upstart crow" beautified "with other birds' feathers."
For, mark it well, imitation is often the first charge brought against
real originality. Why this is so, there is not space to set forth here.
You must have plenty of sea-room to tell the Truth in; especially, when it seems to have an aspect of newness, as America
did in 1492, though it was then just as old, and perhaps older
than Asia, only those sagacious philosophers, the common sailors,
had never seen it before; swearing it was all water and moonshine
there.

Now, I do not say that Nathaniel of Salem is a greater than William of Avon, or as great. But the difference between the two men
is by no means immeasurable. Not a very great deal more, and
Nathaniel were verily William.

This, too, I mean, that if Shakespeare has not been equalled,
give the world time, and he is sure to be surpassed, in one hemisphere or the other. Nor will it at all do to say, that the world is
getting grey and grizzled now, and has lost that fresh charm which
she wore of old, and by virtue of which the great poets of past
times made themselves what we esteem them to be. Not so. The
world is as young today, as when it was created; and this Vermont
morning dew is as wet to my feet, as Eden's dew to Adam's. Nor
has Nature been all over ransacked by our progenitors, so that no
new charms and mysteries remain for this latter generation to find.
Far from it. The trillionth part has not yet been said; and all
that has been said, but multiplies the avenues to what remains
to be said.[5] It is not so much paucity, as superabundance of material that seems to incapacitate modern authors.

Let America then prize and cherish her writers; yea, let her
glorify them. They are not so many in number, as to exhaust her
good-will. And while she has good kith and kin of her own, to
take to her bosom, let her not lavish her embraces upon the
household of an alien. For believe it or not England, after all, is,
in many things, an alien to us. China has more bowels of real
love for us than she. But even were there no strong literary
individualities among us, as there are some dozen at least; nevertheless, let America first praise mediocrity even, in her own
children, before she praises (for everywhere, merit demands acknowledgment from every one) the best excellence in the children of
any other land. Let her own authors, I say, have the priority of
appreciation. I was much pleased with a hot-headed Carolina cousin
of mine, who once said,—"If there were no other American to

5. At 15½.28 in the manuscript is one
of Mrs. Melville's more striking misreadings. A very faint "x" in the margin signals her doubt about "brilliant
part"—and she has marked out "brilliant" and inserted the correct "trillionth".

stand by, in Literature,—why, then, I would stand by Pop Emmons and his 'Fredoniad,' and till a better epic came along, swear it was not very far behind the 'Iliad'." Take away the words, and in spirit he was sound.

Not that American genius needs patronage in order to expand. For that explosive sort of stuff will expand though screwed up in a vice, and burst it, though it were triple steel. It is for the nation's sake, and not for her authors' sake, that I would have America be heedful of the increasing greatness among her writers. For how great the shame, if other nations should be before her, in crowning her heroes of the pen. But this is almost the case now. American authors have received more just and discriminating praise (however loftily and ridiculously given, in certain cases) even from some Englishmen, than from their own countrymen. There are hardly five critics in America; and several of them are asleep. As for patronage, it is the American author who now patronizes his country, and not his country him. And if at times some among them appeal to the people for more recognition, it is not always with selfish motives, but patriotic ones.

It is true, that but few of them as yet have evinced that decided originality which merits great praise.[6] But that graceful writer, who perhaps of all Americans has received the most plaudits from his own country for his productions,—that very popular and amiable writer, however good, and self-reliant in many things, perhaps owes his chief reputation to the self-acknowledged imitation of a foreign model, and to the studied avoidance of all topics but smooth ones. But it is better to fail in originality, than to succeed in imitation. He who has never failed somewhere, that man can not be great. Failure is the true test of greatness. And if it be said, that continual success is a proof that a man wisely knows his powers,—it is only to be added, that, in that case, he knows them to be small. Let us believe it, then, once for all, that there is no hope for us in these smooth pleasing writers that know their powers. Without malice, but to speak the plain fact, they but furnish an appendix to Goldsmith, and other English authors. And we want no American Goldsmiths; nay, we want no American Miltons. It were the vilest thing you could say of a true American author, that he were an American Tompkins. Call him an American, and have done; for you can not say a nobler thing of him.—But it is not meant that all American writers should studiously cleave to nationality in their writ-

6. An "x" in the margin at 16.10 indicates Mrs. Melville's uncertainty. She left a space after "as yet have", and later filled it in with "evinced". It *appears* that "decided" was also added later, but it may not have been.

ings;[7] only this, no American writer should write like an Englishman, or a Frenchman; let him write like a man, for then he will be sure to write like an American. Let us away with this leaven of literary flunkyism towards England. If either must play the flunky in this thing, let England do it, not us. While we are rapidly preparing for that political supremacy among the nations, which prophetically awaits us at the close of the present century; in a literary point of view, we are deplorably unprepared for it; and we seem studious to remain so. Hitherto, reasons might have existed why this should be; but no good reason exists now. And all that is requisite to amendment in this matter, is simply this: that, while freely acknowledging all excellence, everywhere, we should refrain from unduly lauding foreign writers, and, at the same time, duly recognize the meritorious writers that are our own;—those writers, who breathe that unshackled, democratic spirit of Christianity in all things, which now takes the practical lead in this world, though at the same time led by ourselves—us Americans. Let us boldly contemn all imitation, though it comes to us graceful and fragrant as the morning; and foster all originality, though, at first, it be crabbed and ugly as our own pine knots. And if any of our authors fail, or seem to fail, then, in the words of my enthusiastic Carolina cousin, let us clap him on the shoulder, and back him against all Europe for his second round. The truth is, that in our point of view, this matter of a national literature has come to such a pass with us, that in some sense we must turn bullies, else the day is lost, or superiority so far beyond us, that we can hardly say it will ever be ours.

And now, my countrymen, as an excellent author, of your own flesh and blood,—an unimitating, and, perhaps, in his way, an inimitable man—whom better can I commend to you, in the first place, than Nathaniel Hawthorne. He is one of the new, and far better generation of your writers. The smell of your beeches and hemlocks is upon him; your own broad prairies are in his soul; and if you travel away inland into his deep and noble nature, you will hear the far roar of his Niagara. Give not over to future generations the glad duty of acknowledging him for what he is. Take that joy to yourself, in your own generation; and so shall he feel those grateful impulses in him, that may possibly prompt

7. At 17.7 in the manuscript Mrs. Melville copied "studiously cleave to nationality in their"—leaving a space about as long as that taken up by the word "writers" in the line above. There is an erased "x" in the margin, but the space is not filled in. Presumably the erased "x" means that she had thought that there might be another word in the manuscript; she *may* have left a much longer space and filled in "nationality", though that word does not appear to be added at a later time.

him to the full flower of some still greater achievement in your eyes. And by confessing him, you thereby confess others; you brace the whole brotherhood. For genius, all over the world, stands hand in hand, and one shock of recognition runs the whole circle round.

In treating of Hawthorne, or rather of Hawthorne in his writings (for I never saw the man; and in the chances of a quiet plantation life, remote from his haunts, perhaps never shall) in treating of his works, I say, I have thus far omitted all mention of his "Twice Told Tales," and "Scarlet Letter." Both are excellent; but full of such manifold, strange and diffusive beauties, that time would all but fail me, to point the half of them out. But there are things in those two books, which, had they been written in England a century ago, Nathaniel Hawthorne had utterly displaced many of the bright names we now revere on authority. But I am content to leave Hawthorne to himself, and to the infallible finding of posterity; and however great may be the praise I have bestowed upon him, I feel, that in so doing, I have more served and honored myself, than him. For, at bottom, great excellence is praise enough to itself; but the feeling of a sincere and appreciative love and admiration towards it, this is relieved by utterance; and warm, honest praise ever leaves a pleasant flavor in the mouth; and it is an honorable thing to confess to what is honorable in others.

But I cannot leave my subject yet. No man can read a fine author, and relish him to his very bones, while he reads, without subsequently fancying to himself some ideal image of the man and his mind. And if you rightly look for it, you will almost always find that the author himself has somewhere furnished you with his own picture. For poets (whether in prose or verse), being painters of Nature, are like their brethren of the pencil, the true portrait-painters, who, in the multitude of likenesses to be sketched, do not invariably omit their own; and in all high instances, they paint them without any vanity, though, at times, with a lurking something, that would take several pages to properly define.

I submit it, then, to those best acquainted with the man personally, whether the following is not Nathaniel Hawthorne;— and to himself, whether something involved in it does not express the temper of his mind,—that lasting temper of all true, candid men—a seeker, not a finder yet:—

"A man now entered, in neglected attire, with the aspect of a thinker, but somewhat too rough-hewn and brawny for a scholar. His face was full of sturdy vigor, with some finer and keener attribute beneath; though harsh at first, it was tempered with the glow of a large, warm heart, which had force enough to heat his powerful intellect through and through. He advanced to the Intelligencer, and looked at him with a glance of such stern sincerity, that perhaps few secrets were beyond its scope.

" 'I seek for Truth,' said he."

* * * * * *

Twenty-four hours have elapsed since writing the foregoing. I have just returned from the hay mow, charged more and more with love and admiration of Hawthorne. For I have just been gleaning through the "Mosses," picking up many things here and there that had previously escaped me. And I found that but to glean after this man, is better than to be in at the harvest of others. To be frank (though, perhaps, rather foolish), notwithstanding what I wrote yesterday of these Mosses, I had not then culled them all; but had, nevertheless, been sufficiently sensible of the subtle essence, in them, as to write as I did. To what infinite height of loving wonder and admiration I may yet be borne, when by repeatedly banquetting on these Mosses, I shall have thoroughly incorporated their whole stuff into my being,—that, I can not tell. But already I feel that this Hawthorne has dropped germinous seeds into my soul. He expands and deepens down, the more I contemplate him; and further, and further, shoots his strong New-England roots into the hot soil of my Southern soul.

By careful reference to the "Table of Contents," I now find, that I have gone through all the sketches; but that when I yesterday wrote, I had not at all read two particular pieces, to which I now desire to call special attention,—"A Select Party," and "Young Goodman Brown." Here, be it said to all those whom this poor fugitive scrawl of mine may tempt to the perusal of the "Mosses," that they must on no account suffer themselves to be trifled with, disappointed, or deceived by the triviality of many of the titles to these Sketches. For in more than one instance, the title utterly belies the piece. It is as if rustic demijohns containing the very best and costliest of Falernian and Tokay, were labeled "Cider," "Perry," and "Elder-berry Wine." The truth seems to be, that like many other geniuses, this Man of Mosses takes great delight in hoodwinking the world,—at least, with respect to himself. Personally, I doubt not, that he rather prefers to be generally esteemed but a so-so sort of author; being willing to reserve the thorough and acute appreciation of what he is, to that party most qualified to judge—that is, to himself. Besides, at the bottom of their natures, men like Hawthorne, in many things, deem the plaudits of the public such strong presumptive evidence of mediocrity in the object of them, that it would in some degree render them doubtful of their own powers, did they hear much and vociferous braying concerning them in the public pastures. True, I have been braying myself (if you please to be witty enough, to have it so) but then I claim to be the first that has so brayed in this particular matter; and therefore, while pleading guilty to the charge, still claim all the merit due to originality.

But with whatever motive, playful or profound, Nathaniel Hawthorne has chosen to entitle his pieces in the manner he has, it is certain, that some of them are directly calculated to deceive —egregiously deceive—the superficial skimmer of pages. To be downright and candid once more, let me cheerfully say, that two of these titles did dolefully dupe no less an eagle-eyed reader than myself; and that, too, after I had been impressed with a sense of the great depth and breadth of this American man. "Who in the name of thunder" (as the country-people say in this neighborhood), "who in the name of thunder," would anticipate any marvel in a piece entitled "Young Goodman Brown"? You would of course suppose that it was a simple little tale, intended as a supplement to "Goody Two Shoes." Whereas, it is deep as Dante; nor can you finish it, without addressing the author in his own words—"It is yours to penetrate, in every bosom, the deep mystery of sin." And with Young Goodman, too, in allegorical pursuit of his Puritan wife, you cry out in your anguish,—

"Faith!" shouted Goodman Brown, in a voice of agony and desperation; and the echoes of the forest mocked him, crying —"Faith! Faith!" as if bewildered wretches were seeking her all through the wilderness.

Now this same piece, entitled "Young Goodman Brown," is one of the two that I had not all read yesterday; and I allude to it now, because it is, in itself, such a strong positive illustration of that blackness in Hawthorne, which I had assumed from the mere occasional shadows of it, as revealed in several of the other sketches. But had I previously perused "Young Goodman Brown," I should have been at no pains to draw the conclusion, which I came to, at a time, when I was ignorant that the book contained one such direct and unqualified manifestation of it.

The other piece of the two referred to, is entitled "A Select Party," which, in my first simplicity upon originally taking hold of the book, I fancied must treat of some pumpkin-pie party in Old Salem, or some Chowder Party on Cape Cod. Whereas, by all the gods of Peedee! it is the sweetest and sublimest thing that has been written since Spenser wrote. Nay, there is nothing in Spenser that surpasses it, perhaps, nothing that equals it. And the test is this: read any canto in "The Faery Queen," and then read "A Select Party," and decide which pleases you the most,— that is, if you are qualified to judge. Do not be frightened at this; for when Spenser was alive, he was thought of very much as Hawthorne is now,—was generally accounted just such a "gentle" harmless man. It may be, that to common eyes, the sublimity of Hawthorne seems lost in his sweetness,—as perhaps in this same "Select Party" of his; for whom, he has builded so august a dome of sunset clouds, and served them on richer plate, than Belshazzar's when he banquetted his lords in Babylon.

But my chief business now, is to point out a particular page in this piece, having reference to an honored guest, who under the name of "The Master Genius" but in the guise "of a young man of poor attire, with no insignia of rank or acknowledged eminence," is introduced to the Man of Fancy, who is the giver of the feast. Now the page having reference to this "Master Genius", so happily expresses much of what I yesterday wrote, touching the coming of the literary Shiloh of America, that I cannot but be charmed by the coincidence; especially, when it shows such a parity of ideas, at least, in this one point, between a man like Hawthorne and a man like me.

And here, let me throw out another conceit of mine touching this American Shiloh, or "Master Genius," as Hawthorne calls him. May it not be, that this commanding mind has not been, is not, and never will be, individually developed in any one man? And would it, indeed, appear so unreasonable to suppose, that this great fullness and overflowing may be, or may be destined to be, shared by a plurality of men of genius? Surely, to take the very greatest example on record, Shakespeare cannot be regarded as in himself the concretion of all the genius of his time; nor as so immeasurably beyond Marlowe, Webster, Ford, Beaumont, Jonson, that those great men can be said to share none of his power? For one, I conceive that there were dramatists in Elizabeth's day, between whom and Shakespeare the distance was by no means great. Let anyone, hitherto little acquainted with those neglected old authors, for the first time read them thoroughly, or even read Charles Lamb's Specimens of them, and he will be amazed at the wondrous ability of those Anaks of men, and shocked at this renewed example of the fact, that Fortune has more to do with fame than merit,—though, without merit, lasting fame there can be none.

Nevertheless, it would argue too illy of my country were this maxim to hold good concerning Nathaniel Hawthorne, a man, who already, in some few minds, has shed "such a light, as never illuminates the earth, save when a great heart burns as the household fire of a grand intellect."

The words are his,—in the "Select Party"; and they are a magnificent setting to a coincident sentiment of my own, but ramblingly expressed yesterday, in reference to himself. Gainsay it who will, as I now write, I am Posterity speaking by proxy—and after times will make it more than good, when I declare—that the American, who up to the present day, has evinced, in Literature, the largest brain with the largest heart, that man is Nathaniel Hawthorne. Moreover, that whatever Nathaniel Hawthorne may hereafter write, "The Mosses from an Old Manse" will be ultimately accounted his masterpiece. For there is a sure, though a secret sign in some works which proves the culmination of the powers (only the developable ones, however) that produced them. But I am by no means desirous of the glory of a prophet. I pray Heaven that Hawthorne may *yet* prove me an impostor in this prediction. Especially, as I somehow cling to the strange fancy, that, in all men, hiddenly reside certain wondrous, occult properties—as in some plants and minerals—which by some happy but very rare accident (as bronze was discovered by the melting of the iron and brass in the burning of Corinth) may chance to be called forth here on earth; not entirely waiting for their better discovery in the more congenial, blessed atmosphere of heaven.

Once more—for it is hard to be finite upon an infinite subject, and all subjects are infinite. By some people, this entire scrawl of mine may be esteemed altogether unnecessary, inasmuch, "as years ago" (they may say) "we found out the rich and rare stuff in this Hawthorne, whom you now parade forth, as if only *yourself* were the discoverer of this Portuguese diamond in our Literature." —But even granting all this; and adding to it, the assumption that the books of Hawthorne have sold by the five-thousand,— what does that signify?—They should be sold by the hundred-thousand; and read by the million; and admired by every one who is capable of Admiration.

Melville's Letters

[*At the Time of* Moby-Dick] †

To Richard H. Dana, Jr.

NEW YORK, MAY 1, 1850

* * * About the "whaling voyage"—I am half way in the work, & am very glad that your suggestion so jumps with mine.[1] It will be a strange sort of a book, tho', I fear; blubber is blub-

† These excerpts from Melville's letters, together with the footnotes, are taken from *The Letters of Herman Melville*, edited by Merrell R. Davis and William H. Gilman (New Haven: Yale University Press, 1960), pp. 108–46. Copyright 1960 by Yale University Press; reprinted by permission of the publish- ers. The excerpts given here include Melville's own references to *Moby-Dick* at the time of its composition and publication. The anomalous spellings are Melville's own.
1. Melville's first reference to the composition of *Moby-Dick*.

ber you know; tho' you may get oil out of it, the poetry runs as hard as sap from a frozen maple tree;—& to cook the thing up, one must needs throw in a little fancy, which from the nature of the thing, must be ungainly as the gambols of the whales themselves. Yet I mean to give the truth of the thing, spite of this. * * *

To Richard Bentley

NEW YORK, JUNE 27, 1850

* * * In the latter part of the coming autumn I shall have ready a new work; and I write you now to propose its publication in England.

The book is a romance of adventure, founded upon certain wild legends in the Southern Sperm Whale Fisheries, and illustrated by the author's own personal experience, of two years & more, as a harpooneer.[2]

Should you be inclined to undertake the book, I think that it will be worth to you £200. Could you be positively put in possession of the copyright, it might be worth to you a larger sum— considering its great novelty; for I do not know that the subject treated of has ever been worked up by a romancer; or, indeed, by any writer, in any adequate manner. * * *

To Evert A. Duyckinck

PITTSFIELD, MASS., DECEMBER 13, 1850

* * * I have a sort of sea-feeling here in the country, now that the ground is all covered with snow. I look out of my window in the morning when I rise as I would out of a port-hole of a ship in the Atlantic. My room seems a ship's cabin; & at nights when I wake up & hear the wind shrieking, I almost fancy there is too much sail on the house, & I had better go on the roof & rig in the chimney.

Do you want to know how I pass my time?—I rise at eight— thereabouts—& go to my barn—say good-morning to the horse, & give him his breakfast. (It goes to my heart to give him a cold one, but it can't be helped) Then, pay a visit to my cow—cut up a pumpkin or two for her, & stand by to see her eat it—for it's a pleasant sight to see a cow move her jaws—she does it so mildly

---

2. At best Melville's claim to two years' experience as a harpooner is an exaggeration. There is no evidence that he ever hurled a harpoon in the eighteen months he spent on the *Acushnet* or the six or seven weeks on the *Lucy Ann.*

On his third and last whaling voyage aboard the *Charles & Henry* he may possibly have been a boat-steerer and harpooner, but the trip lasted only six months. (Howard, 63–4.)

& with such a sanctity.—My own breakfast over, I go to my work-room & light my fire—then spread my M.S.S on the table—take one business squint at it, & fall to with a will. At 2½ P.M. I hear a preconcerted knock at my door, which (by request) continues till I rise & go to the door, which serves to wean me effectively from my writing, however interested I may be. My friends the horse & cow now demand their dinner—& I go & give it them. My own dinner over, I rig my sleigh & with my mother or sisters start off for the village—& if it be a Literary World day, great is the sat-isfaction thereof.—My evenings I spend in a sort of mesmeric state in my room—not being able to read—only now & then skimming over some large-printed book.—Can you send me about fifty fast-writing youths, with an easy style & not averse to polishing their labors? If you can, I wish you would, because since I have been here I have planned about that number of future works & cant find enough time to think about them separately.—But I dont know but a book in a man's brain is better off than a book bound in calf—at any rate it is safer from criticism. And taking a book off the brain, is akin to the ticklish & dangerous business of taking an old painting off a panel—you have to scrape off the whole brain in order to get at it with due safety—& even then, the paint-ing may not be worth the trouble. * * *

To Evert A. Duyckinck

PITTSFIELD, MASS., FEBRUARY 12, 1851

* * * After a long procrastination, I drove down to see Mr. Hawthorne a couple of weeks ago. I found him, of course, buried in snow; & the delightful scenery about him, all wrapped up & tucked away under a napkin, as it were. He was to have made me a day's visit, & I had promised myself much pleasure in getting him up in my snug room here, & discussing the Universe with a bottle of brandy & cigars. But he has not been able to come, owing to sickness in his family.—or else, he's up to the lips in the *Universe* again.

By the way, I have recently read his "Twice Told Tales" [3] (I hadnt read but a few of them before) I think they far exceed the "Mosses"—they are, I fancy, an earlier vintage from his vine. Some of those sketches are wonderfully subtle. Their deeper meanings are worthy of a Brahmin. Still there is something lack-ing—a good deal lacking—to the plump sphericity of the man. What is that?

3. Melville borrowed *Twice-Told Tales* (Boston, 1837) from Duyckinck on or after 20 July, 1849, and received two inscribed copies from Hawthorne (First Series, Boston, 1845, and Vol. 2, Sec-ond Series, Boston, 1842) on 22 Janu-ary, 1851 (Sealts, "Melville's Reading," Nos. 258, 259, and 260).

—He does'nt patronise the butcher—he needs roast-beef, done rare.—Nevertheless, for one, I regard Hawthorne (in his books) as evincing a quality of genius, immensely loftier, & more profound, too, than any other American has shown hitherto in the printed form. Irving is a grasshopper to him—putting the *souls* of the two men together, I mean. * * *

To Nathaniel Hawthorne

PITTSFIELD, MASS., APRIL 16, 1851

* * * "The House of the Seven Gables: A Romance. By Nathaniel Hawthorne. One vol. 16mo, pp. 344." [4] The contents of this book do not belie its rich, clustering, romantic title. With great enjoyment we spent almost an hour in each separate gable. This book is like a fine old chamber, abundantly, but still judiciously, furnished with precisely that sort of furniture best fitted to furnish it. There are rich hangings, wherein are braided scenes from tragedies! There is old china with rare devices, set out on the carved buffet; there are long and indolent lounges to throw yourself upon; there is an admirable sideboard, plentifully stored with good viands; there is a smell as of old wine in the pantry; and finally, in one corner, there is a dark little blackletter volume in golden clasps, entitled "Hawthorne: A Problem." It has delighted us; it has piqued a re-perusal; it has robbed us of a day, and made us a present of a whole year of thoughtfulness; it has bred great exhilaration and exultation with the remembrance that the architect of the Gables resides only six miles off, and not three thousand miles away, in England, say. We think the book, for pleasantness of running interest, surpasses the other works of the author. The curtains are more drawn; the sun comes in more, genialities peep out more. Were we to particularize what most struck us in the deeper passages, we would point out the scene where Clifford, for a moment, would fain throw himself forth from the window to join the procession; or the scene where the judge is left seated in his ancestral chair. Clifford is full of an awful truth throughout. He is conceived in the finest, truest spirit. He is no caricature. He is Clifford. And here we would say that, did circumstances permit, we should like nothing better than to devote an elaborate and careful paper to the full consideration and analysis of the purport and significance of what so strongly characterizes all of this author's writings.

4. Melville had visited Hawthorne in Lenox on 11 April, bringing a bedstead and clock with him (Leyda, *Log*, 409). Hawthorne gave him a copy of the newly published *The House of the Seven Gables*, inscribing it: "Herman Melville from Nath[el] Hawthorne," to which Mrs. Hawthorne added "April 11th 1851 Friday evening."

There is a certain tragic phase of humanity which, in our opinion, was never more powerfully embodied than by Hawthorne. We mean the tragicalness of human thought in its own unbiassed, native, and profounder workings. We think that into no recorded mind has the intense feeling of the visable truth ever entered more deeply than into this man's. By visable truth, we mean the apprehension of the absolute condition of present things as they strike the eye of the man who fears them not, though they do their worst to him,—the man who, like Russia or the British Empire, declares himself a sovereign nature (in himself) amid the powers of heaven, hell, and earth. He may perish; but so long as he exists he insists upon treating with all Powers upon an equal basis. If any of those other Powers choose to withhold certain secrets, let them; that does not impair my sovereignty in myself; that does not make me tributary. And perhaps, after all, there is *no* secret. We incline to think that the Problem of the Universe is like the Freemason's mighty secret, so terrible to all children. It turns out, at last, to consist in a triangle, a mallet, and an apron,—nothing more! We incline to think that God cannot explain His own secrets, and that He would like a little information upon certain points Himself. We mortals astonish Him as much as He us. But it is this *Being* of the matter; [5] there lies the knot with which we choke ourselves. As soon as you say *Me*, a *God*, a *Nature*, so soon you jump off from your stool and hang from the beam. Yes, that word is the hangman. Take God out of the dictionary, and you would have Him in the street.

There is the grand truth about Nathaniel Hawthorne. He says NO! in thunder; but the Devil himself cannot make him say *yes*. For all men who say *yes*, lie; and all men who say *no*,—why, they are in the happy condition of judicious, unincumbered travellers in Europe; they cross the frontiers into Eternity with nothing but a carpet-bag,—that is to say, the Ego. Whereas those *yes*-gentry, they travel with heaps of baggage, and, damn them! they will never get through the Custom House. What's the reason, Mr. Hawthorne, that in the last stages of metaphysics a fellow always falls to *swearing* so? I could rip an hour. You see, I began with a little criticism extracted for your benefit from the "Pittsfield Secret Review," and here I have landed in Africa.

Walk down one of these mornings and see me. No nonsense;

5. Is this a mistaken reading of Melville? Perhaps Julian Hawthorne's transcription is an error for Melville's "Being that matters" or "Being that maddens." This would suppose that Julian read Melville's "that" as "of the" and that he did not recognize Melville's final "s," both of which are possible and understandable mistranscriptions of Melville's hand. Either of the two readings proposed here would be more appropriate in the context.

[The original letter is not available; it is printed by Davis and Gilman from Julian Hawthorne's transcription, hence their above conjectures—*Editors*.]

come. Remember me to Mrs. Hawthorne and the children.

H. Melville.

P.S. The marriage of Phoebe with the daguerreotypist is a fine stroke, because of his turning out to be a *Maule*. If you pass Hepzibah's cent-shop, buy me a Jim Crow (fresh) and send it to me by Ned Higgins.

To Nathaniel Hawthorne

PITTSFIELD, MASS., JUNE 1?, 1851

* * * I should have been rumbling down to you in my pine-board chariot a long time ago, were it not that for some weeks past I have been more busy than you can well imagine,—out of doors,—building and patching and tinkering away in all directions. Besides, I had my crops to get in,—corn and potatoes (I hope to show you some famous ones by and by),—and many other things to attend to, all accumulating upon this one particular season. I work myself; and at night my bodily sensations are akin to those I have so often felt before, when a hired man, doing my day's work from sun to sun. But I mean to continue visiting you until you tell me that my visits are both supererogatory and superfluous. With no son of man do I stand upon any etiquette or ceremony, except the Christian ones of charity and honesty. I am told, my fellow-man, that there is an aristocracy of the brain. Some men have boldly advocated and asserted it. Schiller seems to have done so, though I don't know much about him.[6] At any rate, it is true that there have been those who, while earnest in behalf of political equality, still accept the intellectual estates. And I can well perceive, I think, how a man of superior mind can, by its intense cultivation, bring himself, as it were, into a certain spontaneous aristocracy of feeling,—exceedingly nice and fastidious,—similar to that which, in an English Howard, conveys a torpedo-fish thrill at the slightest contact with a social plebeian.[7] So, when you see or hear of my ruthless democracy on

6. Melville seems to have had in mind the quality pointed out in Menzel's criticism of Schiller as quoted by Longfellow in *The Poets and Poetry of Europe* (Philadelphia, 1845), p. 308: "We turn now to the second secret of the beauty belonging to Schiller's ideal characters. This is their nobleness,—their honorableness. His heroes and heroines never discredit the pride and dignity which announce a loftier nature; and all their outward acts bear the stamp of magnanimity and inborn nobleness. Its perfect opposite is the vulgar character, and that conventional spirit which serves for a bridle and leading-strings to the vulgar nature." "Elevation of mind" was called typical of Schiller's characters in "Aeschylus, Shakespeare, and Schiller," *Blackwood's Edinburgh Magazine, 32* (June 1851), 651.

7. Melville may have meant any one of a number of members of the English Howard family, like Charles, the commander-in-chief of the fleet that destroyed the Spanish Armada, or Henry, collaborator with Wyatt and others in the songs and sonnets that achieved fame when published as *Tottel's Miscellany*. This family, which held the earldoms of Surrey, Effingham, and Carlisle, was a symbol of the English aristocracy.

all sides, you may possibly feel a touch of a shrink, or something of that sort. It is but nature to be shy of a mortal who boldly declares that a thief in jail is as honorable a personage as Gen. George Washington. This is ludicrous. But Truth is the silliest thing under the sun. Try to get a living by the Truth—and go to the Soup Societies. Heavens! Let any clergyman try to preach the Truth from its very stronghold, the pulpit, and they would ride him out of his church on his own pulpit bannister. It can hardly be doubted that all Reformers are bottomed upon the truth, more or less; and to the world at large are not reformers almost universally laughing-stocks? Why so? Truth is ridiculous to men. Thus easily in my room here do I, conceited and garrulous, reverse the test of my Lord Shaftesbury.[8]

It seems an inconsistency to assert unconditional democracy in all things, and yet confess a dislike to all mankind—in the mass. But not so.—But it's an endless sermon,—no more of it. I began by saying that the reason I have not been to Lenox is this,—in the evening I feel completely done up, as the phrase is, and incapable of the long jolting to get to your house and back. In a week or so, I go to New York, to bury myself in a third-story room, and work and slave on my "Whale" while it is driving through the press. *That* is the only way I can finish it now,—I am so pulled hither and thither by circumstances. The calm, the coolness, the silent grass-growing mood in which a man *ought* always to compose,—that, I fear, can seldom be mine. Dollars damn me; and the malicious Devil is forever grinning in upon me, holding the door ajar. My dear Sir, a presentiment is on me,—I shall at last be worn out and perish, like an old nutmeg-grater, grated to pieces by the constant attrition of the wood, that is, the nutmeg. What I feel most moved to write, that is banned,—it will not pay. Yet, altogether, write the *other* way I cannot. So the product

8. Julian Hawthorne prints "revere the test of my Lord Shaftesbury." Shaftesbury maintained that one test of truth was its power to survive ridicule. "Truth," he wrote in "An Essay on the Freedom of Wit and Humour," " 'tis supposed, may bear *all* Lights: and *one* of those principal Lights or natural Mediums, by which Things are to be view'd, in order to a thorow Recognition, is *Ridicule* it-self, or that Manner of Proof by which we discern whatever is liable to just Raillery in any Subject. So much, at least, is allow'd by All, who at any time appeal to this *Criterion*. The gravest Gentlemen, even in the gravest Subjects, are suppos'd to acknowledge this: and can have no Right, 'tis thought, to deny others the Freedom of this Appeal; whilst they are free to censure like other Men, and in their gravest Arguments make no scruple to ask, *Is it not ridiculous?*" *Characteristicks of Men, Manners, Opinions, Times* (6th ed. 1737), *I*, 161. He cites, too, the fact that Socrates' character and doctrines seemed only the more "solid and just" after they had "stood the Proof" of Aristophanes' ridicule (*I*, 31). But whereas Shaftesbury is saying that you can know a thing is true if it survives ridicule, Melville is saying that you can know a thing is true because it is considered ridiculous. Melville may have revered Shaftesbury's test, but here he is reversing it.

is a final hash, and all my books are botches. I'm rather sore, perhaps, in this letter; but see my hand!—four blisters on this palm, made by hoes and hammers within the last few days. It is a rainy morning; so I am indoors, and all work suspended. I feel cheerfully disposed, and therefore I write a little bluely. Would the Gin were here! If ever, my dear Hawthorne, in the eternal times that are to come, you and I shall sit down in Paradise, in some little shady corner by ourselves; and if we shall by any means be able to smuggle a basket of champagne there (I won't believe in a Temperance Heaven), and if we shall then cross our celestial legs in the celestial grass that is forever tropical, and strike our glasses and our heads together, till both musically ring in concert,—then, O my dear fellow-mortal, how shall we pleasantly discourse of all the things manifold which now so distress us,—when all the earth shall be but a reminiscence, yea, its final dissolution an antiquity. Then shall songs be composed as when wars are over; humorous, comic songs,— "Oh, when I lived in that queer little hole called the world," or, "Oh, when I toiled and sweated below," or, "Oh, when I knocked and was knocked in the fight"—yes, let us look forward to such things. Let us swear that, though now we sweat, yet it is because of the dry heat which is indispensable to the nourishment of the vine which is to bear the grapes that are to give us the champagne hereafter.

But I was talking about the "Whale." As the fishermen say, "he's in his flurry" when I left him some three weeks ago. I'm going to take him by his jaw, however, before long, and finish him up in some fashion or other. What's the use of elaborating what, in its very essence, is so short-lived as a modern book? Though I wrote the Gospels in this century, I should die in the gutter.— I talk all about myself, and this is selfishness and egotism. Granted. But how help it? I am writing to you; I know little about you, but something about myself. So I write about myself, —at least, to you. Don't trouble yourself, though, about writing; and don't trouble yourself about visiting; and when you *do* visit, don't trouble yourself about talking. I will do all the writing and visiting and talking myself.—By the way, in the last "Dollar Magazine" I read "The Unpardonable Sin." [9] He was a sad fellow, that Ethan Brand. I have no doubt you are by this time reponsible for many a shake and tremor of the tribe of "general readers." It is a frightful poetical creed that the cultivation of the brain eats out the heart. But it's my *prose* opinion that in most cases, in those men who have fine brains and work

9. Hawthorne's story was printed in *Holden's Dollar Magazine* for May 1851.

them well, the heart extends down to hams. And though you smoke them with the fire of tribulation, yet, like veritable hams, the head only gives the richer and the better flavor. I stand for the heart. To the dogs with the head! I had rather be a fool with a heart, than Jupiter Olympus with his head. The reason the mass of men fear God, and *at bottom dislike* Him, is because they rather distrust His heart, and fancy Him all brain like a watch. (You perceive I employ a capital initial in the pronoun referring to the Deity; don't you think there is a slight dash of flunkeyism in that usage?) Another thing. I was in New York for four-and-twenty hours the other day, and saw a portrait of N.H. And I have seen and heard many flattering (in a publisher's point of view) allusions to the "Seven Gables." And I have seen "Tales," and "A New Volume" announced, by N.H.[1] So upon the whole, I say to myself, this N.H. is in the ascendant. My dear Sir, they begin to patronize. All Fame is patronage. Let me be infamous: there is no patronage in *that*. What "reputation" H.M. has is horrible. Think of it! To go down to posterity is bad enough, any way; but to go down as a "man who lived among the cannibals"! When I speak of posterity, in reference to myself, I only mean the babies who will probably be born in the moment immediately ensuing upon my giving up the ghost. I shall go down to some of them, in all likelihood. "Typee" will be given to them, perhaps, with their gingerbread. I have come to regard this matter of Fame as the most transparent of all vanities. I read Solomon more and more, and every time see deeper and deeper and unspeakable meanings in him.[2] I did not think of Fame, a year ago, as I do now. My development has been all within a few years past. I am like one of those seeds taken out of the Egyptian Pyramids, which, after being three thousand years a seed and nothing but a seed, being planted in English soil, it developed itself, grew to greenness, and then fell to mould.[3] So I. Until I was twenty-five, I

1. Melville might have seen some such announcement as early as 10 May, in the *Literary World,* when the "Publisher's Circular," an editor's column, noted that "Ticknor, Reed & Fields have in Press . . . [a] New Volume of Stories by Hawthorne" and "a new volume by Hawthorne." A Ticknor, Reed and Fields advertisement containing these two items ran from 17 May to 9 August.
2. See *Moby Dick:* "The truest of all men was the Man of Sorrows, and the truest of all books is Solomon's, and Ecclesiastes is the fine hammered steel of woe. 'All is vanity.' ALL. This wilful

world hath not got hold of unchristian Solomon's wisdom yet." (Mansfield-Vincent, 42.)
3. At about this time, G. P. R. James carried on an experiment at Stockbridge south of Pittsfield of planting some Egyptian wheat seed taken from the inside of a mummy case. His son, Charles Leigh James describes the planting, saw it come up, and observed that "it did not seed 'worth a continental.'" See S. M. Ellis, *The Solitary Horseman, or the Life and Adventures of G. P. R. James,* as cited in *American Notes and Queries, 7* (December 1947), 41.

had no development at all. From my twenty-fifth year I date my life. Three weeks have scarcely passed, at any time between then and now, that I have not unfolded within myself. But I feel that I am now come to the inmost leaf of the bulb, and that shortly the flower must fall to the mould. It seems to me now that Solomon was the truest man who ever spoke, and yet that he a little *managed* the truth with a view to popular conservatism; or else there have been many corruptions and interpolations of the text. —In reading some of Goethe's sayings, so worshipped by his votaries, I came across this, *"Live in the all."* [4] That is to say, your separate identity is but a wretched one,—good; but get out of yourself, spread and expand yourself, and bring to yourself the tinglings of life that are felt in the flowers and the woods, that are felt in the planets Saturn and Venus, and the Fixed Stars. What nonsense! Here is a fellow with a raging toothache. "My dear boy," Goethe says to him, "you are sorely afflicted with that tooth; but you must *live in the all,* and then you will be happy!" As with all great genius, there is an immense deal of flummery in Goethe, and in proportion to my own contact with him, a monstrous deal of it in me.

H. Melville.

P.S. "Amen!" saith Hawthorne.

N.B. This "all" feeling, though, there is some truth in. You must often have felt it, lying on the grass on a warm summer's day. Your legs seem to send out shoots into the earth. Your hair feels like leaves upon your head. This is the *all* feeling. But what plays the mischief with the truth is that men will insist upon the universal application of a temporary feeling or opinion.

P.S. You must not fail to admire my discretion in paying the postage on this letter.

---

4. Melville's exact source remains to be discovered. The idea is general in Goethe; the particular thought is doubtless a translation of a phrase in stanza four of "Generalbeichte":

Willst du Absolution
Deinen Treuen geben,
Wollen wir nach deinem Wink
Unablässlich streben,
Uns von Halben zu entwohnen
Und im Ganzen, Guten, Schönen
Resolut zu leben,

Carlyle, in whom Melville was well read, translates it "To live . . . in the Whole. . . ."—"Death of Goethe," *Critical and Miscellaneous Essays* (Boston, 1839), 3, 205, and John S. Dwight renders it ". . . living" "In the Whole . . . ."—George Ripley, ed., *Specimens of Foreign Standard Literature*, Vol. 3 . . . *Select Minor Poems from the German of Goethe and Schiller* (Boston, 1839), p. 48. One of Ripley's notes on Goethe may have helped give currency to the idea Melville was lampooning: "Total occupation of himself, heart and soul, in the subject nearest him,—living *in* it, and identifying himself with it for the time,—left no room for sick yearnings, made each little sphere a world, each moment an eternity. This is evidently what he meant by 'Living in the Whole,' by finding 'All in One, and One in All'" (ibid., p. 365).

To Nathaniel Hawthorne

PITTSFIELD, MASS., JUNE 29, 1851

* * * The clear air and open window invite me to write to you. For some time past I have been so busy with a thousand things that I have almost forgotten when I wrote you last, and whether I received an answer. This most persuasive season has now for weeks recalled me from certain crotchetty and over doleful chimearas, the like of which men like you and me and some others, forming a chain of God's posts round the world, must be content to encounter now and then, and fight them the best way we can. But come they will,—for, in the boundless, trackless, but still glorious wild wilderness through which these outposts run, the Indians do sorely abound, as well as the insignificant but still stinging mosquitoes. Since you have been here, I have been building some shanties of houses (connected with the old one) and likewise some shanties of chapters and essays. I have been plowing and sowing and raising and painting and printing and praying,— and now begin to come out upon a less bustling time, and to enjoy the calm prospect of things from a fair piazza at the north of the old farm house here.

Not entirely yet, though, am I without something to be urgent with. The "Whale" is only half through the press; for, wearied with the long delay of the printers, and disgusted with the heat and dust of the babylonish brick-kiln of New York, I came back to the country to feel the grass—and end the book reclining on it, if I may.—I am sure you will pardon this speaking all about myself,—for if I *say* so much on that head, be sure all the rest of the world are thinking about themselves ten times as much. Let us speak, though we show all our faults and weaknesses,—for it is a sign of strength to be weak, to know it, and out with it,—not in [a] set way and ostentatiously, though, but incidentally and without premeditation.—But I am falling into my old foible— preaching. I am busy, but shall not be very long. Come and spend a day here, if you can and want to; if not, stay in Lenox, and God give you long life. When I am quite free of my present engagements, I am going to treat myself to a ride and a visit to you. Have ready a bottle of brandy, because I always feel like drinking that heroic drink when we talk ontological heroics together. This is rather a crazy letter in some respects, I apprehend. If so, ascribe it to the intoxicating effects of the latter end of June operating upon a very susceptible and peradventure feeble temperament.

Shall I send you a fin of the *Whale* by way of a specimen

mouthful? The tail is not yet cooked—though the hell-fire in which the whole book is broiled might not unreasonably have cooked it all ere this. This is the book's motto (the secret one), —Ego non baptiso te in nomine—but make out the rest yourself.[5] * * *

To Richard Bentley

PITTSFIELD, MASS., JULY 20, 1851

* * * I promptly received your note of the 3[d] Inst: in reply to mine concerning the publication of my new book.[6]

I accept your offer for the work; but not without strong hope that before long, we shall be able to treat upon a firmer basis than now, & heretofore; & that with the more assurance you will be disposed to make overtures for American books. And here let me say to you,—since you are peculiarly interested in the matter—that in all reasonable probability no International Copyright will ever be obtained—in our time, at least—if you Englishmen wait at all for

5. The phrase appears in fuller form when Captain Ahab uses the blood of the pagan harpooneers to baptize the harpoon with which he plans to kill Moby Dick and speaks the words "Ego non baptizo te in nomine patris, sed in nomine diaboli" (Mansfield–Vincent, 485). It also appears in even more detail in a sketch labeled "Devil as Quaker" which Melville jotted down, apparently in 1849, in Volume 7 of his set of Shakespeare:

Ego non baptizo te in nominee Patris et
Filii et Spiritus Sancti—sed in nomine
Diaboli. Madness is undefinable—
It & right reasons extremes of one.
Not the (black art) Goetic but Theurgic magic—
seeks converse with the Intelligence, Power, the
Angel.

Thus Melville associated the Latin phrase with various forms of seeking illicit power, presumably including the Sabbat, or perverted worship of the devil, in which infants and others were baptized: Montague Summers, *The History of Witchcraft and Demonology* (New York, 1926), pp. 84–5.
6. On 3 July Bentley had written Melville offering him £150 on account of half profits for his new work. "I think," he added, with obvious misgivings, "that, as we shall be in the same boat, this mode of publication is the most suitable to meet all the contingencies of the case" (Jerman, "More Corre-

spondence," 310).
[From Bentley's point of view these misgivings proved justified. On May 5, 1852 he wrote Melville: ". . . If you will give me permission to make or have made by a judicious literary friend such alterations as are absolutely necessary to "Pierre" being properly appreciated here, I would undertake this; and I will add that I think that you would have no reason to regret this course. Perhaps somebody ignorant of the absolute failure of your former works might be tempted to make a trifling advance on the chance of success; but I learn this in consequence of the reception by the English public of your later works, any new book would have an uphill fight of it and would require a considerable outlay of advertisements to make it pay, much more to yield a profit. I have ventured to speak with great frankness, because I know you will appreciate it. Rely upon it, that if I could reconcile it with prudence, I should not hesitate a moment; but I cannot. I have only to repeat my offer, to publish the New Work if I may be allowed to make such alterations as are actually necessary, not to charge you commission but account for the books at the prices I obtain for them, and to yield you one half of all the net profits.
Believe [me], to be my dear Sir with all truth, with real admiration of your genius and entertaining a sincere value for your friendship . . ." (Jerman, "More Correspondence," 313) *Editors' Note*].

the first step to be taken in this country. Who have any motive in this country to bestir themselves in this thing? Only the authors.—Who are the authors?—A handful. And what influence have they to bring to bear upon any question whose settlement must necessarily assume a political form?—They can bring scarcely any influence whatever. This country & nearly all its affairs are governed by sturdy backwoodsmen—noble fellows enough, but not at all literary, & who care not a fig for any authors except those who write those most saleable of all books nowadays—i e—the newspapers, & magazines. And tho' the number of cultivated, catholic men, who may be supposed to feel an interest in a national literature, is large & every day growing larger; yet they are nothing in comparison with the overwhelming majority who care nothing about it. This country is at present engaged in furnishing material for future authors; not in encouraging its living ones.

Nevertheless, if this matter by any means comes to be made nationally conspicuous; and if you in England come out magnanimously, & protect a foreign author; then there is that sort of stuff in the people here, which will be sure to make them all eagerness in reciprocating. For, be assured, that my countrymen will never be outdone in generosity.—Therefore, if you desire an International Copyright—hoist your flag on your side of the water, & the signal will be answered; but look for no flag on this side till then.

I am now passing thro' the press, the closing sheets of my new work; so that I shall be able to forward it to you in the course of two or three weeks—perhaps a little longer. I shall forward it to you thro' the Office of the Legation. And upon your receipt of it, I suppose you will immediately proceed to printing; as, of course, publication will not take place here, till you have made yourself safe. —You say you will give me your notes at three & six months; I infer that this means from the time of receiving the book. * * *

To *Nathaniel Hawthorne*

PITTSFIELD, MASS., JULY 22, 1851

This is not a letter, or even a note—but only a passing word said to you over your garden gate. I thank you for your easy-flowing long letter (received yesterday) which flowed through me, and refreshed all my meadows, as the Housatonic—opposite me—does in reality. I am now busy with various things—not incessantly though; but enough to require my frequent tinkerings; and this is the height of the haying season, and my nag is dragging me home his winter's dinners all the time. And so, one way and another, I am not yet a disengaged man; but shall be, very soon. Meantime, the earliest good chance I get, I shall roll down to you, my good fellow, seeing

we—that is, you and I—must•hit upon some little bit of vaga-
bondism, before Autumn comes. Graylock—we must go and vaga-
bondize there. But ere we start, we must dig a deep hole, and bury
all Blue Devils, there to abide till the Last Day.

Goodbye,
his x mark.

To Sarah Huyler Morewood [7]

PITTSFIELD, MASS., SEPTEMBER 12, 1851

* * * The "Hour & the Man" is exceedingly acceptable to me.[8]
"Zanoni" is a very fine book in very fine print—but I shall endeavor to surmount that difficulty.[9] At present, however, the Fates
have plunged me into certain silly thoughts and wayward speculations, which will prevent me, for a time, from falling into the reveries of these books—for a fine book is a sort of revery to us—is it
not?—So I shall regard them as my Paradise in store, & Mrs Morewood the goddess from whom it comes.

Concerning my own forthcoming book [1]—it is off my hands, but
must cross the sea before publication here. Dont you buy it—dont
you read it, when it does come out, because it is by no means the
sort of book for you. It is not a peice of fine feminine Spitalfields
silk—but is of the horrible texture of a fabric that should be woven
of ships' cables & hausers. A Polar wind blows through it, & birds
of prey hover over it. Warn all gentle fastidious people from so
much as peeping into the book—on risk of a lumbago & sci-
atics. * * *

To Evert A. Duyckinck

PITTSFIELD, MASS., NOVEMBER 7, 1851

* * * Your letter received last night had a sort of stunning
effect on me. For some days past being engaged in the woods with
axe, wedge, & beetle, the Whale had almost completely slipped
me for the time (& I was the merrier for it) when Crash! comes

7. Sarah Huyler Morewood (1824–1863), the wife of John Rowland Morewood (1821–1903). Sarah Morewood was a lively and volatile person whose energies often directed the parties, picnics, and excursions of the Melvilles' Pittsfield years. She died of tuberculosis before she was forty. Her oldest son, William Barlow Morewood (1847–1923), married Melville's niece, Maria Gansevoort Melville (1849–1935), Allan Melville's oldest daughter.

8. Harriet Martineau's historical romance *The Hour and the Man* was published in 1841 and not republished until 1855.
9. *Zanoni* was another historical romance, by Bulwer-Lytton. The edition is probably that of Harper's, 2 vols. 1842. The type would probably not have seemed "very fine print" to the average reader.
1. *Moby Dick.*

Moby Dick himself (as you justly say) [2] & reminds me of what I have been about for part of the last year or two. It is really & truly a surprising coincidence—to say the least. I make no doubt it is Moby Dick himself, for there is no account of his capture after the sad fate of the Pequod about fourteen years ago.[3]—Ye Gods! What a Commentator is this Ann Alexander whale. What he has to say is short & pithy & very much to the point. I wonder if my evil art has raised this monster.

The Behrings Straits Disaster, too, & the cording along the New Foundland coast of those scores & scores of fishermen, and the inland gales on the Lakes.[4] Verily the pot boileth inside & out. And woe unto us, we but live in the days that have been. Yet even then they found time to be jolly. Why did'nt you send me that inestimable item of "Herman de Wardt" before? [5] Oh had I but had that pie to cut into! But that & many other fine things doubtless are omitted. All one can do is to pick up what chips he can buy[?] round him. They have no Vatican (as you have) in Pittsfield here. * * *

2. Duyckinck had obviously enclosed in his letter a newspaper or magazine clipping that described the sinking of the *Ann Alexander* by a whale on 20 August in the Pacific. Originally printed in the Panama *Herald* of 16 October the story was reprinted in the New York *Daily Tribune* (2 November), and in other papers. Melville's excitement about the disaster is easy to understand in view of its similarity to the sinking of the *Pequod* in *Moby Dick*. One of the *Ann Alexander's* boats had harpooned a whale, which turned and crushed it in its huge jaws to fragments the size of a chair. When another boat joined the chase it turned and crushed that also. Captain Deblois got the survivors of each boat into his own and continued the pursuit from the ship. He avoided one attack, but as he stood in the bow ready to harpoon the whale he suddenly discovered it approaching at the rate of fifteen knots. "*In an instant,*" the story reads, "*the monster struck the ship with tremendous violence, shaking her from stem to stern.*" She sank quickly, barely giving the men a chance to flee into the remaining boats. Unlike the doomed crew of the *Pequod*, however, the sailors of the *Ann Alexander* lived to tell the story.

3. No ship named *Pequod* appears in the records of the American whaling industry prior to the writing of *Moby Dick*. Nor has Melville apparently transferred the name of his fictional ship to a real one, for the only other vessels known to have undergone the *Ann Alexander's* fate were the *Essex* in 1820 and the *Parker Cook* in 1850 (cf. Alexander Starbuck, "History of the American Whale Fishery," in *Report of the Commissioner* [of Fish and Fisheries], *Part IV, 1875–1876*, Washington, 1878). What Melville has apparently done is to pretend, though without deceptive intent, that the imaginary *Pequod* was just as real as the *Ann Alexander*, even assigning its "sad fate" to a point in historical time, just as he insists in *Moby Dick* upon the reality of the story he is telling.

4. The New York *Daily Tribune* of 18 October reported that the whole northern whale fleet, in attempting to make its spring passage through Behring Straits, had got caught in the ice, with loss of or damage to nearly seventy ships. The same issue and others described a gale near Prince Edward Island which sank many vessels and piled up nearly a hundred on the shore (no such disaster at Newfoundland was reported in the New York papers in October or early November). On 23 October a succession of hard gales on Lake Erie sank the *Henry Clay* and did much damage to shipping, but there seem to be no reports of gales in the Great Lakes generally.

5. The allusion is unlocated. Leyda conjectures a reference to Wynkyn de Worde's "Booke of Kervynge," from which an extract appears in *Moby Dick* (Leyda, *Log*, 431).

To Nathaniel Hawthorne

PITTSFIELD, MASS., NOVEMBER 17, 1851

* * * People think that if a man has undergone any hardship, he should have a reward; but for my part, if I have done the hardest possible day's work, and then come to sit down in a corner and eat my supper comfortably—why, then I don't think I deserve any reward for my hard day's work—for am I not now at peace? Is not my supper good? My peace and my supper are my reward, my dear Hawthorne. So your joy-giving and exultation-breeding letter is not my reward for my ditcher's work with that book, but is the good goddess's bonus over and above what was stipulated for—for not one man in five cycles, who is wise, will expect appreciative recognition from his fellows, or any one of them. Appreciation! Recognition! Is love appreciated? Why, ever since Adam, who has got to the meaning of this great allegory—the world? Then we pygmies must be content to have our paper allegories but ill comprehended. I say your appreciation is my glorious gratuity. In my proud, humble way,—a shepherd-king,—I was lord of a little vale in the solitary Crimea; but you have now given me the crown of India. But on trying it on my head, I found it fell down on my ears, notwithstanding their asinine length—for it's only such ears that sustain such crowns.

Your letter was handed me last night on the road going to Mr. Morewood's, and I read it there. Had I been at home, I would have sat down at once and answered it. In me divine magnanimities are spontaneous and instantaneous—catch them while you can. The world goes round, and the other side comes up. So now I can't write what I felt. But I felt pantheistic then—your heart beat in my ribs and mine in yours, and both in God's. A sense of unspeakable security is in me this moment, on account of your having understood the book. I have written a wicked book, and feel spotless as the lamb. Ineffable socialities are in me. I would sit down and dine with you and all the gods in old Rome's Pantheon. It is a strange feeling—no hopefulness is in it, no despair. Content—that is it; and irresponsibility; but without licentious inclination. I speak now of my profoundest sense of being, not of an incidental feeling.

Whence come you, Hawthorne? By what right do you drink from my flagon of life? And when I put it to my lips—lo, they are yours and not mine. I feel that the Godhead is broken up like the bread at the Supper, and that we are the pieces. Hence this infinite fraternity of feeling. Now, sympathizing with the paper, my angel turns over another page. You did not care a penny for the book. But, now and then as you read, you understood the pervading thought that impelled the book—and that you praised. Was it not so? You were archangel enough to despise the imperfect body, and embrace the soul. Once you hugged the ugly Socrates because you saw the flame in the mouth, and heard the rushing of the demon,—the familiar,—and recognized the sound; for you have heard it in your own solitudes.

My dear Hawthorne, the atmospheric skepticisms steal into me now, and make me doubtful of my sanity in writing you thus. But, believe me, I am not mad, most noble Festus! [6] But truth is ever incoherent, and when the big hearts strike together, the concussion is a little stunning. Farewell. Don't write a word about the book. That would be robbing me of my miserly delight. I am heartily sorry I ever wrote anything about you—it was paltry.[7] Lord, when shall we be done growing? As long as we have anything more to do, we have done nothing. So, now, let us add Moby Dick to our blessing, and step from that. Leviathan is not the biggest fish;—I have heard of Krakens.[8]

This is a long letter, but you are not at all bound to answer it. Possibly, if you do answer it, and direct it to Herman Melville, you will missend it—for the very fingers that now guide this pen are not precisely the same that just took it up and put it on this paper. Lord, when shall we be done changing? Ah! it's a long stage, and no inn in sight, and night coming, and the body cold. But with you for a passenger, I am content and can be happy. I shall leave the world, I feel, with more satisfaction for having come to know you. Knowing you persuades me more than the Bible of our immortality.

What a pity, that, for your plain, bluff letter, you should get such gibberish! Mention me to Mrs. Hawthorne and to the children, and so, good-by to you, with my blessing.

Herman.[9]

P.S. I can't stop yet. If the world was entirely made up of Magians, I'll tell you what I should do. I should have a paper-mill established at one end of the house, and so have an endless riband of

6. See Acts 26:24–25, "And as he thus spake for himself, Festus said with a loud voice, Paul, thou art beside thyself; much learning doth make thee mad. But he said, I am not mad, most noble Festus; but speak forth the words of truth and soberness."
7. "Hawthorne and His Mosses," *Literary World* (17, 24 August, 1850).
8. Cf. Joseph C. Hart, *Romance of Yachting: Voyage the First* (New York, 1848), p. 209: "Oh Shakespeare—Immortal bard—Mighty genius—Swan of Avon—thou Unapproachable! Are there no more fish, no more krakens in that wondrous sea from which thou wert taken? Shall there be no more cakes and ale?" See Perry Miller, *The Raven and the Whale* (New York, 1956), pp. 241–2, and Mansfield–Vincent, *Moby Dick*, 277 and n. 753: "There seems some ground to imagine that the great Kraken of Bishop Pontoppodan may ultimately resolve itself into Squid."
9. The one occasion in his letters, except those to members of his family, when Melville signs his first name only.

foolscap rolling in upon my desk; and upon that endless riband I should write a thousand—a million—billion thoughts, all under the form of a letter to you. The divine magnet is on you, and my magnet responds. Which is the biggest? A foolish question—they are *One*.

H.

P.P.S. Don't think that by writing me a letter, you shall always be bored with an immediate reply to it—and so keep both of us delving over a writing-desk eternally. No such thing! I sh'n't always answer your letters, and you may do just as you please.

To Sophia Hawthorne [1]

NEW YORK, JANUARY 8, 1852

* * * I have hunted up the finest Bath I could find, gilt-edged and stamped, whereon to inscribe my humble acknowledgment of your highly flattering letter of the 29th Dec:—It really amazed me that you should find any satisfaction in that book. It is true that some *men* have said they were pleased with it, but you are the only *woman*—for as a general thing, women have small taste for the sea. But, then, since you, with your spiritualizing nature, see more things than other people, and by the same process, refine all you see, so that they are not the same things that other people see, but things which while you think you but humbly discover them, you do in fact create them for yourself—Therefore, upon the whole, I do not so much marvel at your expressions concerning Moby Dick. At any rate, your allusion for example to the "Spirit Spout" [2] first showed to me that there was a subtle significance in that thing—but I did not, in that case, *mean* it. I had some vague idea while writing it, that the whole book was susceptible of an allegoric construction, & also that *parts* of it were—but the speciality of many of the particular subordinate allegories, were first revealed to me, after reading M[r] Hawthorne's letter, which, without citing any particular examples, yet intimated the part-&-parcel allegoricalness of the whole.—But, My Dear Lady, I shall not again send you a bowl of salt water. The next chalice I shall commend, will be a rural bowl of milk.[3] * * *

---

1. Sophia Amelia Peabody (1811–1871) married Nathaniel Hawthorne, 9 July 1842.
2. Cf. *Moby Dick*, chapter 51, "The Spirit Spout."

3. The first reference to *Pierre*. The phrase might have been appropriate to an early stage of the story. Applied to the full novel it could only be ironic.

Analogues and Sources

RALPH WALDO EMERSON

[Journal Entry on a White Whale] †

Boston, Feb. 19 [1834] A seaman in the coach told the story
of an old sperm whale which he called a white whale which was
known for many years by the whalemen as Old Tom & who
rushed upon the boats which attacked him & crushed the boats to
small chips in his jaws, the men generally escaping by jumping overboard & being picked up. A vessel was fitted out at New Bedford,
he said, to take him. And he was finally taken somewhere off Payta
head by the Winslow or the Essex.

J. N. REYNOLDS

Mocha Dick:

OR THE WHITE WHALE OF THE PACIFIC:
A LEAF FROM A MANUSCRIPT JOURNAL. ‡

We expected to find the island of Santa Maria still more remarkable for the luxuriance of its vegetation, than even the fertile
soil of Mocha; and the disappointment arising from the unexpected shortness of our stay at the latter place, was in some degree
relieved, by the prospect of our remaining for several days in safe
anchorage at the former. Mocha lies upon the coast of Chili, in
lat. 38° 28′ south, twenty leagues north of Mono del Bonifacio,
and opposite the Imperial river, from which it bears w. s. w. During the last century, this island was inhabited by the Spaniards,
but it is at present, and has been for some years, entirely deserted.
Its climate is mild, with little perceptible difference of tempera-

† From *The Journals and Miscellaneous
Notebooks of Ralph Waldo Emerson,*
Volume IV, edited by Alfred R. Fer-
guson (Cambridge, Massachusetts: Bel-
knap Press of Harvard University Press,
1964), p. 265. Copyright © 1964 by the
President and Fellows of Harvard Col-
lege; reprinted by permission of Harvard
University Press.
‡ From J. N. Reynolds, "Mocha Dick,"
*The Knickerbocker, New York Monthly
Mazagine,* XIII (May, 1839), 377–92.
This is the chief printed account before

Melville's *Moby-Dick* of the great white
whale of oral legend. For further discussions see Howard P. Vincent, *The Trying-out of Moby-Dick,* and also Janez
Stanonik, *Moby-Dick: The Myth and
the Symbol,* where scattered reports, including one in French in 1837, are
brought together. It has not been shown
that Melville actually saw or used
Reynolds' present account, though he
may have done so; it is useful chiefly as
illustrating the kind of whalemen's
stories he made use of.

ture between the summer and winter seasons. Frost is unknown on the lowlands, and snow is rarely seen, even on the summits of the loftiest mountains.

It was late in the afternoon, when we left the schooner; and while we bore up for the north, she stood away for the southern extremity of the island. As evening was gathering around us, we fell in with a vessel, which proved to be the same whose boats, a day or two before, we had seen in the act of taking a whale. Aside from the romantic and stirring associations it awakened, there are few objects in themselves more picturesque or beautiful, than a whale-ship, seen from a distance of three or four miles, on a pleasant evening, in the midst of the great Pacific. As she moves gracefully over the water, rising and falling on the gentle undulations peculiar to this sea; her sails glowing in the quivering light of the fires that flash from below, and a thick volume of smoke ascending from the midst, and curling away in dark masses upon the wind; it requires little effort of the fancy, to imagine one's self gazing upon a floating volcano.

As we were both standing to the north, under easy sail, at nine o'clock at night we had joined company with the stranger. Soon after, we were boarded by his whale-boat, the officer in command of which bore us the compliments of the captain, together with a friendly invitation to partake the hospitalities of his cabin. Accepting, without hesitation, a courtesy so frankly tendered, we proceeded, in company with Captain Palmer, on board, attended by the mate of the Penguin, who was on his way to St. Mary's to repair his boat, which had some weeks before been materially injured in a storm.

We found the whaler a large, well-appointed ship, owned in New-York, and commanded by such a man as one might expect to find in charge of a vessel of this character; plain, unassuming, intelligent, and well-informed upon all the subjects relating to his peculiar calling. But what shall we say of his first mate, or how describe him? To attempt his portrait by a comparison, would be vain, for we have never looked upon his like; and a detailed description, however accurate, would but faintly shadow forth the *tout ensemble* of his extraordinary figure. He had probably numbered about thirty-five years. We arrived at this conclusion, however, rather from the untamed brightness of his flashing eye, than the general appearance of his features, on which torrid sun and polar storm had left at once the furrows of more advanced age, and a tint swarthy as that of the Indian. His height, which was a little beneath the common standard, appeared almost dwarfish, from the immense breadth of his overhanging shoulders; while the unnatural length of the loose, dangling arms which hung from them, and which, when at rest, had least the appearance of ease, imparted to his uncouth and muscular frame an air of grotesque awkwardness, which defies description. He made few pretensions as a sailor, and had never aspired to the command of a ship. But he would not have exchanged the sensations which stirred his blood, when steering down upon a school of whales, for the privilege of treading, as master, the deck of the noblest liner that ever traversed the Atlantic. According to the admeasurement of his philosophy, whaling was the most dignified and manly of all sublunary pursuits. Of this he felt perfectly satisfied, having been engaged in the noble vocation for upward of twenty years, during which period, if his own assertions were to be received as evidence, no man in the American spermaceti fleet had made so many captures, or met with such wild adventures, in the exercise of his perilous profession. Indeed, so completely were all his propensities, thoughts, and feelings, identified with his occupation; so intimately did he seem acquainted with the habits and instincts of the objects of his pursuit, and so little conversant with the ordinary affairs of life; that one felt less inclined to class him in the genus *homo*, than as a sort of intermediate something between man and the cetaceous tribe.

Soon after the commencement of his nautical career, in order to prove that he was not afraid of a whale, a point which it is essential for the young whaleman to establish beyond question, he offered, upon a wager, to run his boat 'bows on' against the side of an 'old bull,' leap from the 'cuddy' to the back of the fish, sheet his lance home, and return on board in safety. This feat, daring as it may be considered, he undertook and accomplished; at least so it was chronicled in his log, and he was ready to bear witness, on oath, to the veracity of the record. But his conquest of the redoubtable MOCHA DICK, unquestionably formed the climax of his exploits.

Before we enter into the particulars of this triumph, which, through their valorous representative, conferred so much honor on the lancers of Nantucket, it may be proper to inform the reader who and what Mocha Dick was; and thus give him a posthumous introduction to one who was, in his day and generation, so emphatically among fish the 'Stout Gentleman' of his latitudes. The introductory portion of his history we shall give, in a condensed form, from the relation of the mate. Substantially, however, it will be even as he rendered it; and as his subsequent narrative, though not deficient in rude eloquence, was coarse in style and language, as well as unnecessarily diffuse, we shall assume the liberty of altering the expression; of adapting the phraseology to the occasion; and of presenting the whole matter in a shape more succinct and connected. In this arrangement, however, we shall leave our adventurer to tell his *own story*, although not always in his own words, and shall preserve the person of the original.

But to return to Mocha Dick—which, it may be observed, few were solicitous to do, who had once escaped from him. This renowned monster, who had come off victorious in a hundred fights with his pursuers, was an old bull whale, of prodigious size and strength. From the effect of age, or more probably from a freak of nature, as exhibited in the case of the Ethiopian Albino, a singular consequence had resulted—*he was white as wool!* Instead of projecting his spout obliquely forward, and puffing with a short, convulsive effort, accompanied by a snorting noise, as usual with his species, he flung the water from his nose in a lofty, perpendicular, expanded volume, at regular and somewhat distant intervals; its expulsion producing a continuous roar, like that of vapor struggling from the safety-valve of a powerful steam engine. Viewed from a distance, the practised eye of the sailor only could decide, that the moving mass, which constituted this enormous animal, was not a white cloud sailing along the horizon. On the spermaceti whale, barnacles are rarely discovered; but upon the head of this *lusus naturæ*, they had clustered, until it became absolutely rugged with the shells. In short, regard him as you would, he was a most extraordinary fish; or, in the vernacular of Nantucket, 'a genuine old sog,' of the first water.

Opinions differ as to the time of his discovery. It is settled, however, that previous to the year 1810, he had been seen and attacked near the island of Mocha. Numerous boats are known to have been shattered by his immense flukes, or ground to pieces in the crush of his powerful jaws; and, on one occasion, it is said that he came off victorious from a conflict with the crews of three English whalers, striking fiercely at the last of the retreating boats, at the moment it was rising from the water, in its hoist up to the ship's davits. It must not be supposed, howbeit, that through all this desperate warfare, our leviathan passed scathless. A back serried with irons, and from fifty to a hundred yards of line trailing in his wake, sufficiently attested, that though unconquered, he had not proved invulnerable. From the period of Dick's first appearance, his celebrity continued to increase, until his name seemed naturally to mingle with the salutations which whalemen were in the habit of exchanging, in their encounters upon the broad Pacific; the customary interrogatories almost always closing with, 'Any news from Mocha Dick?' Indeed, nearly every whaling captain who rounded Cape Horn, if he possessed any professional ambition, or valued himself on his skill in subduing the monarch of the seas, would lay his vessel along the coast, in the hope of having an opportunity to try the muscle of this doughty champion, who was never known to shun his assailants. It was remarked, nevertheless, that the old fellow seemed particularly careful as to the portion of his body which he exposed to the approach of the boat-steerer; generally presenting, by some well-timed manœuvre, his back to the harpooner; and dexterously evading every attempt to plant an iron under his fin, or a spade on his 'small'. Though naturally fierce, it was not customary with Dick, while unmolested, to betray a malicious disposition. On the contrary, he would sometimes pass quietly round a vessel, and occasionally swim lazily and harmlessly among the boats, when armed with full craft, for the destruction of his race. But this forbearance gained him little credit, for if no other cause of accusation remained to them, his foes would swear they saw a lurking deviltry in the long, careless sweep of his flukes. Be this as it may, nothing is more certain, than that all indifference vanished with the first prick of the harpoon; while cutting the line, and a hasty retreat to their vessel, were frequently the only means of escape from destruction, left to his discomfited assaulters.

Thus far the whaleman had proceeded in his story, and was about commencing the relation of his own individual encounters with its subject, when he was cut short by the mate of the Penguin, to whom allusion has already been made, and who had remained, up to this point, an excited and attentive listener. Thus he would have continued, doubtless, to the end of the chapter, notwithstanding his avowed contempt for every other occupation than sealing, had not an observation escaped the narrator, which tended to arouse his professional jealousy. The obnoxious expression we have forgotten. Probably it involved something of boasting or egotism; for no sooner was it uttered, than our sealer sprang from his seat, and planting himself in front of the unconscious author of the insult, exclaimed:

'*You!*—you whale-killing, blubber-hunting, light-gathering varmint!—*you* pretend to manage a boat better than a Stonington sealer! A Nantucket whaleman,' he continued, curling his lip with a smile of supreme disdain, 'presume to teach a Stonington sealer how to manage a boat! Let all the small craft of your South Sea fleet range among the rocks and breakers where I have been, and if the whales would not have a peaceful time of it, for the next few years, may I never strip another jacket, or book another skin! What's taking a whale? Why, I could reeve a line through one's blow-hole, make it fast to a thwart, and then beat his brains out with my seal-club!'

Having thus given play to the first ebullition of his choler, he proceeded with more calmness to institute a comparison between whaling and sealing. 'A whaler,' said he, 'never approaches land, save when he enters a port to seek fresh grub. Not so the sealer. *He* thinks that his best fortune, which leads him where the form of man has never before startled the game he's after; where a quick eye, steady nerve, and stout heart, are his only guide and defence, in difficulty and danger. Where the sea is roughest, the whirlpool wildest, and the surf roars and dashes madly among the jagged cliffs, there—I was going to say there *only*—are the peak-nosed, black-eyed rogues we hunt for, to be found, gambolling in the white foam, and there must the sealer follow them. Were I to give you an account of my adventures about the Falkland Isles; off the East Keys of Staten Land; through the South Shetlands; off the Cape, where we lived on salt pork and seal's flippers; and finally, the story of a season spent with a single boat's crew on Diego Ramirez,[1] you would not make such a fuss about your Mocha Dick. As to the straits of Magellen, Sir, they are as familiar to me, as Broadway to a New-York dandy; though *it* should strut along that fashionable promenade twelve dozen times a day.'

Our son of the sea would have gone on to particularize his 'hair-breadth 'scapes and moving accidents,' had we not in-terposed, and insisted that the remainder of the night should be devoted to the conclusion of Dick's history; at the same time as-suring the 'knight of the club' that so soon as we met at Santa Maria, he should have an entire evening expressly set apart, on which he might glorify himself and his calling. To this he assented, with the qualification, that his compliance with the general wish, in thus yielding precedence to his rival, should not be construed into an admission, that Nantucket whalemen were the best boatmen in the world, or that sealing was not as honorable and as pretty a business for coining a penny, as the profession of 'blubber-hunting' ever was.

The whaler now resumed. 'I will not weary you,' said he, 'with the uninteresting particulars of a voyage to Cape Horn. Our vessel, as capital a ship as ever left the little island of Nantucket, was finely manned and commanded, as well as thoroughly provided with every requisite for the peculiar service in which she was engaged. I may here observe, for the information of such among you as are not familiar with these things, that soon after a whale-ship from the United States is fairly at sea, the men are summoned aft; then boats' crews are selected by the captain and first mate, and a ship-keeper, at the same time, is usually chosen. The place to be filled by this individual is an important one; and the person designated should be a careful and sagacious man. His duty is, more particularly, to superintend the vessel while the boats are away, in chase of fish; and at these times, the cook and steward are perhaps his only crew.

1. Diego Ramirez is a small island, lying s. w. from Cape Horn.

His station, on these occasions, is at the mast-head, except when he is wanted below, to assist in working the ship. While aloft, he is to look out for whales, and also to keep a strict and tireless eye upon the absentees, in order to render them immediate assistance, should emergency require it. Should the game rise to windward of their pursuers, and they be too distant to observe personal signs, he must run down the jib. If they rise to leeward, he should haul up the spanker; continuing the little black signal-flag at the mast, so long as they remain on the surface. When the 'school' turn flukes, and go down, the flag is to be struck, and again displayed when they are seen to ascend. When circumstances occur which require the return of the captain on board, the colors are to be hoisted at the mizzen peak. A ship-keeper must farther be sure that provisions are ready for the men, on their return from the chase, and that drink be amply furnished, in the form of a bucket of 'switchel.' 'No whale, no switchel,' is frequently the rule; but *I* am inclined to think that, whale or no whale, a little rum is not amiss, after a lusty pull.

'I have already said, that little of interest occurred, until after we had doubled Cape Horn. We were now standing in upon the coast of Chili, before a gentle breeze from the south, that bore us along almost imperceptibly. It was a quiet and beautiful evening, and the sea glanced and glistened in the level rays of the descending sun, with a surface of waving gold. The western sky was flooded with amber light, in the midst of which, like so many islands, floated immense clouds, of every conceivable brilliant dye; while far to the northeast, looming darkly against a paler heaven, rose the conical peak of Mocha. The men were busily employed in sharpening their harpoons, spades, and lances, for the expected fight. The look-out at the mast-head, with cheek on his shoulder, was dreaming of the 'dangers he had passed,' instead of keeping watch for those which were to come; while the captain paced the quarter-deck with long and hasty stride, scanning the ocean in every direction, with a keen, expectant eye. All at once, he stopped, fixed his gaze intently for an instant on some object to leeward, that seemed to attract it, and then, in no very conciliating tone, hailed the mast-head:

' 'Both ports shut?' he exclaimed, looking aloft, and pointing backward, where a long white bushy spout was rising, about a mile off the larboard bow, against the glowing horizon. 'Both ports shut? I say, you leaden-eyed lubber! Nice lazy son of a sea-cook *you* are, for a look-out! Come down, Sir!'

' 'There she blows!—sperm whale—old sog, sir;' said the man, in a deprecatory tone, as he descended from his nest in the air. It was at once seen that the creature was companionless; but as a lone whale is generally an old bull, and of unusual size and ferocity, more than ordinary sport was anticipated, while unquestionably more than ordinary honor was to be won from its successful issue.

'The second mate and I were ordered to make ready for pursuit; and now commenced a scene of emulation and excitement, of which the most vivid description would convey but an imperfect outline, unless you have been a spectator or an actor on a similar occasion. Line-tubs, water-kegs, and wafe-poles, were thrown hurriedly into the boats; the irons were placed in the racks, and the necessary evolutions of the ship gone through, with a quickness almost magical; and this too, amidst what to a landsman would have seemed inextricable confusion, with perfect regularity and precision; the commands of the officers being all but forestalled by the en-thusiastic eagerness of the men. In a short time, we were as near the object of our chase, as it was considered prudent to approach.

' 'Back the main-top-s'l!' shouted the captain. 'There she blows! there she blows!—there she blows!'—cried the look-out, who had taken the place of his sleepy shipmate, raising the pitch of his voice with each announcement, until it amounted to a downright yell. 'Right ahead, Sir!—spout as long an 's thick as the main-yard!'

' 'Stand by to lower!' exclaimed the captain; 'all hands; cook, steward, cooper—every d—d one of ye, stand by to lower!'

'An instantaneous rush from all quarters of the vessel answered this appeal, and every man was at his station, almost before the last word had passed the lips of the skipper.

' 'Lower away!'—and in a moment the keels splashed in the wa-ter. 'Follow down the crews; jump in my boys; ship the crotch; line your oars; now pull, as if the d—l was in your wake!' were the successive orders, as the men slipped down the ship's side, took their places in the boats, and began to give way.

'The second mate had a little the advantage of me in starting. The stern of his boat grated against the bows of mine, at the in-stant I grasped my steering-oar, and gave the word to shove off. One sweep of my arm, and we sprang foaming in his track. Now came the tug of war. To become a first-rate oarsman, you must under-stand, requires a natural gift. My crew were not wanting in the proper qualification; every mother's son of them pulled as if he had been born with an oar in his hand; and as they stretched every sinew for the glory of darting the first iron it did my heart good to see the boys spring. At every stroke, the tough blades bent like willow wands, and quivered like tempered steel in the warm sunlight, as they sprang forward from the tension of the retreating wave. At the distance of half a mile, and directly before us, lay the object of our emulation and ambition, heaving his huge bulk in unwieldly gambols, as though totally unconscious of our approach.

' 'There he blows! An old bull, by Jupiter! Eighty barrels, boys, waiting to be towed alongside! Long and quick—shoot ahead! Now she feels it; waist-boat never could beat us; now she feels the touch!—now she walks through it! Again—*now!*' Such were the broken exclamations and adjurations with which I cheered my rowers to their toil, as, with renewed vigor, I plied my long steering-oar. In another moment, we were alongside our competitor. The shivering blades flashed forward and backward, like sparks of light. The waters boiled under our prow, and the trenched waves closed, hissing and whirling, in our wake, as we swept, I might almost say were *lifted*, onward in our arrowy course.

'We were coming down upon our fish, and could hear the roar of his spouting above the rush of the sea, when my boat began to take the lead.

' 'Now, my fine fellows,' I exclaimed, in triumph, 'now we'll show them our stern—only spring! Stand ready, harpooner, but do n't dart, till I give the word.'

' 'Carry me on, and his name 's *Dennis!*' [2] cried the boat-steerer, in a confident tone. We were perhaps a hundred feet in advance of the waist-boat, and within fifty of the whale, about an inch of whose hump only was to be seen above the water, when, heaving slowly into view a pair of flukes some eighteen feet in width, he went down. The men lay on their oars. 'There he blows, again!' cried the tub-oarsman, as a lofty, perpendicular spout sprang into the air, a few furlongs away on the starboard side. Presuming from his previous movement, that the old fellow had been 'gallied' by other boats, and might probably be jealous of our purpose, I was about ordering the men to pull away as softly and silently as possible, when we received fearful intimation that he had no intention of balking our inclination, or even yielding us the honor of the first attack. Lashing the sea with his enormous tail, until he threw about him a cloud of surf and spray, he came down, at full speed, 'jaws on,' with the determination, apparently, of doing battle in earnest. As he drew near, with his long curved back looming occasionally above the surface of the billows, we perceived that it was *white as the surf around him*; and the men stared aghast at each other, as they uttered, in a suppressed tone, the terrible name of MOCHA DICK!

' 'Mocha Dick or the d—l,' said I, 'this boat never sheers off from any thing that wears the shape of a whale. Pull easy; just give her way enough to steer.' As the creature approached, he somewhat abated his frenzied speed, and, at the distance of a cable's length, changed his course to a sharp angle with our own.

2. A whale's name is "Dennis", when he spouts blood.

' 'Here he comes!' I exclaimed. 'Stand up, harpooner! Do n't be hasty—do n't be flurried. Hold your iron higher—firmer. Now!' I shouted, as I brought our bows within a boat's length of the immense mass which was wallowing heavily by. '*Now!—give it to him solid!*'

'But the leviathan plunged on, unharmed. The young harpooner, though ordinarily as fearless as a lion, had imbibed a sort of superstitious dread of Mocha Dick, from the exaggerated stories of that prodigy, which he had heard from his comrades. He regarded him, as he had heard him described in many a tough yarn during the middle watch, rather as some ferocious fiend of the deep, than a regular-built, legitimate whale! Judge then of his trepidation, on beholding a creature, answering the wildest dreams of his fancy, and sufficiently formidable, without any superadded terrors, bearing down upon him with thrashing flukes and distended jaws! He stood erect, it cannot be denied. He planted his foot—he grasped the coil—he poised his weapon. But his knee shook, and his sinewy arm wavered. The shaft was hurled, but with unsteady aim. It just grazed the back of the monster, glanced off, and darted into the sea beyond. A second, still more abortive, fell short of the mark. The giant animal swept on for a few rods, and then, as if in contempt of our fruitless and childish attempt to injure him, flapped a storm of spray in our faces with his broad tail, and dashed far down into the depths of the ocean, leaving our little skiff among the waters where he sank, to spin and duck in the whirlpool.

'Never shall I forget the choking sensation of disappointment which came over me at that moment. My glance fell on the harpooner. 'Clumsy lubber!' I vociferated, in a voice hoarse with passion; '*you* a whaleman! You are only fit to spear eels! Cowardly spawn! Curse me, if you are not *afraid* of a whale!'

'The poor fellow, mortified at his failure, was slowly and thoughtfully hauling in his irons. No sooner had he heard me stigmatize him as 'afraid of a whale,' than he bounded upon his thwart, as if bitten by a serpent. He stood before me for a moment, with a glowing cheek and flashing eye; then, dropping the iron he had just drawn in, without uttering a word, he turned half round, and sprang head-foremost into the sea. The tub-oarsman, who was re-coiling the line in the after part of the boat, saw his design just in season to grasp him by the heel, as he made his spring. But he was not to be dragged on board again without a struggle. Having now become more calm, I endeavored to soothe his wounded pride with kind and flattering words; for I knew him to be a noble-hearted fellow, and was truly sorry that my hasty reproaches should have touched so fine a spirit so deeply.

'Night being now at hand, the captain's signal was set for our return to the vessel; and we were soon assembled on her deck, discussing the mischances of the day, and speculating on the prospect of better luck on the morrow.

'We were at breakfast next morning, when the watch at the fore-top-gallant head sung out merrily, 'There she breaches!' In an instant every one was on his feet. 'Where away?' cried the skipper, rushing from the cabin, and upsetting in his course the steward, who was returning from the caboose with a replenished biggin of hot coffee. 'Not loud but deep' were the grumblings and groans of that functionary, as he rubbed his scalded shins, and danced about in agony; but had they been far louder, they would have been drowned in the tumult of vociferation which answered the announcement from the mast-head.

' 'Where away?' repeated the captain, as he gained the deck.

' 'Three points off the leeward bow.'

' 'How far?'

' 'About a league, Sir; heads same as we do. There she blows!' added the man, as he came slowly down the shouds, with his eyes fixed intently upon the spouting herd.

' 'Keep her off two points! Steady!—steady, as she goes!'

' 'Steady it is, Sir,' answered the helmsman.

' 'Weather braces, a small pull. Loose to'-gallant-s'ls! Bear a hand, my boys! Who knows but we may tickle their ribs at this rising?'

'The captain had gone aloft, and was giving these orders from the main-to'-gallant-cross-trees. 'There she top-tails! there she blows!' added he, as, after taking a long look at the sporting shoal, he glided down the back stay. 'Sperm whale, and a thundering big school of 'em!' was his reply to the rapid and eager inquiries of the men. 'See the lines in the boats,' he continued; 'get in the craft; swing the cranes!'

'By this time the fish had gone down, and every eye was strained to catch the first intimation of their reäppearance.

' 'There she *spouts!*' screamed a young greenhorn in the main chains, 'close by; a mighty big whale, Sir!'

' 'We'll know that better at the trying out, my son,' said the third mate, drily.

' 'Back the main-top-s'l!' was now the command. The ship had little headway at the time, and in a few minutes we were as motionless as if lying at anchor.

' 'Lower away, all hands!' And in a twinkling, and together, the starboard, larboard, and waist-boats struck the water. Each officer leaped into his own; the crews arranged themselves at their respective stations; the boat-steerers began to adjust their 'craft;' and we left the ship's side in company; the captain, in laconic phrase, bidding us to 'get up and get fast,' as quickly as possible.

'Away we dashed, in the direction of our prey, who were frolicking, if such a term can be applied to their unwieldly motions, on the surface of the waves. Occasionally, a huge, shapeless body would flounce out of its proper element, and fall back with a heavy splash; the effort forming about as ludicrous a caricature of agility, as would the attempt of some over-fed alderman to execute the Highland fling.

'We were within a hundred rods of the herd, when, as if from a common impulse, or upon some preconcerted signal, they all suddenly disappeared. 'Follow me!' I shouted, waving my hand to the men in the other boats; 'I see their track under water; they swim fast, but we 'll be among them when they rise. Lay back,' I continued, addressing myself to my own crew, 'back to the thwarts! Spring *hard!* We'll be in the thick of 'em when they come up; only *pull!*'

'And they did pull, manfully. After rowing for about a mile, I ordered them to 'lie.' The oars were peaked, and we rose to look out for the first 'noddle-head' that should break water. It was at this time a dead calm. Not a single cloud was passing over the deep blue of the heavens, to vary their boundless transparency, or shadow for a moment the gleaming ocean which they spanned. Within a short distance lay our noble ship, with her idle canvass hanging in drooping festoons from her yards; while she seemed resting on her inverted image, which, distinct and beautiful as its original, was glassed in the smooth expanse beneath. No sound disturbed the general silence, save our own heavy breathings, the low gurgle of the water against the side of the boat, or the noise of flapping wings, as the albatross wheeled sleepily along through the stagnant atmosphere. We had remained quiet for about five minutes, when some dark object was descried ahead, moving on the surface of the sea. It proved to be a small 'calf,' playing in the sunshine.

' 'Pull up and strike it,' said I to the third mate; 'it may bring up the old one—perhaps the whole school.'

'And so it did, with a vengeance! The sucker was transpierced, after a short pursuit; but hardly had it made its first agonized plunge, when an enormous cow-whale rose close beside her wounded offspring. Her first endeavor was to take it under her fin, in order to bear it away; and nothing could be more striking than the maternal tenderness she manifested in her exertions to accomplish this object. But the poor thing was dying, and while she vainly tried to induce it to accompany her, it rolled over, and floated dead at her side. Perceiving it to be beyond the reach of her caresses, she turned to wreak her vengeance on its slayers, and made directly for the boat, crashing her vast jaws the while, in a paroxysm of rage. Ordering his boat-steerer aft, the mate sprang forward, cut the line loose from the calf, and then snatched from the crotch the remaining iron, which he plunged with his gathered strength into the body of the mother, as the boat sheered off to avoid her onset. I saw that the work was well done, but had no time to mark the issue; for at that instant, a whale 'breached' at the distance of about a mile from us, on the starboard quarter. The glimpse I caught of the animal in his descent, convinced me that I once more beheld my old acquaintance, Mocha Dick. That falling mass was white as a snow-drift!

'One might have supposed the recognition mutual, for no sooner was his vast square head lifted from the sea, than he charged down upon us, scattering the billows into spray as he advanced, and leaving a wake of foam a rod in width, from the violent lashing of his flukes.

' 'He's making for the bloody water!' cried the men, as he cleft his way toward the very spot where the calf had been killed. 'Here, harpooner, steer the boat, and let me dart!' I exclaimed, as I leaped into the bows. 'May the *'Goneys'* eat me, if he dodge us *this* time, though he were Beelzebub himself! Pull for the red water!'

'As I spoke, the fury of the animal seemed suddenly to die away. He paused in his career, and lay passive on the waves, with his arching back thrown up like the ridge of a mountain. 'The old sog's lying to!' I cried, exultingly. 'Spring, boys! spring *now*, and we have him! All my clothes, tobacco, every thing I 've got, shall be yours, only lay me 'longside that whale before another boat comes up! My *grimky!* what a hump! Only look at the irons in his back! No, do n't *look*—PULL! Now, boys, if you care about seeing your sweethearts and wives in old Nantuck!—if you love Yankee-land—if you love *me*—pull ahead, *wont* ye? Now then, to the thwarts! Lay back, my boys! I feel ye, my hearties! Give her the touch! Only five seas off! *Not* five seas off! One minute—*half* a minute more! Softly—no noise! Softly with your oars! That will do——'

'And as the words were uttered, I raised the harpoon above my head, took a rapid but no less certain aim, and sent it, hissing, deep into his thick white side!

' 'Stern all! for your lives!' I shouted; for at the instant the steel quivered in his body, the wounded leviathan plunged his head beneath the surface, and whirling around with great velocity, smote the sea violently, with fin and fluke, in a convulsion of rage and pain.

'Our little boat flew dancing back from the seething vortex around him, just in season to escape being overwhelmed or crushed. He now started to run. For a short time, the line rasped, smoking, through the chocks. A few turns round the loggerhead then secured it; and with oars a-peak, and bows tilted to the sea, we went leaping onward in the wake of the tethered monster. Vain were all his struggles to break from our hold. The strands were too strong, the barbed iron too deeply fleshed, to give way. So that whether he essayed to dive or breach, or dash madly forward, the frantic creature still felt that he was held in check. At one moment, in impotent rage, he reared his immense blunt head, covered with barnacles, high above the surge; while his jaws fell together with a crash that almost made me shiver; then the upper outline of his vast form was dimly seen, gliding amidst showers of sparkling spray; while streaks of crimson on the white surf that boiled in his track, told that the shaft had been driven home.

'By this time, the whole 'school' was about us; and spouts from a hundred spiracles, with a roar that almost deafened us, were raining on every side; while in the midst of a vast surface of chafing sea, might be seen the black shapes of the rampant herd, tossing and plunging, like a legion of maddened demons. The second and third mates were in the very centre of this appalling commotion.

'At length, Dick began to lessen his impetuous speed. 'Now, my boys,' cried I, 'haul me on; wet the line, you second oarsman, as it comes in. Haul away, ship-mates!—why the devil do n't you haul? Leeward side—*leeward!* I tell you! Do n't you know how to approach a whale?'

'The boat brought fairly up upon his broadside as I spoke, and I gave him the lance just under the shoulder blade. At this moment, just as the boat's head was laid off; and I was straitening for a second lunge, my lance, which I had 'boned' in the first, a piercing cry from the boat-steerer drew my attention quickly aft, and I saw the waist-boat, or more properly a fragment of it, falling through the air, and underneath, the dusky forms of the struggling crew, grasping at the oars, or clinging to portions of the wreck; while a pair of flukes, descending in the midst of the confusion, fully accounted for the catastrophe. The boat had been struck and shattered by a whale!

' 'Good heaven!' I exclaimed, with impatience, and in a tone which I fear showed me rather mortified at the interruption, than touched with proper feeling for the sufferers; 'good heavens!—had n't they sense enough to keep out of the red water! And I must lose this glorious prize, through their infernal stupidity!' This was the first outbreak of my selfishness.

' 'But we must not see them drown, boys,' I added, upon the instant; 'cut the line!' The order had barely passed my lips, when I caught sight of the captain, who had seen the accident from the quarter-deck, bearing down with oar and sail to the rescue.

' 'Hold on!' I thundered, just as the knife's edge touched the line; 'for the glory of old Nantuck, hold on! The captain will pick them up, and Mocha Dick will be ours, after all!'

'This affair occurred in half the interval I have occupied in the relation. In the mean time, with the exception of a slight shudder, which once or twice shook his ponderous frame, Dick lay perfectly quiet upon the water. But suddenly, as though goaded into exertion by some fiercer pang, he started from his lethargy with apparently augmented power. Making a leap toward the boat, he darted perpendicularly downward, hurling the after oarsman, who was helmsman at the time, ten feet over the quarter, as he struck the long steering-oar in his descent. The unfortunate seaman fell, with his head forward, just upon the flukes of the whale, as he vanished, and was drawn down by suction of the closing waters, as if he had been a feather. After being carried to a great depth, as we inferred from the time he remained below the surface, he came up, panting and exhausted, and was dragged on board, amidst the hearty congratulations of his comrades.

'By this time two hundred fathoms of line had been carried spinning through the chocks, with an impetus that gave back in steam the water cast upon it. Still the gigantic creature bored his way downward, with undiminished speed. Coil after coil went over, and was swallowed up. There remained but three flakes in the tub!

' 'Cut!' I shouted; 'cut quick, or he'll take us down!' But as I spoke, the hissing line flew with trebled velocity through the smoking wood, jerking the knife he was in the act of applying to the heated strands out of the hand of the boat-steerer. The boat rose on end, and her bows were buried in an instant; a hurried ejaculation, at once shriek and prayer, rose to the lips of the bravest, when, unexpected mercy! the whizzing cord lost its tension, and our light bark, half filled with water, fell heavily back on her keel. A tear was in every eye, and I believe every heart bounded with gratitude, at this unlooked-for deliverance.

'Overpowered by his wounds, and exhausted by his exertions and the enormous pressure of the water above him, the immense creature was compelled to turn once more upward, for a fresh supply of air. And upward he came, indeed; shooting twenty feet of his gigantic length above the waves, by the impulse of his ascent. He was not disposed to be idle. Hardly had we succeeded in bailing out our swamping boat, when he again darted away, as it seemed to me with renewed energy. For a quarter of a mile, we parted the opposing waters as though they had offered no more resistance than air. Our game then abruptly brought to, and lay as if paralyzed, his massy frame quivering and twitching, as if under the influence of galvanism. I gave the word to haul on; and seizing a boat-spade, as we came near him, drove it twice into his small; no doubt partially disabling him by the vigor and certainty of the blows. Wheeling furiously around, he answered this salutation, by making a desperate dash at the boat's quarter. We were so near him, that to escape the shock of his onset, by any practicable manœuvre, was out of the question. But at the critical moment, when we expected to be crushed by the collision, his powers seemed to give way. The fatal lance had reached the seat of life. His strength failed him in mid career, and sinking quietly beneath our keel, grazing it as he wallowed along, he rose again a few rods from us, on the side opposite that where he went down.

' 'Lay around, my boys, and let us set on him!' I cried, for I saw his spirit was broken at last. But the lance and spade were needless now. The work was done. The dying animal was struggling in a whirlpool of bloody foam, and the ocean far around was tinted with crimson. 'Stern all!' I shouted, as he commenced running impetuously in a circle, beating the water alternately with his head and flukes, and smiting his teeth ferociously into their sockets, with a crashing sound, in the strong spasms of dissolution. 'Stern all! or we shall be stove!'

'As I gave the command, a stream of black, clotted gore rose in a thick spout above the expiring brute, and fell in a shower around, bedewing, or rather drenching us, with a spray of blood.

' *'There's the flag!'* I exclaimed; 'there! thick as tar! Stern! every soul of ye! He 's going in his flurry!' And the monster, under the convulsive influence of his final paroxysm, flung his huge tail into the air, and then, for the space of a minute, thrashed the waters on either side of him with quick and powerful blows; the sound of the concussions resembling that of the rapid discharge of artillery. He then turned slowly and heavily on his side, and lay a dead mass upon the sea through which he had so long ranged a conqueror.

' 'He 's fin up at last!' I screamed, at the very top of my voice. 'Hurrah! hurrah! hurrah!' And snatching off my cap, I sent it spinning aloft, jumping at the same time from thwart to thwart, like a madman.

'We now drew alongside our floating spoil; and I seriously question if the brave commodore who first, and so nobly, broke the charm of British invincibility, by the capture of the Guerriere, felt a warmer rush of delight, as he beheld our national flag waving over the British ensign, in assurance of his victory, than I did, as I leaped upon the quarter deck of Dick's back, planted my wafe-pole in the midst, and saw the little canvass flag, that tells so important and satisfactory a tale to the whaleman, fluttering above my hard-earned prize.

'The captain and second mate, each of whom had been fortunate enough to kill his fish, soon after pulled up, and congratulated me on my capture. From them I learned the particulars of the third mate's disaster. He had fastened, and his fish was sounding, when another whale suddenly rose, almost directly beneath the boat, and with a single blow of his small, absolutely cut it in twain, flinging the bows, and those who occupied that portion of the frail fabric, far into the air. Rendered insensible, or immediately killed by the shock, two of the crew sank without a struggle, while a third, unable in his confusion to disengage himself from the flakes of the tow-line, with which he had become entangled, was, together with the fragment to which the warp was attached, borne down by the harpooned whale, and was seen no more! The rest, some of them severely bruised, were saved from drowning by the timely assistance of the captain.

'To get the harness on Dick, was the work of an instant; and as the ship, taking every advantage of a light breeze which had sprung up within the last hour, had stood after us, and was now but a few rods distant, we were soon under her stern. The other fish, both of which were heavy fellows, lay floating near; and the tackle being affixed to one of them without delay, all hands were soon busily engaged in cutting in. Mocha Dick was the longest whale I ever looked upon. He measured more than seventy feet from his noddle to the tips of his flukes; and yielded one hundred barrels of clear oil, with a proportionate quantity of 'head-matter.' It may emphatically be said, that 'the scars of his old wounds were near his new,' for not less than twenty harpoons did we draw from his back; the rusted mementos of many a desperate rencounter.'

The mate was silent. His yarn was reeled off. His story was told; and with far better tact than is exhibited by many a modern orator, he had the modesty and discretion to stop with its termination. In response, a glass of 'o-be-joyful' went merrily round; and this tribute having been paid to courtesy, the vanquisher of Mocha Dick was unanimously called upon for a song. Too sensible and too good-natured to wait for a second solicitation, when he had the power to oblige, he took a 'long pull' and a strong, at the grog as an appropriate overture to the occasion, and then, in a deep, sonorous tone, gave us the following professional ballad, accompanied by a super-annuated hand-organ, which constituted the musical portion of the cabin furniture:

I.

'Do n't bother my head about catching of seals!
To me there's more glory in catching of eels;
Give me a tight ship, and under snug sail,
And I ask for no more, 'long side the sperm whale,

In the Indian Ocean,
Or Pacific Ocean,
No matter *what* ocean;
    Pull ahead, yo heave O!

II.

'When our anchor's a-peak, sweethearts and wives
Yield a warm drop at parting, breathe a prayer for our lives;
With hearts full of promise, they kiss off the tear
From the eye that grows rarely dim—never with fear!
    Then for the ocean, boys,
    The billow's commotion, boys,
    That's our devotion, boys,
        Pull ahead, yo heave O!

III.

'Soon we hear the glad cry of "Town O!"—there she blows!'
Slow as night, my brave fellows, to leeward she goes:
Hard up! square the yards! then steady, lads, so!
Cries the captain, 'My maiden lance soon shall she know!'
    'Now we get near, boys,
    In with the gear, boys,
    Swing the cranes clear, boys;
        Pull ahead, yo heave O!'

IV.

'Our boat's in the water, each man at his oar
Bends strong to the sea, while his bark bounds before,
As the fish of all sizes, still flouncing and blowing,
With fluke and broad fin, scorn the best of hard rowing:
    'Hang to the oar, boys,
    Another stroke more, boys;
    Now line the oar, boys;
        Pull ahead, yo heave O!'

V.

'Then rises long Tom, who never knew fear;
Cries the captain, 'Now nail her, my bold harpooner!'
He speeds home his lance, then exclaims, 'I am fast!'
While blood, in a torrent, leaps high as the mast:
    'Starn! starn! hurry, hurry, boys!
    She's gone in her flurry, boys,
    She 'll soon be in 'gurry,' boys!
        Pull ahead, yo heave O!'

VI.

'Then give me a whaleman, wherever he be,
Who fears not a fish that can swim the salt sea;
Then give me a tight ship, and under snug sail,
And last lay me 'side of the noble sperm whale;

'In the Indian ocean,
Or Pacific ocean,
No matter *what* ocean;
Pull ahead, yo heave O!'

The song 'died away into an echo,' and we all confessed ourselves delighted with it—save and except the gallant knight of the
seal-club. He indeed allowed the lay and the music to be well
enough, considering the subject; but added: 'If you want to hear
genuine, heart-stirring harmony, you must listen to a rookery of fur
seal. For many an hour, on the rocks round Cape Horn, have I
sat thus, listening to these gentry, as they clustered on the shelving
cliffs above me; the surf beating at my feet, while——'

'Come, come, my old fellow!' exclaimed the captain, interrupting
the loquacious sealer; 'you forget the evening you are to have at
Santa Maria. It is three o'clock in the morning, and more.' Bidding
farewell to our social and generous entertainers, we were soon safely
on board our ship, when we immediately made all sail to the
north.

To me, the evening had been one of singular enjoyment. Doubtless the particulars of the tale were in some degree highly colored,
from the desire of the narrator to present his calling in a prominent
light, and especially one that should eclipse the occupation of
sealing. But making every allowance for what, after all, may be considered a natural embellishment, the facts presented may be
regarded as a fair specimen of the adventures which constitute so
great a portion of the romance of a whaler's life; a life which, view-
ing all the incidents that seem inevitably to grow out of the
enterprise peculiar to it, can be said to have no parallel. Yet vast
as the field is, occupied by this class of our resolute seamen,
how little can we claim to know of the particulars of a whaleman's
existence! That our whale ships leave port, and usually return, in
the course of three years, with full cargoes, to swell the fund of national wealth, is nearly the sum of our knowledge concerning them.
Could we comprehend, at a glance, the mighty surface of the
Indian or Pacific seas, what a picture would open upon us of unparalleled industry and daring enterprise! What scenes of toil along
the coast of Japan, up the straits of Mozambique, where the
dangers of the storm, impending as they may be, are less regarded
than the privations and sufferings attendant upon exclusion from
all intercourse with the shore! Sail onward, and extend your view
around New-Holland, to the coast of Guinea; to the eastern and
western shores of Africa; to the Cape of Good Hope; and south, to
the waters that lash the cliffs of Kergulan's Land, and you are ever
upon the whaling-ground of the American seaman. Yet onward, to
the vast expanse of the two Pacifics, with their countless summer

isles, and your course is still over the common arena and highway of our whalers. The varied records of the commercial world can furnish no precedent, can present no comparison, to the intrepidity, skill, and fortitude, which seem the peculiar prerogatives of this branch of our marine. These characteristics are not the growth of forced exertion; they are incompatible with it. They are the natural result of the ardor of a free people; of a spirit of fearless independence, generated by free institutions. Under such institutions alone, can the human mind attain its fullest expansion, in the various departments of science, and the multiform pursuits of busy life.

OWEN CHASE

[The *Essex* Wrecked by a Whale] †

I have not been able to recur to the scenes which are now to become the subject of description, although a considerable time has elapsed, without feeling a mingled emotion of horror and astonishment at the almost incredible destiny that has preserved me and my surviving companions from a terrible death. Frequently, in my reflections on the subject, even after this lapse of time, I find myself shedding tears of gratitude for our deliverance, and blessing God, by whose divine aid and protection we were conducted through a series of unparalleled suffering and distress, and restored to the bosoms of our families and friends. There is no knowing what a stretch of pain and misery the human mind is capable of contemplating, when it is wrought upon by the anxieties of preservation; nor what pangs and weaknesses the body is able to endure, until they are visited upon it; and when at last deliverance comes; when the dream of hope is realized, unspeakable gratitude takes possession of the soul, and tears of joy choke the utterance. We require to be taught in the school of some signal suffering, privation, and despair, the great lessons of constant dependence upon an almighty forbearance and mercy. In the midst of the wide ocean, at night, when the sight of the heavens was shut out, and the dark tempest came upon us; then it was, that we felt ourselves ready to

† From Owen Chase, *Narrative of the Most Extraordinary and Distressing Shipweck of the Whale-Ship Essex, of Nantucket; Which Was Attacked and Finally Destroyed by a Large Spermaceti-Whale in the Pacific Ocean* * * *. (New York, 1821), pp. 23–41. The selection is all of Ch. 2 and the beginning of Ch. 3, which is given to show how, for dramatic effect, Melville made the *Pequod* sink much faster than did the *Essex*. Melville's extended reference to the *Essex* disaster in *Moby-Dick* is in Ch. 45. His manuscript notes, inserted in his own copy of Chase's *Narrative* are given in the next selection.

exclaim, "Heaven have mercy upon us, for nought but that can save us now." But I proceed to the recital.—On the 20th of November, (cruising in latitude 0° 40' S. longitude 119° 0' W.) a shoal of whales was discovered off the lee-bow. The weather at this time was extremely fine and clear, and it was about 8 o'clock in the morning, that the man at the mast-head gave the usual cry of, "there she blows." The ship was immediately put away, and we ran down in the direction for them. When we had got within half a mile of the place where they were observed, all our boats were lowered down, manned, and we started in pursuit of them. The ship, in the mean time, was brought to the wind, and the main-top-sail hove aback, to wait for us. I had the harpoon in the second boat; the captain preceded me in the first. When I arrived at the spot where we calculated they were, nothing was at first to be seen. We lay on our oars in anxious expectation of discovering them come up somewhere near us. Presently one rose, and spouted a short distance ahead of my boat; I made all speed towards it, came up with, and struck it; feeling the harpoon in him, he threw himself, in an agony, over towards the boat, (which at that time was up alongside of him,) and, giving a severe blow with his tail, struck the boat near the edge of the water, amidships, and stove a hole in her. I immediately took up the boat hatchet, and cut the line, to disengage the boat from the whale, which by this time was running off with great velocity. I succeeded in getting clear of him, with the loss of the harpoon and line; and finding the water to pour fast in the boat, I hastily stuffed three or four of our jackets in the hole, ordered one man to keep constantly bailing, and the rest to pull immediately for the ship; we succeeded in keeping the boat free, and shortly gained the ship. The captain and the second mate, in the other two boats, kept up the pursuit, and soon struck another whale. They being at this time a considerable distance to leeward, I went forward, braced around the main-yard, and put the ship off in a direction for them; the boat which had been stove was immediately hoisted in, and after examining the hole, I found that I could, by nailing a piece of canvass over it, get her ready to join in a fresh pursuit, sooner than by lowering down the other remaining boat which belonged to the ship. I accordingly turned her over upon the quarter, and was in the act of nailing on the canvass, when I observed a very large spermaceti whale, as well as I could judge, about eighty-five feet in length; he broke water about twenty rods off our weather-bow, and was lying quietly, with his head in a direction for the ship. He spouted two or three times, and then disappeared. In less than two or three seconds he came up again, about the length of the ship off, and made directly for us, at the rate of about three knots. The ship was then going with about the same velocity. His appearance and attitude gave us at first no alarm; but while I stood watching his movements, and observing him but a ship's length off, coming down for us with great celerity, I involuntarily ordered the boy at the helm to put it hard up; intending to sheer off and avoid him. The words were scarcely out of my mouth, before he came down upon us with full speed, and struck the ship with his head, just forward of the fore-chains; he gave us such an appalling and tremendous jar, as nearly threw us all on our faces. The ship brought up as suddenly and violently as if she had struck a rock, and trembled for a few seconds like a leaf. We looked at each other with perfect amazement, deprived almost of the power of speech. Many minutes elapsed before we were able to realize the dreadful accident; during which time he passed under the ship, grazing her keel as he went along, came up alongside of her to leeward, and lay on the top of the water, (apparently stunned with the violence of the blow,) for the space of a minute; he then suddenly started off, in a direction to leeward. After a few moments' reflection, and recovering, in some measure, from the sudden consternation that had seized us, I of course concluded that he had stove a hole in the ship, and that it would be necessary to set the pumps going. Accordingly they were rigged, but had not been in operation more than one minute, before I perceived the head of the ship to be gradually settling down in the water; I then ordered the signal to be set for the other boats, which, scarcely had I despatched, before I again discovered the whale, apparently in convulsions, on the top of the water, about one hundred rods to leeward. He was enveloped in the foam of the sea, that his continual and violent thrashing about in the water had created around him, and I could distinctly see him smite his jaws together, as if distracted with rage and fury. He remained a short time in this situation, and then started off with great velocity, across the bows of the ship, to windward. By this time the ship had settled down a considerable distance in the water, and I gave her up as lost. I however, ordered the pumps to be kept constantly going, and endeavoured to collect my thoughts for the occasion. I turned to the boats, two of which we then had with the ship, with an intention of clearing them away, and getting all things ready to embark in them, if there should be no other resource left; and while my attention was thus engaged for a moment, I was aroused with the cry of a man at the hatchway, "here he is—he is making for us again." I turned around, and saw him about one hundred rods directly ahead of us, coming down apparently with twice his ordinary speed, and to me at that moment, it appeared with tenfold fury and vengeance in his aspect. The surf flew in all directions about

him, and his course towards us was marked by a white foam of a
rod in width, which he made with the continual violent thrashing
of his tail; his head was about half out of water, and in that way
he came upon, and again struck the ship. I was in hopes when I
descried him making for us, that by a dexterous movement of
putting the ship away immediately, I should be able to cross the
line of his approach, before he could get up to us, and thus avoid,
what I knew, if he should strike us again, would prove our inevitable destruction. I bawled out to the helmsman, "hard up!" but
she had not fallen off more than a point, before we took the second
shock. I should judge the speed of the ship to have been at this
time about three knots, and that of the whale about six. He struck
her to windward, directly under the cathead, and completely
stove in her bows. He passed under the ship again, went off to
leeward, and we saw no more of him. Our situation at this juncture
can be more readily imagined than described. The shock to our
feelings was such, as I am sure none can have an adequate conception of, that were not there: the misfortune befel us at a moment
when we least dreamt of any accident; and from the pleasing anticipations we had formed, of realizing the certain profits of our labour,
we were dejected by a sudden, most mysterious, and overwhelming
calamity. Not a moment, however, was to be lost in endeavouring
to provide for the extremity to which it was now certain we were
reduced. We were more than a thousand miles from the nearest
land, and with nothing but a light open boat, as the resource of
safety for myself and companions. I ordered the men to cease
pumping, and every one to provide for himself; seizing a hatchet
at the same time, I cut away the lashings of the spare boat, which
lay bottom up across two spars directly over the quarter deck, and
cried out to those near me, to take her as she came down. They did
so accordingly, and bore her on their shoulders as far as the waist of
the ship. The steward had in the mean time gone down into the
cabin twice, and saved two quadrants, two practical navigators, and
the captain's trunk and mine; all which were hastily thrown into
the boat, as she lay on the deck, with the two compasses which I
snatched from the binnacle. He attempted to descend again; but
the water by this time had rushed in, and he returned without
being able to effect his purpose. By the time we had got the boat to
the waist, the ship had filled with water, and was going down
on her beam-ends: we shoved our boat as quickly as possible from
the plank-shear into the water, all hands jumping in her at the
same time, and launched off clear of the ship. We were scarcely
two boat's lengths distant from her, when she fell over to windward,
and settled down in the water.

Amazement and despair now wholly took possession of us. We contemplated the frightful situation the ship lay in, and thought with horror upon the sudden and dreadful calamity that had overtaken us. We looked upon each other, as if to gather some consolatory sensation from an interchange of sentiments, but every countenance was marked with the paleness of despair. Not a word was spoken for several minutes by any of us; all appeared to be bound in a spell of stupid consternation; and from the time we were first attacked by the whale, to the period of the fall of the ship, and of our leaving her in the boat, more than ten minutes could not certainly have elapsed! God only knows in what way, or by what means, we were enabled to accomplish in that short time what we did; the cutting away and transporting the boat from where she was deposited would of itself, in ordinary circumstances, have consumed as much time as that, if the whole ship's crew had been employed in it. My companions had not saved a single article but what they had on their backs; but to me it was a source of infinite satisfaction, if any such could be gathered from the horrors of our gloomy situation, that we had been fortunate enough to have preserved our compasses, navigators, and quadrants. After the first shock of my feelings was over, I enthusiastically contemplated them as the probable instruments of our salvation; without them all would have been dark and hopeless. Gracious God! what a picture of distress and suffering now presented itself to my imagination. The crew of the ship were saved, consisting of twenty human souls. All that remained to conduct these twenty beings through the stormy terrors of the ocean, perhaps many thousand miles, were three open light boats. The prospect of obtaining any provisions or water from the ship, to subsist upon during the time, was at least now doubtful. How many long and watchful nights, thought I, are to be passed? How many tedious days of partial starvation are to be endured, before the least relief or mitigation of our sufferings can be reasonably anticipated. We lay at this time in our boat, about two ship's lengths off from the wreck, in perfect silence, calmly contemplating her situation, and absorbed in our own melancholy reflections, when the other boats were discovered rowing up to us. They had but shortly before discovered that some accident had befallen us, but of the nature of which they were entirely ignorant. The sudden and mysterious disappearance of the ship was first discovered by the boat-steerer in the captain's boat, and with a horror-struck countenance and voice, he suddenly exclaimed, "Oh, my God! where is the ship?" Their operations upon this were instantly suspended, and a general cry of horror and despair burst from the lips of every man, as their looks were directed for her, in vain, over every part of the ocean. They immediately made all haste towards us. The captain's boat was the first that reached us. He stopped about a boat's length off, but had no power to utter a single syllable: he was so completely overpowered with the spectacle before him, that he sat down in his boat, pale and speechless. I could scarcely recognise his countenance, he appeared to be so much altered, awed, and overcome, with the oppression of his feelings, and the dreadful reality that lay before him. He was in a short time however enabled to address the inquiry to me, "My God, Mr. Chase, what is the matter?" I answered, "We have been stove by a whale." I then briefly told him the story. After a few moments' reflection he observed, that we must cut away her masts, and endeavour to get something out of her to eat. Our thoughts were now all accordingly bent on endeavours to save from the wreck whatever we might possibly want, and for this purpose we rowed up and got on to her. Search was made for every means of gaining access to her hold; and for this purpose the lanyards were cut loose, and with our hatchets we commenced to cut away the masts, that she might right up again, and enable us to scuttle her decks. In doing which we were occupied about three quarters of an hour, owing to our having no axes, nor indeed any other instruments, but the small hatchets belonging to the boats. After her masts were gone she came up about two-thirds of the way upon an even keel. While we were employed about the masts the captain took his quadrant, shoved off from the ship, and got an observation. We found ourselves in latitude 0° 40′ S. longitude 119° W. We now commenced to cut a hole through the planks, directly above two large casks of bread, which most fortunately were between decks, in the waist of the ship, and which being in the upper side, when she upset, we had strong hopes was not wet. It turned out according to our wishes, and from these casks we obtained six hundred pounds of hard bread. Other parts of the deck were then scuttled, and we got without difficulty as much fresh water as we dared to take in the boats, so that each was supplied with about sixty-five gallons; we got also from one of the lockers a musket, a small canister of powder, a couple of files, two rasps, about two pounds of boat nails, and a few turtle. In the afternoon the wind came on to blow a strong breeze; and having obtained every thing that occurred to us could then be got out, we began to make arrangements for our safety during the night. A boat's line was made fast to the ship, and to the other end of it one of the boats was moored, at about fifty fathoms to leeward; another boat was then attached to the first one, about eight fathoms astern; and the third boat, the like distance astern of her. Night came on just as we had finished our operations; and such a night as it was to us! so full of feverish and distracting inquietude, that we were deprived en-

tirely of rest. The wreck was constantly before my eyes. I could not,
by any effort, chase away the horrors of the preceding day from my
mind: they haunted me the live-long night. My companions—
some of them were like sick women; they had no idea of the extent
of their deplorable situation. One or two slept unconcernedly,
while others wasted the night in unavailing murmurs. I now had
full leisure to examine, with some degree of coolness, the dreadful
circumstances of our disaster. The scenes of yesterday passed in
such quick succession in my mind that it was not until after many
hours of severe reflection that I was able to discard the idea of the
catastrophe as a dream. Alas! it was one from which there was no
awaking; it was too certainly true, that but yesterday we had existed
as it were, and in one short moment had been cut off from all the
hopes and prospects of the living! I have no language to paint out
the horrors of our situation. To shed tears was indeed altogether
unavailing, and withal unmanly; yet I was not able to deny myself
the relief they served to afford me. After several hours of idle sorrow and repining I began to reflect upon the accident, and endeavoured to realize by what unaccountable destiny or design,
(which I could not at first determine,) this sudden and most
deadly attack had been made upon us: by an animal, too, never before suspected of premeditated violence, and proverbial for its in-
sensibility and inoffensiveness. Every fact seemed to warrant me
in concluding that it was any thing but chance which directed his
operations; he made two several attacks upon the ship, at a short
interval between them, both of which, according to their direction, were calculated to do us the most injury, by being made
ahead, and thereby combining the speed of the two objects for the
shock; to effect which, the exact manœuvres which he made were
necessary. His aspect was most horrible, and such as indicated resentment and fury. He came directly from the shoal which we had
just before entered, and in which we had struck three of his companions, as if fired with revenge for their sufferings. But to this it
may be observed, that the mode of fighting which they always
adopt is either with repeated strokes of their tails, or snapping of
their jaws together; and that a case, precisely similar to this one, has
never been heard of amongst the oldest and most experienced
whalers. To this I would answer, that the structure and strength of
the whale's head is admirably designed for this mode of attack;
the most prominent part of which is almost as hard and as tough
as iron; indeed, I can compare it to nothing else but the inside of a
horse's hoof, upon which a lance or harpoon would not make the
slightest impression. The eyes and ears are removed nearly one-third
the length of the whole fish, from the front part of the head, and are
not in the least degree endangered in this mode of attack. At

all events, the whole circumstances taken together, all happening before my own eyes, and producing, at the time, impressions in my mind of decided, calculating mischief, on the part of the whale, (many of which impressions I cannot now recall,) induce me to be satisfied that I am correct in my opinion. It is certainly, in all its bearings, a hitherto unheard of circumstance, and constitutes, perhaps, the most extraordinary one in the annals of the fishery.

November 21st. The morning dawned upon our wretched company. The weather was fine, but the wind blew a strong breeze from the SE. and the sea was very rugged. Watches had been kept up during the night, in our respective boats, to see that none of the spars or other articles (which continued to float out of the wreck,) should be thrown by the surf against, and injure the boats. At sunrise, we began to think of doing something; what, we did not know: we cast loose our boats, and visited the wreck, to see if any thing more of consequence could be preserved, but every thing looked cheerless and desolate, and we made a long and vain search for any useful article; nothing could be found but a few turtle; of these we had enough already; or at least, as many as could be safely stowed in the boats, and we wandered around in every part of the ship in a sort of vacant idleness for the greater part of the morning. We were presently aroused to a perfect sense of our destitute and forlorn condition, by thoughts of the means which we had for our subsistence, the necessity of not wasting our time, and of endeavouring to seek some relief wherever God might direct us.

HERMAN MELVILLE

[Manuscript Notes on Owen Chase] †

[2]   *General Evidences*

This thing of the Essex is found (stupidly abbreviated) in many compilations of nautical adventure made within the last 15 or 20 years.

The Englishman Bennett in his exact work ("Whaling Voyage round the Globe") quotes the thing as an acknowledged fact.

Besides seamen, several landsman (Judge Shaw & others) acquainted with Nantucket, have evinced to me their unquestioning faith in the thing; having seen Captain Pollard himself, & being conversant with his situation in Nantucket since the disaster.

[3]   *What I Know of Owen Chace &c*

When I was on board the ship Acushnet of Fairhaven, on the passage to the Pacific cruising-grounds, among other matters of forecastle conversation at times was the story of the Essex. It was then that I first became acquainted with her history and her truly astounding fate.

But what then served to specialise my interest at the time was the circumstance that the [4] Second mate of our ship, Mr Hall, an Englishman & Londoner by birth, had for two three-years voyages sailed with Owen Chace (then in command of the whale-ship "William Wirt" * (I think it was) of Nantucket.) This Hall always spoke of Chace with much interest & sincere regard—but he did not seem to know any thing more about him or the Essex affair than any body else.

Somewhere about the latter part of A. D. 1841, in this same ship the Acushnet, we spoke the [5] "Wm Wirt*" of Nantucket, & Owen Chace was the Captain, & so it came to pass that I saw him. He was a large, powerful well-made man; rather tall; to all appearances something past forty-five or so; with a handsome face for a Yankee, & expressive of great uprightness & calm unostentatious courage. His whole appearance impressed me pleasurably. He was the most prepossessing-looking whale-hunter I think I ever saw.

——Being a mear foremast-hand I had no opportunity of conversing with Owen (tho' he was [6] on board our ship for two hours at a time) nor have I ever seen him since.

But I should have before mentioned, that before seeing Chace's ship, we spoke another Nantucket craft & *gammed* with her. In

† Melville inserted several pages of manuscript notes in his copy of Chase's *Narrative*, procured for him in March or April 1851 by his father-in-law, Chief Justice Lemuel Shaw. Just when the notes were written is not clear, but evidently at several successive times. The book, with the notes bound in at the end, is now in the Houghton Library of Harvard University, by permission of whose Librarian, William H. Bond, they are transcribed for publication here. They have been previously published, most fully and notably by B. R. McElderry, Jr., together with a photofacsimile of the original manuscript pages, in an edition of Chase's book titled *Shipwreck of the Whaleship Essex*, Corinth Books, New York, 1962. In our transcription here we have not tried to reproduce Melville's erratic hand exactly; except when there are clear misspellings we give the words with normal spelling. The bracketed page-numbers occur in the manuscript.

Melville's notes contain some errors of fact: it is impossible that the "prepossessing-looking whale-hunter" who came aboard the *Acushnet* was Owen Chase, for he was not at sea at the time; also Chase's son whom Melville met was not the son of the unfaithful wife, and Chase's divorce from her (Justice Shaw presided in the case) had occurred in 1840, before Melville sailed on the *Acushnet*. Melville regularly spells Chase's name Chace.

For discussion of Melville's use of the *Essex* matter, see, besides McElderry's introduction, the article by Henry F. Pommer, "Herman Melville and the Wake of the *Essex*," *American Literature*, XX (November 1948), 290–304, and Vincent's *The Trying-Out of Moby-Dick*.

* See p. 19. of M. S. [*Melville's note; he meant 16, not 19. See p. 599.*]

the forecastle I made the acquaintance of a fine lad of sixteen or thereabouts, a son of Owen Chace. I questioned him concerning his father's adventure; and when I left his ship to return again the next morning (for the two vessels were to sail in company for a few days [7] he went to his chest & handed me a complete copy (same edition as this one) of the *Narrative.* This was the first printed account of it I had ever seen, & the only copy of Chace's Narrative (regular & authentic) except the present one. The reading of this wondrous story upon the landless sea, & close to the very latitude of the shipwreck had a surprising effect upon me. [*Pages 8-13 are blank.*]

[14]   Authorship of the Book

There seems no reason to suppose that Owen himself wrote the Narrative. It bears obvious tokens of having been written for him; but at the same time, its whole air plainly evinces that it was carefully & conscientiously written to Owen's dictation of the facts.—It is almost as good as tho' Owen wrote it himself.

[15]   Another Narrative of the Adventure

I have been told that Pollard the Captain, wrote, or caused to be wrote under his own name, his version of the story. I have seen extracts purporting to be from some such work. But I have never seen the work itself.—I should imagine Owen Chace to have been the fittest person to narrate the thing.

[16]   Note

Vide ante p.p. 4-5, M.S.
    I was doubtful a little at the time of writing whether this ship was the Wm. Wirt. I am now certain that it was the *Charles Carroll* of which Owen Chace was Captain for several voyages.

[17]

Since writing the foregoing I—sometime about 1850-3—saw Capt. Pollard on the island of Nantucket, and exchanged some words with him. To the islanders he was a nobody—to me, the most [18] impressive man, tho' wholly unassuming, even humble —that I ever encountered. [*Pages 19-20 are missing.*]

[21]   Sequel

——I can not tell exactly how many more pages the complete narrative contains—but at any rate, very little more remains to be related.—The boat was picked up by the ship, & the poor fellows were landed in Chili & in timê sailed for home. Owen Chace returned to his business of whaling, & in due time became a Captain, as related in the beginning.

Captain Pollard's boat (from which Chace's had become separated) was also after a miserable time, picked up by a ship, but not [22] until two of its crew had died delirious, & furnished food for the survivors.

The third boat, it does not appear, that it was ever heard of, after its sub-separation from Pollard's.

Pollard himself returned to Nantucket, & subsequently sailed on another whaling voyage to the Pacific, but he had not been in the Pacific long, when one night, his ship went ashore on unknown rocks, & was dashed to peaces. The crew, with Pollard, put off in their boats, & were soon picked up by [23] another whale-ship, with which, the day previous, they had sailed in company.—I got this from Hall, Second Mate of the *Acushnet*.—

Pollard, it seems, now took the hint, & after reaching home from this second shipwreck, vowed to abide ashore. He has ever since lived in Nantucket. Hall told me that he became a butcher there. I believe he is still living. [*Added in pencil and underlined three times:* A night-watchman]

Concerning the three men left on the island;—they were taken off at last (in a sad state enough) by a ship, which [24] purposely touched there for them, being advised of them, by their shipmates who had been previously landed in Chili.

——All the sufferings of these miserable men of the Essex might, in all human probability, have been avoided, had they, immediately after leaving the wreck, steered straight for Tahiti, from which they were not very distant at the time, & to which, there was a fair Trade wind. But they dreaded cannibals, & strange to tell knew not that for more than 20 years, the English [25] missionaries had been resident in Tahiti; & that in the same year of the shipwreck—1820— it was entirely safe for the mariner to touch at Tahiti.

——But they chose to stem a head wind, & make a passage of several thousand miles (an unavoidably roundabout one, too) in order to gain a civilised harbor on the coast of South America.

[26]   *Further Concerning Owen Chace*

The miserable pertinaciousness of misfortune which pursued Pollard the Captain, in his second disaster & entire shipwreck, did likewise hunt poor Owen, tho' somewhat more dilatory in over-taking him, the second time.

For, while I was in the *Acushnet* we heard from some whale-ship that we spoke, that the Captain of the "*Charles Carrol*"—that is

Owen Chace—had recently received letters from home, informing him of the certain infidelity of his wife, the mother of several children, one of them being the lad of sixteen, whom I alluded to as giving me a copy of his father's narrative to read. We also heard that this receipt of this news had told most heavily upon Chace, & that he was a prey to the deepest gloom.

HOWARD P. VINCENT

[Sources of "The Try-Works"] †

"Looking into the red heat of the fire"

In "The Try-Works" (96), Melville takes up the most spectacular of all the operations in the sperm whale fishery: the trying-out of the blubber in the try-pots resting in a great brick oven built on the deck. Into these two great try-pots the crew tossed the chunks of blubber, the "bible-leaves" minced into thin slices by the "archbishoprick" in his strange cassock. Frederick Debell Bennett described the entire process succinctly in *A Whaling Voyage Round the Globe:*

> Previous to being boiled, or "tryed-out," the blubber is cleared from adhering flesh, and cut with spades into slips, or "horsepieces," which, (after they had been "minced," or scored by a broad and thin knife, upon an elevated block of wood, termed the "horse,") are consigned to the boilers of the try-works. The "head" is first boiled, and its produce kept as distinct as possible from the "Body"; since the one is considered as Spermaceti, or "head-matter," and the other as Sperm-oil.
>
> It must be regarded as a curious circumstance, and as one highly essential to the economy of these ships, that the process of boiling the oil supplies also the fuel required for that purpose; the "scraps," or refuse from which the oil has been extracted, burning, when placed in the furnace, with a fierce and clear flame and intense heat, and being sufficient in quantity to render any other fuel unnecessary; the scraps remaining from one affair of oil being reserved to commence a second.
>
> In a dark night, the process of "trying out" in the open ocean presents a spectacle partaking much of the grand and terrific. The dense volumes of smoke that roll before the wind and over the side of the vessel, as she pursues her course through the water— the roaring of the flames, bursting in lofty columns from the

† From Howard P. Vincent, *The Trying-Out of Moby-Dick* (Boston: Houghton Mifflin Company, 1949), pp. 329–36. Copyright 1949 by Howard P. Vincent; reprinted by permission of the author.

works, and illuminating the ship and surrounding expanse of sea—
and the uncouth garb and implements of the crew, assembled
around the fires—produce a peculiarly imposing effect; though
one that is not altogether to be reconciled with the ordinary
character of marine scenery.

Bennett's description, especially in the last paragraph, probably
contributed to Melville's account of the try-works; it is almost certain that Melville had read it. More important borrowing is to be
found in comparing the words of *Moby-Dick* with J. Ross Browne's
description in *Etchings of a Whaling Cruise*. Writing with a fuller
feeling for the picturesque qualities of the scene than had Bennett,
Browne exploited the sensational possibilities of his material at
greater length and with more imaginative sweep, the allusions to
Salvator Rosa and Dante, for instance, adding considerably to the
superiority of his version:

> A "trying-out" scene is the most stirring part of the whaling
> business, and certainly the most disagreeable. . . . We will now
> imagine the works in full operation at night. Dense clouds of
> lurid smoke are curling up to the tops, shrouding the rigging
> from the view. The oil is hissing in the try-pots. Half a dozen
> of the crew are sitting on the windlass, their rough, weather-
> beaten faces shining in the red glare of the fires, all clothed
> in greasy duck, and forming about as savage a looking group as
> ever was sketched by the pencil of Salvator Rosa. The cooper
> and one of the mates are raking up the fires with long bars of
> wood or iron. The decks, bulwarks, railing, try-works, and wind-
> lass are covered with oil, and slime of black-skin, glistening with
> the red glare from the try-works. Slowly and doggedly the vessel
> is pitching her way through the rough seas, looking as if enveloped
> in flames. . . .
>
> . . . A trying-out scene has something peculiarly wild and
> savage in it; a kind of indescribable uncouthness, which renders
> it difficult to describe with anything like accuracy. There is a
> murderous appearance about the blood-stained decks, and the
> huge masses of flesh and blubber lying here and there, and a
> ferocity in the looks of the men, heightened by the red, fierce
> glare of the fires, which inspire in the mind of the novice feelings
> of mingled disgust and awe. But one soon becomes accustomed
> to such scenes and regards them with the indifference of a veteran
> in the field of battle. I know of nothing to which this part of the
> whaling business can be more appropriately compared than to
> Dante's pictures of the infernal regions. It requires but little
> stretch of the imagination to suppose the smoke, the hissing
> boilers, the savage-looking crew, and the waves of flame that
> burst now and then from the flues of the furnace, part of the
> paraphernalia of a scene in the lower regions.

Browne's passage is excellent—compact and vivid, alive to surfaces and lights. To improve on it was a challenge to Melville's subtlest skill. How he met and surpassed Browne may be seen by studying this short sample from *Moby-Dick*:

> The hatch, removed from the top of the works, now afforded a wide hearth in front of them. Standing on this were the Tartarean shapes of the pagan harpooneers, always the whale-ship's stokers. With huge pronged poles they pitched hissing masses of blubber into the scalding pots, or stirred up the fires beneath, till the snaky flames darted, curling, out of the doors to catch them by the feet. The smoke rolled away in sullen heaps. To every pitch of the ship there was a pitch of the boiling oil, which seemed all eagerness to leap into their faces. Opposite the mouth of the works, on the further side of the wide wooden hearth, was the windlass. This served for a sea-sofa. Here lounged the watch, when not otherwise employed, looking into the red heat of the fire, till their eyes felt scorched in their heads. Their tawny features, now all begrimed with smoke and sweat, their matted beards, and the contrasting barbaric brilliancy of their teeth, all these were strangely revealed in the capricious emblazonings of the works. As they narrated to each other their unholy adventures, their tales of terror told in words of mirth; as their uncivilized laughter forked upwards out of them, like the flames from the furnace; as to and fro, in their front, the harpooneers wildly gesticulated with their huge pronged forks and dippers; as the wind howled on, and the sea leaped, and the ship groaned and dived, and yet steadfastly shot her red hell further and further into the blackness of the sea and the night, and scornfully champed the white bone in her mouth, and viciously spat round her on all sides; then the rushing Pequod, freighted with savages, and laden with fire, and burning a corpse, and plunging into that blackness of darkness, seemed the material counterpart of her monomaniac commander's soul.

Stirred by his personal memories and by the graphic accounts in Browne and Bennett,[1] Melville has deepened his description by developing the Dantesque associations suggested in *Etchings*. Melville etches every detail with the sharpness, and the feeling for

1. And also, possibly by *Ribs and Trucks* (Boston, 1842): "but one thing, I pray thee forget not to honor with a parting glance—a night-scene around the 'try-works';—it is too like purgatory, to be neglected. Three ovens, amidships, surmounted by three huge cauldrons of oil; the oil boiling, the ovens lapping out tongues of flickering flame; the watch clustering and flitting and gibbering, in a light now lurid, now livid—some feeding the gaping furnaces with fuel, some couchant on the windlass, 'spinning yarns'; one brandishing a mighty fork, another 'spairging about the brumstane cootie,' with a long, long ladle, and occasionally anointing the fire, till it makes the rigging and the sails and the weltering waters gleam again in its blaze; and each busy, smutty, diabolical-looking figure at hand flash into second daylight;—all, together, afford a spectacle 'beautiful as rare,' and leave nothing to be guessed at, would you fancy to yourself a 'situation' in the freehold of 'auld Nickie-Ben.' "

chiaroscuro, of a Rembrandt, and to the photographic fidelity of his words he adds a haunting suggestiveness Ryderesque in quality. What shows Melville's skill most completely, however, is the way in which he subordinates and unites his word-painting to the characterization of Ahab and to the emotional-philosophical currents of *Moby-Dick*. Interesting though it is in itself, the description is fused with the total structure of the novel. Here, certainly, is a single fact described not only for itself but also for its implications—a fact seen in its totality.

Although such an unforgettable bit of wit as the description of the smoke from the try-works, "It smells like the left-wing of the day of judgment," may possibly have been inspired by Browne's down-Easter who, choking with the fumes, swore: "if this warn't he–l on a small scale, he didn't know what to call it"; nevertheless, Melville's entire chapter reaches heights of meaning independent of, although extended from, fish documents. From the masterly exposition of the trying-out process Melville modulates back to his original theme, Selfhood, and to his original character, Ishmael.

Ishmael's vantage point from which he had seen the trying-out had been the tiller of the ship, apart but not far from the flaming try-pots. The physical separation suggests spiritual separation as well, which Melville subtly points up by having Ishmael describe the crew as capering fiend shapes much like flickering shapes moving about a great cauldron of evil. Watching the whalemen's sabbath, "that night, in particular, a strange (and ever since inexplicable) thing occurred to me." Ishmael fell into a doze.

I was half conscious of putting my fingers to the lids and mechanically stretching them still further apart. But, spite of all this, I could see no compass before me to steer by; though it seemed but a minute since I had been watching the card, by the steady binnacle lamp illuminating it. Nothing seemed before me but a jet gloom, now and then made ghastly by flashes of redness. Uppermost was the impression, that whatever swift, rushing thing I stood on was not so much bound to any haven ahead as rushing from all havens astern. A stark, bewildered feeling, as of death, came over me. Convulsively my hands grasped the tiller, but with the crazy conceit that the tiller was, somehow, in some enchanted way, inverted. My God! what is the matter with me? thought I. Lo! in my brief sleep I had turned myself about, and was fronting the ship's stern, with my back to her prow and the compass. In an instant I faced back, just in time to prevent the vessel from flying up into the wind, and very probably capsizing her. How glad and how grateful the relief from this unnatural hallucination of the night, and the fatal contingency of being brought by the lee!

The episode is dramatic, arising naturally but suddenly out of the rich painting of the preceding paragraphs. We may never know whether Melville was transferring journalistic fact to his novel, but it is possible to suggest that the scene may have been built from one which he had already used. The narrow escape of the *Pequod* suggests a similar event in *White-Jacket*, in which the *Neversink* is saved just in the nick of time when "Mad Jack" mutinously countermands the previous orders of Captain Claret. In *White-Jacket* Melville uses the scene to point up his contrast between the efficiency of the subordinate as against the bungling stupidity of the superior. Melville adapted this scene from a little volume entitled *Scenes in "Old Ironsides."* Possibly the idea of the ship saved at the last minute by a reversal of controls, which we have here in *Moby-Dick*, was Melville's second adaptation of an episode which had already served him well.

But whatever the source of the narrative section of "The Try-Works," Melville's manipulation of the episode is of course uniquely his own. What is the secondary meaning of the event? Ishmael, remember, said that it was "inexplicable." May it not illustrate the folly of isolation from the social norm, the sinfulness of what Hawthorne has called the Unpardonable Sin, when man has "lost his hold of the magnetic chain of humanity"? Melville makes the point obliquely through symbolism:

> Look not too long in the face of the fire, O man! Never dream with thy hand on the helm! Turn not thy back to the compass; accept the first hint of the hitching tiller; believe not the artificial fire, when its redness makes all things look ghastly. To-morrow, in the natural sun, the skies will be bright; those who glared like devils in the forking flames, the morn will show in far other, at least gentler, relief; the glorious, golden, glad sun, the only true lamp—all others but liars!

Without the capacity to sense our relatedness to our fellows we cut ourselves off from the capacity for change, and starve or destroy ourselves. One needs an awareness of one's separate identity but too complete a separation cuts us from human growth.

In the chapter on "The Mast-Head" Melville had satirized the neo-Platonic idealist, his identity lost in the infinite, dreamily unable to keep a sharp eye for the physical and harsh facts (symbolized by the whales) and therefore in imminent danger of plunging from the masthead into the Descartian vortices of the sea. If Transcendentalism errs in too great an insistence on unity and too little heeds multiety, it also errs in too great an insistence on self-reliance. Too great an emphasis on self, he says implicatively, may lead to self-destruction just as surely as too great a disregard for appearances had done. Ishmael looking at the whalemen, his fellow crew members, pitchforking the blubber, saw them pictorially and then metaphorically as devils from hell—but himself at the tiller as none. (Such confidence in his own selfhood was almost suicide —and the destruction of the crew.) These devils in the forking flames will show in the next morning's sun as human beings like himself. Man—Ishmael—may look into the fire to see the demonic shapes, but he must also recognize them as his own companions also.

The flame into which Ishmael stares resembles the lime-kiln fire into which Ethan Brand, in Hawthorne's story of that title, had too long gazed and by which he is destroyed. In both "Ethan Brand" and *Moby-Dick* the fire symbolizes the demonic and irrational forces to which Freud gave the name the "Id"; the bawdy, mae-nadic, and orgiastic foundations of the human personality. Amiel describes his fear at facing these terrifying, subterranean forces: "I too have been reduced to nothingness, and I shudder on the brink of the great abysses that yawn within my being, in the grip of a longing for the unknown, weakened by a thirst for the infinite, humbled before the ineffable." Ethan Brand and, momentarily, Ishmael were guilty, in Hawthorne's words, of "the sin of an intellect that triumphed over the sense of brotherhood with man and reverence for God, and sacrificed everything to its own mighty claims!" Melville had already indicated his awareness of the abysses of the human soul [2] when he wrote in *Mardi*: "To scale great heights, we must come out of lowermost depths. The way to heaven is through hell. We need fiery baptisms in the fiercest flames of our own bosoms," a passage similar in insight to Milton's famous dictum:

> The mind is its own place and in itself
> Can make a heaven of hell, a hell of heaven.

Here, in "The Try-Works," Melville implies again the necessity of the fiery baptism, for, as he says, "the sun hides not Virginia's Dismal Swamp, nor Rome's accursed Campagna, nor wide Sahara, nor all the millions of miles of deserts and griefs beneath the moon. . . . So, therefore, that mortal man who hath more of joy than sorrow in him, that mortal man cannot be true—not true, or undeveloped." The fire of the primitive Self must be recog-nized, but abandonment to it means spiritual death; Melville's warning is specific:

2. Compare Nietzsche's Apothegm 146 from *Beyond Good and Evil:* "He who fights with monsters should be careful lest he thereby become a monster. And if thou gaze long into an abyss, the abyss will also gaze into thee." Some student might well study Melville's markings in his volumes of Nietzsche (written of course long after *Moby-Dick*) to see how Melville was im-pressed by the German writer and also to see how Melville had anticipated his thought.

Give not thyself up, then, to fire, lest it invert thee, deaden thee; as for the time it did me. There is a wisdom that is woe; but there is a woe that is madness. And there is a Catskill eagle in some souls that can alike dive down into the blackest gorges, and soar out of them again and become invisible in the sunny spaces. And even if he for ever flies within the gorge, that gorge is in the mountains; so that even in his lowest swoop the mountain eagle is still higher than other birds upon the plain, even though they soar.

"Art," Fauré wrote, "is therefore a game, as the philosophers have called it. It is a matter of dancing on the edge of the abyss, or hiding it with flowers." And so, implies Melville, is Life; it is a mean between unfettered Selfhood and regimented sociality. But looking into depths of the try-works Ishmael found what Gerard Manley Hopkins later discerned:

> . . . O the mind, mind has mountains; cliffs of fall
> Frightful, sheer, no-man-fathomed.

Into these blackest gorges of Life only Catskill eagles like Shakespeare and Melville dive to explore the depths of tragic horror, then soar to the heights of human—individual and social—experience, recorded for us in ambiguous symbol.

DAVID H. BATTENFELD

The Source for the Hymn in *Moby-Dick* †

In Herman Melville's *Moby-Dick*, before Father Mapple preaches his now famous sermon, he leads his congregation in a hymn which, as Yvor Winters remarks, "contains the essence of the sermon." [1] A critical edition of *Moby-Dick* notes:

> No original has been found for this hymn. Its aptness for Melville's artistic purposes and the imaginative freedom with which it was written (notably in the avoidance of the conventional rhyme in the fourth stanza) suggest that Melville himself was the author. [2]

Nevertheless, an original does exist. The source is the rhymed version of the first part of Psalm 18, as found in the psalms and

† From David H. Battenfeld, "The Source for the Hymn in *Moby-Dick*," *American Literature*, XXVII (November, 1955), 393–96. Reprinted by permission of Duke University Press.

1. *In Defense of Reason* (Denver, 1947), p. 206.
2. Edited by Luther Mansfield and Howard Vincent (New York, 1952), p. 616.

hymns of the Reformed Protestant Dutch Church, the Church in which Melville was brought up.[3] Needing an appropriate hymn for his artistic purposes, Melville may have remembered this psalm from his youth, or he may simply have gone looking through the hymnal. In any case, the subtitle, "Deliverance from despair," surely caught his attention, for Jonah's plight is parallel to that of the psalmist. The Psalm, however, speaks only of a very generalized situation; Melville's problem therefore was to alter it to fit the specific reference to the story of Jonah. How well he succeeded may be best seen in a line-by-line comparison of the two versions.

Psalm 18. First Part. L.M.
Deliverance from despair.

Melville's version.

1 Thee will I love, O Lord, my strength,
My rock, my tower, my high defence:
Thy mighty arm shall be my trust:
For I have found salvation thence.

2 Death, and the terrors of the grave,
Spread over me their dismal shade;
While floods of high temptations rose,
And made my sinking soul afraid.

"The ribs and terrors in the whale,
Arched over me a dismal gloom,
While all God's sun-lit waves rolled by,
And left me deepening down to doom.

3 I saw the opening gates of hell,
With endless pains and sorrows there,
Which none but they that feel, can tell;
While I was hurried to despair.

"I saw the opening maw of hell,
With endless pains and sorrows there;
Which none but they that feel can tell—
Oh, I was plunging to despair.

4 In my distress I call'd my God,
When I could scarce believe him mine;
He bow'd his ear to my complaints;
Then did his grace appear divine.

"In black distress, I called my God,
When I could scarce believe him mine,
He bowed his ear to my complaints—
No more the whale did me confine.

3. *The Psalms and Hymns . . . of the Reformed Protestant Dutch Church in North America* (Philadelphia, 1854), pp. 34–35. This book was compiled by Dr. John H. Livingston in 1789, and was expanded in 1830 and 1846. The volume cited was approved by the General Synod in 1846.

5 With speed he flew to my relief,
　As on a cherub's wings he rode:
　Awful and bright as lightning shone
　The face of my deliv'rer, God.

"With speed he flew to my relief,
　As on a radiant dolphin borne;
　Awful, yet bright, as lightning shone
　The face of my Deliverer God.

6 Temptations fled at his rebuke,
　Dispell'd by his almighty breath:
　He sent salvation from on high,
　And drew me from the depths of death.

7 Great were my fears, my foes were great,
　Much was their strengh, and more their rage,
　But Christ, my Lord, is conqu'ror still,
　In all the wars that devils wage.

8 My song for ever shall record
　That terrible, that joyful hour;
　And give the glory to the Lord,
　Due to his mercy and his pow'r.

"My song for ever shall record
　That terrible, that joyful hour;
　I give the glory to my God,
　His all the mercy and the power."

Melville omits the first stanza of the Psalm. Since it sums up the theme, his narrative purpose is thereby enhanced, and he is able to fit his hymn to the Jonah story from the beginning. The second stanza is almost completely rewritten to state Jonah's situation, though both the meter and rhyme scheme are adhered to. The use of "ribs" makes natural the substitution of "arched" for "spread." The rest of the changes were probably suggested by the Book of Jonah: "For thou hadst cast me into the deep, in the midst of the seas; and the floods compassed me about: all thy billows and thy waves passed over me." [4] The rhyme change may be only for assonance and the alliteration in the last line,[5] but it should be observed that the Bible makes no mention of Jonah's fear, only of his state of despair. It is interesting that Melville rejects the natural word "floods" in the Psalm, even though it also appears in the

4. Jonah: 2:3 (King James version).
5. It seems to me conclusive from the tense of the source that Melville's verb should be "left," as in the first English edition, rather than "lift," as most commonly reprinted.

Jonah story.

The change of "gates" to "maw" in stanza three of the Psalm is in keeping with the whale imagery, and the changes in the final line of the stanza heighten the emotional quality and substitute a more vividly specific image. Melville's substitution of "black" for "my" in the fourth stanza is also an improvement, and his revision of the final line is most skilful, enabling him as it does to keep the rhyme. Likewise, in the next stanza the change from the cherub to the dolphin is ingenious. "Borne" eliminates the partial rhyme of "rode" and "God," but manages to get another partial rhyme with "shone." The substitution of "yet" for "and" may be explained by the change in meaning of "awful" from the older "filling with awe" to the more modern "terrible," the sense that Melville usually gives it.

The sixth and seventh stanzas of the Psalm are rejected by Melville. They deal with "temptations" and "wars that devils wage," and as such are not apt for the Jonah story. Jonah is not subject to temptations, but rather suffering just punishment for his sin. In the final stanza, Melville changes "Lord" to "God," avoiding a rhyme, and revises the final line to get rid of the awkward initial trochaic foot.

We observe that Melville's changes and revisions are of two kinds. Substantially, they are to change the generalized theme of the Psalm to attain specific correspondence to the story of Jonah. The omission of three stanzas is fairly automatic, but the revisions within the stanzas used demonstrate a very real ability to keep within the framework of his source while substituting particularized relevant material. Also, a number of changes are purely stylistic, and in every case I believe they are an improvement on the original. Thus, this single example of poetic revision from a given source shows the same kind of imaginative re-creation as do those prose revisions that have been studied at length, in *Moby-Dick* and elsewhere, and again raises the question whether sources as yet undiscovered exist for many other key Melville passages—possibly even Father Mapple's sermon itself.

Criticism

Contemporary Reviews:
1851–1853

EVERT A. DUYCKINCK

[An Intellectual Chowder] †

A difficulty in the estimate of this, in common with one or two other of Mr. Melville's books, occurs from the double character under which they present themselves. In one light they are romantic fictions, in another statements of absolute fact. When to this is added that the romance is made a vehicle of opinion and satire through a more or less opaque allegorical veil, as particularly in the latter half of Mardi, and to some extent in this present volume, the critical difficulty is considerably thickened. It becomes quite impossible to submit such books to a distinct classification as fact, fiction, or essay. Something of a parallel may be found in Jean Paul's German tales, with an admixture of Southey's Doctor. Under these combined influences of personal observation, actual fidelity to local truthfulness in description, a taste for reading and sentiment, a fondness for fanciful analogies, near and remote, a rash daring in speculation, reckless at times of taste and propriety, again refined and eloquent, this volume of Moby Dick may be pronounced a most remarkable sea-dish—an intellectual chowder of romance, philosophy, natural history, fine writing, good feeling, bad sayings—but over which, in spite of all uncertainties, and in spite of the author himself, predominates his keen perceptive faculties, exhibited in vivid narration.

There are evidently two if not three books in Moby Dick rolled into one. Book No. I. we could describe as a thorough exhaustive account admirably given of the great Sperm Whale. The information is minute, brilliantly illustrated, as it should be—the whale himself so generously illuminating the midnight page on which his memoirs are written—has its level passages, its humorous touches, its quaint suggestion, its incident usually picturesque and occasionably sublime. All this is given in the most delightful manner

† From Evert A. Duyckinck, "Melville's *Moby-Dick; or, The Whale*," New York *Literary World* 9 (Nov. 22, 1851) 403–04.

in "The Whale." Book No. 2 is the romance of Captain Ahab, Queequeg, Tashtego, Pip & Co., who are more or less spiritual personages talking and acting differently from the general business run of the conversation on the decks of whalers. They are for the most part very serious people, and seem to be concerned a great deal about the problem of the universe. They are striking characters withal, of the romantic spiritual cast of the German drama; realities of some kinds at bottom, but veiled in all sorts of poetical incidents and expressions. As a bit of German melodrama, with Captain Ahab for the Faust of the quarter-deck, and Queequeg with the crew, for Walpurgis night revellers in the forecastle, it has its strong points, though here the limits as to space and treatment of the stage would improve it. Moby Dick in this view becomes a sort of fishy moralist, a leviathan metaphysician, a folio Ductor Dubitantium, in fact, in the fresh water illustration of Mrs. Malaprop, "an allegory on the banks of the Nile." After pursuing him in this melancholic company over a few hundred squares of latitude and longitude, we begin to have some faint idea of the association of whaling and lamentation, and why blubber is popularly synonymous with tears.

The intense Captain Ahab is too long drawn out; something more of *him* might, we think, be left to the reader's imagination. The value of this kind of writing can only be through the personal consciousness of the reader, what he brings to the book; and all this is sufficiently evoked by a dramatic trait or suggestion. If we had as much of Hamlet or Macbeth as Mr. Melville gives us of Ahab, we should be tired even of their sublime company. Yet Captain Ahab is a striking conception, firmly planted on the wild deck of the Pequod—a dark disturbed soul arraying itself with every ingenuity of material resources for a conflict at once natural and supernatural in his eye, with the most dangerous extant physical monster of the earth, embodying, in strongly drawn lines of mental association, the vaster moral evil of the world. The pursuit of the White Whale thus interweaves with the literal perils of the fishery—a problem of fate and destiny—to the tragic solution of which Ahab hurries on, amidst the wild stage scenery of the ocean. To this end the motley crew, the air, the sky, the sea, its inhabitants are idealized throughout. It is a noble and praiseworthy conception; and though our sympathies may not always accord with the train of thought, we would caution the reader against a light or hasty condemnation of this part of the work.

Book III., appropriating perhaps a fourth of the volume, is a vein of moralizing, half essay, half rhapsody, in which much refinement and subtlety, and no little poetical feeling, are mingled with quaint conceit and extravagant daring speculation. This is to be taken as in some sense dramatic; the narrator throughout among the personages of the Pequod being one Ishmael, whose wit may be allowed to be against everything on land, as his hand is against everything at sea. This piratical running down of creeds and opinions, the conceited indifferentism of Emerson, or the run-a-muck style of Carlyle is, we will not say dangerous in such cases, for there are various forces at work to meet more powerful onslaught, but it is out of place and uncomfortable. We do not like to see what, under any view, must be to the world the most sacred associations of life violated and defaced.

We call for fair play in this matter. Here is Ishmael, telling the story of this volume, going down on his knees with a cannibal to a piece of wood, in the second story fireplace of a New-Bedford tavern, in the spirit of amiable and transcendent charity, which may be all very well in its way; but why dislodge from heaven, with contumely, "long-pampered Gabriel, Michael and Raphael." Surely Ishmael, who is a scholar, might have spoken respectfully of the Archangel Gabriel, out of consideration, if not for the Bible (which might be asking too much of the school), at least for one John Milton, who wrote Paradise Lost.

Nor is it fair to inveigh against the terrors of priestcraft, which, skilful though it may be in making up its woes, at least seeks to provide a remedy for the evils of the world, and attribute the existence of conscience to "hereditary dyspepsias, nurtured by Ramadans"—and at the same time go about petrifying us with imaginary horrors, and all sorts of gloomy suggestions, all the world through. It is a curious fact that there are no more bilious people in the world, more completely filled with megrims and head shakings, than some of these very people who are constantly inveighing against the religious melancholy of priestcraft.

So much for the consistency of Ishmael—who, if it is the author's object to exhibit the painful contradictions of this self-dependent, self-torturing agency of a mind driven hither and thither as a flame in a whirlwind, is, in a degree, a successful embodiment of opinions, without securing from us, however, much admiration for the result.

With this we make an end of what we have been reluctantly compelled to object to this volume. With far greater pleasure, we acknowledge the acuteness of observation, the freshness of perception, with which the author brings home to us from the deep, "things unattempted yet in prose or rhyme," the weird influences of his ocean scenes, the salient imagination which connects them with the past and distant, the world of books and the life of experience—certain prevalent traits of manly sentiment. These are strong powers with which Mr. Melville wrestles in this book. It would be a great glory to subdue them to the highest uses of fiction.

It is still a great honor, among the crowd of successful mediocrities which throng our publishers' counters, and know nothing of divine impulses, to be in the company of these nobler spirits on any terms.

GEORGE RIPLEY

[A Pregnant Allegory] †

A new work by Herman Melville, entitled *Moby Dick; or The Whale,* has just been issued by Harper and Brothers, which, in point of richness and variety of incident, originality of conception, and splendor of description, surpasses any of the former productions of this highly successful author. *Moby Dick* is the name of an old White Whale; half fish and half devil; the terror of the Nantucket cruisers; the scourge of distant oceans; leading an invulnerable, charmed life; the subject of many grim and ghostly traditions. This huge sea monster has a conflict with one Captain Ahab; the veteran Nantucket salt comes off second best; not only loses a leg in the affray, but receives a twist in the brain; becomes the victim of a deep, cunning monomania; believes himself predestined to take a bloody revenge on his fearful enemy; pursues him with fierce demoniac energy of purpose; and at last perishes in the dreadful fight, just as he deems that he has reached the goal of his frantic passion. On this slight framework, the author has constructed a romance, a tragedy, and a natural history, not without numerous gratuitous suggestions on psychology, ethics, and theology. Beneath the whole story, the subtle, imaginative reader may perhaps find a pregnant allegory, intended to illustrate the mystery of human life. Certain it is that the rapid, pointed hints which are often thrown out, with the keenness and velocity of a harpoon, penetrate deep into the heart of things, showing that the genius of the author for moral analysis is scarcely surpassed by his wizard power of description.

In the course of the narrative the habits of the whale are fully and ably described. Frequent graphic and instructive sketches of the fishery, of sea-life in a whaling vessel, and of the manners and customs of strange nations are interspersed with excellent artistic effect among the thrilling scenes of the story. The various processes

† Anonymous review. "Review of *Moby-Dick,*" *Harper's New Monthly Magazine,* 4 (Dec., 1851), 137.   Ascribed to George Ripley by Hetherington (1961), pp. 212–13.

of procuring oil are explained with the minute, painstaking fidelity of a statistical record, contrasting strangely with the weird, phantom-like character of the plot, and of some of the leading personages, who present a no less unearthly appearance than the witches in Macbeth. These sudden and decided transitions form a striking feature of the volume. Difficult of management, in the highest degree, they are wrought with consummate skill. To a less gifted author, they would inevitably have proved fatal. He has not only deftly avoided their dangers, but made them an element of great power. They constantly pique the attention of the reader, keeping curiosity alive, and presenting the combined charm of surprise and alternation.

The introductory chapters of the volume, containing sketches of life in the great marts of Whalingdom, New Bedford and Nantucket, are pervaded with a fine vein of comic humor, and reveal a succession of portraitures, in which the lineaments of nature shine forth, through a good deal of perverse, intentional exaggeration. To many readers, these will prove the most interesting portions of the work. Nothing can be better than the description of the owners of the vessel, Captain Peleg and Captain Bildad, whose acquaintance we make before the commencement of the voyage. The character of Captain Ahab also opens upon us with wonderful power. He exercises a wild, bewildering fascination by his dark and mysterious nature, which is not at all diminished when we obtain a clearer insight into his strange history. Indeed, all the members of the ship's company, the three mates, Starbuck, Stubb, and Flask, the wild, savage Gayheader, the case-hardened old blacksmith, to say nothing of the pearl of a New Zealand harpooner, the bosom friend of the narrator—all stand before us in the strongest individual relief, presenting a unique picture gallery, which every artist must despair of rivaling.

The plot becomes more intense and tragic, as it approaches toward the denouement. The malicious old Moby Dick, after long cruisings in pursuit of him, is at length discovered. He comes up to the battle, like an army with banners. He seems inspired with the same fierce, inveterate cunning with which Captain Ahab has followed the traces of his mortal foe. The fight is described in letters of blood. It is easy to foresee which will be the victor in such a contest. We need not say that the ill-omened ship is broken in fragments by the wrath of the weltering fiend. Captain Ahab becomes the prey of his intended victim. The crew perish. One alone escapes to tell the tale. Moby Dick disappears unscathed, and for aught we know, is the same "delicate monster," whose power in destroying another ship is just announced from Panama.

WILLIAM A. BUTLER

[A Prose Epic on Whaling] †

Moby-Dick, or the Whale, is the narrative of a whaling voyage; and, while we must beg permission to doubt its authenticity in all respects, we are free to confess that it presents a most striking and truthful portraiture of the whale and his perilous capture. We do not imagine that Mr. Melville claims for this his latest production the same historical credence which he asserted was due to "Typee" and "Omoo;" and we do not know how we can better express our conception of his general drift and style in the work under consideration than by entitling it a prose Epic on Whaling. In whatever light it may be viewed, no one can deny it to be the production of a man of genius. The descriptive powers of Mr. Melville are unrivalled, whether the scenes he paints reveal "old ocean into tempest toss'd," or are laid among the bright hillsides of some Pacific island, so warm and undulating that the printed page on which they are so graphically depicted seems almost to palpitate beneath the sun. Language in the hands of this master becomes like a magician's wand, evoking at will "thick-coming fancies," and peopling the "chambers of imagery" with hideous shapes of terror or winning forms of beauty and loveliness. Mr. Melville has a strange power to reach the sinuosities of a thought, if we may so express ourselves; he touches with his lead and line depths of pathos that few can fathom, and by a single word can set a whole chime of sweet or wild emotions into a pealing concert. His delineation of character is actually Shakspearean—a quality which is even more prominently evinced in "Moby Dick" than in any of his antecedent efforts. Mr. Melville especially delights to limn the full-length portrait of a savage, and if he is a cannibal it is all the better; he seems fully convinced that the highest type of man is to be found in the forests or among the anthropophagi of the Fejee Islands. Brighter geniuses than even his have disported on this same fancy; for such was the youthful dream of Burke, and such was the crazy vision of Jean Jacques Rousseau.

The humor of Mr. Melville is of that subdued yet unquenchable nature which spreads such a charm over the pages of Sterne. As illustrative of this quality in his style, we must refer our readers

† From the review of *Moby-Dick* in the Washington *National Intelligencer,* (Dec. 16, 1851). Ascribed to William A. Butler by Hetherington (1961), p. 214.

618

to the irresistibly comic passages scattered at irregular intervals through "Moby Dick," and occasionally we find in this singular production the traces of that "wild imagining" which throws such a weird-like charm about the Ancient Mariner of Coleridge; and many of the scenes and objects in "Moby Dick" were suggested, we doubt not, by this ghastly rhyme.

ANONYMOUS

[Cause for a Writ *de Lunatico*] †

In all those portions of this volume which relate directly to the whale, his appearance in the oceans which he inhabits; his habits, powers and peculiarities; his pursuit and capture; the interest of the reader will be kept alive, and his attention fully rewarded. We should judge, from what is before us, that Mr. Melville has as much personal knowledge of the whale as any man living, and is better able, than any man living, to display this knowledge in print. In all the scenes where the whale is the performer or the sufferer, the delineation and action are highly vivid and exciting. In all other respects, the book is sad stuff, dull and dreary, or ridiculous. Mr. Melville's Quakers are the wretchedest dolts and drivellers, and his Mad Captain, who pursues his personal revenges against the fish who has taken off his leg, at the expense of ship, crew and owners, is a monstrous bore, whom Mr. Melville has no way helped, by enveloping him in a sort of mystery. His ravings, and the ravings of some of the tributary characters, and the ravings of Mr. Melville himself, meant for eloquent declamation, are such as would justify a writ *de lunatico* against all the parties.

WILLIAM HARRISON AINSWORTH

[Maniacal Style and Furibund Story]‡

For so successful a trader in "marine stores" as Mr. Melville, "The Whale" seemed a speculation every way big with promise.

† *The Southern Quarterly Review*, 5 (Jan., 1852), p. 262.
‡ "Sir Nathaniel," "American Authorship, No. 4: Herman Melville." *New Monthly Magazine* [London], 98 (July, 1853), 307–8. The reviewer is identified as William Harrison Ainsworth by Hetherington (1961), p. 202.

From such a master of his harpoon might have been expected a prodigious hit. There was about blubber and spermaceti something unctuously suggestive, with him for whaleman. And his three volumes entitled "The Whale" undoubtedly contain much vigorous description, much wild power, many striking details. But the effect is distressingly marred throughout by an extravagant treatment of the subject. The style is maniacal—mad as a March hare —mowing, gibbering, screaming, like an incurable Bedlamite, reckless of keeper or strait-waistcoat. . . .

When he pleases, Mr. Melville can be so lucid, straightforward, hearty, and unaffected, and displays so unmistakable a shrewdness, and satirical sense of the ridiculous, that it is hard to suppose that *he* can have indited the rhodomontade to which we allude. Surely the man is a Doppelganger—a dual number incarnate (singular though he be, in and out of all conscience):—surely he is two single gentlemen rolled into one, but retaining their respective idiosyncrasies—the one sensible, sagacious, observant, graphic, and producing admirable matter—the other maundering, drivelling, subject to paroxysms, cramps, and total collapse, and penning exceeding many pages of unaccountable "bosh". . . . Writing of Leviathan, he exclaims, "Unconsciously my chirography expands into placard capitals. Give me a condor's quill! Give me Vesuvius' crater for an inkstand! Friends, hold my arms!" Oh that his friends had obeyed that summons! They might have saved society from a huge dose of hyperbolic slang, maudlin sentimentalism, and tragicomic bubble and squeak.

His Yankeeisms are plentiful as blackberries. "I am tormented," quoth he, "with an everlasting itch for things remote." Remote, too frequently, from good taste, good manners, and good sense. We need not pause at such expressions as "looking a sort of diabolically funny;"—"beefsteaks done rare;"—"a speechlessly quick chaotic bundling of a man into eternity;"—"bidding adieu to circumspect life, to exist only in a delirious throb." But why wax fast and furious in a thousand such paragraphs as these:—"In landlessness alone resides the highest truth, indefinite as the Almighty . . . . Take heart, take heart, O Bulkington! Bear thee grimly, demigod! Up from the spray of thy ocean-perishing—straight up, leaps thy apotheosis!"—"Thou (*scil.* Spirit of Equality) great God! who didst not refuse to the swart convict, Bunyan, the pale, poetic pearl; Thou who didst clothe with doubly hammered leaves of finest gold the stumped and paupered arm of old Cervantes; Thou who didst pick up Andrew Jackson from the pebbles; who didst hurl him upon a war-horse; who didst thunder him higher than a throne!"—"If such a furious trope may stand, his (Capt. Ahab's) special lunacy stormed his general sanity, and carried it, and turned all its concentrated cannon upon its own mad mark. . . . then it was, that his torn body and gashed soul bled into one another; and so interfusing made him mad."—"And the miser-merman, Wisdom, revealed (to a diving negro) his hoarded heaps; and among the joyous, heartless, ever-juvenile eternities, Pip saw the multitudinous, God-omnipresent, coral insects, that out of the firmament of waters heaved the colossal orbs. He saw God's foot upon the treadle of the loom, and spoke it; and therefore his shipmates called him mad.'

The story itself is a strange, wild, furibund thing—about Captain Ahab's vow of revenge against one Moby Dick. And who is Moby Dick? A fellow of a whale, who has made free with the captain's leg; so that the captain now stumps on ivory, and goes circumnavigating the globe in quest of the old offender, and raves by the hour in a lingo borrowed from Rabelais, Carlyle, Emerson, newspapers transcendental and transatlantic, and the magnificent proems of our Christmas pantomimes. Captain Ahab is introduced with prodigious efforts at preparation; and there is really no lack of rude power and character about his presentment—spoiled, however, by the Cambyses' vein in which he dissipates his vigour. . . . The amiable cannibal Queequeg occasions some stirring and some humorous scenes, and is probably the most reasonable and cultivated creature of the ship's company. Starbuck and Stubb are both tiresome, in different ways. The book is rich with facts connected with the natural history of the whale, and the whole art and process of whaling; and with spirited descriptions of that process, which betray an intense straining at effect. The climax of the three days' chase after Moby Dick is highly wrought and sternly exciting—but the catastrophe, in its whirl of waters and fancies, resembles one of Turner's later nebulous transgressions in gamboge.

Interim Appraisals: 1893–1913

ANONYMOUS

[A Marvellous Odyssey] †

It was not until this remarkable romance came out, over forty years ago, that Herman Melville, that strange compound of Dutch, English and Huguenot blood, merited the name of the American prose Victor Hugo. In fact it was after the publication of "Moby-Dick" that Hugo's really great romances of the sea and land came out; so that one might truthfully turn the tables and almost say that Victor Hugo was the French Melville. So striking, so suspicious is the resemblance between "Moby-Dick" and "Les Travailleurs de la Mer," that one is sorely tempted to the enticing accusation of a certain sort of plagiarism on the part of the Sage of Guernsey, of that general and diffusive kind which critics love to point out between Swift and Lucian, Goethe and Marlowe, Faust and Manfred, and Coleridge and Mme. de Staël. A gigantic devilfish is one of the *dramatis personæ* of "Moby-Dick" as it is of "The Toilers of the Sea," and the fantastic learning, the episodic style, the wonderful picturings of the sea in all its beauty and terror, and the peculiar manipulation of imaginative effects in both books, emphasize the fact of their essential kinship. Hugo was familiar enough with English literature to command it completely, and it is far from incredible that he knew the works of Melville. Hawthorne paid the warmest tribute to Melville's surpassing imagination, and to him "Moby-Dick" was very appropriately dedicated.

Indeed there is no romance of Hawthorne's that surpasses this whaling-story in witching power, in grasp on the pulse, in almost supernatural strength of description, and in ability to quicken the blood. The undreamt poesy lying in the lives of Nantucket whalers in the fifties has for once received epical treatment, and the result is a marvellous Odyssey of adventure in warm seas and in icy, in halcyon and in purgatorial latitudes, over such a range of sunlit or storm-smitten billows as could occur only in actual experience before the mast in search of real whales on the real deep. Hugo never travelled; and therefore his lovely poems of the sea or his "Hans

† "*Moby-Dick;* or, *The White Whale,*" *The Critic,* 22 (1893), 232.

d'Islande" are conceived from the shore—powerful but shadowy idealizations of things he had never really seen. His empty shells Melville fills full of the living breath, the roar, the music, the vibration of the living sea, Whitmanesque in its intensity and realism, the memories of one who had lived years in the troughs or on the mountain-crests of Homeric waves, and who therefore in his work simply transcribed ineffaceable impressions. Mohammedanism has been described as mere "paint"; even so Hugo's seas are painted seas as compared with the streaming or starlit or surging oceans of this real mariner. To depict the guillotining of Louis XVI. it is not necessary indeed to feel the actual flash of the axe itself across one's arteries, but a certain amount of actual knowledge is always welcome if not indispensable in depicting the mighty phenomena of great voyages, great emotions or great deeds. This Hugo did not possess, and his phantom romances are mere husks, mere *larvæ* or *simulacra*, illumined by an unnatural interior light, like a jack o' lantern, as compared with the healthy, wholesome, rude but terrible realities of such books as "Moby-Dick."

In this story Melville is as fantastically poetical as Coleridge in the "Ancient Mariner," and yet, while we swim spellbound over the golden rhythms of Coleridge feeling at every stroke their beautiful improbability, everything in "Moby-Dick" might have happened. The woe-struck captain, his eerie monomania, the half-devils of the crew, the relentless pursuit of the ever-elusive vindictive white whale, the storms and calms that succeed each other like the ups and downs of a mighty hexameter, all the weird scenery of the pursuit in moonlight and in daylight, all are so wonderfully fresh in their treatment that they supersede all doubt and impress one as absolutely true to the life. Even the recondite information about whales and sea-fisheries sprinkled plentifully over the pages does not interfere seriously with the intended effect; they are the paraphernalia of the journey. The author's extraordinary vocabulary, its wonderful coinages and vivid turnings and twistings of worn-out words, are comparable only to Chapman's translations of Homer. The language fairly shrieks under the intensity of his treatment, and the reader is under an excitement which is hardly controllable. The only wonder is that Melville is so little known and so poorly appreciated.

WILLIAM P. TRENT

[Melville's Flawed Masterpiece, and his Decline] †

[Melville] published, in 1851, his masterpiece, *Moby Dick, or the White Whale*. If it were not for its inordinate length, its frequent inartistic heaping up of details, and its obvious imitation of Carlylean tricks of style and construction, this narrative of tremendous power and wide knowledge might be perhaps pronounced the greatest sea story in literature. The breath of the sea is in it and much of the passion and charm of the most venturous of all the venturous callings plied upon the deep. * * * Moby Dick, the invincible whale, [is] a creation of the imagination not unworthy of a great poet. In this uneven, but on the whole genuine, work of genius, Melville probably overtasked himself. He published several other books while * * * attending to his duties in the custom-house, but nothing comparable to his earlier works. One, *Israel Potter*, deserved Hawthorne's praise because of its spirited portraits of Franklin and Paul Jones, but no revival of their author's fame will justify the republication of these productions of his decline.

W. CLARK RUSSELL

[Melville's Finest Performance] ‡

"Moby Dick" * * * is generally and with justice regarded as Melville's finest performance. It is, indeed, taken on the whole, a very noble piece. Some of the conversations among the sailors remind one for their strength, sweetness and courage of such passages in Dekker, Webster, Massinger, Fletcher, and other old dramatists as Charles Lamb loved to select. The opening chapters of this book are extraordinarily impressive. He gives a picture of New Bedford by night. His sketch of the Spouter Inn, its hoarse, salt landlord, its delicious clam chowder, the frightful Mowrèe harpooner whose bed the hero has to share, enchant the imagination and chisel the

† From William P. Trent, *A History of American Literature, 1607–1865* (New York: D. Appleton, 1903), pp. 390–91.

‡ From W. Clark Russell, "Preface" to *Typee* (London: John Lane, 1904), pp. vii–viii. Reprinted by permission of The Bodley Head Ltd.

memory with the delights and impressions produced by a masterpiece in Dutch painting. Yet it is easy to understand why "Moby
Dick" should never reach the popularity of "Typee" or "Omoo." In
parts it is too obscure. The reader, moreover, is harassed by the
frequent interpolation of a transcendental mysticism which often
ill-fits the mouths of the rough tarpaulins who are made to deliver
their minds of the sublimated fancies which appear to oppress
them even more than the brine-hardened food they consume.

WILLIAM J. LONG

[A Group of Minor Fiction Writers] †

With the tales of Irving, Cooper and Poe we have considered
all the fiction of the period that seems destined to a permanent
place in our literature. There were many other romancers, however, some with ten, others with fifty volumes to their credit. A
few of their works, such as Miss Sedgwick's *Redwood* (1824), were
more widely read in Europe than were the works of Poe or Irving;
many others were as dear to our grandmothers as are the romances
of Crawford or Louisa Alcott to the present generation. Among
these dust-covered books one may still find many suggestive pages.
Susanna Rowson's *Charlotte Temple* is a type of the early novel
of "sensibility," once extremely popular but now forgotten.
Catherine Sedgwick's *Redwood*, *Hope Leslie* and *The Linwoods*
contain excellent pictures of American home life, and are notable
as the beginning of the novel of character and manners, so finely
developed in our time by Miss Jewett and Miss Wilkins. And here
are the stirring *Typee*, *White Jacket*, *Moby Dick* and other stories
of the deep by Herman Melville, of whom a modern sea novelist,
Clark Russell, writes enthusiastically:

"A famous man he was in those far days when every sea was
bright with the American flag, when the cotton-white canvas
shone star-like on the horizon. * * * * Famous he was; now he is
neglected; yet his name and his work will not die. He is a great
figure in shadow; but the shadow is not that of oblivion."

Better known than Melville's work is a veritable classic of the
sea written by R. H. Dana, Jr., and called *Two Years before the
Mast* (1840). * * *

† From William J. Long, *American
Literature: A Study of the Men and
the Books That in the Earlier and
Later Times Reflect the American Spirit* (Waltham, Massachusetts: Blaisdell
Publishing Company, 1913), p. 247.
Reprinted by permission of Ginn and
Company.

Revival and Reaction:
1917–1936

CARL VAN DOREN

[The Originality of *Moby-Dick*] †

Ahab, not Melville, is to blame if the story seems an allegory, which Melville plainly declared it was not; but it contains, nevertheless, the semblance of a conflict between the ancient and scatheless forces of nature and the ineluctable enmity of man. This is the theme, but description can hardly report the extraordinary mixture in *Moby Dick* of vivid adventure, minute detail, cloudy symbolism, thrilling pictures of the sea in every mood, sly mirth and cosmic ironies, real and incredible characters, wit, speculation, humour, colour. The style is mannered but often felicitous; though the book is long, the end, after every faculty of suspense has been aroused, is swift and final. Too irregular, too bizarre, perhaps, ever to win the widest suffrage, the immense originality of *Moby Dick* must warrant the claim of its admirers that it belongs with the greatest sea romances in the whole literature of the world.

RAYMOND WEAVER

[Melville's Composite Achievement]‡

Born in hell-fire, and baptized in an unspeakable name, "Moby-Dick, or the Whale" (1851), reads like a great opium dream. The organizing theme of the book is the hunting of Moby-Dick, the abhorred white whale, by the monomaniac Captain Ahab. To Ahab,

† From Carl Van Doren, *Cambridge History of American Literature*, Vol. 1 (New York: Macmillan, 1917), pp. 322-23. Copyright 1917 by The Macmillan Company; reprinted by permission of the publishers.

‡ From Raymond Weaver, "The Centennial of Herman Melville," *The Nation* [New York], 109 (August 2, 1919), 146. Reprinted by permission of Sidney A. Burrell.

this ancient and vindictive monster is the incarnation of all the vast moral evil of the world; he piles on the whale's white hump the sum of all the rage and hate of mankind from the days of Eden down. There are in "Moby-Dick" long digressions, natural, historical, and philosophical on the person, habits, manners, and ideas of whales; there are long dialogues and soliloquies, such as were never spoken by mortal man in his waking senses; . . . perhaps a fifth of the book is made up of Melville's independent moralizings, half essay, half rhapsody; withal, the book contains some of the most finished comedy in the language. If one logically analyzes "Moby-Dick," he will be disgusted, just as Dr. Johnson, who had no analysis but the logical, was disgusted with "Lycidas." And so with Melville's novel. If one will forget logic and common sense, and "abandon himself"—as Dr. Johnson would contemptuously have said—to this work of Melville's, he will acknowledge the presence of an amazing masterpiece. But neither "Lycidas" nor "Moby-Dick" should be read by philistines or pragmatists. * * *

"Like a frigate," Melville once wrote of himself, "I am full with a thousand souls; and as on, on, on, I scud before the wind, many mariners rush up from the orlop below, like miners from caves; running shouting across my decks; opposite braces are pulled and boisterous speaking trumpets are heard, and contending orders, to save the good ship from the shoals. In my tropical calms, when my ship lies tranced on Eternity's main, the many, many souls in me speak one at a time, then all with one voice, rising and falling and swaying in golden calls and responses." Because of this multiplicity of personality, Melville eludes summary classification. In his composite achievement he is severally a gentle Smollett, a glorified Whitman, an athletic Coleridge, a dandified Rabelais, a cynical Meredith, a doubting Sir Thomas Browne. Essentially was he a mystic, a treasure-seeker, a mystery-monger, a delver after hidden things spiritual and material. The world to him was a darkly figured hieroglyph; and if he ever deciphered the cabalistic sign, the meaning he found was too terrible, or else too wonderful, to tell. Whenever he sat down to write, at his elbow stood ever the chosen emissary of Satan, the Comic Spirit—a demoniac familiar that saved him in many a trying pass. The versatility and power of his genius was extraordinary. If he does not eventually rank as a writer of overshadowing accomplishment, it will be owing not to any lack of genius, but to the perversity of his rare and lofty gifts.

A WAYFARER

[A Deposition from a New Reader] †

It is clear that the wind of the spirit, when it once begins to blow through the English literary mind, possesses a surprising power of penetration. A few weeks ago it was pleased to aim a simultaneous blast at the direction of a book known to some generations of men as "Moby Dick." A member of the staff of *The Nation* was thereupon moved in the ancient Hebrew fashion to buy it and to read it. He then expressed himself on the subject, incoherently indeed, but with signs of emotion as intense and as pleasingly uncouth as Man Friday betrayed at the sight of his long-lost father. While struggling with his article, and wondering what the deuce it could mean, I received a letter from a famous literary man, marked on the outside "Urgent," and on the inner scroll of the MS. itself "A Rhapsody." It was about "Moby Dick." Having observed a third article on the same subject, of an equally febrile kind, I began to read "Moby Dick" myself. Having done so I hereby declare, being of sane intellect, that since letters began there never was such a book, and that the mind of man is not constructed so as to produce such another; that I put its author with Rabelais, Swift, Shakespeare, and other minor and disputable worthies; and that I advise any adventurer of the soul to go at once into the morose and prolonged retreat necessary for its deglutition. And having said this, I decline to say another word on the subject now and for evermore.

J. ST. LOE STRACHEY

[Melville's Enduring Reputation in England] ‡

* * * Before I leave the subject of Melville I should like to point out that the latest biographer [Weaver] of the great American does not seem to realize how strong the feeling about Melville has always been in England. I well remember some thirty years ago writing a review in the *Spectator* on a new edition of Melville's works

† From *The Nation* [London], 28 (January 22, 1921) 572. Reprinted by permission of the *New Statesman*.
‡ From J. St. Loe Strachey, "Review of *Herman Melville: Mariner and Mystic*," *The Spectator*, 128 (May 6, 1922), 559–60. Reprinted by permission of *The Spectator*.

which had just appeared. A reference thereto shows that a Melville boom was then proceeding. But this is not all. I remember that when my article appeared a lady of letters who could remember the 'fifties remarked to me that she was glad to see people were reading Melville again, and added: "I can't tell you how enthusiastic we all were, young and old, at the end of the 'forties and beginning of the 'fifties, over *Typee*, *Omoo*, and *Moby-Dick*. There was quite a furore over Melville in those days. All the young people worshipped him."

As a further proof of that, I have just been turning over a reprint of *The Whale*, issued as a three-volume novel by Bentley in 1851. It is interesting, though rather sad, to note that in this seventy-year-old book the paper is for the most part spotless, firm, and crisp, and the print exquisitely clear. It is to be feared that our post-War, and even many of our pre-War novels will not be anything like as legible at the beginning of the twenty-first century.

Melville, I venture to say, will never be forgotten either here or in America. So long as the English language survives—and who dare prophesy its extinction?—so long will people read and wonder at the eccentric mariner, who described a whale-hunt in the terms of Urn Burial. He was an uncanny throw-forward, and did not in his day quite fit into either the life or the literature of his age. If he were living and writing now, he would be one of the world's greatest-sellers and would thoroughly deserve his success.

LEONARD WOOLF

[Execrable English and Fantastic Grandeur] †

Melville is a very remarkable writer, but I think that, as is nearly always the case when books are suddenly and at the last moment rescued from oblivion, his rescuers and their followers have loaded him with a good deal of indiscriminate praise. It is time that we began to discriminate. For this purpose "Typee" and "Omoo" can be neglected; they are good, plain, vigorous stories of adventure, and in style, construction, and conception they differ materially from the books which followed them. It is with these, or rather with "Moby Dick" and "Mardi"—for "White Jacket," though interesting, is on a lower level—that Melville's reputation must stand or fall. The division between the books which preceded and those which followed "Mardi" is, I think, of great importance, because I hazard the

† From Leonard Woolf, *The Nation & The Athenaeum*, 33 (September 1, 1923) 688. Reprinted by permission of Hogarth Press Ltd. and the author.

conjecture that between writing "Omoo" and writing "Mardi" Melville read Dickens. I base this conjecture solely upon internal evidence, but it seems to me that after 1846 Dickens had a deep, and in some respects a disastrous, influence on Melville. From Dickens he derived the exaggerated, and in his case unspontaneous, humour which disfigures so many pages of "Moby Dick," some very marked features in the form of the conversations and interminable soliloquies, the repetitive style of the loose torrent of his unending sentences. Unfortunately, I have no space here for quotations, but I would ask anyone to read such a paragraph as that in Chapter 22 of "Moby Dick," which begins: "It was curious and not unpleasing . . ." [, or] speeches of Stubb and Starbuck, in that book, or the long conversations in "Mardi" between Yoomy, Babbalanja, and Mohi; let him compare the style of these with the narrative and conversations in "Typee" or "Omoo"; let him then read a chapter or two in which Dickens is really letting himself go; and he will, I think, see for himself where the impetus came from which changed the author of "Omoo" into the author of "Moby Dick."

The first thing which must be said of Melville is that he writes the most execrable English. Take a sentence like the following: "That certain sultanism of his brain, which had otherwise in a good degree remained unmanifested; through those forms that sultanism became incarnate in an irresistible dictatorship." This is a thoroughly bad sentence, and its badness is quite pointless, and there are thousands like it in "Mardi" and "Moby Dick." (The use of the semi-colon in this sentence is worth noting; it is characteristic of Melville, who bespatters his sentences with semi-colons without regard to meaning or convention.) His second great vice is rant or rhetoric. When he wants to say that a sailor looked angrily at the mate, he describes him as "stabbing him in the eye with the unflinching poinard of his glance." I cannot see the slightest point in this kind of bombast, and, when it raves on for page after page, I almost pitch the book into the waste-paper basket and swear that I will not read another line, however many people vouch for the author's genius.

Almost—for Melville is undoubtedly one of those strange geniuses, peculiar to English literature and unintelligible to classicists like the French, who perversely produce masterpieces out of their most glaring vices. If you care for language, you will be bored and exasperated by Melville in "Mardi" and "Moby Dick" for some three hundred pages, but if you can stand this for so long, then suddenly something happens: the book—and its very imperfections and corruptions—suffers a sea-change into something rich and strange. The same thing happens once or twice and for brief moments in Mr. Joyce's "Ulysses," a book which, both in style and

conception, continually recalls "Moby Dick." * * * I do not know
exactly what the symbolism of Captain Ahab or Yillah means, but
in each case the book seems to me at a certain moment to be lifted
on to a higher plane of fantastic grandeur and poetry where even
the intolerable rantings and ravings find a proper place.

So in the end one has to admit that "Moby Dick" attains, and
that "Mardi" is on the verge of, greatness. But if I had to "place"
Melville, to find him his niche in the hierarchy of English
literature, I should have to double on my tracks, return to his
imperfections and vices, and introduce qualifications for which
unfortunately I have left myself no space. Thus I must leave Melville see-sawing between his semi-colons on the one side and greatness on the other.

LEWIS MUMFORD

[*Moby-Dick* as Poetic Epic] †

Moby-Dick is a poetic epic. Typographically, Moby-Dick con-
forms to prose, and there are long passages, whole chapters, which
are wholly in the mood of prose: but in spirit and in actual rhythm,
Moby-Dick again and again rises to polyphonic verse which resembles passages of Webster's in that it can either be considered
as broken blank verse, or as cadenced prose. Mr. Percy Boynton
has performed the interesting experiment of transposing a paragraph in Pierre into excellent free verse, so strong and subtle are
Melville's rhythms; and one might garner a whole book of verse
from Moby-Dick. Melville, in Moby-Dick, unconsciously respects
Poe's canon that all true poetry must be short in length, since the
mood cannot be retained, unbroken or undiminished, over lengthy
passages, and if the form itself is preserved, the content nevertheless is prose. But while Poe himself used this dictum as an excuse
for writing only short lyrics, Melville sustained the poetic mood
through a long narrative by dropping frankly into prose in the
intervening while. As a result, he was under no necessity of clipping
the emotions or of bleaching the imaginative colours of Moby-
Dick: like a flying-boat, he rises from the water to the air and
returns to the water again without losing control over either medium. His prose is prose: hard, sinewy, compact; and his poetry is
poetry, vivid, surging, volcanic, creating its own form in the very

† From Lewis Mumford, *Herman Melville* (New York: Harcourt, Brace &
World, Inc., 1929), pp. 123–24. Revised edition, copyright 1929, by
Harcourt, Brace & World, Inc.; copyright © 1957, 1962, by Lewis Mumford.
Reprinted by permission of the publishers.

pattern of the emotional state itself, soaring, towering, losing all respect for the smaller conventions of veracity, when the inner triumph itself must be announced. It is in the very rhythm of his language that Ahab's mood, and all the devious symbols of Moby-Dick are sustained and made credible: by no other method could the deeper half of the tale have been written. In these poetic passages, the phrases are intensified, stylized, stripped of their habitual associations. If occasionally, as with Shakespeare, the thought itself is borne down by the weight of the gold that decorates it, this is only a similar proof of Melville's immense fecundity of expression.

Both Poe and Hawthorne share some of Melville's power, and both of them, with varying success, wrought ideality and actuality into the same figure: but one has only to compare the best of their work with Moby-Dick to see wherein Melville's great distinction lies. The Scarlet Letter, The House of the Seven Gables, William Wilson, like most other works of fiction, are melodic: a single instrument is sufficient to carry the whole theme; whereas Moby-Dick is a symphony; every resource of language and thought, fantasy, description, philosophy, natural history, drama, broken rhythms, blank verse, imagery, symbol, is utilized to sustain and expand the great theme. The conception of Moby-Dick organically demands the expressive interrelation, for a single total effect, of a hundred different pieces: even in accessory matters, like the association of the Parsee, the fire-worshipper, with the death of Ahab, the fire-defier, or in the makeup of the crew, the officers white men, the harpooners the savage races, red, black, brown, and the crew a mixed lot from the separate islands of the earth, not a stroke is introduced that has not a meaning for the myth as a whole. Although the savage harpooners get nearest the whale, the savage universe, it is Ahab and the Parsee, the Westerner and the Asiatic, who carry the pursuit to its ultimate end—while a single American survives to tell the tale!

Melville's instrumentation is unsurpassed in the writing of the last century: one must go to a Beethoven or a Wagner for an exhibition of similar powers: one will not find it among the works of literature. Here are Webster's wild violin, Marlowe's cymbals, Browne's sonorous bass viol, Swift's brass, Smollett's castanets, Shelley's flute, brought together in a single orchestra, complementing each other in a grand symphony. Melville achieved a similar synthesis in thought; and that work has proved all the more credible because he achieved it in language, too. Small wonder that those who were used to elegant pianoforte solos or barrel-organ instrumentation, were deafened and surprised and repulsed.

BERNARD DeVOTO

[*Moby-Dick* vs. *Huckleberry Finn*] †

So, though I regard comparisons as worthless in æsthetics, the obligation of a critic of Mark Twain rests on me to point out these selfsame faults in the only American novel which even enthusiasm can offer to dispute the preëminence of "The Adventures of Huckleberry Finn." Much more identity than has ever been noticed in print exists in the careers of Mark Twain and Herman Melville, whose minds were as antipathetic as religion and reality or the subjective and the objective worlds can be. Similarly, Jonathan Edwards's successor, when he came to write his masterpiece, plentifully anticipated the errors of Mark Twain and went beyond them. "Moby Dick" has, as fiction, no structure whatever. Its lines of force mercilessly intercept one another. Its improvisations are commoner and falser than those in Huck Finn. It does not suffer from burlesque (exuberant vitality had no place in Melville's nature) but its verbal humor is sometimes more vicariously humiliating than such passages as Huck's discussion of kings—a miracle, no doubt, withheld Mark Twain from the mere jokes habitual to him. And, though Melville could write great prose, his book frequently escapes into a passionately swooning rhetoric that is unconscious burlesque. He was no surer than Mark, he was in fact less sure, of the true object of his book, and much less sure of the technical instruments necessary to achieve it. That much of weakness the two novels have in common. It is convenient to point out, this much having been said, that they are otherwise antipathies. "Moby Dick" opposes metaphysics to the objective reality of "Huckleberry Finn." It is a study in demonology, bound to the world of experience by no more durable threads than a few passages in the lives of mates, harpooners and sailors who are otherwise mostly symbol or mist. They were the book's disregarded possibility of great realism. Melville preferred to sigh through eternity after the infinite. It is a search which has an eternal value for some minds. Other minds, if they look to fiction for values of time instead of eternity and of the finite instead of the infinite, are likely to relinquish the *Pequod's* voyage toward fulfillment of man's destiny and prefer a lumber raft's voyage down inland waters after no more ambitious purpose than to see what the world is like.

† From Bernard DeVoto, *Mark Twain's America* (Chautauqua: Chautauqua Institution, 1932), pp. 312–13. Reprinted by permission of Houghton Mifflin Company.

LUDWIG LEWISOHN

[Melville: Not Even a Minor Master] †

The final image that arises from all of Melville's work is that of a big bearded violently excited man trying to shout down the whimpering, lonely child in his soul.

It will be seen at once that I consider the recent reëstimate of Melville to have somewhat overshot the mark. Great wits have praised him, but not, perhaps, those of most balanced judgment. He has his superb moments. But are those moments not rare and do they wholly repay the labor necessary to reach them? A younger generation, in search of that "usable" American past which Van Wyck Brooks so earnestly and sagaciously demanded long ago, has fastened its flag to his mast. Has not that generation been both deceived and self-deceived? Has it not substituted its desire and ideal for the reality? Melville was not a strong man defying the cruel order of the world; he was a weak man fleeing from his own soul and from life, a querulous man, a fretful man. * * *

No, Melville is not even a minor master. His works constitute rather one of the important curiosities of literature. He will be chiefly remembered as the inventor of a somber legend concerning the evil that is under the sun. But to embody this legend in a permanently valid form he had only half the creative power and none of the creative discipline or serenity.

† From Ludwig Lewisohn, *Expression in American* (New York: Harper & Brothers, 1932), pp. 188–89, 93. Reprinted by permission of the publishers.

Academic Criticism:
1938–1960's

WILLARD THORP

[Melville's Quest for the Ultimate] †

How is *Moby-Dick* to be read as the allegory of Melville's spiritual state in 1851? To what point has he come in his quest for the Ultimate? He invites us to inquire in the passage which admits his sympathy with Ahab's feud. The wall of the mystery had been shoved menacingly near. He was like a prisoner whose only escape was by thrusting through. The ultimate answer, if it could be reached, would be complex, he now realized, and its quest perhaps dangerous to the sanity. He might have to impute the evil omnipresent in the universe to its ruler. But was this evil the work of principal or of agent? He began to suspect even that the intricate subject of all his speculations might dissolve in nothing, that there was, as he wrote to Hawthorne, no secret, "like the Freemason's mighty secret, so terrible to all children," which turns out, at last, "to consist in a triangle, a mallet, and an apron,—nothing more." In this same illuminating letter he notes that as soon as man begins to objectify the invisible world, to talk of *Me*, a *God*, a *Nature*, he prepares the noose that will hang him, like Ahab who sought to fight the intangible malignities only when he found in the White Whale their tangible incarnation.

Although Ahab was mad, as Melville knew him to be, and though he tried revenge, which is no solution to man's predicament, we must not suppose that Melville, even though defiant, would now choose to follow Ahab into the gulf, as Taji had turned his prow towards the racing tide. It is not merely for the purpose of saving the narrator that Ishmael-Melville survives the White Whale's assault. However much he sympathized with Ahab's Promethean determination to stare down the inscrutableness of the

† From Willard Thorp's Introduction to *Herman Melville: Representative Selections* (New York: American Book Company, 1938), pp. lxxiv–lxxv. Copyright 1938 by American Book Company; renewed 1966 by Willard Thorp; reprinted by permission of the publishers.

universe, Melville hurled, not himself, but Ahab, his creature, at the injurious gods. Like the mountain eagle, though he had swooped into the blackest gorge, that gorge lay within the lofty mountains. He had written a wicked book for which Ahab was made to suffer vicariously, and he felt as spotless as the lamb.

STANLEY GEIST

[Melville's Tragically Great Hero] †

It is obvious * * * that any interpretation of *Moby Dick* which represents the book as a metaphysical drama, or as a systematized scheme in which every character and every incident is carefully integrated in a pattern of thought, becomes absurd. Such a mode of apprehending life or of presenting life was repulsive to Melville: any attempt to reduce life to a set of abstractions, or to impose an ordered system upon an irrational universe, was both presumptuous and heartless. He recognized, deeply if not clearly, that between the metaphysical mind and his own was the same split which has always separated the philosopher from the creative artist: all his thought constituted a mode of perception, all the thought of the philosopher constituted a reasoned scheme. And though philosophy was but the rationalization of vision, the philosopher yet distinguished himself from the creative artist by being concerned with vision as system while the artist was concerned with vision as life. If there was an eternal war of metaphysical Good with metaphysical Evil in the mad gyrations of the spheres, Melville knew nothing about it. But he was obsessed with the eternal drama which he saw within the profoundest men, and within them only: the drama whose Chorus endlessly intoned, "We begin to live when we have conceived life as tragedy."

Grief and Greatness, suffering and heroism: these were, to Melville, inseparable; and they were the theme of his two most ambitious books. Nowhere does *Moby Dick* more nearly become one with the work which inspired it, *King Lear* [1] than in its penetration by this double theme. And nowhere, interestingly enough, does it more nearly approximate the very letter of *King Lear* than in the imagery through which the motive of heroic suffering is expressed. As in *Lear*, the sense of mental suffering is maintained by

† From Stanley Geist, *Herman Melville: The Tragic Vision and the Heroic Ideal* (Cambridge, Massachusetts: Harvard University Press, 1939), pp. 43–51. Copyright 1939 by the President and Fellows of Harvard College. Reprinted by permission of the publishers.
1. See Charles Olson's "Lear and Moby Dick," in *Twice A Year*, No. 1, 1938.

the general floating image, kept constantly before us, chiefly by means of the verbs used, but also in metaphor, of a human body in anguished movement, tugged, wrenched, beaten, pierced, stung, scourged, dislocated, flayed, gashed, scalded, tortured, and finally broken on the rack.[2]

With the first appearance of Ahab on deck the note is struck:

> He looked like a man cut away from the stake when the fire has overrunningly wasted all the limbs without consuming them. . . .

And from that point the image recurs, like a musical phrase with variations, in virtually every scene in which Ahab is mentioned. Tortured by his *blazing brain*, at night,

> with glaring eyes Ahab would burst from his stateroom as though escaping from a bed that was on fire.

Starbuck reads in Ahab's eyes "some lurid woe that would *shrivel* me up;" and Ishmael speaks of "that *burnt-out* crater of his brain." Ahab is driven on in his pursuit of Moby Dick by

> all that most *maddens* and *torments* . . . all that *cracks the sinews and cakes the brain.*

The *jagged* edge of his iron crown of woe *galls* him as he proceeds in his *brain-battering* fight.

> He piled upon the whale's white hump the sum of all the general rage and hate felt by his whole race from Adam down; and then, as if his chest had been a mortar, he *burst his hot heart's shell* upon it.

His *torn* body and *gashed* soul *bleed* into one another. He is

> *gnawed* within and *scorched* without, with the unrelenting *fangs* of some incurable idea.

He stands before his men "with a *crucifixion* in his face."
"God! God! God!—*crack* my heart! *stave* my brain!" he cries in despair. His passion, *like a hawk's beak, pecks* his brain. He is *shrivelled* by his woe.

> The lightning flashes through my skull; mine eyeballs *ache* and *ache*; my whole *beaten* brain seems as *beheaded* and rolling on some *stunning* ground.

A *vulture feeds* upon his heart. He is like the

> lofty trunk of a great tree, when the upper lightning *tearingly darts* down it . . . leaving the tree still alive, but *branded.*

2. Caroline F. E. Spurgeon, *Shakespeare's Imagery*, New York, 1936, pp. 338–40.

But through his suffering Ahab is ennobled. Melville wrote in *Pierre*, "Not to know Gloom and Grief is not to know aught that an heroic man should learn." And he made it plain in both *Moby Dick* and *Pierre* that suffering and heroism were concomitant. Ahab soliloquizes at sunset:

Is then the crown too heavy that I wear? This Iron Crown of Lombardy [which was made of the nails used in the Crucifixion].

And he continues:

Yet is it bright with many a gem; I, the wearer, see not its far flashings; but darkly feel that I wear that, that dazzlingly confounds.

Melville would leave no doubts of Ahab's magnificence. The crown of woe, with its jagged, galling edges, shines "bright with many a gem," its brilliance dazzling and confounding. And Ahab, like Pierre, is exalted far above all common mortals. He is "a lone gigantic elm," a Norse king. He is Prometheus, and he is Adam, "staggering beneath the piled centuries since Paradise."

Melville's firm conviction that man became a hero of gigantic stature by attaining the vision of tragedy, and his equally firm conviction that he was himself among the giants, made his use of the Prometheus symbol particularly appropriate. For if the greatness of the individual, residing wholly within his own vision of the world, was contingent upon no one and nothing outside himself, what distinction remained on the timeless and bodiless spiritual plane between human and superhuman? "To trail the genealogies of these high mortal miseries," he wrote in *Moby Dick*, "carries us at last among the sourceless primogenitures of the gods." [3] What more could the gods themselves know of the depths of the human tragedy than the profoundest men? If no more, why should the hero abase himself before any powers, human or superhuman? He compared Hawthorne (and so himself, for his comments on Hawthorne are habitually self-portraits) [4] to

the man who . . . declares himself a sovereign nature (in himself) amid the powers of heaven, hell, and earth. He may perish; but so long as he exists he insists upon treating with all Powers upon an equal basis. If any of those other Powers choose to withhold certain secrets, let them; that does not impair my sovereignty in myself; that does not make me tributary.

3. Since, in Melville's "theology," pagan terms were so often mingled with Christian concepts, and Christian terms with pagan concepts, this discussion necessarily makes use of figurative rather than literal language.

4. See, for example, the markings in his copy of Hawthorne's *Mosses* (now in Widener Library).

And in another letter to Hawthorne he remarked:

> You perceive I employ a capital initial in the pronoun referring
> to the Deity; don't you think there is a slight dash of flunkeyism
> in that usage?

So Promethean defiance of the gods and intense pride, were other
elements in the nature of the tragic hero. Pierre and Ahab habitually defy all the powers of all the spheres, and the pride of each
is immense. But their pride, and Melville's, springs not out of conceit or vanity but out of suffering; and it must be carefully distinguished from that false pride in external beauty and material
wealth which Pierre finds so revolting in his mother. It has in it, to
be sure, something of the self-reliant spirit, but is, at bottom, a
corollary to the belief that man becomes god-like in attaining the
tragic vision. None but the mighty could look into the heart of darkness, and it was sheer hypocrisy to pretend ignorance of one's own
might. If the sense of sorrowful greatness which accompanied the
tragic vision was illusory, it was yet a clear intuition, rather than a
wishful thought imposed upon experience: there was no mistaking
the fact of sorrow, and no mistaking the instinctive supposition
that sorrow was a nobler emotion than joy.

> For, thought Ahab, even the highest earthly felicities ever have a
> certain unsignifying pettiness lurking in them, but, at bottom, all
> heart-woes a mystic significance, and, in some men, an archangelic
> grandeur. . . . The ineffaceable, sad birth-mark in the brow of a
> man is but the stamp of sorrow in the signers.

Ahab, in his Promethean greatness, is thus "proud as a Greek god."
Soliloquizing upon the "dark Hindu half of nature"—all the blackness which he feels in the world—he cries out:

> Yet dost thou, darker half, rock me with a prouder, if a darker
> faith.

In proclaiming his sovereign power, the hero also proclaimed
his solitude. Ahab, studying the figures stamped upon his doubloon, sees his own nature mirrored in them and says:

> There's something ever egotistical in mountain-tops and towers
> and all other grand and lofty things; look here,—three peaks as
> proud as Lucifer. The firm tower, that is Ahab; the volcano, that
> is Ahab; the courageous, the undaunted and victorious fowl, that
> too is Ahab.

"As proud as Lucifer"—a conventional simile, to be sure; but
Melville, like his hero, admired the rebel archangel for his proud
and heroic defiance. * * *

WILLIAM ELLERY SEDGWICK

[Ishmael vs. Ahab] †

The Dantesque and Shakespearean Actions in Moby Dick

I shall now enter *Moby Dick* in a comparison involving two of the greatest names in all literature. My purpose here is practical. I want to show to what lengths *Moby Dick* escapes all classification, and at the same time to explore a little into its labyrinthine interior. A cosmopolite, it is not to be pinned down by easy definitions. On the other hand, just because it is so thorough a cosmopolite, it lends itself on all sides to illuminating comparisons.

By December, 1850, Melville was well along with *Moby Dick*. When in the summer of this year he wrote his essay on Hawthorne's *Mosses*, he was composing himself for the great task which lay ahead of him. In what he wrote in this essay about Hawthorne and Shakespeare he was, at bottom, envisaging his own development. He was feeling out his own equilibrium in virtue of which all his experience and all the aspects of his consciousness were available to him; to serve, respectively, as his materials and as so many different look-outs over his materials. The essay also shows that of all the forces outside himself which helped him to a full awareness of his own resources, the greatest by far was Shakespeare. What the essay shows in this respect is borne out in abounding measure in *Moby Dick*.

The influence of Shakespeare on Melville was fundamentally a profound and pervasive act of fertilization. There are many indications of this that one can point to, some of them important and others superficial. That is, there are numerous and diverse parallels in language, in emotional effect, in situation and tragic action between *Moby Dick* on the one hand, and, on the other, *King Lear*, *Hamlet*, *Macbeth*, *Othello* and *Timon*. I must repeat what I quoted in the last chapter from Melville's remarks on Shakespeare: "those deep faraway things in him; those occasional flashings-forth of the intuitive Truth in him; those short, quick probings at the very axis of reality;—these are the things that make Shakespeare, Shakespeare." Now look at *Moby Dick*. "Oh God!" cries Ahab, "Oh God! that man should be a thing for immortal

† From William Ellery Sedgwick, *The Tragedy of Mind* (Cambridge, Massachusetts: Harvard University Press, 1944), pp. 84–88, 119–26. Copyright 1944 by the President and Fellows of Harvard College; reprinted by permission of the publishers.

souls to sieve through!" There is Ahab's angry retort to the ship's carpenter, "Thou art as unprincipled as the gods, and as much of a jack-of-all-trades." And I might add any number of other instances where Melville, following Shakespeare, put in the mouths of his own "dark" characters words which probe jaggedly at the very axis of reality.

A point of difference must come up first which is high-lighted by the many similarities between them. This difference might have been expected from the peculiarity of Melville's response to Shakespeare, his response to him primarily as a seer or truthteller. This was Melville's first criterion in estimating a poet's worth. How independent and rigorous he was in applying this criterion of truthfulness can be seen in his letter to Evert Duyckinck of March, 1849, in which he wrote, "Now I hold it a verity, that even Shakespeare, was not a frank man to the uttermost." Shakespeare, he granted, was handicapped by the prejudices of his time when all men were forced to wear a muzzle on their souls. Thereupon Melville added, with an optimism which his own experience was to belie, "but the Declaration of Independence makes a difference."

In *Moby Dick*, as in Shakespeare's tragedies, there is a solid, crowded foreground of material things and of human characters and actions. Yet this solid ground will suddenly seem to give under our feet, so that we feel ourselves hung momentarily over the abyss. We owe this sensation to the fact that solidity has been sacrificed to transparency for the sake of a more immediate view into the ultimate. Shakespeare was satisfied to leave the mysterious background of life to random probings or to inference. Melville could not. He was bound by many diverse considerations—by his inherited and his temperamental Calvinism, by the American pioneer in him as well as the Puritan—to confront the truth as directly and comprehensively as possible. In *Moby Dick* the mysterious background truth looms in the foreground of palpable facts. It articulates itself in those facts and by so doing it confers upon them something of an apocalyptic scale and intensity foreign to Shakespeare's prevailing naturalism.

Melville's headstrong preoccupation with the truth was served by the form he chose for *Moby Dick*, the narrative instead of the dramatic, and by the intervention of Ishmael, the ubiquitous "I" who tells the story. But such shifts are not sufficient. This preoccupation diffuses a settled character throughout *Moby Dick* which, while removing it from Shakespeare's tragedies, relates it to the "visions" of mediaeval literature of which Dante's *Divine Comedy* is the commanding masterpiece.

The comparison of *Moby Dick* with the *Divine Comedy* should not come as a surprise. In *Mardi*, as we know, the harmony of consciousness which Melville aspired to was imaged by "grim Dante" shaking sides with fat Rabelais. In *Mardi*, too, Babbalanja discourses at length on the great poet Lombardo, and his words show that Melville felt a kinship with Dante, if not in the substance, at any rate in the process of his unfolding vision. ("And ere Necessity plunged spur and rowel into him," Babbalanja says of Lombardo, "he knew not his own paces. *That* churned him into consciousness; and brought ambition, ere then dormant, seething to the top, till he trembled at himself.") Moreover, the comparison between *Moby Dick* and the *Divine Comedy* does not rest on the bare fact that both are cosmic visions. There are some further details which add not a little to the light this comparison can shed.

In the *Divine Comedy* the vision focusses ultimately on the will of God in his creation. In *Moby Dick* the vision focusses on the mystery of creation, the chief emblem of which is the terrible White Whale. However, just as in Dante's poem all men are classified as they stand in relation to the will of God, so in *Moby Dick* the characters are classified in relation to the Whale—according to whether they fear him, worship him, or ignore him.

From this view of *Moby Dick*, it would appear that Melville aimed to strike a balance between Dante and Shakespeare. Certainly, there are two actions in the book which although they mesh are distinct from one another, one of which is Shakespearean, the other Dantesque. The Shakespearean or outward tragic action includes Ahab's conflict with forces outside himself and, also, the bitter, agonizing self-conflict which follows on its heels. All the other characters are caught up in this action, but it centers in Ahab. The other action, the Dantesque, lies entirely with Ishmael, who, let me say for the moment, stands to Ahab as the shadow to the object which casts it. Pushing a paradox, I shall call this action passive as well as inward—inward, that is, with respect to the book as a whole. Like the action that extends from first to last in the *Divine Comedy*, it is the action of man's comprehension slowly completing itself. In Dante each incident, each observation that adds to his comprehension gains from the next; each shares in the accruing interest of his unfolding vision, and each participates by undergoing a transfiguration in the completion of the whole. It is much the same in point of action with Ishmael. His every realization gains from the next and each is the more realized by the completion of his comprehension of things. But how appallingly different is the substance of his vision! Dante came at last to the beatific vision and beheld the divine love enfolding the orders of creation as a lordly rose enfolds its own petals. The long accumulation of Ishmael's comprehension of things rolls back along the dark interior windings of *Moby Dick*. From his last word of all Ishmael has seen into a sundered or cloven universe and he ends by calling himself "another orphan." His vision takes a direction opposite to Dante's; it shows him at the core of creation, not love but destruction. His vision has bereft him of all sense of kinship either below, among bodies terrestrial, or on high, among the celestial orders.

* * *

Only Ishmael survived. It so happened that on the last day he was asked to take the part of bowsman in Ahab's boat, left vacant when Fedallah disappeared the day before. In the commotion of the battle he was tossed and left floating on the margin of the final scene, where he just escaped being sucked in after the sinking *Pequod.* All that remained to him was his own lifebuoy and by that means Ishmael kept himself afloat, until picked up by a vessel that chanced to come his way.

This lifebuoy had been a coffin made for Queequeg when he thought himself dying. Upon his recovery Starbuck ordered the carpenter to make it over to serve in the opposite capacity. Observing the transformation, Ahab is given pause; "A life-buoy of a coffin! Does it go further? Can it be that in some spiritual sense the coffin is, after all, but an immortality preserver! I'll think of that. But no. So far gone am I in the dark side of earth, that its other side, the theoretic bright one, seems but uncertain twilight to me." Ishmael escaped then by means of the coffin life preserver which Ahab had rejected as a possible symbol of faith.

The truth we come at by way of Ishmael's story is the final truth about *Moby Dick,*—the truth, I might add, that made it whole. At the beginning, Ishmael explains that he is suffering one of his fits of hypochondria; "a damp, drizzly November" in his soul. His misanthropic hypos are getting the best of him. Therefore—his usual remedy for this condition—he decides to go to sea. That is his substitute for "pistol and ball. With a philosophical flourish Cato throws himself upon his sword; I quietly take to the ship. There is nothing surprising in this. If they but knew it, almost all men . . . some time or other, cherish very nearly the same feelings towards the ocean with me." When, some days later, on the little boat that takes him from New Bedford to Nantucket, he first catches sight of open water, his soul leaps up in him. "How I snuffed the Tartar air!—how I spurned the turnpike earth!—that common highway all over dented with the marks of slavish heels and hoofs; and turned me to admire the magnanimity of the sea which will permit no records." In Nantucket, Ishmael chooses the garish and outlandish *Pequod* as the ship for himself and Queequeg. What he gleans about Captain Ahab when he goes on board to sign affects him deeply; "I felt a sympathy and a sorrow for him, but for I don't know what, unless it was the cruel loss of his leg." It is worth noticing that Ishmael is the only one of those who sailed with Ahab on the *Pequod* who caught sight of shadowy Fedallah being sneaked on board. Of what he felt when Ahab announced his purpose we already know something: "Who does not feel the irresistible arm drag?" "I, Ishmael, was one of that crew; my shouts had gone up with the rest; my oath had been welded with theirs; and stronger I shouted, and more did I hammer and clinch my oath, because of the dread in my soul. A wild, mystical, sympathetical feeling was in me; Ahab's quenchless feud seemed mine."

That is sufficient to show Ishmael's danger. His story turns on his mortal need to maintain himself against the strong drag he feels towards Ahab.

Since there is nothing on which Melville digresses that does not serve his meaning, Ishmael's jeopardy can be put in the picturesque language of the fishery as Melville explains it under the headings, "Fast-Fish and Loose-Fish." A fast-fish is a whale who has been struck and who, presumably, can be brought alongside and made fast to the ship whose harpoon has caught him. A loose-fish is still fair game for anybody: he is still free for anybody to have, himself first of all. Ahab is a fast-fish. The universe has got its barb in him. His humanity is transfixed. Ishmael, on the contrary, is a loose-fish. Will he keep himself so? Or will he like Ahab impale himself on the exasperating inscrutability of things? Will he cease to stand up a "sovereign nature (in himself) amid the powers of heaven, hell and earth"? "If any of those powers choose to withhold certain secrets, let them; that does not impair my sovereignty in myself; that does not make me tributary." But that, directly and indirectly, is what did impair Ahab's sovereignty.

The chapter called "The Whiteness of the Whale" begins with Ishmael saying, "What the White Whale was to Ahab has been hinted; what, at times, he was to me, as yet remains unsaid. . . . It was the whiteness of the Whale that above all things appalled me."

Thereupon he proceeds to follow the meaning of whiteness, tracking it down through all its associations in man's mind from time out of mind—as they appear in pageantry, story and ritual. Whiteness enhances beauty. It is associated with royalty and with royal preëminence, the same in kings and which, among peoples, gives "the white man ideal mastership over every dusky tribe." Whiteness is associated with gladness, with innocence, with the holy of holies. Yet, for all these associations, there is an ambiguity about whiteness; the same ambiguity that in the connotations of the sea seem to identify death with glory, bleached bones and desecration with spirituality. "Is it," Ishmael asks, "that by its indefiniteness it shadows forth the voids and immensities of the universe, and then stabs us from behind with the thought of annihilation, when beholding the white depths of the Milky Way? Or is it, that as in essence whiteness is not so much a colour as the visible absence of colour, and at the same time the concrete of all colours; is it for these reasons that there is such a dumb blankness, full of meaning, in a wide landscape of snows—a colourless, all-colour of atheism from which we shrink? And when we consider that other theory of the natural philosophers, that all other earthly hues—every stately or lovely emblazoning—the sweet tinges of sunset skies and woods; yea, and the gilded velvets of butterflies, and the butterfly cheeks of young girls; all these are but subtle deceits, not actually inherent in substances, but only laid on from without; so that all deified Nature absolutely paints like the harlot, whose allurements cover nothing but the charnel-house within; and when we proceed further, and consider that the mystical cosmetic which produces every one of her hues, the great principle of light, forever remains white or colourless in itself, and if operating without medium upon matter, would touch all objects, even tulips and roses, with its own blank tinge—pondering all this, the palsied universe lies before us a leper; and like wilful travellers in Lapland, who refuse to wear coloured and colouring glasses upon their eyes, so the wretched infidel gazes himself blind at the monumental white shroud that wraps all the prospect around him."

Under the spell of Ahab, yet going his own way, Ishmael catches sight or, better, has a "sensational presentiment" of the cleavage in creation which sprang up an active principle, in Ahab. Not "the time is out of joint" but the very underpinning of creation. "Oh, cursed spite,"—there lies the source "of all those malicious agencies which some deep men feel eating in them. . . . That intangible malignity which has been from the beginning. . . . All that maddens and torments . . . all truth with malice in it" and, "the instinct of the knowledge of the demonism in the world."

The horror of whiteness, is it the soul's fear of death, the fear of extinction after death? Yes, but it goes beyond that. It is more fearful because more intimate. It is the soul's fear of itself. For in its own conscious self lies the seed of its destruction. The preoccupation with truth, with ideality, with "ideal mastership," with "spiritual things," nay, with the Deity itself, which are of the conscious soul, these are of the light principle, which "great principle of light, forever remains white or colourless in itself." In the white light of the soul's preoccupation with truth all its earthly satisfactions seem illusory—all stale, flat and unprofitable. The vital needs of its own earth born humanity are but "coloured and colouring glasses." Refusing to wear these kindly glasses, the soul finds itself in a void. It sees everywhere, as was seen in the White Whale, when he faced the staggering *Pequod*, its own featurelessness, its own colorlessness.

Ishmael felt himself on the verge of the abyss which he saw outwardly in Ahab's lurid light. In that extremity he felt within himself the source of all the tormenting ambiguities of life. What is life to one side of the soul is death to the other, and death at last to both.

Strong as his attachment to Ahab is, Ishmael is open to contrary influences. He is reluctant to share a bed with Queequeg at the inn at New Bedford, but the next morning brings a change. Ishmael is glad to accept Queequeg's offer of friendship and they share a pipe over it. Then Queequeg, according to the custom in his country, makes him a gift of half his possessions in silver and tobacco. Ishmael feels himself restored. He is in the position that Ahab is in, much later, with Pip. Ishmael, however, goes the full length of his more kindly emotions; "I began to be sensible of strange feelings. I felt a melting in me. No more my splintered heart and maddened hand were turned against the wolfish world. This soothing savage had redeemed it."

While Ahab's hunt for the hated White Whale gets hotter, Ishmael's land sense struggles to preserve itself. Whereas Ahab curses "that mortal inter-indebtedness" which makes a man dependent on his fellows, Ishmael submits to the fact that it is "a mutual, joint-stock world, in all meridians." Two thirds of the way through the book comes the chapter, "A Squeeze of the Hand." Ishmael describes the operation of squeezing down lumps of sperm into a delicious aromatic milk. The work is done in tubs, and since many hands are at work in each tub, they often squeeze each other by mistake. "Squeeze! squeeze! squeeze!" cries Ishmael, himself melting down again. "I declare to you, that for the time I lived as in a musky meadow; I forgot all about our horrible oath. . . . I felt divinely free from all ill-will, or petulance, or malice, of any sort whatsoever. . . . Would that I could keep squeezing that sperm forever! For now, since by many prolonged, repeated experiences, I have perceived that in all cases man must eventually lower, or at least shift, his conceit of attainable felicity; not placing it anywhere in the intellect or the fancy; but in the wife, the heart, the bed, the table, the saddle, the fireside, the country; now that I have perceived all this, I am ready to squeeze case eternally."

In the next chapter but one Ishmael's drama reaches its climax. It is night and he is taking his turn at the helm. The rest of the crew are employed in boiling blubber and have gathered around two vast cauldrons under which fires have been kindled. From his place in the stern Ishmael looks on, while "the wind howled on, and

the sea leaped, and the ship groaned and dived, and yet steadfastly shot her red hell further and further into the blackness. . . ."
While he was watching it came over Ishmael that "the rushing
Pequod, freighted with savages, and laden with fire . . . and
plunging into that blackness of darkness, seemed the material
counterpart of her monomaniac commander's soul." Then something happens. There just fails of being a fiery welding between
his soul and Ahab's. He is conscious that something is very wrong.
He cannot see the compass. There is nothing in front of him but a
pit of gloom, "now and then made ghastly by flashes of redness.
Uppermost was the impression, that whatever swift, rushing thing
I stood on was not so much bound to any haven ahead as rushing
from all havens astern. A stark, bewildered feeling, as of death,
came over me. . . . My God! what is the matter with me? thought
I. Lo! in my brief sleep I had turned myself about. . . . In an instant I faced back, just in time to prevent the vessel from flying up
into the wind, and very probably capsizing her. How glad and how
grateful the relief from this unnatural hallucination of the night,
and the fatal contingency of being brought by the lee!"

"Look not too long in the face of the fire, O man!" Fire is idio-
syncratic. It has a capricious, distorting intensity. It is the light of
personal feelings, that take the universal sorrow of life as personal
grievance, and reason for personal rage. And "that way madness
lies." "There is a wisdom that is woe; but there is a woe that is
madness. And there is a Catskill eagle in some souls that can alike
dive down into the blackest gorges, and soar out of them again
and become invisible in the sunny spaces."

The freedom of spirit, alike to plunge and to soar. Here we come
upon the significance of Ishmael's escape in the coffin life-preserver,
which is more directly rendered when Ishmael, or rather Melville,
taking a suggestion from the vapour that hangs about a whale's head
"as you will sometimes see it—glorified by a rainbow, as if heaven
itself had put its seal upon his thoughts"—writes, "And so through
all the thick mists of the dim doubts in my mind, divine intuitions
now and then shoot, enkindling my fog with a heavenly ray. And for
this I thank God; for all have doubts; many deny; but doubts or
denials, few along with them have intuitions. Doubts of all things
earthly, and intuitions of some things heavenly; this combination
makes neither believer nor infidel, but makes a man who regards
them both with equal eye."

Against the strong attraction he feels for Ahab, Ishmael manages
to keep his spiritual balance, his spiritual and intellectual freedom.
Sharing Ahab's perceptions and feeling himself drawn to Ahab's
desperate conclusions, he manages to so hold himself that he keeps
in view the whole circle of life's possible issues. His soul, like
Bulkington's, his sleeping partner, keeps "the open independence

of her sea."

Ishmael escaped. Slowly the suction of the sunk ship reached him and he was slowly drawn towards the closing vortex. But when he reached it it had subsided. "Round and round, then, and ever contracting toward the button-like black bubble at the axis of that slowly wheeling circle, like another Ixion I did revolve. Till, gaining that vital centre, the black bubble burst upward . . . and, owing to its great buoyancy, rising with great force, the coffin life-buoy shot lengthwise from the sea, fell over, and floated by my side."

What are we to understand by Ishmael's escape? Between him and Ahab there is a divergency which repeats the divergency between Babbalanja and Taji at the end of *Mardi*. Babbalanja and Taji stood for opposite pulls in Melville's temperament. We can be more specific and say they stood for opposite exigencies in the religious consciousness which was paramount in Melville's nature. Ahab's last act was like Taji's: "Now I am my own soul's emperor, and my first act is abdication." So saying, Taji, like Ahab after him, disappeared; "and then pursuers and pursued flew on over an endless sea." But while Ishmael is a foil for Ahab as Babbalanja is for Taji, we cannot go the full length and identify his escape with Babbalanja's conversion in Serenia. Indeed, any single conclusion drawn from his escape would be false. It is simply one episode among several that make up Ishmael's own story, the whole force of which, if it can be said to conclude at all, is to conclude against conclusions.

CHARLES OLSON

Ahab and His Fool †

Life has its way, even with Ahab. Melville had drawn upon another myth besides Shakespeare's to create his dark Ahab, that of both Marlowe and Goethe: the Faust legend. But he alters it. After the revolutions of the 18th–19th century the archetype Faust has never been the same. In Melville's alteration the workings of Lear and the Fool can also be discerned.

The change comes in the relation of Ahab to Pip. Ahab does not die in the tempestuous agony of Faustus pointing to Christ's blood and crying for His mercy. He dies with an acceptance of his damnation. Before his final battle with the White Whale Ahab has

† From Charles Olson, *Call Me Ishmael* (New York: Reynall & Hitchcock, 1947), pp. 59–63. Copyright 1947 by Charles Olson; reprinted by permission of City Lights Books.

resigned himself to his fate.

His solipsism is most violent and his hate most engendered the night of The Candles when he raises the burning harpoon over his crew. It is a night of storm. The setting is *Lear*-like. Ahab, unlike Lear, does not in this night of storm discover his love for his fellow wretches. On the contrary, this night Ahab uncovers his whole hate. He commits the greater blasphemy than defiance of sun and lightning. He turns the harpoon, forged and baptized for the inhuman Whale alone, upon his own human companions, the crew, and brandishes his hate over them. The morning after the storm Ahab is most subtly dedicated to his malignant purpose when he gives the lightning-twisted binnacle a new needle. Melville marks this pitch of his ego:

> In his fiery eyes of scorn and triumph, you then saw Ahab in all his fatal pride.

In a very few hours the change in Ahab sets in and Pip—the shadow of Pip—is the agent of the change. Like a reminder of Ahab's soul he calls to Ahab and Ahab, advancing to help, cries to the sailor who has seized Pip: "Hands off that holiness!" It is a crucial act: for the first time Ahab has offered to help another human being. And at that very moment Ahab speaks Lear's phrases:

> Thou touchest my inmost centre, boy; thou art tied to me by cords woven of my heart-strings. Come, let's down.

Though Ahab continues to curse the gods for their "inhumanities," his tone, from this moment, is richer, quieter, less angry and strident. He even questions his former blasphemies, for a bottomed sadness grows in him as Pip lives in the cabin with him. There occurs a return of something Peleg had insisted that Ahab possessed on the day Ishmael signed for the fatal voyage. Peleg then refuted Ishmael's fears of his captain's wicked name—that dogs had licked his blood. He revealed that Ahab had a wife and child, and concluded:

> hold ye then there can be any utter, hopeless harm in Ahab? No, no, my lad; stricken, blasted, if he be, Ahab has his humanities!

These humanities had been set aside in Ahab's hate for the White Whale. One incident: Ahab never thought, as he paced the deck at night in fever of anger, how his whalebone stump rapping the boards waked his crew and officers. The aroused Stubb confronts Ahab. Ahab orders him like a dog to kennel. For Stubb cannot, like Pip, affect Ahab. When it is over Stubb's only impulse is to go down on his knees and pray for the hot old man who he feels has so horribly amputated himself from human feelings.

Pip continues to be, mysteriously, the agent of this bloom once it has started. Says Ahab: "I do suck most wondrous philosophies from thee!" He even goes so far as to ask God to bless Pip and save him. BUT before he asks that, he threatens to murder Pip, Pip so weakens his revengeful purpose.

Though Pip recedes in the last chapters, the suppleness he has brought out of old Ahab continues to grow. Pip is left in the hold as though Ahab would down his soul once more, but above decks Ahab is no longer the proud Lucifer. He asks God to bless the captain of the *Rachel,* the last ship they meet before closing with Moby-Dick, the vessel which later picks Ishmael up after the tragedy. The difference in his speech is commented on: "a voice that prolongingly moulded every word." And it is noticed that when, toward the last days, Ahab prepares a basket lookout for himself to be hoisted up the mast to sight Moby-Dick, he trusts his "life-line" to Starbuck's hands. This running sap of his humanities gives out its last shoots in The Symphony chapter: observe that Ahab asks God to destroy what has been from the first his boast—"God! God! God! stave my brain!" He has turned to Starbuck and talked about his wife and child! And though this apple, his last, and cindered, drops to the soil, his revenge is now less pursued than resigned to. His thoughts are beyond the whale, upon easeful death.

In the three days' chase he is a tense, mastered, almost grim man. He sets himself outside humanity still, but he is no longer arrogant, only lonely: "Cold, cold . . ." After the close of the second day, when Fedallah cannot be found, he withers. His last vindictive shout is to rally his angers which have been hurled and lost like Fedallah and the harpoon of lightning and blood. He turns to Fate, the handspike in his windlass: "The whole act's immutably decreed." That night he does not face the whale as was his custom. He turns his "heliotrope glance" back to the east, waiting the sun of the fatal third day like death. It is Macbeth in his soliloquy of tomorrow, before Macduff will meet and match him. On the third day the unbodied winds engage his attention for the first time in the voyage. Even after the White Whale is sighted Ahab lingers, looks over the sea, considers his ship, says goodbye to his masthead. He admits to Starbuck he foreknows his death: the prophecies are fulfilled. In his last speech he moans only that his ship perishes without him:

Oh, lonely death on lonely life! Oh, now I feel my topmost greatness lies in my topmost grief.

He rushes to the White Whale with his old curse dead on his lips.

The last words spoken to him from the ship had been Pip's: "O master, my master, come back!"

What Pip wrought in Ahab throws over the end of *Moby-Dick*

a veil of grief, relaxes the tensions of its hate, and permits a sympathy for the stricken man that Ahab's insistent diabolism up to the storm would not have evoked. The end of this fire-forked tragedy is enriched by a pity in the very jaws of terror.

The lovely association of Ahab and Pip is like the relations of Lear to both the Fool and Edgar. What the King learns of their suffering through companionship with them in storm helps him to shed his pride. His hedging and self-deluding authority gone, Lear sees wisdom in their profound unreason. He becomes capable of learning from his Fool just as Captain Ahab does from his cabin-boy.

In *Lear* Shakespeare has taken the conventional "crazy-witty" and brought him to an integral place in much more than the plot. He is at center to the poetic and dramatic conception of the play. Melville grasped the development.

Someone may object that Pip is mad, not foolish. In Shakespeare the gradations subtly work into one another. In *Moby-Dick* Pip is both the jester and the idiot. Before he is frightened out of his wits he and his tambourine are cap and bells to the crew. His soliloquy upon their midnight revelry has the sharp, bitter wisdom of the Elizabethan fool. And his talk after his "drowning" is parallel not only to the Fool and Edgar but to Lear himself.

A remark in *Moby-Dick* throws a sharp light over what has just been said and over what remains to be said. Melville comments on Pip:

> all thy strange mummeries not unmeaningly blended with the black tragedy of the melancholy ship, and mocked it.

For Pip by his madness had seen God.

WALTER E. BEZANSON

Moby-Dick: Work of Art †

* * * Interest in *Moby-Dick* as direct narrative, as moral analogue, as modern source, and as spiritual autobiography has far outrun commentary on it as a work of art. A proper criticism of

† From Walter E. Bezanson, *"Moby-Dick:* Work of Art," in *Moby-Dick: Centennial Essays,* edited by Tyrus Hillway and Luther S. Mansfield (Dallas: Southern Methodist University Press, 1953) pp. 31–58. Copyright © 1953 by Southern Methodist University Press. Reprinted by permission of the publishers.

Bezanson's paper was read at Oberlin College on November 13, 1951, at exercises to commemorate the one-hundredth year of publication of *Moby-Dick.* The opening paragraph and half of the second are omitted here.

so complex a book will be a long time in the making and will need immense attention from many kinds of critics. In the meantime I am struck by the need just now for contributions toward a relatively impersonal criticism directed at the book itself. The surrounding areas—such as *Moby-Dick* and Melville, *Moby-Dick* and the times in which it was made—are significant just because the book is a work of art. To ask what the book means is to ask what it is about, and to ask what it is about is in turn to ask how art works in the case at hand.

My remarks are therefore in this direction. Beginning with a look at the materials out of which *Moby-Dick* is created, we shall explore the means of activation and some of the forms that contain and define them. The three roadmarks we shall follow are *matter*, *dynamic*, and *structure*.

I

By *matter* I mean here the subject (or subject matter) in the gross sense. *Moby-Dick* has as its gross subject not Indian fighting or railroad building but whaling.

Any book about mid-nineteenth-century American whaling must in some fashion or other deal with certain phenomena, artifacts, and processes. There they are, and they must be used or the book is not about whaling. A rough inventory of data would include at least the following areas:

NATURAL WORLD: *The seas and oceans*, covering three-fifths of the globe: on the surface—tides, currents, winds, and weather; under the surface—countless forms of life of extreme diversity. Marine animals of the order *Cetacea*, ranging from small dolphins and porpoises to whales, the largest form of life in earth history (up to 125 tons). The Sperm Whale (*Physeter Macrocephalus*): one of the larger varieties (up to 75–85 feet), wrapped in a fat blanket (blubber) like other whales but unique in carrying a pool of pure spermaceti oil (up to 500 gallons) in his great square head; protects himself with rows of ivory teeth and the slap of his tail (20 feet across), or dives to the sea bottom; known to attack great objects which threaten him.

HISTORICAL WORLD: *Man*, a prolific, social, land animal constantly in search of animal, mineral, and vegetable resources for survival and use. *Seventeenth century*: discovering the use of whale products especially the oil for lighting, man begins to bring to bear on the pursuit of whales the technologies developed in transportation and war. *Nineteenth century*: the United States, a newly created and powerfully expanding democracy in the early stages of capitalism, builds a whaling fleet of over seven hundred vessels and commits itself to a sea frontier that girdles the globe. New Bedford, Nantucket, and Sag Harbor become the world centers for the pursuit of sperm whales.

ARTIFACTS: *The whale-ship:* a wooden vessel, length about 105 feet, beam about 28 feet; three vertical masts (foremast, mainmast, mizzenmast), each with four horizontal yards (crosspieces); rigged to the yards more than thirty separate sails, each named for identification. *Nautical equipment:* windlass, capstan, chocks, pins, block and tackle, pumps; lines for handling sails, anchors, cargo. *Navigation equipment:* chronometer, quadrant, compass, charts, log and line, wheel or tiller; for finding location and keeping on course. *Spaces:* below decks two levels of compartments, including forecastle bunkroom for the crew and cabins aft for the captain and mates; storage quarters for food, water, whaling gear, casks, shooks (staves and barrel heads); sail and chain lockers, blubber room, holds for the cargo. *Pursuit equipment:* whaleboats of cedar planking, length 25 feet; plank seats for five oarsmen, platforms bow and stern for harpooner and boatsteerer; five pair of oars, steering oar, harpoons, lances, waif poles (for signal flags), line tubs, assorted gear. *Processing equipment:* try-works (deck furnaces), kettles, forks, spades, mincing knives, etc.

TECHNIQUES: innumerable skills demanded by all artifacts, especially ship and boat handling, maintenance, attack, butchering.

SOCIAL ORGANIZATION: *In the background:* Yankee owners who furnish capital and artifacts for voyages, to whom the products of voyages are returnable for sale at a profit. *In the foreground:* a ship's company of about thirty-five men brought aboard under individual contracts giving each a percentage of the profits (lay) according to his skill with men or artifacts. *The hierarchy*, in descending order of authority: absentee owners; captain, three mates, three harpooners, boat crews, blacksmith, cooper, cook, cabin boy. *Politics:* manhandling.

OBJECT OF VOYAGE: in three or four years' time to sight, chase, kill, and process into oil as many whales as possible, returning to port safely with a profitable cargo.

These are the given elements of whaling as a major industry in nineteenth-century America. They may be thought of as simply existing in nature and experience; we have been thinking of them independent of communication, though they are necessarily written down here. In art, however, communication is the heart of the matter; and the subject of whaling, it chances, offers good historical instances of some planes on which the communication problem may be conceived.

Looking back into nineteenth-century Anglo-American history, we find at least four different levels of communication of whaling. The first was that of the typical whaling logbook. A whaleman's log was a record kept for the owners by the mates or captain; it consisted of daily entries giving the ship's position, weather, land-falls, ships sighted or hailed, whales taken and their size (expressed in barrels of oil), crew desertions, injuries, deaths, etc. What any of this felt like or meant, except in terms of navigation and trade, was purposely excluded. The whaler's log was meant to be an abstraction of group experience in terms of pragmatic ends.

A second level was that of the standard histories. The aim here was the compilation of reliable data on the natural history of the whale (as part of the zoölogical record) or on the happenings in the fishery (as a contribution to economic history). Classic examples of the histories that had wide circulation in the second quarter of the nineteenth century include Thomas Beale's *Natural History of the Sperm Whale* (1835, 1839), Frederick Bennett's *A Whaling Voyage Round the Globe, from the Year 1833 to 1836* (1840), and William Scoresby's *An Account of the Arctic Regions with a History and Description of the Northern Whale Fishery* (1820). Empirical knowledge set the aims and limits for such books as these, too; their meaning and function were conditioned by the rise of the life sciences and of inductive historiography.

A third level of communication was the simple transcription of generalized personal experience. Americans who had never been whaling were interested to know something of the representative experiences of the seventeen thousand men engaged in the American fisheries in the 1840's. So came the reports of scenes and adventures, of duties and dangers, in books like J. Ross Browne's *Etchings of a Whaling Cruise* (1846) and the Reverend Henry Cheever's *The Whale and His Captors; or the Whaleman's Adventures and the Whale's Biography* . . . (1849). Such books were records of out-ward experience to whose general validity any ex-whaleman could testify. They were the journalism of the whaling industry, written by the Lowell Thomases and John Gunthers of the day (or perhaps one should say *Jonah* Gunthers, as no doubt he would have called his book *Inside the Whale*).

A generous distance beyond these logbooks, histories, and per-sonal narratives lies the problem of fiction. When Melville was composing *Moby-Dick* in 1850 and 1851 he did not hesitate to make quite shameless use of all the books just named, as well as others, in the preparation of his own. Reading for facts and events, for recall and extension, he took on an enormous cargo of whaling matter. But facts are not fiction. In *Moby-Dick* the inert matter of whaling has been subjected to the purposes of art through a dynamic and a structure.

II

By the term "dynamic" I mean the action of forces on bodies at rest. The whaling matter in *Moby-Dick* is in no sense at rest, excepting as here or there occurs a failure in effect. For the most part the stuff and data of whaling are complexly subject to the action of a force which can be defined and illustrated. So too is the whole narrative base of the book, which is something far more than a record of what anyone aboard the *Pequod* would agree had happened. There is a dynamic operating on both matter and narrative which distinguishes *Moby-Dick* from logs, journals, and histories.

One of two forces, or their combination, is commonly assumed to provide the dynamic of *Moby-Dick*. The first, of course, is Captain Ahab, the dark protagonist, the maimed king of the quarter-deck whose monomania flows out through the ship until it drowns his men—mind and (finally) body. That he is the dominant "character" and the source of "action" seems obvious. The reader's image of him is a lasting one. Is Ahab the dynamic?

The alternative force, it is commonly assumed, is Moby Dick himself, that particular white "spouting fish with a horizontal tail" about whom legend and murmured lore have woven enchantments, so that he looms a massive phantom in the restless dreams of the *Pequod's* captain and crew. His name gives the novel its title. He is prime antagonist of the tale. Is Moby Dick the dynamic?

Both these interpretations have their uses, especially when taken together in a subject-predicate relation. But there is a third point of view from which neither Ahab nor the White Whale is the central dynamic, and I find it both compelling and rewarding, once recognized. This story, this fiction, is not so much about Ahab or the White Whale as it is about Ishmael, and I propose that it is he who is the real center of meaning and the defining force of the novel.

The point becomes clearer when one realizes that in *Moby-Dick* there are two Ishmaels, not one. The first Ishmael is the enfolding sensibility of the novel, the hand that writes the tale, the imagination through which all matters of the book pass. He is the narrator. But who then is the other Ishmael? The second Ishmael is not the narrator, not the informing presence, but is the young man of whom,

among others, narrator Ishmael tells us in his story. He is simply one
of the characters in the novel, though, to be sure a major one whose
significance is possibly next to Ahab's. This is forecastle Ishmael or
the younger Ishmael of "some years ago." There is no question here
of dual personality or *alter ego*, such as really exists, for instance, in
Poe's "William Wilson" or Conrad's "The Secret Sharer." Narrator
Ishmael is merely young Ishmael grown older. He is the man who
has already experienced all that we watch forecastle Ishmael going
through as the story is told.

The distinction can be rendered visual by imagining, for a moment, a film version of the novel. As the screen lights up and the
music drops to an obbligato we look on the face of narrator Ishmael
(a most marvelous face, I should judge), and the magic intonation
begins:

> Call me Ishmael. Some years ago—never mind how long pre-
> cisely—having little or no money in my purse, and nothing par-
> ticular to interest me on shore, I thought I would sail about a little
> and see the watery part of the world. It is a way I have of driving
> off the spleen, and regulating the circulation. Whenever I find
> myself . . .

And as the cadenced voice goes on, the face of the Ishmael who has
a tale to tell fades out, the music takes up a brisk piping air, and
whom should we see tripping along the cobbled streets of New Bedford, carpetbag in hand, but forecastle Ishmael. It is a cold winter's
night, and this lonely young man is in search of lodgings. For very
soon now he plans to go a-whaling.

Meanwhile we hear the voice, always the magic voice, not of the
boy we watch with our eyes, but of one who long since went aboard
the *Pequod,* was buried in the sea and resurrected from it. This
voice recounts the coming adventures of young Ishmael as a story
already fully experienced. Experienced, but not fully understood; for
as he explicitly says: "It was the whiteness of the whale that above
all things appalled me. But how can I hope to explain myself here;
and yet, in some dim, random way, explain myself I must, else all
these chapters might be naught." So we are reminded by shifts of
tense from time to time that while forecastle Ishmael is busy hunting whales narrator Ishmael is sifting memory and imagination in
search of the many meanings of the dark adventure he has experienced. So deeply are we under the spell of the narrator's voice that
when at last the final incantation begins—" 'And I only am escaped
alone to tell thee'. . . . The drama's done. . . ."—then at last, as
forecastle Ishmael floats out of the *Pequod*'s vortex, saved, we look
again on the face of Ishmael narrator. And we realize that for many
hours he has been sitting there and has never once moved, except at

the lips; sitting in profound reverie, yet talking, trying to explain "in some dim, random way" what happened, for "explain myself I must."

The distinction between the function of the two Ishmaels is clear. Yet it would be a mistake to separate them too far in temperament. Certainly young Ishmael is no common sailor thoughtlessly enacting whatever the fates throw his way. He is a pondering young man of strong imagination and complex temperament; he will, as it were, become the narrator in due time. But right now he is aboard the *Pequod* doing his whaleman's work and trying to survive the spell of Ahab's power. The narrator, having survived, is at his desk trying to explain himself to himself and to whoever will listen. The primary use of the distinction is to bring the narrator forward as the essential sensibility in terms of which all characters and events of the fiction are conceived and evaluated. The story is his. What, then, are some of his primary commitments of mind and imagination as he shapes his story through one hundred and thirty-five chapters?

As a lover of laughter and hilarity, Ishmael delights in the incongruities. Of whales, for instance: whales spout steam because they think so much; they have no nose, but don't really need one—there are no violets in the sea; they are very healthy, and this is because they get so much exercise and are always out of doors, though rarely in the fresh air; and they like to breakfast on "sailor tarts, that is whaleboats full of mariners." Ishmael has too a deep belly laugh for the crudities and obscenities that mark the life of animal man, making much more than is proper of some talk about gentlemen harpooning ladies, relishing a Rabelaisian remark about "head winds" versus "winds from astern," and penning a memorable canonization of a rarely discussed part of the anatomy in "The Cassock." But as a purveyor of the "genial, desperado philosophy," his most characteristic humor is that of the hyena laugh: he begins his tale with a mock confession of suicidal impulses; he sends young Ishmael running to his bunk after his first encounter with a whale to make out his will; he reports that some sailors are so neat that they wouldn't think of drowning "without first washing their faces"; and he delights in Queequeg's solemn decision, when he seems mortally ill, whereby the good savage suddenly "recalled a little duty ashore, which he was leaving undone; and therefore . . . changed his mind about dying." Beneath Ishmael's mask of hypochondria is the healthy grimace of a man who stands braced to accept "the universal thump" and to call out: "Who ain't a slave?" To Ishmael "a good laugh is a mighty good thing, and rather too scarce a good thing; the more's the pity."

As narrator Ishmael betrays a passion for all faraway places and things, "Patagonian sights and sounds," imagined cities, fabled heroes, the sepulchers of kings. His rich imagination is stirred by all that is secret, mysterious, and undecipherable in the great riddles of mankind. He both cherishes and mocks the great systems of the philosophers, the operations of "chance, free will, and necessity," the great religions and heresies of the past. His fascination with ancient lore and wisdom runs from Adam to Zoroaster; to help him tell his tale he marshals the great mythic figures of past centuries and all black-letter commentaries thereon.

His temperament is complex. If one of its facets, that of the "Sub-Sub-Librarian," has an antiquarian glint, another glows with the love of action. Each cry from the masthead alerts him from dreamy speculations to the zest of the hunt. Every lowering away starts his blood pounding. He is a superb narrator of the frenzied strivings of the boat crew as they press in for the kill, chanting their terror and competence as they enter "the charmed, churned circle" of eternity. When the death-deed is done, when the whirl slowly widens, he takes up the song of dismemberment. For the weapons of the chase, the red tools of slaughter, the facts of procedure, he has an insatiable curiosity. Cutting in, trying out, stowing down—the whole butcher-slab routine of processing the dead whale he endows with ritual certainty, transforming dirty jobs into acts of ceremonial dignity. Ishmael's voice translates the laughter and wild deeds of the bloody crew into the ordered rites of primitive tribal priests.

Narrator Ishmael has an instinct for the morally and psychologically intricate. He presses close in after the intertwinings of good and evil, tracks down the baffling crisscross of events and ideas, ponders their ambiguities and inversions. He is keen for a paradox and quick to see polarities—so keen in fact that the whole experience seems a double vision of what is at once noble and vile, of all that is lovely and appalling. This two-fold sensitivity marks his probings into the life-images of those he has known—whether in his grand-scale exposition of the "ungodly, god-like man, Captain Ahab" or in the compassionate recollection of little Pip, for a time lost overboard in the "heartless immensity" of the sea, and gone divinely mad from it. Whether noting that Queequeg's tomahawk-pipe "both brained his foes and soothed his soul" or contemplating "the interlinked terrors and wonders of God," he turns the coin both ways. He makes it a crisis of the first order that young Ishmael, both a brooder and a good companion, was drawn with the rest of the crew by the dark magnetic pull of the captain's monomania, wavering between allegiance to that uncommon king—Ahab—and to "the kingly commons"—the crew. Only the traumatic revulsion on the night of "The Try-Works" saved young Ishmael—"a strange (and ever since inexplicable) thing" which the narrator now explains symbolically: "Give not thyself up, then, to fire, lest it invert thee, deaden thee; as for the time it did me."

Above all one notes the narrator's inexhaustible sense of wonder. Wonder at the wide Pacific world, with its eternal undulations; wonder at the creatures of the deep; wonder at man—dreamer, doer, doubter. To him in retrospect the whale has become a mighty analogue of the world, of man, of God. He is in awe before the whale: its massive bulk, tiny eyes, great mouth, white teeth; its narrow throat and cavernous belly; the spout; the hump; the massed buttress of its domed head; the incomparable power and magic of its fanning, delicate tail. It is wonder that lies at the center of Ishmael's scale of articulation, and the gamut runs out either way toward fear and worship.

Enough of evocation. Every reader of *Moby-Dick* can and will want to enlarge and subtilize the multiple attributes of Ishmael. The prime experience for the reader is the narrator's unfolding sensibility. With it we have an energy center acting outward on the inert matter of nature and experience, releasing its possibilities for art. Whereas forecastle Ishmael drops in and out of the narrative with such abandon that at times a reader wonders if he has fallen overboard, the Ishmael voice is there every moment from the genesis of the fiction in "Call me Ishmael" to the final revelation of the "Epilogue" when "The drama's done." It is the narrator who creates the microcosm and sets the terms of discourse.

But this Ishmael is only Melville under another name, is he not? My suggestion is that we resist any one-to-one equation of Melville and Ishmael. Even the "Melville-Ishmael" phrase, which one encounters in critical discussions, though presumably granting a distinction between autobiography and fiction, would seem to be only a more insistent confusion of the point at stake unless the phrase is defined to mean either Melville or Ishmael, not both. For in the process of composition, even when the artist knowingly begins with his own experience, there are crucial interventions between the act that was experience and the re-enactment that is art —intrusions of time, of intention, and especially of form, to name only a few. Which parts of Ishmael's experience and sensibility coincide with Melville's own physical and psychological history and in just what ways is a question which is initially only tangential to discussion of *Moby-Dick* as a completed work of art.

III

But what of structure? That there is a dynamic excitation in *Moby-Dick* sympathetic readers have not denied. Is the effect of Ishmael's energy, then, simply to fling the matter in all directions, bombarding the reader with the accelerated particles of his own high-speed imagination? Is Ishmael's search for "some dim, random way" to explain himself not merely a characterization of the complexity of his task but also a confession of his inadequacy to find form? The questions are crucial, for although readers will presumably go on reading *Moby-Dick* whichever way they are answered, the critical reader will not be encouraged to keep coming back unless he can "see" and "feel" the tension of controlling forces.

To an extraordinary extent Ishmael's revelation of sensibility is controlled by rhetoric. Throughout the tale linguistic versatility and subtle rhythmic patterns exploit sound and sense with high calculation. Almost at random one chooses a sentence: "And ever, as the white moon shows her affrighted face from the steep gullies in the blackness overhead, aghast Jonah sees the rearing bowsprit pointing high upward, but soon beat downward again towards the tormented deep." It is a successful if traditional piece of incantation with its rising and falling movements manipulated to bring a striking force on the qualitative word "aghast." Its mood is typically Gothic-romantic (pictorial equivalents would be certain passages from Poe or the sea-paintings of Ryder), but structurally its allegiance is to the spacious prose of the seventeenth century. Although the passage is from Father Mapple's sermon, it is in no way unrepresentative; there are scores of sentences throughout *Moby-Dick* of equal or greater rhetorical interest.

Of the narrative's several levels of rhetoric the simplest is a relatively straightforward *expository* style characteristic of many passages scattered through the cetological accounts. But it is significant that such passages are rarely sustained, and serve chiefly as transitions between more complex levels of expression. Thus a series of expository sentences in the central paragraph of the chapter on "Cutting In" comes to this point: "This done, a broad, semicircular line is cut round the hole, the hook is inserted, and the main body of the crew striking up a wild chorus, now commence heaving in one dense crowd at the windlass." Whether it cannot or will not, Ishmael's sensibility does not endure for long so bare a diction: "When instantly, the entire ship careens over on her side; every bolt in her starts like the nail-heads of an old house in frosty weather; she trembles, quivers, and nods her frighted mastheads to the sky." The tension is maintained through a following sentence, strict exposition returns in the next, and the paragraph concludes with an emotionally and grammatically complex sentence which begins with exposition, rises to a powerful image of whale flesh hoisted aloft where "the prodigious blood-dripping mass sways to and fro as if let down from the sky," and concludes with a jest about getting one's ears boxed unless he dodges the swing of the bloody mess. Even in the rhetorically duller chapters of exposition it is a rare paragraph over which heat lightning does not flicker.

A second level of rhetoric, the *poetic,* is well exemplified in Ahab's soliloquy after the great scene on the quarter-deck. As Matthiessen has shown, such a passage can easily be set as blank verse:

> I leave a white and turbid wake;
> Pale waters, paler cheeks, where'er I sail.
> The envious billows sidelong swell to whelm
> My track; let them; but first I pass.

Because the rhythms here play over an abstract metrical pattern, as in poetry, they are evenly controlled—too evenly perhaps for prose, and the tone seems "literary."

Quite different in effect is a third level of rhetoric, the *idiomatic.* Like the poetic it occurs rather rarely in a pure form, but we have an instance in Stubb's rousing exordium to his crew:

> "Pull, pull, my fine hearts-alive; pull, my children; pull, my little ones . . . Why don't you break your backbones, my boys? . . . Easy, easy; don't be in a hurry—don't be in a hurry. Why don't you snap your oars, you rascals? Bite something, you dogs! . . ."

Here the beat of oars takes the place of the metronomic meter and allows more freedom. The passage is a kind of rowing song and hence is exceptional; yet it is related in tone and rhythm to numerous pieces of dialogue and sailor talk, especially to the consistently excellent idiom of both Stubb and young Ishmael.

One might venture a fourth level of rhetoric, the *composite,* simply to assure the inclusion of the narrator's prose at its very best. The composite is a magnificent blending of the expository, the poetic, the idiomatic, and whatever other elements tend to escape these crude categories:

> The Nantucketer, he alone resides and riots on the sea; he alone, in Bible language, goes down to it in ships; to and fro ploughing it as his own special plantation. *There* is his home; *there* lies his business, which a Noah's flood would not interrupt, though it overwhelmed all the millions in China. He lives on the sea, as prairie cocks in the prairie; he hides among the waves, he climbs them as chamois hunters climb the Alps. For years he knows not the land; so that when he comes to it at last, it smells like another world, more strangely than the moon would to an Earthsman. With the landless gull, that at sunset folds her wings and is rocked to sleep between billows; so at nightfall, the Nantucketer, out of sight of land, furls his sails, and lays him to his rest, while under his very pillow rush herds of walruses and whales.

The passage is a great one, blending high and low with a relaxed assurance; after shaking free from the literary constrictions of the opening lines, it comes grandly home. And how does it relate to event and character? Ishmael's memory of the arrival at Nantucket, a mere incident in the movement of the plot, is to Ishmael now an imaginative experience of high order; and this we must know if we are to know about Ishmael. The whole chapter, "Nantucket," is a prose poem in the barbaric jocular vein, and it is as valuable a part of the documentation of Ishmael's experience as are the great "scenes." It is less extraneous to the meaning of the book than are many of the more average passages about Captain Ahab. The same could be said for other great passages of rhetoric, such as the marvelous hymn to spiritual democracy midway in "Knights and Squires." The first level of structure in *Moby-Dick* is the interplay of pressure and control through extraordinarily high rhetorical effects.

Beneath the rhetoric, penetrating through it, and in a sense rising above it, is a play of symbolic forms which keeps the rhetoric from dropping into exercise or running off in pyrotechnics. The persistent tendency in *Moby-Dick* is for facts, events, and images to become symbols. Ahab makes the most outright pronouncement of the doctrine of correspondences on which such a tendency depends, and to which almost all characters in the book are committed: "O Nature, and O soul of man! how far beyond all utterance are your linked analogies! not the smallest atom stirs or lives on matter, but has its cunning duplicate in mind." No less sensitive to symbolic values than Ahab is the young Ishmael in the forecastle. It is he who unfolds moral analogues from the mat-making, from the monkey-rope, from squeezing the case. He resembles Ahab in his talent for taking situations "strongly and metaphysically."

So on down the roster of the crew, where symbols and superstitions blend. Can there be any doubt that it is above all the enfolding imagination of the narrator which sets and defines the symbolic mode that pervades the entire book? From the richly emblematic theme of "meditation and water" in the opening chapter, to the final bursting of the "black bubble" of the sea which releases young Ishmael, the narrator sets the symbolic as the primary mode of self-examination and communication. He is predisposed to see events, however incidental, as "the sign and symbol" of something larger. To Ishmael "some certain significance lurks in all things, else all things are little worth, and the round world itself but an empty cipher. . . ."

Most commonly the symbols begin with a generative object: a waif-pole, a coin, a compass needle, a right-whale's head. The symbolic events begin with a chance incident: the dropping of his speaking trumpet by the Captain of the *Goney* (the nameless future), finding ambergris in a blasted whale (unexpected sweetness at the core of corruption), the chasing of the *Pequod* by Malay pirates (the pursuer pursued). Both give the tale solidity, for the objects and events are objects and events before they become meanings. But all the symbols do not rise out of tangible referents. We have to take into account also the narrator's love for "a furious trope" which often far exceeds the simple metaphorical function of comparison; the thing to which analogy is made—a pyramid, an elephant, a Leyden jar, a bird, a mythic figure—may itself enter the circle of symbolic values through recurrent reference. Thus the imagery brings scope to the limited range of symbols available on board the *Pequod*. Whereas the object-symbols in a sense carry the "plot," elucidating the experience of young Ishmael, Ahab, the mates and crew (as well as serving the narrator), the image-symbols chiefly reveal the psyche of the narrator through images of procreation and animality, mechanization and monomania, enchantment and entombment.

Though simpler objects, events, or images may connote primarily some one thing, as a shark means rapacious evil, most symbols which Ishmael develops in his narration express a complex of meanings which cannot easily be reduced to paraphrase and are not finally statable in other than their own terms. So it is with the *Pequod* herself and the ships she passes, with the root metaphors of earth, air, fire, and water which proliferate so subtly; and so it is with the most dynamic word-image-symbol of the tale: "white" (or "whiteness"). Their meanings are not single but multiple: not precisely equatable but ambiguous; not more often reinforcing than contradictory. The symbolism in *Moby-Dick* is not static but is in motion; it is in process of creation for both narrator and reader. Value works back and forth: being extracted from objects, it descends into the consciousness; spiraling up from the consciousness, it envelops objects.

Symbolism is so marked a characteristic of the narrator's microcosm that it is possible to phrase Ahab's tragedy not only in moral, social, and psychological terms, but in "structural" terms as well. Clearly Ahab accepts the symbolic as a source of cognition and of ethics. It was a symbolic vision that brought him on his quest, as no one senses with stronger discomfort than Starbuck, who stands alone in his sturdy, limited world of facts and settled faith. Yet the tragedy of Ahab is not his great gift for symbolic perception, but his abandonment of it. Ahab increasingly reduces all pluralities to the singular. His unilateral reading of events and things becomes a narrow translation in the imperative mood. Unlike young Ishmael, who is his equal in sensitivity but his inferior in will and authority, Ahab walls off his receptiveness to the complexities of experience, replacing "could be" or "might be" with "must." His destruction follows when he substitutes an allegorical fixation for the world of symbolic potentialities.

Ishmael's predilection for keying his narrative in the symbolic mode suggests another aspect of structure. *Moby-Dick* lies close to the world of dreams.We find the narrator recalling at length a remembered dream of his childhood. Stubb attempts a long dream-analysis to Flask after he has been kicked by Ahab. It is not strange, then, that young Ishmael's moment of greatest crisis, the night of the try-works when he is at the helm, should be of a traumatic order. More subtly, numerous incidents of the narrative are bathed in a dream aura: the trancelike idyll of young Ishmael at the mast-head, the hallucinatory vision of the spirit spout, the incredible appearance on board of the devil himself accompanied by "five dusky phantoms," and many others. The narrator's whole effort to communicate the timeless, spaceless concept of "The Whiteness of the Whale" is an act of dream analysis. "Whether it was a reality or a dream, I never could entirely settle," says the narrator of his childhood dream; and so it was with much of what occurred aboard the *Pequod*. Ishmael's tale is to be listened to in terms of a tradition that runs from Revelation to *Finnegans Wake*. Dream sense is an important mood in *Moby-Dick*; and dream form, to the extent there is such a verbal form, is an incipient structural device of the book. At regular intervals the narrator, in his intense effort to explain himself, resorts to a brief passage in which there is a flashing concentration of symbols that hold for a moment and then disappear. It is a night device for rendering daytime experience, and in *Moby-Dick* it happens again and again.

Any rigorous definition of structure must lead us on to consider the nature and relation of the constituent parts. Since the tale is divided into "parts" by the narrator himself (135 chapters, plus prefatory materials and "Epilogue"), one cannot escape considering the extent to which individual chapters themselves are structural units. We shall have to pass over such chapters, probably the largest group, as are devoted to the movement of narrative or to character analysis; the form here falls in a general way within the customary patterns of novelistic structure. Two chapter forms, however, are sufficiently non-novelistic to invite comment, the first of these being the dramatic. The term "dramatic" is here used in a technical, not qualitative sense, and refers to such devices of the playwright's script as italicized stage directions, set speeches with the speaker named in capitals, straight soliloquies, and dialogue without commentary. More than a tenth of the chapters are in this sense dramatic, some ten having strictly dramatic form without narrative intrusion, and another half-dozen or so using some script devices along with the narrative. The most successful of the strict-form group is certainly "Midnight, Forecastle," a ballet-like scene which superbly objectifies the crew in drunken exaltation over the quest. But the two greatest are in the second group. "The Quarter-Deck," Ishmael's curtain-raising treatment of the quest theme, is a triumph of unified structure, conceived with extreme firmness and precision of detail. The powerful dramatic structure of the chapter—prologue, antiphonal choral address, formal individual debate, and group ceremonial—is a superb invention on free-traditional lines, unhampered by stage techniques yet profiting from them. The other great dramatic scene, a counterpart to "The Quarter-Deck" both thematically and structurally, is the massive Ahab-and-his-crew scene late in the book, "The Candles." The chapter is not so firmly conceived as its forerunner; and this, rather than its subject matter, is what brings it dangerously close to seeming overwrought and a bit out of hand. The key to the structure here lies in the narrator's word "tableau," a dramatic device of considerable currency in nineteenth-century America. As the primary symbols of fire and whiteness melt hotly into each other for the first time, we see a series of memorable tableaux lit by storm lightning and corposant flames between "intervals of profound darkness." The piece is a series of blinding kaleidoscopic flashes which reveal the alarmed mates, the primitives in their full demonic strength, Ahab in a fury of ritual power. The "enchanted" crew, which near this same quarter-deck had made its jubilant pledge, now hangs from the rigging "like a knot of numbed wasps"; and when Ahab brandishes his burning harpoon among them (an unstated completion of the image), "the mariners did run from him in a terror of dismay." The two chapters, "The Quarter-Deck" and "The Candles," are twin centers of gravity in ordering the structure of the Ahab theme. The two fields of force are possibility and necessity, and Ahab's shift is from initial ecstasy to final frenetic compulsiveness.

A second unusual element of chapter structure in *Moby-Dick* grows out of the sermon form. Most famously there is Father Mapple's sermon (chapter nine), a piece of sustained eloquence in the idiomatic-composite style. From his *text* in Jonah the old sailor-preacher moves at once to two *doctrines* (the Christian pattern of sin and repentance, and the hardness of obeying God); enters a highly imaginative narrative *explication* of the Biblical story; comes next to *applications* and *uses* (that the congregation shall take Jonah as "a model for repentance" and the preacher shall "preach the Truth to the face of Falsehood"); and concludes with an *exhortation* (the very subtly constructed incantation on the doublethemed coda of Woe and Delight). Somewhat buried away in another chapter, "Stubb's Supper," is the shorter sermon in which Fleece, the Negro cook, one night preaches to the sharks in a seriocomic vein. As he peers over the *Pequod's* side with his lantern at the murderous feasting down below, Fleece addresses his "congregation" first as "Fellow-critters," then as "Belubed fellow-critters," and finally as "Cussed fellow-critters," the final imprecation sharpening Fleece's ominous doctrine that "all angel is not'ing more dan de shark well goberned." The structural pattern, especially in its repetitive address, is clearly derived from the folk tradition of the Negro sermon.

These are not the only two "sermons" in *Moby-Dick*. Although the free essay tradition from Montaigne to Hazlitt provides a more comfortable prototype for the more loosely ordered speculative chapters, most of these have a prophetic or protestant vein that pulls them over toward the sermon tradition. Again and again throughout the narrative a chapter comes to its climax in a final paragraph of moral exhortation (Mapple) or imprecation (Fleece). Nor should we forget that young Ishmael's crisp moral analogues (above) start with symbols and end as parables. It is especially interesting to note that some of the cetological chapters can be analyzed in terms of sermon structure. In "The Line," for instance, the narrator takes hemp for his text, makes a full-scale explication of its history and uses, gives admonitions on its subtleties and dangers, and concludes with a full-scale application of the doctrine that "All men live enveloped in whale-lines." In "The Blanket" the text is whale blubber; and preacher Ishmael comes inevitably to the doctrine of internal temperatures, raising it to a high exhortation (Mapple) and then cutting it down with three lines of wry counterstatement (Fleece). Nor is it hard to identify text, inferences, uses, doctrine, and admonition in the brief "sermon" the narrator preaches over the peeled white body of a whale in "The Funeral." The technique lies midway between the Protestant sermon of the nineteenth century and the tradition of the digressive-antiquarian essay.

Coming to the problem of the mutual relation of the chapters in *Moby-Dick*, we can observe several tendencies, of which *chapter sequences* is one. The simplest sequence is likely to be one of narrative progression, as in "The Chapel," "The Pulpit," and "The Sermon," or in the powerful concluding sequence on "The Chase": "First Day," "Second Day", "Third Day." Or we get chapter sequences of theme, as in the three chapters on whale paintings. Or again sequences of structural similarity: the five chapters beginning with "The Quarter-Deck" all use dramatic techniques, as do the four beginning with "The Candles." More typical than strict sequences, however, are the *chapter clusters* in which two or three (or five or six) chapters are linked by themes or root images, other chapters intervening. For example, chapters xlii, li, lii, and lix make a loose cluster that begins with "The Whiteness of the Whale" and carries through the white apparitions in "The Spirit-Spout," "The Albatross," and "Squid." Similarly, later in the narrative, fire imagery becomes dominant, breaking out in young Ishmael's fire-dream ("The Try-Works") and running intermittently until the holocaust of Ahab's defiance ("The Candles"). In addition to sequences and clusters there are also widely separated *balancing chapters*, either of opposites ("Loomings" and the "Epilogue") or of similars ("The Quarter-Deck" and "The Candles"); here the problem is infinitely complex, for the balancing units shift according to the standard of comparison: theme, event, root image, structure, and so forth. Two points can be made in tentative summary of this complex aspect of structure: there are definable relations between any given chapter and some other chapter or chapters; and these relations tend to be multiple and shifting. Like the symbols, the chapters are "in process."

Looking beyond chapter units and their interrelations we find the most obvious larger structural effect in the narrative line of the book, such as it is, which records the preparations for going on board, leaving port, encountering adventures, and meeting some final consequence. Along this simple linear form of The Voyage occur two sets of events: the whale killings and the ship meetings. The question is whether either of these event groups performs more for the structure than the simple functions of marking the passage of time and adding "interest." Of the whale pursuits and killings some ten or more are sufficiently rendered to become events. They begin when the narrative is already two-fifths told and end with the final lowerings for Moby Dick during which the killers are themselves killed. The first lowering and the three-day chase are thus events which enclose all the whaling action of the novel as well as what Howard Vincent has aptly called "the cetological center," and the main point I wish to make about the pursuits is that in each case a killing provokes either a chapter sequence or a chapter cluster of cetological lore growing out of the circumstances of the particular killing. The killings in themselves, except for the first and last, are not so much narrative events as structural occasions for ordering the whaling essays and sermons. Their minimized role is proof enough, if any were needed, that Ishmael's tale is not primarily a series of whaling adventures.

Much more significant structurally than the killings is the important series of ship meetings also occurring along the time line of the voyage. The nine gams of the *Pequod* are important in several ways, of which three might concern us here. First of all, even a glance at the numbers of the chapters in which the gams occur shows a clear pattern: the first two are close together; the central group are well spaced (separated by an average of twelve chapters with not very wide divergences); the last two are close together. The spatial pattern looks like this:

1 2   3   4   5   6   7   8 9

This somewhat mechanical pattern is a stiffening element in the structure of the book, a kind of counterforce, structurally, to the organic relationship of parts we have been observing. The gams are bones to the book's flesh. Secondly, their sequence is meaningful in terms of the Ahab theme. The line of Ahab's response from ship to ship is a psychograph of his monomania showing the rising curve of his passion and diagraming his moral hostility. The points on the graph mark off the furiously increasing distance between Ahab and the world of men. And thirdly, their individual meanings are a part of the Ishmael theme. Each ship is a scroll which the narrator unrolls and reads, like a prophet called to a king's court. They provide what Auden calls "types of the relation of human individuals and societies in the tragic mystery of existence," though his superbly incisive reading of each type is perhaps too narrowly theological and does scant justice to either the tone of the episodes (are not the *Jungfrau* and *Rosebud* accounts hilariously comic and ironic?) or their rich amplitude of meanings. The ships the *Pequod* passes may be taken as a group of metaphysical parables, a series of biblical analogues, a masque of the situations confronting man, a pageant of the humors within men, a parade of the nations, and so forth, *as well as* concrete and symbolic ways of thinking about the White Whale. Any single systematic treatment of all of the ships does violence to some of them. The gams are symbolic, not allegorical.

It is time in fact to admit that our explorations of structure suggest elaborate interrelations of the parts but do not lead to an overreaching formal pattern. For the reader predisposed to feel that "form" means "classical form," with a controlling geometric structure, *Moby-Dick* is and will remain an aesthetically unsatisfying experience. One needs only to compare it with *The Scarlet Letter*, published a year and a half earlier, to see how nonclassical it is. If this is the sort of standard by which one tries to judge *Moby-Dick*, he will end by dismissing it as one of the more notable miscarriages in the history of literary lying-in. But surely there is no one right form the novel must take—not the one used by Hawthorne, not even the form, one might wryly add, perfected by

James. For Hawthorne the structural frame of reference was neo-classical; for Melville it was romantic.

To go from *The Scarlet Letter* to *Moby-Dick* is to move from the Newtonian world-as-machine to the Darwinian world-as-organism. In the older cosmology the key concepts had been law, balance, harmony, reason; in the newer, they became origin, process, development, growth. Concurrently biological images arose to take the place of the older mechanical analogies: growing plants and life forms now symbolized cosmic ultimates better than a watch or the slow-turning rods and gears of an eighteenth-century orrery. It is enough for our purposes to note that the man who gave scientific validity to the organic world view concluded the key chapter of his great book, *The Origin of Species*, with an extended image of "the great Tree of Life . . . with its ever branching and beautiful ramifications." It was a crucial simile that exploited not the tree but the tree's growth.

Of course the poets had been there first. Coleridge had long since made his famous definition of organic form in literature. The roots of his theory had traveled under the sea to the continent of Emerson, Thoreau, and Whitman (as Matthiessen brilliantly showed in *American Renaissance*), where they burst into native forms in the minds of a few men haunted simultaneously by the implications of the American wilderness, by the quest for spiritual reality, and by the search for new literary forms. *Moby-Dick* is like Emerson's *Essays* and *Poems*, like *Walden*, like *Leaves of Grass*, in its structural principles. In the literature of the nineteenth century it is the single most ambitious projection of the concept of organic form.

Recharting our explorations we can see now where we have been. The matter of *Moby-Dick* is the organic land-sea world where life forms move mysteriously among the elements. The dynamic of the book is the organic mind-world of Ishmael whose sensibility rhythmically agitates the flux of experience. The controlling structure of the book is an organic complex of rhetoric, symbols, and interfused units. There is no over-reaching formal pattern of literary art on which *Moby-Dick* is a variation. To compare it with the structure of the Elizabethan play, or the classical epic, or the modern novel is to set up useful analogies rather than congruous models. It is a free form that fuses as best it can innumerable devices from many literary traditions, including contemporary modes of native expression. In the last analysis, if one must have a prototype, here is an intensively heightened rendition of the logs, journals, and histories of the Anglo-American whaling tradition.

Organic form is not a particular form but a structural principle. In *Moby-Dick* this principle would seem to be a peculiar quality of making and unmaking itself as it goes. The method of the book is unceasingly genetic, conveying the effect of a restless series of morphic-amorphic movements. Ishmael's narrative is always in process and in all but the most literal sense remains unfinished. For the good reader the experience of *Moby-Dick* is a participation in the act of creation. Find a key word or metaphor, start to pick it as you would a wild flower, and you will find yourself ripping up the whole forest floor. Rhetoric grows into symbolism and symbolism into structure; then all falls away and begins over again.

Ishmael's way of explaining himself in the long run is not either "dim" or "random." He was committed to the organic method with all its possibilities and risks. As he says at the beginning of one chapter: "There are some enterprises in which a careful disorderliness is the true method." And at the beginning of another chapter we have an explicit image whose full force as a comment on method needs to be recognized: "Out of the trunk, the branches grow; out of them, the twigs. So, in productive subjects, grow the chapters."

IV

From our considerations of *Moby-Dick* a few simple, debatable propositions emerge. More accurately they are, I suppose, the assumptions which underlie what has been said. The first is that *nature*, ultimately, is chaos. Whatever order it has in the mind of God, its meaning is apparent to man only through some more or less systematic ordering of what seems to be there. The second is that *experience* is already one remove from nature; filtered through a sensibility, nature begins to show patterns qualified by the temperament and the culture of the observer. And the third is that *art*, which is twice removed from nature, is a major means for transforming experience into patterns that are meaningful and communicable. As in part it is the function of religion to shape experience for belief and conduct, and of science to organize nature for use and prediction, so it is the business of art to form man's experience of nature for communication. In art the way a thing is said is what is being said. To the maker the form is completion; to the receiver it is possibility. Art is an enabling act for mankind without which life may easily become meager, isolated; with it the mind can be cleared and the spirit refreshed; through it memory and desire are rewoven.

The great thing about fiction, which is simply the telling of a story in written words, is that it is fiction. That it is "made up" is not its weakness but, as with all art, its greatest strength. In the successful work of fiction certain kinds of possibilities, attitudes, people, acts, situations, necessities, for the first and last time exist.

They exist only through form. So it is with *Moby-Dick*—Ishmael's vast symbolic prose-poem in a free organic form. From *olim erat* to *finis* is all the space and time there is.

CHARLES FEIDELSON, JR.

[*Moby-Dick* as Symbolic Voyage] †

Like Hawthorne and Whitman, Melville in his way is deeply concerned with this question of "approach." The first chapter of *Moby-Dick* is the statement of a point of view. Ishmael opens his narrative by identifying voyage with vision: the field of man's vision is the sea. Like the island city whose avenues all radiate "waterward" and whose shores are thronged with "crowds of water-gazers," the sensibility of the individual man opens onto the ocean. And the "thousands upon thousands of mortal men fixed in ocean reveries," who come from far inland, "north, east, south, and west," are united in their silent brooding upon the waters. Beneath the jocular tone these initial paragraphs create an effect of irrepressible need. The attraction of the mind to the sea is life itself as a quest for knowledge. "Why did the old Persians hold the sea holy? Why did the Greeks give it a separate deity, and own brother of Jove? Surely all this not without meaning." The meaning is rendered more fully at the end of the chapter on "The Mast-Head," where another watergazer, lulled into reverie "by the blending cadence of waves with thoughts,"

> at last . . . loses his identity; takes the mystic ocean at his feet for the visible image of that deep, blue, bottomless soul, pervading mankind and nature; and every strange, half-seen, gliding, beautiful thing that eludes him; every dimly-discovered, uprising fin of some undiscernible form, seems to him the embodiment of those elusive thoughts that only people the soul by continually flitting through it.

Here the voyaging mind is fused with the world in a flux of wave-like forms; the identity of the self is lost in a pantheistic sea. Yet this attainment of sheer vision—in which, as Emerson described it, "I become a transparent eye-ball; I am nothing; I see all"—is suddenly dangerous. As your foot slips on the masthead, external things become alien, the empty spaces between man and nature

† From Charles Feidelson, Jr., *Symbolism and American Literature* (Chicago: The University of Chicago Press, 1953), pp. 28–35, 240–46. Copyright 1953 by The University of Chicago Press; reprinted by permission of the publishers.

spread to infinity, "and your identity comes back in horror." To submerge in the sea is to drown; the self and the world are two, not one. The voyage of Ishmael, though it lacks the desperation of Ahab's outlook, is crossed by a doubt similar to his. Water-gazing is a paradoxical activity—a search for absolute unity with the objects of thought, only to discover that immediate knowledge destroys the thinker. This is the "still deeper . . . meaning" of the story of Narcissus—to return to the first chapter. "Because he could not grasp the tormenting, mild image he saw in the fountain, [he] plunged into it and was drowned. But that same image, we ourselves see in all rivers and oceans. It is the image of the ungraspable phantom of life; and this is the key to it all." The image is not merely a self-reflection but the embodiment of thought, the matching phantom in the sea of forms. The phantom is ungraspable as long as we stand on the bank; and the ocean is annihilative once we dive into it.

Whatever hazards Ishmael may perceive in the alliance of "meditation and water," the impossibility of resolving the dilemma by simply returning to land is even more obvious in his case than in Ahab's. To send the visionary back home would be to invalidate the whole book. Ishmael is at once a character and the narrator of *Moby-Dick*, and he is a "voyager" in both respects. The concluding paragraphs of the first chapter are not only an explanation of the sailor's motives in going to sea but also a kind of rationale of the book itself as a "voyage." The narrator is immersed in a drama of which the Fates, in a manner of speaking, are the "stage managers," since he performs a part having nothing to do with his own "unbiassed free will and discriminating judgment." Will is the essence of self, and judgment is objective knowledge; but he is governed by the symbolic imagination, which moves in still another plane. Before him swims "the overwhelming idea of the great whale." In the sea, which is the field of his vision, the White Whale is the mightiest image, the summation of all the myriad shapes that succeed one another through infinite change:

> The great flood-gates of the wonder-world swung open, and in the wild conceits that swayed me to my purpose, two and two there floated into my inmost soul, endless processions of the whale, and, midmost of them all, one grand hooded phantom, like a snow hill in the air.

The "endless processions of the whale" are transitive forms that issue out of a fecund center; each procession comes "two and two," for each shape implies an opposite. To go whaling is to entertain these symbolic perspectives. It is significant that the narrator himself is flooded as he sets out to invade the sea. For, properly

speaking, the moment of imagination is a state of becoming, and
the visionary forms simultaneously are apprehended and realize
themselves.

In "The Whiteness of the Whale" the ambiguity of whiteness—
its mingled beauty and horror, as exemplified in countless ways—
repeats the doubleness of the "endless processions," and "whiteness" becomes a synonym for fluid reality, like the "grand hooded
phantom" of the earlier account. In this chapter Ishmael solicits
the reader's understanding of his method; he must explain himself, he says, "else all these chapters might be naught." He is trying
to define not only "what the White Whale . . . was to me" but
also the kind of thinking which generates that ambiguous creature:
"How is mortal man to account for it?" The apparent answer is
that the double meaning of whiteness is a product of imaginative
perception: "To analyze it would seem to be impossible. . . . In
a matter like this, subtlety appeals to subtlety, and without imagination no man can follow another into these halls." He who would
follow Ishmael must exert the symbolic imagination, for Ishmael's
"pursuit" of the whale is the evolution of an image. Although the
meanings that develop are disquieting, and the whole process tends
to become a "fiery hunt," he has no other approach.

Ishmael, unlike most fictive narrators, is not merely a surrogate
for an absentee author. Behind him, always present as a kind of
Doppelgänger, stands Herman Melville. As Ishmael the narrator
enters more deeply into his symbolic world, he increasingly becomes a presence, a visionary activity, rather than a man; we lose
interest in him as an individual, and even Ishmael the sailor almost drops from the story. Ishmael the visionary is often indistinguishable from the mind of the author himself. It is Melville's
own voice that utters the passage on the heroic stature of Ahab.
This apparent violation of narrative standpoint is really a natural
consequence of the symbolic method of *Moby-Dick*. The distinction between the author and his alter ego is submerged in their
common function as the voyaging mind. In fact, the whole book,
though cast in the form of historical narrative, tends to the condition of drama, in the sense that it is a presentation, like Ishmael's
vision of the whale processions, in which both Melville and Ishmael lose themselves. The frequent references to drama and the
actual use of dramatic form in a number of chapters reflect the
visionary status of the entire action. In the sequence of chapters
(xxxvi–xl) from "The Quarter-Deck" to "Midnight, Forecastle,"
there is no narrator, to all intents and purposes; Ishmael has to
re-establish his own identity at the beginning of chapter 41. At
the same time the drama does not take place *in vacuo*; the symbolic
nature of the action depends on its being perceived. This is the

reason why Ishmael is necessary in the book, despite the fact that he and Melville often merge into one. Ishmael is the delegated vision of Melville: he can enact the genesis of symbolic meaning, whereas Melville, speaking solely as an omniscient author, could only impute an arbitrary significance. Unlike Hawthorne, the Melville of *Moby-Dick* does not verge toward allegory, because he locates his symbols in a unitary act of perception. Moreover, the symbolic vision of Ishmael is repeated by the dramatis personae. From Father Mapple's interpretation of Jonah to Ahab's blasphemous rituals, the symbols take on meaning in the course of perception. The pattern of "The Doubloon" is the scheme of the book: under the overhanging consciousness of Ishmael, with Melville looking over his shoulder, the several characters envisage the meaning of the coin. As the various meanings multiply, we hear the chant of Pip: "I look, you look, he looks; we look, ye look, they look."

Melville, first and last, assumes that "some certain significance lurks in all things." There is no other justification for the survival of Ishmael at the end of *Moby-Dick*. "The drama's done. Why then does anyone step forth?" Ishmael survives as the voyaging mind, the capacity for vision, the potentiality of symbolic perception. He floats on the ocean to which he is dedicated, just as the entire narrative assumes the necessity of water-gazing. The white shroud of the sea, the plenum of significance, remains an eternal challenge. Yet the very fact that Ishmael and the sea are left as mere potentiality indicates the deep distrust interwoven with Melville's faith. The translation of man and the world into sheer process, which satisfies Emerson and Whitman, does not content him. The doubloon is evidence of the reality of symbolic meaning; the significance is *in* the world, and the significant world is generated by "looking." But the meaning suffers a fragmentation as it comes into being, and Pip's commentary is an assertion of real multiplicity. The diversity that Emerson and Whitman easily accept as new "frontiers" of exploration presents itself to Melville as a network of paradox. Traveling with Whitman down the open road, "the earth expanding right hand and left hand," Melville notes that right and left are opposites.

Not only does symbolism imply a complex of logical oppositions but it also tends to obscure these real and important differences. While Melville hardly contemplates, except as a lost hope, any return to the substance of the land, he is uncomfortably aware of the irrationality of the fluid sea. The ultimate horror of whiteness is "its indefiniteness," the merging of distinctions in the insubstantial medium. For "whiteness is not so much a colour as the visible absence of colour, and at the same time the concrete of all colours," so that a snowy landscape, though "full of meaning," is "a dumb blankness, . . . a colourless, all-colour of atheism from which we shrink." The totality of symbolic meaning is intensely present, but destroys individuality; its "atheism" is that of transcendentalists like Whitman, who, in order to become God-possessed, deny a personal God. By the same token, in order to unite themselves with nature, they also deny personal identity. Melville follows in evident dismay. Seen rationally, as an object, the world is inaccessible; but, seen as accessible, the world swallows up the visionary. Ishmael's presentiment of the danger of water-gazing is verified by the fate of the "Pequod," which disappears into the ambiguity and formlessness of the sea. Only by self-annihilation does the "Pequod" penetrate the whiteness, which closes above it in "a creamy pool." Ishmael, as though to epitomize Melville's position, almost follows, but does not. He is drifting toward the "vital centre" of the swirling vortex when the "coffin life-buoy" suddenly emerges. Ishmael's status remains provisional. He accepts ambiguity and indefiniteness—he is "buoyed up by that coffin"—and yet somehow manages to retain his own "identity."

If the inconclusive fate of Ishmael evinces a double attitude in Melville—an acceptance of "voyaging" and a fear of its full implications—the fate of Ahab results from a refusal to remain in suspense. Ahab's motives, which are dramatized as vengeance against nature and revolt from God, lie deeper than mere satanic pride. Beneath his ferocious mood is the "little lower layer" which he confides to Starbuck: he seeks a kind of value not to be measured by the arithmetical methods of accountants. Money, the medium of exchange, is for him a symbolic medium; and his repudiation of the "Nantucket market" is a rejection of rational thought, just as Melville's doubloon is opposed to the commerce of Boston. When Starbuck continues to protest this irrational "profit," Ahab counters with a still "lower layer." He draws a contrast between "visible objects" and the world in process—the "event," the "living act," the "undoubted deed." Ahab has taken quite seriously Emerson's dictum, "But man thyself and all things unfix, dispart, and flee." The visible object is only a "pasteboard mask"; the wall should open, as Emerson says, "into the recesses of being"; the living act is fraught with meaning. And in one sense the death of Ahab is the necessary outcome of these premises. For him "the White Whale is that wall, shoved near." He does manage to penetrate, hurling his harpoon, and he disappears into the sea, "still chasing . . . though tied to" the whale. In another sense, indicated by the wreck of the "Pequod." Ahab dies because the object is impenetrable and his assumptions are wrong. As he remarks long before the final chase, "the dead, blind wall butts all inquiring heads at last." He simultaneously carries the voyage to an extreme, losing himself to gain reality, and is forced to accept the rational distinction between the human intellect and the world it explores. In either case he is faced with an "inscrutable" world: a mask whose meaning is enticing but destructive, or a wall without any human significance. "That inscrutable thing," he declares, "is chiefly what I hate." He hates both the ambiguity of the meanings that lure him on and the resistance of objects to the inquiring mind. As the mood of the voyager alters, from love to hate, the world of the Emersonian journey changes from hospitality to malice, and the "living act" becomes an act of defiance.

All this does not imply, however, that Melville washes his hands of Ahab. If Ahab persists in the face of an obvious dilemma, and is thereby destroyed, the dilemma is the same as Melville's own, and Melville has not resolved it for himself. Melville can reprobate Ahab only as part of his self-reprobation, for Ahab's fury is the last stage of Melville's malaise. Actually, no final condemnation is possible. The largest paradox in *Moby-Dick*, prior to any moral judgment, is the necessity of voyaging and the equal necessity of failure. The voyage can accommodate the benevolence of Father Mapple; it is the "apotheosis" of Bulkington, the perfect transcendentalist, who is present as a "sleeping partner" throughout the book; but it issues in the satanism of Ahab, the wilfully destructive pursuit of a knowledge that dissolves into nothingness. Melville feels involved in what happens to Ahab. That is why he could write Hawthorne that Ahab's greatest blasphemy was "the book's motto (the secret one)": "Ego non baptizo te in nomine patris, sed in nomine diaboli!" The diabolism of *Moby-Dick* is more an effect than a cause of Melville's method. Pursuing the symbolic voyage to the utmost, but realizing at the same time its ineffectuality, Ahab is ruined, and Melville discovers that he is potentially an Ahab, the devil's partisan, the nihilist.

R. W. B. LEWIS

[The Try-Works] †

* * * [The last] three paragraphs [of "The Try-Works"] are more nearly three stanzas. * * * The subject of this, one of the richest meditations in all of Melville, is the different degrees of moral alertness—with variations on the realities present in the world and man, on the quality of moral illumination for the perceiver, on

† From R. W. B. Lewis, *The American Adam* (Chicago: The University of Chicago Press, 1955), pp. 132–34.

the states of being accompanying the various perceptions.

There occur (as Ishmael sees it) two dangerous alternative conditions. On the one hand: an empty innocence, a tenacious ignorance of evil, which, granted the tough nature of reality, must be either immaturity or spiritual cowardice. On the other: a sense of evil so inflexible, so adamant in its refusal to admit the not less reducible fact of existent good that it is perilously close to a love of evil, a queer pact with the devil. Each alternative is a path toward destruction; the second is the very embrace of the destroying power. * * *

So "alternative" is a misleading word, in speaking of any characteristic passage in Melville. Indeed, one way to grasp this passage and Melville's achievement in general is to notice that Melville is *not* posing static alternatives but tracing a rhythmic progression in experience and matching the rhythm as best he can in language. This is the way of a Platonist, and not of a polemicist; much more, it is the way of a poet. We still tend, for all the good criticism of our time, to read a poem the way we watch a tennis-match: turning our heads and minds back and forth between what we presume to be unchanging opponents, as though a poem moved between fixed choices of attitude before plumping conclusively for one of them as the unequivocal winner. The best kind of poem is a process of generation—in which one attitude or metaphor, subjected to intense pressure, gives symbolic birth to the next, which reveals the color of its origin even as it gives way in turn by "dying into" its successor. Such a poem does not deal in dichotomies but in live sequences.

Here, then, in "The Try-Works," we have a series of displacements. Artificial light gives way to natural light, darkness to morning, and the imperative to the indicative. Then dawn and sunlight yield to darkness, to the moon and "the dark side of the earth"—to hell, to sickness, and to death. But hell and death are the source at last of a new and loftier life, new "sunny spaces" and new imperatives. Those sunny spaces are not the same bright skies of the opening stanza. The moral imagination which contemplates the sunny spaces in stanza 3 has been radically affected by the vision of hell and death at mid-point. The sunny spaces (tragic optimism) relate to the earlier morning skies (empty-headed cheerfulness) as does the Catskill eagle to "the other birds upon the plain"; it is the sky, as the eagle is a bird—but bird and sky have been raised to a higher power.

What Melville has done here is to accomplish what, in an ugly phrase translated from Nietzsche, has been called "the transvaluation of values": something which Melville had to do in his poet's way, by what we perhaps can call the "transfiguration of figures."

EDWARD H. ROSENBERRY

[Comic Vision and Technique in *Moby-Dick*] †

The Comic Vision

If comedy contributes to ambiguity of meaning in *Moby-Dick*, it contributes no less vitally to the ambiguities of attitude from which the ideas inherent in the story are viewed. Ideas are philosophical; attitudes, psychological. Hence the label I have assigned to the third major category of Melvillian comedy, the philosophical-psychological. The ideas it is concerned with are ideas of value, questions of distinction that were becoming more and more absorbing to Melville's skeptical intelligence. What was the truth about the qualities conventionally defined as merriment and gravity, madness and sanity, good and evil? In each case, he had decided once and for all in *Mardi*, the "question is more final than any answer." Circumstance and point of view are the only determinants with meaning. The spiritual impact of the whale's majestic "peaking of flukes" depends on "what mood you are in; if in the Dantean, the devils will occur to you; if in that of Isaiah, the archangels." Depending on the light in which it is seen, the diamond looks now like "the divinest symbol of the crystal skies," now "like some crown-jewel stolen from the King of Hell." [1] Thus on all questions of significance the prior question becomes: Seen by whom, in what mood, and in what light?

Moby-Dick's philosophical ambiguities, insofar as they are explored by the comic spirit, are explored through three personalities organic to the novel: Stubb, Ahab, and Ishmael. Each of these reflects in his attitude, often by direct verbal echo, some aspect of the ambiguity of merriment and gravity set forth by Babbalanja in his demonic theory of humor. The book is thus shot through with the elusive perversity of Azzageddi; but it is happily not unprovided with a criterion for evaluating the comic vision of its principals. That criterion, based on Melville's primal sea–land metaphor, is highly figurative but unmistakable in its application:

> The sun hides not the ocean, which is the dark side of this earth, and which is two thirds of this earth. So, therefore, that mortal man who hath more of joy than sorrow in him, that mortal man cannot be true—not true, or undeveloped. With books the

† From Edward H. Rosenberry, *Melville and the Comic Spirit;* (Cambridge, Massachusetts: Harvard University Press, 1955), pp. 105–15. Copyright 1955 by the President and Fellows of Harvard College. Reprinted by permission of the publishers.

1. MD 86, 93. [References are to chapter numbers.]

same. The truest of all men was the Man of Sorrows, and the truest of all books is Solomon's. . . But even Solomon, he says, "the man that wandereth out of the way of understanding shall remain" (i.e. even while living) "in the congregation of the dead" . . . There is a wisdom that is woe; but there is a woe that is madness. And there is a Catskill eagle in some souls that can alike dive down into the blackest gorges, and soar out of them again and become invisible in the sunny spaces. And even if he forever flies within the gorge, that gorge is in the mountains; so that even in his lowest swoop, the mountain eagle is still higher than other birds upon the plain, even though they soar.[2]

Here, then, is a standard of sorts (though we can hardly hold Melville to such an exact mathematical accounting): life is two-thirds dark, one-third light; more sorrow than joy. And here are standards by which to gauge the life-views of the three characters whose comic vision we are to examine. First we have the untrue or undeveloped man, the man "who hath more of joy than sorrow in him"; that is Stubb. Next we have the man who is all woe and therefore mad; that is Ahab. And finally we have the balanced man, the man with the Catskill eagle in his soul: Ishmael. It is an alignment recognized in principle by Starbuck, himself the balanced agent of the tragic vision, as he ponders amidships one night on the revelry in the forecastle and the "unfaltering silence aft": "Methinks it pictures life. Foremost through the sparkling sea shoots on the gay, embattled, bantering bow, but only to drag dark Ahab after it, where he broods within his sternward cabin, builded over the dead water of the wake . . ."[3]

The life that it pictures, the essential thing of which Stubb, Ahab, and Ishmael each has his vision, the thing with which each must somehow come to terms, is of course the thing or complex of things symbolized by the white whale himself: "outrageous strength, with an inscrutable malice sinewing it"; "that intangible malignity which has been from the beginning . . . all truth with malice in it . . . all the subtle demonisms of life"; "the heartless voids and immensities of the universe."[4] It is Stubb's role not to understand this thing; or rather, to seek refuge in the negation of thought and defend himself against tragic understanding by a policy of determined levity. It is Ahab's role to understand the thing and to fight it. It is Ishmael's role to understand it, accept it for what it is, and adjust his conduct accordingly.

1

Melville introduces Stubb, his "happy-go-lucky," in his customary symbolic way, carefully using a symbol which he can also apply to Ahab with directly opposite effect:

2. *MD* 96.   3. *MD* 38.   4. *MD* 36, 41, 42.

What, perhaps, with other things, made Stubb such an easy-going, unfearing man, so cheerily trudging off with the burden of life in a world full of grave peddlers, all bowed to the ground with their packs; what helped to bring about that almost impious good-humor of his; that thing must have been his pipe. For, like his nose, his short, black little pipe was one of the regular features of his face. . . I say this continual smoking must have been one cause, at least, of his peculiar disposition; for everyone knows that this earthly air, whether ashore or afloat, is terribly infected with the nameless miseries of the numberless mortals who have died exhaling it; and as in time of the cholera, some people go about with a camphorated handkerchief to their mouths; so, likewise, against all mortal tribulations, Stubb's tobacco smoke might have operated as a sort of disinfecting agent.[5]

This studious immunity to vexation and the sense of evil is soon underscored in Stubb's observation on Ahab: "I guess he's got what some folks ashore call a conscience; it's a kind of Tic-Dolly-row they say—worse nor a toothache. Well, well; I don't know what it is, but the Lord keep me from catching it. . . Think not, is my eleventh commandment." [6]

After Ahab's revelation of the terrible purpose of the *Pequod's* cruise, Stubb is characteristically the first to settle the whole matter comfortably in his own mind, by reducing it to comic terms: "Ha! ha! ha! ha! . . . I've been thinking over it ever since, and that ha, ha's the final consequence. Why so? Because a laugh's the wisest, easiest answer to all that's queer . . . I know not all that may be coming, but be it what it will, I'll go to it laughing. Such a waggish leering as lurks in all your horribles!" [7] This grotesque ambiguity in Stubb's vision is reflected emblematically in his behavior to-wards his men.

He would say the most terrific things to his crew, in a tone so strangely compounded of fun and fury, and the fury seemed so calculated merely as a spice to the fun, that no oarsmen could hear such queer invocations without pulling for dear life, and yet pull-ing for the mere joke of the thing . . . Stubb was one of those odd sort of humorists, whose jollity is sometimes so curiously ambiguous, as to put all inferiors on their guard in the matter of obeying them.[8]

The ironic discrepancy is that the force of destiny which Stubb obstinately interprets as a hoax is in reality no more a hoax than the commands he so waggishly utters in the stern of his whale-boat.

5. *MD* 27.
6. *MD* 29.
7. *MD* 39. Cf. Azzageddi: "It is good to laugh, though the laugh be hollow; and wise to make merry, now and for aye. . . All ends in a shout. . . Ha! ha! how demoniacs shout; how all skeletons grin; we all die with a rattle" (*Mardi*, 183.)
8. *MD* 48.

As the tensions of the story draw tighter, the sterility of Stubb's vision becomes increasingly apparent. His reflections on the cabalistically marked doubloon, which is the symbol of the voyage's significance, are merely a clownish version of some familiar Shakespearean comic philosophy, and the "jolly" moral he draws from it is as inevitable in its way as that of Ahab, who finds it "stout stuff for woe to work on." [9] It is highly significant of the operation of Stubb's mind that he can eavesdrop with equanimity on all the doubloon's commentators except mad Pip, who, in describing him as "two bones stuck into a pair of old trousers, and two more poked into the sleeves of an old jacket," gives him an uncomfortable moment of insight into the spiritual scarecrow he is. "I can stand the rest," he mumbles, "for they have plain wits; but he's too crazy-witty for my sanity." The remark is a valuable contribution to the madness–sanity ambiguity that runs through the novel.

His reaction to the symbol of the sea, like his reaction to the symbol of the doubloon, is pathetic, almost terrible, in its comic uniformity. When the Pacific is mild and Starbuck is grasping at its quiet beauty to bolster his faith, Stubb "takes oaths that he has always been jolly." [1] When the ship is dashed about in a fearful electrical storm, Stubb insists "it's all in fun," and breaks into song. Even Starbuck's taunt that his tune was not quite the same when the corposants struck cannot reduce him beyond a certain querulous defiance of the true state of affairs: "No, no, it wasn't; I said the corposants have mercy on us all; and I hope they will, still. But do they only have mercy on long faces?—have they no bowels for a laugh?" [2]

It is Ahab, finally, who with his diametrically opposite vision spells out the meaning of Stubb's fatal comic bias. Hearing with revulsion the ill-timed joking of his mate over the boat Moby Dick has chewed in the chase, Ahab cries, "What soulless thing is this that laughs before a wreck? Man, man! did I not know thee brave as fearless fire (and as mechanical) I could swear thou wert a poltroon." Soulless and mechanical, or untrue and undeveloped: that in the end is Stubb. [3] Even at the moment of death Stubb jests, once more in terms reminiscent of one of Azzageddi's diabolical paradoxes: "I grin at thee, thou grinning whale! Look ye, sun, moon, and stars! I call ye assassins of as good a fellow as ever spouted up his ghost. For all that, I would yet ring glasses with ye,

9. *MD* chap. 99.
1. *MD* 114.
2. *MD* 119.
3. *MD* 133. W. H. Auden's otherwise admirable analysis of Stubb (*The Enchaféd Flood*, pp. 130, 132) is flawed by the unfortunate error of reading Flask into this scene in place of Stubb and then building a distinction between them on the strength of his erroneous reading.

would ye but hand the cup! Oh, oh! oh, oh! thou grinning whale,
but there'll be plenty of gulping soon!" [4]

2

Ahab, too, is one to "laugh and hoot" at the gods, but whereas
Stubb's laughter is a kittenish evasion of life, Ahab's is a profane
challenge thrown in its teeth. The hellish apparitions in the cave of
Hecate tell Macbeth to "laugh to scorn the power of man," but
when Fedallah prophesies in close imitation of the Weird Sisters,
Ahab's more terrible "laugh of derision" laughs to scorn the power
of God.[5] This is the madness into which his surrender to woe
has plunged him, and his own words, echoing Macbeth's, place
him accurately in the scale of light and dark prescribed by his
author: "So far gone am I in the dark side of earth, that its other
side, the theoretic bright one, seems but uncertain twilight to
me." [6] To make explicit the opposition of Ahab's view to Stubb's,
Melville has Ahab throw away his pipe, again in a mood like
Macbeth's: "What business have I with this pipe? This thing that
is meant for sereneness, to send up mild white vapors among mild
white hairs. . ." [7]

In his very tragic intensity, however, Ahab demonstrates Azzageddi's dictum that "woe is more merry than mirth." For, lugu-
brious as it is, Ahab has among his "humanities" a sense of humor
and makes a number of mirthless contributions to the comedy of
the book. As the *Pequod*'s workmen fashion him a new leg, it
suits his heavy facetiousness to conceive them as "manmaker" and
"Prometheus" and to invent a grim comic recipe for "a complete
man after a desirable pattern."

> Imprimis, fifty feet high in his socks; then, chest modelled after
> the Thames Tunnel; then, legs with roots to 'em, to stay in one
> place; then, arms three feet through the wrist; no heart at all,
> brass forehead, and about a quarter of an acre of fine brains; and
> let me see—shall I order eyes to see outwards? No, but put a
> sky-light on top of his head to illuminate inwards. There, take the
> order and away.[8]

A wicked Christian twist occurs to him, and he cynically plays with
the carpenter's bewildered replies.

> Carpenter? why that's—but no;—a very tidy, and, I may say,
> an extremely gentlemanlike sort of business thou art in here,

4. *MD* 135. Cf. *M* 183—"Ho! let us
be gay, if only for an hour, and Death
hand us the goblet."
5. *MD* 37, 117.
6. *MD* 127. Cf. *Macbeth*, III, iv:
　"I am in blood
Stepp'd in so far that, should I wade
　no more,

Returning were as tedious as go o'er."
7. *MD* 30, Cf. *Macbeth*, V, iii:
　"And that which should accompany
　　old age,
As honour, love, obedience, troops of
　friends,
I must not look to have."
8. *MD* 108.

carpenter;—or would'st thou rather work in clay?

Sir?—Clay? clay, sir? That's mud; we leave clay to ditchers, sir. The fellow's impious! What art thou sneezing about?

Bone is rather dusty, sir.

Take the hint, then; and when thou art dead, never bury thyself under living people's noses.

It is in a final jesting exchange with the carpenter that Ahab lays bare the fatal atheism and nihilism of his vision. The sight of the carpenter converting Queequeg's coffin into a lifebuoy is irresistibly comical to his graveyard humor, and he once more uses this uncomprehending colloquist to his own ends, as Poe's bereaved lover had used the raven.

"Art thou not an arrant, all-grasping, intermeddling, monopolizing, heathenish old scamp, to be one day making legs, and the next day coffins to clap them in, and yet again life-buoys out of those same coffins? Thou art as unprincipled as the gods, and as much of a jack-of-all-trades."

"But I do not mean anything, sir. I do as I do."

"The gods again. Hark ye, dost thou not ever sing working about a coffin? The Titans, they say, hummed snatches when chipping out the craters for volcanoes; and the grave-digger in the play sings, spade in hand. Dost thou never?"

"Sing, sir? Do I sing? Oh, I'm indifferent enough, sir, for that; but the reason why the grave-digger made music must have been because there was none in his spade, sir. But the calking mallet is full of it. Hark to it."

"Aye, and that's because the lid there's a sounding-board; and what in all things makes the sounding-board is this—there's naught beneath. And yet, a coffin with a body in it rings pretty much the same, Carpenter." [9]

3

When the ultimate catastrophe strikes the *Pequod*, death comes to both Ahab and Stubb, and comes in a way appropriate to each. Ahab dies violently, garroted by the superhuman force he so insanely taunted; Stubb, refusing to see in its final gesture anything more than a grin, drowns ignominiously in his drawers. Only Ishmael survives, buoyed up by that remarkable symbol of resurrection, the coffin-lifebuoy. The artistic reason for his survival lies in the careful balance of his comic vision between the fatal extremes of the two characters who are, in this respect, his foils.

The central statement of his comic philosophy—and that is to say the comic philosophy of the book—comes after the first chase of the voyage, a particularly reckless venture in which the high-spirited men virtually run up the whale's back in a storm and are rescued

9. *MD* 127.

only after a damp and cheerless night in a swamped boat in the middle of nowhere. Ishmael's important reflections on that experience echo the Mardian theory of humor in three respects: the first is a verbal echo in the title of the chapter, "The Hyena"; the second is an echo of the philosophical concept that "life is an April day, that both laughs and weeps in a breath"; the third is an echo of the corresponding psychological concept that "mirth and sorrow are kin; are published by identical nerves."

> There are certain queer times and occasions in this strange mixed affair we call life when a man takes this whole universe for a vast practical joke, though the wit thereof he but dimly discerns, and more than suspects that the joke is at nobody's expense but his own. However, nothing dispirits, and nothing seems worth while disputing. He bolts down all events, all creeds, and beliefs, and persuasions, all hard things visible and invisible, never mind how knobby; as an ostrich of potent digestion gobbles down bullets and gun flints. And as for small difficulties and worryings, prospects of sudden disaster, peril of life and limb; all these, and death itself, seem to him only sly, good-natured hits, and jolly punches in the side bestowed by the unseen and unaccountable old joker. That odd sort of wayward mood I am speaking of, comes over a man only in some time of extreme tribulation; it comes in the very midst of his earnestness, so that what just before might have seemed to him a thing most momentous, now seems but a part of the general joke. There is nothing like the perils of whaling to breed this free and easy sort of genial, desperado philosophy; and with it I now regarded this whole voyage of the Pequod, and the great White Whale its object.[1]

Superficially this attitude may seem to embrace both the inflexible levity of Stubb and the inflexible irreverence of Ahab rather than to strike any sort of balance between them. An important distinction is that this mood is a flexible one, coming "only in some time of extreme tribulation" as a kind of psychological safety valve. It comes out of earnestness, whereas Stubb has no earnestness; and the earnestness is grounded on faith, whereas Ahab has no faith. The faith is not explicit in this purely humorous passage, but it is in another of Ishmael's mixed moods, the one that comes on him as he sits pondering the memorial tablets in the Whaleman's Chapel just before the *Pequod* sails.

> Yes, Ishmael, the same fate may be thine. But somehow I grew merry again. Delightful inducements to embark, fine chance for promotion, it seems—aye, a stove boat will make me an immortal by brevet. Yes, there is death in this business of whaling—a speechlessly quick chaotic bundling of a man into Eternity. But

1. *MD* 49.

what then? . . . Methinks my body is but the lees of my better being. In fact take my body who will, take it I say, it is not me. And therefore three cheers for Nantucket; and come a stove boat and a stove body when they will, for stave my soul, Jove himself cannot.[2]

Ishmael saves himself from despair by laughing at what threatens his body; Ahab dooms himself to it by laughing at what threatens his soul. Ishmael's laughter is thus a psychological symbol of a philosophical acceptance, long before a more solemn and less credible symbol was devised in *Billy Budd*.

The voyage that for Ahab is a struggle for a definitive death is for Ishmael a struggle for rebirth. That is the philosophical meaning of the favorite Melville joke with which *Moby-Dick* opens.

Whenever I find myself growing grim about the mouth; whenever it is a damp, drizzly November in my soul; whenever I find myself involuntarily pausing before coffin warehouses, and bringing up the rear of every funeral I meet; and especially whenever my hypos get such an upper hand of me, that it requires a strong moral principle to prevent me from deliberately stepping into the street, and methodically knocking people's hats off—then, I account it high time to get to sea as soon as I can. This is my substitute for pistol and ball.

The sober substratum in this notion is brought out as Melville later applies it to Perth, the *Pequod*'s blacksmith, who, having made a tragic mess of his life ashore, sought the sea as "another life without the guilt of intermediate death." [3] Ishmael's mood, of course, is only whimsically suicidal. Like a "sulky" whale he once saw, he is merely "dispirited," and looking less for a new life than for a fresh start on the old one.

The joke of the thing is that he should choose so radical a remedy for his "hypos." He leaps from schoolmaster to sailor, from the bosom of "an old established family" to the elemental society of the forecastle. To make matters worse, he ships on a whaler; and, as Redburn and White-Jacket had discovered before him, no branch of the maritime profession was held in such uniform contempt as the "blubber-boilers." [4] The total abandon of any landsman who, like himself, would sacrifice comfort, safety, and respectability to go before the mast, especially in a whaler, never failed to arouse in Melville an ambiguous excitement which emerged sometimes in a tragic reflection, as in the case of Perth or Bulkington, sometimes in a comic one, as in the case of Ishmael. The comedy of the situation, even when that aspect predominated in his mind, was never wholly unalloyed with the sympathy that hu-

2. *MD* 7.   3. *MD* 112.   4. *Redburn* 21, *White-Jacket* 4.

manizes true humor. We have already remarked the sympathy that lay behind the comic portrait of Rope Yarn in *Omoo*, whose going to sea to repair his soul sounds so much like Ishmael's: "Ropey went to the sign of the Pipe and Tankard; got fuddled; and over his fifth pot meditated suicide—an intention carried out; for the next day he shipped as landsman aboard the Julia, South Seaman." And there is at least as much sympathy mixed with the laughter when a friend of Redburn's writes of the vanished Harry Bolton, "I cannot believe that his melancholy could bring him to the insanity of throwing himself away in a whaler." [5] This kind of humor, applied to and through the character of Ishmael, is an artistic balance wheel in *Moby-Dick* and one of the symptoms of its spirit of renascence.

Another ambiguity in Ishmael's comic attitude is that it appears to lead him to both acceptance and rebellion: acceptance in the sailor's "genial, desperado philosophy," rebellion in the landsman's urge to go around "methodically knocking people's hats off." Both reactions have a certain reckless Pantagruelism in common, both are deeply imbued with the demoniac temper of Azzageddi, but they are not reactions to the same thing and therefore never conflict. The distinction is related, as so much in Melville ultimately is, to the sea–land metaphor. The perverse hat-knocking mood, in which Ishmael was so precisely anticipated by young Redburn as he defied his supercilious fellow passengers on the river boat—this essentially childish humor is a thing of the land, a petulant revolt against the frustrations of orthodoxy. Redburn is "afterward heartily ashamed" of it, Ishmael applies "strong moral principle" to curb it, and both escape from it to the "open independence" of the sea, though of the two only Ishmael is mature enough to recognize it as a compelling motive for that escape. Once at sea, for him the symbol of physical and spiritual reality, Ishmael's bitterness drops from him and he is ready to play the game with whatever gods there be, in the highest good humor, though he himself may very well be the butt of some "unseen and unaccountable old joker."

This is the sane if somewhat pagan philosophy of "The Hyena." It involves by definition the two ambiguities which most deeply pervade the novel: the motivation of destiny, which is both diabolic and divine; and the reaction of man, which is both laughter and terror. The latter is by now a familiar ambiguity, thematic in all of Melville's books to date. Its recurrence in connection with an occupation as hair-raising as whaling is understandably frequent. One of the standard perils of the chase, for instance, is the whale-line, which is threaded in such murderous vicinity to every oarsman as to make "the very marrow in his bones to quiver in him like

5. *O* 14, *R* 62.

a shaken jelly." Yet "gayer sallies, more merry mirth, better jokes, and brighter repartees, you never heard over your mahogany, than you will hear over the half-inch white cedar of the whale-boat, when thus hung in hangman's nooses." Another "humorously perilous business" is being tied by the "monkey-rope" to a blubber-cutting shipmate as he dodges the multiple disasters of drowning, crushing, and shark-bite. There is mirth in the face of death as Queequeg, in an access of fatalism, orders his coffin and tries it on for size. And there is merriment before the fires of hell as the crew, gathered at night before the symbolic try-works, exchange "their unholy adventures, their tales of terror told in words of mirth." [6]

Whatever force or forces direct the fate of this "merry-mad," "gloomy-jolly" *Pequod* are seen with a corresponding doubleness of vision. The fate that drove Pip mad acted through a sea that "jeeringly kept his finite body up," yet carried his soul "to wondrous depths" where "he saw God's foot upon the treadle of the loom." [7] The aftermaths of Ahab's demonic oaths remind us of Azzageddi's assertion that "there is laughter in heaven, and laughter in hell"; the Faustlike compact calls forth both. As Ahab passes the grog like the Eucharist to pledge his crew to the impious chase, Ishmael hears a low "subterranean laugh" from the hold; and afterwards, when Ahab plunges his barb into the blood of his pagan harpooneers to baptize it "in nomine diaboli," "a light, unnatural, half-bantering, yet most piteous sound was heard" —the mad laughter of Pip, who to Ahab is "holiness." [8]

These facts understood, all the ambiguities of Ishmael's comic vision and the middle course it finds between the polar nihilisms of Stubb and Ahab can be read in their subtle synthesis in a single passage:

> Though amid all the smoking horror and diabolism of a sea-fight, sharks will be seen longingly gazing up to the ship's decks, like hungry dogs round a table where red meat is being carved, ready to bolt down every killed man that is tossed to them; and though, while the valiant butchers over the deck-table are thus cannibally carving each other's live meat with carving-knives all gilded and tasselled, the sharks, also, with their jewel-hilted mouths, are quarrelsomely carving away under the table at the dead meat; and though, were you to turn the whole affair upside down, it would still be pretty much the same thing, that is to say, a shocking sharkish business enough for all parties; and though sharks also are the invariable outriders of all slave ships crossing the Atlantic, systematically trotting alongside, to be handy in case a parcel is to be carried anywhere, or a dead slave to be decently buried; and though one or two other like instances might be set down, touch-

6. *MD* 60; 72, 110; 97. 8. *MD* 36, 113, 125.
7. *MD* 93.

ing the set terms, places, and occasions, when sharks do most socially congregate, and most hilariously feast; yet there is no conceivable time or occasion when you will find them in such countless numbers, and in gayer or more jovial spirits, than around a dead sperm whale, moored by night to a whaleship at sea. If you have never seen that sight, then suspend your decision about the propriety of devil-worship, and the expediency of conciliating the devil.[9]

The genesis of such a vision is obvious enough. We have here in fact the predictable union of *Mardi*'s diabolism and the folk-comedy of hardship which set the tone of the early romances.[1] It is the artistically optimum combination of the two that strips the comic travesty of the narrative to its tragic core of terror and impending evil and death.

Comic Technique

* * *

1

Readers of *Moby-Dick* are generally agreed that the moving literary influence behind it was Shakespearean tragedy.[2] With respect to comic technique the chief point of resemblance between Melville and Shakespeare, though it has been little noted, is fairly obvious. Both writers were given to having flashes of humor in the midst of their earnestness, or (as the case might be) flashes of earnestness in the midst of their humor. Both were profoundly indifferent to the theory and practice of genres and profoundly concerned with the theory and practice of life—a much more vital business, as Dr. Johnson long ago remarked, than anything conceived in the prescriptions of art.

Melville's comic method was of course not altogether Shakespeare's, even in *Moby-Dick* where the two are closest. Melville had largely from French tradition the critical humor that Shakespeare lacks; and he had largely from native tradition that profane and mocking view of "the rim or confines of things, the brink of the abyss, [which] was to Shakespeare dark and terrible altogether,

---

9. *MD* 64.
1. When Constance Rourke writes (*American Humor*, p. 193) that "in *Moby-Dick* this many-sided diabolism reached an ultimate culmination," she unaccountably ignores the fatal predominance of that element in later books; but she does recognize its union here with the folk element in which she is primarily interested.
2. All Melville scholars have made

passing reference to the fact, and two have made partial and impressionistic studies of the Shakespearean influence: R. G. Hughes, "Melville and Shakespeare," *Shakespeare Association Bulletin*, 7:103–112 (July 1932); and Charles Olson, *Call Me Ishmael* (1947). A definitive study of the literary relations of Melville and Shakespeare has yet to be made.

lit up by no grim or ghastly ray of laughter." [3] But it is in the English tradition of Shakespeare (carried down through the works of Sterne and Lamb, whom Melville also admired) that Melville stands in his conception of comedy and tragedy as matters of degree, rather than of kind, as in the French tradition. It is a hallmark of the Shakespearean tradition for notes of agony or merriment to intrude into scenes of essentially opposite emotional tenor. Even tragic heroes like Hamlet, as E. E. Stoll has remarked, "give vent to their wit and their irony in the midst of their sufferings." [4] And Shakespeare's special talent for blending the comic and tragic is perhaps even more remarkable in those low-comedy interludes, such as the grave-digger scene in *Hamlet* and the porter scene in *Macbeth,* where a bloodcurdling irony is achieved through characters in ignorance of the tragic issue of the business they are being droll about. What the comedy appears to do in such scenes is to intensify the tragic potential of the play through the momentary illusion that life is less tragic than it really is. But the object in view, as one critic has put it, "is not so much to depict the confusion of exterior nature as the confusion of the soul at moments when tragic and comic seem to form one indivisible experience." [5] The words could pass for a paraphrase of Babbalanja's theory of humor.

Of the four or five Shakespearean tragedies with which *Moby-Dick* shows some points of affinity, *King Lear* has received the most attention, though a better case might very well be made for *Macbeth.* The point of resemblance that fascinates is the relationship of the madman and the fool to the tragic hero. In *Moby-Dick* the character of Pip was evidently conceived as a composite of the bedlam and the jester who support Lear in his adversity. In building his pathetic figure over those models, Melville passed over their Elizabethan comic surfaces and used their ambiguous dramatic power, as Shakespeare had done, "to emphasize, to contrast with, to comment on the tragic fate of his great protagonist." [6] Moreover, he did this in a conspicuously Shakespearean idiom, complete with stage directions and poetic soliloquies in the grand manner such as were never heard from Negro cabin boy, sane or crazed, on land or sea. The effect, despite the bolder and less sophisticated method, is not unlike that of Eugene O'Neill's New England transposition of the Agamemnon material.

This use of Pip is the key, in both purpose and method, to the use of more frankly comic persons involved in the tragic voyage

3. E. E. Stoll, "The Comic Method," *Shakespearean Studies* (1927), p. 184.
4. *Ibid.,* p. 155.
5. Raymond M. Alden, "The Use of Comic Material in the Tragedy of Shakespeare and His Contemporaries," *Journal of English and Germanic Philology,* 13:298 (1914).
6. Parrott, *Shakespearean Comedy,* p. 304.

of the *Pequod*. Ishmael, central though he is to the comic philosophy of the book, is conspicuously absent from the dramatic level of the story, standing aloof from the conflict as a commentator in the manner of a chorus, and coming in at the end almost as detached as Fortinbras to proclaim the continuity of life. But Stubb, like Pip, is an active participant in scenes which sketch the tragic progress of Ahab toward his damnation. At the dramatic heart of *Moby-Dick*, as on its surface, Stubb is Melville's principal comic agent, though here little of the old Yankee independence is left him. At carefully calculated intervals Melville converts him into a Shakespearean clown to cast the ironic light of comedy on Ahab and the somber meaning of his quest.

Ahab's first speech to Stubb—"Down, dog, and kennel!" [7]— seems a clear enough echo of the fool's speech in *Lear*, I, iv, which, to judge by the marking in his copy, impressed Melville as much as anything in the play: "Truth's a dog must to kennel." Melville's irony is the reverse of Shakespeare's in that the corrective role of the comic character, instead of being recognized by both parties, is recognized by neither. Since the irony is implicit in the allusion, it may even be missed by the reader; but one can hardly miss the explicit use of the dog metaphor in establishing the fatal excess of pride in Ahab and the fatal deficiency of it in his foil. Stubb's resentment has a fleeting moment of manly earnestness, then quickly collapses into comic rationalization, an attitude that makes him the ideal buffoon-commentator on Ahab's granitic immutability. In the same way, Stubb's comic superstitiousness about Fedallah ironically defines the diabolic influence at work on Ahab. As Vincent puts it, "The clown can see what the King will not; one is reminded of the insight of the fool as against the blindness of Lear." [8] Here again, of course, Stubb's irony proceeds less from true insight than from his fixed position of equal and opposite error.

Within the framework of this comic function Melville juggled Stubb's Shakespearean antecedents to suit his convenience. An evident resemblance to such prototypes as Bottom and Launcelot Gobbo has been seen in the highly derivative set-piece called "Queen Mab" (Chapter 31), in which Stubb relates to Flask his comical dream of symbolic capitulation to Ahab.[9] There is something of Falstaff, too, in Stubb's ingenious rationalization in that episode on the honor of being kicked by a great man. In the typhoon scene (Chapter 119) it is again the disarming bravado and "discretion" of the fat knight that are reflected in Stubb's frank disavowal of moral courage. And when Ahab speaks his final rebuke

7. *MD* 29.
8. *MD* chap. 73. Vincent, *The Trying-*   *Out of Moby-Dick*, p. 250.
9. Vincent, p. 113.

to Stubb ("What soulless thing is this that laughs before a wreck?"), we are reminded of the repulse of Falstaff by his former playmate, Henry V:

> *I know thee not, old man: fall to thy prayers;*
> . . . . .
> *Reply not to me with a fool-born jest.*[1]

Stubb's great moment on the stage is a solo performance occupying most of Chapter 99 and investing him with a further variety of Shakespearean guises. This episode shows its genesis, in both style and situation, more clearly than any other in the book. It is a series of soliloquies before the symbolic doubloon by a succession of characters representing the gamut of opinion on the quest for the white whale—a series in which Stubb is himself a participant and on which he reports to the reader through the familiar Shakespearean expedient of eavesdropping and commenting within sight and hearing of the audience. As each man sees in the coin the reflection of his own point of view, so Stubb reads his philosophy in its zodiacal decoration, which he interprets Jaques-like as "the life of man in one round chapter." "There's a sermon now, writ in high heaven," he concludes, shifting lightly to the role of another philosopher in the same play, who had found sermons in stones. His comment on Flask's evaluation of the doubloon ("nine hundred and sixty cigars") is an impeccably antithetic Shakespearean witticism: "Shall I call that wise or foolish, now; if it be really wise it has a foolish look to it; yet, if it be really foolish, then it has a sort of wiseish look to it." Finally, the alternation of Pip's somnambulistic gibberish and Stubb's puzzled asides results in a chilling travesty of the sleep-walking scene in *Macbeth.* In a sense, Stubb's whole performance in this chapter recalls the drunken whimsy of the porter in that play, who also entertained himself with a series of character studies in a fixed situation until the game palled on him. Melville may have had a dozen or a score of Shakespearean scenes and characters in mind as he constructed the episode; he certainly had in mind Shakespeare's controlling artistic purpose.

Whether he gained or lost by writing these scenes in so sedulously Shakespearean a style is an arguable point. Certainly it must be admitted that they are "lumbering enough . . . so derivative in their conception that the humor runs thin." [2] Notwithstanding the occasional advantage—even necessity—of representing Ahab's

1. *Henry IV, Part 2,* V, v. In connection with this passage it is interesting to note that Melville later wrote a humorous poem dramatizing Falstaff's probable rationalization of that repulse: "Falstaff's Lament over Prince Hal Become Henry V," *Collected Poems,* pp. 382–383 [H. P. Vincent's edition].
2. Matthiessen, *American Renaissance,* p. 432.

foils in his own high-Shakespearean terms, it was far more important that the comic structure of *Moby-Dick* remain firmly rooted
in its gross material fishery if the book was to escape being the
"monstrous fable," the "hideous and intolerable allegory" that
Melville wryly disavowed.[3] Accordingly, he was at some pains to
accomplish his dramatic purpose without consistently sacrificing
the comic verisimilitude of his characters. Paradoxically, the very
scenes in which Shakespeare's idiom is abandoned are the most
finished tributes to the exemplar who introduced such figures as
Bottom and Stephano into his airiest fantasies to "link the imaginary with the real world."[4] * * *

RICHARD B. SEWALL

[*Moby-Dick* as Tragedy] †

It is easy to see why Melville, himself a prey to the deepest forebodings about the optimism of his day, recognized at once his kinship of spirit with Hawthorne. "There is a certain tragic phase of
humanity which, in our opinion [he wrote], was never more powerfully embodied than by Hawthorne." A year after Hawthorne published *The Scarlet Letter*, Melville dedicated his own most powerful
embodiment of this tragic phase, *Moby-Dick*, to Hawthorne, his
acknowledged master. Together the two books are witness to the
vitality of the tragic vision, which pierces beneath the "official view"
of any culture to the dark realities that can never be permanently
hidden, and together they mark a recrudescence of the tragic spirit
in what would seem an unlikely time, on unlikely soil, and without
benefit of tragic theater or tragic audience.

Both authors were aware of the untimeliness of their books.
Hawthorne, in the famous letter to his publisher, Fields, spoke of
fearing that his novel would "weary very many people and disgust
some" by keeping so close, and with so little diversification, to "the
same dark idea." Would he have an audience receptive to his peculiar view of things? The Greek and Elizabethan dramatists or
Racine or even the Poet of Job could count on an audience culturally
predisposed through myth, theater, or racial view to accept at once a
drama of direness. Hawthorne had to make his own audience, to
lead it by easy stages, as it were, into the dark idea. Hence the

3. *MD* 45.
4. Parrott, *Shakespearean Comedy*, p.
401.
† From Richard B. Sewall, *The Vision
of Tragedy* (New Haven: Yale University Press, 1950), pp. 92–105. Copyright 1950 by Yale University Press;
reprinted by permission of the publishers.

familiar, reassuring tone of the Custom House introduction, where the only dire events involve a certain goose of tragic toughness and the routine political loss of a job not worth holding. Hence the whimsical apology, in advance, for the "stern and sombre aspect" of Hester's story—"too much ungladdened by genial sunshine; too little relieved by the tender and familiar influences which soften almost every scene of nature and real life, and, undoubtedly, should soften every picture of them"—an apology which we may well regard as almost wholly tactical.

And hence (among other reasons) the long preliminary phase of *Moby-Dick*, introducing Ishmael, the reassuringly normal one who would go to sea now and again to drive off the spleen, or merely to satisfy "an everlasting itch for things remote"; who would take "the universal thump" with equanimity, and cry three cheers for Nantucket—"and come a stove boat and stove body when they will, for stave my soul, Jove himself cannot." The world of Ishmael's setting forth, like the world of the Custom House, was undimmed by the dark idea and seemingly invulnerable to any Jovian thunderbolts. God was above young Ishmael's world as he packed his bag for Cape Horn and the Pacific; and even as he read on the tablets of Father Mapple's chapel in New Bedford the fate of the whalemen who had gone before him, he "grew merry again." The rest of his story shows how shallow his optimism was, as Melville leads him (and the untragic American audience) by slow degrees, but remorselessly, toward tragic truth.

Ishmael has been called the chorus to Ahab as tragic hero, but this is hardly adequate to describe his total participation in the tragic action. To be sure, the Aeschylean choruses became involved, acted, and suffered as the other choruses in Greek drama for the most part did not. But it is significant of Melville's task of rendering his tragedy probable to his age that Ishmael frames and pervades the story as no Greek chorus does. He is a constant link to the known and familiar. He is average, goodhearted humanity, though somewhat more given to meditation than most and (as he says of himself) "quick to perceive a horror." His optimism lies not in his denial that the horror is there but in his hope of being "social with it"— "since it is but well to be on friendly terms with all the inmates of the place one lodges in." Only gradually does this hope come to be fully tested. All the little horrors of the early stages of his adventures are accommodated to his hearty, comic vision. He accepts the wintry and forbidding conditions of his stay in New Bedford with good cheer. The inauspicious omens in Father Mapple's chapel fail to daunt him. He shares his bed with the terrifying Queequeg, and rejoices in the evidence of natural goodness even in this pagan cannibal. Queequeg's rescue of the man overboard on the trip to

Nantucket confirms his faith in his new friend and in this "mutual joint-stock world" where Christians and cannibals live and let live. "Dost know nothing at all about whaling, I dare say—eh?" asks Captain Peleg as Ishmael presents himself at the *Pequod* to sign on for the voyage. "Nothing, Sir," he answers handsomely; "but I have no doubt I shall soon learn." Only Peleg's strange confidences about the captain of the *Pequod*—that "grand, ungodly, god-like man, Captain Ahab"—momentarily shake his confidence that there is no horror he cannot be social with. As he hears the story of Ahab's fierce troubles, he is filled "with a certain wild vagueness of painfulness concerning him"—"a sympathy and a sorrow for him, but for I don't know what, unless it was the cruel loss of his leg." But more than that—"a strange awe of him; but that sort of awe, which I cannot at all describe, was not exactly awe; I do not know what it was."

Such were the first intimations to this young novitiate of mysteries not to be resolved by his philosophy, the first hint (as Stephen Daedalus was later to refine on Aristotle's notion of terror) of "the feeling which arrests the mind in the presence of whatsoever is grave and constant in human sufferings and unites it with the secret cause." So far in Ishmael's experience whatever had been grave had not been constant, and what had been constant had not been grave. Pity, of the sort which he felt for Ahab's misfortune, is a passing thing, as he soon confesses: "However, my thoughts were at length carried in other directions, so that for the present dark Ahab slipped my mind."

But the sense of awe, the intimations of terror, were not to be denied, nor the full terror in store. Queequeg's pagan fanaticisms, his all-day Ramadan, or Fasting and Humiliation, were easy for Ishmael's ready rationalism—"I say, we good Presbyterian Christians should be charitable in these things, and not fancy ourselves so vastly superior to other mortals, pagans and what not, because of their half-crazy conceits on these subjects"—and he pled with his cannibal friend to give over his "prolonged ham-squattings in cold, cheerless rooms" as opposed to "the obvious laws of Hygiene and common sense." But he could not so easily accommodate his second warning about Ahab, this time from old Elijah, whose "ambiguous, half-hinting, half-revealing, shrouded sort of talk begat in me all kinds of vague wonderments and half-apprehensions." He even chided himself for not facing squarely this challenge to his security, but in the busy preparations for the voyage he "said nothing, and tried to think nothing." In such situations, he said, a man "insensibly strives to cover up his suspicions even from himself."

But in spite of himself he was coming ever nearer the vortex. One morning, several days out, "as I levelled my glance toward the taffrail, foreboding shivers ran over me. Reality outran apprehension; Captain Ahab stood upon his quarter-deck." What Ishmael saw for the first time was no Queequeg with his crazy conceits, nor "humbug" Elijah, but a man "with a crucifixion in his face," standing there "in all the nameless regal overbearing dignity of some mighty woe." Ahab had looked on terror, and Ishmael looked on Ahab. Soon he was to stare into it face to face.

Somewhat before this first startling encounter, Melville had begun to shift his method from the narrative mode to the dramatic. It is as if he were confident by now that the bridge was whole and firm between the world of his readers and the tragic world of his imaginings. Ishmael was doing his work; the audience, like him, is almost ready for the full revelation. The "Knights and Squires" of the ship's company have been introduced. Stubb has had his first encounter with Ahab, told not by Ishmael but by Melville as dramatist: Stubb's mild plea that Ahab curtail his nightly deck-walks over the sleeping sailors' heads; Ahab's furious rebuke: "Down, dog, and kennel!"; and Stubb's bewildered ruminations: "He's full of riddles. . . . Damn me, but all things are queer, come to think of 'em." We have met the staid and steadfast Starbuck, "firm in the conflict with seas, or winds, or whales, or any of the ordinary irrational horrors of the world" yet unable (we are told prophetically) to "withstand those more terrific, because more spiritual terrors, which sometimes menace you from the concentrating brow of an enraged and mighty man." We know the "ignorant, unconscious fearlessness" of Flask—"a little waggish in the matter of whales." We have seen Ahab throw away his pipe—his next rejection, after his rebuke of Stubb, of his links with common humanity, which would seek only rest after toil and the solace of creature comforts. We learn of "that certain sultanism of his brain" which the hierarchical situation on shipboard encourages toward "an irresistible dictatorship." We have already accepted the possibility (ch. 16) that out of these old Quaker whalemen might come the "globular brain," the "ponderous heart," the "bold and nervous lofty language," of "a mighty pageant figure"—a Job, an Oedipus, a Lear—"formed for noble tragedies." The stage is set and the characters drawn for "the tragic dramatist" (as Melville now openly calls himself) to present his action.

There is a preliminary lull, but full of portent, in the brief "Masthead" chapter, when Melville returns the story to Ishmael's consciousness (as, occasionally, he does throughout the action) to show the youthful novitiate's view from the crow's nest, how it induces a mystic, Platonic reverie, providing a kind of "asylum [in the whaling industry] for many romantic, melancholy, and absent-minded young men, disgusted with the carking cares of earth, and seeking sentiment in tar and blubber." Here, to the young dreamer at the masthead, the Many merge into One; the watcher, "lulled into such an opium-like listlessness of vacant, unconscious reverie," ceases to watch; the waves blend with his thoughts and the sea with his soul: "he loses his identity." For a moment we hear Ishmael talking: "For one, I used to lounge up the rigging very leisurely, resting in the top to have a chat with Queequeg, or any one else off duty whom I might find there * * *" But it is Melville's voice that dispels this Emersonian dream, the tragic dramatist who prepares for the full revelation. "But while this sleep, this dream is on ye [Melville so addresses the young dreamers], move your foot or hand an inch; slip your hold at all; and your identity comes back in horror. Over Descartian vortices you hover. And perhaps, at mid-day, in the fairest weather, with one half-throttled shriek you drop through that transparent air into the summer sea, no more to rise for ever. Heed it well, ye Pantheists!"

Ishmael was never in greater danger than on his seemingly secure and sunny perch. Here, says the tragic dramatist, was no true wisdom and therefore (in the literal sense) no true poise. Ishmael must return to the common deck and the rigors of whaling. He must know it at its worst as at its best. He must "look in the face of fire." Only then does he learn (in "The Try-Works") that "that mortal man who hath more of joy than sorrow in him, that mortal man cannot be true—not true, or undeveloped." Down from the masthead, on Ahab's own quarter-deck, a major event in Ishmael's development is about to take place.

In the Quarter-Deck scene, when with his demonic eloquence Ahab enticed the crew into his terrifying enterprise, Ishmael was confronted for the first time with a "hero" in action. Ishmael's presence as the percipient narrator is not felt during the scene; we have only his belated comment afterward. In Melville's dramatic presentation Starbuck is given the only role as antagonist to Ahab; but against the "general hurricane" of Ahab's fury, his protest in the name of common sense and respect for God's creatures could not stand. The full drama starts with this thrust of Ahab's against his destiny, against "the unknown but still reasoning thing" (as he sees it) that has worked his woe; and to this heroic fury—terrifying yet somehow appealing—Ishmael could not be a passive witness only. In the turbulent scene, all thought of comic detachment, of being sociable with horror, was for the moment overwhelmed. "I, Ishmael, was one of that crew; my shouts had gone up with the rest; my oath had been welded with theirs; and stronger I shouted, and more did I hammer and clinch my oath, because of the dread in my soul. A wild, mystical, sympathetical feeling was in me; Ahab's quenchless feud seemed mine." All of his old, reassuring categories are burst asunder in this first experience of "the dread in the soul."

But, as the voyage progressed, this dread had its abatements for Ishmael—signalizing, perhaps, how sturdy are the "admirable evasions" of average man, loath to admit his failure to domesticate the universe. Ishmael is normal, unpossessed humanity. There are moments of calm when he detaches himself from Ahab's quenchless feud and returns to his philosophizings. They are still cheerful, even if they have a new somber note, as when making mats with Queequeg, he speculates about "chance, free will, necessity," finds them "no wise incompatible—all interweavingly working together." But chance, he concludes darkly, can rule either one, and has "the last featuring blow at events." Later (ch. 49), speculating on "this strange mixed affair we call life," he slips into a sort of "desperado philosophy." In such a mood, he regards the universe as a "vast practical joke," perhaps on himself, but "with nothing to dispirit a man and nothing to dispute." He simply makes his will. "Now then, thought I, unconsciously rolling up the sleeves of my frock, here goes for a cool, collected dive at death and destruction, and the devil fetch the hindmost." Thus, argues the wise youth, if we cannot be merry, we can at least know the universe for the risky thing it is and be prepared for whatever comes. This is not Ahab's feud; it is a stoic rather than a tragic phase. It is as far, except for one other episode, as Ishmael ever gets.

If, as in *The Scarlet Letter*, there is something archetypal of all tragedy in this steady uncovering, layer by layer, of the hard meaning of existence, it is not through Ishmael's consciousness that Melville uncovers it all. Ishmael recedes as Ahab occupies the foreground. The frankly dramatic episodes (for example, The Quarter-Deck, the nine gams, The Forge, The Carpenter, the chases), like much of the whaling lore, are not controlled by Ishmael as narrator (as, for instance, the narrator Marlow controls some of Conrad's stories), nor do they reveal to us any sustained or intense spiritual struggle. A few times only, as Melville develops the "linked analogies" between whaling and human existence, is Ishmael's voice heard unmistakably. The "Monkey-Rope" episode reminds him of the precarious interdependence of human beings, how one man may innocently perish through another's error—Queequeg's, in this instance —and for a moment we hear the young tyro philosophizing again. Squeezing "case" with Queequeg puts him in mind of the friendly pressure of the hands that should bind all men together in "the very milk and sperm of kindness." But is it Ishmael's voice (or Melville's) which thanks God (in "The Fountain") that "through all the thick mists of the dim doubts in my mind, divine intuitions now and then shoot, enkindling my fog with a heavenly ray"? or, in "The Grand Armada," likens the state of his soul, "amid the tornadoed Atlantic of my being," to the calm center in the midst of the vast encircling herd of whales: "But even so . . . do I myself still forever centrally disport in mute calm; and while ponderous planets of unwaning woe revolve round me, deep down and deep inland there I still bathe me in eternal mildness of joy"? Who dichotomizes all men and nations, nay the great globe itself, according to the categories of Fast-Fish and Loose-Fish? All this may be a measure of Ishmael's deepening stoicism or growing philosophic poise; but actually about this time he ceases to be a fictional narrator with an autonomous spiritual development, and merges into Melville the omniscient novelist, commenting and discoursing without regard for Ishmael's fictional status or his personal point of view, and taking us within the personalities of other characters, especially Ahab and Starbuck, where Ishmael as observer could not penetrate.

Only once more before the very end do we see through Ishmael's eyes. In "The Try-Works" he knows for an awful instant what it actually feels like to be "given up" to fire. As helmsman, staring at night into the flaming try-works, he sees in the "tartarean shapes of the harpooneers," as they pitch and pole the hissing masses of blubber, "the material counterpart of [their] monomaniac commander's soul." He sees the "redness, the madness, the ghastliness," and he sees nothing else. He slips into an hypnotic drowsiness; his hold on the helm loosens, and he comes suddenly to consciousness to find himself facing dead astern. Only barely does he save the ship from being brought by the lee and possibly capsizing. He sees in his temporary distraction a sign of Ahab's moral inversion—Ahab who had looked too long on fire. Ishmael, having learned the "wisdom that is woe," now learns the "woe that is madness"; and he learns it this time on his own pulses. He learns that he is not the "Catskill eagle," nor is Ahab, who can dive down into the "blackest gorges" and rise again into the sun. "Give not thyself up, then, to fire [says Melville-Ishmael] lest it invert thee, deaden thee; as for the time it did me."

This is the last of Ishmael's intimate moral revelations. Here, except for the occasional reflections on the likeness of whaling to human life and except for the Epilogue, where he recounts only in the barest fashion the circumstances of his lone survival, we leave him. With "The Try-Works" his main function in the novel is done. He has cast off his green and dreamy youth and brought us to the edge of the vortex. The drama is now Ahab's (with Starbuck the main but ineffectual human antagonist) and Moby Dick's. The necessary probability has been established for Ahab's final plunge into the vortex itself, carrying all but Ishmael to destruction. And not since Job, as Melville's epigraph reminds us, has the destruction been so complete: "And I only am escaped alone to tell thee." All is gone, the whole "Anacharsis Clootz deputation" for the human race so devilishly misled by Ahab. The sea rolls on undisturbed as it rolled five thousand years ago. No angels sing the hero to his rest; no kingdom remains to be restored to order; only one lad just out of his novitiate lives to tell the story. Even the "bird of heaven," pinned to the mast by Tashtego's hammer, "his whole captive form folded in the flag of Ahab," goes down with the ship, which "like Satan, would not sink to hell till she had dragged a living part of heaven along with her . . ."

Such an ending forces to the limit any definition of tragedy comprehending positive values. We look in vain for precedents, certainly among the "Christian" heroes. Dr. Faustus had defied God and ended in hell. But he had defied God not out of hate but out of boredom or curiosity or restlessness, and in the end he had a vision of God's grace and forgiveness none the less real because he could not (or thought he could not) share in them. Lear railed at the universe but sought instruction even in his madness and learned reconciliation and love in unexpected ways. Hester lived out the dark ambiguities of her existence, with no satisfying resolution either way, but grew toward acceptance and humility rather than hate and denial. Ahab hated and denied. The universe had wronged him; he adjudged it evil and defied it. In this phase, he is a demonic, not a tragic, hero; less a Faustus or Lear or Prometheus than (as Richard Chase describes him) a false Prometheus, with destruction not salvation in his heart. Ahab's is no "puritan drama of the soul," a constant tension between the vision of innocence and the accepted guilt. He rejects guilt, both when he puts himself beyond good and evil as lord and master over all the souls on the *Pequod* ("Talk not to me of blasphemy, man; I'd strike the sun if it insulted me . . . Who's over me?") and in his final conception of "this whole act [as] immutably decreed": "I am the Fates' lieutenant." In the first pose, Ahab is more than man—and more than tragic man; he is a self-appointed God. In the latter, he is less than man, a mere agent of destiny. To the extent that the book glorifies Ahab in these two poses and passes no further judgment on him, Melville was right in telling Hawthorne that in *Moby-Dick* he had written "a wicked book." To this extent also, it is no tragedy.

But the indictment fails to do justice to Ahab and to that in the book which is not Ahab. Ahab is an emblem of no absolute order, and the book is not a "hideous allegory" of the triumph of Evil over Good. Like the tragedies which it recalls, it is more an exploration of mysteries than a rejection of mysteries in a sweeping nihilistic gesture. Much has been made of the book as a document in Melville's personal "quarrel with God," and his rebellious accents ring (or so it would seem) unmistakably in passage after passage. But so do Melville's accents sound in Ahab's melting moods, of which there are many, and in Ahab's passages of introspection and self-doubt, as in his confession to Starbuck: ". . . and then, the madness, the frenzy, the boiling blood and the smoking brow, with which, for a thousand lowerings old Ahab had furiously, foamingly chased his prey—more a demon than a man—aye, aye! what a forty years' fool—fool—old fool, has old Ahab been!" Ahab "has his humanities," as Captain Peleg announced to the novitiate Ishmael at the signing on. He understands and admits (as no demonic and few romantic heroes do) his own ruthlessness—toward Pip ("Thou touchest my inmost centre, boy"), toward Starbuck, toward the captain of the *Rachel* who would engage his help in searching for the lost child. He drops his one salt tear into the great Pacific. But more than this, his feud, like Job's and Prometheus' and Lear's, is not entirely his own. He is no Byronic hero kicking himself loose from the moral universe in ironic bitterness. He took upon himself what he conceived to be the burden of humanity. He faced the darkness as he saw it. Starbuck reconciled it with his traditional beliefs; Stubb and Flask laughed it off; Ishmael saw it and adopted his "desperado philosophy." Only Ahab felt what "some deep men feel": "that intangible malignity which has been from the beginning"—whatever it is in nature that makes these hard hearts, whatever oppresses, bewilders, and bears man down. Like Job and Lear, he saw his own misfortunes as a sign of the common lot; and like them he struck back. "He piled upon the whale's white hump the sum of all the general rage and hate felt by his whole race from Adam down; and then, as if his chest had been a mortar, he burst his hot heart's shell upon it."

Should he or should he not have done what he did? Should he or should he not have followed his "fatal pride," as Melville calls it, to the end? If the book is to be read as saying that he *should*, then it is a "wicked" book, justifying monomania, sultanism, blasphemy, and the all-but-total destruction they wrought. But the book neither justifies nor condemns Ahab. Tragedy is witness to the moral ambiguity of every action, and Melville is true to the witness of *Job*, *Dr. Faustus*, and *Lear* in conceiving of Ahab's action in just this light. Melville keeps the precarious balance in many ways—not only through Ishmael's comments and experience and Ahab's brooding awareness of the ethics of his action, which comes to the surface in some of his calmer soliloquies and in his gentler replies to Starbuck, but in the perspective that Starbuck and the visiting captains in the gams give to Ahab's purpose; in the constant reminder, through imagery and (later) direct comment, of the beauty, the goodness, the truth that make (with the vision of evil) the dual vision of tragedy. Indeed, the "monomaniac" Ahab's own statements of this duality are among the most poignant: "I am damned in the midst of Paradise." "There is that in thee, poor lad, which I feel too curing to my malady." "So far gone am I in the dark side of earth, that its other side, the theoretic bright one, seems but uncertain twilight to me."

But having gone thus far in the uncertain twilight, he does not turn back. If it grows ever darker, we are not left in total darkness. He is aware to the end of "the lovely leewardings" that he views on his last look from the masthead. Starbuck weeps as he clasps his hand for the last time. "Oh, my captain, my captain!—noble heart . . ." In the end, Ahab goes down "death-glorious" like his ship, "ungodly" yet "god-like," demonic in his own hate and vengeance, yet noble in his sense of the community of all unjust suffering. The book does not pronounce him good or evil any more than *The Scarlet Letter* calls Hester Prynne good or evil. But by carrying him through his fatal action in all its tensions, paradoxes, and ambiguities, the book, like a true tragedy, goes deeply into the mysteries of all moral judgments. All categories are put to the sharpest test, not only Ishmael's, Starbuck's, Stubb's, and Flask's but Ahab's own. We see the nature of each, how far toward good-and-evil each can go. The book leaves us, again true to its tradition, somewhere between pity and terror, faith and doubt, heaven and hell; it leaves us in what Ishmael-Melville calls (in "The Gilder") "manhood's pondering repose of If." But we have seen the conditions of pity and terror, good and evil, heaven and hell, more clearly. "Doubts of all things earthly, and intuitions of some things heavenly; this combination makes neither believer nor infidel, but makes a man who regards them both with equal eye."

Ahab himself never achieved such repose or looked on life so steadily, or if he did it was only momentarily. One other momentary insight comes to him in the frenzy of his final battle with the whale, and in a way it is his climactic insight. The perennial sense of injustice, the cry of Prometheus and Job as of Lear and Hamlet, was also Ahab's. Why do the innocent suffer? "O cursed spite / That ever I was born to set it right." This was the "inscrutable thing" that Ahab hated. Ahab never penetrated the mystery nor came to as full an understanding of the meaning in suffering as did Job or Lear. But in the moment of final conflict he senses a new dimension in his suffering, a relatedness to something other than the sheer malice of the universe, the whiteness of the whale.

As Ahab in his whaleboat watches the *Pequod* founder under the attack of the whale, he realizes that all is lost. He faces his "lonely death on lonely life," denied even "the last fond pride of meanest shipwrecked captains," the privilege of going down with his ship. But here, at the nadir of his fortunes, he sees that in his greatest suffering lies his greatest glory. He dies spitting hate at the whale, but he does not die cynically or in bitterness. The whale conquers—but is "unconquering." The "god-bullied hull" goes down "death-glorious." What Ahab feels is not joy, or serenity, or goodness at the heart of things. But with his sense of elation, even triumph, at having persevered to the end, there is also a note of reconciliation: "Oh, now I feel my topmost greatness lies in my topmost grief." This is not reconciliation with the whale, or with the malice in the universe, but it is a reconciliation of Ahab with Ahab. Whatever justice, order, or equivalence there is, he has found not in the universe but in himself. He is neither "sultan" now nor "old fool." In finally coming to terms with existence (though too late), he is tragic man; to the extent that he transcends it, finds "greatness" in suffering, he is tragic hero.

Melville did not dramatize further this final phase of Ahab's course, and therein lies the peculiarly shocking nature of the book. It is as if we left Job at the end of one of his diatribes or Oedipus at his self-blinding or Lear as he curses his daughters and plunges into the storm. Even with this final insight of Ahab's, the ending seems too dire for tragedy. It seems to deny the future; when the *Pequod* sinks, all seems lost; and there is no further comment, no fifth-act compensations to let in a little hope. The only comment is the action itself, the total action from beginning to end, all the good and the evil it uncovers. There is one survivor of the action: the tragic artist to tell about it from beginning to end. In the chapter called "Brit," Melville writes: ". . . man has lost that sense of the full awfulness of the sea which aboriginally belongs to it"; and the sea, he reminds us shortly, covers "two thirds of the fair world." *Moby-Dick* presents this awfulness relentlessly, even wickedly, as Melville hinted to Hawthorne. It is a cruel reminder of the original terror. If the world it presents is the starkest kind of answer to the Emersonian dream, it is not a world for despair or rejection—as long as there is even one who escapes to tell its full story.

WARNER BERTHOFF

[Characterization in *Moby-Dick*] †

* * * Melville's characterizations, as much as any other factor, are what give dramatic life and movement to the structure of his best writing. A successful piece of narrative fiction is a progression of formal events which are persuasive both in their general logic and

† From Warner Berthoff, *The Example of Melville* (Princeton: Princeton University Press, 1962), pp. 103–11. Copyright 1962 by Princeton University Press; reprinted by permission of the publishers.

sequence and also in their constituent parts. The arrangement of the whole must hold together, so as positively to accomplish its large effects; but it will not do so unless there is life and truth in the words and things of each successive part, and a steady return of immediate satisfaction. Style alone is not enough, nor is a system of interlocking analogies, however efficiently worked out. The composition will need some rough, plain, natural shorthand of demonstration and reference which will be quickly intelligible to the reader, and of course sufficiently entertaining in its 'own part, and which will save the writer from having to establish *ab novo* the interest and bearing of each new unit of narration.

In the central mass of *Moby-Dick*—to take the most impressive single case of Melville's compositional skill—the characterizations, and in particular the figures of Stubb and Queequeg, perform a very great part of this tactical service. How, we may ask, would *Moby-Dick* manage without this sturdy pair? Studying the book as a table of ethical types and values, as W. H. Auden has done in *The Enchaféd Flood*, we may see them as subordinate integers at best. So for Auden, Stubb, defined as the man "unable to face suffering," is neither more nor less important than the other mates, who stand for other forms of spiritual cowardice, while Queequeg, held to represent the "unconscious pagan world" of natural appetite, is rather less significant than, say, Pip or Fedallah.[1] But simply following the narrative along, chapter by chapter, we may come to a different rating of their importance. For more than two hundred pages in the middle of *Moby-Dick*, between the first lowering and the ship's climactic emergence into the Pacific, Stubb and Queequeg are, in frequency of appearance, very nearly its principal actors. In that part of the book which is a meditative-heroic poem on the honor and glory, and practical enterprise, of whaling, they are (the narrator apart) the figures of first prominence among the *Pequod's* company, and they are instruments of the first importance in securing the impression of reality on the grand scale of Melville's conceiving.

It would be easy to exaggerate this point. *Someone*, presumably, must be on hand to perform the labors which are to be tabulated and described. Also, the prominence of Stubb and Queequeg is a relative thing; for every passage in which they are called forth in aid of the exposition, there are two or three others in which the narrator's meditative fancy works alone. But it is precisely in counter-

1. In effect, however, this is to judge the events of the book from Ahab's demented point of view—as Melville did not, except when he edged over into mechanical allegory in certain late chapters. To Ahab, Stubb is nothing more than an especially convenient target for his scornful opinion of the ordinary race of "manufactured" men, whom he is compelled to rely on; and Queequeg, too, is of interest to him only as a fine "tool"—or, in the hieroglyphic mysteries of his tattooing, as an equally impersonal "tantalization of the gods."

Auden's comments on Stubb simply ignore the rough vitality and charm of the second mate's nature, and—this is more to the point—Melville's obvious pleasure in it.

pointing this first-person discourse, and underscoring its probings with the natural emphasis of their special prowess, that they repeatedly give pace and vitality to the progress of the narrative—a function for which the quality of character Melville has troubled to establish in them precisely fits them. Of Stubb especially is this true. No more consequential example can be cited—since it is the success of *Moby-Dick* that is at stake—of Melville's way of projecting a character by means of a few explanatory epithets and designations, and then allowing him the freedom of action to convince us of the reality both of his own being and of all that the narrative shows him engaged in.

Stubb's moral type is quickly established. He is "calm," "cool," "off-handed," "indifferent" to danger or the thought of death, a "high liver" attentive to his own rugged comforts, and above all "humorous." From the first we know his ultimate limits of spirit, the something mechanical about his fearlessness, the "almost impious" quality of his good humor. For describing the everyday business of whaling, however, he is the man Melville needs. More than once Stubb's boat is "foremost" in pursuit of the whale; it is he who is most often seen in the chase and at the kill, and who also has the laborious office of overseeing the work of boiling down. He perfectly exemplifies the workaday, democratic skillfulness, on a heroic scale where "dignity and danger go hand in hand," that Melville proposes to celebrate. So we are asked to marvel at Stubb's deftness in decapitating the huge, thick-fleshed, neckless sperm whale, half under a rolling sea, in ten minutes' time; and we are commanded to take special note of his excellence in the fine art of pitchpoling. He exemplifies no less flamboyantly the commercial motive at the heart of the whole business of whaling, as by "unrighteous cunning" (though also by superior knowledge of the details of his trade) he tricks a French whaler out of a cache of ambergris. He is continually presented to us as an ingenious, inventive, devising man, cheerfully at home among the violent necessities of his work.

Now by abstracting this character from the uses Melville puts it to, it is possible to draw up a severe moral indictment of it—as Auden does in stressing Stubb's declared indifference to whatever passes his practical understanding. In the matter of abandoning Pip on the empty ocean, Stubb, according to Auden, is "guilty of destroying an innocent boy's sanity": "He does not guess what the consequences of leaving Pip in the water will be, because he has never really looked at him." To which it can only be answered that though the indictment may well apply, Melville himself does not think to press it. Stubb has already saved Pip's life once, breaking off the chase to do it, and is only speaking the world's plain truth in reminding the slave-boy that one whale is worth thirty Pips on the open market. At another point we see Stubb bedeviling the old negro cook (a figure of fun, be it said, out of the crudest popular tradition); but we also see him forcefully interceding for Queequeg in behalf of his right to a proper ration of grog. The point is that he knows the value of every tool and every man in his hazardous service, and acts accordingly, with impressive dispatch. The cook's remark that Stubb is "more of shark dan Massa Shark hisself" is a just and, in the circumstances of the book, an honorific tribute.

Queequeg does not appear as often as Stubb in these middle chapters of *Moby-Dick*, but plays, in his own even cooler and calmer pagan manner, the same kind of role. He is a comparably heraldic figure in the celebration of the arts and mysteries of whaling. (In these passages we are only incidentally reminded of his relationship to Ishmael in the New Bedford chapters.) He, too, is singled out in the narrative to perform various tasks of professional skill: drawing the whale's teeth, delivering Tashtego out of the well of sperm in its huge head, fencing off sharks from its floating corpse, riding its slippery back to drive in the blubber-hook, managing the delicate and exhausting business of stowing the oil casks in the hold, and so on. To these competences the savage Queequeg adds, naturally enough, some that are all his own. He has a special alertness to physical signs and omens; he it is, for example, who happens to remember that where squid have been seen, sperm whales may be expected. Everything he does is on a prodigious scale, as befits the setting and action of the story, yet is performed with the "indifferent promptitude" of his savage nature. He is a magnificent creature in a world of magnificent creatures, mutually sympathetic. Thus the cannibalism he was bred to corresponds to the "universal cannibalism" of the sea, whose most savage monsters have no spiritual terror for him. But in this, too, civilized Stubb matches him, for it is Stubb's epicurean meal of whale-steak, and his thus devouring "a newly murdered thing of the sea, and . . . by his own light," that leads the narrator to exclaim concerning carnivorous mankind: "Cannibals? who is not a cannibal?"

A sense of Stubb's fitness, in particular, for pointing up certain main themes and emphases seems to have grown on Melville as he worked along, for Stubb's prominence in the narrative does not diminish in the Ahab-dominated climax of it. He makes as good a commentator on certain dramatic incidents as Ishmael, and Melville uses him fitfully all through the last hundred pages as a point of reference for the main action. Stubb's "humorousness" matches one major mood of Ishmael's witness, and provides the same kind of contrasts. In his own habitual style he takes Fedallah's measure, we notice, from the start, and more than once siphons off our own

dangerous sense of Fedallah's ludicrousness as a symbolic agent.[2]
He takes Ahab's measure, too; the carpenter insists, in fact, that
Stubb is the one who knows Ahab "best of all." The narrator of
course "knows" more; yet it may be pointed out that Stubb's quick
response to Ahab's display of concentrated pride and purpose—
"damn me, Ahab, but thou actest right; live in the game, and die in
it!"—speaks as centrally for Melville's multiple apprehension of his
hero's nature as does, say, Father Mapple's glorification of "him
. . . who against the proud gods and commodores of this earth,
ever stands forth his own inexorable self." To the end Stubb's impulsive sympathy for Ahab holds strong, and his rising excitement
as the catastrophe comes on is dramatic vindication of Ahab's conduct—though the mad captain still scorns him.[3]

An especially interesting case of Stubb's accumulating usefulness
as a character is his part in the chapter called "The Doubloon."
Two pages along in this masque-like survey of ways of interpreting
the world's emblematic mysteries, he steps forward and takes over
as impresario and chorus (mad Pip, of course, is given the last
word). In such appearances Stubb comes very near representing
the narrative point of view, or one main element in it. In his
own proper character he perfectly embodies that "free and easy
sort of genial, desperado philosophy" especially bred by whaling,
Ishmael tells us, but also natural to all the "queer times and occasions in this strange mixed affair we call life when a man takes this
whole universe for a vast practical joke. . . ." ". . . nothing dispirits, and nothing seems worth disputing. He bolts down all
events, all creeds, and beliefs, and persuasions, all hard things
visible and invisible, never mind how knobby; as an ostrich of potent
digestion gobbles down bullets and gun flints." "Queer" is Stubb's
"one sufficient little word" for all the mysteries he encounters; and
it is a perfectly accurate word as far as it goes, though schoolmaster
Ishmael can always think of a few more.

The two attempts at full-scale dramatic characterization in Melville's work are Ahab and Pierre. It may seem unnecessary to remark
that the first is on the whole the more effective. Yet if anything
comes near to spoiling *Moby-Dick* it is the presentation of Ahab as a
personal agent in the drama; and if anything comes near to saving
Pierre it is the presentation of the unfolding inward nature, capable
of passional action and change, of its otherwise preposterous hero

---

2. See Chapter 99, "The Doubloon":
" 'But, aside again! here comes that
ghost-devil, Fedallah; tail coiled out of
sight as usual, oakum in the toes of his
pumps as usual.' "

3. It would be less than fair to Stubb
not to point out that he makes the best
end of the three mates. So it seems to
me, at least; Auden, however, considers
his last words evasive and childish.

(who is hardly more preposterous, however, than the type of the free-born young male, on the edge of manhood, in actual life). The characterization of Ahab can succeed because *Moby-Dick* as a whole does not depend on it. Its strength is borrowed from the strength of the whole recital of which it is a part (including the brazenly suspenseful plot of the hunt after a fabulous creature). Its chief artistic virtue is its consistency with what is elsewhere revealed, defined, and rehearsed in this extraordinary book. The characterization of the young Pierre, on the other hand, is in certain ways a more thoughtful and potentially a more interesting undertaking; but there is little else in the book capable of supporting it, or of bringing the crude formal conventions it is encased by back into living reality.

In *Moby-Dick* the essential character of Ahab is established in a rather curious way—well before he puts in an appearance, almost before he is even named. This is done in the much-quoted passage in Chapter 16, "The Ship," which describes the general breed of Nantucket whale-hunter. Here the figure is sketched of a man of "audacious, daring, and boundless adventure," possessing "a globular brain and a ponderous heart," who has been led by his course of life to think "untraditionally and independently," and who now stands forth as "a mighty pageant creature, formed for noble tragedies," but who also exhibits a certain "half wilful over-ruling morbidness at the bottom of his nature." With the addition of two or three further generalizations, a few pages later, by Captain Peleg, the characterization of Ahab is now virtually complete. Successive chapters—describing his appearance on the quarterdeck, the vision of him in Stubb's dream, and his sultanic overlordship on the *Pequod*—amplify it, but mostly by the same kind of type-defining, the same application of descriptive labels and epithets. It is as though some vast and changeless phenomenon of physical nature was being analyzed and explained, according to the logic of its prehistoric formation (so that there is a fine appropriateness to the borrowing of Hotspur's rhetoric that closes out Chapter 33: "Oh, Ahab! what shall be grand in thee, it must needs be plucked at from the skies, and dived for in the deep, and featured in the unbodied air!"). Ahab's first long speeches, in Chapters 36 and 37, have the same essentially explanatory function—though we notice that in their overwrought style and floundering organization they are distinctly less effective, even dramatically, than the strong, well-paced analytic writing in those chapters immediately succeeding (Chapters 41, 44, 46), to which the main exposition of Ahab's case is entrusted.

Mad from the beginning, Ahab makes a strange and awesome figure but not, in the main, one arousing tragic pity and fear. The sublimity of his posture and the astonishing energy of his "monomania" are skillfully indicated. But perhaps the most impressive single paragraph about him is one (Chapter 41) in which the direct rendering of his individual being is abandoned altogether, and the job of suggesting the real presence in him of some "larger, darker, deeper part," that contains his "State-secret" and "whole awful essence," is assigned to an elaborate descriptive metaphor of the spiked Hôtel de Cluny in Paris and the weird, timeless Roman ruins beneath it. The role Ahab is given to play is an earnest of Melville's drive and ambition in the book. But the characterization itself is static in conception, and contrived and mechanical in the actual working out. Ahab acts most of the time in a trance of calculating madness; or, to put it in another way, he stays monotonously within the mold established for him.[4] The vitality and persuasiveness of the narrative are chiefly secured, I have already suggested, by other means. Yet there are moments of genuine poignancy in the presentation of Ahab that enrich the whole book, most notably the touching interlude of Chapter 132, "The Symphony," in which for once he steps briefly out of his appointed role and questions it, in Starbuck's presence, from his "own proper, natural heart." Also, in the final chapters, the theatrical contrivance of this role does emerge as thoroughly in keeping with the splendidly theatrical effectiveness of the long three-act climax.

4. "Thus a man lasts but a very little while, for his monomania becomes insupportably tedious in a few months." (Emerson, "The Method of Nature.")

Biography

LEON HOWARD

[The Composition of *Moby Dick*] †

II

The stimulating events of early August [1850] had a profound effect upon Melville's new book when he returned to its composition after the departure of his guests and meditated its progress during his physical labors in the autumn. For although Duyckinck had described it as being "mostly done," it still lacked copiousness in its treatment of the whaling industry; and Melville evidently intended to extend its length after his usual fashion as soon as his technical library was complete. He already had on hand when he began his work Frederick D. Bennett's *Narrative of a Whaling Voyage round the Globe* and J. Ross Browne's *Etchings of a Whaling Cruise,* and he had borrowed from the New York Society Library on April 29, 1850, William Scoresby's *Arctic Regions* and *History and Description of the Northern Whale Fishery.* He had also ordered at about the same time Thomas Beale's *The Natural History of the Sperm Whale,* but Putnam's had been obliged to import the book from England and it had not arrived until July 10, shortly before he went to Pittsfield, and he had hardly had time to look at it. Since the portion of Melville's own work which had reached a "half way" point at the time of his letter to Dana on May 1 could have contained nothing derived from Scoresby,

† From Leon Howard, *Herman Melville: A Biography* (Berkeley: University of California Press, 1951), pp. 162–79. Copyright 1951 by University of California Press; reprinted by permission of the publishers.

The first section of Howard's Ch. 7, omitted here, tells of Melville's returning from England in February 1850 with plans for a novel that later became *Israel Potter;* of his beginning that spring in New York City to write instead the whaling book that became *Moby-Dick;* of his visit to Pittsfield in western Massachusetts; of his meeting Hawthorne on August 5 at the famous Berkshire picnic where the New York literati had such a vigorous argument with Oliver Wendell Holmes and other Boston literati that Melville carried it on into his essay on Hawthorne and his *Mosses* in Evert Duyckinck's *Literary World* of August 17 and 24; of his buying the farm near Pittsfield which he named "Arrowhead"; and of his settling down there in the middle of October with "nothing to keep him from dividing his time between his book and his harvest or woodpile" (p. 161).

Howard's Preface explains that both the source material and the documentation for his book will largely be found in Jay Leyda's *The Melville Log.*

and the part seen by Duyckinck could not have included much if any material from Beale, it seems most probable that he had been engaged upon a narrative which he expected to supplement in various places rather than upon the progressive composition of the sort of book he later published.

A careful study of the sources of the finished work bears out this conclusion, showing that he interpolated one distinctive chapter, "The Advocate," in his early sourceless narrative and did not begin to draw regularly upon Beale and his other sources of technical information until he reached chapter thirty-two, entitled "Cetology." It is quite evident, however, that when he began to rework his manuscript for the purpose of introducing technical information and description he did not merely add to its substance as he had done in his previous books and as he had started to do in this one. Of the seventy-four chapters which may be described as representing the central section of the finished work, all but twenty-two contain material based upon published sources of information—much of it from Beale—and some of the twenty-two are so intimately linked with chapters influenced by Beale that they must necessarily have been written after their author had access to the *Natural History*. Occasional allusions which have nothing to do with whaling also show that his revision amounted to more than his customary insertions of new material: the reference in chapter seventy-eight to an occurrence at Niagara Falls on June 25, 1850; the identification of "this blessed minute" in chapter eighty-five as "a quarter past one o'clock P.M. of this sixteenth day of December, A.D. 1851" (which seems to be a printer's error for the year before); and the use in chapter ninety of an anecdote which appeared in the *Literary World* for June 29, 1850. Melville may have salvaged large sections of the work in progress, but when he took it up again after the departure of his friends he not only began to enlarge but substantially to rewrite his book.

For this reason, in order to understand what was going on underneath the visible surface of his life, it is necessary to look somewhat closely at the new parts of the book itself in an attempt to uncover the intellectual and emotional stimuli which kept him working at it for another full year and which later affected his whole career as an author. Nothing that had ever happened to Melville in his travels was more important than the activities of his mind between August, 1850, and August, 1851, as he sat before his desk in the privacy of a locked room. Although these activities are recorded in his book, they are revealed there only obliquely; and it is impossible to recognize them at all unless the book is considered in relation to the literary tradition of which it was a part—that is, unless Melville's own work is examined against the background of works by other writers who were in his mind at the time he planned and wrote his own story.

These writers were almost all romantic poets and novelists or earlier writers seen through the eyes of romantic essayists. There seems to be little reason to doubt that in undertaking to write *Moby Dick* Melville, having almost exhausted the autobiographical materials around which he had constructed his successful early books, planned to make his new story a dramatic romance that combined the characteristics of a romantic novel with those of a Shakespearean tragedy. His cast of characters and his description of the work as a romance both indicate the general type of fiction he was planning to produce; and such early hints as his reference to Ahab as "a mighty pageant creature, formed for noble tragedies" and his allusion to the "tragic graces" to be woven around "meanest mariners" anticipate the stage directions, the dramatic form of certain chapters, and the soliloquies in high style which are visible evidences of his calculated intent to dramatize and poetize his fiction.

The romantic tradition in which Melville conceived and began *Moby Dick* is revealed by the opening section of the book itself and by the type of fiction which predominates in the lists of books he brought back from Europe or borrowed during the first few months after his return. In general, he bought Gothic and borrowed transcendental romances. Both had in common a considerable element of mystery and either a hero or a villain driven by some intense emotion—often a desire for power—which kept the entire plot moving. Melville's Captain Ahab, in his early appearances, could have stepped from the pages of either. In his "greatly superior natural force" of brain and heart, in his "queer" state of being neither sick nor well, in his mysterious but somehow extraordinary past, this "grand, ungodly, god-like man" belongs in the tradition commonly called Byronic because Byron—most typically in his verse drama *Manfred*—so perfectly gathered up the strands of romantic mettle, moodiness, and mystery and wove them into an individual pattern which was enormously popular among early nineteenth-century writers and readers alike. Melville evidently intended to follow this pattern and, by drawing a popular type of romantic hero through the curious incidents and "wild legends" of the whale fishery, produced something quite new and entirely different from the realistic story by J. Ross Browne which he had reviewed three years before.

Melville may not have been conscious of one considerable obstacle to his success. The author who had composed the "Old Zack" articles and had made such sport of the Irish captain of the head in *White Jacket* possessed too much humor to take his Byronism straight. The humor is evident enough in *Moby Dick*—in the account of Ishmael's first acquaintance with Queequeg, in sardonic turns of phrase and frequent examples of verbal playfulness, and in the occasional tall stories succinctly slipped into the narrative. Like Thomas Carlyle, Melville could take romantic moodiness seriously but not with entire solemnity; and of all the novels he read during the gestation of his own, Carlyle's *Sartor Resartus* was the one which seems to have made the greatest impression upon him and which was to be most frequently reflected in his writing. Carlyle's manner was to become particularly evident in Melville's use of Scoresby's *History and Description of the Northern Whale Fishery*, which he obtained soon after reading *Sartor Resartus*, for he dipped into it and brought out the raw material of his own book with the same sort of Shandean humor that Carlyle exercised upon the various paper bags from which he extracted the autobiographical and philosophical writings of Professor Diogenes Teufelsdröckh of Weisnichtwo. Scoresby, in *Moby Dick*, was variously Captain Sleet, an Esquimau doctor Zogranda, a famous authority on smells named Fogo Von Slack, and Professor Dr. Snodhead of the College of Santa Claus and St. Potts. The elaborate bibliographical classification of whales and their kindred in the first of the intermediary chapters (where Scoresby is introduced under the first of his comic pseudonyms, Charley Coffin) is entirely in that vein of humor, and the vein is abundant throughout that section. Had something not happened to Melville's original design his humor would have considerably modified the book's high romantic tone.

The dramatic influences upon *Moby Dick* are less clearly traceable from a precise knowledge of the author's reading, but Melville is known to have begun rereading Shakespeare in a new edition with large print and with a new enthusiasm after hearing Fanny Kemble render the part of Lady Macbeth in February, 1849. He had also brought back from England two plays of Shakespeare and editions of Ben Jonson, D'Avenant, Beaumont and Fletcher, and Marlowe. He was even then caught in the net of Shakespearean idolatry and by the middle of 1850 explicitly shared the tendency of such romantic critics as Lamb and Coleridge to despise the "popular" aspects of his genius and admire him primarily as a profound and subtle literary artist who was to be seen at his best in the "dark characters of Hamlet, Timon, Lear, and Iago." How much he actually knew of Lamb's and Coleridge's Shakespearean criticism, however, is not indicated by external evidence. Duyckinck, who was a great admirer of both writers, certainly interested Melville in Lamb before he called on the English publisher Moxon and received Lamb's *Works* and Talfourd's *Final Memorials* of Lamb as a gift; and Melville's markings in the latter of these indicate an interest in Coleridge which may have led to the reading of other works than the *Biographia Literaria* he is known to have acquired in 1850.

Insignificant though this may be, it nevertheless touches up a curious resemblance between Melville's anticipatory references to Ahab as a character who, "dramatically regarded," has "a half-wilful overruling morbidness at the bottom of his nature" and Coleridge's statement, in his famous essay on *Hamlet*, that "one of Shakespeare's modes of creating characters is to conceive any one intellectual or moral faculty in morbid excess, and then to place himself . . . thus mutilated or diseased, under given circumstances." Melville made the resemblance even more striking by adding: "For all men tragically great are made so through a certain morbidness. Be sure of this, O young ambition, all mortal greatness is but disease." Later Ahab's disease was to become more malignant and to be more carefully diagnosed.

But at the beginning Melville gave no indication that his mysterious, queer captain was anything more than an ominous character set up for a bad end by the "ambiguous, half-hinting, half-revealing, shrouded sort of talk" of the water-front prophet Elijah and by the clearer insistence of the squaw Tistig that "his name would somehow prove prophetic." Other characters were almost as ominously queer: the tattooed cannibal harpooner, Queequeg, who was evidently designed to play some major part in the story before he took his "last long dive"; and the tall sailor Bulkington with landscorched feet, an outcast whose tragic fate and "stoneless grave" were foreshadowed by a formal address to his immortal spirit. The other notable outcast, Ishmael, was of course destined by his role as narrator to survive his companions' fate; but at least one other member of the crew, the little Negro Pip, had the finger of death put upon him from the very beginning. Of the mates, the chief officer Starbuck was created for trial by conflict, a man with a spirit to be bent but not broken; and the others were characterized with reference to strife, the happy-go-lucky Stubb being described as "neither craven nor valiant" and the little Vineyarder named Flask as a man of "ignorant, unconscious fearlessness." These, with the Gay Head Indian Tashtego and the gigantic African Daggoo, constituted the crew of the *Pequod* formally introduced in the first thirty-one chapters, although Melville referred incidentally to others such as the gray Manxman and Dough-Boy the steward and placed certain shadowy figures in the hold to be brought above decks later.

If *Moby Dick* had been published serially and Edgar Allan Poe had been alive to review the whole book from the logic of its first installments, as he had successfully reviewed Dickens' *Barnaby Rudge*, he would have had few qualms about anticipating the progress of the narrative. He would have guessed that Melville was preparing for a conflict of wills between a bizarre master and a steady though superstitious mate, a plot of dramatic violence in which the heathen harpooner was to play an active role, and a resolution of the action by catastrophe rather than victory. If he recalled his Bible sufficiently well to know that "king Ahab of old" had been killed by an arrow from "a bow drawn at a venture" and had read Joseph C. Hart's *Miriam Coffin*, Owen Chase's *Narrative* of the sinking of the *Essex*, or any of several other stories that might have been called to his mind by contemporary newspaper accounts of the *Ann Alexander*, he might even have expected to find the catastrophe caused by the very white whale of which Ahab so queerly inquired at the end of chapter thirty-one.

But except for the importance of the white whale, hinted at in only the last hundred words of the opening narrative, the concluding section provides a situation quite different from that toward which the book appeared to be moving at its beginning. Although it contains a minor clash between master and mate which the former does not force to an issue, the officers and crew are completely under Ahab's control. Queequeg has become indistinguishable in importance from Tashtego and Daggoo. Bulkington has disappeared entirely with no more of an accounting than may be explained by a revision of the early proof. Pip has gone mad, but has not preceded anybody before the heavenly throne. The narrator Ishmael has been so completely replaced by the omniscient author that an Epilogue is required to explain his survival. The dramatic conflict is between Ahab and the white whale who is no longer a piece of machinery but a character with a personality and a strange suggestiveness of his own, between Ahab and the great ocean which hides the object of his mad search, and between Ahab and Ahab during a rare moment of humane weakness. The narrative has passed through the seventy-four central chapters like a straw through the surface of water in a glass, and the two segments appear disjointed fragments of the same substance, contiguous but not continuous with one another. Although these incoherences are not so great that an ingenious critic, determined to find some mysterious perfection in every admirable work of art, cannot explain them away, they are evident enough to suggest that something unexpected happened to the book during its composition—something which would have infuriated such a literary artisan and student of craftsmanship as Poe.

What may have happened can be inferred from a consideration of the crucial point at which the second growth of the book began and of Melville's recorded activities at that particular time. The first of the narrative chapters in the central section of *Moby Dick* is the thirty-sixth, "The Quarter-Deck," and the first of such chapters which actually contains materials derived from Beale's *Natural History of the Sperm Whale* is the forty-first, entitled "Moby Dick."

The two are intimately related by the close parallelism of the explanations they offer concerning Ahab's attitude toward the white whale and by a continuity of narration which suggests that Melville's separation of them by the four intervening chapters in dramatic form was an arbitrary act of arrangement having nothing to do with their actual order of composition. The two seem to have been conceived together and written successively. In the second of these Melville was clearly referring to his source book while he wrote, for he borrowed from it some specific testimony concerning the ferociousness of the sperm whale (which Beale, incidentally, did not accept) and followed the *Natural History* in misspelling the name of one of the witnesses by writing "Olassen" for "Olafsen." This chapter in its present form thus could not have been written before July 10, 1850, and was probably not composed until after Melville had returned from his agricultural inspection on the twentieth and had spent the next three weeks in a trip to New York and in the entertainment of his visiting friends in Pittsfield. On the other hand, since both it and its twin are essentially preliminary to chapters forty-two and forty-four and to the main development of the narrative which follows, they are not likely to be late insertions introduced into the early part of the book as afterthoughts. They most probably date from the time Melville began to tinker with his story shortly after his friends departed on August 12 in their fond belief that the book was "mostly done."

This means, of course, that the second growth of *Moby Dick* began immediately after Melville had written his essay on "Hawthorne and His Mosses" and while he was still under the powerful influence of his stimulating conviction that the literature of America could rival that of England. For this essay was more than a generous tribute to a fellow author and a mischievous continuation of a dinner-table controversy over the present state and future prospects of American genius. It was a serious contention that an American writer with the intellectual capacity of Hawthorne could reach, through the medium of narrative prose, the heights of excellence achieved by Shakespeare; and in its serious insistence that Hawthorne had already approached these heights, it was a confession that the author of *Mosses from an Old Manse* possessed some extraordinary power of appeal to him at that special time. Melville had previously read some of the same author's *Twice-Told Tales* and possibly *The Scarlet Letter* without any great enthusiasm, and after the publication of *Moby Dick* he rarely saw him again except on business—although he enjoyed these later visits, bought his books, and, on one occasion, tried to interest Hawthorne in important literary business. The excitement and enthusiasm aroused in him by Hawthorne belonged entirely to the period in which he was reworking *Moby Dick*.

At the beginning of this period, at least, there is no doubt of the genuineness of the excitement and enthusiasm. In the *Mosses from an Old Manse* Melville discovered some stories with a "mystical depth of meaning" and a "profound, nay appalling" moral and others "shrouded in a blackness, ten times black." He found a man capable of mountainous heights of "humor and love" and depths "immeasurably deeper than the plummet of a mere critic." In this "still, rich utterance of a great intellect in repose," he decided, "Shakespeare has been approached": "Not a very great deal more, and Nathaniel were verily William." In the concluding section of the essay, written after an interruption of twenty-four hours or more, he added: "To what infinite height of loving wonder and admiration I may yet be borne, when by repeatedly banqueting on these Mosses I shall have thoroughly incorporated their whole stuff into my being,—that, I cannot tell. But already I feel that this Hawthorne has dropped germinous seeds into my soul."

The explanation of Melville's curious enthusiasm may be readily found in his preoccupation with Hawthorne's "blackness," in his appreciation of Hawthorne as a master "of the great Art of Telling the Truth" which Shakespeare had practiced only "covertly and by snatches," and in the particular stories and sketches that made the most profound impression upon him. Two of the last provide especially good illustrations of the thoughts by which Melville could be deeply moved at this time: "Earth's Holocaust," discussed in the first part, had as its "profound" and "appalling" moral the teaching that even if the follies and affectations and all the vanities and empty theories of the world could be utterly destroyed they would be re-created by the "all-engendering heart of man"; and "Young Goodman Brown," described in the postscript as being as "deep as Dante," taught the ambiguity of appearances, hinted that goodness might be merely a disguise for Satanism, and ended with the representation of a desperate and bewildered young man allegorically crying for "Faith." Either of these deserves the description Melville gave to the second—"a strong positive illustration of that blackness" which so attracted him in both Shakespeare and Hawthorne. The first declared something that the onetime primitivist, the admirer of the noble savage and the denouncer of civilization, had begun to suspect: that man is not innately good but may have the source of the world's evil in his own nature. The second sympathetically portrayed the agony of a young man faced with that belief. The ambiguities of *Mardi*, the increasing tendency to portray such inherently vicious or weak characters as Bland in *White Jacket* and Jackson and Harry Bolton in *Redburn*, and the strong impressions made by the "sane madness of vital truth" in *Lear* and the "great thoughts" in *Hamlet*—all culminated in Melville's excited willingness to accept the black moral of "Earth's Holocaust" as "Truth" and in his sensitive appreciation of the tragedy of "Young Goodman Brown."

Melville, in short, began to revise his romantic narrative of the whale fishery at a time when his reading of Hawthorne's stories and his meeting with their author had just served as a catalytic agent for the precipitation in words of a new attitude toward human nature which his mind had held in increasingly strong solution for some years. Such an experience, like that of a religious conversion, is exciting and stimulating to a high degree; and in his state of excited stimulation Melville was not content merely to feed new raw material into his story, as he may have originally planned, in order to give it a comfortable bulge and enable his English publisher to bring it out as a three-decker. He was emotionally obliged to put into it some of the force of his new philosophical convictions, and he could hardly have avoided thinking of it, in the secret recesses of his mind, as a possible medium through which these convictions could reach Shakespearean heights of expression. The book became, in its essence if not in its superficial design, a different one from the romance he had planned.

Just how the essential imaginative quality of the book revised itself at this critical point may perhaps be revealed by an examination of two short passages from "The Quarter-Deck" and the "Moby Dick" chapters which have often been recognized as crucial in the interpretation if not in the writing of Melville's drama. In the first, Ahab explains himself:

> All visible objects, man, are but as pasteboard masks. But in each event—in the living act, the undoubted deed—there, some unknown but still reasoning thing puts forth the mouldings of its features from behind the unreasoning mask. If man will strike, strike through the mask! How can the prisoner reach outside except by thrusting through the wall? To me, the whale is that wall, shoved near to me. Sometimes I think there's naught beyond. But 'tis enough. He tasks me; he heaps me; I see in him outrageous strength, with inscrutable malice sinewing it. That inscrutable thing is chiefly what I hate; and be the white whale agent, or be the white whale principal, I will wreak that hate upon him.

In the second, from the chapter "Moby Dick," which is so intimately related to "The Quarter-Deck" in its opening lines and in its content, Melville has the narrator explain Ahab to the reader:

> Ahab had cherished a wild vindictiveness against the whale, all the more fell for that in his frantic morbidness he at last came to identify with him, not only his bodily woes, but all his intel-

lectual and spiritual exasperations. The White Whale swam before him as the monomaniac incarnation of all those malicious agencies which some deep men feel eating in them, till they are left living on with half a heart and half a lung. That intangible malignity which has been from the beginning; to whose dominion even the modern Christians ascribe one-half of the worlds; which the ancient Ophites of the east reverenced in their statue devil;—Ahab did not fall down and worship it like them; but deliriously transferring its idea to the abhorred white whale, he pitted himself, all mutilated, against it. All that most maddens and torments; all that stirs up the lees of things; all truth with malice in it; all that cracks the sinews and cakes the brain; all the subtle demonisms of life and thought; all evil, to crazy Ahab, were visibly personified, and made practically assailable in Moby Dick.

What, we may ask of this examination, do these passages signify concerning the imaginative growth of Melville's book?

In the first place, they signify that Melville modified but did not renounce his conception of Ahab as a romantic hero. The captain became less a conventional man of mystery, driven by obscure but powerful impulses, and more like the "half prophet and half fiend" Arbaces in Bulwer-Lytton's *The Last Days of Pompeii*—a man whose superior intellect induced him to practice "goetic, or dark and evil necromancy," instead of "theurgic, or benevolent magic," in his efforts to divert Nature from her "ordinary course" and control the hearts of men. For the Ahab of these new passages was led by his "dark imagination," like Arbaces, beyond the "appointed boundaries" of the ordinary human understanding and "into the land of perplexity and shadow"; and a note on a blank page in one of Melville's volumes of Shakespeare seems to indicate that he was aware of Bulwer's characterization of misguided greatness and may have reflected upon it while considering the "snatches" of dark truth he found in Shakespeare's tragedies.

This Ahab also belongs to the race of "demonical," or demon-possessed, characters discussed by Goethe in the autobiography, *Poetry and Truth*, which Melville had recently purchased in London. But his nearest prototype—the literary hero whose meditations his were made to resemble almost to the point of parody—was the hero of Carlyle's *Sartor Resartus* who believed that "all visible things are emblems; what thou seest is not there on its own account; strictly taken, is not there at all: Matter exists only spiritually, and to represent some Idea, and *body* it forth." Indeed, the Ahab who appears here had many resemblances to the Teufelsdröckh whose "strong inward longing shaped Fantasms for itself" and drove him toward them: he too had come to feel that the Universe, whether hostile or indifferent, was "rolling on . . .

to grind me limb from limb"; he too had heard the words "Behold, thou art fatherless, outcast, and the Universe is mine (the Devil's)" and had replied with his "whole Me," "*I am not thine, but Free, and forever hate thee!*"; and he too came out of his "Baphometic Fire-baptism," as Carlyle had called it, as "a specter-fighting Man" whose "Indignation and defiance" against "things in general" was "no longer a quite hopeless Unrest" but something with "a fixed center to revolve round" and whose tendency to "eat his own heart" did not disguise the fact that he had "a certain incipient method" in his "madness."

But these passages also show that if Melville retyped his romantic hero he retained and made unexpectedly productive use of the dramatic method of creation which Coleridge may have taught him. The reappearance of the Coleridgean language in such words as "morbidness" and "mutilated" in the second quotation indicates that Melville was still thinking of Ahab as a sufferer from some mental disease. In modern terms, he would have been suffering from a "transference neurosis." In the terms of such a contemporary psychologist as Hawthorne's college instructor in "mental science," Thomas C. Upham, who had prepared the *Outlines of Imperfect and Disordered Mental Action* for the Harpers' Family Library, he would have been a good illustration "Of disordered Judgment in connexion with obstinacy of Belief"—that is, of those persons who "attach themselves to a particular object" or "seize upon a particular opinion" and "hold it with a tenacity which neither life nor death can separate" and which makes out-of-place and ridiculous "all appeals to their feelings, to their sympathies, to their common humanity." "Leviathan," Upham had incidentally added of such appeals, "is not so tamed."

Melville's representation of his condition, however, was more literary. Ahab was like Carlyle's Teufelsdröckh, in the passages quoted above, a transcendentalist who had not achieved the Everlasting Yea of optimism although he had passed from depression to defiance. He was a superambulatory rather than inactive case of the disease which the transcendental Coleridge, looking into his own mind, diagnosed as Hamlet's: a man with a "craving after the indefinite," who "looks upon external things as hieroglyphics," and whose mind, with its "everlasting broodings," is "unseated from its healthy relation" and "constantly occupied with the world within, and abstracted from the world without—giving substance to shadows, and throwing a mist over all commonplace actualities." Had Ahab's morbidness remained as ill-defined as it was when Melville first mentioned it, the measure of the drama in *Moby Dick*, like that in Byron's *Manfred*, would have been only the power of the author's rhetoric. By translating it from temperamental moodiness into a describable mutilation of the intellect, Melville gave his book an internal dramatic force which was genuinely Elizabethan in its power and which, incidentally, could sustain a humor that would have destroyed the dramas of Byron.

The third signification of these passages is that they had implicit within them "the pervading thought that impelled the book"— one that Hawthorne might readily have recognized and praised (as Melville said he did, in a letter of November, 1851) although we do not have the words in which he identified it. For Melville moralized his drama by making it a parable after the "germinous" fashion of Hawthorne's stories. Quite clearly, Ahab's "Fire-baptism" was in the name of the devil, not in that of the Holy Ghost. His spirit of defiance led not to the spiritual triumph of Teufelsdröckh but to the destruction of himself and of the *Pequod* and all its crew save one. In the language applied to his Biblical prototype, "king Ahab of old," it was a "lying spirit" which led into the path of undirected vengeance a man who had done evil in the sight of the Lord. The teaching of the parable was that same black "Truth" which had been struggling into Melville's consciousness for years and had been brought to recognition by his excited reading of Hawthorne's *Mosses from an Old Manse*: the human heart engenders its own evil, men seek or can be led to seek their own worst fate, the noblest appearance of heroic manhood may be but a pasteboard mask. It was a "Truth" which went contrary to all Melville's early assumptions, it was opposed to all he had been taught that he ought to believe, and it was one which all the obscure censors of the mind had resisted. But it is always a relief, in the familiar phrase, to "face the worst and get it over with," especially when someone else knows that you have done so. When *Moby Dick* was at last finished and Hawthorne had read it, Melville wrote: "A sense of unspeakable security is in me at this moment, on account of your having understood the book. I have written a wicked book, and feel spotless as the lamb."

The feeling of security was slowly and painfully achieved, however, and all the surviving evidence concerning Melville's activities during the year of unexpected delay in bringing his book to an end bears witness both to the severity of his labors and to the strength of his impulse to seek an additional outlet for his intellectual and emotional energy through direct communication with Hawthorne. In December of 1850, while his cow was dry and his wife and young son were away on a six-weeks' visit to Boston, he described his routine to Duyckinck: rising at eight, he fed his stock, ate his breakfast, and started a fire in the room in which he locked himself up and wrote without interruption until two-thirty. At that time his family had instructions to knock on the door until he was forced to stop, do his afternoon chores, and have his dinner, after which he rigged the sleigh and drove his mother or sisters to the village for recreation and mail. Unable to work at night—although he would sometimes skim over some large-printed book or squint with one eye at the paper while he wrote a letter—he spent the evening "in a sort of mesmeric state" in his room while his mind raced with thoughts of the work in progress or of other books he would like to write in the future. It was a routine which allowed almost as much time for unemployed thought as for thoughtful writing; and his mother and sisters, knowing nothing of the normal state of excitement produced by intellectual activity which outruns its physical expression, may have begun to fear that winter that Herman—like his father, during the last weeks of life, before him—was "peculiar."

But the son was experiencing the excitement of creation rather than of desperation. His mind was swirling with new ideas and old memories. In the early fall he had received a letter from his former companion, the Long Ghost [of *Omoo*], written from California; and, somewhat later, a shipmate from the *Acushnet*, Henry F. Hubbard, had stopped by to see him with a report of what had happened to the voyage and the crew after Melville's desertion. If either of the two old friends had heard reports from the second voyage of the *Acushnet*, they might have discussed another dramatic chapter in the history of that ill-fated ship: the loss of a boat from the attack of a furious whale and the rescue of one of its crew, picked up hours afterward and miles away, swimming through an empty ocean. There was also "a sort of sea-feeling" about the snow-covered country. Melville looked out of his window in the morning as he would out of the porthole of a ship. His room seemed a ship's cabin, and as the wind shrieked at night he almost fancied that there was too much sail on the house and had to resist the impulse to "go up on the roof and rig in the chimney." It was easy to work—but not to work calmly—under such circumstances.

After the return of Lizzie with Malcolm in early January, if her later recollections may be trusted, the pressure of Melville's creative energy mounted until he extended his period of fasting and writing to include the last hour of good daylight. He felt the need of relief through conversation with some understanding spirit, however, and on the afternoon of January 22 hitched up the sleigh and drove over to Lenox in an effort to persuade the Hawthornes to pay him a visit at Pittsfield. But Hawthorne was busy finishing his own new book, *The House of the Seven Gables*, and Melville got only a supper of cold chicken and a gift of the *Twice-Told Tales* for his trouble. Back to his intellectual solitude, he was rudely impatient with Duyckinck when his friend asked him, in February, for contributions to *Holden's Dollar Magazine* and for a daguerreotype portrait to be published in that popular and well-paying periodical. "I am not in the humor to write the kind of thing you need," he explained shortly without attempting to "bore" his friend with his better reasons; and he had too much "intensified vanity" for the common distinction of having his "mug" engraved for the public. Yet he continued to want the companionship of Hawthorne and on March 12 drove again to Lenox and talked him into coming over, with his daughter Una, to Pittsfield for an overnight visit on the following day. Kept indoors by a spring snowstorm, the two friends talked of their first meeting the summer before, of their mutual friends in New York, and of the thoughts that crowded the younger man's brain; for Hawthorne had finished his book while Melville was still wrestling with his, and each realized that it was Melville's enthusiasm which had kept their friendship from hibernating during the winter.

When the snow melted and the Berkshires began to show signs of approaching spring during the next two weeks, Melville took time to escort his boyhood companion, Eli James Murdock Fly (who had become a confirmed invalid), as far as Springfield on his way from Greenbush to Brattleboro; but generally he continued to be too busy writing to get abroad during the daytime. Nevertheless, he paid another visit to Hawthorne on April 11, enriching his friend's poorly furnished cottage with a bedstead and a clock, and afterwards took another day off to read *The House of the Seven Gables*—a book which he found full of "genialities" but also full of the same tragic perception which had so impressed him when he read the *Mosses from an Old Manse*. Hawthorne was an enigma who appeared to lack the normal vitality of a red-blooded writer yet possessed the tough spiritual vitality of a hero who would try to tear through the web of fate. Melville saw him as a quiet version of the hero of Carlyle's *Sartor Resartus*, whispering rather than shouting the "thunder" of his everlasting "No" in defiance of a universe which threatened to crush the individual ego beneath its heavy material weight. The enigma was fascinating, for Melville was feeling the same pressure and had no inclination to confine his response to a whisper. His failure to finish his book on schedule had got him into financial difficulties, and when he was finally driven, late in April, to ask his publishers for another advance he met with a refusal—a refusal which forced him to borrow $2,050 at nine per cent in order to pay off his note to Brewster. Furthermore, the inevitable revolutions of the universe were, as a matter of literal fact, bearing down on his creative activity and suppressing it: with the arrival of May he had to stop writing and plant his corn and potatoes if he wanted to get his family—which was due to increase in October—through the next winter.

Frustrated by the processes of nature, pressed by the march of the seasons, and exasperated by the conflict between his financial and creative necessities, he took advantage of a rainy day that kept him indoors during the planting season and let the turmoil of his mind overflow in a long letter to Hawthorne. It was a rambling and not altogether coherent outburst, filled with the perplexities that beset a man who had been brooding over the peculiar intellectual attraction exercised by his friend, over the contradictions between ideal or moral "truth" and the visible truth of consciously perceived facts, and over the conflicts between philosophy and everyday reality. It was also charged with his emotional distress at his inability to make his book come out right as a practical job:

> In a week or so, I go to New York to bury myself in a third-story room, and work and slave on my 'Whale' while it is driving through the press. *That* is the only way I can finish it now,— I am so pulled hither and thither by circumstances. The calm, the coolness, the silent grass-growing mood in which a man *ought* always to compose,—that, I fear, can seldom be mine. Dollars damn me; and the malicious Devil is forever grinning in upon me, holding the door ajar. My dear Sir, a presentiment is on me,— I shall at last be worn out and perish, like an old nutmeg-grater, grated to pieces by the constant attrition of the wood, that is the nutmeg. What I feel most moved to write, that is banned,—it will not pay. Yet, altogether write the *other* way I cannot. So the product is a final hash, and all my books are botches.

But the story was once more, as it had been almost ten months before, approaching completion. His "whale"—for he had begun to refer to it as an account of a particular animal rather than as a presentment of the "whale fishery"—was "in his flurry" and would soon be finished up "in some fashion or other." "What's the use," he asked, "of elaborating what, in its very essence, is so short-lived as a modern book?" If he should write the Gospels in the nineteenth century, he would die in the gutter; and he was trying to reconcile himself to the "fame" of going down to the next generation of posterity as a "man who lived among cannibals" and then being forgotten. It was the letter of a man who was trying to escape the excitements of intellectual activity and creative emotion and find sanctuary in the belief that his hopes were all vanity and vexation of spirit.

By the fourteenth of June he was actually close enough to the end to return the reference volumes he had borrowed from the New York Society Library in April of the year before. But his publishers were enlarging their plant, the printers were behind schedule, and the city was too hot and uncomfortable for good work. Before the end of the month he was back in Pittsfield, feeling some relief from pressure. The "tail" of the book was "not yet cooked," but he did not expect to be busy very long; and he had enough leisure to rest his eyes by working around the farm, construct a few "shanties of chapters and essays" which would hold his book together more firmly, and add footnotes to completed chapters which he was reading in proof. Although it was "only half through the press," he wrote Hawthorne, he could look forward to talking "ontological heroics" over a bottle of brandy with his friend in the near future; and he was in sufficiently good spirits to make a joke of "the hell-fire in which the whole book" had been "broiled" and to reveal its "secret motto": *Ego non baptiso te in nomine—* but make out the rest yourself." Five weeks were to pass, however, before Melville could write Richard Bentley, to whom he had sold the English rights for one hundred and fifty pounds, that he was passing "the closing sheets" of his new work through the press and would be able to forward a printer's copy "in the course of two or three weeks." And it was to be two and a half weeks longer before he was completely free from entertaining relatives and gathering hay and sufficiently far ahead in his proofreading to bring Hawthorne and his New York friends together for another entertainment like the one of the year before. The finished proof sheets were not to be bundled up and sent to England until September 10, and it was not until after the proof sheets had been sent that he settled upon *The Whale* as his English title and decided to inscribe the book to Nathaniel Hawthorne "in token of my admiration for his genius." But when Evert Duyckinck, on his second visit to Pittsfield, wrote his first letter home on the morning of August 7, 1851, he might have repeated with literal truth what he had so mistakenly written exactly one year before: "Melville has a new book mostly done."

How well he had written Melville did not at the time know. Acutely aware of the way in which he had put his book together and of the nervous strain it involved, he may not have begun to realize its essential coherence until both Sophia and Nathaniel Hawthorne wrote him of its success. Replying to Mrs. Hawthorne on January 8, 1852, he expressed his amazement that a woman had found "any satisfaction" in *Moby Dick* and explained the phenomenon with the theory that her "spiritualizing nature" enabled her to see things that other people did not see and to refine them until they became "things, which while you think you but humbly discover them, you do in fact create them for yourself." "At any rate," he added, "your allusion for example to the 'Spirit Spout' first showed to me that there was a subtle significance in that thing—but I did not, in that case, *mean* it." Of the book in general he wrote: "I had some vague idea while writing it, that the whole book was susceptible of an allegorical construction, and also that *parts* of it were—but the specialty of many of the particular subordinate allegories, were first revealed to me after reading Mr. Hawthorne's letter, which, without citing any particular examples, yet intimated the part-and-parcel allegoricalness of the whole."

Melville was neither the first nor the last writer between Isaiah and Thomas Mann to have such an experience. It is, in fact, a normal one for an author who uses the kind of symbolism found in *Moby Dick*. For a symbol is an imaginative bridge between the general and the particular which may be crossed in either direction; and Melville, having tried without much satisfaction in *Mardi* the method of expressing a general conception in a specific image, had gradually slipped into the practice of letting his mind play around concrete details until they were made luminous with suggestive implications. Part of this was conscious and fairly obvious, as in the short chapter called "The Pipe" in which Ahab tosses the conventional symbol of peace into the sea. Part of it was a mental habit, built up while dealing with "the world in a man-of-war" in *White Jacket*, which had grown upon him more than he knew. It was the energetic burgeoning forth of this habit of mind in every phase of his writing which was the important result of his intellectual excitement while writing *Moby Dick*. The story which he wanted to sell, the whaling details which he wanted to exploit, and the dramatic vigor and heroic characterization with which he wanted to demonstrate the potentialities of American literature —all of these became the material substance that attracted the impulses of his more abstract thought as he brooded upon such questions as the origin of evil, the validity of intuitive perceptions which contradicted common experience, and the mysterious nature of man. Although the meaning of his calculated fable was that of his general observation, in a letter to Hawthorne, on the validity of the transcendentalist's experience—"But what plays the mischief with the truth is that men will insist upon the universal application of a temporary feeling or opinion"—it was a meaning to which he had committed himself with the enthusiasm of a recent convert rather than one which he had accepted with settled conviction. Thus the major "truth" revealed by the book was itself speculative, and its cold morality was humanized by Melville's admiration for Ahab's vigorous heart and his sympathetic awareness that he himself might have made the same intellectual error. He had compared Hawthorne with the hero of *Sartor Resartus*, because Hawthorne had denied intellectually the validity of those appearances which Carlyle's hero had defied emotionally; and he had found in himself a tendency to shout his defiance of the universal illusion even while denying its reality. He was temperamentally closer to the passionate Carlyle than to the intellectual Hawthorne, and thus his attitude toward the seagoing Teufelsdröckh who became the hero of his own book was ambiguous. Intellectually he condemned him. Emotionally he identified himself with him. And some of the dramatic effectiveness of the book comes from the divided attitude which enabled Melville to portray a hero with a tragic flaw and to do so without a feeling of superiority.

He was never, of course, to be made aware of the full power of his creation, for it was not until a generation after his death that his book began to have the same effect upon his readers that his fabulous white whale had upon its pursuers, provoking responses ranging from studied indifference to neurotic obsession. But by the time he wrote Hawthorne his discouraged letter of June, 1851, he was conscious that the book was having a profound effect upon himself as its author. He had been unfolding within himself at regular intervals since the beginning of his development and had "now come to the inmost leaf of the bulb" so that "shortly the flower must fall to the mould." He had been going through a period of artistic development far greater than anything he had ever experienced before. Financial need and commitments to his publishers had prevented him from giving up his original design of a romantic but literal presentment of the whale fishery. But as he worked at it he discovered that he had unwittingly begun to use materials that made their own structural demands because of their own peculiar and unanticipated qualities. The inherent dramatic power of the reconceived Captain Ahab was too great to be matched by the opposition of any individual or individuals among the officers or crew. Such a conflict might do for an episode like "The Town-Ho's Story." But Ahab demanded a more worthy antagonist. The white whale which may have been originally intended as a piece of machinery—a wedge of dissension between captain and mate, or the arrow of fate from a bow drawn at a venture—began to dominate the narrative; and that was why the author's allusions to the book, at the very time that he was writing out his technical descriptions of whaling, came to be references to his story of "the whale" rather than "the whale fishery." The sweep of the drama became too broad and its intensity too great to be presented through the medium of a bystanding narrator, and Melville was forced into an omniscience which made new and severe demands upon the literary craftsmanship of a habitual spinner of pseudo-autobiographical yarns.

Furthermore, "the pervading thought that impelled the book" was one not only at odds with the author's earlier beliefs but at odds with the pervading thoughts of some of the greatest literary minds of his day—with those of Emerson, in whom Melville had become interested the year before; with those of Carlyle, whose book had made such a considerable impression upon his own; and with those of the great Goethe, whose autobiography he was reading with thoughtful regard to this particular point at the time he was writing. Nor, as his chapter on "The Whiteness of the Whale" indicated and his next novel *Pierre* would prove, was Melville wholly and absolutely convinced that the great "Truth" of his parable was true at all. His struggle in *Moby Dick* was a struggle to master the art of reconciling a calculated plan with an independent organic growth, old habits with new techniques of literary craftsmanship, and an unwilling skepticism concerning the goodness of man with his will to believe in man's inherent nobility. Not only the book but its author had been going through a period of imaginative and intellectual second growth, and his allusion to the hell-fire in which his book was broiled was a reference to his growing pains. Although he was to try, in the years that followed, to repeat the popular successes of his earlier books, his interest in literature and philosophy was never again to be as relatively superficial as it had been before he wrote *Moby Dick*.

Selected Bibliography

The bibliography of *Moby-Dick* is enormous. The following are studies especially useful to students. For biographical information the best sources are Howard, Leyda, and Metcalf (cited below) and *The Letters of Herman Melville,* edited by Merrell R. Davis and William H. Gilman (New Haven: Yale University Press, 1960). The Mansfield-Vincent edition of *Moby-Dick* (New York: Hendricks House, 1952) is superseded as to text by the Norton Critical Edition but is still valuable for two hundred pages of explanatory notes. For further study of *Moby-Dick* the most useful volume is *MOBY-DICK as Doubloon,* edited by Hershel Parker and Harrison Hayford (New York: W. W. Norton, 1970). *MOBY-DICK as Doubloon* contains all the known contemporary reviews of *Moby-Dick* and *The Whale,* over seventy pages of commentary during 1853-1925, two hundred pages of the most important and most representative modern criticism, and a twenty-page annotated bibliography of modern *Moby-Dick* criticism. The brief list on this page consists of some standard and readily accessible studies.

Arvin, Newton. *Herman Melville* (New York: Sloan, 1950); reprinted New York: Viking Compass Books, 1957.

Berthoff, Warner. *The Example of Melville* (Princeton: Princeton University Press, 1962).

Bowen, Merlin. *The Long Encounter: Self and Experience in the Writings of Herman Melville* (Chicago: University of Chicago Press, 1960).

Chase, Richard, ed. *Melville: A Collection of Critical Essays* (Englewood Cliffs: Prentice-Hall, 1962).

Fiedler, Leslie. *Love and Death in the American Novel* (New York: Criterion Books, 1960); reprinted New York: Meridian Books, 1962.

Hillway, Tyrus, and Luther S. Mansfield, eds. MOBY-DICK *Centennial Essays* (Dallas: Southern Methodist University Press, 1953).

Hoffman, Daniel G. *Form and Fable in American Fiction* (New York: Oxford University Press, 1961).

Howard, Leon. *Herman Melville: A Biography* (Berkeley: University of California Press, 1951); reprinted, 1958.

Jerman, Bernard R. " 'With Real Admiration': More Correspondence between Melville and Bentley," *American Literature,* Vol. 25 (November, 1953), pp. 307-313.

Leyda, Jay. *The Melville Log,* 2 Vols. (New York: Harcourt, Brace, 1951). Reprinted with a new Supplement, New York: Gordian Press, 1969.

Matthiessen, F. O. *American Renaissance* (New York: Oxford University Press, 1941).

Metcalf, Eleanor Melville. *Herman Melville: Cycle and Epicycle* (Cambridge: Harvard University Press, 1953).

Modern Fiction Studies (Vol. 8, Autumn, 1962): A special Melville issue with a Melville bibliography by Maurice Beebe, Harrison Hayford, and Gordon Roper.

Parker, Hershel, ed. *The Recognition of Herman Melville* (Ann Arbor: University of Michigan Press, 1967).

Rosenberry, Edward. *Melville and the Comic Spirit* (Cambridge: Harvard University Press, 1955).

Sewall, Richard B. *The Vision of Tragedy* (New Haven: Yale University Press, 1959); reprinted as a Yale Paperbound, 1962.

Stern, Milton R., ed. *Discussions of* MOBY-DICK (Boston: Heath, 1960).

Stewart, George R. "The Two *Moby-Dicks,*" *American Literature,* Vol. 25 (January, 1954), pp. 417-448.

Thorp, Willard. *Herman Melville: Representative Selections* (New York: American Book Company, 1938).

Vincent, Howard P. *The Trying-Out of* MOBY-DICK (Boston: Houghton Mifflin, 1949); reprinted Carbondale: Southern Illinois University Press, 1965.

Wright, Nathalia. *Melville's Use of the Bible* (Durham: Duke University Press, 1949).

NORTON CRITICAL EDITIONS